THE WOLVES OF TIME

II
Seekers at the WulfRock

William Horwood

THE WOLVES OF TIME

= II =

SEEKERS AT THE WULFROCK

HarperCollins*Publishers*

HarperCollins*Publishers*
77–85 Fulham Palace Road,
Hammersmith, London W6 8JB

This paperback edition 1998
1 3 5 7 9 8 6 4 2

First published in Great Britain by
HarperCollins*Publishers* 1997

SF
Pbk

A catalogue record for this book
is available from the British Library

ISBN 0 00 649935 X

Printed and bound in Great Britain by
Caledonian International Book Manufacturing Ltd, Glasgow

Contents

Contents

PROLOGUE

I T IS PRUDENT in a man or woman to find out who it is that
leads them, especially on a journey whose purpose may be unclear,
and whose outcome quite uncertain. So, if you are to continue
your journey with the Wolves of Time to the very end, perhaps you
need to know something about your new guide.

My new guide? you say, wondering what can have happened to the
old one?

*Was he not a wolf, a very old wolf, a wolf immortal who could lay
claim to be the last surviving member of the original Wolves of Time
who served under Klimt?*

While some might add: *Was that old wolf not Tervicz himself, first
and most fiercely loyal of all Klimt's followers?*

Well ... yes he was, in *part* immortal, but ...

I hesitate because we have already reached that borderland between
two worlds, and others, through which we humans wander, stray, get
lost, making discoveries and rediscoveries of things that anciently we
knew.

This is the borderland between what we humans think of as our 'real'
day-by-day world, and those Otherworlds it is the shaman's special art
to learn to journey into. To those who think they firmly dwell only in
the real-seeming human world, and dismiss even such obvious evidence as dreams or sudden feelings of Otherworldiness as – well, *mere*
dreams! *mere* feelings! – the notion of Otherworlds seems absurd and
fantastic. It is the talk of fools and madmen, the subject of tricks and
deceit.

But shamans know differently, and so does almost anyone willing
to be still by forest or mountain, to listen, and to wait for the journey
to begin. Those who dwell in the Otherworlds are surprisingly willing
to guide us there, often in the form of some animal or another, whose
spirit has empathy with our own.

For some it is the soaring eagle that leads, for others a dark-dwelling
mole; for him a fleet-footed deer, for her a raging bear. Such familiars

1

talk and guide, leading on through the darkness and shadows, the reflections and the light, by fair paths and foul, through borderland and on to the Otherworld.

We know already from *Journeys to the Heartland* that for the Mann, that personal spirit-guide came in the form of a wolf called Tervicz, who led him to the Wolves of Time.

While you take that in, I pause and stare into the fire here in the forest clearing where we meet.

Which forest clearing? you ask at once, glancing over your shoulder to see what it is that shifts and moves beyond the shadows.

I reply, 'A clearing in the Schwarzwald of what was once Germany, and before that *West* Germany.' I fall silent as I wait for your next question, hoping it will get to the heart of things, which it does.

If Tervicz was our first guide, you say, *and he was the Mann's first guide, was it then the Mann himself who wrote the words of what we know as Journeys to the Heartland, and if he did when could he have done it? In fact, if . . .*

'Yes, it was the Mann who wrote the words,' I reply.

If that is so and you are our new guide now, who are you? And will Tervicz return to take up the tale as well because he's the one we thought was guiding us? But then . . . ?

I know, I know . . . These are questions that also worried me for many years, until I learnt the shaman's art and began to understand a little of their answers. Let us for the moment simply agree that Tervicz was our guide to the Wolves of Time and all their world, and the Mann wrote down the journey they made together.

Humph! you growl, as Kobrin might, or even Klimt himself, listening to some youthful vagrant explaining who he is, and why he's come. *Humph!!*

What I know is this: the Mann knew he would not be able to complete the story of the Wolves of Time and saw to it that one day, long after he had journeyed on, I myself would be able to continue it. Just as Klimt saw to it that his ledrene Elhana had young the pack could raise and nurture that they might one day continue.

The years have passed and now the time has come to take the journey on. Youthful though I must seem compared to the Mann himself as *you* first knew him, I am now, as it happens, rather older than he was when you last met him.

Humph!

It may help you to remember that Klimt's pack was called the Wolves of *Time*, and that they were journeyers in the Otherworlds. *Journeys to the Heartland* ended with the birth of Klimt's sons and a kindly visit from Wulfin Herself. Soon after that telling, the Huntermann caught up with the Mann and he had to abandon his tale. I do not yet know more than you do about how his life ended, or whether it was he or Huntermann who won through to the end and reached the WulfRock.

In fact, I do not even yet know if there was an end.

Some guide! you declare.

Quite so, except for one thing which may help you decide to join me. Last night beyond the shadows of this fire that lights our faces, an old wolf came and called my name. Last night Tervicz came back.

I knew then that my journey to find out the truth of the Wolves, and the truth of the Mann, must now begin. But Wulf knows I need help if I am to bring my quest for the truth of the Wolves of Time, of the Mann, and of Huntermann to a successful conclusion.

It is a journey I prefer to make in your company and which you may prefer to make in mine. It is for this reason I first suggested that you might wish to know a little more about me . . .

I

THE SHAMAN'S STORY

CHAPTER ONE

The Trophy

I WAS BORN in Anno Lupi 12, or AD 2023 by the old Gregorian Calendar, which I believe some communities in Europe still cling to. But since the tribe in which I was raised honours the Wolves and not the flawed Christian god, we mark the passage of our rites and rituals, as we do our seasons, by respectful reference to the year when the God Wulf ended his last mortal life upon this earth and began his journey on the wolfway to the stars, so signalling the end of the Dark Millennium, and our survival.

My tribe is named after the Feldberg mountain which dominates the Black Forest lands that lie to the south and east of Freiburg along the Upper Rhine. Most call us the Feldberg Volk or People, and fear us, for they think us strange and mysterious, dwellers of the upland forest and the crags, mystics of the misty places, and that we are chosen of the Wolves.

It was upon the slopes of the Feldberg that my tribe's founders first paid tribute to the Wolves after the wars were over and the time of hiding, survival and the rediscovery of the pre-Christian ways had begun.

With each month and year that passed after Anno Lupi 1, the tragedies and trials of the period of the final European conflagration began to recede, and a simpler and better life advanced across our earth, our Mother, once again.

Raised as I was at the latter end of those first years of survival and recovery it was inevitable that the evidence of the old life, and its terrible demise, should still be all about us. Inevitable too that amongst us boys, as we approached puberty, there should be a desire to leave the sanctuary of these uplands and risk the journey alone down through the abandoned valleys to prove ourselves by venturing into some ruined town or city and there recover a trophy to mark our passage into manhood.

Usually it was some shiny metal object we brought back, something both portable and durable, dangling about our necks or affixed to our arms. Brass coins were a great favourite for a time, then gold objects such as rings if any could be found that had not been too burnt in the destruction to be usable. Then, as I approached my own time, there was a vogue for the great ball bearings that may be found in broken machinery, and once helped its parts to turn.

Soon after this, in the year before I myself set off, the trophies became more subtle than part of a machine. One boy-man, a friend of mine, brought back a silver watch, quite large, mechanical, golden inside, which ticked and told the time. It dangled from his belt and I envied it. Another had found a cellar full of old things well-stored and in good condition, part of a place that sold 'antiques' as he deduced, and he brought back what pleased him most: not rings or gems, or watches, but a pair of silver clippers, for cutting hair. Perfect to hold. Practical. Desired by the girls and so making him desirable. What might I find to rival that? I had no idea.

There were real dangers in these exploits – from the tribeless vagrants who wandered across Europe at that time, mostly remnants of the believers in Christ. Their cruelty was well known, and the tortures they imposed upon the followers of Wulf were savage, and diabolic in their vileness. It was better to kill yourself, it seemed, than fall into their evil hands.

There was danger too from the packs of feral dogs and other creatures that roamed the urban ruins, whose forebears had escaped the final conflagration and spawned their violent offspring into new life and survival.

There were dangers also within the urban ruins themselves, or along what had once been roads and fields, where long-dead combatants had left a legacy of undetonated bombs, crumbling buildings, treacherous slurry-filled holes, and minefields – the killing debris of an unfinished war and an unmade peace.

Elsewhere – so the elders warned us – were different hazards, which had to do with darker places of reality and of the Otherworlds into which inexperienced male adolescents, trying to prove themselves, sometimes stray and get lost. Little wonder that some of us ventured forth and never came back.

Yet to us growing boys, lying in the long grass of summer, and gazing through the heat-haze to the valleys below, or across to the twists and shimmers of the River Rhine on the far horizon, though these dangers seemed real enough, they were never so fearful that they made us doubt the need to set off alone, and find our trophies, and ourselves; or worry that we might not come back. The danger, the conquering of the fear we felt, was the whole point.

Which our fathers understood very well, marking the time of our puberty with invocations to Klimt's two mortal sons, Solar and Lunar, that the strength of each might be with us when we ventured forth, and knowledge of their weakness too, for we must ever be like wolves and temper our courage with prudence, our pride with compassion, our selfish ambitions with responsibility to our tribe, which was our pack.

When my own time came my mother asked that one of the elders might conduct such a ceremony and invocation for me, for I had no father, nor had she told me who he really was. I often imagined him returning home, and sometimes in the flickering darkness beyond the edge of our circle about the campfire, or in the deeper and more threatening dark beyond our stockade, I fancied that he was there, watching over us, ready to hold me in his arms and help and protect me, for which I had always longed, for which my mother longed.

I did not then know that my father had been Jakob Wald, the first who ran with wolves, the first to journey with the Wolves of Time. Nor did I even guess how important he was to those elders who knew the truth, whose tribe he had helped found; not even when, as the elder helped my mother with the rites of my passage towards manhood, all the others came to listen and to watch, far more than was usual, as if a moment of importance for the whole tribe was happening and needed witnesses. Was I not just another boy whose time had come? In those moments of ritual farewell I knew I was not.

My mother's embrace ended that tribal moment, and as her arms encircled me, and I felt the sweet press of her body to mine, and felt as well the pang of knowing it could never be quite the same again for soon I would leave and come back changed – if come back I did – I knew for certain that whoever he was my father was near and watching, he was there.

I left that dawn, slipping out of the stockade through grass made wet with autumn dew, and began the long journey downslope towards the alien valleys, to find my courage and prove myself; and to bring back a trophy as proof of what I had done.

When I looked back one last time before disappearing into the lowland glades, I saw my mother standing there. Then something more; *him*, or his shadow. For across the fell, in the half-light of dawn, I saw what seemed the running of a wolf, and felt it was propitious, and knew who my guide would be.

'Wulf help me!' I whispered, murmuring the simplest prayer; 'Oh my god, help me!' Just as Klimt had done when he first undertook his journey to the Heartland.

Of that first journey I have spoken many times, and written as well, that others may have some signs and signals along the way when they dare venture forth at last. Such tellings and re-tellings cannot make a boy a man, or a girl a woman, or a frightened person cast off their fear; but they can be a comfort and a companion, a helping hand along the way.

So . . . I journeyed downslope into my own fears and weaknesses, and as I dared confront them, and experienced them, it seemed I took upon myself something of the fallen majesty of the Mennen, which lay all about me, and the Mennen's risen evil, which in those days was still unavoidable.

The tatters of a man's clothes may cling to his rotting bones for fifty years, and still give the semblance of life; a child's cot may still stand where it stood on a floor ten feet up, before half the walls and all the child were blown away.

Though eighty people may have been shot and torched in the corner of a stadium, where only rabbits and rats run among the weeds, the evidence of their dying lives on still in a scatter of mouldering skulls drenched in rain; and some rusting metal that may once have been a flamethrower.

Standing there, a boy from the Schwarzwald feels despair and fear; and turning, startled, he may wonder what it was that had seemed to move across the ruined running tracks and up among the stands, silhouetted by a crumbling entrance, beyond which is the white sky.

That boy is wise to move on quickly, wolflike, finding cover, stopping still, seeking out the danger, moving away from it to find a point of vantage. In doing which that boy discovers he has learnt the techniques of survival, but cannot yet be sure that he will survive.

In two months of journeying through villages and towns, and finally to Freiburg and its forgotten stadium, I found trophies enough: coins of corroded copper and silver, and misshapen rings of gold, one melted into a knuckle bone, which I kept as a reminder of what had been. But I found no trophy that spoke to me; nor the one I felt sure was waiting if only I could find it, and know it for what it was.

So I took the first perfect ring I found, a thick band of gold so big it fitted round my thumb, and knew it would do if I could find nothing better. I was ready to go back, and could return with honour, except that . . . whatever it was I really sought I had not found.

But winter was advancing down the Rhine valley all the way from the Alps, with long bitter nights and foul weather, and feral dogs were coming down from the hills and bothering me. Two or three, even as many as six, and a man with a staff and his knife, who has been taught how to use them, and keeps a retreat or escape route always in his sight, is safe enough.

But then, quite suddenly, even before I knew they had been tracking me, the vagrants came, and found me. They were as cunning at concealment in the ruins as I was in the hills and forest, for they had learnt to skulk like rats, hiding and biding their moment.

There followed a strange and dangerous hunt, they after me and I, in a foolish way, after them. I was cornered only once and killed what I thought was a man from his soiled face and rags, but he turned out to be no more than a boy like me. Not only was he a vagrant but it seemed he was a Christian, for he had a wooden cross about his neck. I pitied him a little more when I saw that his blood was as red as mine, and in his last whimpers of pain and death he tried to cling to me as if I were his brother. I vowed never, ever to kill a man again, Christian or not.

But I did not escape for long. A pack of dogs cornered me, and gave me scars I carry still; and an illness of sweating and diarrhoea made me linger in the ruins longer than I wished, long enough for the vagrants to catch up with me again. Yet my fear was overridden by the lingering sense that I still had not found what I knew was there, my trophy.

Then the tracking of me began in earnest, by vagrants and their dogs; allies, family, tribe of the boy I killed.

Ill as I was I tried now to get out of the city and back to the hills I could see – now receiving their first powdering of snow – but they prevented me, forcing me to turn inward, away from escape, familiar ground and all external help, in towards the broken centre of the city, in towards myself.

Desperate, fugitive, I found cellars and tunnels to survive in. Below ground and in darkness, using the streams and rivers in the broken sewers to cover my tracks and give me sustenance, I began to discover my deepest fears, and call for the help of the father I never knew. I began to wonder if I would ever reach the hills again, and the forest-lands above them, or hear the howling of the Wolves.

In the fear and the filth of hiding and skulking, the killing of rats for food with my bare hands and teeth, the too-hurried washing of my body, the slow decline into my own stench and fatigue, I discovered that my rite of passage was not quite the fine and noble thing I had dreamed of so romantically as a boy in the hills, gazing into this valley, this place that was really a fugitive's hell. But though I was a boy no more, I was not yet a man, and the vagrants and the dogs were showing me the depth of my inadequacies.

Finally, foolishly weakening to the desire for light and fresh air, I emerged for a moment from Wulf knows what subterranean passage-way, tired, bewildered and confused, beginning to despair. There my pursuers cornered me, and cut off my retreat back underground.

Four men and a woman, probably the mother of the boy I had killed, all armed, and at their heels a pack of dogs, growling and baring teeth, awaiting orders. Though I felt that final weakening and relief that precedes the act of surrender, I dodged them and ran off a little way, telling myself as I did so that perhaps death by dog might be better than the tortures the vagrants inflicted on those they caught, better, better, bett . . . and I felt myself fall down; I turned, and saw the baying, barking dogs rush round a corner after me, their filthy masters not far behind, laughing and gesticulating as the first dog slowed, lowered his head, and bared his teeth preparatory to beginning the attack.

'Wulf!' I began to cry, for I could no longer help myself, 'Wulf . . . father . . .'

He came then out of the shadows, the wolf I had seen when I left our stockade, who I had known would be my guide, and he took up a stance between the dog and me. He stood as solid and as huge as a rock, a dark wolf, the slow in—out of his breath telling of his calm, his composure, his lack of fear. His scent was of forests and mountain winds.

One of the dogs barked and the wolf growled in reply, lowering his head just slightly. The dogs whined in response and looked abject, tails dropping in submission, while the vagrants, who had halted abruptly, their laughter cracking in their throats, their mocking ges-tures changing to defensiveness, stared in surprise and fear, as if they faced not one wolf but an entire pack.

Then one by one they retreated, muttering and glancing at each other, until with a whistle or two, and low urgent shouts, they commanded the dogs to follow them. Whether or not these folk worshipped the Christian god I did not truly know, but it was Wulf, and his representative, they feared.

I got up, the remnants of my fear and final abjection giving way to awe. I had never been so close to a wolf, nor dared believe what I had always felt, that Wulf *was* close to me, and so was my father too.

I began to shake, and then to cry, a mere boy again, and the wolf turned to gaze at me. As I passed through the amber light of his eyes, so great and good, and undertook the journey he led me on, I first reached the farther side of fear, and had a glimpse, or a brief taste, of the freedom that lay beyond. I had found not an external trophy but internal knowledge, and I knew from that moment that my way would be the shaman's, and to the Otherworlds.

How long I journeyed thus I do not know but finally, safe now, I came back to my daily self and moved off another way, to sleep in the shadows of sunlight, the dreamful sleep of the journeyer into one of the Otherworlds.

I woke once more, in no hurry now to leave, though knowing I would do so soon, and my wolf-protector shadowed me. While further off across the ruins, their dogs whining in their wake, the vagrants moved on and made their escape from Wulf.

It was in the course of the afternoon that followed, when I wandered half-waking and half in my dreams, that I saw the corner of what seemed a metal box glinting from out of the fresh rubble of a building's recent further collapse. I dug, and dug some more, my wolf guide watching with what I imagined was approval, and uncovered not a box but some drawers of the kind I know now were once to be found in offices, not homes.

The drawers were not much rusted, though their grey paint was bubbled and corroded, and the parts that had once been silver were now green. Plainly, the drawers had been well protected for decades past and now Wulf had let them come to light that I might find whatever was within. I forced the drawers and found inside something the like of which I had never seen before. Better than coins or rings, ball bearings or silver watches that ticked. Better even than hair clippers that attracted the girls. It was wrapped in clear plastic, taped, dry, clean; I was not sure what it was. It was not much bigger than two hands, thin, neither light nor heavy.

I opened it fearfully, as if it might be a mine or bomb, though really I knew it was not. The wolf had guided me to it and Wulf was with me, and my father too. I removed the plastic carefully and there it was, a tarnished metal oval with a handle, a mirror encased in silver that was now black. The mirror was startling in its clarity and it seemed to showed me my face more clearly than I had ever seen it in the metal mirrors that we normally used.

Certainly I had seen glass mirrors before, but most were broken, and always the silvering was puckered and peeling. This was as crystal-clear as seeing trees against morning sky after a night of cleansing rain.

Squatting on the ground with ruins all about, recently starved, and having lived with fear for long days past, I should not perhaps have been astonished at the face that peered out at me. But I was.

It was no longer a boy, but a man. It was something more: it was the face of *the* Mann, as I knew it from my mother's treasured photograph. I was no longer the me I thought I was. I looked like I had a past, and thereby I found the beginnings of a future. For in that moment I not only found the object that would be the trophy that bore witness to my rite of passage into adulthood, I also began my long apprenticeship as a shaman. That mirror showed me the image of a man upon a journey, and gave me such a potent vision into self and time that I have pursued it ever since.

I remained there for a time, utterly still, holding the mirror and thinking about what it was I saw. I felt it had been wrapped up and put in a place of safe-keeping for me decades before. I would not have been surprised to find a label attached to the mirror's handle reading, 'For Matthius, son of Jakob Wald.'

The wolf came back to me. His eyes transfixed me, commanded me to rise and leave now, to journey on, journey back, journey home, to begin my studies as a shaman.

My trophy I took with me, this perfect mirror which survived through the decades before the holocaust, then during it; I took it, this journeyer.

With it safely stowed in the rucksack on my back I followed whoever guided me; Wulf, or the footsteps and shadows of my father, or the Wolves of Time, and was ready to begin my journey home, and from there, one distant day, on to the WulfRock itself and my wolfway to the stars.

The wolf paused briefly before we went, shapeshifting for a moment into a Mann, my father, that I might know who my guide was, and that I could trust the way he led.

I seemed to see myself.

A Youth

My father, who was *the* Mann, the adversary of Huntermann, was born in 1970 in Rinteln, a farming town in the northern part of what was then West Germany.

Rinteln lies in the valley of the River Weser, and the area was then well-wooded, with bridle paths and older forested ways running up into the Wesergebirge which, with the Teutoburger hills, form the uplands that reach out north-westwards into the North European Plain.

Jakob's father was the bailiff of the largest local livestock estate, his mother a teacher in the local *Volkschule*. He had an older brother, Hans, to whom he was very close, who was killed in a farming accident when Jakob was eleven.

The rural location of his home, the deep woods and accessible hills, the powerful River Weser and its shadowed depths, where trout swam and pike lurked, formed the serene backcloth of Jakob's childhood days and wanderings; the drama of a livestock farm, in the days when a pair of carthorses still trod the dung heap in the main yard, and sows were mated by dangerous boars prodded on to their work by men with pitchforks, was the daily foreground.

Perhaps his father, who had served as a middle-ranking clerk in the German Army, and now helped with the day-to-day management of the estate with great efficiency, gave Jakob an early liking for order, and the persistence to carry his schemes through; his mother, a dark, round-faced Bavarian girl with bright eyes and a love of country song and dance, inculcated him with dreams of the Tyrolean hills she always missed, and the mysteries and dangers of the Austrian mountains beyond. Their annual pilgrimage south, to his mother's family's cottage in the hills, was a time of cousins and laughter, of long tramps and late nights listening, with Hans in the bunk above, to the adults singing, and sometimes later still to the sounds of their parents making love.

But after Hans's death, from the summer of 1981 the bunk above was empty, never to be occupied again by the one Jakob had so admired and loved. Jakob began now to take to the hills above the chalet, ascending as far as the snow to sit in the shadows and weep, and rage, watched by the marmots, stock-still but for their blinks, and the chamois, all overflown by eagles; discovering only weeks later the ending of his tears in the raindrops that shone in edelweiss, whose star-like petals sometimes seemed a world, one that rose to become stars at twilight, and fell back to earth at the cries of his anxious parents.

'Jakob! Jakob!'

That summer, and the next few that followed, my father explored the mountains further still, always alone, walking and hiking and never climbing or skiing, which did not interest him. He liked the feel of his feet upon the ground, with as few props and supports as possible. He became what many never become – an adept in the hills, able to find his way about by day and night, self-dependent, glorying in those moments of sudden revelation in solitude, when a storm drives past across the fell, or the sun catches the flanks of the chamois, and the green of the moss by a stream is the very brightness of life itself.

He began to see that he could never again be far from mountains, or live without hope that he might very soon journey among them again; or imagine a world where the creatures that roamed so free about him should be considered less than man. Why, they knew so much more than he did.

As the end of his schooldays approached, the decision about what he should study at college had to be made; he found himself caught between farm management, which Hans would have done and his father wanted him to study, and zoology, for which he had a natural gift, and which his mother was inclined to think might suit him better.

Unable to choose between the practical good sense of his father's advice and the instincts of his mother and himself, he decided to defer the decision for a year. Using his savings from holiday jobs about the farm to buy a small motorcycle, he took a year out to travel in Europe and North America.

It was during those months of his first journeying that my father came across the teachings of wise men and women other than Christians, and though the details of his journeys and the names of those he met are now nearly all lost, he revisited them through the story of the Wolves of Time. Certainly he lived for a time with shamans in Lapland, and later received teachings from elders of the Squamish tribe in British Columbia, the words of whose honorary chief Dan George my father learnt by heart and taught to my mother, that one day she might teach them to me.

I remember her doing so, and telling me that when my father was in Canada he was moved to hear how on the occasion of that country's one hundredth birthday – a white man's celebration – Chief Dan George told an audience in Vancouver: 'Canada . . . I have known you when your forests were mine; when they gave me my meat and my clothing. I have known you in your streams and rivers where your fish flashed and danced in the sun, where the waters said "Come, come and eat of my abundance." I have known you in the freedom of your winds. And my spirit, like the winds, once roamed your good lands.

'But in the hundred years since the white man came, I have seen my freedom disappear like the salmon going mysteriously out to sea. The white man's strange customs, which I could not understand, pressed down upon me until I could no longer breathe. When I fought to protect my land and my home I was called a savage. When I neither understood nor welcomed this way of life, I was called lazy. When I tried to rule my people, I was stripped of my authority. Oh God in heaven! Give me back the courage of the olden Chiefs . . .'

My father's journey through that long year of his youth was like my own, when I went in search of an easy trophy and took up something that proved much harder than coins to carry and keep hold of. He took to heart the words the wise men spoke and the teachings he received, understanding that though he himself might be called 'white man', he was Indian too, or Lappish, or aboriginal.

Just as the Squamish Chief played with time, and saw himself as all the Chiefs that had been, and their journey his own and continuing, so my father began to understand the tragedy of the European lands in which he was raised, and the possibilities. The shamans taught him that the salmon might come back, and abundance with them; the olden Chiefs, that he was of them too, however sullied the history of his race might be; and that the earth, our mother, had not died, not even through the Dark Millennium, and that her wounds were not yet mortal if the life she had made could learn again to give life back to her.

At the time of my father's first journey to meet the Nordic gods, and hear the shamans and elders of the northern lands, he seemed to be doing no more than following the interests and fashions of many young travellers at the time. It was just that while most in those days made their way to the ashrams of gurus in India, it was to the huts and tipis of Nordic and North American shamans he felt his heart drawn.

But it was not only to wise people that he went, but to wise places too, or places of power where he first felt the spirits of our ancestors calling to him, the whispering of wind, and cries out of silence.

My mother said that of all the places he went, two stood out, seeming to reach into his heart and soul, giving him that same sense out of which Chief Dan George spoke, which is that we are the incarnation of people past, and the land lives on, whispering its history and warnings to us, and its wisdom too, if only we can hear.

Both places reappear in that part of *Wolves of Time* he was able to complete. The first is the forest of Bialowieza on the boundary of what was once Poland and Russia, to where we too must soon go . . .

The second was Oradour, in central France, to where we shall go first. For it was in Oradour that my father's young-man's journey came to an abrupt end in early summer 1990 when he was forced to confront the darkness at the very heart of his own nation's past.

In Oradour, where he paid his money like any other wondering tourist, entered through the gates into that closed and infamously ruined village, and began the slow, curved ascent into its very heart, which was a portal for him, as for all the Mennen of Europe, into that war, that ruin, that final conflagration yet to come.

A few yards into the village, with the church's blackened tower just coming into view, he paused for a moment to stare at the simple word the French Government had ordered should be inscribed upon a board, and erected after the war, to stand for ever, or until the last stone of that place should crumble, and Oradour be no more: SILENCE.

Oradour

My father's war was yet to come, and he would be over forty when it did, but in Oradour-sur-Glane he had his first sight and smell of what war might be, and first began to hear its screams, and know its clinging odours too.

On 9 June 1944, the 2nd Panzer Division of the German Army

arrived at St-Junien, a village some twelve kilometres from Oradour. It was on its way north, to add strength to German defences along the Normandy coast.

Afterwards nobody was able to give a good reason why, not even at the official enquiry, but on the morning of June the tenth, a detachment from the Panzer Division, the 3rd Company of the 1st SS Regiment, arrived at Oradour. The reason was probably that the Germans had suffered French mockery on the way from the south, and some of their men had been attacked.

On arriving at Oradour the German soldiers, led by Commander Dickman, aided by Captain Kahn and Lieutenant Barth, rounded up the village's entire population of 642 people and held them on the Champ de Foire, the village square. There were 197 men, 240 women, and 205 children.

Some said it was just an identity check, others something else, but only one then acted on his fear that what was about to happen might be something worse than a mere checking of names: something so terrible, so final, that a whole nation would be shocked when they knew what happened in the hours following.

The solitary doubter was eight-year-old Roger Godfrin, an evacuee from Lorraine, which was near enough to Germany, and other horrors, that he had been warned that if ever the Nazis came he was to hide himself at once. He hid himself away when the summons to the Champ de Foire came, and was the only one of the 205 schoolchildren to survive.

Once in the village square the men were separated from the women and children, who were marched off to the church and confined within, and the door locked. Meanwhile the men were divided into smaller and more manageable groups and marched off to three barns – named Bouchoule, Milord and Laudy – two garages, a wine warehouse, and a shed. Amidst the mounting fear life struggled to go on. Monsieur Compain, one of the town's *pâtissiers*, asked one of the soldiers if he might go and remove some cakes from the bakery's oven, lest they burn.

'Ne t'inquiète pas . . .' said the soldier in strongly accented French, 'don't worry . . .'

But worry Monsieur Compain did . . .

After hours of waiting and the shifting of feet, and the buzz of flies, and a hundred thousand glances at the impassive faces of the German soldiers, and the silent decision by some as to what they must do if they were to survive the hail of bullets that might soon come, there was a sudden explosion from one of the streets. It was the signal all the soldiers watching over their various prisoners had waited for.

Without a moment's pause they trained their machine guns on the groups of men and fired, and immediately raked the fallen and falling men with more fire. Then, as the shocked screams and shouts began to die, as bodies moved over others that lay still, the soldiers walked among the dead and finished off the living with shots to head and body.

Yet even then some survived, and from them the world learned what had happened. The soldiers in the Laudy barn were less efficient than those elsewhere, or they had a bigger group of men to shoot: the victims fell and five men found themselves still alive, and not so badly wounded that they could not crawl away one by one in the barn's gloom, first into some adjacent stables, and then through other outbuildings.

The last out was Robert Hebras who made his way to a little yard a few steps away and there found four others: Marcel Darthout, Yvon Roby, Clement Broussaudier and Matthieu Borie. As they lay there wondering what to do they heard the sounds of more shooting, and then of repeated explosions, and the acrid smell of burning drifted into their grubby sanctuary.

They waited and watched, and when the only two patrolling soldiers they could see were not looking, with the whole helping the wounded they fled out of the village into nearby fields whose contours they knew well, for they had played there as children, just as their own children recently had.

Those children were now in the church, along with their mothers, their aunts, their sisters, their grandmothers, their cousins. Soon after the shooting began outside the church doors were opened and two soldiers silently hurried in carrying a large wooden box from which several fuses trailed; they placed it near the altar. The box looked heavy, and smelt of kerosene.

The soldiers lit the fuses and ran back to the doors, which were opened for them; once they were safely outside, the doors were slammed shut by their companions, and locked.

Seconds later there was an explosion and 240 women and 205 children began to die, some killed by debris, some bleeding to death from their wounds, many burnt by the kerosene flames, all screaming, all panicking, the children crying, clinging, or shocked into stillness.

A group of women broke down the vestry door but the Germans

had thought of that and were ready with machine guns at the windows, raking those trying to escape the fire with a storm of bullets. Those that survived this second assault fled back into the thick smoke and flames, and such as still lived saw the church doors open and men standing there, shooting at them too . . .

Yet even from this hell there was a survivor, just one. A Madame Rouffanche, her two daughters and grandson already dead in the church, found her way to the back of the altar and from there was able to climb up to one of the three windows that pierced the thick walls behind it. Though badly wounded, she clambered up, crawled through, and tumbled into the vegetation beneath.

Another mother, her child in her arms, saw her and followed and called out to Madame Rouffanche to catch her child; but her desperate shouting only attracted attention, gunfire shattered into the windows and the mother and child fell to the ground, already dead. Madame Rouffanche crawled away round the corner of the church and into the presbytery garden and laid herself down, shielded by rows of peas.

Drifting in and out of consciousness she heard soldiers killing their last victims, and their colleagues systematically destroying Oradour with explosives and incendiaries; she heard the soldiers drinking and laughing in the two houses they had left unharmed and intact – probably because their cellars were well stocked with wine.

A few yards behind Madame Rouffanche the church burned on, the holy statue of St Bernadette and the altars of St Joseph and St Anne utterly destroyed by the fierceness of the fire, while the sacristy collapsed and took its burden of shot and burnt corpses into the crypt below.

At 7.30 p.m. that evening, with smoke rising into the darkening skies, the tram from Limoges reached the nearby bridge over the River Glane where it was halted. Those from Oradour were separated and kept waiting by a barn wall, guns trained on them, while the others were sent back to Limoges.

For two and a half hours the returning villagers waited, not knowing what had happened, but certain they were to be shot. But at ten o'clock they were freed and told to find accommodation elsewhere: no one was allowed into Oradour.

The Germans' evening continued into the night, the wild, drunken night of men who have done and seen things no human being can without a madness coming into them. Finally, in the early morning, having set ablaze the two houses that had been the venue for their partying, the men of the SS Regiment left, and the silence before a June dawn fell over the ruined village.

Within minutes of first light, with the Germans gone, surviving villagers, including Robert Hebras who had escaped from Laudy barn, dared venture into what had been their home and source of life, leaving lookouts posted lest the Germans returned.

The horrors they found were beyond belief, sights beyond imagining: their church destroyed; streets of houses roof-less, door-less, window-less; the Renault garage, its little stock of cars burnt out; ruined barns, the hay still smouldering; the bakery, its ovens destroyed and Monsieur Copain's cakes mere scraps of cinder, yet still recognizable as *gougères*, *éclairs*, and *jalousies*, his sweet ones, which the children always liked.

While in barn and house, street and church, the survivors ran back and forth, the hell that had been their less fortunate fellow-villagers' pyre hours before, now burning into their memories for evermore, to be repeated, re-told, re-enacted, never exorcized.

By a quirk of fire and flame one man, searching the church, saw his wife and one of her relatives seeming still intact, unhurt, alive though covered in fine ash, their arms entwined. He hurried forward to seize his wife's shoulder and it crumbled in his hands, dust. While the wooden confessional, tucked away in a corner of the church, showed no sign of the flames at all. But on opening its latticed doors the searcher found two little children, holding hands and standing upright, both shot, both dead.

Only when the survivors, shocked and crazed by what they found and kept on finding, searched about the presbytery did they finally hear the weak and dying cries of Madame Rouffanche, sole survivor and witness of the massacre in the church.

Then the bodies, and parts of bodies, in sheets, in curtains, on burnt doors, on shutters, row after row; and the visitors; and the enquiries; and the excuses in the cold light of another day, one after another, for outrages Mennen have always committed; and the photographers; and the survivors to whose doors people beat a path in the years and decades ahead and listened to a tale that needed no embellishment, nor much comment, except for sighs and a head shaken in disbelief.

Souviens-toi, read the notices the French Government later put up; REMEMBER.

While with a simplicity that stood in stark contrast to the complexity of what seemed to have happened, and its aftermath, the President of France, General de Gaulle, later stood in the village cemetery, before the memorial to those murdered by *les monstres*, and decreed that Oradour-sur-Glane should be left just as it was, untouched, ruined, for ever, or until its last stone crumbled into dust.

There were other town and village massacres at that time: Lidice, Czechoslovakia, June 1942, 476 victims; Marzobotto, Italy, September to October 1944, 1836 victims; Distomon, Greece, June 1944, 239 victims; Maille, France, August 1944, 126 victims; and others, many others yet to come in other continents in the years ahead.

But for the student Jakob Wald, Oradour was the first massacre, the first taste of a cruelty that always seems irrational and aberrant, and surely never likely to happen again, until it does; and as the first, its sight and memory, the story of its victims, burnt into his heart and soul as surely as they burnt into the hearts of the first people to get back into the village that June in 1944. He stood finally quite still, staring in silence, shocked, and was ashamed to be a German, ashamed to be a man, knowing at last the void into which Mennen could fall.

Finally, a bell tolling to mark the closing of the gates, Wald walked down the village street towards the bridge over the River Glane where he had left his beloved motorcycle.

He did not pause to stare at the water's flow, nor turn to go to his machine, but carried on walking, leaving it and all the little valuables and souvenirs he had collected on his first travels just where they were. He walked on through the night, on into the dawn, sleeping in a ditch on the far side of Limoges only when he could finally walk no further.

Wald later counted his long walk home as his first shamanic walk, if not as a true shaman then as a novitiate and a seeker after truth. On this extraordinary walk, he crossed the High Causses of the Auvergne's limestone country – later the location he gave as the home territory of Lounel, the most mystic of the Wolves of Time – and from there travelled by way of the Rhone Valley up into the Jura Mountains, where he lingered for a time, living rough.

Something finally moved him on and took him to the Upper Rhine Valley, and thence, evading all crossing and custom points by way of higher ground, he reached that part of Germany that became his *Alma Mater*, the place to which much later, with Europe in chaos and the final wars of the years of 2011–2013 in progress, he retreated and helped found the Feldberg Volk: the Black Forest.

Here too he lived rough, avoiding contact with anybody who came near, living like an animal that fears all other life: living out some angst that the experience of Oradour had provoked within him, hiding himself in the forest deeps, studying the birds and animals, lying for days upon the ground to watch the great red forest ants at work and finding in them a model of new order out of the chaos of his mind.

Then, self-healed, changed, his pre-university travels done, he began the final part of his trek home, to a different chaos. The police picked him up on the *Autobahn* outside Stuttgart and hauled him off into custody. He was, it seemed, a 'missing person', and his parents were summoned to identify him, since his documents were long gone.

Not so his once-beloved motorcycle, his souvenirs, the material things he had tried to leave behind – the French police had the bike and all else, traced his parents' home, raised the alarm, put out calls requesting that he contact home, and finally sent his things ahead of him back to Rinteln.

His mother's relief that he was still alive confronted his father's anger at his poor explanations – 'A massacre? Do you think the French never did the same? Or the English? As for . . .' – and his gentle mother won. He wept for Oradour in her arms, a man weeping with a child's abandon, and saw a vision of two small boys, terrified and hand-in-hand, hiding in a confessional as bullets ricocheted about, and punished them with death.

God is dead, the Christian God does not exist.

It was then that Jakob Wald decided to turn to animals and study zoology, and he knew already that it would be but a stage upon a journey whose destination was still unknown.

Huntermann

First and foremost Huntermann was a survivor; the rest was always secondary to that. Those who thought they had finally seen the last of him – then, and later, even now perhaps – will do well to remember it.

Huntermann was born of Ruthenian stock in Uzghorod, the capital of the obscure Transcarpathian province which lies at the mountainous south-western part of the Ukraine. His birth-name is unknown, and his first recorded name merely a nickname: Bozgor, a Romanian term of abuse meaning a bastard without a homeland, usually used of Hungarians. A bastard without a home; perhaps it is the best description possible of the nature of Huntermann and what he finally became.

The Ruthenians were an east-Slavonic people who lived in the Carpathian mountains and never had a state of their own. Their 'state' was that extraordinary nexus of forested mountains and foothills that is formed by the mountain borders of five states – the Ukraine, Romania, Hungary, Slovakia and Poland – in all of which groups of Ruthenians live.

They had no truly common literary language, most speaking the language of their adopted country intermingled with a common east-Slav dialect; the more intelligent spoke several languages.

Huntermann was not raised in Uzghorod itself, where his parents lived, but by one set of his grandparents in an obscure Carpathian village, surrounded by mountains, lost in pine forests, secretive, parochial, and even in the seventies, when he was growing up, without electricity, piped water, television, supermarkets, metalled roads.

But for his real education, and a creation of a view of the world that would inform all he later did, Huntermann had two tutors: one was his grandmother, a German raped and abducted by his Ruthenian grandfather in a raid out of the mountains on a small colony of Germans who lived in Bukovina – a tale enjoyed and embellished by the grandmother herself.

'After all,' she would say with a shrug, her eyes still filled with gratified desire fifty years on, 'if he had not taken me the Russians would have done so a few years later and I would have been killed and your father never born.' She taught him the fluidity of history, and something of its repetitions, and of Hitler, of whom she spoke with pride; and she taught him German, of a curious sing-song kind which, married to his other languages and accents, meant that he could pass for almost anything.

His second 'tutor' was the country, the forests and mountains in which he grew up, warm and gay in the summer, freezing cold in the winter. So cold indeed that his grandfather would test the safety of a winter's day for his grandson by spitting from the back door at the frozen ground outside. When the spittle reached the ground, and cracked into fogged icy splinters, it was all right to go out, provided he had a fur hat on; when it got no further than a gob on the mouth, freezing fast even as it dribbled on a stubbly chin, the boy stayed in and helped grandma with the chores as she talked, and taught him all she knew.

But the forest was his true teacher, and the wolves therein were the teacher's reluctant assistants, for the boy learned to follow them, and know their ways, and control the fear and superstition the other villagers, including his grandparents, felt for them.

Control, not conquer, the fear he always felt. The wolves looked at him with eyes that were less clouded than his own, with neither liking nor dislike, but with indifference. He fancied the wolves felt superior, and *that* he could not stand. So he controlled his fear, and nurtured a hatred for the quiet efficiency of their ways, and their communal howling, and for their life in a community of trust such as he, a human, did not know.

The boy learnt to trap and hunt, and found a thrill in outwitting any living creature that crossed his path, or whose path he crossed. His knowledge of the Forest, and its rivers, and the mountain heights above – of flesh and fish and fowl – was as great as any village man's and his stocky certainty was something his peer group feared, less for his strength than for his utter ruthlessness. He never hesitated to hurt if hurting would win, nor to inflict further pain if his victim's submission lay that way; yet nor did he ever forget who his allies were, and to meet their needs that they might continue to serve him.

Along with other village boys he abused the life they found and learned to know: to make a whirling mill of a beetle, to have a race of crippled ants, to see if it was true that butterflies screamed if you burnt off their wings. Games, briefly played by boys who moved on to other and better things, who could see no point in continuing them.

Except Huntermann; on his secret forays into the forest deeps, he did continue them. He reduced to a science the art of cutting the legs off the huge forest ants so that the stronger crossed his notional finishing lines at the same time as the weaker. He established beyond doubt that butterflies do not scream, in any circumstances, however painful. He watched through a magnifying glass the final antennal movement of blackfly, long after their bodies were crushed.

In these small pursuits he found a greater pleasure, which was the thrill of control, of knowing as he held the sharp blade of his knife above a creature's leg that he could choose the moment when to make the cut, and so change life irrecoverably. Now? Now? *Now?*

Rooks did not scream either, rather they gave a curious, muted squawk.

Huntermann, just thirteen, enjoyed his first orgasm the day he cut the legs off a squawking rook and released it into the air, watching it flapping upward among the pine trunks, knowing it could never land.

A week later he drowned the boy they said had Jewish blood in the mill pond, and came again, this time in his Sunday best. After church, before a formal lunch, pants still wet, knowing what he had done, waiting for the cries, knowing they could not possibly guess it was him; and better still, knowing that they would not even ask the questions because everybody wanted the little bastard to be no more, seeing that he was stupid as well as being different from the rest. So stupid no one would doubt that he fell under the mill wheel of his own accord.

One night the following winter his grandmother extended his sexual education a little more. When Grandpa stayed up drinking too late in a neighbour's house to be able to get himself home, Grandma let her grandson share her for the night with the Alsatian dog. He enjoyed it, and learnt at last where the sighs he had heard many times before when Grandpa was not around came from, and how a dog shuddered to completion much like a wolf, and more than a man, though like a man he too soon fell asleep.

His grandfather sent him back to Uzghorod at fourteen to join his parents and find a better education in books. He was bright, and as ruthless in his studies as in all else, ruthless and quite unstoppable.

In 1984, as the Communist world was just beginning to show the signs of flagging before later disintegration, he reported his father to the police, for practice, and advantage. It worked for eighteen months until someone reported him and he faded out of town, back up into the mountains, and found them waiting there for him.

Mother was the traitor, grandfather indifferent, grandmother the saviour. Huntermann was sent up into the forest with directions to cross the Carpathians and seek out Ruthenian relatives on his father's side in Poland. Along the way, hunted by Slovakian police, he stumbled on a German community of the kind his mother had come from, and for a few days was safe. He betrayed them all but one, a young boy, and saved his own skin and that of his protégé and made off into the mountains again. The boy's real name is not recorded, but later, Huntermann's shadow and bodyguard, he was known as Schlitz, after the beer that Huntermann drank for a time.

Huntermann and Schlitz were the political and military wings of a

two-man outcast union of minor forgotten nations that would grow
like a cancer and conquer Europe.

Huntermann ended his schooling in Warsaw and moved on to college in Dresden, East Germany. Thence to Prague, with God knows
whose papers he had obtained by murder and extortion, and with
Schlitz always at his side. Engineering was his subject, student politics
his fascination – give him a committee and he could dominate it, give
him a group and he could lead it, give him an institution and he could
take it over.

Schlitz learnt his military skills in Yugoslavia, as it once was, as
Huntermann's spy; and by the nineties he, like his master, was prepared for the chaos that arose, and ready to move as the wolves began
to, from battlefield to killing ground, from front to front, border by
border, collecting contacts, taking control, amassing wealth and laun-
dering it all in the safer havens of Germany and France, and Spain,
though that was one language Huntermann did not enjoy. Too flowery
for him, the *rrr*'s too difficult, the gestures too feminine, the passions
too fragile: still, he could speak it well enough to deposit cash and
withdraw it and weave such a web of complex confusions behind him
that even had he left behind sufficient reason for others to wish to
follow him, they could not have done.

Homes in Bonn, in Brussels, and in Prague. Sudden absences; three
passports, one of which was Dutch; a marriage in Düsseldorf, the
child a cot death the same night Huntermann left again. The mother
later disappeared. Hunting trips in east Poland, fishing in Brazil, and
hunting for more human prey on an estate in Nigeria, to where an
arms deal took him; Schlitz ever at his side, and needed too, for a
man like Huntermann provoked hostility.

Then, after two years of quiescence cleaning up his past, in Prague,
in 1994, he formed the Nationalists' Alliance, which was all things to
every man who had ever felt angry that he had been dispossessed,
which one way or another might be anybody, east or west, north or
south. So it was, appealing to the aggressive envious nationalism that
corrupted so many at the end of what some have called the Dark
Millennium, the Huntermann the world now knows was born. A cancer
that would not stop growing until it destroyed the body that gave it
life, and so itself.

Though perhaps, had not Huntermann allied his party to the Christian cause, for what seemed sensible expediency, and changed its name
to the Nationalists' *Christian* Alliance, he and those who followed him

might possibly have survived. For Christ proved the false god he had been throughout that grim Millennium, and the cancer itself put a cancer in its own lungs.

Disintegration

The full horror and implications of the Neo-nationalist Christian Alliance's Crusade (as it was finally called) that Huntermann led from his Prague base and imposed upon Europe in the early years of the twenty-first century, and the decline into final anarchy and disintegration it presaged, were not generally recognized at the time.

When a few individuals like my father began to understand what was happening and tried to speak out, and to act within the old infrastructures of opinion and power, they were impotent – the populations of Europe were already broken and fragmented, their refugee peoples wandering in shock from pillar to post, from ruined house to charnel pit.

In truth, even had there still been a public widespread and general enough to form a view and an understanding of what had happened, and structures in place to do something about it, it was already too late. The destructive process begun by Huntermann, quite deliberately, had become irreversible, a spiralling down into a nightmare void of war and internecine feuding, of landscape degradation and ruination, of plagues and disease that ravaged fauna and flora, breaking the already fragile food chain so absolutely that by the years 2011–2013, as the old calendar had it, Europe's earth had become a hell for those who tried to live upon it.

In every city, every town, every village, it seemed, along every road and lane, within the confines of every house, every apartment, the horror was played out, its witnesses killed, or traumatized and set adrift.

In Paris, Köln, Dortmund, León, Amsterdam ... whole communities were wiped out in a flash of heat and atomic wind; the few survivors may be found still in compounds here and there, often blind, fingers welded to the palms of hands, teeth black and untended, their hoarse words a pathetic remembrance of a world completely lost, betraying their incomprehension of the long decades when they were the prey of hatred and superstition, herded and corralled, outcast with other unfortunates of those times.

In Stuttgart, in Stockholm, in Munich, Marseille and Madrid ... almost anywhere a person cares to name, or picks out at random from a torn and tattered atlas of that world gone by, women were raped, men mutilated, fathers forced to kill their sons, mothers to torture daughters, old men and women burnt by children, children forced ...

Worse still, and so widespread and general that these events went unremarked, usually in obscure places, the Oradours of the early twenty-first century began to take place ... and become worse as Huntermann increased the boldness of his terrorism, and gained access to nuclear power.

Amsterdam, April 2004, 3200 dead and over 15,000 injured; Toulouse, southern France, November 2004, 1432 dead, 745 of them in one school, and 8,000 injured; Venice, April 2005, the city half destroyed and 123,000 dead – and then the outrage that demonstrated that matters were out of control and led to a quickening of the breakdown into anarchy in so many other countries – the simultaneous mass destruction in Düsseldorf, Dortmund and Köln, at the heart of so much of Germany's industry and administration, not to mention the loss of life.

No wonder that the smaller massacres, the local feuds that were now fuelled into outright bloody confrontation, the resurrection of ancient hatreds and rivalries, the routine of rape and torture, of violence for its own sake, and the pitiful lines of refugees feeling this way and that and finding no respite anywhere – no wonder most of it is unrecorded and forgotten, save for the fields of bones, and the gaunt ruins that survived the holocaust.

A situation in which the wolves were able to expand once more, feeding on the Mennen corpses, and the livestock that roamed untended out of fields, and lumbered down the *Autobahnen* and *autostrade*, leading their lupine predators on, as herding beasts always do.

While my father, so deeply imbued with horrible memories of Oradour, whose job took him further afield than most and for a time gave him an immunity which politicians did not have because the claim to love animals is universal, saw for himself what the Huntermann creed meant. Yet though deep was the shock my father felt in those chaotic years of Europe's disintegration – the years before the Wolves came to guide him back to spiritual safety – he was to experience worse yet than these modern Oradours.

In the year 2009, not long before the final years of the anarchy, plagues and disease swept across Europe like poisonous death-dealing winds across a vast plain of dying people, finishing them off. Weakened by the stress and famine of those years, lost and wandering, their rivers polluted by their own dead, their foodstuffs lost to drought and flood, fire and fungal disease, and swarms of insects so numerous that whole fields crawled with them, the peoples of Europe succumbed to a neo-plague that first took hold in the Portuguese port of Lisbon, carried there by a refugee boat that drifted in from the west coast of Africa.

Perhaps it might have been contained had local doctors had the experience to recognize the nature of the disease they were dealing with, and the staff numbers and technical support they needed; and had that boat's few survivors stayed where they were, rather than stowing aboard ships that sailed south and east into the Mediterranean, and, in one case, northward and then along the north European seaboard to Rotterdam.

A pity the device that destroyed that great city in November 2010 did not explode five months earlier, for then the Ebola pandemic of that time might not have taken hold in those parts as it had already begun to do in Portugal.

As for the rest of the world, this too was ravaged and struggling, for Huntermann was not unique, and the brewing stew of trouble and evil in which he had been made and which he now began to dominate produced other gobbets and bits and morsels of perverse humanity as bad as he: their skins were a different colour, their first languages different too, their outward semblances different again, but inside, in their hearts and minds, in the vile morass of their thoughts, and in their greedy seeking after power and control, and their need to destroy that they might thrive, they were the same. Dark is dark wherever it is found, and light is light.

Those of my own generation were born just too late to remember those dark and terrible years, or to quite believe the tales their elders told; while those born later still, like my own children, cannot comprehend such foulness and evil, of which Huntermann was not the cause but the focus. Nor can they comprehend such dreadful suffering, when the world they see is made of small communities, living close to the land and nature once again, struggling and surviving with the aid of the spirits all about, and the knowledge that the Otherworld is here, that the Wolves are benign. Knowing also that men and women

– the Mennen once upon a time – are merely part of something greater and more lasting than themselves which it is their duty to honour, to nurture and to which must be given back something equal to what is taken if the Earth is to become whole and balanced once again.

In my father's time, when the tragedy of Huntermann's assumption of power in Eastern Europe had become manifest, and his final acts of folly were causing a complete disintegration of the infrastructures across all of Europe, events and personalities were still so fresh in the survivors' minds that they needed no explication in the tale he told. Perhaps, as well, he was then unwilling or unable to give any, so horrible had been his experiences, so revolted were those to whom the story of the Wolves was addressed, and who might follow the trails it blazed. A beaten child needs no reminder of the rod and fist to understand that the recent past might have a bearing on his future.

Today, with most of those to whom my father would have wished to tell his tale long dead – dying or killed before ever they knew of the Wolves of Time – there is a need to describe something of the background, unpleasant though the task will be. Even the foulness of Huntermann is beginning to be glossed over with myths that threaten to make a hero even of a creature such as he was, and the complications of the European wars that climaxed so cataclysmically through the years 2010–2013, as community after community, and people after people, declined and disappeared before the ravages of plagues unstoppable and revenge unthinkable, have been all but forgotten. Simplistic accounts are given of how the Eastern European states rose up, and how the fatted calves of old capitalism and debauched Christian democracy bloated and died as messily as the corpses that lay untended through the hot droughts of 2011, in city after city, village after village, refugee camp after camp . . .

Europe as it had been known died a rapid death in those years. Like a king rat fighting other vermin for dominance over a body their own attacks had killed, Huntermann survived, and seemed to triumph. Like an air-borne seed that is driven before the forest fires which have destroyed its parent plant, my father survived as well.

The one had all the militant Christian virtues of greed, power, weaponry, hypocrisy and self-righteousness to help him to a final victory.

The other found the Wolves of Time.

My Father's Legacy

My father, then, was Jakob Wald, the Mann in the stories of the Wolves of Time, the enemy of Huntermann . . .

We know that now, but he did not know it at the time. He was a Wanderer trying to find an order in the chaos about him, trying to find a way forward, following the vague hints and clues to a future not yet born.

He did not know that I would ever exist, to carry on his tale. He did not yet dare believe he would ever find the woman who would be my mother. He was a Wanderer in a world of chaos, and achingly alone. In seeking out the heartland of the wolves, he sought as well a heartland for himself, only slowly realizing where it might be, and that he must go to it to find himself.

It was near to Freiburg that he finally returned, to the uplands of the Black Forest, in whose dark depths he had found sanctuary and survival in the months of his turmoil and upset after the experience of Oradour.

Here in Feldberg, where I write these words.

But let me try to explain why the narrative of the Wolves of Time was so brutally interrupted, and why it is that I have now taken up the tale – and trail – which my father was forced to abandon, and to which he never returned.

Jakob Wald's only material legacies to me were the manuscript of the story whose words you have read, and a worn, oiled, leathern bag, drawn to with a knotted cord, which I left unopened, its contents undisturbed until last Longest Night, the winter solstice, which is at the heart of Samhain, our year's beginning, the coming of the dark; the night of the beginning of its end.

I kept these things which are my father's legacy to me for more than forty years until last year, which was Anno Lupi 61, the sixty-first year since the coming of the Wolves. By then, of course, I had come to understand that my father had been a shaman, the first of the modern age to dedicate himself to the Wolves, and that I too had been trained, without at first knowing it, in the shaman's arts.

It was a good many years before I realized that the bag my father left me was his crane bag[1] and a long while after that before I fully understood the significance of his leaving it for me, rather than carrying it with him on his last journey.

Finally, with all due ceremony, and with the elders of the tribe I serve about me, their journey drums sounding, whose pulse became the rhythm of my step, their urging the impulse of my waking dream, their call a singing to my soul, I opened up the crane bag that was his, and his last legacy to me.

The tooth of a wolf, a curl of hair, a child's, my own, his portal to this future; a broken stone, black-green, partly smoothed and striated by an ancient glacier's flow, partly broken and rough, from which the tundra's Nordic winds blew and flew, ruffling my hair even in my tent; a knuckle-bone from a deer's foot, his first kill probably, first offering to Wulf, that he might be as fleet of foot as the prey he took; and a rune text on brittle parchment, that told of past fruition, present harvest, and the need for future stillness: his legacy to me. So many riches for a man-child to receive, bound together by a father's care, and love.

There were two reasons why he left for his final journey to the Heartland before finishing his tale of the Wolves of Time. First, there was the practical imperative that if he had stayed here in the encampment amongst the trees that rise over an ancient river terrace above the Rhine near Freiburg – where I now write these words – the Mennen sent by Huntermann would have found and taken him, and finally killed him. He had escaped them twice already, and might not be so lucky a third time.

Second, to him perhaps more importantly, the Wolves had come for him, howling him back from the journey of the tale, that he might run with them towards an end brought forward from the future to a present that loomed darkly up about him then, and made him see that he must set forth as a Seeker at the WulfRock far sooner than he had thought.

So he was forced to leave his tale unfinished, embracing me for a

[1] The crane bag or shamanic pouch, which in Nordic countries is usually made of leather, is used by a shaman to carry objects of special personal significance to him or her. Such objects are imbued with magical energy and serve a shaman much as a bag of tools might serve a craftsman; but for a shaman each item in his crane bag will almost certainly represent a spiritual reference point, and a portal to the powers and secret places in the Otherworld – or worlds. For a shaman to deliberately leave his crane bag behind him, as Jakob Wald did, is of great significance, and means perhaps that he believes he is setting forth upon the final wolfway to the stars.

final time, and my mother too, and leaving behind the manuscript and crane bag as I have mentioned, that I might one day take them up and set forth on his final journey and complete it; complete it for those who have travelled with him and the Wolves from the beginning . . .

As it was he escaped with only moments to spare, having entrusted me to the care of my mother and the thickets nearby, offering up an invocation that the Wolves might leave one of their number to protect us after he had escaped, which they did. Now, these decades later, I take up the threads of his dream-journey with the Wolves with all due care and prudence, honouring his memory, and honouring the Wolves, dead and living, whose spirits animated his life and showed him the way to go.

Now, before I begin my own journey to the Heartland, in pursuit of the end of the Wolves' story and his own, let me repeat here the words he wrote before he left, which were words meant for me alone.

With these words, I, Jakob Wald of the Feldberg Volk, dwelling in the Black Forest above the Upper Rhine, in what was once called Germany, bequeath the story of the Wolves of Time to my son Matthius. My account is as I have journeyed it with the Wolves as my mentors and guides . . .

A slow, consuming darkness has beset our earth this past millennium. A thousand years of clearing, taming and contaminating the land we should have loved. Our fathers did it, their fathers before them, all our forefathers; and our foremothers too.

And the wolves are part of what we tried to kill, which was our first Mother, and our Father.

If you have known something of that shameful darkness, and felt it, then perhaps you too have wept real tears upon the breast of our poor desecrated land, and let the impoverished earth run through your trembling fingers in despair.

If you have known the dead silence of the forests of the North whose trees stand stiff and still where they were poisoned and slowly died a century past . . .

Oh, hold my hand while I remember what you may never see – the black waters of a thousand ruined lakes, and the birds that flock in hundreds and seek a resting-place where once thousands filled the skies with colour, flight and song.

If you have stood alone amidst a ruined city's manmade cliffs, and stared in horror along roads made too wide and long for

*feeling men, where now only the dry litter of last year's plants
journeys on the wind . . .*

If you . . .

Heuren Sie! *Listen now!*

*Even if you have let these things touch your heart and soul
but once, it will have been enough, for you will know that with
the coming of the Wolves of Time the earth which bore us showed
us at last that it had heard our cries, and knew our tears.*

The dying earth knew then that it might turn to us for help.

*You will know as well that the coming of the Wolves turned
the world a better way than we could ever do, to bring to us a
rising sun, whose rays begin to bathe the memories of the Dark
Millennium in light, and soothe them, and rid us of them; a sun
whose continuing warmth will ease the chill that has so long beset
our communal heart.*

*We, who were once so arrogant that we called ourselves wise,
sapient, Homo sapiens, are not men, nor women, nor human at
all.*

*Truly, we are what the Wolves of Time chose to call us, and
what the wolves call us still: Mennen, things without gender. I,
Jakob Wald, am a Mann. You, if you are a woman, are also a
Mann so far as the wolves are concerned; and believe me, they
do not often speak the word with much respect.*

Together we may call ourselves the Mennen.

*Dare not to call yourself human again who are the living link
with so much that brought betrayal and death to its source of
life.*

We are all Mennen, no more.

And I! I, too!

*Homo sapiens is dead; long live Lupus sapiens, wise wolf! For
the earth, our Mother and our Father, beginning then to die, sent
the Wolves of Time to save us, and to be our Gods.*

Well then . . .

*I am older now and have but one task left to complete before
I say farewell to this life, and seek out the wolfway to the stars
and the everlasting protection of our lupine gods: Wulf help me,
but I must set down the story of your birth.*

*As you know, I have already set down as much as I can of the
story of the Wolves of Time. This was after years of wandering
the old wolfways, recovering the story, living it again. Eventually*

I returned to unwelcome celebrity and much fuss and bother. Until, that over, the headman of our community took it into that head of his that I should set down all I knew. It was no good saying I was a teller, not a writer, for he and his Council only shook their heads and said, 'And who will tell it when you die?'

'You,' I replied. 'You will tell it as I have done, and others like me. There will always be people like us . . .'

'There will never be another like you, Jakob, who knows and remembers so much,' my headman said.

I nodded, beaten. It was so. There would not, could not be another like me, unless it were my own son. But then I had none.

'Tell it for our children who are not yet born,' he said.

I laughed and said, 'Not for the children who run at my heels when I venture out among the steadings? The children who mock and laugh at a strange man like me.'

He did not laugh but instead he said, 'Tell it for all of us.'

'You command it?' I asked.

Did he guess how much depended on his reply? I think he did, and for that I was proud that the Mann who had fought and ousted me as leader was finding the way towards the hard-won wisdom a true leader needs.

'No,' he replied, shaking his head with a smile, 'I command nothing. I ask that you consider what I have said for all of us, and seek the guidance of Wulf himself for what you must do. And to help you . . .' and here he had the grace to smile again, 'we shall grant you sanctuary and remission from the tasks that elders should perform.'

'Remission,' I whispered.

'Yet not respite,' he added. 'Your task will be hard. Harder by far than being leader!'

We gazed into each other's eyes as only men who have led communities can do once their differences are restored, and old enmities have died, leaving respect, and empathy.

'It will be hard,' I replied, 'and I must ask for remission in one other thing: I shall be storyteller no more. Find others to fulfil that task. To write in private as you have asked, I must be silent in public.'

'But the rituals . . .'

'Ah, yes, there is a place for me there. The older ones must serve that the youngest may learn.'

He looked relieved and said, 'But maybe a few tales here and there? But say no more now; tell us, when you have thought more of this, what else you'll need . . .'

I interrupted him and said, 'I have no need to ponder more – I have done so on my journeys and the spirit of Klimt himself told me what I must do, and where I must begin. I need peace, I need a place of my own at the stockade's edge where I may see the forest above, and the valley below. Then, too, as well as the youth who helps with my healing preparations I need a girl to help me about my home, and to sleep in my bed; and more of this paper and suchlike things.

'And if there be days when I do nothing, weeks perhaps, I need to know that no one will ever question what I do. You see, I need to be given the community's space and silence as well as my own. As for children who dance and mock at my heels, let them be. They remind me of myself when young, which is where we all begin this brief life, which is far nearer the wolfway to the stars than we adults ever know.'

'It shall be so,' he said. 'You shall have sanctuary and peace, and the time you need; and none shall judge you.'

'Come out with me to the forest now,' I said impulsively, for some instinct told me that while a leader might say one thing, a community will do another. I wanted him to understand something of the nature of the task he had so lightly set me, though he had the wisdom to see that it might indeed be hard. It was auspicious that as we went out from my steading and up towards the stockade's forest gate there came out of the darkening forest heights above the howl of a solitary wolf, and then, further off still, some answering howls.

I took his hand as I had when he was young and, in silence, and watched no doubt in awe by those who saw us go, led him out through the gate, and up among the trees and into the forest depths.

'Heuren Sie,' I said in the old tongue of our forebears: 'listen now . . .'

I drew him into a silence of meditation upon the forest sounds, as I had often drawn the young ones of our community, as I myself when young had been drawn. 'Heuren Sie . . .' I whispered, and I offered up the journey prayer to Wulf Himself. Then our leader, remembering the training of his youth, answered with the prayer of intercession to Wulfin, that She might see that Her mate was disposed to hear our call. We pulled our furs about us against the bitter cold, and entered into that different world of time where there is finally no waiting.

Into that deep silence, full as it was of the stresses and appeals, sighs and shouts of the trees and rocks of the forests of the Rhine, the howl of the lone wolf entered in once more, gyring above us, closer now.

I pulled my crane bag nearer and opened it, and in the darkness let my right hand feel those sacred, hallowed objects I had been collecting all my life. One by one they slipped between my fingers back into their dark silence, until one alone sought my spirit out and my hand held on to it: it was the tooth of wolf I held.

I placed it on the forest floor between us and if it caught the light of the rising stars and seemed to shine brighter even than the moon that was still out of our sight, well then, such was its nature and its power.

'Touch it, Mann,' I ordered him.

He reached out his hand, which seemed made fire by the tooth's great light, and he gasped and said, 'I cannot! I can . . . not!'

'Such,' I whispered, 'is how I feel when you and our community command me to set down the sacred story of the coming of the Wolves of Time. I feel I cannot, I can . . . not – and yet I feel perhaps I must. So . . . we shall wait and see what the gods decide.

So we sat in the forest through the night, we talked, we journeyed into the eternities of our hearts and minds to explore like children the wolfways of our souls until dawn came.

When it did so, and the early spring sun cut through the forest glades and we returned to where we were, he said, 'I shall decree that you are left in peace, and none ever demands that you show us what you do. May the Wolves of Time show you the way.'

He continued with other practical things that would ease my path and concluded by saying this: 'I shall send my youngest daughter for your steading and your bed.'

But I shook my head immediately. It was a high honour indeed, and I knew the girl and liked her, but . . .

I took up the tooth of wolf and returned it to the darkness of my bag. As I did so I found myself trembling and gasping, for my hand, in the darkness of the pouch, touched my mother's amber brooch. Near to us now, from where she had watched so long through the night in the shadows beyond the trees that encircled us, the vagrant wolf howled.

'Send to me the vagrant woman who shall come in three days time,' I said, in a shaman's voice. 'She shall be my helpmeet and companion.'

'But . . .'

He nodded and said no more, and I knew myself well enough not to ask further from where my words, my small prophecy, came. A shaman is wise not to ask himself too much in the conscious world. She was unseen, but the wolf I had known to be nearby turned and was gone off to seek out that woman whose coming I had felt, and to guide her to our community.

Wulfin was that wolf, and the one she would find would be my last companion. Our work was done.

Three days later the vagrant woman came, with Wulf knows what despair and hopelessness upon her face and worn body.

'This woman?' my headman said. For what companion could so drawn and thin a woman be when what I needed . . .

'Surely my daughter . . . ?'

I waved one hand to dismiss him, and with the other I reached out to touch one who had been touched by Wulfin herself, and whose eyes told me she had journeyed further by far than me, perhaps from the very beginning of the Dark Millennium and the fall of wolves. Had this present life of mine always been her destination? Had I been waiting for her to find me once again? Wulfin and Wulf . . . the light and shadows of their lives are us.

I tended her, and healed her. Then first in gratitude, and then in love, she gave me comfort and companionship and I found a fulfilment I had never known before.

That was three years ago. Three years in which I struggled with my tale. Long years in which, I think, even my leader began to have his doubts. But how could I set down the story of the Wolves of Time when I did not know to whom I told it? How hard indeed was the journey I was on! In all that time I set down barely more than a few words, and those I burnt as meaningless. Only my beloved, and the youth I trained, were there to see my struggle.

I thought that perhaps Wulf cursed me with this silence for daring to presume I could tell His story and that of all His pack. Yet there was a single, wonderful, saving grace in that long search:

Wulfin comforted me by blessing my woman with a child, a son.

Heuren Sie mein Sohn, *my son, listen now . . .*

You were born eight months ago, and from the day of your first cry I began to write down the Wolves' story. It was you I had waited for before I could begin. A week ago I decreed that you should be weaned: nervously, I may say, for your mother was not well pleased, and knew in any case what I must do once the weaning was complete. She pleaded with me not to, but her heart was not in her pleas. She knew well what I must do, what Wulf demanded I must do. So yesterday I took you, my only child, up into the forest, and offered you up to the Wolves of Time: that they might take you back unto themselves, or bless you and grant you your life with us. All fathers must do this, for how else shall they know that what they have is blessed? How else, too, can parents learn the true honour of what they are given in a child, but in the searing hours of a night when the Wolves may take that child away? For the child should be the whole earth to us and in its honouring we learn to honour the earth that is our Mother and our Father. During the terrible journey of a night of offering, parents learn again that the earth which was once their parents, has become their child.

I confess that I was more fearful than I have ever been as I set you down on the forest floor, wrapped up in the warm clothes and furs your mother had prepared, to stare at the darkling sky, to watch the coming of the stars.

Out of sight, but within earshot of your cries, I sat down to begin a night of prayers perhaps more heartfelt than any I have ever offered up. I soon heard the hushed sliding patter of the wolf pack's paws and their growls and barks. Yet I knew I must stay seated where I was. I heard your cries grow faint, I heard a sudden cry of fear, I heard your silence after that as if it was the very dying of my heart. Yet I knew I must not move.

I heard their rough-and-tumble play, and the growls of their practice fights; I heard the growling, panting, tearing of their feeding time. I heard your cries no more and I was still and lost as death.

Then, in the darkest hour of that dark night, when the pack was still, He came to me: Wulf was there, and Wulfin at his side.

I wept, and they nuzzled me and I felt their huge presence all about, their yellow-amber eyes upon me.

'Begin with my father Klimt,' Wulf seemed to say, 'begin with him, just as he told you to.'

He picked me up in his jaws as tenderly as I had laid you down upon the forest floor, and then he took me through the night back to Helsingborg, and Klimt. Then, bit by bit I saw it all, all of the story of the Wolves of Time, the gaps in my understanding filled at last, until as a new dawn came the pack drifted off, and you cried out for me once more, and Wulf returned with me.

Only with the sun's first rays did I go to you, and pick you up, and knew that you had been blessed, and spared to live a mortal life.

You reached up to touch my face, and you stroked it as you never had before, as if you learned to do it by stroking the fur of Wulf himself. Holding you I wept, and knew why Wulf had prevented me from writing down His tale until then.

My son, listen now, listen to the meaning of my tale.

I carried you out of the forest and from out of the dawn I brought you back to the community, back to your waiting, tearful, relieved mother. But I would not give you up, not for a little while more. I took you to my room, and sat you on the floor and we smiled at each other. I was certain in that moment that one day when the time was right you would have the strength to take up my half-finished tale.

I knew I would not have time to teach you all a father should: the prayers and invocations of the days and seasons; the names of the healing herbs; the rituals. Nor would I now have time to show you the places I had explored when young, and the trees and mountains I had climbed . . .

One day, when you are old enough to read, perhaps you will take up these pages and understand what it was I made for you, and look up at the night sky, and on among the stars, and know that in our time the Mennen strove to be wise, by learning how to run with wolves and listen to their howls.

Therefore, heuren Sie!

Listen now . . .

Jakob Wald
Upper Freiburg
Anno Lupi 13

Well, well, I am old enough to read my father's words now. Old enough, indeed, to know when not to read, but rather to think and act, to dream and journey, to learn to be at home wherever the Spirit – or the One, or the Wolves, or Wulf Himself, or whatever name you choose to give to that of which we are each one an essential part – chooses to guide me.

Now, let me take up once more the narrative my father left unfinished so long ago, and journey as he tried to do to its very end. If you will accompany me then I shall not finally be alone as he was, as he had to be. He ran with the Wolves before us, and led the way.

Let us now follow him . . .

Departure

The son of Jakob Wald began his famous journey at dusk, deciding to travel but a short distance up into the adjacent forest from the Feldberg People's main stockade before he encamped for the night.

His friends and family thus had an opportunity to accompany him a little on the way, to talk into the night and wish him well, and offer him such gifts as a shaman traveller, wishing to carry next to nothing, might choose to take: smoked deer meat as sustenance for the first few days, a fold or two of waterproof material against the rain, some paper on which to leave a poem or two along the way – invocations to the wolves perhaps, or thoughts to share with another passing traveller.

> From this day forth
> I shall be called a Wanderer,
> Leaving on a journey
> That follows the shadows of wolves.

He took with him a young and sturdy assistant, to help along the way and to act as porter should there be a need; he took as well certain items from his father's crane bag to carry in his own, and suspended from his belt, protected by a leather pouch, was the hand mirror he had found as a youth, whose reflections were a source of truth.

It was late in the night when the Feldberg elders left, and his family and children, and friends, carrying torches to light their way back to the stockade, their farewells bleak yet celebratory, filled with awe. They knew that Jakob Wald's son's journey was to a kind of death and the Mann who left them would not be the one who came back.

As their torches bobbed and ducked and weaved away downslope amongst the trees and off into the night, Wald's assistant wept, homesick already, while his master simply turned over and slept.

They moved off the following dawn, journeying for three days and nights with barely a word said between them. Then, on the fourth evening, as dusk approached once more, Wald lay on his back on the Forest floor, the pine scent strong, and his assistant covered him with a light cotton blanket, weighted down at its edges by stones.

Then his assistant took up his journey drum and began to drum steadily, as he had been taught, that Wald might journey on the hoofbeats of sound to the threshold of the Otherworld in the hope that one might be there to greet him, and guide him on.

An old one, far past his years, his fur patched and white, his face etched and wrinkled with the trials of time and patient faith, his paws worn and scratched from many lifetimes' worth of journeying.

He came through the Forest, this old one, down through the trees, pausing to listen now and then, hearing the drum that summoned him, listening to the whisper of the wind, his eyes wet with old tears that the last part of his own journey was now beginning, his long task nearly done. For he was a Bukov wolf, who first dared summon the Wolves of Time, the last survivor of those who first journeyed to the Heartland, come now to guide a Seeker forward.

Wald stood at the threshold and saw the coming of his guide, who stared at him with eyes that were blind with age, yet seemed to see his very soul.

'Come,' said Tervicz to the son of Jakob Wald, 'follow me and I shall take you far ahead of the journey you are to make, to the Heartland, back to the time when the sons of Elhana were beginning to find their destiny.'

Ahead and back he went, the son of Jakob Wald, as the drumming grew louder for a moment, then receded into far places, other times, where wolves looked up in wonder, and raised their heads to howl the feeling that they had that now, at last, Wulf Himself was getting ready to journey back to the stars.

II

WANDERERS OF THE WOLFWAYS

CHAPTER TWO

*The coming of winter brings a renewal of the Mennen war,
heralding danger to the Heartland, and the Wolves of Time*

IT WAS MID-OCTOBER, and a dull wet autumn was reaching
its end across the High Tatra mountains of Slovakia, with a few
bright, clear days. The sky was pale blue, the air just turning raw,
while down on the flatter ground a few remaining heather bells and
bilberries clung on against a brisk, cold breeze that whispered and
hissed the unwelcome news of the arrival of an early winter.

To the south of the highest peaks stretched the Scarpfeld, the high
terrace of ground that was the summer territory of the Wolves of
Time. Here and there across its broken rocky ground, the last of the
rock pipits darted about uneasily, their final feeding over before they
migrated to the lower ground of the Fell, which stretched off southward, all still and cold, and powdered with a brief flurry of snow from
the previous night.

The sheer, dark cliffs of the Tatra loomed over the Scarpfeld itself,
deeply gulleyed and creviced, already pocketed with snow, home
now only to ravens, and overflown that morning by a solitary eagle,
whose summer mate had died. He had come back again and again
in the days past, in rain and mist, and now in the sun, making
a forlorn search for the mate he had lost. His wings were bronze-
golden in the sun, his tail feathers white, and as he gyred higher
and higher his yellow bill caught the light momentarily with each
slow, sad turn.

Upon the Scarpfeld, its rock outcrops interspersed with rough
sward, peaty and waterlogged, the dark, reflective surface of the pools
of water shivered with the rising wind, and began to freeze.

The Wolves themselves were scattered about, barely visible, but
mostly huddled out of the wind against rocks or sward banks enjoying
such warmth from the sun as they could find, and waiting for their
leader Klimt to announce the final departure to the lower wintering

grounds of the Forest and Vale, which lay out of sight, beyond the high col which marked the eastward end of the Scarpfeld.

They might leave later today, possibly tomorrow, but for now there was time to be at ease, to enjoy the view of cliffs and blue sky, to narrow their eyes against the wind, to take in the fading scents of decaying summer vegetation, of rabbits long gone, and of marmot lying low in their deep rocky homes.

The pack was only eleven strong – six established adults, including Klimt and Elhana, the leader and ledrene, and the five youngsters born to Elhana eighteen months before, and now full-grown members of the pack.

All were now silent but for two of the senior wolves, who were talking in low voices: Tervicz, the stringy, still youthful-seeming Bukovian wolf who had been the first to join Klimt in the uncertain dream and quest that *was* the Wolves of Time; and Kobrin, a huge wolf, but old now, once warlord of all the Russian packs, who had come to the Heartland to serve a leader in whose destiny he believed.

'Klimt will probably decide we should stay another night and leave tomorrow if this weather holds,' Tervicz was saying. 'He's finding it hard to talk things through with Elhana, but talk those two must if they are to lead the pack together in some semblance of harmony through the coming winter.'

Kobrin nodded, his wide face wrinkled and grey-furred, his rough, worn paws nearly twice the size of those of Tervicz.

All seemed peaceful, all at ease, all –

Kobrin started, for the eagle high over the cliffs had turned suddenly, and begun a steep and angled stoop to cover amongst the crags; while a raven came suddenly out of its cliff-side home, turned on its back, grunted darkly, and swerved into a deeper and more protective gulley in the cliff.

'What . . . ?' growled Kobrin rising.

With a whine and an ear-splitting roar, the autumnal peace was shattered by the arrival overhead of Mennen jet planes. Sudden, and absolute, the jets were there upon them, looming in the sky, massive, frightening as they went darkly surging past, leaving in their wake ear-shattering noise, and angry, rebounding echoes in the cliffs all about.

Then, as the roaring faded, and the Wolves began to think they knew what it was had so destroyed their peace, there came the first sound of rock-falls nearby and far off, the result of the new and alien vibrations in the air intruding in the clefts and gulleys of the crags.

But before the Wolves could draw breath, worse followed. No sooner had the jet planes faded into the distance and disappeared from sight, than there came the deep and resonant BOOM-BOOM of Mennen bombs, far off beyond the Scarpfeld, down in the Vale where the Wolves had been about to go, where the Mennen jets had now preceded them.

A BOOM-BOOM!

. . . and a *CRUMP!!!!! BOOM-CRUMP!*

Like a heart that has missed a beat and now painfully tries to catch up with itself, making a wolf suddenly feel his age, and remember how frail is his mortality.

Then BOOM-BOOM! again, so huge now, and terrible in its impact, that the cliffs above seemed to shake, and the Wolves, already startled into alarm, could only stand and stare about themselves, ears pricking this way and that, for the danger seemed to come from no one place, but to be endemic to the earth itself.

But before their leader Klimt could summon them together, or their warlord Kobrin could make sense of what had happened, or Elhana, the pack's ledrene, could instinctively call the younger wolves to the denning ground, the jets came back overhead as suddenly and violently as they had gone by before.

Whoooooooo-WHOOOOS-SSSSSH!

. . . causing a black, angry violence in the ears, an instinctive cowering down, as wild eyes followed the disappearance of the dark, malevolent shapes away once more to the peaceful, eastern, autumn sky.

Then it was over, and as the last of the rock-falls faded, and the ravens and rock pipits settled back to the perches from which they had fled, the Wolves looked at each other with an awed wonder mixed with despair, and sensed – no, *knew* – that their world might never be quite the same again.

Klimt summoned Kobrin and Tervicz at once to investigate what the sound of bombing they had heard from the Vale might mean for the pack, and despatched them on their task immediately. Both were well used to reconnaissance, and with no more than a word of acknowledgement to Klimt and to each other, they were off – Tervicz taking the lead as he usually did on such ventures, with the stolid Kobrin just behind. As they left, the familiar montane silence began to return across the Scarpfeld, but it was accompanied now by the unfamiliar and unwelcome scent of the fumes of the low-flying aircraft, choking and acrid.

'Where's Lounel?' Klimt demanded, trying to turn his mind to other things. Lounel was his adviser in matters of the spirit, and a wolf who often went missing for a time – sitting and thinking, some said, or merely sitting, according to others.

'He's fetching Merrow,' replied Elhana, Klimt's consort and the mother of the pack's five youngsters, two males and three females, all now adult enough to be involved in all the pack's daily hunting, guarding and reconnaissance duties.

Merrow was one of the females, and still the weakest of them all. She had not been strong from birth, without the physical strength to deal with Tare, the most aggressive of the females, and the one most likely to become ledrene when Elhana grew too old for that task. Nor did Merrow have the easy good humour of her other sister, Rohan, whom everybody liked.

Yet Merrow had survived, and the pack began to see she had other qualities, one of which was a spiritual strength which came with having been frail for so long, and having dug deep into inner resources some of her siblings had never had need to explore.

She liked to wander by herself – dangerously so perhaps, for the evil Magyar wolves who lived out on the Southern Fell were a constant threat, and the Mennen had always been a lurking danger. But when pack life became too much for her she would find a place to be alone, and there pursue her study of the stars, or the movements of the clouds. Among the adults she was close to the eccentric Lounel, and he often watched out for her – as he did that day the jets overflew them and all began to change . . .

'There they are, they're coming now,' said Elhana, still relieved to see her young back safe within the pack, though her role as mother had been over since the spring.

Klimt relaxed, for the others were all accounted for. Of his two sons, Solar was standing protectively over Raute, the old blind Magyar female whom the pack had taken into its heart and protection at the time of the youngsters' birth; for she had much lore to impart, and disapproved of the ways and means of the new generation of Magyars. Her consort had been the brutal Hassler, whom Klimt had defeated and killed before he led the Wolves to the Heartland; old though Raute now was, the pack valued her highly.

Solar was the strongest of the siblings, and their natural leader, and no one could doubt that when the time came for Klimt to give way to a younger wolf, that of his two sons it would be Solar who would take his place. He was strong and dependable, and had taken on his adult pack responsibilities sooner than any of his siblings – and long before his erratic brother Lunar, Klimt's second son.

'And where has Lunar got to now?' asked Klimt testily, for though he had been about somewhere moments before he seemed now to have disappeared.

'Gone off to greet Merrow and Lounel,' said Solar a shade wearily, for he took after Klimt in being not much interested in such displays of affection.

Merrow and Lunar got on together best of all the siblings, and the sound of their laughter came into the pack's circle now as Lounel led them back.

'Lunar . . . *Lunar!*' barked Klimt, for after the shock they had all just had, and the seriousness of the reconnaissance that Kobrin and Tervicz had just embarked on, laughter seemed inappropriate. Lunar winked at Merrow and went immediately to sit with Solar, alongside whose darkly impressive form he looked inconsequential – his fur was lighter and rougher, and his ears never seemed to quite prick up with the purpose and solidity of a true-born leader.

Merrow smiled after him and went to Elhana's side, though she settled further off than she would have liked to do because Tare would not give way, and snarled when she came near. Tare was the least prepossessing of them all, but among her sisters she was dominant, though she rarely bullied the stronger Rohan in the way she did the frail Merrow.

'We'll stay within denning limits until Kobrin and Tervicz return, which will probably not be until tomorrow,' said Klimt. 'Solar, you take the eastern watch, with Tare to back you up. Lounel, you take the western side, for you know those routes well. Merrow, you can stay with your mother, and Lunar . . .'

'Mmmm?'

'You can stay with me, where I can see you. This is not a time to go a-wandering. You and I will take up a place near the Great Cleft, for the Magyars may hope that sounds of Mennen bombing from our territory mean we have suffered harm, and come along to investigate.'

The plan Klimt had outlined was a familiar one, employed often enough before when a threat had appeared and the pack strength was depleted while its most experienced males went off to reconnoitre. It was a matter of watching out with care, and keeping close together. Klimt never betrayed the slightest alarm in such situations, and the fact that he had chosen to stay up in the Scarpfeld indicated that, for the moment at least, he felt the threat up there was slight, and that Tervicz and Kobrin could find out what he would need to know – which might, when it came to it, be nothing at all.

In any case, the summer had been a long one, and the hunting hard, and Klimt had wanted these last days of what had been a dispiriting autumn to talk to Elhana – to *really* talk to her – about their future, now the youngsters were full-grown.

The issue, as Tervicz's words with Kobrin earlier had suggested, was a familiar one to the Wolves, and concerned them. No one necessarily expected a leader and ledrene to get on personally, for their roles were decided solely by their success in dominating their own sex within the pack – a liking for each other was merely a bonus. Duty to the pack, and then to themselves, and only finally the effort to like each other was the order of priorities.

But mutual liking helped a pack in troubled times, and love between a leader and ledrene, that rarest of commodities, made it a pack blessed indeed. Yet even for a pack as fortunate as that, let leader or ledrene be defeated by another and though the love might still be there, duty would force the losing partner down in the hierarchy, and perhaps out of the pack altogether.

By now even the most dreamy and impractical of the youngsters – and Lunar and Merrow might claim to be those – knew what Klimt had had to do when Elhana gained predominance over the females by defeating Jicin, the Magyar wolf he had loved, and loved deeply.

Jicin had been exiled, and with her had gone two others: Stry, a wolf who needed change to heal himself from the loss of his brother beneath an avalanche in the Scarpfeld, and mighty Aragon, briefly leader of the Wolves, and once the lover of Elhana.

Wise Klimt had sent all three into exile together, commanding them to explore the wolfways of western Europe until the youngsters were full-grown, to give him and Elhana time and space to raise the cubs without let or hindrance, or needless conflict. Whether the youngsters knew, or guessed, that they were the product of Aragon of Spain's mating with Elhana rather than Klimt's none knew, for it was not a subject about which the Wolves spoke.

In any case, it was not quite certain, for Solar was physically very like Klimt, while Lunar, rough and ready though he so far was, and unkempt though he kept his fur, had a touch of the pride and style of Aragon, who despite his moods, and weakness in leadership as the pack remembered it, had something of the southern sun about his nature, and the light of good humour in his handsome eyes.

Be that as it may, Aragon, Stry and Jicin had left the Heartland in the first weeks after the youngsters' birth, and nothing had been heard of them since, nothing at all.

But with the youngsters' second summer successfully over, and a new winter just beginning, Klimt's and Elhana's duty had been done. Now, with more time to themselves, they had begun to rediscover the true nature of the loveless void between them, which had deepened the day Jicin and the others had departed into exile.

For Elhana it was not so much that she missed Aragon, for the truth was that theirs had been the sudden excitement of discovered passion rather than the slow, reassuring realization of deep love. Aragon had given her all the laughter and sense of ease a southern wolf finds in summer sunshine, and their mating had satisfied her longing for such a sensual love.

But when she had got with cub, though probably by him, her priorities had changed and she had found quiet and simple pleasure in the ledrene's role as mother of the pack's young. As they had grown, she had felt disappointment that not one of them seemed much like Aragon in temperament, unless it be Lunar, who was a disappointment in so much else. In any case, her young, as young will, had grown away from her and now the emptiness she felt was as much to do with missing the cubs they had been, as with missing Aragon.

Aragon? Why, in memory he seemed so young to her now, and their secret moments – and there had been many – half forgotten, no more than the fleeting of summer light in a stream, or the waving of cotton-grass at summer's end, or the drift of seeds upon the autumn winds.

Now, though she was growing old, and perhaps only retained the ledreneship because there had been no female opposition since Jicin's departure (her daughters were still too young to seriously contest her place), Elhana wanted to get with cub one more time. Then, surely, she would have done her duty by the pack, and contributed the most she could towards the destiny of the Wolves of Time. It would be enough, and she could yield at last to the aches and pains she had begun to feel with the onset of the winter winds.

Meanwhile, if only Klimt could satisfy her need and mate with her, she would let him be, and not mind if next year Jicin returned, for her own place in the history of the pack would be secure and she would not begrudge Klimt time with the one he loved.

Love . . .

Sometimes Elhana wondered what the word truly meant, unless it be love for those she had borne. As for the memory of her hopes of it – of being ledrene to a leader she loved and felt passion for, a dream that had first driven her out of Italy to the Heartland – it was nearly gone.

Love? There was a bleakness to Elhana's eyes, a coolness to her love even for her young, a giving-up of hope for all of that . . . If only she could get with young again, so . . .

Klimt approached the pack, his watching duty done, and told Tare to take up his place at the Great Cleft. Lunar was still there.

'Klimt . . . ?'

Great Klimt eyed her uneasily, and let his gaze shift to the pale cold sky, as if prompted by her call to think of the Mennen jets that had so disturbed their day.

'Klimt?'

'Elhana?'

He went to her, ignoring the pack's curious stares and unspoken questions as to what he would do.

'We need to talk, my dear,' she said coolly.

'Yes, we do,' he replied and led her off, knowing what she wanted and not yet willing to give it. Too soon. Let the winter deepen, let them get off the Scarpfeld down into the Forest and then, perhaps, in darkest winter, in a moment's forgetting of how she chilled his heart and in remembrance of another who still stirred it, he might do his duty and mate with her once again. Then, at least, if she should get with young, he would know they were his.

He led her off, out of sight of the others, aware of the burdens on him – his duty to the pack, and satisfaction of her need. Somewhere or other he turned towards her and stared into her eyes. There was no watching duty to be done, no food to be found, no young to chastise, or encourage. There was just what lay between the two of them and he saw how deep, how dreadful, was its void.

'You miss her, don't you Klimt?' she said quietly.

He nodded, expressionless. There was a kind of comfort in her acknowledgement.

'And Aragon, do you miss *him*?' he asked.

She shook her head with a slight smile and murmured that she did not.

They faced each other in silence, the void deep, and to Klimt at least, very dark indeed. The loss of Jicin felt as sharp and painful to him now as it had been the day she left.

'I want more young, Klimt,' Elhana said. 'It is my right, and the pack's right too.'

She seemed calm enough, but as she spoke something in her voice quailed. She was a strong ledrene, and even had there been far fiercer female opposition than Jicin, in whom the lust for ledreneship had never been very real, Elhana would still have emerged triumphant, just as she had in her home pack years before in southern Italy.

Yet . . . before Klimt she always finally quailed, knowing him to be a stronger leader, and more awesome, than she had thought a leader could ever be. She feared him, she respected him, and deep in her heart perhaps she might have found love for him, if only . . . if only he could have been easier with her, smiled with her, and found time to laugh, and play, as Aragon had done. But that Klimt had never been able to do.

She had had a dream of the Wolves of Time, and her place with them; but Klimt had had a vision, compelling and powerful, and his role as leader was as nothing compared to his vision – too distant for her – of the pack's holy destiny.

'It is the pack's right, Elhana, but . . . I am weary with the summer and uncertain where we must next turn.'

'More young, my dear, that was ever a pack's way. And we are weak in number, you know we are. Eleven of us now, but with Raute near her time. Who knows what injuries the winter might bring? Death lives longest in the winter months, as my mother Lauria used to say.'

She smiled at the memory of Lauria, and might have smiled more had Aragon been there, or any wolf who knew how to touch such memories and bring them forth. But the smile faded before Klimt's bleak gaze, and bleakness came into her own face, which was a reflection of his.

'We shall go down to the Forest the moment Kobrin and Tervicz report back, providing they judge it is safe to do so. Perhaps in the winter months we can . . . we shall . . . I . . .'

'Yes, Klimt.'

'But in truth, I want no more young with you, Elhana.'

'It is your duty, Klimt, and it need be no more nor less than a single mating.'

Klimt stared at her and for the briefest of moments she fancied she saw hatred, but in that she was mistaken. It was not hatred his face showed but the sudden, painful stab of loss and longing, and loneliness. There were days and moments he might have wept – why, there were moments when he almost did weep. This was one of them.

'My dear . . .' she said, moving towards him.

He shook his head slightly, trying to disguise his flinch at her approach, and she stilled and retreated once again, understanding him, pitying him, afraid of him; another part of her dying before him.

'But you are right, Elhana,' he conceded, 'the pack is vulnerable and needs more young. We shall make them as we must, though my instinct says that we should not. We have done our duty by our young and they are wolves to be proud of.'

Neither moved, as they thought of the five youngsters, and the grass trembled unnoticed before them with the rising winter wind.

'Solar will take the leadership from me one day and then . . .' said Klimt.

'And Tare has her eyes on the ledreneship, but it would be better to have new blood,' his ledrene added.

'The gods will decide such matters,' said Klimt.

'The gods . . .' whispered Elhana, musing bitterly.

When her young had been born a She-wolf had come among them to gaze on the cubs, and none had doubted it had been Wulfin Herself. She had said that one of the males was Wulf incarnate, born into mortality one final time and destined to bring the Dark Millennium to its end, though whether to renewal for wolfkind, or its final extinction, She did not know or say. Nor did She then indicate which of the two would be Wulf, and which but mortal, though time had told them clearly enough that Solar was the one.

'We have raised Lunar equally with him,' said Klimt, his voice a little brighter, for in all of that he felt pride and fulfilment. 'We gave Lunar every chance, but it has been Solar who has proved himself.'

'There is no rancour between them,' said Elhana, a little brighter too, for here they always found common ground. Anyway, her leader had conceded that they would mate until she got with young, and at such a season as late autumn that was as far as a tactful ledrene could expect a reluctant leader to go. Klimt would take her when the time came, and might even come to enjoy it. She would have a final litter and when Solar took over the leadership there would be a bigger pack for him to lead than Klimt now ruled.

'No rancour at all,' said Klimt. 'The only rancour comes from Tare, who has the eyes of one who wants things a little too soon and hopes to displace you before she should.'

'She'll try and mate with you, Klimt,' said Elhana matter-of-factly.

Klimt smiled briefly; 'She won't succeed. She has not her mother's charms.'

Elhana smiled, glad he could make light of such things, and having no doubt at all that unlike some leaders, in that department he meant exactly what he said.

'If you do get with young, the problem will be to keep Tare with the pack,' he said, 'but . . . we shall manage that. For better or for worse we are a good team, Elhana, good leaders of the Wolves. I am sorry that I . . . disappoint you.'

'And I that I am not other than I am,' said Elhana.

Astonishingly, he came forward and bent down to touch her face with his muzzle, bleak still, but affectionate, respectful, and in his own way understanding.

'I would defend you to the death, Elhana,' he said.

'And I do not think that any other leader but you would have so gained my respect, or so often made me tremble, Klimt.'

They stood in silence together a little while, and stared about the Scarpfeld and the distant cliffs, above the highest of which the solitary eagle had returned.

'Change is with us now, terrible change,' said Klimt, 'and I do not know what to do for the best, or which way to turn. I sense danger too. I –'

There was a signal bark from the eastern cliff.

'That's Lounel,' said Klimt. 'Kobrin and Tervicz back already . . . ?'

They both turned back towards the denning ground, breaking cover only when they reached slightly higher terrain, and stilled immediately. It was distant, the boom-boom of guns, and strangely frail, the rat-tat-tat. The Mennen once again . . .

'Come, my dear, and do not worry, you shall have your cubs. That at least is my clear duty, reluctant though I am.'

Again the brief bleak smile, again duty to the fore, and again for Elhana the flush of respect and sympathy but no love for a wolf who was a leader before all else.

57

'Wulfin,' she whispered as he went off to join the pack, 'grant that he finds happiness one day . . .'

Lounel had indeed summoned Klimt, but not to say that Tervicz and Kobrin were on the way back.

'What then?' growled Klimt a shade impatiently, for Lounel had about his face a vague, searching expression, like a wolf who feels he has something important to say but is not altogether sure what it is; or if he knows, is very uncertain what the reception of it might be.

'I caught a scent, and one I thought you should know about,' said Lounel, pacing about. He was an ungainly wolf, long of leg, slight of body, and with eyes that could be wild and agitated at times, and were on the way to being so now.

'Mennen?' suggested Klimt, who knew that at moments such as this his friend needed helpful prompting rather than a show of impatience, which would only send him wandering off.

Lounel shook his head.

'Magyar?' said Klimt, for he had half expected them to show up, though not in this part of the Scarpfeld. The Great Cleft, which marked the southern boundary between the two territories, was where they would appear.

'I think not,' said Lounel. 'Now, Klimt, *there* . . .'

The two wolves raised their muzzles to the wind, which came from the west, and Klimt was surprised to find that it did have a strange scent, not especially alien, but not one he could identify.

'What is it, wolf?' he asked.

'Thyme and tarragon,' said Lounel faintly. There was a certain awe in the way he said it.

'Herbs?' said Klimt. 'A strange time of year for such scents as those, though I suppose that the sun might have been warm enough to seek out and release some plants in late bloom . . .'

'Like herbs, but not herbs,' said Lounel. 'The legends say that these are the scents of holy wolves, travellers, teachers, those who journey out of the past to bring news to the wolves in the present.'

'Hmmph!' said Klimt, turning back to the pack. 'When these ghosts appear, Lounel, be so kind as to tell me, for I wouldn't want us to be taken by surprise. Meanwhile, continue your watch for Tervicz and Kobrin, will you, and let me know when they return.'

'I will,' said Lounel vaguely, not at all put out by Klimt's irony. 'Things are changing, Klimt, and will change more.'

His words were caught in the sudden chill of the winter breeze, and the elusive scent of thyme and tarragon seemed suddenly gone as he turned back to do his duty.

CHAPTER THREE

*The Wolves of Time return to the wintering grounds
and find their world has changed for ever*

AS THAT MEMORABLE DAY advanced, and darkness came, the
pack began to worry for the safety of Tervicz and Kobrin. The
sky stayed clear, so that as the wind died, the cold grew deeper
about them and the pools began to ice over. The Wolves said little,
but all were thinking of Kobrin and Tervicz, for the sound of guns
had continued, distant and faint but ever more persistent until final
darkness came, when they fell silent.

Typically, Klimt was calm. Where some leaders might have been
inclined to send others out to see if they could find the first two, he
did not. When he gave wolves a task he expected them to accomplish
it. He only broke his silence in the dark of evening to observe, lest
any doubted it, that the two wolves could be trusted to find out the
position of the Mennen guns they had all heard, and come back by
dawn.

'Kobrin's not one to dally, unless he's got very good reason, and he
and Tervicz know the Vale as well as any of us, and far better than
Mennen. So rest, Wolves, rest and keep warm, for tomorrow, if it is
judged safe, we shall journey back to our wintering grounds. Lunar,
take the last watch on the east instead of Merrow and Lounel, for
those two are looking tired.'

Lunar nodded, glancing at Solar, who always preferred to be given
these extra tasks. He guessed that Solar might be needed for more
onerous work on the morrow.

'Do you mind taking my place?' whispered Merrow, coming to settle
by Lunar.

Lunar shook his head, staring at the winking of the stars, which
grew ever more bright as night advanced.

'They always look brighter up here,' he said, 'bright as berries, bright
as sun-filled dew . . .'

'. . . bright as new snow, bright as your laugh,' she continued, laughing softly.

It was a game they played, of a kind they always had, and the others ignored them, preferring to try to settle into sleep.

'Look!' said Merrow, her voice full of awe, pointing to the constellation of Mistur, and of Hrein, the first a million milky stars, the second seven powerful ones that formed an ellipse in the eastern sky.

Lunar nodded silently, eyes wide and mouth open, oblivious of the cold. Brother and sister shared the same wonders, and needed little talk to do so.

'They say that Mistur and Hrein loved each other,' said Merrow softly.

Love . . .

As the summer had advanced Lunar had begun to understand what it might mean, and that he felt it for his sister Merrow. He was rarely so happy as when sharing with her such things as stars and sun, the gyre of eagles and the shift-sound of rock.

'Are you tired?' he asked.

She nodded.

'But I'm happy,' she added a little later, her eyes less bright now upon the stars at which Lunar still stared, for she was growing sleepy. He felt her flank warm against his, breathing in and out, and he wished nothing would change from this moment, and that all would be the same. He shivered and saw the stars and the moon had shifted and turned.

'Change is in the air,' he said, and he felt afraid.

He looked at Merrow and saw she was asleep. He felt suddenly uneasy and restless. He rose and went to Raute and lay beside her.

'Lunar?' she rasped, her voice so old. She was just making sure it was him.

'Mmm,' he said, nodding. There was a time when she would not have needed to ask, but she was getting older by the day and her senses were failing her.

'Talk down the stars to me, my dear, if you can't sleep,' she said.

'Got to take a watch later,' he said, by way of explanation.

'Wolves should rest when they can, for who can tell when the gods will need their strength? Eh?'

'Not me,' said Lunar, shifting his flank closer to hers.

Love . . . He supposed he loved old Raute too.

'Talk down the stars for me, my dear,' she repeated, 'for I'm restless too.'

'I'll begin with Mistur,' said Lunar, 'which . . .'

So he began, softly talking down the stars across the sky, not knowing that his voice was a comfort to others, nor guessing that it lulled his bigger brother Solar into sleep. Lunar liked to talk, to see, to play games with words, to re-tell the stories he had been told, especially at night.

Of them all, Lunar was most a wolf of the night.

'Go *on* . . .' said Raute.

So Lunar did, star after star, constellation after constellation, making of them a mandala in the night, as Raute and Lounel had taught him, in a way only frail Merrow had learned better; until, at last, all the Wolves slept but he, and his voice faded into silence with the speaking of the name of the furthest, the faintest, the most distant constellation of them all, which ancient wolves called Tio, and which present wolves know as Time.

Then he went to watch, and drift in his mind, to watch, to try not to sleep, to . . .

VROOMOOOO . . . ! CHSSSSK . . . ! *RrRrRrRrRrRRRRRRRRR!*
The sudden, shattering roar of low-flying jets broke the pre-dawn sky wide open, and brought the whole pack to its feet in alarm. Then, as the roaring began to fade towards the Forest and Vale just as it had the day before there came once more the BOOM-BOOM! and the CRUMP! and rat-tat-tat of Mennen bombs and guns. Once again, but now in freezing darkness, there was the sound of rock-slides, and this time the continuing sound of guns and shells was accompanied by flashes of light at the base of high cloud, some flashes bright, some faint, some brief, some slow to fade.

'Lunar, watch over the pack,' barked Klimt. 'Lounel, Solar, come with me. We shall go to the top of the col and see what we can.'

'Not in search of Kobrin and Tervicz?' said Solar.

Klimt shook his head. 'They know their task well enough, and will keep their heads down if there is danger. The job of those who reconnoitre is to avoid being killed, and to return in one piece and make a report. Those two know their job – none better. Now come, for we need to see if our pack can remain here in safety.'

RRRRRRRrRrRrRrRrRrRrRRRRR . . . ! *CRUMP!*

Nearer this time, somewhere beyond the col above them, a sudden white-blue flash, briefly lighting the eastward faces of the cliffs like a thousand moons.

'Come,' growled Klimt . . .

They were back in under an hour, just as the sun began to rise. There had been no more sounds of Mennen war nearby, but further off the growl and crackle of guns and shells had continued unabated through the dawn.

'We could not see much, just the flashes and sudden light,' Solar told his siblings a little later. 'And there was the acrid smell of Mennen smoke.'

'Is father not going to search for Kobrin and Tervicz at all?' said Rohan, her warm voice troubled.

'No he is not,' said Klimt's deep voice as he joined them. 'I said before, Kobrin and Tervicz know their work well. Never be panicked into sending others after those on a reconnaissance, unless you have very good reason to do so.'

'Like you've got new information they might not have?'

'Exactly, Solar,' said Klimt approvingly.

'So we'll just have to wait?' said Rohan.

It was not just her siblings who awaited Klimt's reply, but senior wolves as well. All were worried about the fate of the two who had been gone nearly a whole day now.

'Wait, *and* rest,' said Klimt, settling down and closing his eyes.

He was so calm, so at ease, such an example to the pack, that when, a short while later, the jets overflew them yet again, the first of a series of such flights that morning, he pricked his ears but barely bothered to open his eyes.

But seeing that others there were growing alarmed, and likely to become more so, he said simply, 'Let the Mennen do to each other what they must, and let us Wolves have faith in each other.'

For three long days did the Mennen battle continue, and for three days did the Wolves wait for the return of Kobrin and Tervicz, kept calm by Klimt alone, for towards the end even the normally imperturbable Lounel betrayed signs of uneasiness, while Elhana grew visibly concerned. She knew, perhaps, that if Kobrin and Tervicz were lost, the pack's vulnerability to incursion by the Mennen, and attack by the Magyars, would be greatly increased. Which, if it were so, might mean that her chances of having young in the coming spring would be much less, for stress was the enemy of conception.

Then, on the fourth morning of waiting, as suddenly as the sight and sound of the Mennen air and land battles had begun, they ceased; and not long afterwards, as suddenly as Kobrin and Tervicz had departed, they appeared within sight of the col, and Rohan, who was on watch just then, was able to bark the welcome news of their return. She made her welcome all the warmer because, of late, she had shown more than a simple interest in Tervicz, though not, as yet, he in her.

Both looked tired, and their fur was filthy with dust and oil, but though they had a few scratches and bruises neither had suffered any hurts or injuries that some good food, a good wash, and a rest could not heal. Indeed, both seemed excited by what they had seen, and relieved to have escaped – and as details of their story emerged through the day, the Wolves began to feel that their general sense that something significant had changed in the wider world about them was well founded.

The moment the two wolves had crested the eastern col after that first overflight of jets four days before, they had been assailed by the sound of heavy guns from across the Vale below.

'Not that we can see much from just above here, as you know,' said Tervicz, who told most of the story, with Kobrin adding bits here and there, and making a commentary on strategy as well, which was his special expertise.

'We took the usual route down to the Forest, and there was no sign of Mennen until then. But Kobrin warned against advancing through the Forest towards the Vale too fast, and he was right. There were Mennen with guns all along its lower, eastern edge. The deer who might normally have been there had taken fright and had long since retreated up into the gulleys of the cliffs above.'

'We passed several groups of deer on the way down,' growled Kobrin, 'and might have made a pleasant meal or two of them for the entire pack had we not had work to do!'

'And all the bird-life had fled,' continued Tervicz. 'We had the Forest to ourselves and soon found the Mennen were too intent on activities of their own kind in the valleys below to look out for the likes of us . . .'

The Mennen later moved downslope under the cover of night, and the two wolves followed them.

'More jets came over from the Scarpfeld with the dawn,' continued Tervicz, 'and we knew you must have seen and heard them. We decided to continue following the Mennen to see what we could find, but as bombs began to fall further down in the Vale Kobrin decided we should stay our ground and keep out of sight. A wolf cannot out-run a bullet. For a day and a half we stayed where we were, watching, listening, smelling such smoke and fumes as drifted our way, hearing and seeing bombs and gunfire, and towards the end of that phase hearing the shouting and screaming of the Mennen.

'We finally used the cover of night to advance further, and sometime then, low down in the Vale, we came across the first of the Mennen bodies, black with blood, and crawling with maggots, and stinking. After that we made our way through a small settlement, and then another, all in darkness, all deserted, all smelling of death.

'We followed in the wake of the Mennen we had first come across in the Forest and it seemed that it was they who were the bringers of death through the Vale, and that the jets that overflew us, dropping their bombs further and further down the Vale, were their allies in war.

'Not all the Mennen we found were dead, nor were all full-grown, for some were like our youngsters when they were cubs, crying in soft voices for their mothers, or screaming with fear and pain, their bodies bloody and blackened, screaming and whimpering until they died.'

'Or were killed by the Mennen who came back,' added Kobrin.

'Yes . . .' said Tervicz darkly. 'That was when we became trapped.'

'Not quite trapped, wolf,' said Kobrin sharply. 'I ensured we had more than one way of escape from beneath the stone structure where we hid, but with Mennen and guns about it seemed most prudent to stay just where we were.'

From their hiding-place the two wolves had been witness to a massacre of Mennen by Mennen, by shooting and by fire. So close to where they lay hidden did this happen that the blood seeped downslope to them, and the heat from the flames that followed the shooting singed their fur.

'We lay low in the same place for another day and night, and might have become weak from thirst and hunger had not the Mennen most obligingly killed cows and pigs as well as themselves, right above our heads, and in an enclosure nearby,' said Tervicz with a grim smile.

'Had to stop him gorging himself,' said Kobrin wryly. 'But . . .'

'Yes, wolf?' said Klimt, sensing there was something more.

'We had discussed the possibility of using the dead Mennen as food if –'

There was a gasp from the youngsters, for this was against the traditional lore of wolfkind.

'. . . if it had come to that. But we were reluctant to do so, or rather our squeamish friend here was. For myself, I have tasted Mennen flesh before, on my long journey to the Heartland years ago, as well you know Klimt, and if we had had to maintain our strength I would have done so again.'

'Humph!' said Tervicz, before continuing. 'After that the Mennen left the settlement in vehicles, leaving behind them nothing alive. Not a chicken squawked, not a pig grunted, not a –'

'Just your farts, my friend,' said Kobrin heavily, 'because you ate too much!'

The two wolves lay low a few hours longer and then made a slow and careful return up the Vale and across into the Forest.

'Kobrin feared there would still be a few outposts of the Mennen about, just as we wolves would leave watchers behind in such a place, and he was proved right,' said Tervicz, 'and that's why we took a long time to get back, for we had to lie low again. In any case, it seemed sensible to pause above the Forest and wait and see if the Mennen left the places where we knew they were, so that we could advise you when and whether to return, now that winter is upon us.'

'An alarming report,' said Klimt, 'which will need much thought and discussion, and demands further reconnaissance. Meanwhile, we have been fortunate that the weather has remained dry so long.'

The clear blue of the days just past had been replaced by high cloud cover, and still conditions that were bitterly cold at night. They could survive on the Scarpfeld a while longer easily enough, but deer and rabbits had all but gone to ground, so their most familiar source of food had deserted them and the frozen pools suggested that the streams as well would turn to ice before long. They would soon have to leave.

'But then,' said the resourceful Kobrin, 'because so many animals have fled the Forest for the higher ground we will find food easier to locate on the eastern side of the col, rather than here across the Scarpfeld.'

'You're suggesting we move over to that side, but delay complete return to the Forest itself until we are sure it is clear?' said Klimt.

Kobrin nodded, and the other senior wolves concurred.

So it was agreed, and with this dramatic end to their summer sojourn on the Scarpfeld, and no further sign of the Mennen War for now, the Wolves shortly afterwards left the Scarpfeld altogether, following Klimt up the steep screes towards the col, even as the air grew colder still, and behind them, right across their home for so many months past, the sky's high pale grey cover began to descend, and turn to the swirling darker-mottled colour that presages the first heavy snowfalls of the year.

For the youngsters, crossing the col once more seemed like a passage into adulthood, for though they had been that way from time to time through the summer, they had all matured in the weeks just past, and followed Klimt now more as leader than as 'father'. Elhana, sensing the moment, distanced herself from all of them, signalling that they no longer had her special protection, and must find their own place in the pack – as indeed they had already begun to do.

So it was that as they journeyed Solar was up there with the leaders, and Lunar some way further down, his sister Tare ostentatiously taking a place ahead of him, and snarling when he dared come too close. He affected indifference to her, but did not feel it, and had not Rohan been nearby to smile at him, and Merrow ready to return his grin and wink, he might have felt lonely and displaced.

But such thoughts were soon dispelled when, some hours of trekking later, the col itself now far behind them, they came to the gulley route that would take them safely down to the Forest, and saw stretching before them the vast expanse of the lower lands where they chose to spend the winter.

Although they knew it had now been defiled by Mennen conflict they could not at first see much sign of that, or of Mennen – though a blue-grey haze in the air above the lower ground to the north suggested that some of the fires Kobrin and Tervicz had reported seeing were still burning.

°　°　°

The wintering grounds of the Wolves of Time lie north-eastward of the High Tatra, in isolated vales which are forested in their higher parts, but which lower down have been cleared over the centuries by the Mennen to form pasture lands.

Traditionally, before the Mennen's persecution drove them from those parts a century before, wolves roamed the forested slopes, for they offered good cover from which to raid on the prey on the lower ground. From here the wolves could follow the deer out of the Forest, or, occasionally, in hard seasons, take the Mennen's sick and dying livestock.

Under Klimt's leadership the Wolves of Time rediscovered these forested grounds, and by degrees, as the first months and years passed by, the pack came to refer to the forest parts simply as the 'Forest', and the lower parts as the 'Vale'. The Mennen rarely disturbed them there.

Between the higher edge of the Forest, and the great dark cliffs which tower over it and mark the beginning of the High Tatra, is rugged and broken ground of great fallen boulders, scree, and rough sward. This is the site for the innumerable rills and streams that flow over (and sometimes under) the scree, all of which originate from the cliffs above. Their sources are the springs and waterfalls, some large, many small, and a few no more than drippings and runnels, which come down all along the cliffs, themselves fed by the precipitation that falls upon the mountains above.

A few are large enough to be landmarks in themselves when viewed from the far side of the Vale, their height and width so great that they appear as jagged white slashes running from top to bottom of the cliffs. When the wind blows northerly, along the cliffs' many faces, these larger falls are sometimes blown bodily off course, their white water scattering into spray, and the spray spreading southward as fine mist.

A wolf might watch for hours as a waterfall struggled thus against the wind, its lower part sent flying across the cliff-face, its water finding refuge on some new area of rock and flooding down in sudden streams and rivulets to the scree and sward below. Until finally the wind began to die, and the waterfall reclaimed its rightful place in the darker clefts it had worn away through the ages.

But mostly the bigger falls were stronger than the winds, and fell stolidly and eternally down, their thunderous sound, at the time of spates especially, as impressive as the sight of them. Up there, amongst the rocks and screes and waterfalls, a wolf could not hear himself, or his enemies; nor easily pick up scent of friend and foe in the shifting winds. So the quieter Forest ways below offered better sanctuary, and it was there the pack preferred to live.

Above that part of the Forest the Wolves frequented, a little to the north and taken as a marker of the beginning of the outskirts of their territory, the greatest fall in those parts came down. Though not the biggest along the cliffs – there were greater falls a good deal further north – it was the only one in their territory whose roar could be heard from the far side of the Vale, even on a windy day when sound travelled badly.

This they simply called the Fall, though Lounel had said that he was sure – and the imaginative Lunar was very willing to agree with him – that in times gone by the wolves who lived in those parts before the Mennen first drove them out and destroyed their pack memory, must have had a better name for it.

Klimt himself was little given to such flights of fancy, though even he agreed when he first surveyed it, in the autumn of the year of the cubs' birth, that it had a dark, deep resonance of mood which strongly suggested that it was once part of a wolfway. From across the Vale the higher parts of the Fall could more easily be seen, its white water so abundant in places that it verged on grey-green.

Over the aeons of its formation the Fall had carved a deep and complex chasm in the cliff, an overhanging, dripping gulley of such height and dark immensity that any wolf who ventured into it could not but feel awe, and unease. Deep, deep within this cavernous place the Fall tumbled to its foot, forming a pool of water which rushed and raged at itself and all the rocks about, before spewing over the jagged, rocky lips of its edge and tumbling down between gulley cliffs, finally emerging in a rush of spume and spray on to the rough ground above the Forest, and then pouring down between banks of rock and grass that could hardly contain it, and through the Forest itself; then on, ever-raging and roaring and out to the pastures below, and down to join the river that flowed in the bottom of the Vale.

Lounel had little doubt that a brave wolf, or a foolhardy one, might make his way deep into the Fall's gulley, and there find caverns and secret places where once giant wolves of legend had no doubt lived, though now only ravens and dippers dared fly and dart there.

Lunar had always been much inspired by such thoughts, but since the Wolves only journeyed to those parts after the autumn, when the rains made the Fall too large and dangerous to allow a wolf very far into its secret confines within the cliff, and left in spring, when the thaw was still in full spate, he had never had the opportunity to explore it very far.

'The only time we'll ever really get there is in summer, in a drought,' shouted Solar against the noise of the place one winter's day when they had entered the gulley; Solar shared Lunar's fascination with the place, but not his yearning to explore it.

'Or if it ever froze,' said Lunar softly, peering up at the dripping walls and remembering that once when he had come to see the place those walls had been shiny with grey rime, and the rocks treacherous with verglas; but still the Falls had roared, and none believed that they would ever freeze; or cared to suggest that even if they did, a wolf should venture anywhere near the place . . .

The cliffs were actually part of the great escarpment which formed the western edge of this part of the Tatra mountains, and it was through passes south of the Fall that the modern wolfways to the Scarpfeld led. Those paths were seldom used by the Mennen, for the Scarpfeld was more easily reached from across the Fell to the south and east, over which a few roads ran.

But in summer, shepherds made their way up the valleys of the Vale, to live in high huts there and tend their flocks. But it was usually the return of the summer walkers which signalled to the Wolves that it was time to return to the Scarpfeld. In the winter few Mennen were ever seen there, and those that were travelled only in ones or twos, trekking, searching, looking, thinking. These isolates rarely saw the Wolves, though the Wolves always saw them.

This vast and broken upland, this place of scree and raging falls, of winter snow and ice, of bright green sward and moss, of yellow spring-time tormentil, and the brilliant blue of early gentian, was where the youngsters had first learned to hunt – chasing marmot, startling the deer, and taking at last their rabbit and hare, to feel the beat of alien hearts beneath their paws, fluttering and ceasing, to hear the squeals of panic and pain, and know the soft warm flow of blood between their teeth.

This place of heights and mountain sound, of life and death, of dangerous ways, was where Lunar first learned to love nocturnal climbs, and Solar learned that foolish though his brother was, and wild and fickle too, up there, amidst the lonely silence of the cliffs,

Lunar could assume command, and pretend to lead a pack of a thousand unseen wolves.

'Lunar, turn back for Wulf's sake!'

'No, Solar, come *on* – for Wulf's sake and mine!'

While the Wolves of the pack did those things all adults must, and marked and hunted their territory, and watched and guarded it against the Magyar and the Mennen, the youngsters had roamed the ground above the Forest, and first learned to see beyond themselves, and each other.

The Vales were adult territory, for they were more easily reached by road, and to them the Mennen came by vehicles and tractor, keeping their livestock as high as they could as late as possible, and just before the first snows came, bringing manure to spread across the fields, and fodder to keep the livestock high as the pasture grasses began to fail. Then, when winter settled in, with shouts and curses, and barking dogs, the shepherds drove the stock back down into the valley bottoms.

The Wolves came and went and returned again in tune with these pastoral rhythms, watching from a distance at the foot of the cliffs above the Forest as the Mennen marked the last of their cattle drives with fires and feasts of cheese and wine, and baked bread in crude and ancient ovens on the slopes.

Such had been the pattern since Klimt and the others first came to the Heartland and began to overwinter in the Forest, and hunt downslope into the Vale for food. This was the wintertime tradition that the youngsters knew, their first memories of snow being associated with the Forest conifers, and explorations to huts, and ovens, and other such places which Mennen made, and which for a time they had deserted.

But that uneasy October, when the Wolves of Time arrived back above the Forest for what must be the final winter together of the youngsters they had nurtured towards adulthood – for soon some would leave, or some might die, and the pack would be changed for ever – they knew at once that Mennen had done something grim and terrible thereabout, and not long since. The heavy guns they had heard firing four days before had not, it seemed, been firing at nothing.

The livestock was gone already, though the winter was still mild; and there was the drifting stench of fire and death across the Vale, carried on winds made foul by the odour of rotting Mennen flesh. Several of the huts in which some of the Mennen lived in summer, and which in previous years they had so carefully closed and sealed up for winter, now stood open to the elements, some burnt, some wilfully destroyed. The hill-fires were still dead from last year, never having been lit to celebrate the passing of the autumn. The ovens smelt of the excrement of bats and birds, not of Mennen bread; and in one a Mann had been thrust head first, and burnt alive. The Vale had clearly been abandoned in haste and panic, and what Klimt's Wolves scented was not just death, but change, and the approach of a darkness that went deeper than a few early winter days.

So strange did all this seem, and so menacing, that at Klimt's suggestion all thought of a pack council to discuss what had so recently happened was set to one side in favour of some further investigation. The moment the Wolves had re-established themselves in their winter quarters in the Forest, and made sure by scent-marking out their winter territory once again that the Magyars would not lightly stray that way from off the Fell, Klimt ordered further rapid reconnaissance of the Vale.

Initially this was to go ten miles to the south, which took them to the Fell, and a similar distance northwards where the ground rose up into the High Carpathians once more, the Vales and Forest swinging westward, and broken by roads. This wider survey was brief and cursory, but it confirmed the impression of destruction and death given by what they had initially found. Huts burnt, rooks and ravens pecking at corpses, untended cows dead and swollen in the fields, others hoarse and weak with bellowing and starvation in shelters and pens.

Mennen lying dead, naked to the sky, mutilated, stinking, struck down where they lay; Mennen still alive, crawling, whispering, blinded to the world of the living, unaware that wolves had come to watch them and sniff at them as, mumbling and crying out, they died. Mennen wandering, strange Mennen, who seemed to see nothing, and bellowed like cattle, and screeched like frightened badgers.

This new reconnaissance done, the pack met together early one morning down by the road that ran the length of the Vale, to discuss what they should do; whether they should stay on in the Forest, or move further away from these parts, to which the Mennen might return.

'What I think . . .' Tervicz was saying, for Klimt had just then asked him for his contribution – but none ever heard what Tervicz thought.

For suddenly Lounel was up in alarm and peering upslope towards the Forest, while Klimt was standing, staring strangely, scenting at the wind, and whispering, 'It is the scent of thyme and tarragon.'

Then Lounel was off and running in the lolloping, eager way he had, upslope, towards what he had seen approaching them.

Out of the light of the rising sun he came, the old wolf, straight to where Lounel stood waiting.

'You are restless, my friend,' the old wolf said.

'I have known you were coming,' whispered Lounel, the light of a new morning of hope in his eyes. 'I knew you were near.'

'I have been nearby for days, for weeks, awaiting my moment. What is your name, wolf? Are you the wolf Lounel?'

'I am,' he replied, as the others rose slowly in wonder, and saw the old wolf there.

Pale his fur, paler than any they had ever seen, pale as passing dust upon a wolfway in summer; and warm was his ancient gaze.

'Lounel,' the old wolf repeated, pondering the name before looking at the others and shaking his head as if they were not quite what he sought. 'And the name of your leader?'

'Klimt,' said Lounel softly.

'Ah,' sighed the wolf, and it seemed a stillness came upon him such as he had taken a lifetime to find.

'What wolf are you?' asked Lounel. 'And what do you seek?'

'I am a Wanderer . . .' the wolf replied, and Lounel gasped, for he had always thought that Wanderers were but wolves of myth and legend and that none lived now.

'I am a Wanderer, and it is to speak to Klimt of Tornesdal that I have journeyed these long years,' the old wolf said, his voice like the whisper of wind through the ancient trees of the far-distant land whence he had come. 'Therefore, lead me to him now . . .'

CHAPTER FOUR

*The Wanderer tells of his origins, and the great
event which marked the beginning of his journey*

THE WOLVES watched in silence as the stranger advanced into their very midst, straight to where Klimt stood. Old though he evidently was – his fur was dry and thin, his face wizened, his flanks and legs all skin and bone – he walked with grace and ease, seeming unaware of, or unconcerned with, the impact his sudden arrival had upon them all. All, that is, but Lounel, who seemed almost matter-of-fact about it.

Even the normally calm and imperturbable Klimt seemed unable to comprehend what the coming of so old and venerable a wolf might mean, or whether he should so readily allow a stranger, whose origin and intentions were quite unknown to him, to join them without any questioning at all. Yet so powerful was the sense of wisdom and right-purpose that the wolf exuded it would have seemed wrong to interrogate him, or make him stay on the outside of their circle for a time, as they would have done with any other alien wolves.

However, Klimt quickly recovered his composure, and evidently deciding that the wolf should be honoured and made welcome, offered him food and water, and a place to rest awhile.

The wolf shook his head.

Would he then perhaps like to know the names of the pack, and after that to . . . ?

Again he indicated there was no need, not yet at any rate, and kept his grey eyes fixed on Klimt's.

'What wolf are you?' said Klimt, astonishing the pack by yielding up his own place of honour to the old wolf, by which action a new and yet more awed and sombre mood came over the Wolves, for if their leader so acknowledged him, he must be a great wolf indeed.

'You are Klimt of Tornesdal, leader of the Wolves of Time whose territory is now the Heartland?'

He spoke in a clear mellifluous voice which was only a little cracked with age.

'I am,' said Klimt, 'and you . . . ?'

'I am a Wanderer,' responded the wolf firmly but courteously, 'and I thank you for your offer of food and water, and a place to rest. These I accept, for I have need of them. But far though I have travelled to find you, and hungry and fatigued though I now am – and not a little troubled too by the Mennen violence, through the middle of which I have had to wend my way in recent days – I must tell you at once the news I bring to you and all those who follow you . . . and give you a warning too. Then, my most important task done, I shall feel better able to accept your pack's hospitality.'

'Wanderer,' said Klimt respectfully, 'you said you would speak to all the pack, but they are not all here. Two are on watching duty, and a third, Raute, is old and near death and seeks rest and respite in a place deep in the Forest. Your words sound urgent, but please delay your telling awhile to let us all have opportunity to hear you. Solar and Lunar, go and get the watchers while I lead this venerable wolf to Raute's resting-place, for surely she should hear what it is he has to say.'

'But surely you should leave the watchers where they are for safety's sake?' replied the Wanderer quizzically.

Klimt smiled, hesitating only briefly before he replied.

'I have taught the younger members of the pack that good leadership should combine prudence with risk, and reverence for the past with belief in the future. I know not your name, wolf, but I sense that the gods themselves must have sent you – or if not, that their blessings must be on you. They shall protect us from danger while you tell *all* the pack this news and warning you have travelled so far to bring.'

'That is well said, Klimt,' said the Wanderer, and the pack could not but notice that there was respect for their leader in his voice.

'Come then . . .' said Klimt, and he led the old wolf into the Forest, to the clearing where Raute lay.

No sooner was the whole pack gathered, and Raute told what was happening, than the Wanderer began to speak. None of them had ever heard the like before – for his talk was strangely rhythmic and beautiful, and melded soon into a discourse and finally a howling none of them would ever after likely forget.

Listen now, listen wolves, for I have travelled the wolfways from the past to help guide you to the future. This is the Wanderer's way, this his purpose and intent. Listen now.

I come from a place so far distant that most of you will imagine it to be a place of myth and legend rather than reality, though Kobrin here may have heard of it from others, and Tervicz may have heard tell of it in the howlings he was taught when young . . .

Both the wolves mentioned looked astonished that the old wolf knew their names, and yet more astonished still when he named the place from which he had travelled. Indeed, Kobrin, not a wolf inclined to be taken unawares, let out a little grunt of surprise.

I come from the Springs of Lake Baikal, in southern Siberia . . .

'But Wanderer,' cried Kobrin, 'I tried myself to reach the Springs many years ago and the distance proved too far, the going too difficult, so how . . . ?'

Whilst Tervicz said, 'All I know of the Springs, which indeed I had thought was a place of myth and legend, is that it was there that the daughter of Smilodon shed tears for the death of her father, who was God of All. But more than that . . .'

The Wanderer nodded, thought a bit, stayed silent a little longer, and then began once more.

. . . I come, then, from the Springs, which is that territory north of holy Lake Baikal whose highest point is Gora in'aptuk, formed when Smilodon's daughter lay down her head in grief at His death. His passing brought to an end the time before wolfkind. Her tears formed the rivers that run to north, west and east, and flow endlessly in acknowledgement of the time of peace and tranquillity that seemed to pass for ever with Smilodon, the sabre-toothed one.

To the south of where she lay, and lies still in mountain form, her tears filled the chasm that Smilodon's right paw made in his death throes. The chasm is Lake Baikal, and her tears, which were as crystal-clear as light, form the purest water on the Earth. Baikal's water gave birth to all new life after Smilodon's death, and from it Wulf, our lord, first emerged. But of that, and His

*later incarceration in what we now call the WulfRock, we shall
talk together another time.*

*The story of my journey here begins with the birth of a female
cub upon the sacred slopes of Gora in'aptuk, the first birth of a
wolf in the region of the Springs for a whole millennium.*

*Know this: that great upland territory admits of no breeding
wolves. To its hills of shimmering spruce and thin pale birch trees
the wolves that would be Wanderers, male and female as I have
said, journey to dwell in peace; to learn, to think, and finally, if
so it must be, to be anointed Wanderer in the river of tears of
which I have spoken, and set forth.*

*I myself first came to the Springs many years ago, having felt
a vocation for that life from youth, having been raised a Yakut
wolf in the northern reaches of the Siberian tundra, upon the
frozen shores of the River Lena . . .*

'A Yakut wolf!' exclaimed Kobrin, once more unable to contain himself. 'But I had heard they were wolves of legend, wolves who in
far-gone times served the ancient frost giants.'

The Wanderer laughed, not minding Kobrin's interruption one bit
– indeed, rather welcoming it, for evidently he liked the ebb and flow
of trusting talk.

'Well, Kobrin, you can see that I am very much alive. As a matter
of fact I was brought up to believe that Pechoran wolves, of which I
believe you are one, were also wolves of legend – wolves who once
hunted down and killed the last of the ice giants, who were Kaldr's
sons. But it seems we were both wrong, and labouring under the
delusions and prejudice that isolation and the death of wolfkind's
collective memory bring about.'

'A Yakut!' Kobrin could not help repeating. 'Well I'm damned!'

'I hope not, Kobrin,' said the Wanderer, making them all laugh.
'Now, as I was telling . . .'

*. . . The north part of the River Lena was my home territory. I
soon heard tellings of the fact that its source rose at Gora in'aptuk,
or the Holy Mountain, as our shamans called it. Such wolves, I
should explain, for I see you youngsters know not of what I speak
at all, are wolves in touch with the spirits of the gods. They help
and heal us, they guide us, and sometimes they frighten us.*

Their stories inspired me, but when I learned that not one of them had ever journeyed up the River Lena to its source because they were afraid, I decided they too must be fallible. They did not want me to leave but when you lose fear of something it has no more power over you, and therefore I bid my kin farewell and began the journey that only much later I understood served as my apprenticeship to be a Wanderer.

Of that long travail I shall say no more than this: I learned that a journey is only as long and as hard as you make it; I learned that one step through the verdant vale of wisdom serves a wolf a great deal better than foolhardy leaps up at the mountain of knowledge.

I learned too that even in the furthest and most secret places, far from their roads and towns, the Mennen make incursions on our mother earth. Wonderful they are to fly in machines – wonderfully ignorant therefore of the wisdom learned by taking the same route by foot. A wolf respects the virgin forest he enters, because he has made the effort to travel through the old, worn forests, and has learned what they can give him; he respects the mountain-tops because he has reached them from the slopes below, whose vales and streams have given him sustenance. Mennen go too far and fast to learn the deeper things.

A wolf respects the far-distant place, because by the time he arrives it has begun to feel familiar, to feel like home, and therefore to be of value to him. Give a wolf food all his life and he will grow fat and ignorant and die young. Make him hunt for it and he will appreciate it more, stay lean, gain wisdom, and live.

Once, the Yakut legends teach, Mennen were the same. But then they learned to make roads, to make rails, to fly, and journeyed too fast to pick up the wisdom that awaits them on the way.

These were the things I learned on my way up the River Lena. Remember them.

When I reached the Springs I was made welcome by the wolves living there. Most were older than me, some very old; those that chose to speak taught me with words; those that remained silent taught me to learn from silence.

The wolves about Gora in'aptuk are celibate, and lead separate lives. There is no pack as you know it, nor leader either – though usually one or other of the older wolves becomes the Elder, and is respected and listened to with care. In my early days at the

Springs there was no great Elder, but in more recent years, and until the day I left to make the journey that brings me here, the Elder was a venerable female, Zajsan, born of the lake-territory of that name, to the southeast of Lake Baikal.

Of those that came to Gora in'aptuk, many found the life too hard, the disciplines too severe, and left, wiser than when they came. Others stayed, but somehow shrivelled up, worthy to keep the traditions alive, but never finding courage or vision enough to set off once more as Wanderers. They always found good reasons to stay behind.

For myself, I desired to leave but had no special vocation that made me do so, no overriding purpose, for wandering by itself is not quite enough. Zajsan advised me to be patient, and as the years passed by and she grew older, I came to see that in the waiting was much learning.

During that time I became her helper, and in some sense her companion. She would often ask me if I had yet found a reason to leave and when I shook my head she would say I should not worry, a reason would come along one day.

'And what of you, Elder Zajsan? Did you never find a reason for becoming a Wanderer?'

She laughed – she had a happy, gentle laugh – and told me that she had been – once. She had wandered far and wide after many years at Gora in'aptuk, but then she found a reason to come back, which few Wanderers ever do, very few.

What that reason was she would not immediately tell me, except to say that she felt sure that one day her help would be needed by a wolf who was coming to the Springs.

'He or she may already be here – you may be the wolf yourself! I do not know, but . . . when it happens I will know, just as when your time has come to leave and journey forth as a Wanderer, you will know, wolf, truly you will know. Therefore, stay attentive to the whispering of the wind, for it is the voice of God and will tell you what to do. Attend to it and not yourself!'

So much for my coming to the Springs. Now I must come to that momentous event which resulted in my hearing the divine whispering of the wind, and accepting at last my fate as a Wanderer.

It was springtime, three years ago, the time when in the Springs the ice and snow of winter begin to melt and the streams and *rivers begin to run in spate. The air is filled with the sound of water, and the sky with watery light.*

Then the spirits of those of us by the Holy Mountain are lifted, for the winter is over and we can share once more in the new life of land and water, of sky and water, and of the land and sky. It was then, in April, that the Elder Zajsan summoned me to her. She was ill, but for another, not herself.

'No, no, do not concern yourself with me. Hasten now off the watershed and down through the vales to the shores of Lake Baikal. You will find a wolf there who needs my help. I feel her tiredness in my breast, and her age in all my limbs. Go at once to find her, wolf, and lead her here.'

I did as I was bid, running by the torrential streams, leaping the thaw-wet boulders, dazzled by the marsh marigold, dancing with the birdsong of the woods, feeling the lightness of my limbs and the joys of all my senses.

Never in my life had I ever been so at one with the land on which I ran, and the water whose song was my accompaniment, or the sky which was my only horizon! I knew then, as the shining waters of Baikal came into view, that my time at Gora in'aptuk was nearing its end, and my life as a Wanderer was beginning. As for the purpose and vision I still needed, I had little doubt that I would find it in the wolf the Elder had sent me to guide back to the watershed.

Only after many days of searching did I find her, and she was right at the water's edge, where I had already looked, which was the first of many strange things connected with her coming.

She proved to be old, older by far than the Elder Zajsan, and her paws and lower legs were worn and scarred from a lifetime of travel, her fur pale yellow in places, like the wolves of the Mongolian deserts, yet darker and flecked with grey like the wolves of the north; and in yet others there was still the fresh russet tinge of the legendary wolves of the temperate eastern plains, of whom I had heard only in stories, but whom I had often imagined meeting.

Well then, this was a strange wolf, born of many places, and to add to her strangeness there was a look in her eyes of brightness, even brighter than the water of Lake Baikal I found her trying to drink.

'Wolf,' I began on seeing her . . .

She turned and welcomed me, and used my name, which none had used for many years. I felt awed by her presence, but she did not make me feel fear; I felt deep respect, yet still she made me feel I could be myself; I felt humble before her, yet still felt I had importance.

'You have come to guide me to Gora in'aptuk,' she said. 'Is Zajsan there?'

I said I had, and she was, and then began to lead her away from Lake Baikal and back up into the mountains. I think it was then, as I saw her struggle up the slopes, as I watched as she stopped from breathlessness, as she seemed ill and sick within herself, that I began to think that she was more than mortal wolf, though Wulf knows her difficulties were mortal. I do not call them suffering, for of that she gave no sense at all. It seemed to me that she was fending death itself from her body.

Yet, for all that I was alone with her for several days, I did not once guess what ailed her, nor what I might soon be witness to.

She answered none of my questions on our journey to the Holy Mountain, yet talked willingly of other things, and told me a great deal I did not know. Of the Dark Millennium, and how, with Wulf's fall, wolfkind gave up their divine inheritance, which was the land, to Mennen.

'They inherited the earth from us, you see, and might have been our gods but . . . they despoiled it. Like cubs without a sense of responsibility they are, or like senile wolves to be pitied and helped because they know no better.

'But you have journeyed up the River Lena, and seen the things the Mennen do.'

I nodded, those memories etched upon my mind like the scars across the land where Mennen ravaged the tundra, and stole the taiga trees.

'I have travelled many lands and seen what Mennen do. Like a cub urinating into water it then seeks to drink, they pollute all water they come near; like an old wolf suffering incontinence of the bowels they defecate their filthy spoil upon the very land on which they live and sleep. No wonder they are poisoned and dying now, for they ingest their own filth.

'The Mennen's time has come, the Dark Millennium is nearly done, and now wolfkind must rediscover the faith in their own

kind which will let them be lords of the earth again. But ... but I fear we may not succeed. The centuries have seen too many of us lost, too many traditions gone, and reverence for the gods has all but melded into fear and ignorance, and wolfkind now has a spirit made too subjugate by the daily imperative of survival to take time to see beyond itself to where the sky is blue, the mountains rise, the sun sets towards another day, and the stars shine bright with hope and awe.'

With such words did the old female inspire me in those few days we journeyed alone. That sense of purpose and renewal I had first had while journeying down to find her, found added strength as she spoke to me, though I still did not know in what direction my vocation as a Wanderer might take me.

Then, too soon for me, we reached Gora in'aptuk, and came to where Zajsan awaited us.

The old female gave herself up to Zajsan's care, and I believe that all of us Wanderers understood that something momentous was happening. The Springs seemed verdant, more alive than any I had ever known. The waters of the streams and rivers ran ever more clear; the skies seemed ever brighter by day, and by night the stars and the moon shone brighter still. Quite when we first guessed at the extraordinary event that was to take place among us I do not know, but Zajsan sent word to me to come quickly.

I was instructed to find a sheltered place near one of the bigger streams; a place within easy reach of water, of food, and facing south that it might be warm.

I presumed that the old female was about to die, and that Elder Zajsan wanted to make her last day, or even hours, as comfortable as possible. In one sense I was right, but in another as wrong as I could be ...

Anyway, I did as I was asked and soon led Zajsan and the old one to the spot. By then she had changed – she seemed to have put on weight, she seemed peaceful, she seemed ... but what she truly seemed was not possible – not here, not for one so old, not for the one I had found but a week or two before.

The place I had chosen was a low cavern, dry and warm and facing south. The stream was not far off, and I could hunt for food nearby if that was what they wanted.

What happened that same day I had best put into as few words as possible. What more should a wolf say when his whole world shifts, and his perception of all he ever knew is changed for ever in a day? Therefore, I shall say no more than this of what then happened . . .

With my own eyes I saw the old one go into the cavern, with Zajsan helping her. I saw a sun shine bright that day, and spring-time at its brightest and most beautiful. I watched as suddenly the skies darkened before they should, and all became still and hushed; I felt the flanks of Gora in'aptuk tremble, and saw evening come. Then, to the light of the stars, and lying fearfully in the moon's shadows near the cavern, I heard the sounds of birth.

Howling I heard; scuffing I heard; and the urging and encouragement of Zajsan's voice; groaning I heard and then, finally, a sigh . . . long it was, and stranger than all that had gone before, for it told of release and death even as it spoke of birth and new life.

That night may have been many nights; that night perhaps time stood still; that night, as I now know, the old one died and journeyed to the stars in giving birth to the new.

She who came to Lake Baikal, who spoke so stirringly to me as we ascended the Holy Mountain, and who went into the cavern I had found, gave birth to her own self . . .

The Wanderer seemed suddenly overcome with emotion and fatigue, as if reliving these events left him as overwhelmed as when they first occurred.

'Perhaps,' he said with a weary sigh, 'I should now take up Klimt's offer of food, water and sleep and only then continue. But now you know that I was witness to nothing less than the re-birth of a god – and one whose name I know, and I believe you must know.'

'It was the She-wolf Wulfin who came to the Springs, and whose re-birth you witnessed that day and night,' whispered Elhana. 'Did She not come among us at the birth of our own cubs and tell us, as this Wanderer plainly knows, that one of our two males would one day be re-born as Wulf Himself? And did not that same She-wolf suggest that She must depart from us, that She too might re-born and be ready for when Wulf would need Her once again?'

The senior wolves nodded, Klimt especially. They were silent, struck dumb by what they had heard, which confirmed something which perhaps they had sought to hide and half forget in these recent years;

that they had made, and raised, a god ... While upon the faces of the younger wolves was disbelief, not of the Wanderer's tale, but that one of them, most likely Solar, was ... was Wu ... was ...

No, it could not be believed.

'Humph!' said Tare, turning from Solar with disdain.

'Well ...' muttered Rohan.

'Curious, if you ask me, which nobody has,' observed Lunar, grinning at Solar with sympathy.

'I don't believe it,' said Solar, in an indifferent un-godlike way.

'I do,' said Merrow softly, her voice breaking, for looking at her brothers as she then did, she could only weep.

The Wanderer shrugged, as if any and all of these responses were quite reasonable.

'So ... I have said all I want to for the moment. Now I shall try to recover something of my strength, and then, if I may, tell you how after that holy cub's birth I came to depart the Springs, to seek out this pack whose destiny was always to be given the task of serving wolfkind by seeking a way to lead them safely beyond the end of the Dark Millennium.'

CHAPTER FIVE

The Wanderer concludes his telling with a warning,
and a difficult challenge to Klimt that he will not be able to ignore

THE WANDERER SLEPT for three days after his first telling, and when he awoke he ate but little of the food the pack found for him. But he did declare himself to be thirsty and that he would welcome the clearest, coldest mountain water they could find. Klimt commanded Lunar and Lounel to lead him through the Forest to where the outwaters of the Fall ran as a torrent amidst the mossy rocks and trees.

Here he sat watching the rushing stream alone for a time, down among the dank and dripping rocks at the water's very edge, seemingly lost in its endless noise, his fur pale against its broiling depths and shadows, his body seeming frail against its boundless strength. Lounel and Lunar watched over him, choosing to look away for most of the time, as if to gaze upon him was to disturb his contemplation.

When he had done, they led him back to Raute's clearing, and spoke to her for a time as the pack quietly gathered together once again. When they were all settled once more he fell silent as if wishing to recommence his telling without more ado. Then his gaze fell from the Wolves to the Forest floor, and he nodded his head a little, he frowned somewhat, and it seemed that shadows crossed his face and eyes, and from the joy of that remembered birth he was journeying on to a time of anxiety and concern.

But he did not immediately resume the howling, preferring for a time to ask questions of the Wolves, and to listen to their replies. In this way, and with remarkable perspicacity, he extracted from them the essentials of the situation – that since the youngsters' birth the Wolves had been so involved in rearing them they had had no time for outward exploration, or for much thought about the future; and that in this introspective and reclusive phase they had been greatly aided by the continuing absence of Magyars, whose leaders and main pack seemed to have all but deserted the Southern Fell that stretched out south of the Scarpfeld.

He learned too of the exile of Aragon, Jicin and Stry, and seemed to know its reasons, though he displayed some disappointment that they had not returned, and brought news of the outside world. He was told enough – or observed enough – to understand the hierarchy of the pack, and that Solar was the strongest of the younger males, and Tare seemed set to be a dominant female in the future.

He listened to such things benignly, and heard the Wolves' talk of their knowledge of the lore of gods and myth – or rather their lack of it – without comment, though his quizzical expression occasionally betrayed his feeling that perhaps in some areas they should know more.

Finally, with a brief nod to indicate that for the time being he felt their talk was done, he resumed his own telling . . .

I spoke a few days ago of a birth into mortality, and suggested it was not a mortal birth. How else could it be that I never saw the old one again, alive or dead? No body was there in the cavern when, later, I was permitted to enter it.

I said that during that extraordinary day and night, time seemed to stand still. Perhaps it was my memory that played tricks with me, I know not – though I know no other Wanderer or seeker in those parts who had memories any different from mine. An old one died, and a new one came among us, cubbish, without speech, without much strength, as yet; but strangely ready for life, like a bird that had come out of its egg fully-fledged and nearly set to fly.

I who had been witness to the birth, or as near as a male might be in such a circumstance, was first witness too to that cub's emergence into the light of day. I swear this was no new-born scrap of life, still blind, wet with afterbirth, mewing for a mother's milk.

I tell you: she was a lively growing cub already: her head, full and soft with a cub's fur; her eyes, gentle and trusting as only a cub's can be; her paws, seeming too big and full-furred, as cubs' usually do; her curiosity for life (and timid first steps out) . . . her sudden fear of it (and rush back in); these came so soon. How she ran for the protection of Zajsan's flanks and, as I feel, the protection of the ancient flanks of Gora in'aptuk.

I was appointed companion to the cub, and her protector. She was given no name, or if she was she answered to none but 'Ngu-hur' – 'No-name'!

I watched No-name grow. I knew her trials and tribulations, not least of which were the slights the older Wanderers showed her, for they did not all share my sense of wonder at her birth, thinking her to be part of a deception of some kind.

A year passed and she was a gawky juvenile, another year and she began to pass into adulthood. I do not say that she was as beautiful as the sunshine on the day she began to be born, or the light of the moon and stars on the long night of her birth. I do not say she was as bright in beauty as that first spring. I do say that another wolf, on seeing her and not knowing her origin, would at first think nothing more than that she was female, youthful, not much different from any other.

But I also say that it took but a short time in her presence to learn that she was different from all others, and utterly remarkable. She had – she has – the capacity to make another feel they have come home, and their journeying is done. The world she represents is the home wolfkind seeks . . .

Soon, amongst the Wanderers, the doubters doubted not; the reserved were no longer shy; the timid no longer afraid; the silent in no need of words to converse with her; the talkative no longer gabbling; the ones who rarely laughed, began to dare laugh; the ones who felt anger and bitterness, in her presence felt only peace. All of us, without exception, and perhaps myself most of all, fell in love with her, and learned that, Wanderers though we were, we might feel such passion.

Therefore, when this last spring we sensed she was no longer happy, nor content, all those who lived about the Springs suffered with her, and wondered what was wrong.

For two years we had called her No-name – and so I still think of her. Yet sometime last winter, when the night grew long and cold, and she began to howl of her own accord to the stars, I came finally to see and believe what Zajsan must already have known and what I have already suggested to you: this young female, so god-like in the sense of love she gave and engendered in others, was Wulf's consort Wulfin, re-born.

Amongst us she had been born, amongst us raised, and with us now she had begun to no longer wish to dwell. I believe her

*growing dismay at life, that burden of suffering and doubt, duty
and a growing purposefulness beyond any we had ever felt, that
we all began to sense come over her, marked the beginning of
her own realization of who she was, and what she was: and, more
than that, her realization that her birth, this life of hers, marked
the end of the Dark Millennium, and the beginning of a trial of
life and faith upon which all of wolfkind would depend.*

*It was then that She, whom we called No-name, began to talk
differently to each of us. But day and night she talked and listened,
garnering all she could of the collective experience of the Wanderers. I accompanied her wherever she went, so I alone of all of
them, including even Zajsan, heard the questions that she asked,
and listened to what was told her.*

*When did I finally believe who she truly was? I do not know
– only that it was with the fall to mortality of Wulf she seemed
most concerned, and stories of the Wolves of Time, and finally –
though wolves in the far-off region of Lake Baikal were ill-placed
to know much of this – she wanted to know about the Heartland,
and the Bukov wolf whose destiny it was to howl down the fabled
Wolves, and so begin the great drama and struggle for spiritual
power between the Mennen and wolfkind, which would mark the
end of the Dark Millennium.*

*Well . . . when she began to talk about journeying to the Heart-
land, and when I found her seeking out the western heights of
the Springs as if to be better able to stare across the infinite
distances of Krasno and the Vales of Ob, which are but the prelude
to the journey from Baikal to Carpathia, I began to fear that it
would not be long before she insisted that we set off a-wandering.*

*Too late! I went to consult with Elder Zajsan, we talked too
long, I pondered too much, I listened to my heart too little, and
when I returned to where I had left No-name, she was already
gone, her trail in the early summer dust already fading and disappearing. A wind that whispered to me then was surely the voice
of the gods: 'Now, wolf, now you must journey, now you shall
take up your true vocation.'*

*I did not hesitate, and began my journey west from Baikal in
search of one who went before, a wolf I loved, the nearest I ever
had, or ever will have, to a daughter. But soon I realized I would
not find her, nor see her again in this mortal world, and to try
to do so was but a futile attempt to cling on to a past that I could*

*not re-live. What is, is now, and in the present I have journeyed
on to find the Heartland, to find the Wolves of Time, and tell
them what I know, and warn them as I must.*

*I came here several weeks ago and have been among you,
learning your names, and your strengths and weaknesses. Worry
not that you have not seen me – though I believe that Lounel
here was aware of the scent of thyme and tarragon, which is the
scent of Wanderers.*

*I began my journey as a Wanderer the spring before last sum-
mer when I was not yet old, hardly middle-aged. Now you see a
wolf turned old with wandering: I have become a Wanderer, and
have no name – just like the holy she-wolf I helped to raise.*

I have no place but where I am.

I have no time but now, now, now . . .

The Wanderer had reached the end of his present howling and he
fell silent, to give the Wolves time to ponder what he had said. This
they certainly wanted to do, for there was not one among them who
was not awed and humbled by all they had heard, and confused by
the many questions raised. They shared the sense that the very world
itself was changing about them, and might never seem the same again.

'Klimt, I do not doubt,' added the old wolf a little later, 'that you
lead the pack which legend has called the "Wolves of Time". Nor is
there any question in my mind that one or other of your sons here
may well be He who will once more become Wulf Himself.

'Be not surprised if, until then, he seems mortal, and ordinary – a
god may not know he is a god, just as a wolf may not know he is a
leader of wolves until that moment comes. Then see the change!

'I am pleased, very pleased, to see that these two, Solar and Lunar,
and their sisters Rohan and Tare, continue to look at me with astonishment and doubt, their awe of me quite properly tainted with simple
disbelief. Long may it remain so, for the first thing wolves need,
whether or not they may one day become gods, is that their four feet
are firmly on the ground; the *last* thing they need is the corruption
of pride and vanity . . .'

He paused and looked at the open, honest faces of the youngsters,
whose eyes in fact were now rather more respectful than when he
had first come, for even Tare seemed to have taken him to her heart.
His gaze settled finally on Solar and Lunar, seeming to find no difference between them, for he observed, 'They both seem well raised,

one a doer perhaps and the other a dreamer, but neither the worse for that! Both qualities are needed in a god, so which will prove the mortal one and which the immortal only time will tell! They seem the least concerned of you all upon that matter, which is as it should be and suggests that Klimt and Elhana, as leader and ledrene of this remarkable pack, have done their work well!'

Elhana smiled and said ironically, 'It is good, Wanderer, to know you approve me as a mother ... and my leader as a father, seeing as you have such wide experience in such matters!'

The old wolf laughed, as they all did, and he shrugged ruefully, looking at Solar and the others.

'Remember those words of your mother, wolves, and forgive my presumption. It is a fault that Wanderers sometimes have – talking too much of things they know but little. Still, I must speak what is in my heart and mind, for there is nothing else I can do.'

Elhana's good-humoured moment of irreverence towards the stranger encouraged others to express their doubts and fears about what he had said more openly, Kobrin among them.

'Wanderer,' he began respectfully enough, 'Lake Baikal is a long way from the Heartland. Why, for some, it would be a lifetime's journey just to reach the Urals, let alone to then continue the trek across the fastness of Kazakhstan and the Ukraine.'

'It may seem so,' said the Wanderer mildly.

'I myself have trekked in the northern reaches of the Russias, from Pechora my home territory eastward across the Urals, and thence to the River Ob, and onward for a time but ...'

'It proved too far?'

'It was very far, yes, and took me years,' said Kobrin, 'so to have made your journey here having only started in the spring ...'

The Wanderer nodded his head, not at all put out by Kobrin's questioning.

'Distance is not real,' he said, 'but imagined. A cub thinks the distance to his mother's flank is far, very far, when she is out of sight. So far indeed that if she is out of sight for long enough he may quite soon give up the idea of getting back to her, and begin to grieve for her loss. Yet we, who are adults, know she may be no distance at all. Distance may seem far, very far, if the one you love is not nearby when you want and need them.

'But distance may seem short if you are fit and well, yet interminably long if you are ill, or injured.

'When I was young, and began my trek up the River Lena to Gora in'aptuk, I had no idea how far it would be, or how long it would take. Believe me, Kobrin, it felt far! As a matter of fact, it *was* far!'

The Wolves chuckled at the Wanderer's self-deprecation.

'Yet – and here is something strange – the more I travelled upriver, and the fitter I became, *and* the less I expected to arrive the next day, the quicker the days passed by, and the further I travelled on oblivious of time. The second half of that great journey to the Holy Mountain took half as long as the first part, the last quarter half as long as the third quarter . . . and so on.

'Which brings me to your question, Kobrin. Wulf created the wolf-ways, and taught us to know them in the stars. This was a great teaching, much of it now lost, for he showed wolves that travel and distance were as much in the mind and heart as in the body and upon the feet. A wolf who thinks somewhere he seeks is "far" has added distance to his journey even before he begins. Have you not noticed how the trek there always seems to take longer than the journey back? Eh?'

The Wolves nodded. Indeed they had, except when they had lost the way coming back and then . . .

'And then,' rejoined the Wanderer, 'it suddenly feels "far" once more, though you may be lost for only a few moments. Yes . . . if we know where we are going, and can trust that we will get there, and think it is not far then it will *not* be.

'I mentioned the wolfways. Those on the ground guide our bodies, those in the stars guide our minds. Bring them together, have trust in both, know them, and suddenly travelling far will not seem to take as long as you expect. In addition to which, a wolf is wise who travels the way that Wulf Himself travelled when He made the wolfways.

'As the Elder Zajsan put it, "You must travel as weather travels across the Steppes: by rain and by the river's flow; by the drifting of snow and by the sliding of ice; now as bold as thunder, next with the sudden impulse of lightning – so a Wanderer travels, and distance becomes a matter of the mind."

'When I left the Holy Mountain, at first to find my lost ward Wulfin, then to come to the Heartland, I journeyed with the shooting of new spring growth, then upon the sway of summer trees. I paused a lifetime to watch the Volga's flow, and knew a lifetime in my body too, but that time passed in a moment, in a day or two, and then on I went with the driving, scattering autumn leaves, on I travelled, until goaded by the sharp points of the first winter frosts, which once were giants but which we choose no longer so to name – though it was their giant strides that speeded me – I ascended the Carpathian mountains in Moldavia and came finally here. No wonder a journey that might have taken you years, Kobrin, took me but months; and might take a god but moments.

'So does a Wanderer deal with distance, and with time, and with "far". So must the Wolves of Time learn to travel if they are to fulfil their destiny, and wolfkind's.'

'But how *far* was it?' asked Solar, when the Wanderer had finished and none had said a word for quite a time. The point plainly bothered him.

The Wanderer chuckled sympathetically, saying, 'I know, I know, wolf, it doesn't make much sense. I fear there are some things, perhaps most things, that a wolf can only learn by experience. I see from the eyes of those older wolves here who have travelled much, or travelled far to get here, that they can make sense of what I have said. You younger ones, who know only your own territory, will need to wander the wolfways rather longer to get your paws to understand the feel of time. It won't take long!'

'Is it like the stars and moon circling at night?' said Lunar. 'I mean that sometimes, when the night is deep and beautiful, the stars circle overhead in no time at all, or seem to. I have wondered where that time went and now I see it never was. Perhaps, in that circling, I might have travelled very far if only I had tried to do so.'

The Wanderer nodded, his eyes full, and still, on Lunar's.

'It *is* like that,' he said, 'very like that, and a wolf of faith might very well travel all the wolfways of the world in a few days and nights. Not much point going any faster for he might not see very much!'

Again they all fell silent until the Wanderer, now very tired once more, said, 'Well then, here I am amongst you. There will be time enough for further talk. You know now what impelled me to leave the Springs and become a true Wanderer, but now that I am here it will be for you to decide what to make of me. I can talk. I can be silent. I can stay. I can go. A Wanderer is no more than what you make of him – just like time in fact! So . . . if you have any more to ask me today, then ask it before I fall asleep!'

Lounel said, 'Forgive me for prolonging things more than you might wish, but you were going to give us a warning, wolf, and I wondered what it was?'

The Wanderer nodded his head, shifted where he sat, stretched, got up, looked about and turned back to them.

'Let me give a warning to you all, issue a challenge to Klimt and finally make a suggestion that Kobrin, as a Russian wolf, may best understand. What you make of these things is up to you.

'The warning is this: understand that your true enemy is the Mennen, not other wolves, and in particular not the Magyar wolves. Only by making the Magyars your friends, and uniting wolfkind to a common destiny can you regain ascendancy over the Mennen.'

He paused and let this startling assertion sink in before moving on to the challenge: 'The greatest leaders recognize when one task is complete, and that to move on to the next they may need to change their ways, to let go some old habits and learn new. If you fail to do this, Klimt, you will disappear into time's forgetting, and fail to lead the Wolves of Time to their destiny. Remember the original vision that brought you here, and inspired the others to follow you. Grasp it anew now that you have gained a foothold in the Heartland, and raised young successfully with Elhana. To let go, to move on, will be no easy thing.'

'To let go *what*?' growled Klimt. 'To move on *where*?'

'*That* is your challenge, wolf!'

'Humph!' said Klimt, not entirely pleased by the Wanderer's unwillingness to say more. 'And the suggestion you were going to make – the one you think Kobrin will understand?'

'Ah . . . yes! I have said little of my journey here, but know this. In Kobrin's day, as I understand it, the main power of the Russian wolves was to the north, not so far from his home territory of Pechora. This has changed. From what I saw and learned the power of the Russian wolves lies further south, in the hills that lie between the great rivers Volga and Don. There lives a great pack, or rather a clan of packs, whose name I am sure Kobrin knows . . .'

'The Kazans,' said Kobrin, his eyes narrowing, and his voice hard. 'They are cruel wolves and in my day were never subdued, *never*. Did you meet their leader, Wanderer?'

The Wanderer shook his head. 'That I did not, though I think I came near to him.'

'They call him Kazan, do they not?'

'Like Wanderers, the one who leads those wolves loses his name. The present Kazan is, from what I heard, a powerful wolf, but one who welcomes strangers if they make obeisance to him.'

'But we are the Wolves of Time,' said Klimt, 'and we make obeisance to none.'

The Wanderer shrugged and said matter-of-factly, and in a way that made it quite plain that he was thinking of the challenge he had set Klimt earlier, 'It is always wise to honour those who may have something to teach you, Klimt. The Kazan rules over a territory ten times the size of the Heartland but with not that many more wolves than are here today, and he seems to achieve this peacefully. You might learn something from him which will stand you in good stead when it comes to dealing with the Magyars. Nor is Khazaria so very far – a wolf whose mind was on the wolfway could reach it in a few weeks. But it is only a suggestion, no more than that!'

'Humph!' said Klimt again. 'Now, Wanderer, you look tired, and we feel tired after all you have told us, and warned us about, and suggested; so let me lead you to a place of rest.'

'The will of the gods be yours,' said the Wanderer, and with that he followed Klimt to a resting-place of peace and warmth, where sleep might again soothe his old body, and ease his mind.

CHAPTER SIX

*As the Wolves survey the environs of their territory, Tervicz
discovers the bewildering landscape of love*

THE WOLVES' MOVE to their wintering grounds, and the
arrival of the Wanderer, combined to create new patterns of
watching, of hunting, and especially of evening pack-talk, which
very soon became the norm, and would remain so until the spring.

Not that the weather was yet as cold across the Forest and Vale as
it had already become in the Scarpfeld. Down in the sheltered Forest
the winds stayed mild, even as across the mountain heights above the
advance of winter showed itself in the gradual spread of snow on the
peaks and high cliff-faces, of which they had a view.

At the same time the roaring of the gulley falls, and of the Great
Fall itself, abated somewhat, as the rain that was their perennial source
in the unvisited heights above turned into settling snow.

Klimt naturally gave much thought to what the Wanderer had said
about the birth of Wulfin, and the necessity of reconsidering just who
their prime enemy might be – the Mennen or the darker elements
of wolfkind. But try though he and such advisers as Lounel and Kobrin
did to focus upon the threat of other wolves, it was hard to do so
when it was the Mennen, and their continuing violent skirmishes of
bombing, gunfire and fighting down in the lower vales, that preoccupied them all.

Indeed, Klimt might reasonably ask, *what* other wolves, for it was
plain enough that the Magyars were still thin on the ground across
the Fell, as they had been for two years past. They were not entirely
absent, as successive scouting parties by the Wolves always showed,
for it was never long before they found themselves spotted and
harassed by two or three Magyars if they ventured too far from their
own boundaries at the high, southern end of the Vale.

There, where the ground reached the rising-point of the springs
that fed the rivers of the Vale to the north, the steep drop of an

escarpment marked the line between the territories. But, as along all such boundaries, there were areas of ambiguity, and Klimt saw to it that the Wolves took it in turns to push their patrols as far as they could.

'There's not many of them about,' observed Kobrin more than once, 'but the Magyars are well organized and disciplined, and over the decades have worked out a good series of watching-points so that we are very soon seen or scented. So whoever has led them since Hassler's death has inherited a system established over decades, perhaps even centuries.'

The clashes between the two groups were never more than snarling matches, and the harassment of howling at night, for Klimt had ordered his own Wolves never to take the differences between the two groups into open conflict. He was conscious of the vulnerability of his small pack to the Magyar hordes if ever their larger and looser federation of packs came under the rule of a bold, ambitious leader.

'It's a matter of reminding them where their territory ends and ours begins . . . and, too, of finding out more about their leadership before we decide on our future strategy. But I also want our Wolves to get used to keeping their eyes open, and to the sight and scent of the Magyars, for one day things may very well become more serious.'

Naturally, it was a source of considerable interest to the Wolves, and to the youngsters in particular, as to which wolf had taken over leadership of the Magyars following Klimt's defeat of Hassler, whom he had killed when they took the Scarpfeld two years before.

They knew a good deal about the Magyar ledrene, the notorious Dendrine, whom the Wolves had met on their first ascent of the Great Gulley after Hassler's death. Descriptions of her foul language, of her haggard haunches, and of the power she seemed to have over her monstrous and depraved son, fuelled in their minds images of a wolf that frightened them, and in younger days had occasionally turned cubbish dreams into nightmares.

But despite all their watching of the Fell, and their cautious advance into that part of it to the south that Klimt made them regularly patrol, none of them had ever had a sight of Dendrine. However, Raute, herself a Magyar, had little doubt that if Dendrine was still alive she must be ledrene still, despite her age; and again and again, until they were tired of hearing it, Raute had warned them of Dendrine's evil need to dominate the weak and destroy the good. The Magyars' absence from the Fell in significant numbers and their seeming nonaggression meant only that Hassler's defeat by Klimt had pushed Dendrine and the Magyars into a period of quiescence rather than decline.

'They'll be back, and back in force, and with the sole purpose of destroying you,' warned Raute. 'Dendrine's a lust for power, that one, and she's a wolf who will swear and curse and fight to cling on to it to the very end; and she's sadistic, and enjoys hurting others in any way she can.'

But as for the Magyar *leader*, or Führer as the Magyars referred to him, the matter was a mystery, the more so because the last time Dendrine had been seen, which was by Tervicz, and at a distance in the cubs' first winter, she had been leading wolves with only her son alongflank, and no other male leader in sight.

The Wolves might have felt inclined to investigate the matter further had they not been so preoccupied with raising young for nearly two years past, and had not wished to provoke the Magyars by unnecessary reconnaissance and exploration at a time when their pack strength was so low.

'We'll wait until our youngsters are full-grown and able to fend for themselves,' Klimt had always said, and the other seniors agreed with him.

Now that time was almost on them, and had not the Mennen wars flared up locally, and right across the Vale, Klimt might have ventured out into the Fell more forcefully this winter, to find out what he could about the new Magyar leadership, and what its plans and purposes might be.

'We could ambush one or two of them and force them to tell us what's afoot across their territory,' said Tervicz, but Kobrin and Klimt were both against it. Let them build up their strength a little more yet . . .

'When spring comes we can become more active,' Klimt declared finally.

So it was that while the Wolves did not quite ignore the Wanderer's warning about concentrating on the threat of other wolves locally with the aim of uniting wolfkind in a common purpose against the Mennen, they had what seemed good reasons for not acting on it more firmly immediately.

In any case the Mennen skirmishes continuing to the north, in the lower valleys of the Vale, were now an almost daily distraction. The Wolves could hear the gunfire, and at night see the flashes and fire of warfare flaring up, and when the wind came from the north, they caught the smell of woodsmoke and burning oil.

Occasionally, as well, the noisome jet aircraft that had so shocked them when they first flew over the Scarpfeld came roaring over again, though by now the Wolves were getting used to them, so far as that was ever possible with a noise so loud that it gave a wolf a headache that lasted a good while after its cause had gone.

But the Mennen themselves rarely showed their faces in the upper Vale near the Wolves' main winter territory, and never climbed up to the Forest itself, which was now more deserted of Mennen than it had ever been.

There was, however, one change, and that concerned the road that came from the Fell and ran northward down the Vale towards the settlements where the warfare now continued, forming the effective eastern boundary of their territory. Until the previous summer the Road, as the Wolves referred to it, had been used summer and winter by the Mennen who worked the land. Their slow vehicles, carrying livestock and foodstuffs, chemicals and waste, were often to be seen upon it, as were the dogs that frequently accompanied them. Now these were all gone, and in their place came bigger and more noisy khaki-coloured vehicles which had to do with war, some belching diesel fumes. Most travelled northward and did not return; many carried Mennen in large numbers; very few ever stopped.

Indeed, when they did and Wolves were patrolling nearby, they would watch with interest to see what might transpire, but nothing much ever did. Often Mennen got out and urinated on the grass by the road, or smoked, the smelly smoky bits left behind them with their piss, for the Wolves to scent at, and move back from, disgusted. Once a vehicle stopped and several Mennen sat on the verge for a time, and left food behind them. One of them shat behind a tree, leaving behind paper that stank of it and blew out on to the Road in the days that followed, and then northward along it, as if it wished to return to where it belonged.

Another time a vehicle stopped and started all along the road, until finally it pulled on to the grass and another came by and took away the Mennen and the things which had been in it. As the days went by others stopped by this vehicle, pored over it, banged at it, and slowly bit by bit took things from it before they too journeyed on, until, abandoned off the road, the rooks took turns to settle on it, and the Wolves dared venture to it at night, and sniff about at Klimt's orders to learn the scent of Mennen and their gear. He believed wolves must learn not to be panicked by the Mennen scent and stenches, and encouraged all the youngsters to learn of such things.

So it was that in the weeks that followed the Wanderer's coming, though the Wolves talked much of the Mennen and the war, they did no more than observe, their primary thoughts and purpose turning on the Magyars, and the possibility of coming threat. While the Wanderer himself, his warning given, did not press the point, but slumbered through the winter days and nights, answered such questions of lore and legend as others asked him, sallied forth to high ground with Lounel on days when the snow allowed it, and softly wove for Raute his howlings and his tales.

Then one night at the end of December, when the days were short and bitter, and the nights long and dreary, the first heavy snow began to fall, so that by morning the Vale was draped in white, and all was tranquil. The sounds of war could still be heard, but muffled now and more distant. It was the time of the winter solstice, a quiet time for wolves and Mennen alike, a time for tales and sleep. The Wolves now kept mainly to the Forest, for the snow had drifted deep and such prey as there was to catch was Forest-bound, as they were.

It was about then that the Mennen war appeared to stop, becoming only sporadic at first, and then finally the distant gunfire ceasing. Vehicles still travelled on the road but they were smaller now, and did not carry so many Mennen, whilst overhead the jets now came but infrequently, and flew much higher than before. They were replaced by helicopters, whose buzzing, softer sound gave the Wolves much better warning of their approach.

Feeling that the Magyar threat, whatever form it finally took, was now in abeyance, Klimt decided it was a good time to carry through a more extensive reconnaissance of the environs of their territory than they had ever carried out before. He wished to establish how far the Mennen war had spread northward along the Vale, and anything more of the Magyar they could discover. Now that the youngsters were older and more experienced such a project would use their energy and interest to good effect, and push harder at the limits of the pack's territory in all directions.

'We are ready now to look beyond ourselves,' he said, seeming to have taken to heart the warning of the Wanderer. 'We shall wait until the present snows thaw, as first snows usually do, and take the opportunity wet ground and running streams offer reconnoitrers –

the different sounds, the disruption of normal winds and scents, the disinclination of Mennen and Magyars to show their snouts in unpleasant and inclement weather, will combine to make our task safer and easier.'

The prudent Klimt decided that they should only go out on these longer journeys in pairs, a senior with a youngster, and only one pair at a time, though with a second pair travelling some way with the first to establish a staging-post where they could wait, ready to offer help if need be, or to warn the main body of the pack if an emergency arose. There was nothing unusual in this, but Klimt's thoroughness in planning it, and his desire to complete a survey of all sides of their territory, with the exception of the Scarpfeld, aroused excitement and curiosity. What would they find in those areas where the Mennen had been fighting for so long? Would the mystery of the Magyar leadership now be solved?

When a thaw occurred two weeks later, already a good way into January, the first pair, Kobrin and Solar, were ready and eager to head northward along the Road.

This initial venture went well, taking the two wolves as far as Kobrin had gone before with Tervicz; they brought back accounts of derelict settlements, and the destruction of buildings and machinery, as well as sightings of many more abandoned vehicles of the kind the Wolves had as a solitary example upon the Road in their immediate territory, though this time some had Mennen corpses in them. Of the Mennen themselves the two had little to report, but that at regular intervals along their roads there were shelters and Mennen watchers, and out on some of the hills and passes as well.

Klimt decided to follow up this initial venture with one out on to the Fell, this time choosing Tervicz to lead it, with Rohan at his flank – a decision that angered Tare, who felt it her right to go as the strongest of the females.

'I decide who goes, with whom and when,' said Klimt firmly, beginning to advance upon his daughter most menacingly when she continued to object. He knew well enough that Tare's time would come, and though the ledreneship was not his concern he did not want the disruption and unpleasantness that a struggle for it would cause through the winter. In any case, reluctant though he had been, he had mated with Elhana and she might already be pregnant.

The reconnaissance that Tervicz and Rohan undertook did not produce anything new at all – there was an absence of Magyars in numbers, but their patrols were as alert as ever. However, something did happen during the short time that the two were together, and it was all too clear that it had left one of them – Rohan – frustrated and displeased.

'What was I to do?' exclaimed poor Tervicz, though choosing the unworldly Lounel as his confidant in matters of the heart and female desire suggested he was not on ground he understood at all. It seemed that Rohan, who had let her warm feelings for Tervicz be known in the past, had taken the opportunity of enforced togetherness to press herself upon him.

'Er . . . quite literally, as a matter of fact,' he said, glancing around lest the female subject of his anxiety hear his words and bear down upon him once more. 'The thing is, Lounel, I have never had strong feelings that way, or not since Klimt saved my life all those years ago and I dedicated my service and loyalty to him. Now I'm far too old for behind-the-nearest-rock dalliance – I mean I'm not exactly an Aragon, am I? – and I would not be much good at it if I tried; and. . . she's Klimt's daughter as well, which doesn't help. She has put me in a most embarrassing position and I cannot think what she means by it.'

Lounel chuckled and his pale eyes wrinkled into cheerful thought.

'What she must mean by it, Tervicz, is that she likes you or, as the younger element in this pack puts it, she *fancies* you.'

'But, for Wulf's sake –' began Tervicz wildly.

'Well I am certainly surprised, Tervicz,' continued Lounel, scratching himself, 'for as you suggest, you are not exactly an Aragon. Now there *was* a wolf who knew how to make a female feel she might be attractive to another . . .'

'But –'

'. . . and one who might have something worthwhile to give . . .'

'But Lounel, I never –'

'. . . yes, he was a wolf could make a female feel, well, likeable and . . .'

'I did not for a moment suggest that Rohan –'

'. . . but, of course, if your object is to undermine that young wolf's confidence, to make her feel unloved and unlovable . . .'

'Lounel, I really . . . I did not mean . . . *Lounel!?*'

'Yes, wolf?' said Lounel, with a twinkle in his eyes.

'I simply observed that it did not seem quite possible or appropriate –'

'Appropriate?'

'. . . not at the present moment, no, not quite.'

'I see,' said Lounel judiciously. 'For a moment I thought that you were saying that you of all the males in this pack were the one who does not find so fine and well-made a female as Rohan attractive.'

'Well I suppose . . .' said Tervicz, who was finding this conversation with Lounel a lot less easy and supportive than he had hoped, 'that she *is* attractive. I mean she is well-made, she is intelligent, she is all those things, but I just don't think of her *that* way.'

'Aaah . . .' said Lounel ambiguously.

'So there it is,' said Tervicz.

'Is it?'

'I . . . think so, yes, I really do. It's just not possible.'

'Isn't it?'

'You just don't understand, Lounel!' declared the irritated Tervicz, stalking off in a huff.

As a matter of fact, Lounel did understand, very well. For Rohan had already been to see him, upon the very same subject, searching him out the moment they had returned from their reconnaissance, anxious to ask his advice about Tervicz.

'What about him?'

'I think I love him. I think I love him very much.'

Lounel had looked at her then, and remembering the warm and affectionate cub she had been, he saw the beautiful and loving female she had become; wise as well, for if there was a wolf in the pack most worth setting her heart upon, it was the modest, the loyal, and the courageous Tervicz. The two were made for each other, however insurmountable the difficulties might seem.

For things were changing for the pack, and changing fast, and who could say that circumstance and destiny would not bring these two together in a union which might one day bring fortune, and honour, to the Wolves of Time?

'What shall I do?' Rohan asked Lounel, when she had explained Tervicz's seeming dislike of her.

'Be patient, my dear, for it may be hard for such a wolf as he to know he is loved, or to dare return the feeling. Yet be persistent, for wolves who wait for the sun to shine upon them before they act sometimes wait for ever. Tervicz is a wolf worth waiting for, Rohan, and fighting for as well I dare say.'

'I think I've always loved Tervicz,' she said softly. 'Ever since I can remember.'

She had gone then, leaving Lounel watching after her with tears in his eyes, for she was open and honest, and if the future of the Wolves depended on such as her, the years of Klimt's fretting and worrying had been worthwhile.

Soon after the return of Tervicz and Rohan, Klimt despatched Lounel northward up the Road once more, together with Tare, and this time Solar and Tervicz acted as a back-up.

The pack knew well that of all the males, Lounel was the one Tare liked least, principally because she could not understand his moments of abstracted thought, his inclination to wander off the mark, and his pleasure in such things as stars, running water, and the way a cloud shadow might pass from one end of the Vale to another.

'He's so . . . so impractical!' she grumbled to Rohan, before they left. 'He makes me feel so . . .'

'Stupid?' offered Lunar, who like Merrow was concerned less with being selected before others to go abroad the territory than with where he might be sent. It was the Fell that interested him, and the prospect of meeting the foul Dendrine and her ghoulish son – ghoulish in his eyes because it was known that he had eaten, or at least tortured to death, his sibling.

'Not stupid, no,' spat Tare; though she dominated Lunar in spirit by virtue of the fact that he could not be bothered, she was very cautious about actually attacking him, for when roused he could move fast and furiously, and nip another if he had to. 'But he's so . . . dreamy!'

'That's why we like him,' observed Merrow, speaking for Lunar as well.

'Hmmm, well, I suppose it might be interesting,' conceded Tare finally, in that offhand, indifferent way she had, not at all concerned that Lounel must have heard some of this. Respect for senior wolves she judged weak was not Tare's way.

But the two had gone off, and interesting it *had* been, for they had ventured further than any of the others into Mennen war territory, and there discovered how extensive was the damage caused by the war, and how widespread the desertion of the countryside by the resident Mennen who had been there before.

'East of the Road, up in the hills where the Carpathians continue,' reported Lounel on their return, 'much livestock from the farms is loose. The Mennen shoot them, like they shoot deer and wolves, but there's food there, Klimt. It is only a matter of time before other predators move in, if they have not done so already. Indeed, we saw some evidence of wolf, but were not able to track it down for it went beyond the range you had set for us.'

'Smelt mean-spirited,' said Tare dismissively, 'more like foxes than wolves if you ask me. But anyway, that was not what was important.'

'What *was* important?' asked Klimt, exchanging a weary glance with Lounel, whose patience had been considerably tried by two days alone with Tare. But then, getting used to each other was one of the purposes of the exercise.

'We nearly got killed by bombs we could not see,' began Tare dramatically.

Klimt silenced her and turned to Lounel, whose account of such an event he was more likely to have reason to trust.

'Yes,' said Lounel, 'I was coming to that. Strange, and dangerous, and Tare is right to say it may be important. We might indeed have been killed.'

He said this last with some emphasis, glancing at Tare as he did so, and it was plain enough he thought that it was in some way Tare's fault that they had both nearly been killed.

It seemed that they had got as far as a railway track that the Wolves knew emerged from a tunnel far down the Vale – a place Klimt himself had once visited, and which he had suggested should be the furthest limit of the exploration the two made. As they advanced through some scrubland towards the clear ground before the tunnel entrance Lounel had paused, scenting uneasily at the air, and then at the ground as if, as if . . .

'Tare, stop! *Stop at once!*'

He sensed danger here, new danger. It was for just such discoveries that Klimt had sent them to survey ground beyond their territory.

But Tare had seen two plump rabbits, out in the open before the railway line, which without benefit of immediate cover, and evidently off their home territory, were ripe for the taking. She had started rapidly forward on a low stalking movement in the hope of catching one.

'Tare!'

It was Lounel's warning shout that alerted the two rabbits and caused them both to startle up at once. They stood stock-still for a moment, and then were off on a jumping, darting, erratic flight towards the railway embankment, and perhaps the tunnel, whose dark mouth was off to their left.

'For Wulf's sake, Lounel, look what you've done!' shouted Tare angrily, as she continued her run on to the flat ground.

'Tare!'

BANG! PEWOOOM...BANG!

Where one of the rabbits had jumped a sudden, violent explosion occurred, enough to hurl the other across the grass where it lay still for a moment as clods and debris spattered back on to the earth, right to where Tare, shocked and winded, stood staring.

'Don't move, Tare, for Wulf's sake!'

BANG! PEWOOOM...BANG!

And the other rabbit, rising to its paws, turning and seeing Tare, desperate to escape, had dragged its injured body straight into a second explosion, or caused it. Both rabbits were no more, or no more whole.

Again the debris, and this time, oddly shocking, among the dirt and gravel that fell back to the earth, a rabbit's head, bloody, eyes staring wide, and both ears intact, one of them slowly moving forward, as if the head itself were still alive.

'The bombs are in the ground,' said Lounel, advancing cautiously, and so they were, the Mennen ground-bombs, flat and smelling of plastic and almonds. It was clear that Tare was too shocked now to beat a safe retreat, and she could not keep her eyes off the staring rabbit's head.

'Come, my dear, follow me back,' said Lounel, who had advanced slowly out to her, conscious of the death-dealing hidden ground-bombs all about; carefully he guided her foot by foot back to the safety of the scrub.

For a time after that Tare had held Lounel not only in respect, but also felt eternal gratitude – or rather gratitude that seemed it might last an eternity but evaporated the moment Tare decided that it had all been his fault anyway because had he not told her to chase those rabbits?

'We found other such ground-bomb fields after that, or scented areas of ground, often flat and disturbed, and smelling of almonds and Mennen,' observed Lounel.

So the general reconnaissance continued, until towards the end of January the weather brought freezing snow and ice and such ventures grew too difficult. But by then a great deal of the ground had been covered in all directions to Klimt's satisfaction, and all the Wolves but Raute and Merrow had gone forth to test their nerves in alien places, and prove that they could follow the strict orders that Klimt gave.

There had been no serious injuries, nor after Tare's experience had any wolf found themselves caught out in a field of ground-bombs. Kobrin was shot at twice, Solar caught his belly on barbed wire and the wound had festered for a time before beginning to settle down and heal, whilst Tervicz and Rohan had confirmed there was no change as yet in the Magyar situation.

As the pack settled back into its Forest retreats there was a general satisfaction at all that had been achieved. None of the Wolves, except perhaps Lunar, had transgressed the boundaries set by Klimt, and much had been learned of the Mennen, and the nature and dangers of their warfare and weaponry, even if the Magyar leadership remained as much a mystery as it had been before.

The error Lunar had made was to wander too far away from Kobrin when the two had been paired to explore the area that lay immediately north of the Forest on their side of the Road. In his vague and dreamy way, Lunar had become bored with the pastures and wandered up into more forested areas, where he had been captivated by the sight of a Mennen building, high and dark, and ruined some time before the present wars. The scars it had suffered were weathered now, the fallen stones long since lichened and moss-covered.

A peat-stained stream ran under part of the building and Lunar could not resist exploring this intriguing tunnel, quite losing himself in it for a time, but temporally rather than spatially. In short, he had quite forgotten his duty towards Kobrin and the pack, so intrigued was he by the sense of a different age, along with something he could not define, which he found in the damp water-tunnel the Mennen had made.

Mid-afternoon was already upon them before he heard Kobrin's by now desperate call and emerged once more into reality, which included the drubbing that old Kobrin gave him once he had got over the relief he felt at not losing one of Klimt's sons.

But that was a small price to pay for the exhilarating sense that Lunar had that he had found a place with a history not only of Mennen but wolves as well, and that in some way he himself had been in that place before, and would be again.

'Come on, wolf, we're late,' insisted Kobrin, 'and Klimt will not be well pleased.'

'But Kobrin, can't you feel something special about this place – something holy?'

'Holy!' exclaimed Kobrin, looking about him with distaste. 'Ruined in times gone by, but . . .'

Great Kobrin had paused then and fallen silent, for there was a special light to the place, and a sense of age. He poked about the ruins for a time.

Then, to Lunar's pleasure and surprise he had turned upslope, ferreted about a bit, broken through the undergrowth to a point where they could see the cliffs above – much as they were able to at the upper edge of their part of the Forest – and said, 'You're right, Lunar, there is something special about this place: it feels to me like part of one of the lost wolfways . . .'

'Yes?' whispered Lunar excitedly, for the moment Kobrin said it he recognized that was the feeling he had had – wolves had been this way in ancient times, trekking upslope and downslope from this place. Oh yes, wolves had once run this way, old wolves, wolves whose drumming paws he could almost feel, whose lives and deaths he felt he might almost have been part of . . .

'Steady, wolf,' said Kobrin, not unkindly, for he knew Lunar well enough to guess the way his mind was running. 'Did your father never tell you that the wolfways often ran by ways settled by the Mennen, for some go back in time to before the Mennen were here, and perhaps the wolves of ancient days guided the Mennen.'

'Guided them?'

'Yes, led them, or perhaps they were at one with them.'

'Kobrin,' said Lunar seriously, 'I feel I have been here before, and that I will be again one day . . . I feel the run of this wolfway right through my body as if . . . as if past, present and future are all one.'

Kobrin was silent, nodding his head; then he said, 'You know, Lunar, though I do not regret chastising you earlier, I am glad your folly led me to explore these ruins. To speak the truth, I envy you. When I was young, and being raised in Pechora, there were such wolfways as these, and I too stood upon them and thought about the wolves that had been and would be. There was one place, at the far end of our territory, where it abutted the Urals, where –'

'Was there a ruin there?'

'No, wolf, there was not,' said Kobrin, puzzled.

'But . . . there was a river, you could hear a river or . . . no, yes, you could hear a fall, a great fall . . .'

'Er . . . *yes* . . . ?' said Kobrin, puzzled.

'I was there,' said Lunar, 'I can feel that wolfway like a throbbing vein of life in my body.'

It seemed to Kobrin that their excursion from the present to the past had gone far enough, and that Lunar was perhaps overwrought from being lost earlier. Wulf knew what visions and nightmares he had seen in that Mennen-made underground place.

'Come on, wolf, we'd best get back, and if you take my advice you'll not talk of these imaginings of yours to others.'

'But there was a great fall where you were in Pechora on the wolfway, and the driving of a wind through the trees and up into the mountains . . .'

Lunar narrowed his eyes and looked far off when he said this, and he did so with such intensity that Kobrin suspected he thought his fur was being pulled and pushed this way and that by the imaginary wind.

Except that . . .

'There *was* a waterfall nearby,' he conceded, 'but there are a good many of those in the Pechora uplands! As for a driving wind – I do not remember any such thing.'

Except that he *did*, for there had been a wind, a strange and powerful wind, first in the trees where Kobrin had stood on a wolfway all those years ago, and later up in the mountain cliffs, almost as if gods had been calling to him.

'Come on!' roared Kobrin, annoyed at letting himself become embroiled in Lunar's youthful imagination. 'Come on, wolf, and we'll treat your little escapade up here as best forgotten. Wolfways are strange places and where they are time can seem different than it really is.'

'Or else more real than it usually seems,' said Lunar, quoting something that Lounel had once said.

Obedient now, he followed after Kobrin, but the pulse and line of the wolfway he had found was in him now, and one day would draw him back, or drive him on . . .

CHAPTER SEVEN

*In which Lunar journeys into the dark void of loss and
makes a telling that is a cry to the gods for help*

ALTHOUGH Kobrin kept little from his leader, he felt that he
did not need to labour the real reason for his late return that
day with Lunar. No doubt something of his son's foolish escapade was mentioned and Klimt decided not to press the point, though
next time . . . It was one of the wonders of Klimt's leadership that he
said so little that might intimidate another wolf, and yet all felt in awe
of him, and knew what limits he set them before he punished them.

Perhaps, after all, Klimt appreciated that the youngsters he helped
raise would all be different from each other, and was wise enough to
know that a pack's solidarity was a combination of the strengths and
interests of its individual members.

He himself was not much interested in matters divine and spiritual,
for they seemed to have no practical application to the task of leadership, but he knew that Lounel valued Lunar, and from that reasoned
that he should leave well alone.

So it was that, as so often in the past, it was Merrow who showed
the greatest interest in Lunar's excited talk of wolfways, of his strange
feeling of identity with them, all the more so because of them all she
alone had not been allowed to help in the great survey Klimt had
planned, which was now all but completed. She understood the reason
why, for the winter had brought to her an undue share of aches and
pains, and there were now days when she was so incapacitated that
it was all she could do to rise from her sleeping-place and go to drink,
and complete her ablutions. Her frailty had not yet the name of illness,
but it seemed that she was getting worse, not better.

In less settled circumstances the pack might have been more brutal
with her, and certainly had they been travelling she would have been
left behind, and lost. But there was no need for this in a time of
over-wintering in a territory as abundant in prey as the Forest, and

so apart from cruel jibes from Tare about Merrow's general useless-
ness, the pack gave her their support.

In any case most of them enjoyed the soft murmur of her talk with
Lunar, their companionship and laughter, and, increasingly, Lunar's
confidence in route-finding up among the cliffs and screes, which he
did partly in response to Merrow's demands. For there was no doubt
that though she was at times too frail to travel very far in body, in
spirit she often did so – staring at the cliffs, and telling the willing
Lunar that she wondered what that waterfall up there might sound
like were a wolf to go close to it . . .

In addition to which, the odd and quirky instruction in matters
spiritual that Lounel gave, more by what he did not say than anything
else, and his nearly complete indifference to the hierarchical fights
and struggles that were the daily fare of all the other Wolves, male
and female, found ready empathy in Lunar and Merrow, who enjoyed
his company, and such talk as he indulged in.

In this respect, Lunar's growing liking for following Lounel up into
the isolated places, to sit and contemplate, and to dream, as well as his
own inclination for night-time journeying, was a response to Merrow's
interest in such things, and frustration that she herself could not
indulge in such exploration.

'I wish you were stronger, Merrow,' Lunar would say, 'for then you
could come with us both. What's wrong with you, anyway?'

Merrow could only shake her head and say she did not know why
she was thin, why her fur was lacklustre, or why her cheerful and
eager spirit bounded so far ahead of her body.

It was therefore no surprise to Lunar that his sister found so much
to be interested about in his whispered account of his absence without
leave in the tunnel under the Mennen ruin he had found while recon-
noitring with Kobrin beyond the northern boundary of their territory.

'Did it go anywhere?'

'No, it was just a structure made by the Mennen over a stream,
open at either end, and dank and dripping in the middle.'

'And there was nothing else in there?'

'The sound of water, greatly increased by echoes and vibrations,
and a smaller ginnel, into which some of the water streamed, but
which was pitch-black and too dangerous to go into. From the sound,
it went into a fall or torrent of some kind right under the Mennen
buildings. But . . .'

'Yes, Lunar?'

'It did not interest me so much as the feeling I had there that though the place was Mennen-made, wolves had been that way in the long-distant past. And, too, it felt like the holy kind of place that Lounel has talked of, and the Wanderer too, where once Mennen and wolves were at one with each other.'

'Won't you take me there, Lunar?' she asked eagerly, not for the first time.

'It's more than my life's worth,' said Lunar, shaking his head. 'Anyway, you're not at your best in this cold weather and –'

'When I get better! When the next spell of mild weather comes! *Will* you?'

'No,' said Lunar, 'I won't.'

'I don't like you very much.'

Lunar laughed affectionately, for he knew she did, and that more than liking, *he* loved her best of all his sisters. With her he was something near himself. With her . . . and he felt sombre, for he feared that once spring came and the pack moved back to the Scarpfeld, or yet further away now that the survey had broadened their horizons, poor Merrow would finally be left behind.

'*Will* you? Now the weather's better? I'm really able to run again now and . . .'

Three weeks had passed, and it was one of those seductive late February days when the air is suddenly warmed by unexpected sun, which lights the streams with the hope, though not yet the full promise, of new life, and soft yellow catkins blow in the wind on the swaying alder branches above the snowdrops. The time in winter when wolves, and Mennen too perhaps, are sometimes lulled into a false sense that spring is almost on them, and it is safe to venture abroad once more.

'I mustn't.'

'But will you?'

'I shouldn't.'

'I'll go alone!'

'Well . . .'

'Come on Lunar, let's *do* it, just like we used to explore the cliffs in the old days. You said it isn't far – if we go now we'll be back before we're even missed.'

On such a winter day as that, mild and sunny, what wolf sees, or wishes to see, the dark cloud that looms, or how up on the higher ground, old heather shivers and shakes as a new wind, cold and bitter, heralds a return to bleak midwinter?

His resistance finally broken, Lunar led her away surreptitiously, through safe Forest routes he knew well, and upon which no watchers were likely to wend their way that day. Finally, he brought her to the northern boundary of their familiar territory, and then beyond, to find again the ruins he had found before.

'Just a quick look,' he said, 'and if the weather starts to break before we get there we'll turn straight back.'

'Yes, Lunar,' said she, hurrying on as best her frailty allowed. For though she had said she was well again, she was slow, and had to pause, pretending when she did that it was just to enjoy the view, though Lunar noticed she was puffing a bit too much.

'We really shouldn't, Merrow,' he muttered halfheartedly. But the real truth was he wanted to go back to the place himself.

'Come on!' she commanded, and he laughed as he followed her, and could not but feel that had her health been better she would have been the strongest of the females, the most resolute and the most imaginative and the one who might after all have one day claimed the ledreneship from Elhana.

He felt too, as he now ran ahead of her, that it was right for her to see the ruined wolfway place, for she might not ever get a better chance, and the memory of it haunted him and he wanted to see if its impact was the same on her. Past, and present, and future had been there . . . and it was the future that they were running now . . .

The ruins suddenly loomed before them amongst the forest trees, beyond the stream over which they were partly built, and they both paused to stare. The buildings were in a clearing and elevated on a terrace above the stream, and the whole place had a hush, and timeless peace.

'I'm glad you brought me, Lunar,' whispered Merrow, slowing to a halt. 'Where's the tunnel you went into, where . . . ?'

They ran forward together, splashing a short way through the stream and then, when it grew suddenly deeper and slippery, they veered up on to the bank. They turned a corner, climbed a little upslope, nearer to where the ruins rose, and there ahead of them was the tunnel's arch right across the stream into which Lunar had explored.

'That's it!'

Only as his sister started forward Lunar saw a brief movement through the trees to their left, and caught the sudden scent of Mennen.

'Mennen? *Merrow!*'

He shouted out her name instinctively, for there were Mennen somewhere down there amongst the trees, whilst above them . . . above them . . .

'Merrow, *stop!*'

Perhaps the noise of the stream drowned his cry, or perhaps she had seen something in the tunnel, or a light at the far end of it. Whatever it was she ran forward and on, and as she did Mennen jets roared over the cliffs above and down upon them, over them, overshadowing them, the noise jagged on the senses, massive all around them, and even as it faded, and Lunar stared, there came a shrill, encroaching, whistling whine, sharp as thorns, and . . .

BOOM-BOOM! *CRUMPPPPPPPPPpppppppp!*

. . . and Lunar could only stare aghast as the world changed for ever before his eyes. The ruins shuddering, exploding, walls rising, stones and bricks slowly going up, and up, earth and grit rising in great spumes, and bright blue-red light overcoming him as the rising debris slowed and stopped for a time somewhere above the highest trees, a long time as it seemed, before it began to fall, and fall and fall as the noise returned, louder and louder, and earth and rock were falling on to him.

'Merrow!' he cried as something hit him in the chest and pulled his feet right off the ground, and the earth turned and whirled about him and the stream's cold water surged over him, hot now, and red with blood.

'Merr . . . !'

Where she had been was nothing now but a crater, from whose smoking walls the white-red torn roots of fallen conifer trees hung, ready now to die. Where the ruins had been the ruins remained, but changed, smoking, dust settling. The walls were less high, and where a tower of a kind had been two fingers of Mennen structure remained, rising in futility to the sky.

Slowly, so slowly, the cawing of disturbed ravens up in the cliffs above and beyond the trees came to Lunar's ears, and more slowly still, the trill and the rill of the stream about him, resuming normality, beginning to clean and erode away the mess.

Though dazed and shocked he pulled himself from the stream-bed, shook the worst of the water out of his fur, tried his body and found himself uninjured, and ran forward to find where she had been going – which was now only where she had been.

'Merrow!'

There was no reply, not then, nor later when he had wandered desperately about and tried to find places he had known before. But though the tunnel was there it was all but blocked by trees and rocks over-rushed at one end by water, surging and bubbling out the other. And . . .

And there were dead Mennen, caught in the water, or Mennen heads and limbs, half in the tunnel and half out, killed where they had been hiding; killed where Merrow would have run to them; and she . . . she was no more, no more . . .

'*No more . . .*'

It was there that Kobrin and Solar found him that night, his leg broken, his face torn.

'I thought I was not injured . . .'

He had searched for Merrow not noticing his pain.

'Come, wolf,' rasped Kobrin, 'come with us.'

'She is here on this old wolfway, Solar, Merrow is here still, but we cannot reach her. I can feel the run of the wolfway, I can feel the throb of her life, oh she is here, brother, our sister is here . . .'

'She was killed,' Solar whispered, 'she died as the Mennen died.'

'Where, Solar, *where?*'

Solar looked helplessly at the great crater and could only whisper, 'She was killed, Lunar, she has died.'

'But . . .' whispered Lunar, 'this is a wolfway, this is a holy place, and here, here, I had been before and so had she. It was . . . it is . . . it for ever will be . . . and she will come again . . .'

'Come on, Lunar, come on, brother,' and Solar led Lunar from where they had lost a sister that the pack had loved so well.

Grief, riven with guilt, became a blizzard that overtook Lunar's heart that terrible day when frail Merrow was caught by chance in Mennen warfare, and so suddenly lost to the Wolves of Time. They had nurtured her, encouraged her, raised her, supported her, and finally loved her – none more than Lunar, none more than him. Now she was lost. Now she was no more, and though the winter wind might turn mild with spring and balmy with summer sounds and scents, it would not bring Merrow back to him. Though he might roam a thousand forests through, he would not hear her laughter there, nor answer her welcoming call, as he had here, where her Forest had been.

No comfort, no words, and least of all the vicious punishment of assault and pack exclusion for a time that Klimt himself visited on his foolish and errant son, broke the black ice of Lunar's emotions. First of tears, then of anger at the Mennen, then of anger at himself, and finally, and worst of all, the crippling ice of silence upon the subject of Merrow and her passing, final and complete.

Not even when the pack forgave him, or said they did – Klimt himself now saying that no wolf could have predicted such a thing happening, nor any pack have expected Lunar to resist the pleas of Merrow to visit the ruins, which they had all heard – not even then did the bleakness of mourning for one he had loved more than any other leave Lunar's eyes, or lift from the set of his body. Head low, fur unkempt, tail curled beneath him in utter dejection, he who had so often given the pack its lightness and laughter in the past, now became its sad shadow, its gloom.

For a time even the seasons seemed to share the grief of Lunar, and the pack as well. Winter stayed later and when spring finally showed its face and the thawing of highland ice and snow turned the streams into torrents, and the rivers into ragings of dirty, gritty water, it seemed that the Forest and Vale, cliff and mountain wept loud and long, wept for them all. The face of spring that year wept tears of mourning.

But finally nature's weeping stopped, and the sun grew brighter and warmer with each day as life returned to the skies and the trees; yet Lunar mourned still. He felt responsible for what had happened, and most of the pack felt so too and while the words of forgiveness and forgetting might be spoken, for this was not the way Klimt and the other senior wolves wanted to enter a new spring, until the pall of sadness left him it would continue to affect the pack.

A sadness made all the worse by the fact that old Raute, who had clung on to life throughout the coldest months, now seemed about to give it up, and surely could not last out those final few days of March. And Raute was the one wolf Lunar could now bear to be near, and to serve, as if in keeping her alive he somehow assuaged something of the guilt he felt for Merrow's death.

'Well, he can't go on blaming himself for ever, can he?' said Klimt to the others one day just then. 'If he does he'll become a liability to us all. In other circumstances I might suggest he goes off to wander the wolfways for a time – it seems it was the call of them over by those ruins that first led him into trouble, and was the lure to them both to return, with such terrible consequences. Perhaps that would be a way out of his present darkness.

'But . . . well, he's one of only two new males we have, and the fact is . . . the fact is that it's only now that he is cast down that I begin to see the nature of the contribution to us he had made.'

The others nodded their agreement, for all had thought or said as much in the weeks past. The truth was that something more than Merrow had died that day by the ruins, something of the pack's inner being, and now that Lunar seemed to have left them too, they saw that in some way he was an essential part of what they were.

'He was always so cheerful,' observed Rohan, whose offer of consolation and comfort he had rejected along with all others, 'and I didn't ever realize it before. The way those two used to chatter into the night, talking of the stars, telling each other old stories! The way Merrow would get him to explore places up amongst the cliffs and then come back and tell her what he had found that she might believe for a while that she had been able to be there.'

The others nodded, even Tare, for self-centred and ambitious though she was, she could feel the pack loss as well.

'Well, at least he finds comfort in helping poor Raute,' she said finally, 'and I suppose that's something. Not that *that* old thing'll last much longer, the way she looks. Why, she's beginning to mess herself now and –'

'And Lunar's helping her to the stream, and cleaning her,' said Rohan sharply, for she did not like Tare's tone, 'and that's more than the rest of us are doing. I think we should accept Lunar back.'

'We have already, my dear,' said Elhana with feeling, for his exclusion was long past, 'it's he who must find a way back to us now from the dark place in which he is lost.'

They all nodded and Klimt said, 'Solar, you are his brother and you found him that day . . . Lounel, he has always trusted you . . . Wanderer, is there no tale or teaching you can give him that might make him understand he is long since forgiven for something that was more an accident of chance than anything?'

'It is himself he must forgive, Klimt, only himself, and then he will be healed.'

They might have said more but their talk was interrupted by a howling, not loud, nor one of distress, but the howling that accompanies a telling, and it came from the Forest depths where old Raute lay. Drawn to its haunting sound, and by the meanings they all understood more clearly the nearer they came, the pack went there silently, and gathered at the edge of Raute's clearing, to listen to the telling of grieving Lunar made. Of Merrow it was, and all she had been; of a sister he had adored; of a sibling he had protected; of one he had loved, and of a wolf he now missed.

'My dear,' they heard Raute whisper, 'my dear, you must stop. This telling I know, I know so well, and would wish you to make another, for it is time, for there comes a time when each one of us must move on from where we are, and let go of what has been, and what we were. I . . .'

'Is there anything you want, Raute?' they heard him say. 'Some food, some water or –'

'I shall very soon move on, my dear, and before I do I want to know that you have heard the wise words of the Wanderer, for he too must soon leave. Yes, yes, he must – winter is over and his warnings given, his time approaches as does mine. Therefore, Lunar, give me a telling you have learned from him, give it me now.'

Lunar grew still and said, 'Which would you hear?'

Raute nodded appreciatively, her blind eyes smiling, her paw to his.

'The first telling I ever heard was of how wolfkind first came to be – of Hrein and Mistur and their love. I like that telling; has the Wanderer taught it to you?'

The other Wolves, back in the shadows still, looked at the Wanderer, but his face had no expression at all, and he only stared upon Lunar, waiting what he might say or tell.

'I know some of it,' said Lunar, 'but –'

'Then begin it, wolf,' said Raute, 'and let's pray the gods will help you journey to its proper end.'

Then Lunar raised up his head, and began to howl down the telling old Raute wanted most to hear, which is of gods, and the coming of wolfkind; and as he told that most ancient of tales, what wolf there who heard him did not begin to understand that his telling was also a prayer to the gods who seemed to have forsaken him, to show him a way back from his grief.

Far, far to the east of here, across the Siberian plain, there is the holy lake called Baikal, of which the Wanderer has taught us.

North of it are the uplands wherein the secret sources of its waters rise, and other springs as well, which flow to north, and

*east and west. That upland is called the Springs, and its highest
point is Gora in'aptuk, formed when the daughter of Smilodon,
the Sabre-toothed One, lay down her head in grief at His death.
Smilodon was God of All, the Ineffable, who is the Light that
comes from Darkness, who made the sun, who made the stars
and moon, who made the earth.*

*His passing brought to an end the time before mortal creatures
came to earth, amongst whom were our own ancestors. The tears
of Smilodon's daughter formed the rivers that run to north, west
and east, and flow endlessly in acknowledgement of the time
of peace and tranquillity that seemed to pass for ever with the
Sabre-toothed One.*

*To the south of where she lay, and lies still in mountain form
as Gora in'aptuk, her tears filled the chasm that Smilodon's right
paw made in his death throes. This tear-filled chasm is Lake
Baikal, the greatest lake in all the world, and her tears being as
crystal-clear as the light of her father's love, they formed the
purest water on the earth.*

*It was Baikal's water that gave birth to mortal life after Smilo-
don's death, and from it the first creatures of sky, and sea and
land emerged, the creatures from whose unions and battles new
forms would successively evolve.*

All this has the Wanderer taught us.

*But we should not forget great Smilodon. In days gone by all
wolves must have known the tale of how his struggles with Death
flattened the very earth itself, forming the vast lands we know as
the deserts of Mongolia.*

*Then, when he was vanquished, he lay down upon the earth
at that great desert's south-eastern edge. His head formed the
massive Mishmi Hills; his left shoulder Everest, the highest mountain in the world; his curving spine became the Himalayas, and
his tail the Tien Shan range.*

*As for his two great sabre teeth, they form the great glaciers
that some know as Qinghai and Tsinghai. There, forming the
frozen heights to the desert depths, Smilodon sleeps, and will
sleep until the last living thing on earth begins to die, and calls
for his help. Then will the God of All awake, and carry the earth
back to the place of peace where he first made it, where all things
are at one. For aeons after Smilodon had gone to eternal sleep
the world turned into trouble and madness as creatures great and*

small, old and new, fought in the shadows of the ages for precedence one over another, like over like, alien over alien. Dark
came across the lands, and gods awoke or were new-born.

Into this strife, upon the flanks of the mountain Gora in'aptuk,
which was Smilodon's daughter in earthly form, the first wolves
came to be, born of the life that came from Lake Baikal. These
ancient wolves came before the Wanderers, before even them . . .

Upon her flanks they made their life, keeping themselves to
themselves, and taking to the shadows of the mountain when
trouble came their way.

Wise they became to ways of avoiding hardship; wise to only
taking from the earth what they must; wise to finding consolation
in the stars for the troubles of the earth below.

A leader rose among them whose name was Wulf; young,
strong, and wise as well. He saw the dangers of the world, and
knew that if ever his pack journeyed forth from the tranquillity
of Gora in'aptuk their peace would be riven by the world's strife,
and lost; and they would be no better than the creatures who
strove only to fight each other and never looked up towards the
stars. Wulf and his ledrene wept to think their offspring would
suffer in a world where there was no peace or order.

Wulf did what no animal had ever done before: he climbed to
the top of the mountain on whose flanks he and his pack had
been nurtured, and he called to the stars for help. Not knowing
of Smilodon, Wulf asked that if there was a God of All, he might
take pity on him and his pack.

The daughter of Smilodon heard him and took pity on him,
for she knew that he was right: once the first pack of wolves
journeyed beyond the mountain they would find no peace, only
trouble and decline. Her breast heaved in sadness for him; and
the rocks were riven, and the first volcano began to form. The
warning sound of its coming was her whispering voice, and she
said to Wulf, 'Of all the creatures who have risen from the waters
of Lake Baikal you and your kind alone have stayed close by me,
and avoided the trouble and strife of the world; and you alone
have asked for my father's help.

'Your time is not yet, Wulf, but will one day be . . . Will you
give yourself and your pack into my protection?'

'I shall,' said Wulf.

'Are you and your kind ready to know forgetting, that you may *survive the coming years until the time is right for you to be again?'*

'We are,' said Wulf.

'Then have no fear, for you shall be re-born in better times, when the world is ready for your compassion and your faith in the God of All. But be warned, do not leave the protection of my flanks in the conflagration and destruction that is coming. Trust me, and you and yours alone will be saved. Do not flinch or show fear . . .'

Then did the first volcano erupt, and the first fire come to be, and the smoke and dust and fumes, and the pouring forth of lava, the earth's own blood.

Wulf kept his pack near him, and all might have been well had not one of the youngest wolves become afraid and fled from the erupting slopes of the mountain which had so long given them protection.

Wulf's ledrene ran after the youngster to bring him back, but she ran too far and began to return too late and both wolves were caught in the destruction and lost their lives.

Even as Wulf howled for that loss, and the remaining members of his pack howled as well, Smilodon's daughter engulfed them in the smoke of the volcano, and gave them the blessing of oblivion; with the fire she granted them endurance; with the molten rock there came protection, for each wolf was encased in it, unknown, unseen, forgotten and finally, with the last eruption, scattered far and wide; and with the flooding rains that brought the eruption to an end she gave to the lost and forgotten wolves the healing waters of compassion.

This eruption, this explosion, was the beginning of mortal time, after which all living creatures might know that they are mortal and their end will come. By this, and the fear of it, Smilodon's daughter hoped that peace would one day be established.

Many the creatures that died out then, including as it seemed the peaceable wolves who had lived on the slopes of Gora in'aptuk. But they were safe, lost in the oblivion of sleep, given the power to endure the passing of the ages, protected by the rock in which each was encased, waiting, waiting . . .

Meanwhile, with old Smilodon's passing new gods came to be. Jord, the earth, was woken by the maelstrom that beset those times – female by night and male by day, never still, always

*turning in pursuit of self, those two halves only ever finding a
brief moment of stillness at dawn and dusk.*

*Jord, who was alternately mocked by Dagr, the god of day,
and by Nacht, the god of night, turned and turned and sought
to destroy both day and night. But they responded by bringing
forth their love child, Fiur or fire. Fiur is born and dies and is
born again one hundred thousand times each day and every night,
and in as many forms, born to irritate Jord with the volcanoes
from which she comes.*

*Now Dagr and Nacht only mocked Jord more. So Jord grew
angry with them and laboured and sweated to produce Sjar, the
sea, to quench Fiur's life for ever. But though the currents of the
sea chased Fiur endlessly, and still do, always she found sanctuary
and re-birth somewhere new.*

*In this endeavour, and to irritate Jord still more, Fiur herself
gave birth to Vindr, the wind, that she might hurry Fiur along
and out of reach of the currents of the sea.*

*But Jord grew cunning, and encouraged Vindr to mate with
Sjar to give birth to Regan, the rain, that she might finally quench
mischievous Fiur. Then, just as Fiur knew how to take on a
hundred thousand forms, so Regan learned to do, but she never
could quite match Fiur's cunning, and failed to quench her . . .*

Lunar paused as old Raute laughed, for she had heard this telling as
a cub and remembered those times of happiness and laughter, when
the tales of the gods had first been told her.

'You make this telling well, very well, Lunar. Now, can you tell me
what happened when Vindr and Regan decided to journey north?'

'I can,' said Lunar . . .

*One day Vindr and Regan grew tired of their hopeless chasing
after Fiur and journeyed to the north, and there they discovered
the slumbering giant Kaldr, the cold. Vindr loved Kaldr for his
silence and Regan loved him for the stillness he brought her.
Many are the stories told of how their union came to be, and how
Kaldr the slow giant seduced both mother and daughter, who in
time gave birth to the two races of frost giants – which are snow
and ice . . .*

*But the daily struggle between Jord on one hand, and Dagr
and Nacht on the other, continued unabated, until the peace-*

loving Kaldr journeyed south to seek a harmony between them. It was then the earth began to freeze. He talked with each alone, and all three together, patiently, for tens of thousands of years. But failing to find a way to unite them he turned his face towards the sun, and wept.

Only when they saw the chaos caused by the great flood of his tears did the combatants Jord and Dagr and Nacht each agree to yield up something of themselves. In this way did Scuwa, the sky, come to be.

Oh Scuwa! Most fickle yet most beautiful of all the gods! Scuwa brought harmony to Jord and Dagr and Nacht, now light, now dark, now clear, now cloudy, that each of her three parent gods might find something of themselves in her, and feel satisfied.

Whilst Scuwa herself, dissatisfied in all, found love and peace in only one, who was Kaldr, who made his sons by Vindr and Regan, the frost giants, her servants. So, one by one, waking to trouble and strife, born of the lust for dispute and the desire for harmony, each of the gods came into being.

Meanwhile the creatures that roamed Jord's great realm fought each other still, each turning for support to the god whom they thought might give them greatest sanctuary. The birds to Scuwa, the fish to great Sjar, the reptiles to Kaldr, the mammals to Fiur for warmth, each to his own, but each still arguing with the others.

The gods grew tired of the constant strife of the creatures of the earth, and of the demands they incessantly made for their protection against each other. But even wise Kaldr, and great Jord, could think of no way to control the incessant conflict.

It was then that Hrein, god of mischief and cunning, who had long desired as his consort Kaldr's daughter Mistur, whom mortals know as mist, said he might find a way to keep earth's unruly creatures under control, though it would not be easy, and might take time.

'We gods live too much in the stars to easily understand earth's creatures. Only by living with them, and being one of them, will a way of controlling them be found. If I am to do it I shall need the help of Mistur, for of all the gods she is the one who most confuses the creatures of the earth and she will be helpful to me.'

'But . . .' began Kaldr, who did not want to part with Mistur. Hrein shrugged and feigned indifference, saying, 'You can

hardly expect me to become a miserable mortal all alone, and without any help. So I shall undertake my task with Mistur or not do it at all . . .'

Many are the stories of how Hrein overcame Kaldr's reluctance to agree to the arrangement, though in the end all agree that wise Kaldr gave his assent when Mistur herself declared that she wished to be Hrein's consort.

'She will take the form of mist upon the earth,' said Kaldr, 'so what form will you take?'

'We shall see,' said Hrein, who kept his secrets to himself.

A short while later Hrein and Mistur slipped away together, journeying down the stars into mortality at daybreak, to begin their life upon the earth – mischief, courage, mystery and laughter, calm purpose and loyalty – here were the beginnings of a purpose for wolfkind . . .

Here, to the disappointment of those listening in the shadows, Lunar brought his telling to a premature end. Old Raute was sleeping peacefully now, though the afternoon had hardly begun, and he saw no need to continue. If he was aware of the other Wolves' presence he did not show it.

Nearby, amongst the wet rocks of the Forest stream which ran by Raute's place, a dipper sang, darting into view for a moment and then away into shadows again, upstream towards the Forest edge, and light. The trees above swayed suddenly at some coming weather change, and the oval of sky beyond the tree-tops seemed blue, and the few drifting clouds a little brighter. Lunar stared at them, turned to where the Wolves stood, and looked away indifferently. Then he turned his back on them, his sudden silence deafening.

Then, something more – something beyond them all. A distant vibration, a shudder in the ground, and far off through the Forest, down in the Vale and beyond to the lower valleys, the sound of gunfire, the first they had heard for many a long week.

'It's only Mennen,' they heard Lunar whisper as he moved nearer Raute, and stood guard over her.

Merrow he had lost, and weak though Raute's hold on life now was he would rather give up his own for her than have her life torn from him while she still had it to live.

Then the guns again, and from the other side of the Forest, from the direction of the Fell, the buzz of an approaching helicopter. Lunar turned briefly to look that way, and up at the sky, and he saw the Mennen thing fly over, sunlight bright and shining from its windows and guns; he saw as well that by then all the other Wolves had gone. At Klimt's orders, no doubt.

Lunar turned back to watch over Raute, who for now was the only reality he cared to know.

CHAPTER EIGHT

The exiled Aragon of Spain decides to return to the Heartland,
but he must leave Jicin, beloved of Klimt, behind

THAT AUTUMN found Aragon of Spain, exiled wolf of the
Heartland, Elhana's former lover and the likely father of her
young, amidst the Mennen's city and industrial wastes of
southern France's lower Tarn valley.

For days he had been uneasy and restless, and those with him had
begun to think him ill. Then, after three days of silence, Aragon
astonished those accompanying him, which was less a pack than a
mere band of vagrant wolves, by declaring that he must begin to
journey back towards the Heartland once again.

'I think you can all guess the reason why,' he said, 'and that recent
events in these parts may have a significance that goes beyond southern
France to affect not only the Mennen, but wolfkind as well. The hour
is coming when we who care for wolfkind's future, and have some
hope of influencing it, should be back at the centre of things.'

The 'events' to which Aragon referred were the Mennen war
that had recently erupted in those parts. From time to time in past
months Aragon and his friends had come upon Mennen fighting one
another, or grim evidence that they had recently done so, but this was
different.

They had been in the French Pyrenean foothills when the war had
started a month before, in the river lowlands but fifty miles north of
where they had spent much of the summer. It had been no simple
matter of a burst or two of gunfire, or an hour or two of shelling and
bombs. This had been a series of explosions so massive that before
their very eyes (as they discovered when they later went forth to
investigate) the entire region of the lower Tarn was affected, and the
city of Toulouse all but annihilated. Aragon and the others had seen
some grim things in their time, but nothing like the streams of
Mennen, many sick and wounded, many dying on the way, who fled

the burning city, and entered a countryside that until then had been the preserve of a few farmers and grazing livestock.

Day after day the wolves had wandered the smouldering wastelands, the shocked Mennen easy to avoid, their dogs often so burnt and wounded that killing them was charity. Day after day they had wondered at the nature of what they saw, and its cause, and begun to feel that here was a change that must finally affect all life, before which a wolf could not be idle.

Then they had come to the Tarn itself, overflowing its banks because the weir over which it ran was blocked and dammed by human rubbish and human corpses; the air was thick with flies, and hundreds of rooks had flocked to feed on the bodies, and clean their bills by dunking them in water that was the colour of human shit; then the rooks too had begun to die.

It was after that Aragon had fallen silent, and because of it that he had decided a time of change had come whose moment he must catch, and respond to.

'Though I shall not make the journey back to the Heartland in haste,' said Aragon, 'the wind whispers and makes me restless, and I sense the time has come to return. There are other places to see before approaching the Heartland itself once more, places upon which great Klimt will expect me to report, and that will take time. But I shall be happier to begin the long journey back and see if Klimt of Tornesdal will now accept me back into the pack.'

What surprised most of those with him was his choice of who would journey with him and who would not, until he began to explain why and to what purpose, and succeeded in putting excitement into all their hearts for the new tasks he was giving them, and new resolution too.

All of which Jicin, once Klimt's mate and for that reason exiled with Aragon some years before, observed and rejoiced to see: yes, she told herself, at last Aragon has matured and so is ready to return, which means that a new challenge may be coming to the Wolves of Time. To Jicin, the trials and tribulations that they faced, and the moments of decision and change, were in the movement of the stars and the will of the lost gods, rather than in wolves' own paws.

'How you have changed, my dear,' she said to Aragon later that evening, when he was done with speeches and orders, 'how you have grown.'

He smiled wryly and shrugged, his eyes dancing with self-mockery, and she laughed aloud. She might have lost Klimt those years ago, lost a love she might never be allowed to know again, but in Aragon she had found a friend.

'So have you,' he began, coming companionably close, 'you have grown and matured.'

She shushed him affectionately, for it was of him she wanted to speak, or rather of his decision to go back, and why he had chosen only some of them to go with him and not certain of the others.

Oh yes, Aragon of Spain had changed, and as a leader he was wiser now, and his words carried more authority. Looking at him by the greying light of the autumn evening, against the dark vertical lines of the power station in whose fenced and secret ditches they had found a resting area for several days past, she could see how he had aged since first she met him. From a distance, and on first meeting, Aragon seemed eternally young: but one who knew him, and crouched close by as she now did, saw that there were lines of worry and responsibility about his eyes and mouth, which belied that impression of youth, of pride, of lightness that he generally gave. They were lines such as come to those who find themselves caring for others more than for themselves.

'When shall you depart?' she asked.

He stared at her and said, 'You are not going to question my decision that you do not come?' He seemed both relieved and surprised.

She shook her head sombrely and looked down at the ground.

'It is for the best,' she said, 'and you have decided rightly. You and Elhana – that is over now. That is past. But Klimt and I, that will always be, *always*. One day, perhaps, when none shall be harmed by our being together again, I shall go to him. In any case, you rightly think that I have more work to do here; but we can talk of that later.'

Aragon nodded, his thoughts on slightly different lines. No female but this one had ever resisted him, not one. But Jicin, what a wolf, what a female, she was! How well matched to Klimt, and how abiding was her love for the wolf whose power and strength had bound them all to a dream and a longed-for destiny. How often during their exile had Aragon prayed to the gods that whatever might happen to him, they would at least grant that one day Jicin and Klimt could be together again, with time to love.

'Jicin,' he began, 'if you really want . . .'

Aaah, still the signs of weakness. She sighed and shook her head, and saw that even now Aragon still had not quite the ruthlessness that a great leader needs. He would let her come with him if she insisted.

'No, Aragon, you are quite right to say I should not go. I would not be happy in Elhana's shadow, and nor would Klimt be to see me there. I have not Elhana's strength to be ledrene – you saw how she defeated me, and might have killed me. To go back, even after so long, would be disruptive. In any case, we have work to do here, or at least a task to fulfil that might suggest a new direction.'

She smiled and looked away, a little shy that Aragon could read her mind so well.

'You are not too old yet to have some cubs,' he said, 'and these wolves I'm putting in your charge, if they are to become a true pack, will need a ledrene. There are males here might take up the task of leader.'

'There are not!' she said softly. 'Nor any that I fancy! But there might be in time, I suppose . . .'

Behind them, beyond the power station whose lights had failed three days before, and whose sounds had all begun to die, they heard the now ever-present *CRASH!* and *CRUMP!!!!* and deep thumping clatter of Mennen guns. The warfare started up each evening, and lit the sky with violent light.

At the renewed sound of war the ragbag of wolves about them glanced Aragon's way, ready to rise and move to full watching-stations if he wished them to. But he stayed still and calm, and they settled back again. He moved closer to Jicin, rubbing his flank to hers with a pleasing sensual roughness, and said, 'Why not, Jicin, just for old time's sake!'

There was good humour in his voice and she laughed again, saying, 'There was never an "old time" with you and me, Aragon, desirable though you are, and were, and probably always will be. But you see . . .'

Flank to flank now they stilled and talked, and Aragon sighed with mock tragedy, and then he chuckled and looked for a time at the darkening sky, and the flashes of war-light. The guns sounded heavily far off, and then near. His face became serious as he felt the push and pull of her flank breathing against his own. He had never had such a friend as her, nor known a female so well, but for his mother, Jimena, who had been his first inspiration.

'Do you miss her much?' said Jicin softly.

He nodded and was quiet for a time before saying, 'It has been an exciting time, this exile of ours, not what I expected at all.'

'We are all changed wolves . . .' she began.

'Who's changed?' a friendly voice rasped out of the gloom. It was Stry, the Polish wolf who had been exiled with them, and he was grinning. He settled down opposite them, his body smaller and more wiry than Aragon's, and his fur ruffled and patchy here and there.

'Some of our friends here are still nervous of the guns so I've cheered up those who will be coming with us with stories of the giants and dragons that live on the far side of the Alps, more dangerous by far than any Mennen guns; while to those who are staying behind I said that where Mennen guns blast at each other wolves can take heart in the knowledge that for once *they* are not in Mennen sights. Then again, where Mennen war with each other there's always the prospect of a Mennen corpse or two to chew at!'

'Oh, Stry!' exclaimed Jicin, who shuddered at such talk. She was of the old traditions and regarded Mennen flesh as taboo.

Stry chuckled and finally said, 'So ... who has changed? I heard you saying –'

'All of us,' said Aragon, 'you and I, and Jicin here, in the time we've been away.'

'Do you mind not going back yet?' Stry asked of Jicin.

She shook her head. 'I understand why I cannot,' she said, 'and I agree. I'm only glad that Aragon's found a task for me. So ... tell Klimt when you see him that I ... that ...' She stared at the stars as Stry nodded.

He knew what to say, and he guessed Klimt would be glad to hear it. He might not be entirely happy that Aragon and he had decided against letting Jicin return, but Klimt was always a wolf who put the pack's needs before his own in the end.

The time for Jicin and Klimt had not yet come round again, though Wulf knew that he, Stry, hoped that one day it would. He had never suffered a broken heart, though when his brother Morten was killed in an avalanche in the Scarpfeld he knew grief for a time, and knew it well.

But a broken heart, that terrible longing for another without whom life is not complete – he had seen its black infection take over Jicin, he had lived with it those first months of the exile, he had watched her struggle to find balance and purpose once again. Oh yes, he knew what a broken heart was, and what a wolf Jicin must be to have survived it, and made it mend.

'Yes, we've all had to change and grow,' he said, 'and Klimt knew we must, if we were to give something more to the pack in the future.

He was wise to exile us, but now we have much to tell them when we get back, for we have seen much, so much . . .'

They nodded together in silence, as those others that travelled with them watched respectfully from a distance. Some would be travelling on with Aragon and Stry on the morrow, and they felt nervous and excited; others would be staying behind with Jicin, and after their initial disappointment, Aragon had made them see that they had a purpose, and important work to do, dangerous work indeed, in the course of which some of them might die.

So as darkness deepened about them, and the Mennen guns growled and barked out across the ruins of Toulouse in the night, each one of them took pause to think of the months or years that had led them to where they were now, and where they might soon be.

Aragon, Stry and Jicin had left the Scarpfeld in the month of the birth of Elhana's cubs, at the start of spring, with Klimt's instructions ringing in their ears.

'Your task shall be to learn all you can of Mennen ways and places, to try to understand things which so far we have only thought of in passing. Just as wolfkind is in change, so too do the Mennen seem to be and we must find out all we can when the time comes to stand up to them.

'I do not know what you will discover during your exile, but I do know it is important. I believe that the time is coming when we shall all have to become wanderers of the wolfways, to try to re-build our knowledge of the lands which the Mennen took from us. In doing that they destroyed the pattern of the wolfways, and made us lose our ancient memory of them, which is patterned in the stars.

'For each earthbound wolfway is but a mortal echo of a way among the stars, now lost to us, just as the gods are all but lost to us. Yet in our joint memory, and in the memories of wolves and packs we may yet find, that ancient lore will still survive.

'Therefore, though you go into exile now, you do not go purposeless, nor in disgrace. You shall be the first of the pack's wanderers and what you do, what you achieve, what you bring back in the course of time shall be the standard by which others of us will follow in your steps.

'Aragon, you know that it is best for you to leave, but you are too great a wolf, and have too much to give the pack, for it to be wise of

me to so vanquish you that you never return. Be gone for at least a year and then ask yourself if you are ready to return and truly accept my leadership. Stry will go with you, for alone you may soon perish, or be lost, and it is wise that he finds himself again in journeying. He must recover from Morten's death if he is to be able to help the Wolves of Time again.

'Finally, Jicin shall go with you, for reasons you know well. With Elhana you have been my rival, Aragon, and it may be that her heart is still with yours. A leader shall not, must not, concern himself with such things. With Jicin you shall have at your flank one who has taught me more than any other wolf, one I . . . do not wish to see go. But she cannot stay, for she will cloud my judgement, and undermine Elhana's authority. I entrust her to your protection – give it and she shall repay you with a friendship, and a wisdom, you would know no other way. By asking this of you I end for ever talk of mistrusting you. Is that understood?'

Aragon had nodded his head, though it was only as the months, and then the years, passed that he had come to truly understand the depth of the trust Klimt had placed in him, and the wisdom he had shown in doing so in such a way.

'As for how you journey,' Klimt had continued, *'where you go, what you do, I have only this to say – your survival is paramount and comes before pride, vanity, other wolves, all things. You are the harbingers of the future of the pack I lead with Elhana, and if you are to return with the knowledge our pack will need,* you must survive. *Therefore avoid confrontation with Mennen and other wolves. If you must meet them, and you will need to, to complete the task I have set, do so prudently: run rather than fight; demean yourselves rather than take risks to stay proud; skulk rather than walk tall. Which, Aragon, may be difficult for a Spanish wolf!*

'Above all, learn and learn to learn! Learn so much that it shall take a lifetime for you to tell us all you have learnt. Learn!'

Klimt had spoken this last with almost terrifying passion, so that mixed and confused though their feelings at departure were, it was that single word 'learn' that became the constant star they followed.

It was as well that Klimt had stressed the importance to them of survival and avoiding confrontation, for otherwise, in the first few days, all might have been lost almost from the start. For somewhere below the Scarpfeld, out upon the Fell which they had each trailed across at different times their scent was picked up by the vile enemies of the Wolves of Time, the Magyar wolves.

Last time they had met the Magyars had been during their assault upon the Scarpfeld by way of the Red Lake, by whose edge Hassler, the Magyar leader, had been defeated and killed by Klimt with the help of Jicin and Kobrin. In their final passage to the Scarpfeld they had come upon the foul life-staining wolves Dendrine, Hassler's violent mate, and her perverse son by him, whose name was then unknown.

This incestuous pair seemed to have taken leadership of the Magyar in the time since then, the son being preternaturally large, and as violent as his parents. It was the scouts of this unsavoury couple who came upon the three wolves Klimt had sent into exile, and followed them, harried them, and slowed them. So much so that there was time for a message to be sent back to Dendrine, and for her and her son to catch them up.

Aragon, who had yet to learn how best to follow Klimt's instructions, was inclined to turn and fight, thinking perhaps that if he won such a fight so soon then he might cut short their exile and win Klimt's favour once again. As Jicin said, and was to say again many times in the months ahead, Aragon had much to learn.

It was her words of warning, born of experience of the Magyar pack, and of the foul Dendrine, that persuaded Aragon to think again: and it was the single brief sight they caught of Dendrine's son and mate, by moonlight, above them on the fell, that caused them to turn and run, pride or no.

He was already large of shoulder and head, and if his eyes caught the shine of starlight, the corrupting power of his warped and twisted mind turned it the red shade of victim's blood, and the yellow of a weeping, infected wound. The wolf they saw was Klimt's enemy, and Klimt's burden. He had killed the father, and in time, before too long they hoped, Klimt might find the strength and cunning to kill the son. But not Aragon, who saw at once that this was a battle and a fight he could not win. So they fled at the sight of their enemy, and were glad they did.

'Magyars!' said Stry with disgust some days later when pursuit finally let up and, clear of the Tatra mountains and heading now towards the Bavarian forests, the three could look back and know they would be followed no more by Magyars. Magyars were the Heartland's enemy and no longer their responsibility; for the rest, whatever form the 'enemy' might take, it all lay ahead, for them to find, for them to learn about, above all for them to survive.

'Mennen, and Mennen's pollution, they are our greatest enemies now,' said Aragon, considerably chastened by their brief encounter with the Magyars.

'Or other wolves like the Magyars, whose existence we do not yet know of,' suggested Stry.

'We should not make enemies of wolves if we can avoid it,' said Jicin. 'Our task is to make them friends and find ways to unite them against the Mennen.'

Aragon, so far wary of Jicin, was inclined to agree with her in this, and said so, which was the first time the two had found some common ground.

'Make wolves friends,' he muttered, 'and unite them,' he sighed. 'I hope you'll be able to suggest ways of doing so.'

Jicin smiled, and Stry chuckled, and Aragon, so long beset by troubles of one kind or another, felt as if the southern sun had begun to shine once more. For in that moment, when Aragon asserted himself over them by the charm of his ease and grace and not by force or threat, they all began to feel they might be friends, and each followed the other on the long trail with lighter and more trusting step.

That slow summer they journeyed eastward and southward, by way at first of the high forests that lie between Germany and Czechoslovakia, thence across the Erzgebirge to the Harz Mountains, where they confirmed observations made by Klimt himself when he had come that way from Sweden several years before.

But remembering his injunction to them to learn, and learn to learn, they did not tarry in the safe heights of the Harz, tempting though it was to do so. Having ascertained that there were no wolves there at all and remembering what they could of what Elhana had told them about how she had travelled the Mennen roadways of northern Italy, and how to exploit the wastelands of industry and polluted rivers for safe journeying, they began a long trail west across the North European plain, city by city, road by road, learning to use such places to their best advantage.

In this, at first, they had naturally been inexperienced but that, as

Jicin said over and again, was the whole point: to learn about the Mennen and their places, to discover what wild wolves had never known, that safety from the Mennen lay under their very noses, in the concrete forests that they made, in the steel thickets of construction and decay, in the filthy waters, in the endless, shifting shadows of the Mennen's artificial lights.

What they found more difficult to understand, because the dangers to wolves were more insidious and harder to see, was that the chemical dust and vapour that hung across the crop-field and the waters of some dykes and rivers might be dangerous. Sometimes, so great was their thirst that they were forced to drink water that experience rather than instinct warned them against, and such forced errors caused each of them sickness. But when they were in doubt they learned to make sure that only one of them indulged in what felt dangerous, so that two of them would remain fit and well.

So they journeyed across the northern plains, learning to work together, and making out a pattern in the stars above of what they saw and scented, so that they might pass it on to others when the time came. Places of safety and places of danger, places of plenty and places where all paths led to fences too high to jump, and lights that came on suddenly, and dogs that hunted and tried to kill.

Slowly and steadily they journeyed through that first summer into autumn, until an encounter came their way which turned their growing trust and understanding into common purpose, and made Aragon decide that it was time now to abandon the Mennen ways and seek out the wilderness again.

It was in the industrial heartland of the Ruhr Valley that they came upon their first zoo, in the deer park of a great estate. Of zoos they had heard from Kobrin, who had spoken darkly of the Russian zoos and how kin of his had been confined in such a place for many years until he and some others of the Pechora pack had freed her. So when they heard the roarings and rantings of exotic animals from behind a line of trees, and scented the tired and foetid odours of animals unable to keep themselves properly clean, they guessed it might be a zoo they had found. They had come upon such scents before but never so strongly, nor ever at a time when they were all fit and healthy and felt inclined to investigate.

Not that the place proved easy to get into, not at all. Though they skirted its whole perimeter by night, their silent slinking presence making the animals in the peripheral cages so restless and uneasy that lights went on and Mennen came out to investigate, they could find no way in.

For two days they lingered, searching for safe access, but eventually Mennen lights and dogs, and the high walls and metal fences, made it too dangerous to risk further attempts. Yet how much they would have liked to try, for on the second night they heard from within the perimeter fence the brief howling of wolves.

'It is too dangerous,' said Aragon finally, and decisively, forcing Jicin back from trying again. 'Klimt's instructions to us were quite clear: learn all we can, but let our watchword be survival. But I swear by the name of my mother Jimena, that I, Aragon of Spain, or another in my stead, will come back to this grim place and try once more to contact the wolves within. Jicin, Stry, remember well the pattern of the stars above here, for we shall pass its location on, that others will know where to come.'

They journeyed on after that, but as if to make recompense for what they felt as their failure at the zoo, they began to watch out for such places, and to learn to follow up such maladorous and stricken scents, discovering caged creatures in the most unexpected places.

Along the Rhine in Germany, town after town seemed to have its zoo or visiting circus of wild defeated animals. A brown bear, its eyes a Mann's eyes, staring uncomprehending for a time at the reflection in their eyes watching in the night, before – not their intention at all – it was overtaken by blind panic, as some distant memory from its ancestral past, lingering down the caged generations of its forebears, offered up the notion of 'wolf pack', and it sought to escape the wood and bars that hemmed it in.

They had meant the creature no harm and, after its display of self-destructive terror, and the way the Mennen came and pronged and beat it into tortured stillness, they swore never again to go so carelessly to such cages. They would stay downwind if they could, observe, stalk, seek to be unseen and unscented.

From that time on they felt their exploration of each cityscape they came upon was not complete until they found the animals caged therein, and sought them out in the hope that they might once again find wolf. Then, somewhere across the plains of Belgium, they did so.

It was upon a wild winter night of noisy errant winds that made their approach much easier. If Mennen were about they stayed locked up indoors, their homes but dimly lit, whose chimneys sent up whipped and fretful smoke that scented of steelworks country.

They had discovered the zoo earlier and lain low, waiting for night. Now, entering without difficulty, they found a line of cages, most terrible – in each an animal or two of different kinds. From most came the odour of unclean straw, of rotten flesh, of limbs dying on the bodies they tried to support; of defeat utter and total, of animals alive that should have been allowed to die.

And finally a wolf, *the* wolf, staring at them out of white-blind dead eyes, whiffling its snout as one by one they tiptoed near. Old, so old he was, and he seemed now to think he had scented the gods coming to take him off to a better place. He showed no fear.

'Wolf,' they said, 'can you hear us?'

Yes.

'Wolf,' they whispered, 'can you scent us?'

He nodded bleakly from a place that stretched back into a whole lifetime of confinement.

'Can you see us?'

No.

'What are you?' he asked, turning momentarily to his right at the sound of some heavy, hidden creature in the next-door cage. His voice was a broken whisper.

'Wolves,' they said, 'like you.'

'Have you come to take me on my journey to the stars? I cannot see the stars, but I can remember them.'

'How long have you been here?'

'Here? Two years, since I grew too old for the Mennen to show me to their young. Blindness came and I think I began to smell.'

'How long have the Mennen held you?'

'Since I was weaned. There was a forest, I was taken from there. I travelled the Mennenways many years ago.'

'What was the name of the Forest where you were born?'

'Bialowieza. Do you come from there? What wolves are you?'

'We are . . .' began Stry who had done most of the talking but now could not continue. There were tears in his eyes to see a wolf so caged, so blind and weak, so utterly lost.

'We are of the Wolves of Time,' said Aragon, coming forward. He spoke more kindly, more gently, than Jicin had ever heard him speak. In that moment she felt that Aragon would be her friend for life.

'The Wolves of Time,' whispered the wolf; 'I was told that one day you would come to earth. We have been waiting for you.'

'Who has?'

'Those wolves caged with me, all dead now, and the generations caged before them. Others I have met upon the Mennenways. So many. Though I cannot see you, I can still see *them*. . . I can remember them and their names. Uvale, Adige, Vesdre, Ostia, Gers . . . all the wolves who were my friends. They live still in my head and are my ancestors and kin, my peers and my future, the only world I have. For all of them, for *all* of them, the Wolves of Time were their only hope. I would like them to see me now with you. But there is something I would like more: to be free again, to walk, to –'

As if imagining that the cage was no longer there he came forward too suddenly and his head hit the bars and his face winced with pain.

They looked at the cage, and at the rows of cages of which it was part. Stry and Jicin checked back and forth for sign of Mennen. There was none, but nor was there any way to free the wolf.

'Free me,' said the wolf.

'We cannot free you,' said Aragon.

'You come all the way from the stars, but you cannot free a wolf when you get here!'

The wolf did not say it bitterly, but rather with a certain irony. He winced again, adding as he struggled to lie down, 'Pain is my only friend.'

There was the sound of doors opening back at the entrance to the zoo, and a light went on somewhere, its weak rays caught in the branches of some ornamental trees across an artificial lake.

'Wolf . . .'

'If you cannot free me, kill me,' said the wolf.

His blind eyes stared at them, white as snow, and they knew he meant what he said. Death would be better than the life he had, which would now be all the worse for their coming.

'Wolf . . .'

'Kill me,' he said, and it was a plea, quite terrible.

'Even if we were willing,' said Aragon, 'we could not, for we cannot reach you.'

'No, you cannot. But –'

'Yes, wolf?'

'Can I touch you? Can I . . .'

He reached a paw through the cage. It was twisted with disease, and fleas glistened on its nearly furless skin.

'Yes wolf, yes you can,' said Jicin.

Then one by one they touched their paws to his, and as they did he said, 'You will remember me. You will not forget?'

'Never!' said Jicin.

This moment of touching, of sharing with him all they thought they could share, which was sympathy, might have gone on had he not suddenly started back, as if he remembered something long forgotten.

He pulled his paw from them and lowered his head and said most diffidently, 'Would you howl down the stars for me at least?'

Jicin glanced for guidance at Aragon, for they very rarely howled. Nothing brought the Mennen to them quicker than that. Yet Aragon nodded, for here perhaps the Mennen were used to animal calls and noise and might be slow to show their faces. In any case, there were almost as many escape routes in the place as cages.

'We shall howl down such stars as we can see,' said Aragon, 'for there is quite heavy cloud cover.'

'And what we know,' added Stry, 'for we do not know all the stars.'

'Is the sky clear to the east?' said the old wolf, pushing his face through the bars once more as if to see all the better. 'Howl down what you can see of that part to me, for it is the place where I was born and I can remember its patterns as I was taught them, and as I watched them in the long years after I was born. They were my only comfort, but in blindness I have lost them.'

There in the eastern sky that night, most strangely, the stars shone bright, and there too Stry, a Polish wolf, knew some of the constellations, and began to howl. Slow and quiet at first, as such howling should be made, then a shade more strongly.

Following his lead Aragon and Jicin joined him, and then, finally, cracked and hesitant, the caged wolf did the same.

'Yes!' they heard him interrupt himself. 'Oh yes!'

Soon his howl wove in amongst theirs, finding out stars they could barely see, taking them amongst the constellations by paths they had not known or guessed had links until then.

'Yes!' cried Stry at one moment, suddenly shown a pattern he had never understood before, though of all of them, that part of the sky was most familiar to him. 'Oh yes . . .'

They paused awhile and spoke of the night sky, pleased that the Mennen did not come. The wolf knew more than they could ever know of his own territory's stars.

'And my birth star, is it out tonight?'

'Which is it, wolf?' asked Jicin.

'I shall lead you to it,' he said suddenly, and he began to howl again, his head rising eastward as he picked out a pattern they had touched on before, his voice taking them along the lines and arcs of stars until it led to one whose name they knew not, and which none of them had noticed before.

'Yes!' he sighed as they howled it down, louder and louder, bringing it to the centre of the constellations their howling journeyed through. 'Oh . . . yes!'

Louder his voice then, louder still, and it made them stretch their necks and seek to go with him, further and louder, forgetting the Mennen, nearer and nearer to that star, which seemed as they howled it down to brighten, to come nearer, to be there before them then . . .

Mennen shouts.

Doors opening.

Lights coming on along the cages even as their voices faded and that old wolf's continued on above their heads, out into the liberty of the night sky, out towards the freedom of a star of birth, and re-birth.

'Jicin! Stry! We must –'

'*Aragon!* Look!'

Jicin pointed at the wolf, who lay now, his head along his twisted paws, and his blind eyes open and staring at a distant star. His flanks and belly were still now, still with death.

'Oh wolf, now you are more free than all the Wolves of Time,' whispered Jicin, before she too turned and slunk away to escape the zoo, whilst behind them the noise of the animals swelled and grew ugly. Above them the clouds drove on across the sky and a million stars and one went out. No, now, they would not forget.

After that none of them had any desire to stay long upon the northern plain or seek out more places of caged animals, except that one place they had been unable to find a way into which Aragon swore one day he would find again.

Southwards into France they went then, to find the Auvergne where Aragon and Lounel had first met. There they over-wintered until, when spring came, they began their long journey into Spain, back to Aragon's home pack. A time of brief fighting, of defeats for old wolves and unions with new, and a time of plenty.

They stayed a year along the Cabrera, and saw a new leader in, before departing with four wolves back across the Meseta and over the Pyrenees to the foothills from where they saw the Mennen war begin. All they had done and seen in Spain they would report to Klimt; so much to report, so much . . .

Then, when the war around Toulouse began, they had a new encounter, meeting another wolf whose extraordinary story, combined with the widespread evidence of Mennen war, had made Aragon sense that the time had come for his return to the Heartland. For there was now a great deal to report, and here in France a task with the strange wolf that he could leave Jicin to perform.

Dawn had not yet broken when the wolves about them began to stretch and yawn, ready now to leave.

'Come,' said Aragon to Stry, 'we must go. Gather those who shall travel with us.'

Stry had no need to, for they were all nearby and up and ready for Aragon's command.

'You others,' he said, turning to those who would be left behind, and most of all to Jicin, 'you . . .'

But he had already said all he could say.

'May Wulf be with each of you, and may we meet again at the Heartland, or upon the wolfways as Wulf wills.'

'May He be with you, Aragon, and you, Stry,' said Jicin, going to each of them one last time.

Then Aragon and the others had turned and were gone into the dawn light, leaving Jicin to her new task.

'And which of you shall fight me for the leadership!' she said.

She meant it ironically, for had they been a proper pack either of the two wolves might have wrested physical power from her. But they were not, nor would be yet, and were content for now to be led by her.

'Come,' she said.

Then they too were gone and where all those wolves had been none were now left at all, just the curving rise of the coolers of a dead power station, and the scrape of broken cables high up, where the breeze caught them now and then.

While off across the fallen city, the sound of the guns began to die as the sun's light broke through the dark of night and put the colour of blood to the eastern clouds, and across the fat belly of the billowing smoke of war.

CHAPTER NINE

Jakob Wald observes Huntermann enjoying his sport,
but begins to realize he is part of it

I T WAS as Jakob Wald began the last few hundred metres of his
three-week trek up into the Forest that he became finally certain
that he had allowed himself to become the plaything of
Huntermann; and that each further step he took exposed him to that
murderer's whim.

Back at the beginning of June Huntermann had granted him an
audience in Ostrava, the Czech mountain provincial capital he had
made his headquarters, by then the headquarters of Eastern Europe,
and the rest. He realized that he had been light relief from affairs of
dictatorship and state, but then he was aware that Huntermann knew
more at first-hand about Carpathian wolves than any man alive, and
guessed the madman would be curious to meet him.

So it proved.

'Ah . . . Herr Doktor Wald . . . ah . . .'

The firm handshake, the pale green eyes, the curious blank stare of
assessment before the smile; the dark wiry looks of a mountain man,
and only the slightest of tremors in the left eyelid betraying the stress
and strain under which Huntermann must live, and had surely lived
for ten years past during his rise to power that still had a great deal
further to go.

'Please . . . yes, please sit down.'

Wald had taken good note of the fear and respect that Huntermann
commanded in all those he had to pass through before he finally
reached him. This was the man who had shot the Premier of Slovakia
in front of his own parliament, personally. This was the man who had
strung up the right-wing Croatian writer 'Trpimir' in Vojvodina, for
daring to assume such a historic and inflammatory nom de plume for
his political writings – strung him up personally, and began the clever
speech that launched his own career in the troubled province with a

141

video camera on hand to record the scene, the hanged man's legs still twitching as the body swung to and fro behind his executioner.

This was . . .

'Please Herr Wald, you can sit down.'

Huntermann had seen Wald's hesitation, rightly guessing that Wald had heard stories of men who took Huntermann's proverbial politeness rather too literally and sat down too soon, and were nailed to the chair into which they had so ill-advisedly slumped. Huntermann was polite, but he expected deference. Nevertheless, his shocked visitors, their hands nailed, would find Huntermann talking to them then, no differently than if they had taken his iced water, the cameras recording their curious desperate grimaces and ghastly smiles though never showing the nails through their wrists, or the crawling and clutching of their fingers at the wood. It is astonishing what men will say in such situations to a man like Huntermann.

His show of doubt verging on fear, Wald decided, was the deference Huntermann needed and he duly sat down in the famous wooden chair, its arms all too clearly showing evidence of recent nails. A sham, arranged for visitors? Wald wished it might be so, but an animal instinct told him it was not.

'Now, let us talk of wonderful things,' began Huntermann, signalling for iced water to be given to his visitor, 'let us talk of wolves . . .'

Huntermann's German was quite excellent, good enough for him to have passed for a native of the old south-west of West Germany. They talked, or rather Huntermann questioned and Wald answered. It was the test Wald had expected, and he was not surprised that Huntermann seemed to have read every one of the eighteen papers he had published in Nature and other learned zoological journals in recent years.

It was half an hour before Huntermann, satisfied it seemed that Wald's reputation was well deserved, advanced an opinion of his own, which had to do with the interesting case of the Pechoran wolves in northern Russia. He seemed to have accepted Wald's thesis that wolves all across Europe were enjoying a resurgence due as much to something endemic to themselves as to the reduction in persecution from hunters that had followed the end-of-century economic declines right across Europe.

'But in Pechora, my friend,' opined Huntermann, 'you will find something altogether more proactive from the wolves, more even than your Factor X, if I may so unscientifically call it!'

The two shared a laugh – Factor X was the label coined by a German newspaper for Wald's notion that wolves were obeying a call of their own, and it was a label Huntermann had cleverly adopted for the purposes of his intra-state political party, whose influence was increasing daily, and now looked set to sweep him into power far beyond the limiting borders of Eastern Europe.

'Mr President?' said Wald.

'I believe you will find that the Pechoran wolves moved north from the Khazarian uplands a century ago, following bounty-hunting and persecution there. Now – I am told they are moving back. If birds can migrate, and salmon, why not wolves? Back to their very heartlands, eh?'

Huntermann's eyes narrowed and chilled, waiting. It was the invitation Wald had been waiting for, the one he had come in search of.

'President Huntermann,' he began carefully, and dared venture to talk of Carpathian wolves, about which Huntermann was the expert, having been raised in those parts, and lived among them, and hidden among them in the years before his emergence to the valleys, and to power.

Half an hour more and Huntermann was being pressed to leave for a meeting. The helicopter was burring and roaring outside to take him. He rose, nodded to a subordinate once more to indicate that he was coming, and said, 'Herr Doktor, you have given me pleasure today. For an hour you have taken my mind off matters of state and made me journey back to where my heart is. I shake your hand and tell you I will help you. I will give you the passes you need to get to the Forest I have told you about, but . . . you will have to walk there. It will do you good. Get there in one piece by . . .' He gave a date, and a map reference, and ordered a subordinate to get Wald the maps. '. . . and I will finish telling you about the true heartland of the wolves, and show you what you need to know if you are to understand their journeys.'

Wald allowed himself to look surprised. 'You mean you yourself will be there, Mr President?'

It was a risk to sound surprised, to express slight doubt, but it paid off.

Huntermann laughed, the laugh of a nearly forgotten ten-year-old boy before corruption came, the laugh of one pleased to have surprised someone he respected.

'I'll be there, Herr Doktor ... I hope you will be. It will be a pity if you let anything cause you to hesitate.'

There was clear menace in these last few words, and the whiff of it lingered in the air as Huntermann left, and Wald was shown out another way, with a promise that the passes and maps would be with him within the hour, which they were.

Now, almost a month later, it was nearly time for his meeting with Huntermann, and here he lay waiting in the undergrowth in which he had hidden himself two days before. He wanted to see Huntermann before Huntermann saw him, but it had not been easy. The journey up through the valleys had been a nightmare, a hell of massacres, and he had had to be a shadow passing through, a flitting thing of darkness and the twilight hours: an observer of flames, of distant rapes, of men's screams.

An observer of Mennen, just as Huntermann had known he would have to be if he was to make their rendezvous.

Now it was the morning before their meeting and he waited unseen, watching the guards who had appeared at first light on the road below, issuing forth from an armoured troop carrier with four prisoners, one of whom Wald immediately recognized, as would anyone who had read the newspapers in recent months and weeks.

It was Milo Kervic, brave man, Polish democrat, last hope of a kind of order and old sensibilities, falling to the ground when he got out of the truck and prodded up again.

Wald studied the scene as an ornithologist studies the corner of a lake where migrating waders have just arrived. Back and forth, slowly, taking it all in. Then he saw why Milo Kervic had tripped. It seemed he had been blinded, and recently; the blood seemed barely congealed upon the untreated wounds in his upper face.

From that moment some final hope and truth began to die in Jakob Wald's heart. He was witness to the death of an old world, to the final conflagration of the Dark Millennium. And he knew that Huntermann had put him there to be a witness, to soften him up before their rendezvous.

Wald watched on, waiting as those below him waited, until at last they heard the distant roar of a helicopter from beyond the mountains that rose far across the valley, above the tree-line of the Forest. Wald backed further into the gloom of vegetation so that when he raised his binoculars to watch no glint of sky would show in them for those below to see, and bring his vile odyssey to a premature conclusion.

The Presidential helicopter flew slowly over the Forest's tree-tops and Huntermann, sighing nostalgically, stared down at ground he knew so well.

To his right the famous Fall thundered down, though with less spray than he remembered, which probably meant the wind along the cliffs was light. His grey eyes, a hunter's eyes, searched along the hard, steep shepherd tracks up amongst the cliffs and over towards the Scarpfeld, searched as a hunter always searches – for signs of life, for movement, for anything strange.

Then he saw the ancient, solitary mountain ash he had called the 'Tree', when he had hiked over this way from the Scarpfeld when he was fifteen, crossing the border and so risking his life. He had sat beneath its gnarled shade for a whole day, watching the mist drift up the Vale and a lone wolf at the Forest edge, lazy and old. That day Huntermann had decided what he would one day become, and what he must do to become it.

That day, he told himself, marked a moment when the history of Europe changed. Screw chaos theory and how the flutter of butterfly wings in the Amazon caused an earthquake in Japan: he, Huntermann, decided he wanted power over men one day here, when he was fifteen, and twenty-eight years later Europe was slipping into controlled anarchy as a result.

'That's chaos theory,' muttered Huntermann with satisfaction.

The Tree was beneath them now, and his mind moved back to all those years ago.

'Fucking shepherds,' he muttered, grinning the grin of the triumphant, malevolent sadist that he was, his head made grotesquely misshapen by the curve of the plastic window, 'fucking peasants.'

They had found him asleep, the last time he ever let himself make that mistake; but the wolf had slept and so had he. They had taken him to the Forest and tied him to a tree, and left him overnight to soften him up a little before they killed him with the knives they had shown him with such pleasure; and all his father had ever said of that bastard nation seemed confirmed. No doubt they thought he would be afraid of the Forest spirits in the night, or the wolves, or whatever superstitions made them think that the place would frighten him.

But it had not. Night-time and wilderness were his meat and drink, his true turn-on, and the fools would have had to secure him a lot better than they had to keep him safe until the dawn.

As the helicopter slowed over the Forest, and circled around so that he might get better views, beads of sweat appeared on Huntermann's sleek temples. He was recalling the details of his first killings (except for the boy he drowned near school): four grown men – the shits had brought another with them next morning to watch the sport – and Huntermann had lain in wait for them down at the Forest edge and killed them one by one, just like he had always dreamed he might since the day he saw the American film Deliverance, *about men hunting men in the Appalachian mountains.*

The last one, the one who had held a knife to his eyes the evening before, he felled and tortured, letting his screams and animal cries of disbelief ring out through the trees, right down to the nearest village, that his friends and family might find him too late. Only when they came blundering up through the trees did Huntermann choose to leave, ending his work on the man with a deep thrust into the femoral artery, just below the groin, so that the shit-head's friends might watch his pathetic life pumping out on to the Forest floor.

Then Huntermann had headed off upslope, taking the escape route he had long since worked out, which was the stream-bed of the Fall, and up into the Gulley, and thence by way of a scramble that came dangerously close to being a climb to the terrace route high above. They had been great days, but afterwards he was different and people were afraid of him, for after that he exuded from his very pores the possibility that those who mixed with him might die.

Now, overflying the place, he did not bother to look for signs of the destruction down these valleys he had ordered months before, for he knew his orders had been carried through. The farmers who had resisted him, cowmen, milkmen, cheese-makers, dung-carriers, ignorant arseholes, were dead or taken to the camps north of Ostrava, where some of them were still being kept alive, for they might have a use.

He had considered bringing Borvic up here with him, and dropping him on to his own land from a height low enough that he could clearly see the rocks and grass and streams he said he loved so much, and high enough to have time as he fell to think about what he was losing.

But no, Huntermann had come up with something better in mind, something more sporting, which gave him an opportunity too rare in these busy militant days to put on his boots and be in the wilderness, near the wolves he envied so much.

Aaaah . . . he grinned across the seats at Porsin, who had delivered Borvic to him, and saw the moment of white fear in the silly old sod's eyes.

'Good day for hunting!' he said, not bothering to shout, and contemptuous of a man so shit-eager to nod his head and half raise a hand in pretence he understood what he could not possibly hear. Why else do pilots in these craft speak through headphones?

Huntermann put his own on and flicked a switch, and gave an order: 'We're early. Overfly the Scarpfeld to the east, keep to its northern edge a little above the cliffs.'

Oh yes, Huntermann knew this ground, and knew this part, where he had lain low while they searched for him after the murders, just about as well as he knew the contours and the cavities, the rough parts and the smooth of his own cock and scrotum, and the routes to pain and pleasure deep therein.

The craft turned slowly, gently, for the pilot knew well President Huntermann's preferences, and that he had killed the last pilot but two for giving him a rough ride and causing him to vomit over his white Schnabel suit. The name of the game around Huntermann was doing the job excellently. Yes, he liked the notion of excellence, and the sanction of death for those who failed.

In any case, the pilot should have known that President Huntermann had a delicate stomach and was prone to air-sickness, sea-sickness, and to secret terrors in the deep of the night, which only the naked hands and arms and breasts of his daughter could soothe away.

The high col where once Huntermann had wanked out of the sheer exuberance of feeling that he might thus possess such a vast terrain, as the Ashanti wanked over African hills and made them fertile in their name . . . and then the black, bleak cliffs of the Scarpfeld came into view.

'Shit!' he muttered ruefully, but with a certain resigned pleasure.

There was a secret gulley in these cliffs, whose entrance was marked by a small outcrop that stood proud of all the screes could hurl at it. He had pored over the army maps of the place, unconvinced. He did not believe the surveyors had been up it. Nor had he himself ever done so, except once, in the mist which was always there and was there now.

In among the gulleys there, deep within, hidden and unvisited, legend had it the WulfRock stood, and would give immortality to any who found it. Only one account of a visit to the place existed that he knew of, by the eighteenth-century wandering priest Askol'd, who spoke of the misty terrors of a gulley wherein 'a great stone or stones arose and put such fear into me that I advanced no further, sensing the presence of the Devil or of God, I know not. This stone, or rock, is known thereabout as WulfRock, and believed to be home and origin of an ancient and profane cult.'

Huntermann had first heard of this when he was ten, and with his father's help was able to study large-scale maps few others had ever seen. He made a papier-mâché model of the terrain around the Scarpfeld and so his explorations had begun. But models don't have mist, and Huntermann laughed down at the land that it could mock him so, for he had never once been to this place when there was no mist about.

As for Askol'd's terror, and talk of devils and of gods, it had been real enough to Huntermann when he was there, and he was grateful for the mists because they flowed in across the Scarpfeld at just the right time to save his life.

'Had they not,' he told himself as the helicopter started its slow swing back towards the Forest, 'Europe might be a very different, and more peaceful, place than it is today. Perhaps all history depends upon such chances as mists helping the resolute when they most need it.'

Now he needed more than mist to keep himself alive – he needed armies, and personal bodyguards, one of whom . . .

'We've four minutes to spare, Mr President,' said Schlitz, the guard whom he rarely let leave his side in public.

'Good,' said Huntermann, searching the Forest as it came into view once more and following the stream up above the trees, and thence towards the Fall.

The land he respected, and the wolves as well, those too, those too . . .

The 'copter landed north of the Fall stream, just above the tree-line of the Forest, and Huntermann climbed out and waited for the rotors to stop and the mountain silence to return before he breathed deeply of the clear, cool air, and felt his feet firm on the ground and slowly looked about.

With a whispered 'Sir . . .' Schlitz proffered a pair of binoculars and stood well clear. His master wanted space. Huntermann slowly raised the binoculars to his eyes, adjusted them, and in a leisurely way *examined the view westward across the tree-tops to a part of the pastures in the Vale that he knew would be visible from here. He did it slowly, taking in the ground to right and left of the area in which he was most interested, as a man does who knows his wilderness, who knows how to look.*

Then Huntermann surveyed the nearer pasture slopes once again and grunted with satisfaction: he had found what he wanted: four men in civilian clothes, hands tied behind their backs, watched over by two fit and tough-looking special troops in dark green uniforms.

Schlitz spoke briefly into a mobile, and one of the distant soldiers answered, each raising their gaze to look across the Forest at each other, far though the distance was. Schlitz nodded, his eyes catching Huntermann's, and said, 'They're ready, sir.'

'I doubt that anyone's ever quite ready for death, eh?'

Schlitz remained expressionless, but Shit-scared grinned and nodded, his face pale and shiny with sweat, his eyes eager and hungry for killing, his thin dry lips wetted quickly by a flick of his tongue.

'Now . . .' said Huntermann rhetorically, and he raised the binoculars again and examined the men they were going to try to execute from a distance of four hundred and fifty metres, 'now . . .'

The moment the helicopter had veered from above the Forest and up towards the cliffs, and thence away and out of sight in the direction of the Scarpfeld, Klimt led the pack out of the Forest and up towards the Tree. He left Kobrin and Tare behind to watch over Lunar and Raute, who could not, or would not, be moved.

It was a strategy long since talked through, for the Wolves felt safer up among the cliffs and screes, where they could watch the Mennen unseen and with impunity, for there were many escape routes to use if need be. If they stayed down in the Forest, to remain undetected immediately became harder, especially if the Mennen had dogs.

So up there they waited, anxious that Raute's weakness meant the others had to stay but happy to return the quick confirmation bark Kobrin gave from the Forest edge once they were beyond the Tree and out of sight, so that he knew roughly where they were. Then they saw him retreat back into the Forest shadows to safety and his watching duties.

Shortly afterwards a truck came along the Road and pulled over alongside the one that had long since been abandoned there. Two

Mennen got out, climbed into the back, and threw out four others before themselves jumping down to the ground. The four struggled upright, their hands tied behind them, and were pushed and shoved protesting across on to the pastures and then upslope.

The shouts and grunts, and a cry of pain when one was hit and fell down, were so loud that Klimt had no doubt that Kobrin and Tare would have gone down through the trees to investigate.

The Mennen continued upslope until they reached a flatter part. If they had continued much further they would have dropped out of sight behind the Forest tree-line. There they waited, the four bound Mennen made to stand some way off from the other two, who took slightly higher ground. The four continued to shout for a time, and then fell silent.

Soon after this Klimt heard the helicopter returning as it swung back from the direction of the Scarpfeld, this time almost above their heads, following the line of the Great Fall and its stream, alongside which, sufficiently above the tree-line to have the six Mennen in view, it landed, and Mennen got out.

The Wolves scented the air, recognizing the thick, oily smells of the helicopter, and watched its whirling wings slow, and finally stop. One of the Mennen stood clear of the others and Klimt scented at the air to catch his odour.

Klimt nodded at Tervicz to take over responsibility for the pack while he slipped away downslope amongst the scree to get a better scent. He lay low down there for a time; then, when the Mennen began to talk, he turned away, and slipped back up to the others.

'Not the Mann,' said Klimt, whose scent he had met with twice in his life, and knew to be benign. 'But possibly, possibly . . . we'll have to wait until they've gone and we can investigate better.'

'Huntermann?' suggested Tervicz, remembering well Huntermann's acrid, cloying scent from his urination on the Fell some years before.

'Possibly . . . now, let's see why they've come.'

Huntermann looked the way of his shit-scared companion in sport and said, 'See them? The last one, the fat one, is mine. You understand?'

'Yes, of course,' said Shit-scared.

They were handed their rifles and both men checked them through.

'Use the rocks to their right for your sighting shots,' said Huntermann, raising his weapon and firing a single round. The noise

echoed briefly among the black cliffs behind them, and there was a spurt of dust and splintered rock near the men, who turned and peered upslope. Huntermann adjusted his sights very slightly, raised his gun and swung it round towards the men and then slowly let it fall, not yet firing.

Shit-scared went through the same process, but nervously, with more fumbles, and he took three shots to get it right.

'Remember Borvic is mine,' breathed Huntermann, lining up his sights once more on the last of the four men they had brought out to the Vale for the purposes of sport and execution . . .

Huntermann was not yet the most powerful European leader, but the more his strategy of chaos-terrorism worked, the more he headed that way. The seventies and eighties European terrorists had been so small-minded, so limited – why blow up an office block and kill three hundred when the new technology, linked to tactical bombing devices, made blowing up whole city quarters and thirty thousand people just as easy?

Yes, they had all been so parochial, and more concerned to change policies than governments. He and his people had thought bigger, and thought longer and applied to European politics what the Mafia had once applied to North American crime: control, fear, power, corruption, all nicely dressed up and packaged, and the mess, and therefore the blame, cleared up behind them.

Better, Huntermann had long since decided, to control a chaotic Europe, and ruined states and peoples, than to control nothing. Already the east European states, part of Austria and what had been Croatia were his, or in the power of the 'Wolves', the federation of Democratic Liberals that he led, whose symbol was the animal he loved, the wolf. A symbol whose dark image, all eyes and snout and ears, he had first sketched that day under the Tree.

Now the DL image was everywhere, and spreading to those towns and cities where his people were assuming power as they gained a footing in the ruins their tactical bombing had caused: Milan, Marseille, Freiburg, Toulouse, and ruined Madrid. More than that, it was in people's hearts now and the Year of the Wolf was nigh.

That was what was so clever about Huntermann – the symbol, the fact that he kept his own zoo and played with wolves, and his promise that the Year of the Wolf was coming, was nigh – and so it would, when he decreed it. People, he knew, chased after hope, and so long as they thought that year was coming, when all their problems would be solved, they would help him make it happen.

Meanwhile, Huntermann was allowing himself a day of fun, and indulging Mr Shit-scared Porsin, who had helped him so much, by letting him shoot personally three of the four patriots who were now running about in panic on the grassy slopes before them.

Porsin was not a bad shot after all, but he was not perfect – or perhaps he liked winging them and letting them suffer a little before aiming for the chest. Milo Kervic had just fallen to Porsin's latest shot. Men fall quicker than deer, and more untidily too, but those had been good shots.

'Your turn, Mr President,' said Porsin, looking at him. His face was flushed, his eyes alight, and Huntermann let his eyes drop to see if Shit-scared had an erection, but there was no sign of it.

Huntermann's eyes narrowed as he framed the last man in his sights. A green shirt, no jacket. Mr Borvic. A prematurely grey head, slightly bald: Borvic the chemist, as they called the multi-millionaire.

Huntermann knew for what he should aim, the chest, but the head was a more appealing target, more difficult, bumping up and down as he ran for cover. Borvic would do better to dodge or –

'He's dived,' said Porsin.

'He fell,' said Huntermann. 'They've been told that if they dive, if they do not run, their deaths will not be pleasant.'

Schlitz's eyes narrowed fractionally, and the grip of his right hand on his left wrist tightened momentarily. He would quite like to have had Borvic at the zoo, where Huntermann kept people on hold for his private pleasures and pursuits, and those of his animals, for Borvic had once bankrupted him.

Borvic came up on to his hands and knees, half looked behind him, and rose up suddenly to begin another run downslope, towards the stream that coursed down there and would give him cover.

'Right idea, wrong approach,' said Huntermann, suddenly very still, his breathing steady. Borvic just behind his sights, steady, steady, and Borvic moving forward, pausing to turn and look back, plumb centre and motionless, fool.

Huntermann lowered the gun a fraction, for tempting though that pig face was, it was the body that was the best target. There were a few things more pleasurable than having prey in a rifle sight like this, just before the squeeze, a moment before the shot when he was in *control and could choose whether to let the animal live or die . . . a few things, but not many.*

He squeezed the trigger with a sigh.

Was Borvic truly frightened in that final moment before he fell, Huntermann wondered? Was the last thing he felt before darkness came on him the acid stickiness of his own shit down his thighs? Huntermann laughed silently, and hoped it had been. The trouble was . . . while his friend might think this kind of hunting was the greatest in the world he knew it was not: animals are more of a challenge than men.

Porsin was about to say . . . and he stilled, suddenly, for Huntermann had. There was movement upslope which tugged at the corner of his eye.

'Ssshh! Shut up!'

Porsin shut up. When Huntermann spoke like that an ever-increasing part of Europe was beginning to shut up.

Huntermann shook his head: if it was wolves, which it probably was, they would stay out of sight now, and there was no time to stalk them. He read the cliffs above north to south and remembered them. The Mann had almost certainly come this way, so there must be a way through into the Scarpfeld. Clever bastard. Perhaps, after all, not all men are inferior to animals as prey. Perhaps some are worth the chase.

'I'll get him in the end,' Huntermann told himself with the easy assurance of a man who had achieved everything he had set his sights on, so to speak. Everything.

'Your daughter will be waiting for us,' said Porsin evenly, very evenly. Huntermann was dangerously sensitive, possessive and jealous where his daughter was concerned and it paid not to betray any feelings about her of any kind.

Huntermann felt the brief thrill that the words 'your daughter' gave him, and let it linger. His love-child; his daughter; his everything.

'And my wife,' he said, savouring the hypocrisy he put into these three words as if it were a fine muscadet.

He rose, and unzipped himself to pee across the world below, as he always did after he had killed something. He had stags' heads as trophies, and salmon, and a wolf's head too, and he had peed after all of them.

He contemplated the idea of Borvic's head and decided that were he alone he would cut it off himself. Failing that, and thinking it was time he had a human head as a trophy, Huntermann decided he would force his fat friend Porsin here to do it. Squeamish? Tough shit.

Huntermann had a pretty use for that head. It would be placed so that it might watch from the mantelpiece in the master bedroom of the palace stolen by the people Porsin led while Huntermann fucked the wife of Borvic, whom he would prefer was not as willing as she seemed likely to be.

Huntermann laughed, and Porsin followed suit, though most uneasily as he followed him back down through the trees to where the men lay, three dead, one dying.

Huntermann thought, 'This idiot doesn't know how to move through trees, nor over rough ground. He can't smell that wolves are here. If this fool was not here, and I did not have to go down, I would go on up, and further up, and seek out wolves. Then I would track that clever Mann down. But . . .'

Huntermann laughed lazily as they reached the guards who had been watching over the four victims before ordering them to run.

'A time to work and a time to play, my friends. My father taught me that. What did yours teach you?'

Power brought out the philosopher in Huntermann, as it brought out the weakness in others about him.

He drew out a hunting knife and took pleasure in Porsin's attempt not to flinch.

'Cut off Borvic's head, Porsin. Now!'

Porsin went white, and cold sweat ran down his spine.

'I . . . can't . . .' he managed to say before he bent down and vomited.

Huntermann smiled and nodded to Schlitz, who went to Porsin and held him fast.

'I'll show you how it's done,' said Huntermann, and Porsin began to struggle and scream as the knife went in below his ear.

'Two heads are better than one,' grunted Huntermann a little later, 'that's what my grandfather used to say.'

CHAPTER TEN

*Klimt and his fellow Wolves observe the Magyars
with disgust; and Jakob Wald finds sanctuary in the Forest*

KLIMT AND THE OTHERS watched as the helicopter suddenly lifted off, skimmed briefly over the tree-tops, and settled down again just above where the Mennen had walked down through the Forest to the bodies of the four they had shot. The living Mennen climbed into it, and the helicopter took off once more, and flew back to the spot where it had first landed, where the Mennen got out once more and seemed to be waiting. For more Mennen?

The two Mennen who had walked up with the four who had been shot walked slowly back down to their truck, and sat and smoked.

All was suddenly silent, but for the roar of the Great Fall behind them, but Klimt ordered them to stay where they were, and gave Kobrin to understand the same when he appeared once more below them at the Forest edge, to indicate that all was well with Lunar and the others.

Klimt eyed the bodies that had been left behind on the pastures, or those that could be made out. But a breeze rising up the slopes caught at something white, which flapped up now from one of them, seeming to warn them to stay clear awhile, and lie low: Mennen and all their works were unpredictable . . .

'Klimt, look!'

Rohan had seen them first, far across to the south-west, at the top of the Vale, where it rose the short way towards the Fell: two wolves, no, three . . . and one of them . . .

'Dendrine's son . . .'

'. . . and Dendrine.'

'The Magyars . . .'

They came with the utmost leisure along the Road, almost ambling, the son in front and horribly unmistakable, the second, a male, in the middle, and the thin and raddled Dendrine behind. Three in a row and silent, scenting the Road occasionally, and raising their heads to the wind, a westerly, and so blowing Klimt's way.

'Look at him!' muttered Tervicz. 'Just *look* at him!'

Dendrine's son stopped and stared their distant way, as if he had heard the comment, which was impossible.

'I thought for a moment he'd seen us,' said Klimt, 'but he'd probably heard the Fall, even against the wind, and now he's seen it.'

'He's . . . he's . . .' whispered Elhana with a shiver of horror.

He was, for one thing, bigger by a head than the other male with him, and seemed almost twice the size of his mother. Bigger by a head – and what a head. It was huge and faceted like rock, the eyes deep and askew, and though they could not possibly be made out in any detail from so far away there was the sense that the wolf's – the monster's – stare was ruthless and cruel.

Yet, in contradiction to the raw malevolence his large, dark presence seemed to radiate when still, and staring, his movements were strangely fluid, as if the ground moved away under him, rather than he over it. His limbs were long, grotesquely long, and his flanks muscled and strong.

In his coming, in the way he walked upon the Road, fearless of the Wolves on whose territory he trespassed, he said without a word, without the need to fight, confront or show his strength, that he, Dendrine's son, was the Magyar leader now, and there was no other.

He stopped, scented at the ground, raised his head and stared in that resolute and fearsome way down the Road towards the abandoned vehicle, and then turned his gaze from it on to the slopes of the pastures, and up to where the bodies lay. Then suddenly, shocking in his speed and power, he accelerated forward and ran straight, fast and straight, off the Road and up the slope towards the Mennen dead, his legs powering back and forth, his whole body rhythmic in its movement, young and fit, and bold as summer sun. It was, in its way, beautiful, but it was a beauty flawed, corrupted, in some way foul, an evil whose nature and meaning were not yet clear to the Wolves, but which they sensed, and their hearts chilled.

Dendrine's huge son ran right to the Mennen, round them, flicking his head down at one as if to smell and taste it, and then back, back downslope, back to his ledrene, his mother, his dam, his . . . flaw. He neared and she advanced on him; his huge dark brutal head bent down to her, and so far as a giant can defer to a dwarf he deferred then to her.

'My sweetling,' she had called him years before when Klimt had first come to the Scarpfeld and that couple had been there in the Great Cleft, 'my darling'.

In the way he talked to her now, waited on her words, watched as she went past him and peered upslope towards the Mennen bodies the making of his life seemed revealed. She who had borne him, who had nurtured him and who had taught him, controlled him. He was leader of the Magyars, but she was his universe.

Klimt had no need to warn his companions to stay still, and he knew they could not be seen. Nor had he need to explain why he was simply observing and not setting off to drive the three Magyars from their territory. They had talked so often of Dendrine and the Magyar leadership, and wondered so much about Dendrine's son that the sudden sight of him – and it could only be him – held them still, and fascinated. Three Magyars could do little harm against their pack, and they might learn much from watching one so bold as to trespass openly in this way.

Klimt was more concerned about Kobrin, for it was inevitable that he would head down out of the Forest and investigate the corpses.

Kobrin appeared silently below them at the Forest edge.

'He's checking if we've seen them. He's indicating that Tare is down there watching. He's . . .'

The Magyars resumed their advance along the Road, not yet returning to where the bodies were. It seemed that Dendrine wished to look at the vehicle first.

'Follow me,' said Klimt, taking this opportunity of the Magyar interest in the vehicle to slip from the cover of the screes and quickly down the open ground to the shelter of the Forest below. They moved in a line and in such shadows and depressions as Klimt could find that they might not be seen.

The Magyars were just reaching the vehicle and the second male turning to look about when the Wolves dropped far enough down to be out of their sightline. Klimt immediately speeded up, and ran into the Forest where Kobrin was awaiting him.

'Lunar is with Raute, and has moved her nearer the stream where she is hard to find and easily protected; Tare is down at the far Forest edge watching the Magyars.'

The Wolves followed him down through the trees, going fast but carefully so they made no noise, and did not disturb the wood pigeons which had begun to return to parts of the Forest, and soon they joined

Tare. She had chosen her watching-spot well, for it lay in deep shadow a little back from the last of the trees, with a few low branches in front to break up the view inward, making their detection by sight nearly impossible, and more likely by scent or sound – but that the wind came from off the pastures, and they knew to keep absolutely silent.

The spot was directly upslope from the abandoned vehicle; off to the right, on nearly the same contour as where the Wolves were hidden, lay the bodies of the Mennen. The white rising and falling thing they had observed earlier from the cliffs above was part of one of the Mennen's garments, fluttering in the updraught on the slope.

The Mennen lay strewn about untidily, their hands and heads pink-grey, except that with two of them, where the heads once were, was nothing but the red-white of torn flesh and bone, and the sheen of muscle tissue.

The Magyars darted in and out of the open vehicle, though never more than one at a time, the others watching, and staring most often up towards the Forest edge.

'They know we're here, Klimt,' breathed Kobrin. 'We could take them – or give them a fright at least.'

Klimt shook his head slowly. He wanted to take this first opportunity to study the leader and ledrene of the Magyars at close quarters.

'Elhana, Tervicz, Tare – fall back to a spot between us and Lunar and Raute. We may need a second line of defence if we retreat.'

Klimt was ever-cautious in such matters and was almost immediately proved wise to have given that order, reluctant though all three were to miss a direct view of the extraordinary and loathsome wolves on the Road below; for just then Dendrine's son turned to face back down the Road the way they had come and raised his head and let forth a curious harsh, staccato signal bark.

Almost immediately three more Magyars broke the southern horizon, where they had evidently been lying in wait, and came trotting down the Road to join their companions.

When they were some distance away one of them called out, 'So the legendary Wolves of Time are skulking in their little wood are they, Führer?'

Dendrine's son, Führer, laughed deeply, nodding his great head, and then glancing at his mother for confirmation. She laughed as well, and they all looked up boldly towards the Forest as if they knew, or suspected, that they were being watched. Kobrin growled his irritation, and frustration.

'We stay right where we are and watch,' said Klimt, lest there was any doubt about it. 'Remember, Solar, a study of your enemy is the best way to learn how to master him. I do not intend to be goaded into a fight with the Magyars which might very well lure us along the Road and into the Fell, which is their ground, quite apart from giving this ... this Führer and his mother an opportunity to assess our strengths and weaknesses.

'Equally, I rather doubt that he will risk entering the Forest, which is our ground, without knowing where we are and how many of us there are. Therefore stay your ground each of you, do not move or make a sound, whatever these bold wolves may do – not unless I specifically command it.'

Solar and the others nodded in silence, impressed by his calm, and the sense he gave of being in command of the situation.

The Magyars talked a little in low voices, eyes on the Forest, and then raised their snouts towards the corpses. One of the males made to advance that way but with a great swing of his head Führer buffeted him off track and on to his side. With an extraordinary twist and leap he was on top of the miscreant, mock-savaging him.

'Mine,' they heard him say, and then he shouted, 'Dendrine, mine!'

'Of course, beloved,' they heard Dendrine rasp, her voice not only thin and shrill, but carrying a curious maternal whine, 'why don't you go and pleasure yourself with food ...'

Führer nodded, looked eagerly towards the bodies, advanced a step or two, and then was off, bounding upslope with the same astounding power and speed he had shown before, like a cub given permission by his mother to go and play awhile.

Up, and up, bound after bound, and then with a high jump landing at the corpse nearest to where the Wolves watched in silent, morbid fascination.

Führer licked at the wound left where the head had been, and seemed to suck. He stepped back, his misshapen head tilted to one side as he considered where to start. He dived again towards the white flapping cloth and tore and tore, and tore again, moving around methodically as he did so, stripping the Mann of his covering, and revealing torn and bloodied flesh.

One of the Mann's arms rose as Führer thrust his head under it, to tear cloth out from beneath the corpse, rose and bent about Führer's neck, the hand seeming to grasp his fur. The dead gesture was strangely gentle, as if the Mann were greeting him with the semblance of a hug. They heard Dendrine's laugh, and saw the other Magyars had advanced a little upslope, but sat now at a respectful distance, waiting for their leader to find a choice morsel, before they dared join the feast.

Führer bit into the Mann's bloated stomach and tore at it, turning away for a moment as if he had tasted something he disliked. Then, as the arm with its hand slipped across his face he turned on it suddenly and with a roar, as if going for the kill, he grasped the arm at its upper part near the body in his jaws, crunched on it, crushed it, and with a mighty turn and wrench, tore the whole thing off as if were a young limb.

Then he threw it in an obscene gesturing arc up into the air before catching it length-on, the lower arm and hand sticking straight out of his great jaws. Crunching and chewing as he went so that the hand moved, and jerked as if alive, he swung round once more, and charged towards the Forest, straight to where the Wolves watched.

There he halted, standing huge and frightening, the Mennen hand jerking still, and faced the shadows, and his enemy.

Then for the first time they saw his eyes, as they stared out of the deep recesses where they hid. They were dark, their whites were red-rimmed, they were as brutal and unkind as horrid death. His strange head caught more dark than light in its sheer sides and wide angles, bigger than Kobrin's, expressive of a whole world of wanton destruction and contempt.

Then he frowned briefly, stopped chewing, and spat out the hand on to the ground, as if it were an offering to wolves he knew were there, and a challenge to wolves he would one day return to fight.

He turned away indifferently, careless of being attacked, and ambled back to the corpses for more. Then his friends and companions, and his haggard mother, came slowly to the bodies, tore at the garments as he had done, and began to gorge themselves, their heads more grisly and bloodied each time they raised them to look about.

While in the shadows the Wolves watched frozen to the ground, staring at the horrors that were now the Magyar leadership, talking and laughing as they enjoyed their feast, like a pack that has success-fully killed a stag. Some ate so much that towards the end they vomited up gobbets of the Mennen they had half consumed.

Sometime then Dendrine detached herself from the others, came over to where Führer had been and stood staring into the Forest, into the unseen eyes of the Wolves. There was blood on her face fur, and the watching Wolves saw that her whole body was thin and worn, and old, while her eyes held a look of cold cruelty, contempt for life, unadulterated lust for power and control.

Suddenly she spoke, her voice harsh and loud enough for the Magyars to pause in their greedy work to turn and listen.

'See us? See *him*?' she said. 'Eh, Klimt of Tornesdal, who skulks in the shadows of broken trees? If you're not in there, watching, and shitting your hindquarters with fear, you should be. You killed Hassler, who was my consort and my leader, my leader and my love. Well then, you must be punished for it, eh? Yes . . . Oh yes . . .'

Here she grinned in a foul way, suggesting that for her punishment was a pleasure, and an expression of a need and lust which he could never satisfy enough.

'Your sons, Klimt, and my best son, my cubling, ought to play. They should gambol on the grass together – eh, Führer? Hear that? Your dam wants you to play with Klimt's male cublings, whose names, I am reliably informed, are Solar and Lunar. Very pretty. Would you like to play with them?'

Führer nodded his head, rolled his eyes, spat out a Mann's vertebra and leaped over, one, two, three to where she was.

'Play with them? I'll eat their legs so they hobble comically.'

Dendrine nearly laughed herself sick at this jolly joke, and wheezed and coughed, her eyes streaming tears.

'I'll kill Klimt's sons most horribly, mother, just for you.'

'There, my dears, now you know what lies in wait across the Fell for you: me, my son Führer, and the Magyar hordes. We are coming soon, and you will die. Eh?'

It was all Klimt could do to restrain those with him from rushing out of the protective darkness upon the foul she-wolf, but he knew it was what these Magyars wanted, and that with numbers such as this serious injury or death would be the consequence for one or more of his pack. It was not worth it. A wise wolf bides his time.

Slowly then, carelessly, trailing Mennen blood, Dendrine and Führer returned to the others by the chewed and torn corpses. Then the Magyars went back down the slope, talking and laughing their way along the Road towards the Fell, where, on the horizon, they were met by others who had been waiting out of sight there – waiting without doubt for the Wolves to show themselves and reveal their strength. Klimt had been right to show restraint.

'Let them go, let them be . . .' growled Klimt, and not a single one of the Wolves moved as the Magyars drifted out of sight.

'And who the fuck's that, sir?' growled Schlitz at Huntermann's side as Wald finally emerged from the undergrowth on the far side of the valley and headed down towards the road, and then towards them.

Radios crackled, orders were given, and Huntermann smiled. 'He can approach unhindered,' he said, 'he is quite unarmed.'

'But who is it, Mr President?' pressed Schlitz, whose job it was to ask, and who alone of all those close to Huntermann dared be persistent when the need arose.

'The greatest living expert on the European wolf,' said Huntermann softly, raising his binoculars to study Wald's arrival at the corpses, 'but for me.'

Wald saw the head of Porsin at the same moment it saw him from its perch on the tussock of grass where Huntermann had thoughtfully placed it. One eye open, the other half open, the mouth sagging. It was not the most sickening thing he had ever seen but it came very close. Wald blinked and swallowed, but paused only momentarily. On his journey here he had seen worse, far worse, than this and was already beyond shock. But as his heart beat harder and he pushed on up the slope leaving the first obscenity behind him, he was suddenly certain that he was now in the sights of someone's gun, Huntermann's probably. Pausing betrayed weakness and fear, and those two spelled death where Huntermann was concerned.

The head of Borvic was pointed another way, half fallen on its side, its jagged neck the reds and nearly-white of flesh and bone and sinews. The bodies . . . Wald pressed on once more, knowing that Huntermann could shoot him whenever he wished, but probably would not. Huntermann's pleasure seemed to come from being in control, knowing what he could do and choosing not to do it now but later. His pleasure was also in the timing, the timing. Huntermann liked to believe he might be God.

Suspecting all this, Wald pressed on with this final ghastly trek, past the indifferent guards, past the heads, past the bodies, watching now for lines of retreat, on through the rocky heights above, through the Forest, and here below it. He had kenned the ground intimately from the maps he had been given, and now systematically fleshed out his knowledge with rocks and vegetation growth, and individual trees.

He watched where the rooks dived and were lost within the Forest; and looked now to see exactly which routes the wolves he had seen must have taken to get back into the territory of the Fell he had observed them coming from in the last two days. Then there were the wolves in the wood, watching, a different pack. Wolves – he doubted Huntermann had seen them, but he himself had. They were there now, he could feel them.

'Herr Doktor!' Huntermann called down from his vantage point above, his voice smug and half mocking. 'Your journey was untroubled I trust?'

The eyes were colder than before, and triumphant now, and could not help flicking past Wald to where the corpses lay. Huntermann's cheeks were flushed, his eyes watchful. Wald had absolutely no doubt that Huntermann intended to kill him: he knew too much about wolves, more than he should, and now . . .

'Now, let me take you for a ride.'

There was no refusing it without the henchman Schlitz shooting him then and there, and as he climbed aboard the helicopter Wald had images of being thrust out, fifteen thousand feet up, not so far above the Tatra that he would not see every nook and cranny of the rocks as he accelerated towards them.

The sweat on his back turned cold as they took off.

But then Huntermann talked, of wolves and of men, and overflew that misty area within which, he said, the fabled WulfRock might be found.

'My heartland, Wald, my very own, if only I had time to find it; but affairs of state . . .'

The helicopter turned back the way they had come and Wald now doubted that he had more than ten minutes to live unless he got his timing right. There was a resolution to the way Schlitz held his weapon.

As they returned Huntermann told him about his first journey here as a lad, and of how he had killed those shepherds who had captured him, all those years ago.

'Do you remember the tree to which they tied you?' asked Wald as they landed.

Huntermann shrugged, losing interest now that the sport was almost done; 'Perhaps.'

Huntermann glanced at Schlitz who glanced at Wald. It was all *about timing and Wald thought about wolves and tried to keep calm.*

'It is a historic tree, Mr President, the one they tied you to, and it would be good to touch it.'

Huntermann shrugged again and smiled slightly, relishing the indirect flattery, and impulsively led the way downslope into the trees.

'Forests change,' he muttered, his curiosity aroused, his eyes glancing from left to right, 'but I remember the few rocks just above, not far, just . . .'

He turned past an old pine whose roots pierced rocks and scrambled down, using the tree to keep his balance. He even turned to proffer a hand to Wald to help him down.

Was this to be his moment of execution, with Schlitz behind?

'Thank you Mr President!' said Wald, jumping down, his hand momentarily in Huntermann's; most strange. It felt like saying thanks and shaking the hand of one's own murderer before the deed itself.

'Shall we spread out and find the rocks?'

Even as he said these words Wald saw from Huntermann's repeated smile and weary glance at Schlitz that he was thinking that their victim really should not take them for such fools, and followed with what he had long since planned to say: 'Wolves, Mr President, there are wolves nearby.'

Huntermann froze and whispered dreamily, 'Wolves, oh yes . . .'

It was as if they could both smell them. The tree to which Huntermann had once been tied was quite forgotten.

'Mr President,' whispered Wald, beginning to slide his feet to one side, 'I'll try to see . . .'

Schlitz pointed his gun but Huntermann signalled him to leave well alone, for wolves take precedence over murdering a man, if only for a few moments, and once he had time to enjoy the wolves, before . . .

Wald was no more than three metres from his would-be killers when he saw a wolf he knew, downslope and half obscured by trees, looking his way, gaze steady, head quite still, ears alert: a wolf he had seen many more times in imagination than he had in life.

The Baltic wolf, the wolf he later found again.

Klimt. The name came to him then from Wulf knows what labyrinth of association and memory.

'Klimt, help me now as once I . . .'

The wolf stared upslope at him, absolutely still, and then, turning to lead the way, offered Wald a cleft in a great wall of time which he must slip through now or die.

Huntermann was still, Schlitz uneasy, both for a moment looking another way as if to find the wolves. The time had come.

The time was now . . .

. . . and Jakob Wald cast off all his past and faded away downslope, finding it finally so simple to leave everything, every person, all he had ever known, behind. One moment he was there and the next he was off and circling, round and downslope and up again, over towards the torrent and then back, even as above him, and far below, radios crackled.

He fancied he heard Huntermann's laughter of appreciation that he had so ably faded into the Forest's confusing murk, just as he felt the angry pointing of Schlitz's gun at the trees which told no tale of men or wolves, and the absolute strength of Huntermann's intention of finding him again one day.

But not today: a wise hunter does not waste energy chasing the eagle that has flown, or the fish that has leapt into another pool, or the wolf that has fled. Rather he waits, and Huntermann would wait, and stalk, and wait, and stalk again until one day he had Wald in his sights once more.

Later Wald lay down and knew the warmth of the wolf's belly that had been there before him, and his scent. Wald dared close his eyes and wait for the helicopter to depart, and then wait two more days to be sure that Huntermann had departed with it.

When Wald finally moved he knew he was the only Mann in a Forest possessed by benign wolves, and that they would give him the freedom of the heights above. He had left everything behind him now, and had everything yet to come. While here and now, where he was, he was still, waiting for the whisper of the wind, and the wolves, to signal which way their newest cub, their weakest brother, should go.

It was the moment Jakob Wald became a Wanderer, the first of the Mennen to show humility, and the first to wish to run with wolves and find a new wolfway to the stars.

III

THE DEMISE OF THE DARK MILLENNIUM

CHAPTER ELEVEN

*Raute begins her journey to the stars, and Lunar
discovers a wolfway that was, and is, and may still be*

THE RAVENS from the cliffs above the Forest finished the meal the Magyars had begun, and it took them three weeks, on and off. By then little was left of the bodies, and the Wolves were glad when other Mennen came and removed the remains. As for the Mann who had come among them, they were indifferent to him, but for Klimt, who would watch him from a distance as if to find the answer to a question he had not yet quite worked out.

The Magyars themselves, and in particular Dendrine and Führer, as the Wolves now called him, had come and gone and had not returned. For as the Wolves soon found from watching the Fell, the Magyars had not yet come back to it in numbers. Their leaders' purpose must have been reconnaissance, but it might very well be – probably was, in Kobrin's view – that the Magyars had observed them unseen and the strange venture along the Road and its horrible finale had been designed as a simple and diabolic warning to the Wolves that the Magyars were alive and well, thank you very much . . . and biding their time.

The incident had one particular result, however, which was to divert Klimt yet again from the warning the Wanderer had given and seem to make him incapable of deciding whether to choose to focus the pack's efforts on dealing with the Magyars or confronting their fear of the Mennen.

The Mennen, like the Magyars, had come and gone, and the Wolves seemed to have no direction or purpose, as if they were waiting, but knew not for what.

Nor was the Wanderer helpful. He had been with them now throughout the winter, and had talked to them, howled down legends for them, taught those who wished to learn what he could; but now, with the approach of warmer weather he seemed to grow silent, and to age, and his interest in them began to fade.

Not that he wanted to move on, though he wandered sometimes up to the icy slopes towards the col that led down to the Scarpfeld, alone but for the wolves Klimt invariably sent out as watchers over him. He spent a good deal of time with Raute, which meant with Lunar as well, and the pack began to feel that nothing would change, could change, until Raute's death. Perhaps, after all, that was what the pack was waiting for.

They discussed their future all the time.

'Perhaps she'll never die!' declared Tare irritably one day during one such discussion. 'If she does not do so soon Klimt will be beginning to think of returning us to the Scarpfeld once more except that . . . except . . .'

What she hesitated to add was, 'What was the point?'

Elhana had not got with cub so the pack were going to have no young to raise, which meant that more than likely Tare would make a bid for the ledreneship when summer came. Was that what they were waiting for?

Or was it that it was surely time for Aragon, Stry and Jicin to return, supposing they were still alive?

Or . . . or . . .

It was some days later, a warm day, and Klimt had declared after due investigation of the snow situation up on the Scarpfeld that it was now just a matter of a week or two before they returned there for the summer; meanwhile they must be patient.

'Patience,' cried Tare, 'will be the death of me and all my hopes!'

'And what might your hopes be, my dear?' wondered Elhana, also irritable, and growing tired of her daughter's verbal hints and challenges. 'Eh?'

And Elhana nipped Tare's flank and stood staring expressionlessly at her to see if she was ready yet to respond, and fight.

'*Mother!*' expostulated Tare, retreating; but her anger was fuelled. She had already decided she would choose her own time and place and that would be up on the Scarpfeld, when Elhana had hunted or trekked all day and was tired. Tare was not a fool.

'*Daughter!*' mimicked Elhana, her eyes unsmiling, and she turned indifferently away.

It was just then that Lunar appeared among them, which was most unusual – they hardly saw him at all these days. Silence fell, for his eyes were even bleaker than usual.

'I think,' he said, 'that Raute is near death. She is calling for you, her ledrene, Elhana, and for Klimt; and I think she would like the Wanderer to talk to her.'

He turned from them without waiting for a response, and went back through the narrow way that led to the hidden place, deep in the wood near the Fall stream, where she had her resting-place.

In the case of a dying female, and one who has been ledrene or counsellor in her time, and has mothered a leader's young, all things that Raute had done, it is the tradition that the pack's ledrene spends time alone with her before the leader takes his leave.

But it was evident enough, when these two and the others came quietly to where Raute lay, with Lunar nearby in attendance and themselves staying their distance, who she most wanted to talk to. For though she seemed to listen to Elhana's words, and to Klimt's as well, the way she sought to nod her head as if to encourage them to get their farewells done with, looked about with her blind eyes and whispered to Lunar 'Is he here? You said the Wanderer would come', showed clearly enough which wolf she most wanted to see.

That she was finally very near death was painfully obvious. Her breathing was racked and sporadic, one side of her jaw seemed to have sagged, and those who had not seen her for several days noticed at once how much more weight she had lost, and that her left flank and hinderparts were raw and running with an open sore. There was a tenderness of trust and feeling between her and Lunar, plain in every movement the two wolves made – she grew anxious if he moved away from her, whilst he did all he could to ease her limbs, and aid her breathing with a gentle nudge to reposition her head, and a shifting of earth and litter behind her back to give her more support.

The Wanderer, who had not been with the pack when Lunar had come to fetch them, had now been found, and he joined them quietly, and with his usual ease and grace, as if such a scene as this was familiar to him, and natural too.

He went straight up to her; the relief she felt was quite apparent from the way her face relaxed, and she almost smiled. Indeed, when he reached a paw to hers she nodded her acknowledgement, and moved her own after his as if to tell him to keep touching her; as if, in fact, his touch was her last link with life.

'Wanderer,' she whispered, 'you know I am near death.'

He nodded.

'I can almost see my wolfway to the stars, and that's the first thing I've seen for many a year!'

The listening pack gave out a collective sigh, both at the sadness of the moment, and the reminder that her wry and self-deprecating humour gave them of what a loss she would be. Her life had been extraordinary and taken her from the heights of Magyar leadership in the days of Hassler, to isolation and out-casting at the command of Dendrine, to rescue and an honoured place among the Wolves, and now, finally, to the ordinariness of death in a clearing amongst conifers, on the bank of a forest stream.

Old, past her time, nearly useless, to the last she displayed grace, good humour, courage, experience that could not be replaced, and wisdom that would be hard to find again.

'Wanderer,' she said, her voice racking again into a choking cough, 'W . . . W . . . Wanderer, you have done so much for this strange pack of destiny of which I have been honoured to be a member. You have told us of places we did not know existed, and are seeking to guide us from preoccupation with wolves to preoccupation with the Mennen.'

Again, he nodded his head and pressed her paw.

'You have howled down a good many things, starting with your own life's story as it took you to Lake Baikal, and from thence to the Heartland in search of a wolf you believe to be Wulfin. But . . . I have not heard you howl down the story of wolfkind's creation as I heard it when I was young, and as I have howled parts of it on occasion for the youngsters here. It is the first true howling I remember and I beg you now, as my last wish, to howl it for me, that in its story I may find strength to put my paws at last upon the starry wolfway I seem to see, and begin my journey of mortality. Will you do this for me?'

'I will, Raute,' he replied, 'I will.'

'Take up the story which we all heard Lunar here begin to howl down, of when Hrein and his beloved Mistur came to earth, and found wolfkind . . . It would give me pleasure, and I think it something these . . . youngsters . . .'

'They are youngsters no more, wolf,' said the Wanderer softly.

'They are to me, Wanderer. Perhaps they will enjoy this tale as I did, and learn from it. Will you howl it for me?'

'Yes,' said the Wanderer.

Absolute silence fell among them, and in the Forest as well, but for a flock of starlings which broke suddenly into smaller flocks to dive out of the blue sky and settle in the adjacent trees, chattering briefly before they too fell silent but for an occasional flutter of wings and scrabble of claws.

'You remember then how Hrein decided he might find a mortal creature to whom all others would pay homage?'

'Yes,' whispered Raute, 'we certainly do!'

The others nodded as the Wanderer began that howling . . .

Hrein and Mistur slipped away from the gods and the stars amongst which they dwelt, journeying down the stars into mortality one daybreak, and so beginning their life upon the earth. Hrein first took the form of a scrap of minute life floating in the sea, with Mistur about and above the sea's surface, watching over him.

In this form, invisible to the naked eye, Hrein allowed himself to be consumed by a creature bigger than himself, though still minute, which he then became; that creature in turn was consumed by one yet larger, and so Hrein again transformed himself into something new.

Thus, turn by turn, Hrein experienced the lives of all the creatures of the sea, great and small.

'There is none among them that could rule all other animals of the earth,' he finally declared, 'and so my search has failed.'

'Yet in the seas alone,' said Mistur, 'which creature is the wisest of them all, and most powerful?'

'The whale,' said Hrein promptly.

'Then when I return to immortality I shall ask my father Kaldr to let the whale be the ruler of the seas.' And so it came to be.

Hrein finally left the sea when the whale form he had become began to die, and he allowed himself to be consumed by a sea eagle that fed upon the dying whale's flesh.

In this new form, and with Mistur for company, he began his exploration of the avian world, once more allowing himself to be transformed through all the forms of bird-life on land and sea.

'There is none among them that could rule all the other animals,' he said finally.

Again Mistur asked which of the birds was wisest and most powerful.

'The golden eagle,' said Hrein.

'I shall ask my father for it to be so,' said Mistur.

Finally, Hrein became a creature of the land, taking as his first form the snow leopard which fed upon the body of the eagle he had been.

Many the years that Hrein, with Mistur for company, tried out the different life-forms of the land – so many that the gods above began to miss him, for his mischief amused them; and to feel the loss of Mistur, too, for hers was a form of changing beauty no other god quite had.

But at last Hrein had tried every animal form there was, and finding himself in his final incarnation, which was as a Mann, who by then was old and ill and would soon die, he said wearily, 'Mistur, I have tried all forms of creature upon the land but none is fit to rule all the animals of the earth. All fear each other too much to accept leadership of another, or to dare offer it themselves.'

'Yet the creatures of the sea have found a new order under the domination of the wise whale,' declared Mistur. 'And in the sky the golden eagle reigns supreme, and all know where they are. So, Hrein my dear, just tell me which of the animals is best fitted to bring order to creatures of the land.'

'I wish I knew!' cried Hrein. 'But I do not. And now I am near death as a Mann and have no other form of life to turn into so that I might continue my quest. Then, no doubt, your father Kaldr will summon me back into immortality and will not be much pleased to discover I have failed.

'Each land creature I have known could make a claim for precedence for one reason or another but none will accept dominance from another. The only thing they agree on is what the gods already know – that some creature must be found that the others will accept as lord of them all.'

'You are god of mischief and cunning,' said Mistur. 'Who better to make them find a way if they cannot find it for themselves?'

Hrein nodded his agreement and sat down. His human body ached and felt tired, and his spirit was low.

'I must sit down and think,' he said, 'but in so wild a place as this an old Mann such as I will fall prey to some creature or another. Therefore Mistur, use your arts to guide me to the place where no other creature lurks, and keep me safe within your swirling wreaths until I have found a way.'

Mistur led her beloved Hrein north.

'I am tired,' he said, 'let me rest here . . .'

But Mistur shook her head, for a strange wind of destiny drove her on, taking her this way and that, and Hrein in his dying human form as well.

Mistur led them east of where they had reached, and again Hrein said, 'Let me rest here, this will surely do . . .'

But Mistur shook her head, the wind persistent still.

Then somewhat south they turned, to higher ground.

'Surely, here will do,' sighed the weary Hrein, hardly able to put one human foot in front of the other.

'Not yet,' whispered Mistur, turning on the wind, understanding that where she finally led him he must find the end to this quest.

At last, with the setting of the sun, and climbing amidst mountain heights, she turned westward and saw a gulley in the cliffs into which no creature had ever ventured before. Deep it was, turning and twisting, its sward as green as emeralds, its sky as blue as azure, its air as crystal-clear as Lake Baikal's water.

'Here . . .' she whispered as the wind drove her higher and higher up the secret gulley.

'I cannot see,' cried poor Hrein, beset now by human age and infirmity, 'for you dim my eyes with your wreaths, Mistur, and you confuse my eyes where darkness finds you, and where the last rays of the sun come down and turn you rose-pink and . . .'

But Hrein stopped speaking, for the wind of destiny had slowed and died, and as Mistur faded this way, and slid off that way, he caught a glimpse of a rising rock, dark and jagged in its strange forbidding shape, huge between the gulley sides as if it reached up the cliff, and then further still towards the skies.

It was against this that the dying Mann whom Hrein had become rested his old head, seeking a way to bring leadership and order to the manifold chaos of life upon the land.

Then it was that for three long days, each dawn and each dusk, did Mistur come to Hrein to see if he had found a way. Each time he shook his head and she saw that he was growing weaker.

Upon the dawning of the fourth day, which was her seventh visit, he was visibly near death as a Mann, and sought to answer the question she asked.

'Is there no animal on earth that can lead the others?'

'I think there cannot be,' he said, 'for he must be prudent, that others bigger than himself do not get the better of him.'

'But there are plenty such, my dear,' said Mistur, puzzled.

'Yes, but he must be bold as well, that others respect him when they must.'

'Prudent and bold . . . well, I can think of a great many that have those qualities.'

'And a vision clear enough to see the far horizon?' said Hrein.

'I could name a good few creatures who have all those qualities.'

'So could I,' said Hrein, 'and so I have, but in addition to those qualities the creature that I seek should have the power to smell so well that he can understand the scents of life, of danger and of death, and so survive by night as well as day.'

'Even so,' said Mistur, 'there are a few with all those qualities!'

'And, as well, he should love his kin more than himself, that thereby all he leads will put their trust in him.'

'Prudence, boldness, clear vision, a sense of smell, and selflessness,' said Mistur. 'Why, my dear, there are still a few who have each and every one of those five attributes.'

'But two more yet are needed,' said the unhappy Hrein. 'First, he must have patience that he can give time to those who need it.'

'Even so,' persisted Mistur, 'there must be –'

'And a sense of awe, that he may raise his eyes to the stars and teach others to dream dreams of what may be.'

At this Mistur was silent, for she saw that no animal whose form Hrein had ever taken had all these virtues together at one time.

Then, too, she saw that Hrein the Mann was sinking into death without succeeding in his quest, and she would lose him when she returned to immortality.

'Dagr,' she cried, speaking to the god of day, 'I beg you to make time stand still and keep Nacht at bay to give Hrein more time.'

'I shall try,' whispered Dagr.

Then she turned her prayers to Jord, god of the earth.

'For many years has Hrein laboured on this quest, while you have not helped him at all. Help him now!'

'I shall try,' said Jord.

Then she turned to Kaldr her father, and cried, 'Father, in your wisdom you sent me upon this quest with Hrein, and ever have I stayed with him because I love him. Therefore, for my sake whom you love, help him now.'

'I shall try,' said Kaldr.

Then as Dagr and Nacht fought over time, the one seeking to stop it, the other seeking to start it up again, thunder and lighting came down where Hrein lay caught between mortal life and death. Then Jord cried to them to be quiet that he might think, and when they continued he soon became enraged, shaking and groaning so that the very cliffs began to move, and even the great rock upon which Hrein had rested cracked and weakened so that Mistur feared that he would soon be crushed.

Seeing which Kaldr, who ever liked to bring calm to those who fought, sent the giants of frost and snow, and ice as well, to cover the rocks and silence them.

But Kaldr's ice crept into the cracks of the great rock, and made them larger still so that even as Dagr and Nacht gave up their struggle as hopeless and let time march on again, and Jord calmed down, and all grew still once more, the rock continued to groan and shake, the great gulley in whose midst it rose echoing with the sound of its strains and harsh cracks.

Now, Mistur could see, she could not save Hrein from the forces of mortality, now he must surely die, his quest still unfulfilled.

Yet if it be true that the whispers of the wind carry the voices of the gods, then it was never more true than in those perilous moments when the great rock began to break, and Hrein, as Mann, lay in the orbit of its collapse.

For about the rock the same wind of destiny that had led Mistur there, stirred and spoke to her, saying, 'Be not afraid, be not afraid, be not afraid . . .'

Ancient it was, and pure, coming out of the far reaches of time, across the aeons, the voice of the daughter of Smilodon. Then as Mistur clung to Hrein, to comfort herself even if she was powerless against a greater and more ancient god to protect him if he was to die, the rock began to shatter.

Down came the confines in which he had been safe, great was the noise and dark disintegration, overwhelming the winds of destiny that swirled and blew. Day turned into night, and later, night to day, as Smilodon's daughter mocked them for struggling over time.

Then the winds began to die, the last rocks to fall, dawn to come.

There, in the ruins of the rock, each piece larger than a mountain-top, a wolf stood blinking at the coming of the day.

In oblivion he had been, and in a time of all forgetting, but now he remembered what he was, and who he was, and why Smilodon had sought to favour him. Though he remembered that his pack was to have been favoured as he was, yet only slowly did the memory return that his ledrene, and a frightened son, had been lost when the first volcano woke.

Then did Wulf raise his head to howl out his loss, for the aeons of time had made it no less painful than the day he was put into the protection of the rock, and cast forth, as the rest of his pack had been, to await this moment of new awakening.

But as he wept and howled he saw upon the ground at his feet a creature he did not know: old, and pale, and weak, and nearly dead. Not a wolf, nor any creature that he knew, for the Mennen had come to be long after Wulf had been cast into the rock.

Wulf saw the creature needed help, and sought to give it warmth.

He saw that it needed life, and sought to give it breath.

He saw it needed a reason to live, and sought to give it words of hope.

He saw that it despaired, and sought to make it know it was not alone.

From dawn to dusk for three long days Wulf forgot his own despair and tried to save the creature's life, as if it was part of his lost pack.

From prudence, he dragged the creature to lower and more protected ground.

With boldness, he repelled the wild beasts that sought to take the creature as their prey.

With vision clear he told the creature what lay ahead, if only he might find strength to recover and journey there.

With his sense of smell he found the creature food, and ways to avoid the dangers of the night.

Selflessly Wulf disregarded his own well-being to bring the creature back to health.

With patience he stayed by the creature through the slowest, longest hours of his recovery.

'There,' whispered Mistur in Hrein's ear, 'you are still mortal, still alive, and this must be the creature that you sought. What is his name, for his is a form you never took upon yourself, although you journeyed to every land in every creature's guise?'

'I know not,' said Hrein, astonished, 'yet still there is one thing I must know. For though he has the first six qualities I sought, the last is most important in the one who would be leader of all the rest.'

Then, as Mann, Hrein rose up, and as Mann he spoke to Wulf saying, 'Creature, you have saved my life and must surely be the most powerful creature of them all . . . ?'

Wulf shook his head and pointed at the stars, saying with awe in his voice, 'Long, long ago I prayed to the stars that I and my kind might be saved, and that prayer was answered. If I was most powerful of them all it would be I myself I saved. But another saved me whose name I know not but who must be God of All. He and his kind, I believe, must be in the stars, ever watching, ever caring. Thank them and not myself. I have a dream that one day I might journey to the stars and meet them, one day . . .'

'Is that a dream I too can share?' said the Mann who was Hrein.

'If you can only dream it as I do then you will surely share it.'

Then Hrein saw that his quest was over, and that he had found at last the one that might by his leadership bring order to the creatures of the earth.

'What is your name?' asked Hrein.

'Wulf.'

'Follow me, Wulf, for you have won the right to see a little of the dream you have.'

Then, as Hrein spoke he cast off his mortal form, and asked Mistur to do the same, and Wulf began to see it was a god he had saved.

'Follow me ...' whispered the wind of destiny, and through the mist Wulf followed, back to the rock where he had been reborn, and there amidst the rising ruins he saw Hrein and Mistur journey home once more upon a wolfway to the stars.

'As you taught me to trust your dream, so shall your name be made immortal when your tasks on earth are done. See the wolfway named after you, and know that one day you shall fulfil your dream,' the wind said.

'Go forth, Wulf, and find your destiny before you join your life to our eternal one. But do not be too long, for we may have need of you ...'

Such is the story of the coming of Wulf to the WulfRock, and it is our greatest tale.

'Yes,' whispered Raute, 'this was the howling that I heard, this is where my memory begins, and now this is ... Oh *yes* ...' she repeated, as the Wanderer's paw touched hers, and Lunar held her close, to keep her warm, that she might know that in the end as in her beginning, as in all wolves' beginnings, whatever their later lives may bring, she was not alone.

It was to Lunar that she now spoke, a few final simple words: 'My dear, you have learned to listen and to learn, and been my comfort, just as one I loved so much learned before.'

'Jicin?' said Lunar softly, looking up at his father.

How often had Raute mentioned Jicin, to whom she had been so close, and to whom she owed Klimt's decision that Tervicz and Kobrin should set forth to rescue her in the months before the youngsters were born! How often had Lunar begged her to talk to Klimt about the one he loved as well!

'Yes, Jicin. I stayed alive hoping she would return; but it matters not, my love, for she is here, today, and now she is with us, in the story of the gods and the beginning of wolfkind she is with us, for the wolfways are the past and the present, the future. It was our destiny to be upon them together for a time. She will come back. Tell her that she gave me happiness when she brought me to the Wolves of Time.'

'I will,' said Lunar, his voice breaking with sadness now to see her fade so fast.

'Always learn, my dear, as she did, as Klimt strives to do, and the others. Do not let yourself be caught in grief too long, for Merrow, for me, for . . .'

Her paw reached out once more for the Wanderer's; he took it with a gentle, rueful smile and a nod of his head.

'Lunar, learn it and teach it to others who do not know it yet. It was the desire to know that drove you and Merrow to that ruin, and so what happened cannot be all bad and must have meaning. Learn through your grief, learn what the Wanderer teaches, learn from your sadness to go beyond it so that you too can see what I see . . . and Wanderer?'

'Yes, Raute?' he said.

'Take me to the WulfRock now, help me begin my journey to the stars for I can almost see them . . .'

Her voice faded into silence then as her blind eyes seemed to begin to see again, to see the mischief and laughter of life, and the courage needed to live, to see the nature of its mystery and the worth of purpose and of loyalty, to see that these beginnings gave the mortal world its value and majesty, and gave to a wolf who learned to live them her foothold towards the stars.

Hushed, the day ending, the wind dying, the trees stilling, with only the endless roaring of the Fall stream for sound, the pack retreated from the place where old Raute lay now, in the sleep that takes a wolf beyond death's moment to its eternity.

A final look, a glance about the place where her old body lay, grey as beech roots, a yellow pine needle already fallen in among her fur; they took their leave, began to depart, one by one.

'Stay with her, Lunar, and you Wanderer too, be the pack's guardians over her.'

The two wolves nodded, settling by her, until only Klimt stayed watching from the edge of the clearing.

Raute had lived past her time, she had given much, and she had waited until she knew, or felt, that one she loved had come to her upon a wolfway of the spirit to say goodbye.

'Jicin,' whispered Klimt, only then his voice breaking, for suddenly he sensed, as Raute had done, that Jicin was near, she was here, she was there by Raute, watching over her, beginning a night of vigil and prayer.

'Jicin,' whispered Klimt with love and gratitude, for he knew then that what Raute had said was true: she would return to him, and her journey back would soon begin.

'Jicin, my dear . . .' he whispered as he too turned away, able to do so because he knew his love would stay with Raute awhile, to see the old one to the stars, to see that to the very last, on the journey through the night of stars and into immortality she was not forgotten, nor alone.

A new dawn, and Lunar awoke. He lay still, listening to the race and roar of the Fall stream through the Forest, listening to the sounds of spring and approaching summer, listening and knowing that with Raute's death something had eased in his troubled heart, and a darkness was no more.

He stretched and opened his eyes and saw . . . nothing.

Nothing?

Lunar started up and stared about the clearing wildly, his heart thumping. Raute was not there, nor the Wanderer nor . . . nor . . . there was just the scents of thyme and tarragon, quite strong, quite clear, leading him away from where Raute was no more, where no-wolf was now, leading him upslope.

'Wanderer?' he whispered, and he ran and ran up through the Forest, feeling that no-wolf was everywhere and he alone, and at peace, except that he wanted to follow them, to be with them, where they had gone.

Up and up he ran, on and on, following their scent which was of thyme and tarragon, knowing where they had gone and hoping he might get there as they did for he wanted –

'Lunar! Stop wolf, *stop!*'

It was Solar, that dawn's watcher, by the Tree.

'Did you see them, Solar? They must have come this way not long ago! I was asleep and they've gone upslope towards the Scarpfeld. Did you see them?'

'For Wulf's sake, Lunar, no wolf has been this way, none at all, and I –'

'But they have, brother, they have!' cried Lunar, and he was off past Solar, on upslope, up the steep and winding path, after the scent he knew was there.

'Where are you going, wolf?' cried Solar.

'To where the Wanderer has taken Raute, for she could not go alone and did not want to.'

'Which is where?' asked Solar, advancing upslope towards Lunar.

'To the WulfRock,' said Lunar simply, 'follow me!'

Then he laughed, really laughed, just as he used to before Merrow died, before he began to look after Raute, before he found that wolfway in the ruins.

'I'm coming,' said Solar, laughing too, and wondering how it might be that his brother seemed suddenly so beloved to him, so precious . . . and how it might be that on the route he followed, going so fast that Solar could not quite catch him, were the scents of thyme and tarragon, and the sense that time was becoming other than it was.

'Wait for me!' cried Solar, forgetting his watch, abandoning his senses, and feeling this was a way he knew, and feared, but he did not know whether from some experience long past, or a sense of something yet to come.

CHAPTER TWELVE

*As Klimt despairs of their return, Solar and Lunar seek
out the WulfRock too soon, and seem lost in time*

THAT SPRING morning, when so much finally changed for the
Wolves of Time, and their leader Klimt was pushed towards
new and difficult decisions, the first scent of trouble had come
with the shifting dawn wind, and Solar's cry. Not a warning bark, nor
a howl, nor like any cry they had heard him make before: distant,
surprised, wandering . . .

When the others went up to the Tree to see what ailed him he was
not there. Just the scents of thyme and tarragon, and when Tervicz
finally hurried on upslope towards the col above, to see if there was
sign of his having gone that way, he found paw-prints in pristine snow,
the last that fell that year. Four sets of them, one after another, some
in-filled, some fresh, and all leading towards the Scarpfeld.

'But after that, nothing, Klimt, nothing at all. It was as if they
reached the Scarpfeld, whoever they were, and disappeared to
nowhere, as if they had never been.'

'Lunar's gone,' said Klimt urgently, 'and the Wanderer too,
and –'

'Yes, leader?' said Tervicz in a hushed voice, for he saw something
in the others' eyes apart from the fact that they already knew what
he was about to be told.

'Raute's body's gone.'

'Raute? But . . . ?'

'Show me these paw-prints you found, wolf,' said Klimt.

But the sun was already bright and warm and by the time they had
got back to where Tervicz said he had found them they had gone, as
if they had never been, and the scent of thyme and tarragon with
them. Only a wind across the high Scarpfeld, a cold one, but not so
cold that the pools of water amongst the rocks and peat had not
already begun to thaw beneath the sun.

184

Then came the scent that Klimt had noticed on waking, which was of Mennen and the oil and fumes of their vehicles, approaching from across the Fell. Convoys appearing as the morning wore on, travelling down the Road in the opposite direction to which they had gone at the beginning of the winter.

The Mennen war was beginning again and WHOOOSHHHH . . .
. . . the jet planes were back and suddenly it seemed that all the Wanderer's warnings and suggestions, and his challenge to find a new way forward, were spinning round and round in Klimt's head.

'For Wulf's sake, Lunar, settle down and enjoy the *view*,' Solar said, rising suddenly as if to nip his restless brother's flank.

'Can't, won't, shan't, mustn't . . . oh, all right,' said Lunar finally, tired of his own games. He settled briefly but then started up again as the sun faded behind weak cloud, and the Fell below darkened at its loss. Colour drained from the rocks about them, and the snow to right and left, glaring white before, turned blue-grey and chill.

A wind whispered up through the rocks of the scree below them, and far above, in the cliffs that loomed behind, there was the *crunk* of falling rock in one or other of the thousand clefts and ginnels there.

'Mist's coming,' Solar muttered, 'and it feels like winter's starting all over again, and the spring's all gone.'

'Or all yet to come,' said Lunar vacantly.

Solar considered this in silence with his eyes shut, and a slight frown on his face. He was feeling nervous, very; and confused, considerably.

They had not found the tracks of the Wanderer or of 'Raute', if it had been she. In fact, they had lost track of everything, and now even time itself seemed to be slipping away and out of their control. They were perched up on the screes on the north side of the Scarpfeld, by the rock that marked the entrance to the WulfRock gulley, the forbidden place.

Solar opened his eyes and found that Lunar had moved, and now stood out on the scree a little below. Solar felt a sudden and unexpected wave of sorrow that Merrow had been lost to them: it came from nowhere, like a Mennen jet . . .

WHOOOOOOSHHHHHHH*SHHHHHH!*

Shit! Just like that!

If Solar missed Merrow it was because Lunar still grieved for her and had in some way been weakened by her loss, as if the wound of it had never healed. Solar loved Lunar with a passion quite undiminished by the fact that he never, ever showed it, though Lunar surely knew it.

Then again . . .

ROARCHRRRRRRRR!

. . . and Solar ducked instinctively as they roared overhead.

'See how the mist has come!' cried Lunar histrionically, not turning round, and pretending he had not heard a thing. 'Mist always amazes me with the speed at which it comes. *Faster than deer, faster than wolves, the mist comes down the hills . . .*'

It was a scrap of one of the cub songs Elhana used to sing to them and Solar smiled at the memory, envious that Lunar could not only remember such things, but knew just when to repeat them.

Moments later, quite suddenly, the mist thickened and the view below was gone and they were above it, the air flowing cold from the north-east. A double bark, the signal to rejoin the pack immediately – but from whom? Not Klimt, though it sounded like him . . . no, it didn't. *Shit!*

Solar, ever calm and responsible, rose and said, 'Come on Lunar, there's danger here; come *on* . . .'

But then, even as they began to move, rocks shifted off to the north-east, and the turning wind brought the sudden sweet scent not of alien wolves but Mennen. The mists swirled below and Lunar turned suddenly on his approaching brother, not himself at all. His eyes were fierce and his stance as bold as if they were playing one of their moon-time games.

'There's Mennen coming, up here, *now!*'

Even as they both instinctively huddled down the mist shifted and they saw the silhouettes of Mennen, one, two, three, four . . .

RAT-TAT-TATATATATAT!

The mounting, shattering crash of the echoes, and the rocks they fractured all about, was louder than the shots themselves. Neither Lunar nor Solar had ever heard anything so frightening, nor smelt before the harsh odour of cordite that the wind brought to them as the last rock fell, and the last echo faded.

The mist shifted, the Mennen were gone, the two wolves stood up scenting, scenting at the wind.

'They're coming nearer, Lunar, I can hear them!'

RAT-TAT-TATATATATAT!

The shattering repetition of the sound seemed to cleave the very mist, and there they were, the Mennen, just along the scree, their sweet smell rancid now with the odour of fear.

'Solar, follow me. It is our last and final chance.'

'But Lunar, we cannot go up there . . . !'

For the only way to avoid the Mennen and their guns was up towards the cleft in the rocks above them, up into the secret and forbidden gulley that led to the sacred WulfRock.

'Come . . .' and Lunar's paw, though firm and gentle at his brother's, was the stronger now. 'You always wanted to venture a little up the forbidden valley towards the WulfRock and I promised to take you when the opportunity arose. The mist will hide us, the wind's shift shall be our excuse that we did not hear the command to return, and anyway . . . anyway, it was too late to go down.'

As Solar hesitated, Lunar stared into the mist that surged and billowed across the scree about them. He was absolutely still but for the wind at his errant fur which now, Solar saw, had droplets of condensation upon it which caught the light and made him seem as pale as the mist itself. He sought to calm himself, and let his breathing ease and slow.

'The Mennen are moving nearer,' he whispered. His fear had gone, but there was new urgency in his voice. 'Follow me, Solar,' he said.

He spoke so softly that it was as if he merely breathed the words, but Solar felt no doubt that he was right. Something seemed to move darkly in the swirl below, and rock crunched under Mennen feet.

Lunar turned and leapt upslope past Solar who continued for only a moment more to stare below before he was sure he saw the dark shadow of a Mann rising from rock where he should not have been, could not be.

'Solar . . .' the wind whispered from somewhere above him as he followed after his brother, along the only way they could go if they were to fade and disappear and not be seen. Long-standing desire to visit the forbidden valley had been displaced by an imperative to do so. Solar ran, searching the shifting mist above and ahead for Lunar. For a long time as it seemed, though it was probably but moments, he could see only the criss-cross of scree rocks ahead, even the nearest made indistinct by the mist.

'Solar!'

The guiding call came from higher ground off to the left and it was as well that it did, and that it came then, for Solar was losing direction and already going back downslope towards outcrops, and perhaps

Mennen, and inevitable retreat to danger. He was never at his best in mist, especially such sudden mist. It confused and slowed him.

'*Solar . . . over here!* It's the way Raute went, and the Wanderer, on their journey to the stars . . .'

The rocks gave way to sudden grass and the vent of a gulley. Then more rocks to run between and there stood Lunar, lightly balanced on three paws, the fourth, his right front, poised to turn and push forward for a foothold.

'Follow me, wolf.'

In game after game, in fantasy and dream, Lunar had practised this moment of command, and it came easily to him now as if this was still a game, and Solar followed him as he always finally had at moments such as these.

Except that now Lunar knew it was no longer a game, but real, and the path they now followed was dangerous and unpredictable and might take them to places and regions far beyond anything his imagination had power to control.

RAT-TAT-TATATATATAT!

The thunder of the Mennen came shooting up from behind them, ricocheting back and forth amongst the rocks. They heard the Mennen's curses, and heard them laugh, and then they heard no more, for the twists and turns of the gulley took them; and the strange thick mists embraced them as their flight slowed, and they moved to what felt like a different place, and a different time.

That day, when his sons were lost and the Mennen war began again, Klimt decided to lead his pack up into the Scarpfeld in the hope of finding Solar and Lunar, and escaping the Mennen.

But neither hope was anything like achieved.

There was a drear, thin mist up in the Scarpfeld and no sooner had they got there than it thickened and spread about them, and they all smelt the odour of Mennen.

'Where?' began Klimt, rising urgently.

'Dangerously near,' said Lounel softly, rising also.

As Klimt barked a warning, Kobrin appeared out of the mist and then Elhana and then . . .

RAT-TAT-TATATATATAT!

The sharp and brutal thunder of Mennen guns, near enough to

cause reverberation in the rocks. It came from upslope of them, up on the screes.

'It's from where Solar and Lunar are,' said Kobrin, starting that way.

RAT-TAT-TATATATATAT!

And bullets cracked and thudded, ricocheted and echoed all about them.

Klimt did not pause a moment more before doing what all leaders must do when a pack is scattered in the face of danger. He barked another warning, ordered brave Kobrin back, for in a situation like this the youngsters must fend for themselves, waited briefly for those members of the pack he knew would get to him in moments, and led them away to find somewhere safe to hide.

It was night, or nearly night, three days later, and the pack huddled in a state of utter desolation upon the Scarpfeld. The mist lingered still, but would one day surely go; but the dark mood of despair that had settled upon Klimt and the others seemed as if it never would.

There had been the shooting, the pack had scattered, the bulk of them with Klimt, and they had come together again only after the Mennen had gone, and Klimt had howled out the all-clear. How swiftly they had come then, and how full of trepidation, for none had seen Solar and Lunar since they had disappeared, and now it seemed that they might have been endangered, and lost.

Klimt now stood apart from the pack, terrifying in his distress, forbidding in his fear, unapproachable. In what world of loss and failure he now dwelt they could only guess at, though each of them dwelt in part of it as well.

Elhana, her shock and weeping over, her keening yet to begin, for how can a mother grieve aloud who has not seen proof her sons are dead?

Kobrin, brooding, angry with himself, impotent. Had it been the Magyars then perhaps their grief could have been diverted to action, but it had not been. No chance of it. It must have been the Mennen who came this way through the mist the day they scented them. Yet . . . no tracks, no blood, no evidence at all that Solar and Lunar had been slain: only their appalling absence, and the feeling they had gone to another place utterly and were no more. Like freezing fog that feeling was, raw and undeniable.

Rohan, near her mother; Tare, angry, the least affected, for she felt they were fools to have strayed, foolish as Merrow had been.

Tare, calculating, seeing what might now be, which, first, was when to challenge her mother, for to lose two males in this way was too much. Elhana was too old. What had happened might not be the fault of her age, but others might well feel that as a ledrene she was cursed and a wolf who was younger and more fecund was now needed. So the disappearance of her brothers seemed to Tare to be an opportunity.

Lounel, silent, scenting the air as he always did as if he might find things there others could not.

Solar and Lunar were gone, not seen for days now, and even less likely to be found alive after that group of Mennen came shooting through, rat-tat-tat, again, and again, and again.

Three days of searching, of howling, of clambering, even up into the entrance of the gulley that led towards the WulfRock, down to the Forest, out and some way across the Fell. But it had all produced nothing, nothing – nothing but the fear that despite Klimt's earlier instincts that they were alive, they were really gone for ever, and the chill that brought to the pack's collective soul.

Klimt turned mutely towards the pack in the gloaming, a wolf who stared at them out of such agony; his eyes, his ears, all his senses were oblivious to everything but the torment he was in.

Then Rohan began to howl, slowly and softly, to howl the agony she saw in her father's eyes, to howl it up to the rising stars and moon, to howl it across the Scarpfeld east and west, to howl it north and south. One by one they joined her, raising their heads, widening their throats, opening their mouths to add their howls to hers, until only Lounel and Klimt had not joined in.

Suddenly Klimt spun round and Lounel cried out, 'No wolf, *no!*' and moved to stop the charge he made upon his own pack.

Klimt turned his anger upon Lounel, and ripped his chest and threw him terribly. The howl stopped abruptly as Klimt stood over Lounel as if to kill him, and he might have done so had not mighty Kobrin charged at him in his turn, wrestling with him, calling to others to help. Tervicz came and then Rohan too and all of them struggled to hold Klimt down as he fought, and bit, and swore and raged out his agony upon them. Until finally he did what none of them had ever seen in all the years he had been their leader.

Klimt wept before them, and though they might subdue his assault upon Lounel and on them all, his grief they could not touch, nor reach.

Night came at last and he turned from them and, with Kobrin following to watch over him, and finally Tervicz too, Klimt wandered and staggered blindly about the Scarpfeld, pausing at the pools where once Solar had played, climbing amidst the screes where once Lunar had laughed, and finally stopping and huddling down far from Elhana and the others, as if the only relief he might find was to die.

Night, and the moaning hours of grief and loss, and a pack's ultimate despair.

Night, and time for each to visit their own agonies and losses, and know that none was worse than this.

Night, and the sound of a great wolf weeping, and knowing not which way to turn.

A black night, when the gods were not in the stars, and the moon's light was a wreath of death.

Dawn, and mild moist winds.

Dawn, and a wolf stretching, and licking at his wound.

Dawn, and Lounel rises in the mist, sore and aching yet still scenting at the wind as if to find, as if . . . as if . . .

Advancing dawn, and across the eastern skies the light of the rising sun, and a clear sky.

Lounel's ear pricking, his wound forgotten, stepping forward as if to greet the sun; scenting as he always did, searching as he always must, dawn . . .

. . . and the clear scents of thyme and of tarragon, clearer than before, the scent of a Wanderer, until . . . it was gone, *he* was gone, and Lounel knew then that Klimt had been right: Solar and Lunar were alive, somehow alive, and would come back to them.

'But it will not be the same. The Wanderer made a challenge to Klimt and now he must rise to meet it . . .'

'What are you muttering about, Lounel?'

It was Kobrin, emerging from sleep and feeling himself somehow altogether better in his mind, as if a cloud of darkness had begun to lift.

'I'm muttering about *things*,' said Lounel, his head on one side as he stared absently at Kobrin.

'You're a strange one, Lounel. You never seem to do anything when you are here among us, and when you're not, which is a lot of the time, I've no idea what you do.'

'I think. I wander. I feel. I stop.'

'Stop?'

'Still and silent, mostly still. I was taught to do it by those who raised me in the High Causses of the Auvergne. These years that we've been here, they've been *doing* years, years of raising, so there's not been much for me to contribute. But now that phase is over.'

'Over and done with,' said Kobrin grimly. 'Three out of five young lost, and both the males –'

'Lost, yes; for ever, no. They're coming back.'

'Oh yes? When?' said the practical Kobrin doubtfully.

Lounel shrugged and did not quite answer the question: 'It won't seem they've been gone long when they return.'

'And the Wanderer's coming back too, I suppose. And Raute?'

Lounel shook his head. 'No, not those two. They're on their wolfways to the stars now, leaving Solar and Lunar behind.'

Kobrin looked at him hard. 'You're talking crap, Lounel, you know that?'

'Except you don't think so, do you?' replied Lounel calmly. 'You're feeling quite cheerful today in fact.'

Kobrin grinned and said, 'Well . . . in a way I do, but –'

'They'll be back,' said Lounel, 'you'll see. Meanwhile I must talk to Klimt, for he's got some hard decisions to make, as we all have.'

'Decisions?'

'What to do. Who to do it with. Whether to stay or go. When to come back. That kind of thing.'

'But you think Solar and Lunar are safe?'

Until that moment Lounel had not been so sure they were. But he remembered the scent of the Wanderer leaving, and knew it was the scent of reassurance, of the shifting of wolves in and out of time. Klimt's sons were making a journey, one ordained by the gods, and now Klimt must do the same, and help them all see the way to go, separately and together. As for Solar and Lunar . . .

'I know they are safe,' said Lounel softly, staring across the cold and misty Scarpfeld, and up to where the screes disappeared towards the secret gulley that led to the WulfRock, which no living wolf had ever seen. 'I'm sure of it.'

Which Kobrin found strangely reassuring then and in the days and weeks that followed, when Klimt wrestled with the grief of loss, and sought to turn it into a wolfway of hope, and new purpose.

CHAPTER THIRTEEN

*Klimt turns to his pack for guidance and support
in his time of grief, and finds a new direction*

B Y APRIL, and already a full month after the disappearance of
Solar and Lunar, the strangest and most critical of moods had
descended upon the Wolves.

For one thing, Lounel's simple faith that the two missing wolves
would come back had in some extraordinary and inspirational way
replaced the pack's earlier despair at their loss. As springtime advanced
across the Scarpfeld bringing the snow's final thawing, and the first
montane flowers began to show – the white and pink of the snow
rose, the anemone, and the first cushions of moss campion which
would flower in May – a new youth seemed to come to Lounel, who
was like a wolf whose time had come. He too was awaking from a
long winter – one that was of the spirit, and stretched back a good
deal further than the five coldest months.

His eyes were bright with spring light, and his mutterings and
wanderings, and sense of gentle fun, were far more noticeable. Even
his fur, always pale and patchy, had a certain ageing shine to it, and
his gawky legs and paws, a certain grace.

So it was that under this most unexpected of spells, one by one the
Wolves had come to believe what Kobrin had first felt – that Lounel
was in touch with something they were not, and was right to be hopeful
of the lost wolves' return.

'But it'll be different than you think, and challenging, and you'll
have to adjust, Klimt, and see a way forward for us all, together and
separately.'

'What do you mean "together *and* separately"?' rasped Klimt. 'We're
a pack, and together, aren't we?'

'We're the Wolves of Time, Klimt, and that may not be quite the
same thing. Packs need to be close in space and time to be called
such; but the Wolves of Time – their proximity is measured by the

power of their vision, by their trust in each other, and by the purposefulness of the spiritual journeys they make; and, if I understand what the Wanderer said rightly, by the inspiration they give others to follow them. Did not the Wanderer say –'

'The Wanderer said a lot of things,' said Klimt testily, 'though not when he was leaving us! He said I'd have to make decisions, true! And go on a journey of some kind, but not where. Yet more than ever my task lies here, does it not?'

He might very well have thought so, given that as well as the loss of his two sons, the Wolves were beset by another unpleasant uncertainty: a renewal of the Magyars' strength across the Fell. Klimt had not entirely discounted the possibility that the disappearance of Solar and Lunar was the Magyars' doing, though Lounel said he was sure it was not. However, since the disappearance, more or less, the Magyars had not only rapidly increased in number but were beginning to make incursions into the Wolves' territory with ever greater frequency and boldness.

It was now surely only a matter of time before they made a major assault upon the Scarpfeld itself. It was easily defended against numbers similar to themselves, but not against a larger force, and one so disposed that it approached the Scarpfeld not only from the Great Cleft down into the Fell, but from the Vale to the west, and the foothills to the east. It was Kobrin's judgement, having seen the Magyars' vile leaders at close quarters when they trespassed down the Vale and made a feast of the Mennen dead, that such was likely to be the nature of their attack.

Now, on a bright April day, the winter mists almost entirely gone but for a few wisps and wreaths up by the WulfRock gulley entrance, the Wolves had been surveying the Fell since the morning from the top of the Great Cleft, and the Magyars below seemed like flies infesting carrion, and coming in ever-increasing quantities. The threat they posed was almost palpable.

'With our limited numbers we *must* be defeated, Klimt,' declared Kobrin. 'Now we can see the Magyars' true strength, which they must have been building up and preparing for a year or two, hence their quiescence, we can also see that the Wanderer was right to suggest we have need of allies. While we have been raising young, the Magyars have been raising an army of wolves.

'There is no shame in retreat, particularly if it leads to a later victory. In my Russian days I allowed myself to lose many a battle with the intention of winning the war. I retreated before a stronger force and then successfully counter-attacked when they had become weak and complacent.'

Klimt considered this without much evident enthusiasm.

'The trouble is,' he said eventually, 'if it is ever known that the Wolves of Time retreated before the Magyars our ability to inspire others to follow us may be considerably reduced.'

'If you have a better alternative, Klimt . . .' growled Kobrin, who could see none himself.

'I shall think upon it. Your task is to watch over the Magyars' moves, delay and confuse any further advance if you can, while I . . . think. The matter will not be easy.'

'Think by all means, Klimt, but I beg you not to be too long about it. Meanwhile, I shall check lines of retreat, as I have done in the past, and ensure that the old routes amongst the screes and cliffs above are still open. We must never forget that Führer was raised by Dendrine up here, and knows the ground as well as we do, if not better. He will have a desire to get back to it, and a will to win it. The slowness of the Magyar preparation, and the scale of their return, suggest to me they will be a formidable enemy.'

Klimt grunted and scowled, his pack all about him, except for those who had been deployed by Kobrin on watching duties. The time for decision had been coming nearer and nearer, and now he knew instinctively it was upon him, and he did not like it.

'Where's Lounel?' he asked peremptorily.

'Here, Klimt,' said Lounel, appearing as if from nowhere, his voice cheerful.

'Come wolf, you've been muttering and mumbling for days past.'

'Weeks, Klimt, and possibly years.'

'No need to sound so pious about it, wolf, nor so pleased with yourself.'

'Not with myself, but for the pack.'

'Come with me, wolf, somewhere where these others won't want to yatter on as well as you. You're my adviser in matters spiritual, for Wulf's sake, and it looks as if we need a miracle of the spirit if we are to recover from the situation we are in. Solar and Lunar lost, the Magyars closing in and our numbers down to seven. Come . . .'

They went but a little way off, only so far that their voices became an indistinct murmur to the others, who waited now restlessly, for they felt suddenly as if there was change in the air, decision, a turning, such as precedes the coming of a storm.

But the sky was clear, and the sun most beautiful upon them.

'Lounel,' Klimt said quietly, glancing for a moment at the others, 'I am afraid. I . . . am . . . afraid.'

'I know, Klimt. You have been for days and weeks now, perhaps even –'

'I am mortally afraid, wolf,' whispered Klimt, and a tear moved slowly down his face.

Lounel was silent.

'It is not the fear that they are dead, for I know they are not, I know that one of them will lead us forward, as the She-wolf said just after they were born. They cannot be dead.'

'Not dead,' said Lounel, 'yet you are afraid . . .' His voice was the echo of Klimt's soul.

'I am afraid of what will be when they return, what we must do, the challenge the Wanderer set.'

'It is a fearsome thing, Klimt, a journey to a place unnamed, a place as yet unseen, a place we may never know we have reached.'

'The journey here was easy, Lounel, wasn't it? Eh? So easy . . .'

He sniffed and wiped his face, first on one paw and then another, and sniffed again.

'You have been my adviser and yet I have never had the grace to ask your advice, not seriously.'

'And now?'

'I need it, wolf, oh I need it.'

'Trust yourself to lead us, Klimt.'

'I miss her.'

'Jicin?'

'Where is she?'

'She is . . . they are . . . she . . .'

Klimt raised his head and turned southwards, towards where the others were, scenting at the air, frowning at the sky, his eyes softening with thoughts of the wolf he had sacrificed for the well-being of the pack, but whose absence was the black void in his life.

'She will come back. She . . .'

'Does she know you think of her, wolf?'

'It is ridiculous to talk so, Lounel.'

'Does she know, eh, wolf?'

Lounel's voice was suddenly harsh, and he half-charged Klimt, buffeting him as a father might a recalcitrant cub who does not want to admit what's good for him.

'She knows,' growled Klimt. 'And Aragon, and Stry, we need them and they are coming, they are coming home, they are coming back . . .'

His head dropped and he was suddenly tired and worn; Lounel stood over him protectively, their heads close, their thoughts closer still.

'The Wanderer warned . . .' began Lounel.

'. . . he was right,' said Klimt at once, almost with excitement. 'I am afraid, and must turn to face my fear, turn from what I have done to what we must yet do.'

'Now . . .' whispered Lounel.

'Now,' said Klimt.

He turned then and looked back towards Kobrin and called out to him, 'Wolf!'

'Klimt? Leader?'

Great Kobrin ran forward a step or two and then stopped, for there was something about the way Klimt stood and stared at him, something in the way he had called, something about them all just then, and about the Scarpfeld – a sense that time was standing still for them up here, with the Fell stretching away into a blue haze below and far beyond.

'What do you feel rising in you?' asked Lounel of Klimt in a low voice, for Klimt's eyes were bright and strange, and held all the Wolves still in their power. '*Be* it, and not afraid of it.'

'A new age is beginning,' whispered Klimt, 'here, now, *now*. . . and we, we are at its very centre, the beginning of its beginning and I can feel . . . I . . .'

His voice broke, his limbs began to tremble, and all that grief and loss with which he had fought and struggled was in his face, in his body, in all of him, but outward now, visible, held back no more.

'Kobrin,' he said again, his voice worn and torn with time, 'I shall have need of all thy strength, wolf, I shall demand much of thee.'

'Demand it, Klimt; it is what I have journeyed my long life to find and achieve.'

'And you Elhana, to whom I have been hard and cold, you who have suffered so much and complained so little, I shall need more from thee yet.'

'I know it, Klimt,' she said, coming nearer.

'Rohan, Tare, daughters of my pack, will you obey the commands I give thee, whatever they may be?'

'Yes, father,' said Rohan.

Only Tare was silent, staring, calculating, wondering.

'And you?' demanded Klimt.

'Yes, father,' said Tare evenly; and though the sky was clear, and early summer coming, yet even in that moment it held a distant cloud, a memory of winter past perhaps, a hint of a winter yet to come.

'Tervicz?'

'Leader?' said that most faithful of wolves, coming to Klimt.

'A new age is beginning, wolf, can you feel it?'

'I feel something, leader. I felt it when I first met you, the day you saved my life. I felt it when I disobeyed my father Zcale and tried to howl down the Wolves of Time.'

'You are the Bukov wolf . . .'

'I am from Bukov.'

'Tervicz, listen. What can you hear?'

All was still; not a shimmer of wind in the faces of the Scarpfeld pools, not a tremble of the oldest, frailest husk of grass.

'I hear . . . I can hear . . .'

They all heard it then, what Klimt had heard first, the howling of wolves from right across the Fell; a howling of Magyar wolves; a howling of one pack and a hundred, of ten wolves and a thousand, a howling for revenge and retribution, a howling dark and threatening.

'What do you hear, Tervicz?'

'I hear . . .' Tervicz looked from one to another of them, his thin face gentle, his eyes warm. 'I hear . . . *nothing*! Or nothing that matters. Nothing that will last. Nothing that –'

He turned from them all then and ran to the edge of the Scarpfeld where it looked down across the Fell, and stood where the howling, threatening wolves below might see him dark against the sky.

'For I am the Bukov wolf,' he cried, almost laughing, almost young again as when he first left Bukovina, and his father Zcale, his sister Szaba and his crippled brother Kubrat said farewell, and wished him well.

Then he turned towards Klimt, indifferent to the intimidation of the howling of advancing wolves and asked, 'What would you have me do? Only ask it.'

How strange the light then, how magical a spring across the Scarpfeld the day, the hour, the moment it turns towards the summer.

'A new age is beginning,' said Klimt once more, advancing with the others towards where Tervicz stood, that the Magyars below might see them. 'Howl down the power that we have made, wolf, howl back my sons to me, howl back the future we so nearly lost, now wolf, *now!*'

Then Tervicz raised his head to howl, to howl as no other wolf could howl, and though a whole pack of Magyars might try to howl him down, or ten packs, or a hundred, right across the Fell, across Carpathia, he was the Bukov wolf, and his voice was the light that time remembers through their darkness.

He howled then, and one by one the others joined their voices to his, up and up, echoing down the Great Cleft and out across the Fell, reverberating and potent, across and up, back and up, and on, on towards the northern cliffs, in amongst the screes, pure as the gold on the eagle that gyred over the cliffs, as the sky in the still Scarpfeld pools, as the hearts of the Wolves who howled.

Then, slowly, across the Fell, the dark cloud of the Magyar howling faltered and grew faint and much afraid, for there high above them, silhouettes against a rising sky, howled the Wolves of Time, and it was as if they summoned the very gods themselves to come and stand with them in that moment for all time.

And Tervicz, wolf of Bukov, began to howl the lost wolves down.

Solar followed Lunar up into the forbidden gulley, up where only the dead and dying came to begin their journey to the stars. They had been told that Elhana's travelling companion Ambato of the Benevento, or his spirit perhaps, had come this way the night he died. And Morten too, the night *he* died.

'Lunar!' muttered Solar as he followed, expressing both admonition and resignation, for he knew there was no turning back, and thus far at least no harm had been done. But ... *'For Wulf's sake don't go too far!'*

The mist lightened, and the sun that had been lost across the Fell began to recover itself up here, shining down into the vapours through which they ran, surrounding them with bright sliding shafts of light, the air all mild again.

'Solar!'

'Lunar!'

They called and played at half seeing each other in the strange, echoing, high rocky place they found themselves in, whose outer limits they could not quite see, and whose whole narrow winding form was never quite defined. Rock walls and rising screes loomed at them out of the radiant flowing mist, and sometimes above their heads great juts of rock momentarily showed, now near, and now far, far above them: huge, seeming to shift and take life against the flow of the mist, as if to look down upon them like the heads of benign wolves; then becoming darker, and more malevolent.

'Solar!'

'Lunar!'

They emerged from mist towards each other, relieved it *was* each other they found, and as the sun darkened at the mist's re-thickening, and the air suddenly cooled, they felt awed and very much afraid.

'Better get out of here,' said Solar flatly, his thick grey fur spotted with a thousand, a hundred thousand droplets of condensation which caught the shifting greys and darks, lights and pales of the hidden sky above.

'Yes, maybe . . .' said Lunar, not moving, his own much darker fur filled with water drops as well, in which the juttings of rock seemed more reflected than the light. The fur on his face was matted and wet as if he had been in rain, and his eyes were calmer, fuller than Solar's.

'Oh, let's go on!' he said impulsively. 'There must be more than this and we'll not get a second chance.'

He turned and was gone before Solar could call out a warning not to do so, and that he must come back and they must be gone, they must –

A gunshot, far, far away: heavy, echoing, and that sudden cold and desperate fear wolves feel when Mennen come out of the shadows into their own bloody light.

'*Lunar!*'

Solar followed over the grassy ground in what he hoped was the way his brother had gone, the mist thick and swirling now, catching at his throat. He ran on, and on, and time seemed to shift about him, as mobile and uncertain as the mist. So Lunar had been right, the Mennen had come and were out there, down there, where their territory was: where the others were. Here, where Lunar had dared bring them, they were safe; *but* they seemed lost as well.

'Lunar!'

Lunar heard but chose to go on alone, through the dark mist and then towards new light again to a place more jutty, more rocky, more awesome than before. The bones of rabbits lay across the sward. From high above, where the sun was, beyond the veils and skeins of mist, the shrill call of eagles came, and the answering grumbling racket of ravens. The bones of rabbits, as white-grey as edelweiss and . . . bones of a wolf. The skull of a wolf.

Lunar went to it, and scented its picked-out, leached-out purity. It smelt of the sweetest grass, and saxifrage. He nuzzled at it for a moment, looked back for his brother and then knew suddenly that Solar must have passed him by and gone ahead upslope, towards that place to which he knew he had been before or would go, would one day go. He ran on, and on, and about him too time seemed to shift, as mobile and uncertain as the mist.

He ran on, and then on, the sound of his paws seeming to come from ahead of him, as if he were late and they had gone on before, far ahead, and he might never quite catch them up.

'Solar!'

The strange-shaped rocks, all about and many above, were wolflike now, moving against the mist and looming in the light. Then he saw a wolf, he was sure he did. She stared at him and he turned to her and then she moved, she shifted, she was ahead again, on the other side, a male now, older, running . . .

'Solar!' It must be him.

Sunlight from a blue, blue sky, the green sward of a valley, summer flowers yellow and shining, and a wolf lying there, mortally hurt, staring and helpless, worn by injury and strain, helpless and broken, and a river running nearby, blue as the summer sky above.

Lunar knew that wolf.

'No!' he cried, terrified at last, and knowing he had come too far and risked too much. 'No!'

The howling of wolves echoed among the clefts and overhangs above, seeming to come from out of the shifting mists that hid their highest parts. He looked up, the sound of the howl seeking to draw him back from where he was trying to go, back into the mists of earlier time, his rightful time.

'Lunar,' they called, the wolves that howled, and it was a summons back again, to where he was needed now. Ahead the ground seemed to rise, but only a little before it fell away, only a step or two more . . .

Lunar took those steps, he saw the mist break once more, he stared down towards a river shining blue with summer light, and a great ancient forest behind. And he saw something he did not wish to see . . .

The howling came at him from the mists and cliffs above, 'Lunar, Lunar, come back to us, come back . . .' and finally, mortally afraid at last, he strove to turn away.

Solar, tired and bruised from failing to avoid the juts of rock that kept shifting their position in the mist as if they were living wolves, turned at the sound of the howling too, and heard his own name called. Then, seeming to fall into summer sunlight, he was unable to rise. Behind him a river roared, near enough that its spray came sometimes on to him.

He saw a forest, he saw a wolf, old with worry and concern, and from out of the darkness that began to come on him now he felt a pity and an understanding that seemed bigger than the sky itself.

'No,' he cried, 'not *you* . . .'

Then Solar howled for pity, and for love.

Lunar found that he had turned back at last; utterly exhausted, he began to trot downslope through the clefts and ginnels of the place whose end he had never reached, whose rocks he had never quite fully seen.

Until, as suddenly as they had been separated, a lifetime of days ago it seemed, Solar and Lunar found themselves together again, the mist lightening, the path twisting and turning before them, all the way back to the forbidden entrance through which they should never have come. Beyond, between the gulley sides, below, they saw the Scarpfeld stretching out, and the sun of an afternoon.

'For Wulf's sake, Lunar, let's get out of here and never come back. It is not a place for mortal wolves.'

'No,' said the chastened Lunar, 'it is not.'

'Swear you will never come here again!'

Lunar looked back into the place, at its mists and rocks and vagueness. He tried and tried to do as Solar demanded.

'I cannot,' he whispered; dark though the visions it contained, the forbidden valley felt like it might one day lead him home.

As Tervicz brought his howling to an end the Wolves saw Solar and Lunar emerging from the mists that clung about the rock up by the cliffs. Emerging, staring, unsure of where they were perhaps, and then a quick bark to say that they were well, and safe, and here for Wulf's sake, *here*.

'Klimt, look!'

It was Kobrin's voice and they all looked where he pointed.

The Fell below was alive with the advance of wolves, angry wolves, vengeful wolves, and at their head, looking towards the entrance up into the Great Cleft, was Führer, furious it seemed, and Dendrine, shouting, urging, screaming.

'Yes,' whispered Klimt, 'the new age is on us with all its darkness, and –'

... Here he turned back from the cliff towards where Solar and Lunar were picking their way gingerly down amongst the rocks, frightened of the strangeness in the eyes of Klimt and Elhana.

'And all its light,' added Klimt.

Then he led them towards the two returning wolves, running and bounding across the Scarpfeld, full of a joy they had never seen him express, and a lightness of heart he had never showed.

'Solar! Lunar! *Solar!*'

How long did the pack share its joy together then? It seemed like an age for all that Klimt cared for the approach of the Magyars. Perhaps it was moments only.

'*Heuren Sie!*' said Klimt in the old way. 'Listen now! Listen to my commands. Do what I ask of you and the future will be ours. Kobrin, Tare, Rohan, Elhana – you will stay here, or hereabouts. You will skulk and hide, and be all but invisible. Kobrin will teach you to make fools of your enemy, to humble him, to anger him, and yet not be caught; never be caught, for there is none to save you. In constant retreat and constant return, like the mosquito that continues to disturb a great wolf's slumber and makes him turn and turn about in irritation, destroying his peace and making him look foolish, you will harass the Magyars into never enjoying the possession they will seek to make of the Scarpfeld, and the Forest, and the Vale.

'The Fall will be your retreat, for it is a wolfway made for us. It is our safe place. Lounel will help you learn to trust it. There we will find you, all of you, on our return.'

'Your return?' said Kobrin, pleased to be given so responsible if formidable a task, but puzzled still as to Klimt's intentions.

Klimt nodded. 'This is no place now for the two wolves Führer and Dendrine have vowed to kill; Solar and Lunar must leave here, and I must leave with them on the journey the Wanderer challenged me to make.'

'Where to?' asked Tare.

'To Khazaria, to find such allies to help us towards wolfkind's destiny as the Magyars never dreamed we could find.'

'The wolf called Kazan?' growled Kobrin. 'He will not help you.'

'He will,' said Klimt, 'he must. Hold the spirit of this place well for us, Kobrin, and trust that before the first snows of winter fall across the Forest some or all of us will return. *We will be back.* As others will.'

'Others?' said Tare.

'Aragon, Jicin, Stry, and others – a new age is beginning and what Kobrin will teach you few to do, and the resistance you show against the Magyars here, will in years yet to come be remembered, and inspire others with a faith in our destiny to travel to the Heartland, and see Wulf and Wulfin begin their journey back to the stars.'

'Father . . .' whispered Rohan, her eyes showing she was afraid and yet would do her best, 'what of Tervicz? Is he to go with thee?'

Klimt smiled and shook his head. 'He has been at my flank for five years now, wolf, and never once have I doubted his courage, his loyalty, or his common sense. I wish him to come with me but . . . I have a fancy he wishes to stay with you! Eh Tervicz?'

'I shall do as you command,' said Tervicz in a low voice.

'Guard my daughters and my ledrene until you are sure they are safe from the Magyars, Tervicz, as Kobrin will help you all guard the Heartland.'

'So he's to stay?' said Rohan, scarcely believing it.

'As close as close can be,' said Klimt with a laugh, 'but if the time comes when you feel you must return to your home territory and take Rohan with you, do so with my blessing. It will help serve the pack's need to know the Magyars' strength in Bukovina.'

From the direction of the Great Cleft came the sound of slipping scree, as of many wolves steadily climbing up towards the Scarpfeld.

'May the gods be with us all,' said Klimt, 'and bring the Wolves of Time together once again, stronger than they have ever been.'

'Solar! Lunar! Leader!'

It was Elhana to say farewell to all three.

'May Wulf and Wulfin be with you, my dears, and send you back safe to me. Now, go or you will see tears in my eyes.'

Klimt retreated, and Lunar with him, but Solar stayed a moment longer.

'I have never seen tears in your eyes, mother,' he said.

'Then see now, my love.'

And she wept and he saw her tears, before he turned at last and followed his father and brother on their quest to Khazaria.

'Come my friends,' said Kobrin, 'for I have things to teach you if we are to fulfil our task, the first of which is to fade and disappear from view, even from the view of a wolf who is but a short distance off . . .'

Then as the Magyars reached the top of the Great Cleft, and first Führer and then Dendrine came into view, Kobrin and all those he now led faded away and disappeared across the Scarpfeld.

'A new age is beginning,' cried Dendrine as she took possession of a place she had once known so well.

'It is, and it has,' said Führer, staring across at the northern cliffs, and the rock, and the screes in whose secret recesses he had been raised, and wondering why the place seemed now to have eyes, but eyes he could not see.

CHAPTER FOURTEEN

*As Jicin sets forth to rescue the wolves of Brive, she believes
the time is coming when she must return to the Heartland*

IT WAS NOW six months since Jicin had been left in Southern
France by Aragon, six months in which she had learnt much of
the Mennen and their war, but rather less of the real task she
had been set, though now, finally, as a new spring warmed the hills
and vales of Armagnac, a mystery seemed likely to be solved.

For the task she and those with her had been set by Aragon was
twofold: first to establish how widespread was the Mennen war, and
second to track down a lone wolf they had come across some weeks
before, who had told a story of other wolves living in captivity in the
farmlands far to the north of Toulouse.

It was a matter for regret that he had chosen to make contact – he
had tailed them over several weeks through the foothills of the
Pyrenees – only a day or two before the Mennen war had broken out.
In that time he had told them his story in the briefest way, and
mentioned the existence of these captive wolves almost in passing,
and by the time Aragon and Jicin realized the significance of what he
had said the destruction of Toulouse had begun, and their attention
was diverted.

So that it was only when they discovered that the wolf, whose name
was Leon, had disappeared once more, as lone wolves will, that they
realized they should have found out more. None of the three original
exiles had forgotten their experience of the blind wolf in the Belgian
zoo and the thought that there might be more than one wolf in captivity, in a place nearby, both concerned and intrigued them. So Aragon
had set Jicin the task of finding out what she could of that matter,
and of the war as well, and then deciding for herself if, perhaps, it
was time to return to the Heartland.

The confidence with which she commanded those with her would
have astonished those who had known her four years before, when

she was but a lost and broken Magyar wolf in thrall to Dendrine, consort of Hassler, leader of the main Magyar pack. But her escape from the Magyars and acceptance by the Wolves of Time marked the start of her transformation into a wolf to be reckoned with, a process that had taken all of those four years, and in some ways it still continued.

No wolf had had a greater influence upon her for the better than Klimt, with whom she had associated for that period of self-exile from the Wolves, before he wrested back leadership from Aragon, and led them all to the Heartland.

Jicin had been well taught the arts of independence and leadership in the happy days when he and she had been alone together for a time, and then by Kobrin when that great and lovable Russian wolf had joined them. Later, when exiled with Aragon, he had taught her much as well.

Only of the period after Elhana had defeated her for the ledreneship of the Wolves of Time and before she was exiled did she prefer not to think: she had never wanted the ledreneship anyway, but she *had* wanted Klimt, whom she loved as himself rather than as leader of the pack.

'Oh Wulf . . .'

How long and bitter had been her hopeless prayers since her exile, wishing that she might be with him once again; how terrible her grief and loss. In the first years away a day did not go by when she did not think of him, and yearn for him. Until, time passing, the loss felt a little less, and the grief became more bearable. Though sometimes, always unexpectedly, the pain came back sharply to her, at which moments she fancied it was because he thought of her – or, wilder fancy still perhaps, that he needed her.

But, over time, with Aragon she had discovered pleasures she had heard of but never known: companionship, fun, and delight in simple things. The loss and yearning for Klimt she still felt, Wulf knew that, but it was easier now and when it came upon her it was in ripples she could rise above, not engulfing waves.

Now, looking at the three wolves with her, and the way they obeyed her command to follow, she understood how much she had learned. If their numbers grew, as was now her task to achieve, she had no doubt that one or other of the males would take over as leader. Might she then stay on as ledrene, fighting others as Elhana had fought her? She might . . . she might . . .

No. To be ledrene would mean that by the pack's lore she must have cubs, and to have cubs would mean that she must mate, and to mate must mean that her memory of Klimt would fade still more. In any case, she had no wish to take responsibility for carrying and raising cubs: she had done so before, and lost them, and if that was not bad enough, she had later lost one of Elhana's.

Oh Wulfin, do not make me weep again . . .

But for that poor cub she *did* still weep, even if her tears for Klimt were now all gone, leaving only bleakness and loss, and the slow fading of her memory of what he had looked like; for that sweet, lost cub whose death she felt was her own fault, the pain was always sharp.

No, no, she did not think she would want to dare mate again.

Of the frustrations of the winter after Aragon left no more than this need be said: the war affected almost everywhere they visited, with whole towns and cities over in Spain destroyed, though in France the infection seemed to have spread little further northward than Toulouse, where they had first been witnesses to it.

As for the lone wolf, Leon, it had been less a matter of finding him – for they began to realize he had continued to tail them – than of persuading him to join them, and talk. This they had failed to do, until finally, in April, Jicin herself had found him injured by a major Mennen road not far from the ruined Toulouse. He lay there quite unresisting, as if being killed by whoever found him, whether it be Mennen or wolves, might be preferable to living on.

As it was, their company soon cheered him, and with food in his belly and plenty of rest he had begun to develop into a healthy, self-assured individual who could give as good as he got, and undoubtedly would make a useful contribution to any pack, if only he would stay with them.

Then at last he told Jicin briefly about the wolves he knew to be in captivity, and seemed mightily relieved to do so. No sooner had he finished than he confessed that he had been putting off going to find them because . . . because . . .

'You can tell us once we get started,' said Jicin, sensing further prevarication.

'Yes, right, I will,' agreed Leon.

'Let's get going then.'

Thus it was that after a six-month delay Jicin finally found herself doing what she had wanted to do for so very long – going to the rescue of wolves who needed help.

The first morning's journey proved hard, for the territory was all Mennen-made with scarcely a tree for cover, or a natural stream for drink. So she led them cautiously, and lay up from noon to dusk because the grey and rainy skies had cleared, and the only way ahead was too open and exposed.

It had always seemed to her that one of Aragon's few weaknesses was that he was not a good listener, so that in times of enforced idleness such as this, opportunities to learn something of the pack's workings and tensions had been missed. Jicin always remembered how Klimt would make others talk so that listening to them without comment he not only learned things he did not know, but was made to think of matters that might otherwise have eluded him, and was able to gauge the mood of those around him as well.

Now Jicin, free of the constraints that Aragon put upon her, and aware of the disappointment those now following her felt at not having been chosen to travel on to the Heartland, encouraged them to talk by staying silent and grooming herself.

Egro, a male they had brought with them from the Cabrera pack, lunged at her once, just to try it on. She nipped him hard and then, snapping and snarling in a display of pre-eminence, she chased him from the shelter, and chastised him for risking drawing the Mennen's attention to where they lay – though she had checked their position sufficiently to know there was no real chance of that. But he was young and eager and contrite as well, and what he had done showed spirit at least. Later, with a smile, she allowed him to come back into the circle of their group without comment. Indeed, she was grateful that he had given her the chance to affirm who, for the moment, was in charge.

Since his dismissal the other two had felt it prudent to be silent, but with his return they began to open up. Ronera, Egro's sister, began the talk with a complaint, as usual.

'How long are we to be here in this damp place with our stomachs grumbling and our –'

'Until the dusk maybe, until the dawn,' said Leon philosophically. Not quite so big and full of hauteur as Egro, nor even so visible, for he had taken the sensible precaution of pulling some dead undergrowth over his hinderparts to shelter them from the wind.

'I shall shiver and grow cold,' said Ronera a trifle tragically, as if there was nothing to be done about it.

Leon grinned, winking at Jicin, and pulling himself even deeper into the undergrowth as if to show what Ronera might do, if she really wished.

There was silence for a time, for they were all used to Ronera and knew the best thing was to say nothing when she was in a complaining mood, for the slightest response, especially one of disagreement, would start her off again.

'I would feel better if I knew how long this ridiculous journey will take,' she said at last.

'It'll take us longer if you talk like that,' said Leon, winking at no one in particular and making Jicin smile before he added, 'it'll take about three days if we're prudent.'

'Three days,' murmured Jicin.

'The cover's good beyond the River Lot,' observed Egro, glancing at Jicin to see if he was allowed to speak. She remained impassive and he ventured further remark. 'It's wood as far as the eye can see – almost.'

'Done the journey yourself, have you?' demanded Leon, who had.

They were jostling for position, but from their glances at Jicin it was plain whom they considered boss.

'No,' said Egro, 'I was just saying what I had seen when I reconnoitred the ground –'

This would have been more than six months ago.

'It's wooded all right,' said Leon, cutting across him and enjoying verbal ascendancy over a wolf who was, if only slightly, his physical superior, 'but not all the way. There's many a farm, and fishpond, and open fields in lower ground.'

'I'll bet there *is* a route could take us there without breaking woodland cover,' said Ronera, defending her brother.

'Of course there is,' said Egro, sensing he had lost a little ground.

'We can kill time or we can use it profitably,' said Jicin, suddenly weary of their bickering. 'Leon knows more than the rest of us about the place we're heading for so why doesn't he tell us once again.'

'Not *again!*' muttered Egro, who had heard Leon tell something of the story.

Ronera said, 'Well, I haven't heard it yet and I'd like to.'

'Tell us once again how you came to hear of these wolves,' commanded Jicin, 'and what you discovered when you tried to seek them out.'

Leon nodded, all the more willing to do so because each time he told the story a little more of what he knew came to light from the depths in which he had chosen to bury it for so long.

'Tell us again wolf, as best you can . . .' said Jicin warmly.

'I do not know my origin, or my parentage,' Leon began, 'nor what wolf gave me my name. My first memory is of mountains and Mennen, the mountains huge and snow-capped, the Mennen dancing and shouting, and staring from great eyes, and the sweet foetid smell of their breath; and my fear, shivering fear.

'I stared at them, and they seemed to dance horribly past me, along with night and day, winter and spring, and I think now that I was ill, very ill.

'My first clear memory is of eating rotten meat, and drinking sour milk, and of another wolf watching me. That wolf taught me to live. That wolf was my father and my mother. That wolf was all I know of what I was, and where I came from, and where I shall go to, which is and was and always shall be from the stars where Wulf and Wulfin once lived, before wolfkind was cursed; and one day back to them.

'I do not know how long it was before I knew where I was, or that it might not be where I was meant to be, but the wolf who shared my cage with me must have told me: I was in a circus, travelling from the mountains to the plains and back again, summer and winter, spring and autumn, a roundel of places that I got to know.

'His name was Galliard, the wolf who cared for me, and his sister's name was Maladon. I know this, because a day – scarcely half a day – did not pass but that Galliard mentioned her. I learned the nature of affection and love, and of hate as well from Galliard and the sister by whom he was obsessed. Galliard raised me, but it was Maladon, whose presence he so continually evoked, who dominated my life.

'"One day you shall meet her," he would say, "and then you shall know why I speak so often of her!"

'But I was not sure I wanted to. If I dreamed of her, it was in nightmares; and if I had a vision of her, she was always angry, always punishing me . . . For I soon learnt that Galliard himself had been raised in a zoo in a place called Brive, north-east of the Pyrenees. There his sister Maladon was ledrene and to her Galliard owed his escape, his cunning and all he knew. Brutal she may have been, perhaps cruel as well, but it was she who saw to it that he escaped the zoo, and had the skills to survive afterwards.'

'And your own background?' asked Ronera, more curious about the wolf before her than the one he seemed almost as obsessed by as Galliard.

'Me? Well . . . I said that I do not know from where I came, and that is so. But it is likely that I was born within the confines of those circus cages I first remember, and that my mother died in giving birth to me. There was a cage they put us in sometimes when we were moved, and in one corner there was the vestigial scent of female wolf. Perhaps I was born there and that was my mother's scent.

'Galliard told me he had been found years before, weak and wandering, by shepherds in the hills, and taken to the circus. Perhaps they brought him to me because they saw that I was dying and they thought I might benefit from the company of one of my own kind.

'In the cages I grew towards maturity and in all that time was allowed out of confinement only three times, each of which I remember as if it was but yesterday: the first for fear, the second for joy, the last for the death of Galliard.

'The first time it was spring and we had begun the journey back towards the mountains and were already in foothills country. Some of the cages were wheeled into a courtyard of stone walls that smelt of horses and bulls, though none were there. The Mennen came and banged our cage with sticks, and pronged at us. Galliard told me to keep down, and stay at the back of the cage. They opened the doors and there was nothing before us but air. That was the first fear, the open air. I felt if I went out into it I would fall down for ever.

'They pronged at us from the sides of the cage and finally from behind and Galliard led the way out, snarling. I shit myself as I was pushed out into the air. I thought I was going to die. There were two dogs there barking and snarling. They were set free, and they came at us. We could not escape because the doors of the cage were closed clanging behind us by the Mennen and we – or at least I – froze.

'Galliard protected me. Snarling at them, he took up a defensive posture between me and the dogs. That stopped them for a time whilst the Mennen shouted and gesticulated with frustration, for they wanted to see us fight. But then the dogs found new courage and suddenly Galliard was rolling, fighting, snarling, until I heard a dog scream. Even as it screamed the other disengaged and came for me. I opened my jaws. I felt the biting, battering thrust of its teeth to my mouth and tongue, and then its sliding, snapping bite down my right flank and then the Mennen hit it and it fell. Then they hit it again and it tried to crawl. They hit it again and there was blood where its eye was. They hit it some more and Galliard came back to me. The other dog, the one that had screamed, had crawled to a far wall, hunched and yelping.

'Galliard said, "You hesitated. *Never* hesitate once you are attacked – not for one moment. Either fight or flee, but do not hesitate."

'We were put back into the cages and after that Galliard taught me how to fight. He taught me all he knew about that art, though now I have met other wolves I know it was not so much. Enough to defend myself, no more . . .'

He glanced at Egro with whom he had fought and tussled ever since he had been found, and against whom he was more or less equally matched.

'And the second time you were allowed out of the cages?' prompted Jicin.

Before continuing Leon rose from where he had taken his place, and stretched. He stared out over the fields and watched with the others as a farmer drove a tractor across a distant field, seagulls diving in his wake. The air was still and growing colder as the day advanced, and blue smoke hung over the woods that reached away across far hills.

'The second time . . .' sighed Leon in a contented way, 'that was in the autumn of that same year. We were coming back out of the mountain passes and were encamped in fields near a village. One day our cage was moved to a field about which were high fences of barbed wire. We were put in there and Galliard said, "Remember what I have told you. Do not hesitate when the dogs come, or whatever else the Mennen might set to fight us."

'But they put *nothing* against us. There was just a vast blue sky, and the dry, warm scent of herbs, and the waving yellow of autumn hawkweed, and the white slow drift of air-borne seeds. The ground was cracked and dry and they let us roam a field that seemed to me vast though I would have ventured no distance at all had not Galliard led me around its perimeter.

'"Is there danger here . . . dogs?"

'"Can't smell any," he said.

'"What are you doing?"

'"Looking for a way out."

'"Galliard!"

'I remember his laugh then as the happiest I ever heard him give.

'"Found liberty once before, because I had been trained to take my chances when they came."

'The Mennen came and drove us back, though we did not want to go. When we got back to the cage it was dripping wet, cleaned and laid out with new straw, and it smelt of disinfectant.

'"Humph!" said Galliard, and he immediately peed in the corner that was always his.

'But the last time I was allowed out of the cages, which was two years later and in summertime, Galliard was already growing old. By then he had told me as much about his life before coming to the circus as he ever cared to. Mostly, what he talked about was his sister Maladon.'

Jicin rose and stared out of the cover towards the sky. The day had advanced into a dull afternoon and it was time to move.

'You shall tell us of this Maladon when we next rest,' she said.

'And how Galliard came to die?' said Ronera.

'And how you came to escape the circus cages,' said Egro, showing, a little reluctantly perhaps, how interested in Leon's tale he had become.

'His death and my escape were closely linked,' responded Leon, 'and as for Maladon, the fierce and fearsome sister whom he never forgot, and perhaps never quite stopped fearing, I must confess that I am very much afraid of her myself. But when I escaped the circus I felt that the only way I could repay my debt to Galliard was to try to reach Brive and see if I might help her.

'I did so, but help I could not give – not alone at least. The zoo is well-made, the cages and compounds not easily breached – not by a single wolf at any rate. So I retreated southward praying to Wulfin, goddess who helps those who suffer, that I might find other wolves and fulfil my self-ordained task. So it was that Jicin here found me, and when Aragon heard my story he agreed to help.'

'You mean he agreed to leave us behind to help you while he went on to the Heartland!' said Egro heavily, but not without a certain rueful resignation. 'It seems we owe this jaunt to you, Leon!' He was beginning to see a certain depth in Leon.

'Did you – ?' began Ronera, before Jicin interrupted her.

'This is the last question, for we must get started.'

Ronera nodded and rose up, saying, 'Did you find out if Maladon is still alive – and still horrible?'

Leon hesitated before replying, and then said carefully, 'The little

I saw of her before I set off to get help suggested she was not a wolf easy to disobey.'

'What did she look like?'

Again Leon hesitated. 'Well, she . . . I mean . . .'

'Another time,' said Jicin firmly, for it seemed plain that Leon would talk a good deal longer if given half a chance. 'Instead of talking, let's see if we can find a wolfway towards this place called Brive, where you say Maladon and other wolves still live.'

She was surprised to see that Leon looked relieved not to have to talk further of Maladon.

The routes Leon took proved safe and easy, for they were mostly through deep woodland where Mennen rarely went. Jicin had expected him to take the same route he said he had travelled before and was surprised that he did not, for he relied instead on the wolfways in the stars, as Galliard had taught them to him in relation to their destination.

On the second day of travel, when they rested once more through most of the daylight hours, they were all tired and talked little. The nearer they approached to Brive – and Leon declared it was now not far off – the more taciturn he became. He was no longer willing to talk about his past to while away the time, and responded irritably, and finally defensively, to Jicin's requests to know how near they were, and what kind of approach the landscape offered. Then his route began to meander, and to bear no direct relation to the stars above, and Jicin was beginning to suspect that the fear of Maladon engendered in him by Galliard's stories ran so deep that he was reluctant to meet her again.

Egro had a simpler explanation: 'He's forgotten the way, otherwise why would he rely on the stars for a route he has already travelled? You tell me that!'

A night or two later, when the others were beginning to protest louder still, Leon broke his silence. He talked at first of how it was that he had been upon the dangerous Mennenway where Jicin found him.

'I had wandered very far you see, not sure what to do, thinking I would never find other wolves again, never. The loneliness finally began to eat at me, and the pointlessness of existing without anything, or any wolf. Until I found myself upon a Mennenway, ready to be killed or simply to die. I *would* have died had not Jicin found me on that road.'

'But before that you had found the wolves at Brive, eh wolf?' said Jicin. 'So you knew there were others somewhere. I do not understand how a wolf who has evidently endured a great deal should suddenly lose heart.'

'No . . .' said Leon, looking at her a shade shiftily.

'How long was it since you had left Brive before . . .' she began, staring at him in astonishment.

'Brive?' he said vaguely. 'Oh, yes . . .'

Jicin stared at him with a mixture of annoyance and amazement as if she suddenly understood something that she had not wished to suspect before.

'You said, wolf, that you had been there already and that you remembered the way. Upon that promise we have come with you.'

'Did I?' said Leon.

'Yes, you damn well did!' cried Egro, moving aggressively towards him.

'I know the wolfway in the stars that goes that way – or rather this way – only because Galliard taught it me.'

'And you can get us there because you've been there, and remember it on the ground. You said earlier that –'

'You mean . . . ?'

'Don't tell me that . . . ?'

Jicin, Egro and Ronera were gathered round Leon now in a dangerously threatening way.

Leon sighed. 'I lied,' he finally said. 'I have never been there. I could not find the courage to go there alone. I did not have courage . . .'

There was blank astonishment at this, except from Jicin who had had time to recover from her surprise and see something else, something more. But for her restraint Egro might very well have attacked Leon then and there.

As it was she calmed the others down, and said that they had better hear Leon out before they did anything else, and suggested they had food and drink before they talked, finally gathering the little pack together once more when each of them was ready to be reasonable.

'I have not told you how I escaped from the circus, or what Galliard had to do to help make it happen, and now is not the time,' began Leon, speaking in a much less confident voice than before. 'But escape I did, last spring. Once free I found that without Galliard at my flank I did not know what to do. For months I lived in the hills near the

Pyrenees and there I suppose I learnt how to fend for myself. But I was lonely – terribly lonely. If he had been still alive and in captivity I would have gone back to him – and many was the time I skulked at the edge of the circus where I had been captive, and others of its kind, to take in the familiar scents of animals and Mennen, and to give myself up to their care once more. But always I hesitated, remembering Galliard's plea that if ever I found freedom I should seek to find the zoo where Maladon was kept.

'Finally I found strength and courage enough to cross the Pyrenees, using the stars as my guide, and once over them found myself freer in spirit. But as you all know the Mennen are at war in the valleys of Gascony and Armagnac and my progress was slow. I stayed in safe country, frightened of their guns, and only a few weeks since dared venture north to find Brive. But the loneliness returned, and a fear greater still than that I already felt of Maladon – the fear that she would be no more.

'I wandered, desolate, and wishing to die, praying to Wulf that I might. But Galliard often told me that it is when a wolf is low that his prayers are heard, and so it was that Jicin found me.'

He looked at them blankly, at their mercy now.

'Only in your company could I have come so far, but somehow I have lost the way to Brive, and am beginning to doubt that the confined pack that gave Galliard life, and finally liberty, any longer exists.'

'But you are confident that the wolfway that your mentor Galliard taught you to find in the stars was as we have followed it?'

'I am, yes. But . . .'

He shrugged and looked up into the darkness, where few stars were to be seen. It was a grey night and the wind was cold, and the sky cloudy as it had been through the day.

'I thought that having got so near to the end as he described it that if I looked confident, and quartered the ground, we might pick up the scent of these wolves.'

'All this way for nothing!' Ronera said, her eyes contemptuous.

'Us following a wolf who did not know the way!' said Egro angrily, beginning to fret his feet in the moist humus beneath the trees where they sat, eager to prove once and for all the ascendancy he felt over Leon.

'But you're sure this is the area where these wolves might be confined?' asked Jicin judiciously.

'As Wulf is my witness,' exclaimed Leon passionately, 'I have followed the route Galliard taught me, and somewhere here I am sure they must be – upon my faith in Wulf Himself I swear it!'

He had stood up and was panting in anger and frustration, for what more could a wolf do than he had done?

'I swear, Jicin, that what I have told you now is true; it was just that alone I could not find the courage, but with you –'

'Listen!'

It was Ronera who heard it first, and then they all did.

Out of the darkness of the night, across the swaying forest trees, there came a howl, high and haunting.

'It is . . .' whispered Jicin.

A howling, not of one wolf but of many, a howling that did not fear that Mennen might hear.

'It is the wolves of Brive,' whispered Leon in wonder and relief.

'It is a prayer answered,' said Jicin wryly. 'Well then, wolf, having led us this far on a lie you had better lead us the rest of the way upon a howl.'

They ran then through the night, one after the other, up through the woodland trees, down across pasture grounds, out on to Mennen tracks, their paws padding faster and faster as if they feared to lose the sound.

But the howling continued, minute after minute, and then longer still. Pausing sometimes, but only long enough that wolves might catch their breath and begin again: a howl born of a desolate faith that sometime, somehow, eventually, wolfkind might hear it and respond.

Faster ran Leon, the others in close pursuit, feeling that if he paused a moment, if he allowed doubt or fear to beset him, he would lose the courage to go on. For the closer they came, and as they saw that the place whence the howling rose was near a town, where lights shone up and lit the underside of clouds, and roads ran with vehicles on them – the closer they came, the better they were able to hear the individual voices that made the howl. Male and female, young and old, and one louder and finally more fearsome than all the others.

One whose howl led the others.

One whose voice mixed bitterness with hope; anger with faith; and a desire for revenge that seemed as strong as her rising howl for liberty.

'Where now?' rasped Jicin, for they had been forced to stop at a wide road.

'In the shadows along this Mennenway until we find a safer route across?' suggested Egro.

'No, this way, *this* way,' said Leon, pointing straight across, regardless of the coming traffic. His eyes were alight with the street lamps above their heads. He seemed a wolf obsessed and unstoppable, turning and running so powerfully now that it was not so much that the others could not or would not follow him, as that they could not stop themselves. This was a wolf desperate now to reach the end of the route first formed in his mind when he was a cub, and another wolf was still alive; to reach it . . . and move beyond it.

They crossed the road, they ran into the shadows of walls and wire fences on the far side, and of the building beyond which held the scents of animals and Mennen, of oil and artificial food, of meat and of water that had been purified and made dead by Mennen.

The howling ceased. A lion roared, briefly. An elephant coughed and shook his chains.

They followed Leon under a fence and away from the road into the shadows and angles of cages and compounds. Lights a short way off the ground lit Mennen paths, but there were no Mennen to be seen.

Leon paused, scented at the air, and ran towards the darkness that lay beyond a great chain fence. In and out of shadow he went, past one light and another, and then to the fence itself, the others gathering on either side of him.

From the darkness of the compound stared a dozen pair of eyes, some near and some far, deathly still. One pair moved, and then another, retreating. Somewhere a wolf growled.

A short sharp bark of warning, and a scrabbling of paws, and the eyes faded back into darkness until finally only one pair remained. For a moment Jicin had a memory of that old blind wolf she and Aragon and Stry had found in a Belgian zoo years before, and helped reach up towards the stars.

But the wolf that stared out of darkness at them was not dead. The eyes moved, first to one side and then the other, as if unseen paws were chafing at the ground and readying to attack.

Then, suddenly, the eyes moved more quickly, and began to grow, began to charge, and out of the darkness came a wolf. First the fur on her face catching the Mennen lights, then the movement of her legs. Then two great shoulders, and her ears, and her whole body as the eyes turned black in shadow and the she-wolf charged at them. Straight at them with such power that although there was a fence between, and a ditch as well, each one of them flinched and retreated before her.

She stopped only at the last moment, her shoulders bulging to hold her weight against her front legs, her flanks heaving. She stared at them, magnificent. Bigger than any of them, and her coat finer.

'You will help get us out of here,' she said, her voice harsh and uncompromising.

'It is what we came to do,' said Leon, whatever other greeting he might have prepared quite deserting him.

'What wolves are you?' she demanded – there was no other word for it.

Somewhere there was Mennen sound, but she merely glanced briefly that way and then brought her gaze back on them. Behind her other wolves emerged out of the darkness into the light. Jicin had never in her life seen such large and powerful wolves as these.

'Galliard sent me,' said Leon, his voice commendably calm. 'I came in search of the ledrene Maladon.'

Did Jicin see the she-wolf's eyes soften for a moment? Was it possible for one so strong-seeming, so ferocious-looking, with a face so etched by anger and bitterness, to show sentiment?

'Galliard,' she said, and even as she said it the momentary softness passed. By the time she had finished speaking his name whatever feeling it had awakened after so many years was replaced by controlled fury and command, as if he, or his representative, should have got there a good deal sooner.

'He died, but . . .' began Leon, not sure quite what to say.

'But you are here, wolf, and your . . . friends. It will suffice. You will find a place at the back of this compound – a place of shadow and rubbish where you can hide unnoticed. You will remain there until dawn, during which time you will make no sound. I shall instruct you in the lay-out of this place, for we shall have one chance only. One of the Mennen will come at dawn – I shall show you where – and you will attack him once he has opened a certain door, and then opened another – *only then*. We shall do the rest. Come, follow me round the compound to the back.'

'Your name?' demanded Jicin, feeling that one of them ought to insist on the traditional courtesies. This extraordinary female made her feel they were low in her hierarchy, rather than her saviours.

'Maladon,' said the wolf, turning her gaze on Jicin. 'Now follow me round.'

And Jicin knew a compulsive throb of fear such as she had not felt since she last saw her mother Dendrine.

She felt as well a sense of inevitability, as if time had been waiting impatiently for this wolf to be set free. The great she-wolf padded along beyond the ditch inside the fence, one flank in the light, the other in shadow, and Jicin thought of Kobrin, of Klimt and of Elhana. Great wolves, all of them. Here, now, as if the wolfways had always been leading her to this moment, Jicin knew that for better, and for worse as well, Maladon too was one of the Wolves of Time.

Then, as that strange night of waiting in shadows continued, and her sense of fear and trepidation mounted for what the dawn might bring, and what the release of Maladon might mean, Jicin sensed something else, something far, far worse. It came to her quite sharply, like a sudden pain, and overrode even the rapidly mounting fear she felt. It concerned Klimt, it *was* Klimt, calling to her, needing her, wanting her . . .

'*No*,' she whispered in the dark, for that was all in the past, and what she felt were but drowned and broken dreams surfacing upon the sea of her fears and doubts. '*No!*'

Then Jicin put all thought of Klimt aside, and the yearning his seeming call had brought to her heart, and focused on the wire fence above her, and the coming of the dawn.

CHAPTER FIFTEEN

Klimt and his sons journey to Khazaria, and learn
something of journeying, of illness, and of themselves

KLIMT'S FAMOUS EASTWARD JOURNEY in search of the
legendary Kazan wolf, first across the Ukraine and thence into
the uplands of the River Volga, proved of enormous significance for the Wolves of Time, not least because though their search
was for the Kazan wolf, it was a very different saviour that they found,
whose teeth and claws, and loyalty, proved well that when it comes
to a fight, and continuing struggle, reality is more useful than myth.
Then too, the journey is remembered because one of them never
came back . . .

But such shadows were not yet seen by Solar and Lunar, who were
filled with excitement at making their first trek of importance beyond
the confines of their home territory, with all the excitements and
discoveries, and reappraisals of self, pack, and home that such a venture implies. While for Klimt it represented a first release after many
years, years in which he had begun to grow old, from daily responsibility for the welfare of a full pack; and an escape to a land of liberty
whose horizons contained not only new-found personal freedoms, but
also those dark abysses and demons which he had been able to avoid
for so long.

It was with these inner challenges that the three Wolves were at
first most concerned as they journeyed through a Ukrainian summer
towards Khazaria. So it was just as well that they were initially so little
challenged either by the terrain they crossed, or by the Mennen and
occasional wolves who inhabited it. Indeed, rather the opposite, for
it soon became apparent that the warfare they had observed at such
close quarters down the Vale was endemic to the whole of the great
land they journeyed through, with the same constant level of strife
amongst the Mennen and destruction of cities, towns and villages,
which they had until then witnessed only in their own area.

With clear and clement weather, and the Mennen so much preoccupied with themselves, and since food was so readily available amongst the dead and dying livestock that were abandoned and wandering all along the way, the three Wolves could hardly have found conditions more suited to safe and rapid travel. True, for the first week of the great journey Klimt's limbs were stiff, his trekking clumsy, his running strained. It had not been like this when he had first left Sweden on his trek to find the Heartland so many years before.

'I'm getting old,' he grumbled, 'my body begins to ache when I rise up.'

He was only slightly gratified that Solar complained of aches and pains as well, wondering how far Khazaria was, how far, saying that if he knew he could pace himself better. A couple of weeks? A month? A whole summer?

It was Lunar, always the one who had liked finding routes among the crags and passes, who proved fittest and seemed to know best how to travel, and who eventually reminded them of what the Wanderer had told them of what *he* had learnt on his great treks.

'Don't you remember what he said?' called Lunar, pausing for what seemed the umpteenth time so that Klimt and Solar could catch him up.

'He said a great deal,' said Klimt shortly.

'Not all of which I personally can remember,' declared Solar, his chest heaving and puffing as they approached.

'On the subject of making light of a long journey he said: "*I journeyed with the shooting of new spring growth, then upon the sway of summer trees. I paused a lifetime to watch the Volga's flow, but the time passed in a moment and on I went with the scattering autumn leaves."*'

'*Did* he?' said Solar with a wry smile, for he never before remembered Lunar quoting another's words so ably and aptly.

'Or something to that effect,' said Lunar grinning, his eyes pale and clear. 'Now, wolves, what did you see on your way up this steep slope, eh?'

Despite himself Klimt had to smile, for there was something so good-natured and easy about Lunar that it lifted his heart to see it, for there had been times following the loss of Merrow when he had doubted that Lunar could ever be himself again. He had been like this when he was young, but in those days . . . 'In those days', Klimt told himself, 'I was too busy to appreciate him.'

'All I saw coming up this slope were the rocks and dust on the path ahead,' confessed Solar.

'All I could think of was where next to place each aching paw,' conceded Klimt.

'And all *I* saw,' said Lunar, 'were the eastward-racing clouds above our heads, rushing past us in the direction we are going, helping my paws along; and all I thought of was of our arrival in Khazaria, and our first sighting of this wolf Kazan.'

Klimt sat down. 'You are right, Lunar. When I left Sweden all I knew was that I was following a dream of the Heartland, and the pack I would one day lead there.'

'And did it make your journey light and easy?'

'It did, Lunar, it did.'

'Well then, father . . .' And Lunar looked at his father quizzically, and with good humour.

The three Wolves laughed together, feeling in that moment, perhaps for the first time, the freedom they could have together as father to sons, as adults to adults, as Wolves with a shared mission and purpose.

Lunar had paused, as he usually did, at a spot which gave them a view of the prospect ahead. Over the last two days they had journeyed through the eastern foothills of the central Carpathian mountains, the smouldering ruins of Krakow, Przmeysl and Lvov below them to the north, and now they could see the vast stretch of the Ukraine before them, undulating, occupied, inviting.

'You will tell me what place it was you were lost within for those dreadful weeks when I thought you were both killed?' said Klimt once he had got his breath back. His thoughts had often drifted back to the question he had not had the opportunity to ask before. 'In time, you'll tell me?'

He was careful not to make it an order, for he sensed that there was something other-worldly and inexplicable in their disappearance, about which they were reluctant to talk. In any case, now the Heartland was behind them relationships had shifted, and were shifting still, and Klimt felt it wrong to try to invoke his former style of inquisitorial command.

'We *will* answer your question father, but . . .' said Solar, glancing at Lunar and finding there a shadow on his face.

'We will try,' agreed Lunar, knowing it would be hard for a wolf to explain the journey towards the WulfRock, and the secrets half-revealed along the way. 'But for now, father, forget your aching limbs and see that far horizon as just ahead, and we'll be there in no time. No time is the best way to travel!'

Klimt chuckled and rose up, then shook himself as if to shake all thoughts of tiredness away, content to be so journeying, happy to be with Solar and Lunar just then, these more than any other wolves he knew and loved.

But . . .

The Heartland had faded behind him, and all in it, living and dead. Elhana . . . ah, and he could not now quite remember the look of her, the scent of her, she was . . . she had never been as close to him as others. His mother, her scent he remembered; his father, and his affectionate rough touch; and Elsinor, his first mate, and the thrill of their first meeting, and their poor young whom he had failed to protect . . .

'Father, come *on*!' It was Solar calling.

'I'm coming,' he growled, not budging. He wanted to reach the end of these thoughts before he started forward once more, this time eastward across the Ukraine, to a new phase in his life.

. . . their poor young, and that cub the Mann had nailed by her paws to a tree, who had been Klimt's daughter.

'Father?' It was Lunar's gentler voice.

Lunar came back to him and stared into his eyes.

'Why, he's almost as tall as me!' Klimt told himself, but it was the love in Lunar's eyes that was the greater surprise, and the kindness, as if he understood, which he could not. Of those things Klimt had spoken only to Tervicz.

'What is it?' asked Lunar.

Klimt looked away, shaking his head, suddenly vulnerable.

'I was thinking of things I had put away in my mind, and a cub the Mennen killed.'

'What cub?'

'Your half-sister.'

They spoke softly and Klimt felt an urge to weep and howl. First one tear and then another came to his eyes.

'You'll tell us one of these days, won't you? You've never talked about the past.'

'I will . . . I will . . .'

Lunar turned to lead them off and Klimt paused only a moment or two more, moments in which he tried to remember Elhana again, the feel and scent of her, and was hardly able to. Then Jicin, clear as the sky above, firm as the ground below, her scent and touch and being as easy to bring to mind as Elhana's were difficult. He started forward into a new world, a new time, his step confident, for in this new place, though she were so many miles away, and behind, he knew he would find her once again.

'Oh, *Jicin*,' he whispered, and then he knew that Elhana was finally behind him for ever now, but that Jicin was ahead and still to come.

'Oh Wulf, I have missed her,' he sighed.

Thus far their route had been through the foothill country of the eastern flanks of the Carpathians, but now the wolfways in the stars, which the Wanderer had taught them and which Lunar remembered best of all and could howl down with ease, took them eastwards on to the flat Ukrainian steppelands. It was hotter than they were used to, a dry beating heat, and the black soils of the low vales they traversed were dusty, and parching.

Now the view ahead was restricted by the general flatness, and even from the higher ground they found the prospect was hazy and warped with rising heat. Now and then they came across vast tracts of ruined ground, where the natural vegetation seemed to have given up and died, and the winter rains to have eroded deep and complex gulleys that stretched north to south, whose slopes and ribbed beds impeded their progress.

Here there were small groups of Mennen living whose sweet and sour odour on the warm summer breeze gave away their presence from far off; here, too, if they approached too close their own scent was picked up by the dogs the Mennen kept, or which lurked where Mennen were, singly and in dangerous packs – very dangerous packs.

Once they were chased by eight or nine such dogs, all shapes and sizes, all filthy and with bodies tattered and torn, patched and lacklustre with infection and parasites, and most with unhealed wounds, the signs of constant in-fighting and malnourishment. Klimt remembered well Elhana's description of being so chased in North Italy, and how she and Ambato escaped across a river. They did so now, though escape was not difficult, for they found they were fitter by far than the dogs, and for the brief moments when the two groups clashed, before Klimt and the others prudently fled, it was plain enough that the Wolves were better, quicker fighters too. All except Lunar that is, who had never enjoyed fighting much and had usually had the stronger Solar nearby to give him support.

'You're going to have to learn some fighting skills, wolf,' said Klimt later, when they were on the far side of the river they had swum and idly watching and the dog pack trying to make up its collective and fractious mind whether or not to cross.

'You've relied too much on being fast on your feet, Lunar,' said his brother with some justice, 'and one of these days . . .'

Lunar frowned, extending his head along his legs and paws and staring at the vacillating dogs.

'Defeating another is a matter of focus,' said Klimt, 'of seeing nothing but the objective, which is winning, and of seeing your opponent as a part of you which is in the way.'

'A part of you?' murmured Lunar, intrigued.

'I am not very good at putting it into words,' said Klimt, who never had been.

'Like this?' said Lunar, rising and starting forward into the water, straight towards the dogs.

'Shit!' said Solar, rising immediately to follow him, for almost as one the dogs had seen Lunar's move and come forward barking and snarling. 'He always was inclined to do foolish things.'

Klimt rose also, and stood watching impassively as Solar followed Lunar into the water; he called after him, 'Do not be too swift to help him out, Solar.'

Then he watched, impressed that Lunar's foolish impulse showed no sign of abating as he approached the dogs – if anything he seemed spurred on by their aggression. Snarling, he clambered up the river bank, Solar not far behind and calling to him to come back.

Lunar engaged with the second biggest of the dogs, probably the leader, even as the others darted in and out, nipping, teasing, eager for signs of submission, eager to make a kill.

Which they might very well have done had not Lunar locked his jaws, turned one way and another, rolled in the dust even as the others closed right round him in a savagery of barking, and somehow managed to turn and flee back to where Solar stood guard, giving him cover as he limped into the water and swam to the other side.

He was suddenly cold and shivering and when he turned to look behind he was astonished to see Solar standing alone, hackles up, backed up right to the river's edge, the dogs forming a semi-circle about him and one, the same one as Lunar had so briefly fought, beginning to come forward.

'Watch,' said Klimt. '*Watch!*'

Solar suddenly lunged forward, but it was no feint. He went straight for the leader, caught him on one side and turned him, and even as he squealed in pain Solar pulled back to his previous position and seemed to challenge another to come for him. Then, after a few moments, he turned quite leisurely back to the river, and dived in.

'*That's* focus,' said Klimt.

'You're a silly bugger,' said Solar to Lunar when he joined them once more.

'I was . . . frightened,' said Lunar quietly. 'Until I got there I felt I could defeat them all but when I smelt them, when I heard and saw them, something in me . . . I was scared.'

Solar chuckled, and buffeted his brother affectionately. 'You've got a bruising bite on your right flank to show what a fool you are.'

Lunar looked round at it, still shivering with a delayed reaction.

'I need to learn to fight,' he conceded.

'You need to learn some common sense,' said his father. 'Shall we journey on?'

Then suddenly Klimt paused and looked at Lunar with an expression of dawning comprehension on his face.

'The way to fight,' he said, 'is no different from the way you told us to journey – keep the main objective in mind and make light of the obstacles that get in the way.'

'Or neutralize them,' said Lunar.

'And make the most of whatever advantages you find,' added Solar.

The three Wolves looked at each other with a sudden sense that they were at one and each understood something better than they had before.

'You're a wise wolf, father,' observed Lunar, starting forward once again, Solar just behind.

Klimt watched after them, shaking his head and thinking he was not wise at all – it was Lunar who had found his own way to understanding.

'Doesn't mean there aren't things to learn about fighting,' he muttered as he followed them.

'He knows that!' said Solar.

Klimt laughed, a thing he had done so rarely in the past but which now he intended to do a great deal more frequently.

Five days later the wound Lunar had suffered had not healed and he became feverish with it, and strange. He turned on Solar, muttering about fighting, and at the sides of his mouth were white-yellow foam and phlegm; his eyes became watery and bloodshot, and when Solar turned from him upslope, he had no strength to follow.

They holed up in dry gulley ground, a stream nearby for water, vole and the occasional rabbit for food. Lunar grew weak, muttering and forlorn, and for more than a day he wept for Merrow; and another day he wept for Solar.

'I'm here, wolf, I'm here,' whispered Solar. Lunar had given up trying to fight him and now clung to him as if without Solar's constant presence he might drift away and fall into a black void of nothingness. *'I'm here!'*

Lunar would not let Klimt near him, nor even eat food which he saw, or thought he saw, Klimt had killed. He would snarl at him and speak foul words and grin oddly, as if convinced Klimt was evil and meant him harm. Lunar's breath became malodorous and foul, his breathing heavy and laboured, and if ever Klimt had wondered about the affection between those two – for Solar had been brutal to Lunar when they were young – he did not doubt it now.

Only when Lunar slept could Solar get away for a little, and then never far. He would go down to the nearby stream and bathe in its cool waters as if he needed to cleanse himself a little of that infection that had taken hold of his brother. Klimt would join him sometimes and try to say that it seemed to him that Lunar was not merely ill in body, but struggling in mind as well.

'He's wrestling with something, he's fighting something he can't see – perhaps that day he turned back towards the dog pack he was turning towards something else as well, as if he had seen some danger he must confront, something he feared but knew he must conquer, something . . . why, Solar, what is it?'

Solar came out of the water and slumped dripping at Klimt's side. 'We never told you about that time we followed the Wanderer and left you all for a short while.'

'For weeks, wolf, *weeks*. I was terrified.'

'Let me try to tell you what happened . . .'

The two Wolves talked, and when they heard Lunar's moan went back to tend him until, when he slept again, they talked further. Or rather Solar tried to tell Klimt about the shifting mists in the gulley that led towards the WulfRock, and how Lunar went on ahead and

how he had seen, or thought he had, a different place and something
that had terrified him.

'He saw me dying, father, and saw me dead. A forest, mountains,
a river, cooler, lusher, less alien than here. He did not want to go on
alone.'

'And you? What did you see?'

Solar shrugged. 'Him alone. Saw him alone, like he is now, alone
and lost and struggling, trying to find a way forward. I've always seemed
to you others the strongest, but he's stronger than me and more
courageous. Give me a territory and I'll defend it, just as you taught
me to. Give me a pack and I'll dominate it. You taught me that as
well. But show Lunar a country he has not seen before and he'll
conquer it.'

'I'm not sure what you mean,' said Klimt. 'I'm not even sure what
we've been talking about.'

'Nor I,' said Solar. 'Yet . . . he's the one, father, he's the one.'

'What one?'

'The one the She-wolf came to see when we were born, the one
who would be Wulf and find His way back to the WulfRock and the
wolfway to the stars.'

'*Noooo!*' cried Klimt, standing up and glowering, for that could not
be. It was Solar, it had always been him. He looked at the stricken
Lunar, taking in the mucus at his mouth, his clogged-up eyes, the
flies that hovered and darted in and out at his face and body-wound,
and the way his flanks heaved so painfully in and out with each
laboured breath. 'No, not him! He is not the one, you are!'

Lunar's eyes opened, he struggled to fours, saw Klimt standing over
him, and snarled, a broken, rasping snarl.

'Get him away from me, Solar, get the bastard away . . .'

Klimt turned and left them to it.

Not Solar? *Lunar?* Surely not . . .

'What is this journey of ours and where is it taking us to?' he asked
himself. 'Where are we now?'

He eyed the dry, eroded landscape below them which shimmered
in the sun; its southern horizon seemed to part company with itself
and turn upside-down and –

Dogs, four of them, walking upside-down, slowly, stopping.

He lowered his body cautiously, peered, shook the flies from his
cheeks and turned calmly back to Solar. His glance was enough to
indicate that he had seen possible danger, and Solar whispered to

Lunar to stay quiet for there was danger near. 'Shhhhh . . . brother. I'll not be far.'

The dogs paused in their upside-down journey in the shimmering sun, their paws not quite touching the liquid, sliding ground. They turned and seemed to become one, coming nearer, approaching from far downslope, across the crusty, black-grey earth. Then they were close enough to be seen more clearly, and as their feet touched the ground at last they became the right way up, and their bodies gained colour, turning from shadow-grey to mongrel beige and yellow and brown, and the watching Wolves saw that there were four after all, walking in single file towards them, almost wolflike.

Four of them, one of whom they remembered, for he was the leader of the pack they had fought days before.

'Weeks before,' murmured Klimt, 'for time is passing more swiftly than we think.'

The dogs were all achingly thin and haggard, with their tongues lolling out.

'They've come for water from the stream, not for us,' said Solar.

'Humph!' said Klimt, eyes narrow, nostrils flaring.

But they had not. They seemed bent on going nowhere, a strange procession of aimlessness, beginning up the steeper part of the slope now, not yet within scent, then pausing because one of them, the second to last, had slowed, had stopped, had begun to whine. The other three attacked him, the leader first, and if it was liquid they sought to quench their thirst it was blood they got, the thin, weak blood of a dying dog, drying and congealing in the sun.

Klimt stayed watching the motley trio as Solar went back to Lunar, and the sun began to set.

'He wants water,' whispered Solar, returning.

'Take him,' said Klimt firmly, 'for these dogs pose no threat. Anyway, I think they've scented us.'

Certainly the leader looked their way occasionally, growling a little, but not moving from where he had slumped, except to whisk his tail and send a cloud of flies briefly up into the air, thick enough to be seen in silhouette against the clear, remorseless sky.

Solar led Lunar to the water and though the dog leader briefly tried to rise, he soon slumped back again, indifferently. Rather more than night was closing in on him.

Come dawn Lunar was better than for days past, and the three dogs seemed all but dead. The wind had shifted and brought with it their odour, which was the same as Lunar's breath, foul and thick, stenchy and off-putting as shit.

'They're sick like him,' said Klimt.

Morning brought something more, before which Solar and Klimt forced the reluctant Lunar up again and into retreat, to find a cave of sorts in the shaley gulley from where they could watch the dogs dying, and drying in the sun.

Mennen came, very slowly, two of them, upslope as the dogs had done. Perhaps they had tracked the dogs, or maybe they were following the same death trail. The Mennen staggered up, one of the dogs tried to move but failed, and the Mennen cut its throat, its last squeal of terror cut short to a gurgle and silence by the knife. The Mennen stabbed at the other dogs, suddenly, wildly in the rising sun, bloody red and flailing into its light, red with canine blood, laughing and rasping at the same time.

Then they sat, staring, laughing until one got up, and the other followed, laughing, ha-ha-ha up the gulley, ha-ha-ha. Then the second raised his knife and stabbed the other in the back, and both collapsed, laughing, ha-ha-ha, and screaming.

The Wolves stared all day at the stabber, the laughing man, dying, reaching towards water he could not seem to find, and as the upslope wind strengthened the odour of Mennen and dead dogs, of sickness, the foul shit-stench came to them and slowly, quietly, Lunar laughed.

'Better,' he said; 'I *am*. What's that stink?'

'You and them,' said Solar, 'all of you.'

Next day, before the dawn light revealed too much of the scene below, and how the sick surviving man had crawled upslope towards them in the night, which they had heard and ignored, they moved on.

Half an hour, the first day, just across the river to some shade. An hour the next dawn, until it became too warm. More the next day, and more in the day following, on and on, and on now as if they had lost so much time through Lunar's illness they had to catch up with themselves.

'Come on, Lunar, come on!' cried Solar, 'race you to the top!'

After that, and before Khazaria, which is further than most wolves ever travel in one journey in ten lifetimes, they remembered hardly anything. Just snatches of a landscape that was endlessly flat, or endlessly undulating – for soon the slightest slope seemed like a hill – and whose tracts were defined by the rivers that separated them, and the roads they followed.

A whole village of Mennen dead, desiccated in the sun, and the odours of the plague that Lunar had suffered lingering in the shade; what had been bodies, but were only skin and scattered bones now, and jagged-toothed jaws among the fluttering clothes; hour upon hour, alone on the roads; nothing alive but the corvids, and buzzards circling; whole regions devoid of life, but for snakes and, strangely, the rivers croaking with toads, alive with lizards. Whilst across the landscape, for days and days as they travelled through it, the south-eastward drift of smoke from Wulf knew what mighty conflagration north or north-west.

Then, weeks on, Lunar's illness a nightmare past, their talk now almost non-existent, their sense of oneness nearly absolute, the Steppes petered out and ended, and Lunar said, 'Nearly there, nearly there. Let's wait for night and the help of the stars.'

That night Lunar howled, for the wolfways were shifting and changing and he had reached the limit of his memory.

'Ahead's the Volga, an hour or so,' he said, as if the howl, though unanswered, sent back an echo he understood. 'We go north and north-east now towards Khazaria, into Khazaria.'

Klimt was silent and at peace; Solar no longer asked how far. Lunar had learned something about fighting, about focus, which might stand him in better stead than the kind of fighting arts that Klimt knew so well.

'Even so,' said Klimt in the days that followed, as they trotted steadily north, expert now at evading trouble, pleased in a way to see living Mennen and their houses once more, 'you might be advised to let us teach you something of fighting in the time we have left.'

'What time?' asked Solar.

Klimt did not quite know, except there was not much of it.

So in the days that followed they slowed down, and each showed Lunar what they knew; and each day Lunar howled down the route they would follow the day after; and each day those three Wolves cared less and less for what had gone before, or what lay ahead.

'You're thin as a foxglove stem, father,' said Lunar one night, 'your legs –'

Klimt turned, roared, mock-raged and attacked, and Lunar feinted, escaped, turned back and might have had his father by the throat if he had been able to stop laughing; and Solar did have Lunar by the throat *because* he was laughing.

'Pay attention to the others, fool,' said Solar. 'A battle for leadership is one to one, but Wulf knows who may join the fight against you in all other situations.'

Lunar pulled himself free and howled up into the starry, Kazakh night, the wolfways above bounded to the east of them by the great, dark gash through the stars of the pattern that was the Volga.

'Where are we?' Solar wondered.

'Nearly there.'

'Listen,' whispered Klimt, rising, the hackles on his back lifting with strange excitement, 'just *listen* . . .'

It was a howling, distant but clear, along the upland Volga way, not far now, not far; nor was it hostile, nor . . .

'Oh, listen . . .' cried Klimt, howling in answer to what he heard.

For it was the howling of wolves, of a pack, of packs perhaps, who were not afraid to be heard, not afraid at all: the howling of wolves who believed in their own ascendancy.

'We're nearly there!' said Lunar, his voice faltering, his head lowering.

'Why do you weep, brother?' asked Solar.

'Because I never knew the way, the Wanderer never taught it me, not really; I never knew.'

Solar chuckled deeply; 'You're a fool, Lunar, always were and always will be.' It was a compliment, and a declaration of abiding love.

'No – we are there!' said Lunar suddenly alert, his head rising.

For there, in the starry darkness, came a wolf, whose size was impossible to make out exactly. He had come from downwind of them, expertly. They could see the brightness of his eyes, and the gloss of his coat where the moonlight caught it. He was big, very big, yet he did not come too near.

'Who are you?' he asked evenly, and with the kind of confidence that suggested that some way behind him, hidden in the darkness, there were other wolves watching, ready to give support if he needed it.

'Three travellers,' said Klimt, coming forward.

'Evidently so,' said the wolf, 'but from where?'

'From the west – our pack was in trouble and we have come to ask –'

'You admit you are from the west?' demanded the wolf. The point seemed important to him, and indeed, two of those they had suspected were behind him came forward, their eyes and teeth glinting in the dark.

'Is there any reason why we should not be?'

The wolf laughed ironically and turned briefly to glance at his colleagues.

'What is it you want?'

'A meeting with the Kazan, to ask –'

'That is your right, of course, but whether or not –'

One of the other wolves whispered to him for a few moments before he continued.

'We are Kazakh wolves and you have entered the territory we patrol – indeed you did so yesterday and we have been watching you since. You will stay here for four days – there is a stream for water along the way you have just come, and a quarry nearby where rabbits abound. If you are disease-free after that time, and still wish to journey northward to, er, meet the Kazan, as you somewhat disrespectfully put it, we shall guide you on for a time. Understand?'

'But –'

'*Understand?*'

Three more of the wolves came forward, all large, all staring fiercely.

'Yes,' said Klimt, 'I think we do.'

'Now, what territory did you say you were from?'

'We didn't,' said Klimt, 'but we come from the Heartland.'

The Kazakh wolf stared at them in surprise and then relaxed.

'But this *is* the Heartland,' he said chuckling as if Klimt had cracked a joke, 'and there is no other. Rest up a few days, prove yourselves healthy enough to enter our territory, and then we shall return.'

Then he and his colleagues faded into the darkness of the sky behind, and where he had stood shone stars.

CHAPTER SIXTEEN

*Klimt and his sons fight for a place in the Kazakh Pack and
see that escape may prove difficult*

FIVE DAYS after his first appearance before Klimt and the
others, the Kazakh wolf returned, this time with four of his
friends. They all stayed their distance, from where they asked
sufficient questions to satisfy themselves that the Wolves were not ill
or diseased in any way. Only then did they come nearer and examine
them more carefully, seeming not entirely convinced that Lunar's
wound, now healed but still showing red beneath his fur, was merely
the result of 'a fight with dogs', which was only half the truth. They
did not ask for names, or offer any, nor was there any further reference
to 'Heartlands', real or imaginary.

'You seem healthy enough to us,' said the one who seemed always
to speak for the others, eventually. 'You still want to journey to seek
an audience with the Kazan wolf?'

'We do,' said Klimt. 'Our kind needs his assistance.'

'Interesting,' said the Kazakh wolf, 'and original. Plenty come to
find him but we have never heard of any wolf asking for his help.'

Klimt shrugged and said, 'What do they come for then?'

'To worship him of course; to pay their respects and offer up their
lives to his service.'

'Humph!' said Klimt. It was his turn to sound non-committal.

'But you seem different from such wolves . . . so what do you need
help for?'

'We prefer to talk to him direct.'

'Hmmm,' said the wolf, 'no one can stop you seeking an audience,
that's your right. Whether you'll get one is another matter, but one
of the Seniors will sort you out.'

It suddenly became clear that these wolves were little more than
messengers for others more powerful than themselves and that it was
these 'Seniors' they must contrive to reach.

'Let's not hang about then,' said Klimt, assuming that formidable tone of command which he had not used for so many weeks, but which could be so intimidating and full of menace.

'Of course not,' said the wolf, rather more respectfully. 'Today we shall travel until midday and then rest up for the night. We Kazakh wolves prefer night travel in this region if the weather and stars permit it, but for now the route is clear.'

He did not say clear of what, and his colleagues had a final consultation together and then set off, some ahead and some behind, no doubt to take up outpost positions along the way and leaving the Wolves in little doubt there might be no easy turning back.

The Wolves' chance for further conversation with the Kazakh who had done all the talking came only at midday, after a steady northward trek through open mixed pasture and forest country, which like so many other areas the Wolves had seen was woefully lacking in signs of living Mennen or their livestock.

The Kazakh wolf's impassive friends had stayed their distance, appearing now and then ahead and behind and to the flanks.

'They're watching against what?' asked Solar, who did not like mysteries.

'Dangers,' growled the wolf, 'within and without. Be patient, my friends, and ask another, for I am merely your guide.'

'What is your name?' asked Solar, trying to sound patient.

'My name is not important, for I will be with you only a day or two longer. Then one more senior than I will take you on. Call me Six.'

'Six?' said Klimt. 'A strange name.'

'There are only four others of you, where's the fifth?' asked Lunar with a smile.

'There's nine in a patrol,' said Six seriously, 'each more senior than the next. I shall be Seven before long . . .'

The wolf allowed himself a slight smile of satisfaction and added, 'It took only four and a half years to reach the Fifth rank, but you could say I was lucky.'

'Lucky?'

'Mennen killed four above me so I moved up to Five very quickly. Becoming Six took longer, but I am well satisfied. But please, no more questions, for I am not meant to answer them.'

'What happens when you become number Nine?' Lunar could not help asking.

'Then I will have earned the right to join the Heartland Pack, though whether I shall be strong enough to win a place is another matter.'

This was something that plainly weighed on the wolf's mind for he added quietly, 'We must fight for the privilege. If we lose then we are cast out as flawed.'

'Cast out?' said Klimt.

'Into the Quarry; but you shall see, they will show you I expect. *Please*, no more questions.'

The Wolves glanced at each other, thinking that with replies like these which provoked more questions than they answered, it was little wonder that others were curious.

'You get many outsiders like us?' persisted Lunar.

'Not so many now, since three or four years ago when the Mennen wars began,' said Six. 'In my time with this patrol we have never had as many as three together, and never before so many from the west . . .'

He stared at them ruminatively, plainly curious and wanting to ask more but feeling he should not.

Then he said, 'You are celebrities already because of where you've come from and the Seniors will be interested to question you, though dubious. We do not understand how you survived the plague. This is the most responsible assignment I have ever had, but little can go wrong – you will be watched all the way until you reach the Ruined Lands and after that a Senior will take you on, Busak probably. He trained me – he is good with strangers, with new wolves, he – I should not talk so much, for Five will report me. That's *his* task.'

The wolf laughed suddenly and rather bitterly, like one who knows the risks he takes but on this occasion has worked them out and feels he has an advantage of some kind.

'Busak,' murmured Lunar, who was better than either Klimt or Solar at getting others to talk.

'He is a good wolf, a worthy Senior,' said Six.

That night they continued their journey by following a wolfway of stars which Six clearly knew well but would not howl down for them, so it was not easy to tell which stars and star-lines he was using, though Lunar worked it out by deduction as they went.

The second night was cloudy and Six this time relied for his route-finding partly on signal howls and barks with his invisible friends, but also on occasional sightings of the lights, some stationary, others moving back and forth, along the great waterway that lay in the valley to their right.

'The Volga,' he said, and there was wistfulness in his voice.

'Your home territory?' surmised Lunar.

'Yes, until the Mennen destroyed it. My part of it is further upriver than you see there.'

'But there are lights on it – are the Mennen not active there?'

'There, yes, but higher up . . . !' he said sharply. 'Wait until tomorrow, wolf, *then* you may catch a glimpse of what they have made of my home territory!'

The morrow brought some dawn-time journeying and then a rest until late afternoon when they pressed on once more, this time turning north-eastward down a vale that contained a bright and cheerful river, evidently a tributary of the Volga itself. However, the Mennen villages and towns along it were all in ruins, though if war was the reason then it had passed by a long time since, for there were young shrubs growing out of the fallen masonry, and the surfaced roads and ways had grass growing through their cracks.

'Lie low! *Hide here!*'

The Wolves followed their guide's sudden warning, and found themselves above the road they had been following, among the ruins of one of the villages. The wind was upslope, and what the Kazakh wolf had seen came from downslope and down-valley, and they scented it before they saw it, and knew at once what it was.

It was the stench of that same disease that had afflicted Lunar, and those dogs and Mennen whose foul deaths the others had witnessed just before his return to health. But this time it was not dogs and Mennen that appeared, coming slowly up the valley, but two wolves, a pair by the look of them. They were gaunt of flank and their swollen tongues lolled out, all pale and coated with a noxious phlegm, rank evidence of their distemper.

'Keep down,' whispered Six, 'for though their sight is poor in this light they can detect movement and will approach anything they think is living and attack it. A bite from one of them will give you the same plague they suffer from and it will begin to show after three days.'

'Hence the four days you insisted that we waited,' murmured Solar.

'Quite so. Two years ago the Kazakh wolves were decimated by this disease, which came up from the south. Naturally the Kazan wolf himself did not suffer it, for he is pure and knows no ill; but a number of the Seniors died. He decreed we move up into the Barysh Upland, as prophesied in Ancient Time, from where the Diseased Ones were driven off to die, or eke out their life in isolation until their death . . . these two here look near death to me.'

The two wolves had paused, the male having turned back towards the female who had stopped and lain down, as if too tired or ill to continue. How weary the male himself seemed, yet how gently he nudged and nuzzled at his stricken mate, and then – and how desperate and pathetic it was – he uttered up a cracked thin howl for help and succour towards the darkening sky, and to the gods who had forsaken him.

'These tainted wolves are cursed by Wulf and Wulfin,' whispered Six, 'and this is the punishment for their crimes.'

'Which are?'

'Rejection of the Kazan wolf,' said Six shortly.

'Sounds like *he's* rejected *them*,' said Lunar.

Six shook his head. 'They would not be ill if he had, my friend; which is why the prospect for yourselves to become worshippers is good, for you are untainted and must have his protection.'

'What of a wolf that recovers from this plague?' asked Solar, winking at Lunar.

'None has ever recovered, or can recover,' said Six firmly, 'but if he did then surely he would be a Maimed wolf.'

'A "Maimed" wolf?' queried Lunar, who had not missed the peculiarly dark emphasis Six had given to the word.

'A wolf turned and twisted from the Kazan's way, which is of obedience and faith. He, or she, would give themselves away as such wolves always do. "Beware the wolf who doubts the word of one more Senior than he for surely he is Maimed and shall be cursed and cast from out the pack into death itself", as Kazan the Good put it.'

It seemed to his listeners that the more Six talked, the more he seemed to be hedged in by superstition and prejudice, and some twisted and warped faith that emanated from, or depended upon, the office of the Kazan.

While they had been talking thus, each instinctively careful to appear to accept what Six said without question, their pose being that of naive wolves who appreciated any guidance offered them, the stricken female on the slopes by the river below them seemed to have recovered somewhat. But having risen up, and with her mate alongflank to help her, she managed only a few more steps before she collapsed again.

There she lay for a time, the afternoon drawing in, her mate clearly much distressed and uncertain what to do, though he seemed little better than she was.

'We could go on,' said Six, 'for they'll not trouble us now, but you might as well see how we drive such scum to their rightful end.'

He had hardly spoken before the Wolves noticed two of Six's colleagues stalking down-valley towards the sick wolves, and settling down to wait. A strange silence fell, broken only by the stertorous breathing of the female; in growing distress the male looked desperately around for a way to help his consort, seemingly unaware of the two wolves watching nearby, let alone the rest of them.

'Their vision declines rapidly at dusk, which is why we travel in darkness, for they skulk about, their night vision being so poor that they are virtually blind, and their faculty for scent is blurred. It is the easiest time for us to avoid them.'

Three more Kazakh wolves appeared, this time from down-valley, and they quickly and expertly formed a threatening semi-circle of wolves about the plague-ridden pair.

Then, as twilight fell, the attackers began a howl, sinister and strange, and most threatening.

'Watch now and see their punishment,' said Six most fervently, rising up, his tail frisking in excitement, and adding in a curious, zealous tone, 'for thee we do it, our Lord Kazan, to cleanse the land of filth, to free the air of the punishment of plague, to purify the waters of the poison of disease.'

The pair of wolves who were the victims of this assault responded only slowly; the female weakly raised her head, though she plainly had difficulty seeing her attackers. Nevertheless, from the sudden terror in her eyes it seemed she had already guessed what was to come.

Meanwhile her mate, frail though he was, boldly took up a defensive stance in front of her, peering hopelessly towards where he thought their attackers were, though also unable to make out the Kazakhs' rapid and mocking running back and forth.

He did not speak, but only stood his ground, baring his teeth in a display of aggression that spoke more for his courage and loyalty than his strength. Then, as the Wolves watched in horror, the advance of the Kazakhs upon him continued and his mate rose once more to her feet and retreated towards the river bank with a look that seemed to say, 'It is inevitable, my dear, and for the best; come, let us struggle no more, no more . . .'

For his part the male continued to stay his ground, though his lowered tail and desperate eyes showed he expected defeat and death. Then, into the cruel and inexorable silence of the Kazakhs' advance, he spoke.

'Each one of you knows me, for was I not Nine? Was I not your leader for a time?'

'You were, wolf, but now you are damned, proven impure by the mark of disease, the stench of your impurity foul on your breath and oozing from your arse. You are nothing now, nothing. You should have stayed in the Quarry of Redemption.'

'The Quarry of Hell, you mean,' came his reply. 'Spare her the water, at least spare her, for she is not far off her natural end, spare her and I will . . .'

He turned then towards the bank as well, and stood staring down at the river, his flanks trembling with fear.

'Spare her and I will . . .'

'Why is he afraid of the water?' whispered Lunar.

'Its touch is torture to their sores,' said Six.

'Do you know this wolf?' asked Solar, his voice betraying the outrage he felt.

Six nodded, the smug look of righteousness in his eyes. 'He was Nine when I first joined the patrol as One. Now look at him! He fought to join the Heartland Pack but lost and was sent into the Quarry. No doubt he took a vagrant female to mate, which was his right, but caught the plague from her, which is his punishment for crimes of the spirit – pride perhaps, or sloth; or dishonest thoughts. Who knows? Who cares? Now it seems he has tried to escape – which we were warned of, for they said he would come back to the part of the territory he knew best.'

Then the Kazakhs charged, brutally, and though it was hard to say if they actually touched their victims, the two stricken wolves pulled back, fell, and tumbled down towards the river and finally into it, where they screamed in pain, seeming to try to find a way out but only swimming and struggling out of their depth.

'I'm here, I'm he —' was the last they heard the male say as the current took them one after the other, turned them, struggling and crying, so palpable and mortal in their distress that the Wolves could not bear to watch it.

'My so-called brother,' said Six with disgust; and yet, did the Wolves detect regret, and guilt in the way he would not meet their gaze, and an attempt at self-justification in his muttered, 'He was justly punished'; and finally remorse in his moodiness and silence? They thought they did.

Little was said and soon afterwards Six led them down the river valley to where it opened up on to the wide-spreading plain which was the valley of the River Volga – a river greater than any the Wolves had ever seen. It stretched off into the gathering gloom of evening, a vast expanse of grey, flowing water, whose width was made to seem the greater by the presence on the far side of a few tiny Mennen lights. These were in contrast to the lack of lights on the nearside bank, whose terrain bore the black and ruined aspect of a land laid waste by Mennen war, all the more desolate for the remnants of great Mennen industries that once thrived all about.

Here, at least, the Kazakh wolf seemed to know his way with help from stars that were just beginning to show, and he turned north alongside a broken railway track, amidst the ruins of walls and cooling towers, creaking derricks and thin chimneys that rose above all else, sometimes alone and sometimes in serried ranks, sometimes straight and vertical, but as often all bent and blasted to one side.

At first the ground stank of oil and rust, later of acerbic chemicals, later still of desiccated excrement, such as that a wolf knows from fox holes whence the foxes have long since fled and died, but the wind has not yet cleansed away the smell.

Only once did their guide speak in the course of the next few hours of journeying through this desolate terrain, when he paused briefly, surveyed the scene, looked across the wastelands towards the mighty Volga and the few twinkling lights beyond, and said, 'This was once my home territory. Now, not even wolves roam it.'

At dawn they rested awhile in the lee of a gravel terrace, which marked a former course of the Volga in centuries gone by, and saw that not only was the land thereabout ruined, but the edges of the river as well, and the sandbanks that rose out of it, all covered by the black oil and filth and detritus of war. In the far distance, on the other side of the river, a Mennen craft was afloat, but stationary. There was no sign of life, but for birds diving and ducking along the shore, black, grey and nondescript like the land, and like the water, their fractious cries and squawks no happier than the creaks and groans of the ruined Mennen buildings and machines.

They set off once more at noon and finally turned north-west up a smaller valley and away from the river, leaving the desolation of its banks behind. Ahead, across their path, several of Six's friends waited, and from behind them others came.

'So . . . our part of your journey's done,' said Six matter-of-factly. 'Wait here, and do not move.'

With that, and no farewells given or expected, Six and his companions disappeared as suddenly as they had appeared, leaving the Wolves restless and uneasy, yet intrigued as well.

But the wait was not a long one, for soon afterwards they saw a wolf coming slowly down the valley towards them, alone. He had the thick-set look they were getting used to in Kazakh wolves, but his fur was grey, and his head thinning with age.

'My name is Busak and I am one of the twelve Seniors. You are Klimt, I believe? And you others are Solar and Lunar?'

'Correct,' said Klimt shortly.

'Your sons, I presume?'

Klimt smiled and said ambiguously, 'We were all members of the same pack, but now, if you don't mind, we would like –'

'You wish to meet the Kazan wolf? You . . . er . . . wish to seek his help?'

'Yes,' said Klimt. 'Can you take us to him?'

'I can, yes, and I even might – but it is not so simple, you see. We Seniors must leave it for the Pack to decide and they will say that you must join the Pack if you are to have counsel with he who is Kazan.'

'Join the Pack?' said Solar. 'But we are members of a pack already.'

'It is our way,' said the wolf. 'If you do not like it then you can always leave.'

He looked beyond them and when they turned they saw six or seven wolves, stolid Kazakh wolves every one of them.

'Some members of the Pack,' said Busak, 'and they will need to give you permission to leave.'

'It seems we are faced by no real choice,' said Klimt evenly.

'It seems that is so,' said Busak. 'Now, follow me . . .'

A new and more sombre mood settled upon the Wolves, for their earlier doubts were now confirmed: having committed themselves thus far to meet the Kazan wolf they could not now retreat safely, and to escape the devastated lands of the Kazakhs and the increasing grip the Kazan's wolves seemed to be imposing upon them might prove more than difficult.

As they followed Busak they saw the Pack members following *them*, and as they progressed through increasing evidence of the mines and quarries, spoil heaps and ruins of country abandoned by the Mennen, they saw other wolves watching, all as large, all as potentially threatening, all sombre and with the same lack of life to their eyes as the landscape itself. Then the pervading smell, the shifting sickening odours, of that same plague they had now been witness to themselves.

Busak turned and said, 'Look, wolves, to your right flank, and see the Quarry of Redemption, the fate of those who fail in the Kazan's service, or strive to diminish him.'

Ahead was a high, rough arch, blasted through a hillside, and deep enough that its centre was in shadow. Before it prowled five wolves; through and beyond it, where the arch of daylight was, they caught a glimpse of the vast Quarry, its distant walls stepped up and up in sheer cliffs of pale and dusty rock, up and up . . .

'You'll get a better view when we've climbed a bit around the edge – there!'

They all stopped and stared and saw below a terrible sight of wolves and . . . of wolves and . . .

'Are those Mennen corpses there?'

Buzak nodded grimly, not opening his mouth for the stench was foetid and retch-making.

It was the foulest sight the Wolves had ever seen: a thousand, five thousand, ten thousand tangled and broken corpses, white and grey, some only bones, some no more than heads, some less putrid than the others; all tumbled and fallen into a heap from beneath which, their bones of arms striving, their sticks of legs struggling, their heads of matted hair and skulls screaming, the lowest seemed to try to escape the weight of the newest above.

Worse, they seemed to move with smaller life, as from a distance the rotting corpse of badger or deer seems to move with maggots. Here the maggots were rooks that pecked and tore at prey and fellow-rook alike, and skulking, disease-ridden wolves, the outcasts, running and snapping at what their ebbing strength allowed until, failing finally, they lay still, among the dead Mennen, only not yet dead, where, wheeling and screaming up and then darting down again with beak and claw, the rooks attacked their softer parts.

From where the Mennen corpses of this massive pile of dead and dying came was all too plain, for at the highest edge of the quarry, at the beginning of a loathsome chute, there was a structure of some kind, a ramp or concrete edge, and over this they seemed to have been tipped.

'Watch,' said Buzak.

Above the ramp the sky darkened with a thousand rising, squalling corvids, intermixed with lapwings and with gulls, up and up to circle and wheel as the back of a truck came into view, reversing to the very edge. Several Mennen silhouettes appeared, staring down. An arm was raised. There came the whine of machinery, and with a shudder the truck seemed to rise, tilting and tipping towards the void, right up over the chute.

A moment's pause, but for the circling, diving birds above, and then an arm raised again, and lowered. The back of the truck appeared to belch, as a sick cub spits out a gobbet of mother's milk and phlegm, and out they came, turning and tumbling through the air, Mennen falling, some screaming, not quite corpses yet.

They bumped, and thumped and fell and rolled, and never quite lay still. Some moved, one sat up and roared out of the hell he found himself in, alive; and then the watching Wolves saw the birds, the half-mad wolves and – something else.

Like black rolling liquid this last thing seemed at first, too far away to make out easily, until Lunar, squinting his eyes, saw what the liquid was, rolling, running, scurrying up and down the living pile, up through skulls, down corridors of shins, in and out of tunnels of rotting clothes, but always higher, always up to where the new arrivals were, scurrying, running, fighting their way up.

'They are *rats*,' said Lunar, turning away in horror, and pulling himself back from the steep edge of the Quarry which hereabout was not quite vertical, but sloped down in such a way that a wolf falling down it would find it nigh impossible to get back up. In any case, when he looked again, Lunar saw there was a seepage of water out of the walls; their lower parts were slippery and slimy, rendering them unscalable.

'Indeed they are,' said Buzak, 'and those wolves you see down there, cursed and damned, are those who have failed the Kazan, through want of will, or through the mark of disease, which is the same, for it is the punishment of Wulf.'

Such was his passion that his voice had risen suddenly as he spoke, his eyes narrowing and his brow furrowing as white flecks of spittle appeared at the corners of his mouth.

But he was not the only one feeling passionate, or angry. For though Solar and Lunar had seen their father upset before, and angry occasionally, they had never seen him overcome with such an ice-cold rage as that which overtook him now: not that his eyes narrowed, though they grew cold, nor did his brow furrow, though they who knew him so well saw a setting and a hardening in his face that made

them understand why he had been – why he still was – such a formidable leader.

'And what would you like us three wolves to do to avoid such
"punishment"?' he asked quietly.

'Merely win a place for yourselves in the Pack!' declared Busak,
leading them further along the Quarry edge and then into the midst
of a group of buildings and workings around a rutted open space about
which a larger number of wolves than they had seen before were
scattered, staring, growling, dark, malevolent, uneasy with their
coming.

'The Pack?' said Klimt very quietly, running his eye over them,
deliberately moving near one or two to gauge their mettle and reaction
before signalling to Solar and Lunar that they must come close by.

'Most of them,' said Busak. 'You can rest for a day or two, no more.
Choose who you wish to challenge; they are all equal, there is no
precedence among them.'

Klimt looked surprised, for how could a Pack be called so which
had no hierarchy?

'Which is the strongest?'

Busak shrugged.

'It is for you to find out.'

'And we may have a day or two's respite?'

Busak nodded, evidently beginning to lose interest, thinking perhaps
it was up to the Wolves to prove themselves before he need again
concern himself with them, and their desire to meet Kazan.

As he moved off to talk to a couple of the Pack Klimt turned to his
sons, his face still hard, his voice icy in its contempt for what he had
seen.

'What do you say we do, Solar?' asked Klimt.

'Choose three of these wolves now and take them immediately.'

Klimt nodded and said, 'I agree. Surprise and ruthlessness is the
only way. But which ones? And what of Lunar, for he is not born
to fighting and most of these wolves seem well able to look after
themselves.'

Solar turned to his brother and said in a low voice, 'You'll trust
me?'

Lunar nodded. Their trust in each other was absolute. In matters
of dreaming and of wolfways, of travelling and making others feel
better than before, Lunar took precedence; but in matters of fighting,
of packs, of strategy, then surely Solar knew more than he.

'We have little time, Solar,' growled Klimt, 'for I want to act before that wolf Busak leaves us. Surprise is the best . . .'

Solar understood at once, turned from them, paced calmly among the members of the Pack, staring hard at one or two, half confronting some, brushing past others.

When he came back he looked relieved. 'Brother,' he said with a grin, 'there's one over beyond that wall who's lying low. Recently hurt in a fight I'd say, maybe when he joined this so-called Pack.'

'But if he's injured –'

'Lunar, if you're defeated you know where you may end up, and I doubt that we'll be able to stop it. Come, be sure you can see the one I mean.'

They moved a little and brought the wolf concerned into view, beyond some others. He had lighter fur than most other members of the Pack, and was of a slimmer build, though lithe of leg, and certainly no smaller than Lunar who, for all his lack of interest in fighting, was as tall as Solar, and certainly greatly toughened by their recent journey, the debilitating effects of his illness now all but gone.

Klimt saw the wolf as well, and nodded his agreement.

'Do not be diverted in your attack, wolf, and think of nothing but victory.'

'Focus,' breathed Lunar, his heart beginning to race.

'Focus,' said Klimt heavily. 'Do it the moment the others are diverted by the move I am about to make.'

'What move?'

'I have to flush out the first among these "equals", for there will be one; and Solar will take the second or third strongest, eh wolf?'

Solar nodded grimly, his eyes set very much like Klimt's; while Lunar wondered why they enjoyed a fight so much, for surely there were better ways . . . ?

'Now, where's Busak?' said Klimt heavily. He sounded at his most dangerous as he set off.

Then espying him he lowered his head and paced deliberately after him, even as he retraced part of the route they had taken and headed once more along the path that took him to the Quarry's very edge.

'Wolf!' roared Klimt suddenly, bring all to a silent standstill, 'I want a word with *you*!'

Then he charged straight at Busak, straight at the Quarry's edge, and that wolf's eyes widened in surprise, in alarm, and then in fear, which was hardly surprising: his front right paw had stumbled and slipped at the Quarry's lip and turning to save himself he saw the lurching, sickening sight of that void and hell begin to come towards him, and despite all his efforts he could not stop himself beginning his struggling, gasping fall towards it.

Then came a clench of pain at his left rump, the world jerked and shuddered about him, and he was heaved back to level ground and safety, turned and tumbled and felt his neck taken in Klimt's great jaws, which tightened sufficiently to start him choking, eyes weeping, trying to breathe, trying to regain control.

With Busak thus temporarily indisposed beneath him, Klimt calmly released his hold on the Senior wolf and looked up to see which of the Pack had been first to come forward. There were two, both large and growling, advancing on him resolutely, heads low. It was hard to say which took precedence, but certainly these were the two strongest in the Pack, and the ones who regarded themselves as first among equals.

Klimt had no time for niceties, and in any case, the further he let them advance the less his room for manoeuvre. A quick check to see that Solar was poised for attack, a moment's glance to note that Lunar was himself resolutely advancing on that wolf he had been deputed to fight, and that none others there seemed to have noticed, and then Klimt turned sideways and ran off along the quarry's edge as if suddenly afraid, leaving Buzak gasping and beginning to rise to his feet.

It was all very quick, deceptively simple, but the next outcome was utterly shocking. Klimt slowed, let the nearest of the two catch him before he dropped to the ground like a stone in water; then, thrusting his great head forcefully under the surprised wolf's belly, he grasped his further leg at the shoulder, rose up and with a tearing, grunting twist heaved him bodily out over the Quarry's edge as a father sometimes heaves a playful cub in jest.

The wolf's legs struggled in the air, his mouth opened in a howl of surprise and then a scream of fear, and down, down he fell, down . . .

Solar did not hesitate. As all eyes followed the wolf's appalling descent down through the void towards the horrors below, he charged the second wolf, teeth raking his ear and jaw, ripping at the flesh of his face for maximum pain and shock. Then, the wolf's face half hanging off, Solar ducked back and thrust forward into his throat, turned him and hustled him back towards the Quarry's edge –

'Enough! It is *enough*!'

The voice came from behind them all, and though it was strangely weak and thin it carried the sharp edge of natural authority.

'Solar! Let him go! *Solar!*'

This time it was Klimt who spoke, his eyes looking towards where the other voice had come from.

Solar raised himself from off his victim, who lay bleeding and whimpering on the ground, and turned to where Klimt pointed.

The wolf stood on a rise near one of the ruined outbuildings, flanked on either side by others of Busak's age and authority. But this one was different, very different. His fur was more white than grey, and though his face was lined and haggard with illness, his eyes were clear and stern, and shone with cold intelligence.

'Be at peace all of you, and be at *ease . . .*' he said, coming down among them to face Klimt. His voice was little more than a sigh, a sigh of weariness, and it was clear that this was the wolf they called Kazan.

But if Klimt hoped this long-sought meeting could now proceed without further trouble, and Kazan believed that he had stopped short the conflict between the three visitors and his Pack, both were mistaken. For as silence and stillness fell among the main body of the Pack a wolf ran out from nowhere, limping helter-skelter through their midst, and then off down the Quarry edge path, pursued by Lunar.

'For Wulf's sake!' hissed Solar, trying to stop him.

But Lunar seemed not to hear him and, catching up with the wolf, he pounced on top of him, tussled him to the ground, growled and pranced about for show, and ended by snarling in his face. It was at once elegant, well-done, and farcical.

'Lunar!' rasped his father helplessly.

'Where are you from?' asked the defeated but by no means subdued wolf.

'You're to tell me first,' said Lunar, strutting about as he imagined victors did.

'I am of Pechora,' was the wolf's astonishing reply. 'I'm not a *member* of this bloody Pack, for Wulf's sake. And you?'

Deflated, Lunar stilled, suddenly aware that all eyes were upon him, including not only those of Klimt and Solar, but of a wolf whose whole stance and presence told him he was, he must be, the one they called Kazan. Yet, foolish though he had seemed a moment before, strutting about and defeating a wolf already maimed, Lunar turned to that part of himself only Solar knew: the dreamer, the visionary, the one who had taught them how to travel well, the one who had come through an illness few others had survived.

'Me?' he said. 'Us?'

'Yes, all of you, for Wulf's sake?'

Lunar smiled, turned from him and went straight to the centre of the Pack. For the first time ever Klimt saw in the boldness of his stride, the way he let his gaze travel from one wolf to another, that there was a hint of the ability to lead in Lunar, and the touch of stars.

'For good or ill,' said his son calmly, 'we are of the pack the old ones called the Wolves of Time. And this wolf, this great wolf, than whom none is a better fighter, nor a wiser one, is our leader, Klimt of Tornesdal.'

'Wise is he?' said the aged white wolf. 'And great?'

He fell silent and the others backed away from Klimt and his two sons, who stood still dangerously near the Quarry's edge; in the background the roar of Mennen machinery, in their nostrils the stench of death.

Lunar was suddenly uneasy; Solar watchful; Klimt was realizing too late that they had put themselves in danger in some way he could not quite . . . *why were the others backing away? What was – ?*

There was a sudden *phut!*, and Klimt's left shoulder seemed to blow open; he slumped uncomprehendingly, turned and reached for help but found instead only that same void into which he had hurled the wolf but moments before.

'*Father!*'

It was Lunar's cry, for he saw where one of the Mennen stood by the machine across the void, pointing something at them, which had flashed at the same time as Klimt had been shot, '*Father. . . .*'

'That was one of my sons you hurled to his death, wolf,' said Kazan, even as Klimt struggled not to slip and slide away from them; he nodded at the bigger members of his Pack.

'Kill him!'

Caught between trying to reach Klimt and the charge of wolves, Solar had no chance. As his wounded father lost his grip at the Quarry's edge, blood pouring from his shoulder, his front left leg useless now, and rolled away down the steep unclimbable slope towards the detritus of dead and living far below, they descended upon him.

'Lun —!' he began to call, his eyes saying more than his voice could manage before they took him, and telling Lunar to flee, to get away, for he was the only one who had a chance, '*Lunar, I command you to escape!*'

Lunar turned away in shock, in obedience, in panic, in a turmoil of everything and found the only wolf in his path was the Pechoran he had defeated earlier. He started to run as behind him Solar began to die, and his father fell to what must surely be his death as well.

To run, to flee, to hasten from the paw-steps pursuing him, this way and that among the Mennen ruins, on and on, until his chest began to burst and the forest trees he saw ahead seemed to come no nearer, no nearer . . .

Father, Solar, help me . . .

He turned, unable to go on and found himself facing his pursuer, the Pechoran wolf.

'Come on!' said that injured wolf, and Lunar was glad to follow him into the forest, into the night, to try to escape, to try to get help.

'Come *on!*'

And Lunar sobbed, for in his very heart he felt his brother die, and knew his was the future burden now, his alone.

'Wolf, if you do not run they'll catch you. It is your only chance.'

Lunar saw that the Pechoran had weakened now and seemed unable to go on. He looked into his eyes and sensed fear and hopelessness.

'It is *our* only chance,' said Lunar purposefully, buffeting him upright again. 'Come, now, for Wulf and destiny is with us, *come . . .*'

IV

A NEW LEADER RISES

CHAPTER SEVENTEEN

Lunar summons the aid of the Pechoran wolves

LUNAR'S FLIGHT from the Kazakh wolves, in obedience to Solar's last desperate command and his own fear, stopped as suddenly as it had begun. He and the injured Pechoran wolf had reached the safety of some scrubland and, turning about and scenting at the air, they knew they were not pursued.

'We should go on . . .' gasped the Pechoran, his sides heaving with the effort of flight and his faced creased in pain from the sharp aching the running had brought into his injured legs.

But Lunar was not listening. He stood amongst the shifting grass and branches of the undergrowth staring out over the rough ground they had crossed towards the now distant outlines of the Mennen buildings near the Quarry. The only movement he could see was the circling of birds preying on the human corpses that lay in the void of the Quarry beyond; the only sound was the dull roar of machinery, indifferent to the drama and the tragedy of wolves.

'Solar . . . my brother is alive and I must go to him.'

'They will kill you too,' said the Pechoran.

'What's your name, wolf?'

'Utin,' replied the wolf sullenly, his flanks trembling, his tongue out on one side of his mouth.

'Then stay here, Utin, for I shall return, and I shall need your help,' said Lunar. 'Pechoran, are you?'

'What of it? What do you know about us?'

Lunar stared at him seriously and said quietly, 'Enough to know our meeting was to be. Enough to know that once you counted wolves like the great Kobrin amongst your leaders, the courageous Semenov and the contrite Gorodok.'

The Pechoran looked at him in astonishment and half rose, as much in fear as anything else, half suspecting that Lunar was some kind of spy, cleverly sent by the Kazakhs to find out things he might not otherwise have spoken of, even under duress.

'Save your energy, Utin, because most likely you're going to need it all. I know those names because Kobrin himself told me the story of how his sister Yashka came to be saved, and how Semenov –'

'What wolf are you that knows the name of my father?'

'The one you were sent to find, wolf,' said Lunar softly, 'that's who I am. Now, stay here and rest and do not move, otherwise I'll track you down later.'

'I'll stay for Wulf's sake,' said Utin, his fear replaced by awe, 'I'll *stay . . . now . . .'*

Only a moment after Lunar ran out of the undergrowth and back towards the Quarry buildings he heard Solar's fading call, and knew him to be alive, and near.

'Lunar!'

'Solar!'

How strange the call, how nearly lost, and how familiar the loss that Lunar now began to feel. The Mennen buildings gave way to jutting rocks, which loomed before him out of a shifting, mountain mist that obscured nearly everything.

'Lunar!'

Lunar ran on through the darkening mist for quite a time before it thinned and he saw new light again, bringing him to a place more jutty, more rocky, more awesome than before. The bones of rabbits lay across the sward. From high above, where the sun was, beyond the veils and skeins of mist, the shrill call of eagles came, and the answering grumbling racket of ravens. The bones of rabbits, as white-grey as edelweiss and . . . bones of a wolf. The skull of a wolf.

He knew this place, and that he was near the WulfRock, to where his wounded brother was trying to run.

Lunar went to the skull of wolf, and scented its picked-out, leached-out purity. It smelt of the sweetest grass, and saxifrage. It smelt of their Heartland home.

Solar! Lunar felt mortal fear.

He nuzzled at the skull for a moment, looked back for his brother and then knew suddenly that Solar must have passed him by and gone ahead upslope, towards that place to which he knew he had been before or would go, would one day go . . . He ran on, and on, and about him too time seemed to shift, as mobile and uncertain as the mist.

He ran on, and then on, the sound of his paws seeming to come from ahead of him, as if he were late and they had gone on before, far ahead, and he might never quite catch them up.

'Solar!'

The strange-shaped rocks, all about and many above, were wolflike now, moving against the mist and looming in the light. Then he saw a wolf, he was sure he did. She stared at him and he turned to her and then she moved, she shifted, she was ahead again, on the other side, a male now, older, running . . .

'Solar!' It must be him.

Sunlight from a blue, blue sky, the green sward of a valley, summer flowers yellow and shining, and a wolf lying there, mortally hurt, staring and helpless, worn by injury and strain, helpless and broken, and a river running nearby, blue as the summer sky above.

Lunar knew that wolf as Solar, a wolf he knew once long ago, and a wolf he might know in some future time.

'No!' he cried, terrified at last, and knowing he had come too far away from mortality and risked too much. '*No!*'

The howling of wolves echoed among the clefts and overhangs above, seeming to come from out of the shifting mists that hid their highest parts. He looked up, the sound of the howl seeking to draw him back from where he was trying to go, back into the mists of earlier time, his rightful time.

'Lunar . . .' they called, the wolves that howled, and it was a summons back again, to where he was needed now. Ahead the ground seemed to rise, but only a little before it fell away, only a step or two more . . .

Lunar took those steps, he saw the mist break once more, he stared down towards a river shining blue with summer light, and a great ancient forest behind. And he saw something he did not wish to see . . .

The howling came at him from the mists and cliffs above, 'Lunar, Lunar, come back to us, come back . . .' and finally, mortally afraid at last, he strove to turn away . . .

. . . Whilst Solar, torn and bleeding from the Pechoran assault upon him, turned at the sound of the howling too, and heard his own name called. Then, seeming to fall back into summer sunlight, the river's flow nearby, the flow of a life that he was leaving now, he found he was unable to rise. Behind him a river roared suddenly, near enough that its spray came sometimes on to him.

He saw a forest, he saw a wolf, old with worry and concern, and from out of the darkness that began to come on him now he felt a pity and an understanding that seemed bigger than the sky itself.

'No,' he cried, 'not *you* . . .'

Then Solar howled for pity, and for love, as he rose again, lighter now, his body hurting no more, and climbed up a slope too steep as yet for Lunar to be able to follow him.

'No!' wept Lunar, seeing his brother climbing up into the misty mysteries of a looming darkness that seemed like a cliff that moved, a tower that stood still, a thousand clefts that rose into one great Rock, which was of Wulf.

'I shall wait for you, Lunar, until your task is done and you shall take your rightful place again, we shall all wait for you . . .'

'No!' cried Lunar once again, his grief the greater because he knew that one by one he would lose them all, all the Wolves of Time, and he must ride the grief and carry on. '*No!*'

The mists of time and destiny cleared away from him and Lunar found himself standing over his brother's body; its beauty torn, its strength all gone, its eyes which once met his with love and understanding more than any other wolf, white-dead, quite empty now.

Around him the Kazakh wolves sat and scratched themselves indifferently, while beyond them the preying birds wheeled and dived down into the Quarry.

'Stay with us and be obedient, or leave and we'll track you down and punish you,' said Busak with a shrug. 'For now, we choose to rest.'

Lunar understood they thought him too weak to bother with, or too cowardly. He went to the Quarry's edge and stared down, though cautiously lest one or other of them was minded to try to hurl him into the void. He did not like these wolves, nor any longer fear them. He searched for a sighting of his father Klimt down there among the forsaken wolves, and the bodies of Mennen and the rats and saw . . . movement, yes; Klimt, no.

A Mann, alive? Klimt nearby?

He turned and walked away.

'I'll stay,' he said to Busak, 'but let me stand off from your pack awhile. I have lost my kin, I have . . .'

Busak nodded briefly, and turned to other things. The aged wolf, the one they called Kazan, lay in the shadow of a building, sleeping.

Lunar quietly left them to it, passed Solar's body without another glance, though Wulf knew the agony he felt to have to do so, and headed off across the fell towards the undergrowth to find the Pechoran wolf once more.

Utin awaited him, considerably recovered. It seemed that what had ailed him was not so much the injuries he had received some time before so much as reduced stamina; the hope that Lunar's coming now inspired had given him new strength.

'This time we must get well clear, and quickly,' said Lunar, 'for the Kazakh wolves will be coming after me, they made that clear enough. But they are smug and complacent and if we use our wits we can outmanoeuvre them even if we cannot outpace them.'

Utin listened eagerly, for he was a proud wolf of noble stock and had not enjoyed the subjugation the Kazakhs imposed any more than the Wolves themselves. He saw too that he might have more than a mere follower's role to play, for he had had time to ponder Solar's violent defeat and probable death, and the ruthless way that this wolf's father had been wounded and subsequently allowed to fall down into the Quarry.

On that score he could at least give comfort, for he had seen others tricked in the same way in his short time with the Kazakh wolves, including some of his own kind. The Mennen delivered the bodies for dumping on the far side of the Quarry from where the Kazakh wolves had made their home and then shot at any living thing that moved, be it surviving Mennen in the void below, rats, or wolves.

'We have little time,' said Lunar grimly, 'so tell me briefly of how your pack came to be here, and why you alone seem to have been spared. I would have liked to have met more of them.'

'You seemed to know of us Pechorans,' said Utin, 'though we think of ourselves as the most forgotten pack in the whole world.'

Lunar was gratified to see the brightness and intelligence that had come to Utin's eyes, and guessed him to be a worthy wolf. Well, he was going to need some reliable wolves at his flank if he was to . . .

If he was to *what?*

If he was to lead . . . the very last thing he had thought he would ever have to do. Solar was the leader, Solar . . .

But now what had happened had a pattern of growing familiarity about it, and of inevitability, as down the wolfways of the past residual memories were flooding into Lunar's mind, some of action and some of feeling, all to do with leadership, all to do with an ancient destiny which held the future of wolfkind in thrall, and would rely on him alone to see it through.

'Wolf . . .' began Utin, coming forward in sympathy, for the stranger wolf seemed stranger still, his eyes distant, his face troubled. It seemed to Utin that there was about him a quality of sunshine and of stars he had never seen in wolf before, and certainly not the moody, troubled race of wolves of which he was part.

Pechorans?

When Busak the Kazakh wolf had repeated the word so disdainfully and Kazan himself had contrived to look even more indifferent – Utin had for the first time in his life had doubts about his pack's fabled destiny. Fabled amongst whom? Now, with the extraordinary coming of this wolf Lunar, and talk of Heartlands, and the confidence he inspired without trying to, the Pechoran began to feel his pack's sense of destiny was not all self-delusion.

'*Wolf!*' said Utin again, more urgently. He fancied he heard the howling of the Kazakh wolves as they massed to chase after the Heartland wolf.

'Tell me then,' said Lunar softly, his calm astonishing, 'how come you are here, and where you advise that we should go.'

'Tell me how you know of us,' persisted Utin, his true qualities beginning now to show. Tough-minded as well as intelligent, it seemed, not the wolf he had appeared at all.

'A wolf called Kobrin journeyed many years ago from Pechora to join our pack . . .'

Utin sighed, his eyes half closing, in relief and joy to have such affirmation so swiftly given. Lunar told him how Kobrin had served at Klimt's right flank, and even now, in his leader's absence, was keeping watch over the Heartland on the Wolves' behalf, resisting the Magyars' advance in all ways that he knew, keeping those who had stayed behind safe and well.

'He is still alive?' cried Utin.

Lunar nodded. 'And what is he to you?'

'Kin, that's what; and inspiration too. No Pechoran before him or since has ever achieved what he did, and come back in the vale of his years to inspire a new generation. And he is still alive.'

'But old,' said Lunar, who found this wolf easy to talk to. His own age, confident, future hope in the way he talked. 'Now, wolf, time runs out. Tell me about your pack.'

His confidence completely gained, Utin told how after years of waiting for Kobrin's return the Pechorans had finally decided to move south from the icy wastes of the Pechora valley.

'Oil wells, spillage, destruction of our forests and then hunters coming, shooting us and trapping us, and worse things.'

It seemed the ancient cruelties to wolf had been visited upon the Pechorans, with new twists: a trapped wolf tethered and tortured for the pack to hear; cubs nailed high that their squeals of pain and terror might bring the parents within range of Mennen guns; an old male of the pack who had given service to it all his life, caught and tied to a Mennen vehicle and towed until he was not quite dead and then left for other wolves to find.

'His back-flesh was so torn and worn away from the rough road that his spine showed white and bloody.'

'And he was still alive?'

Utin nodded bleakly. 'His ears were gone, one leg torn off, and he bled from every orifice. He could no longer see and only whispered Kobrin's name, again and again, and "Find him . . . Find him now, tell him . . . our time has come." So . . . we are still numerous enough that we range our territory in three packs, one of which, the most threatened by pollution, decided to head south, with representatives from the other two packs. I am one of those – I had to fight for my place, for we all wanted to come – the first fight that I ever won.'

'Not the last, I fancy,' said Lunar, 'and if it is any consolation *you* are the first wolf *I* ever defeated!'

Utin grinned, appreciating the wry comment, and then said, 'Well, wolf, if you're the weak one of your pack Wulf knows what the strongest are like.'

'You have seen them already, and one at least is dead.'

His voice trembled and Utin hastily continued.

'We came south to find the Kazakhs, for we had heard of them, and ten days ago an advance party of us made contact with them. The rest had hidden behind in a place of pits and buildings recently ruined in the Mennen war, awaiting our reports. One of us went back to tell them what we were doing while the rest of us came on, just as you and yours did, with much the same result.

'Four of us were killed, five were pushed down into that same Quarry in which your father now finds himself, and I was spared – partly because I aped compliance, and was wounded, and because the Kazan wolf felt it wise to interrogate me.'

'So the main body of the Pechorans are still nearby, undetected?'

'They are two days off,' said Utin, glancing nervously in the direction of the Quarry and the buildings there. Again, the brief howl of wolves, and then silence, and a darkening sky.

'We have talked too long,' murmured Lunar, 'but not so long that we have not a very good start. Let us go and find the main part of your pack, and see what we can do to return in strength to this place and teach the Kazakh wolves what they should know about their bad destiny!'

Even as Klimt had begun to slip into the Quarry's void, the mounting pain in his shoulder not yet fully felt, he knew that he must not die. What he had thought was dust flying from his fur was blood, but the wound was not mortal, and though he had lost movement in his right front leg he had not lost feeling.

Solar was beyond his help, Lunar even more so, but Wulf was with them, and Wulfin, she would help them when he could not. She would see them right.

Then he was over the edge and beginning to roll, scrabbling a little at first to slow acceleration, trying to guide himself towards the less steep part, by way of scree and rubble, mud flows and . . .

THUMP! Sand; he was winded.

CRACK! THUMP! *CRACK!*

They were shooting at him still.

He strove to keep his head and spine from hitting other outcrops, and as he slowed at the bottom where the debris spread out across the Quarry floor, he tried to see some place to get to out of Mennen sight. The stink hit him as he came to a stop and gulped at the foetid air, and then he flinched at the pain of his shoulder.

THUMP! A wall of pain beyond which all seemed red haze.

Then he was up and hobbling, hurrying across Wulf knew what bones, what desiccated flesh, what pottage of surface water and human remains, and the bodies of creatures that had preyed on them and had died, or lived even now. It was an open, foul sewer of rotting decay . . .

Crack!

The shot was muted by the mess into which he drove just ahead of him as he turned another way, saw a concrete hut wall leaning to one side, cracked at its base and held upright only by the rusted reinforcing rods inside, and hid. Perhaps he drowsed off into the nightmare that had him waking with a sob, or it was the awful throb of his shoulder that caused the images of dark and noisome hell that frightened him, except that what he woke to was worse, far worse.

Night-time, the odours, thick and sickening, the steep, stepped walls of the Quarry rising to a flashing eerie sky, and the cranking roaring of machinery above, all floodlit, which bore the bodies in, and over, falling, flailing down into darkness.

Creatures darted and flitted back and forth in the night, rats, and nocturnal rooks, their feathers sheening darkly with the lights above, their eyes a-shine, their claws and beaks and pointed teeth glinting with the dying flesh and maggot ooze through which they searched and fed. Not far from where he lay an owl wrenched its beak at some thing it had found: a rat, it seemed.

Klimt felt relief to have survived until nightfall, and tried his leg. It moved, but its range was limited, and his shoulder could take no weight. He would be able to explore, to flee to a bolt-hole if he could keep one in sight, or fight for a time if he must.

Shadows loomed and there was the sudden bark of wolf nearby, a patter of paws through the dark, and a wolf's eyes stared at his. Klimt snarled, wary but unafraid. It would take an unusual wolf to get him out of this concrete hideyhole.

'You alive?'

Klimt said that he was.

'Injured?'

'No,' lied Klimt.

'Bruised?'

'And battered,' said Klimt emerging heavily into the lurid, floodlit night.

'There's seven of us down here living, though one's likely to die before the dawn. He's retching up his guts and the rats are ready to move in. He ate them, which is a mistake, and soon they'll eat him.'

'So there's six of you . . .' said Klimt to his interrogator, a wolf a good deal smaller than himself. Others of this most unwilling of packs emerged, and what little he could see of them suggested they were dispirited and ill, yet not quite without hope.

'Is there a way out?' asked Klimt, standing proud as he could, authoritative, sensing that here was a vacuum of command.

'Not that we could find.'

'Which of you is leader?'

They looked at each other, some more boldly than others, but none dared claim that role. One or two began to drift away.

'You!' said Klimt. 'You'll stay here and tell me what you know.'

He turned towards the way they had gone, lurched on his weak leg, half fell, and one of them ran forward.

'And who do you think you are?' said the wolf angrily.

Klimt buffeted him away without difficulty and said, 'Probably your only hope. Now who are you?'

The wolves sulked about a bit before one replied, 'All but one of us were in Pechora raised.'

'Pechora!'

Klimt's voice revealed his astonishment and pleasure at hearing a name he had first heard so many years before when Kobrin had joined the Wolves.

'You know of us?'

It was their turn to be surprised, and delighted too when Klimt quickly told them of how the most renowned member of their pack had successfully reached the Heartland, and was even now keeping a watchful presence there while Klimt and his sons sought the help of the Kazan wolf.

'Except that I believe it is to you that Wulf has directed me!'

For a moment the lights above the Quarry moved and grew brighter still and the wolves retreated to a darker place.

The Pechorans shook their heads and one of them said, 'You've found us too late, Klimt of Tornesdal. Believe us when we say there is no way out of here. Don't you think we've searched?'

'All you find is more rats and more piles of Mennen corpses, the ones on the far side of the Quarry being older and more decayed than that one there,' said another.

'If the Mennen got in here to excavate the place, and build their structures here, then wolves can surely get out,' said Klimt.

'The way out is too steep, or else blocked up.'

'Not too steep for a mountain wolf,' responded Klimt, 'nor are the Mennen so clever with their blocking up of routes that cunning wolves cannot find a way around or through.'

Klimt felt suddenly tired and said, 'I need to rest. Give me a day or two and then take me to the route out of here the Mennen have blocked and I swear that Wulf will help me find a way to unblock it!'

Perhaps Wulf would, but he did not do so immediately. It was a day before Klimt was able to walk more than a few steps, and a further day before he was fit enough to traverse the Quarry under cover of darkness and be shown the old way out. Now, great metal gates covered in razor wire above and to the sides blocked it, and not far beyond the Mennen stood with their guns, ready to shoot at any living thing as vehicle after vehicle arrived at the Quarry head and more Mennen bodies were tipped down.

Klimt hid and watched for many hours, and then explored the rest of the Quarry. The Pechorans were right, it was the only way out.

'Mennen must eventually sleep,' he said, 'or their activities cease for a time. If that happened then I have no doubt we could burrow under that great gate and break out. Before then we can use the dark hours to begin the task, the rest of us staying as near to this exit as we can without being seen. Our opportunity will come.'

The Pechorans were ready to believe him, and there was not one among them who questioned his strength as a leader. No wolf they had ever met commanded such respect or inspired such confidence. He might walk with a limp – now and for ever – but he had given them hope.

'When do we start?' asked one of them.

'Tonight, at dusk, we return to the gate and make ourselves hides from which we can venture out under cover of dark to prepare an escape route out of this vile place. Tonight we shall begin.'

That same night Lunar and Utin reached the scrubland hiding-place of the main pack of the Pechorans who had travelled south. There was some preliminary doubt about the newcomer, but the moment Utin explained Lunar's connection with Kobrin the pack's confidence was gained.

In any case Lunar had about him now such an infectious sense of purpose and inner confidence that it was hard not to believe in him; then too, his evident loyalty to his lost brother, and his intention of finding and rescuing his father, spoke of a wolf who prized pack and familial loyalty above his own ambition. For the Pechorans, caught in an ancient web of hope and uncertainty, a clear direction forward was a welcome inspiration.

The return of one of their number, and news that others were not yet dead, gave them new hope and a purpose, and in Lunar they found a wolf willing to give advice yet not so assertive that he wished to take command.

The pack had been twenty-eight strong when it left Pechora four months before. Of these one had died en route and ten more had gone on to find the Kazakhs, including Utin himself. Assuming most in the Quarry had survived, and counting Lunar and Klimt, it looked as if they might still muster a force of twenty-five or twenty-six at least, if only they could all get together.

Lunar saw that young Utin was liked and respected, and the more he got to know him the more he realized why: his reports were intelligent and to the point. This was a wolf to rely on, and one who had potential.

'The Kazakh wolves are fifty or sixty in number,' reported the youngster, 'of whom thirty or more gravitate about the Quarry while the others patrol a wider territory. They are hostile to newcomers as Lunar and myself know, and I doubt if I would have survived once they had extracted from me whatever information they wanted.'

'But they got nothing?'

'I feigned weakness and foolishness,' said Utin modestly. From his injuries it seemed they had done more than merely talk to him.

Two things about the Pechorans struck Lunar forcibly. The first was that to a wolf they seemed out of place in the high dry heathland of this part of Kazakhstan. Their eyes glanced to the far horizon, as if in search of mountain and snow; their fur, thicker than his own, made them look heavy and cumbersome in the warmth of the evening, though their thin legs suggested they were likely to be swifter of foot than they seemed at first glance.

The second thing Lunar observed, and he found it remarkable, was that they seemed to lack a leader. They spoke of various elders by name, but none seemed more important or respected than another, and as many females were named as males.

These were matters that Lunar wanted to explore further, but there was no time. For now they and he wished only to return to the Quarry, and do what they could to rescue their kith and kin. But Lunar soon saw that they were uncertain how to do it and, lacking clear leadership, might take a good few nights and days of further discussion to decide, which was very different from the way his pack made decisions.

'Look,' he said finally, cutting across their long debate, 'whatever we do if we leave it too long it will be too late. My brother is lost, but my father is not. If he survived the fall into the Quarry, which he probably did, and your own wolves are fit enough to talk with him, then believe me, he will have them organized into a pack in no time at all. It's his way.'

'He's assertive?' one of them said, dubiously.

'Very,' said Lunar boldly, 'and at a time like this it is what you need, what we all need. Therefore . . .'

He hesitated to voice an opinion so soon and so boldly, but they seemed only too happy that one among them, even a stranger, was prepared to give direction.

'. . . therefore, I suggest we do not delay but move off towards the Quarry. It would be better if we do not meet one of their patrols until we have tried to make contact with the wolves in the Quarry, for we do not want to alert the main Kazakh pack to our presence. If we approach from the east, from where the Mennen come with their trucks, then we will not be detected by the Kazakhs.'

'But we will be by the Mennen,' said Utin.

Lunar shrugged. 'Mennen are unobservant, especially of wolves who know how to use the shadows their concrete structures make, and the dykes and gulleys that accompany them. I learned much on my way from the Heartland and most of all I know that wolves are often safest where Mennen are thickest, and even more so if there is a war on, for then it is for their own kind that they look, not for wolves.'

'Shall we follow his advice?' said Utin, grabbing the moment.

The Pechorans nodded.

As they set off Lunar turned to them and said, 'And what of fighting, do you have it in your blood, or . . . ?'

He was not sure that wolves such as these, who seemed so fearful of individual assertion, would know how to fight.

'Do not worry,' one of their elders said disarmingly, 'if there is a fight this pack will protect you, wolf, for you brought Utin to safety. We were not taught how to take deer, or how to tackle a bear, without learning how to fight. We do not like to do it but if we must then we may as well vanquish our foes and kill them.'

There was a stolidity and common purpose to their collective gaze that took Lunar by surprise.

'And is not Kobrin of our race?' one of them murmured to general assent.

'He is,' averred Lunar.

'And what is he?'

'The greatest fighter I have ever known,' said Lunar.

'Greater even than your father Klimt?'

Lunar could not but nod his agreement.

'Then, wolf, lead us to the place where the Kazakhs dwell, and when it comes to it, leave the fighting to us and each one of us will strive to be a Kobrin, and all of us together shall be a pack that honours the name of Pechora, which is a pack of destiny.'

So Lunar found himself leading a pack of wolves who hardly knew his name, and feeling that whatever flaws and weaknesses he might have they would more than make up for them. While behind him Utin followed close, his young heart beating fast, even though his limbs ached with hurt and journeying; for there was a light to Lunar's eyes and fur, and a flow to his limbs, that made Utin dare to believe that the time of his pack had come.

'May Wulf be with us!' cried one of them, and as they followed Lunar into the night there was not a wolf there who did not have the sense that He already was.

The assistant of Matthius, the shaman son of Jakob Wald, slowed the drumming for a moment, then speeded it up more than before, then slowed it once again before stopping.

He removed the blankets covering his master from head to toe, first taking away the twelve holding stones as he had been taught, each in due order that the way back might not be confused.

Matthius Wald rose, exhausted but elated, wanting to walk and walk towards his own tiredness, to seek out immediately the last of the guides who had come to him, even as the drumming faded.

'You did well and you did right,' he told his assistant, 'for it can be dangerous to go on too long.'

'Master . . .'

'But now . . . I must rest.'

'Master . . .'

'Then we shall go on. What is it?'

Wald asked the question indifferently as he sat down. He was so tired.

'I resisted the lure of the drumming –'

'Don't!' said Wald with a grin. 'Because you can't.'

'I thought I saw a wolf.'

'You probably did.'

'A guide!'

The shaman stared hard at him. Perhaps he did.

'You just saw him?'

'He was nearby.'

'Did he have a name?'

'Wald's assistant nodded nervously. 'I think he did.'

Wald laughed. 'He did or he didn't?'

'He did.'

'Which was?'

'Leon.'

Wald grew serious. He knew which one Leon was. He knew as well it had been that wolf, of Spain, saved and taught by Galliard, companion to Klimt's mate Jicin, who had come to him just as his journey had ended with the fading of the drum.

Wald nodded and muttered, 'Leon.'

'You know of him, Master.'

'I do ...'

They made a fire and Wald, too tired to sleep as yet, took his assistant on a waking journey, for the Wolves were on the wolfways now and beginning to need to seek out the Heartland once again, and the WulfRock too. Time was advancing ever more rapidly.

'Master, are you going to tell me?'

'Heuren Sie,' whispered Wald in the old way, 'listen now ...'

CHAPTER EIGHTEEN

*Leon whiles away the night hours with a telling of Galliard's
tale, and how his life came to a heroic end*

LEON AND the other wolves who found themselves at Brive,
voluntarily or otherwise, soon found the night tedious and
stressful. The grey skies of the day before thickened into heavy
cloud cover, and as the air cooled, drizzle began to fall. Yet this was
welcomed by the wolves, for it made their discovery less likely. Though
so enshadowed and overgrown with weeds was the place Maladon led
them to, which was the narrow space between the wire fence of the
compound and a solid wooden boundary fence, that there seemed
little chance they would be seen.

Only dogs perhaps might scent them out . . .

'Dogs rarely come into the zoo grounds,' said Maladon, 'and never
alone and without the Mennen. You will not be seen.'

She had ordered them to be silent, but so well hidden were they,
and so interested were the zoo wolves to hear something more of who
they were, and how they came to be at Brive, that Leon was allowed
to tell his story. Some of it Jicin and the others already knew, but that
part which interested the Brive wolves most, which concerned Galliard, and his death, they had not heard before. Perhaps in the shadow
of that night of cold and drizzle, before a dawn came which might
determine all their fates, was the right time to tell it.

Leon was reluctant at first to answer the question one of the zoo
wolves asked: 'What did Galliard say about his life here and how he
left?'

Only when Maladon insisted on being told, even after Leon had
warned her that the story was not entirely complimentary to herself,
did he begin – and when he did he spoke in a strange sing-song
manner, interspersed with soft rills and howls, just as he remembered
Galliard telling the story so many times, which in some ways was all
he had to tell . . .

*Listen to the story of a wolf who once lived, called Galliard's
story. I howl it in the way he howled it to me and will seek to
honour him by becoming him for this telling . . .*

I was born in a zoo across the Pyrenees in a place called Brive.
Maladon was my sister from a previous litter. Our pack was twelve
strong, including the new young, and though it was confined, it
was not close-caged. The perimeter fence had a ditch on the inside
which we could not cross. Only where there was a little wooden
bridge across the ditch to allow Mennen in was there access to
any part of the fence. Perhaps the Mennen thought that we could
scrabble up the fence and get away, and so made it impossible
for us to even try.

But at least the territory had trees, grass, watching ground, a
solitary hut where I was born, and a clean stream of running
water, which the Mennen turned on in the day. Our leader was
a bully of a wolf called Brantome. He was my father, but only
because he had mated with my mother. He was brutal to all of
us, the weakest most of all. Once Maladon had matured, and
could protect herself against Brantome, she also protected me,
which gave her the right to punish me. I was her protégé and
her victim. She nurtured me to bully me, she taught me that she
might punish me for what I did not know. And she counted the
days until she could be ledrene. I was the beginning of her first
pack, and on me she practised.

One day we will escape, she would say to me, but I will leave
you behind if you do not obey me absolutely until then.

Escaping that zoo, which I now see was well run and kept a
healthy pack, became one of my twin obsessions. The other was
making sure I was not left behind. Escape was not unknown –
three wolves broke out but months after I was born, and two of
them got clean away.

The other, Maladon's brother from her birth-litter, was hung
alive at the entrance to the enclosure by the bridge across the
ditch, and the door was left open and the bridge-way down. Only
his suffering, injured body was between the pack and its liberty.
I was told they had disembowelled him while he was still alive
and put his guts in the pack's feed.

For a time he lived, moaning, hanging by his paws upside-down
from the lintel of the door. Before he died they blinded and
castrated him. They say he made no sound. When they took away

his body the following day they left the door open to see if any of the pack dared try to escape. None tried, not even Maladon. Then they closed the door and fed us well, very well, and after that the pack found it easier to forget the world outside.

Except for Maladon, and therefore me as well, because she would not let me forget. She would hound me to the perimeter fence, and forcing my muzzle and teeth painfully this way and that she would whisper, 'Look! That's freedom and there the air smells sweet and Brantome does not live! Look! I shall not take you there unless you obey me absolutely.'

She would talk to me at night, and teach me to understand the stars, and how to howl down where we were. How many times we escaped into our imaginations during those nights, talking the wolfways in the stars that we thought we could make out. In that art I became more adept than her, so of course she punished me, yet made me play the game of escaping still.

Late one winter she fought for the ledreneship and won, and Brantome took her to mate. All the females made obeisance to her, and half the males as well, myself included. I was not by then the weakest, but . . . life remained hard. Every day I had to fight for food. Every day I had to do my watching duty, growling when the Mennen came to stare, summer, autumn and spring, though not in winter when the zoo was closed.

My opportunity for escape came in my fifth winter. Mennen were replacing units of the fence one by one. They put a temporary fence up beyond the existing one, unbolted the old section, removed it, and then put the new one in. We soon grew used to them and most of us did not even bother to watch any more, and in any case the Mennen smelt.

Only Maladon would go over and stare, and naturally we thought she did it to show she was protecting us. Every day she would go over to where they were working at the fence, settle down and stare, and soon the Mennen grew used to her. They even brought her tidbits of food but she never touched them.

When she did not watch she would sometimes command me to do so.

'Why?' I would grumble, for that winter was cold and the wind by the perimeter biting.

'Do it!' she snarled.

So I did, always grateful when she replaced me, or when night came, the Mennen went away and the fence was fully secured once more. The opportunity for escape came when I was not thinking of it, and nor could she have been.

'Go and watch, I'm going to rest,' she commanded me.

'But Maladon, it's cold. It's freezing.'

'Galliard . . .'

She had only to put that tone into her voice and I obeyed.

It was just as I began the reluctant advance across our territory to where the Mennen worked that day that they lost hold of a section they had just unbolted and it began to fall. Slowly at first, then more swiftly. It made no sound, and the Mennen who had been holding it, or maybe unbolting it, only stood and stared, quite mute. It fell slowly forward into the enclosure, gathering speed and then crashing down to form a bridge right across the ditch. As I said I was advancing towards the place, and had started to trot to keep warm, but as it fell instinct made me speed up, faster and faster, straight at where it lay straddling the ditch.

'Jump, Galliard, jump!'

It was Maladon's voice, and it was not advice but an order, though I hardly needed it. It was as if my whole life had been moving towards this moment and I reached the spot at full speed. As I took off I knew why she had told me to jump, for had I tried to run across one of my paws would most likely have gone through a hole in the mesh and my leg been broken. Even so my leap could not take me right across and my front paws fell short of the further side. But her warning shout was enough to make me look down. I saw the ditch all blurry below, and I saw a thicker strut in the fence. My front paws reached out for it, my back feet came up behind, and I leapt on between the two Mennen, thumping into the temporary fence beyond.

It swayed but held me.

Thump! I crashed into it again. I stopped, stared, and saw a clear gap between that section and the next permanent one. I dived for it, scrabbled, tore my paws and skin and head and then I was through and out. I did not hesitate, nor even look back, for I knew Maladon was watching after me and that she would have punished me if I had. I simply ran, and ran . . .

For four months I remained free, the most terrible and lonely four months of my life. I did not know how to hunt, for I had not been taught, and I only felt myself safest near my enemy the

*Mennen. But . . . I could feed on their rubbish, dangerous though
that was, for the food I found was often tainted and made me
weak and ill.*

*At last I felt myself begin to die, and losing the wish to live. I
dared not go back to Brive where the zoo was, and drifted south
to what I hoped might be warmer weather. But then I found
myself seeking a passage through the passes of the Pyrenees. I
just managed to climb their highest peaks and began the descent
of the other side, not having had a scrap of food for days, before
winter set in.*

*I was forced to seek food from Mennen rubbish dumps; then,
very weak, I was finally caught, and turned over to the travelling
circus where you were, Leon . . . where you gave me reason to
live.*

Such was the story told of Galliard's escape, and by the time he had
finished night was very well advanced, and the drizzle still continued.

Maladon had listened in silence, and she made no comment on
what she had heard. Instead she rose and stretched and then showed
them how the narrow corridor of fences they were in led to the far
end of the compound, and near to the metal gate the Mann, their
keeper, would be opening just after dawn.

'You must come down here and be ready, but no more. Do nothing,
nothing, until you hear my command,' Maladon warned them. 'When
you hear my call, then you must attack the Mann, but do not enter
beyond the second gate. Attack and wait for us outside the compound
– we shall do the rest.'

Which said, Jicin could not help hearing some dissent among Maladon's subordinates about the wisdom of attacking their keeper. Jicin
could not hear all that was said, but she heard enough to know that
some strongly disagreed with the idea of escape – 'We're well off here
and safe, and you know what they did to wolves who tried to escape
before and were caught'; while others felt that attacking the Mann was
a grave mistake – 'I beg you, Maladon, to consider the consequences of
breaking such ancient wolf-lore as that. The Mennen must never –'

'The Mennen must always be mistrusted,' she snarled, her contempt
for her pack even more open than that she had seemed to have for
her would-be rescuers, 'and if killing one of them is what we need to
do, we shall do it. Or *I* shall. As for those who say we should stay
here . . .'

Jicin had heard no more after that, except a sudden heavy movement in the dark of the compound, and the yelp of a male wolf, and then his whimpering. Come the dawn Jicin saw a male wolf huddled down inside the perimeter ditch, the mud about him red with his blood.

They had all settled down into silence after that, the minutes passing but slowly, until, too restless to sleep perhaps, one of the zoo wolves came and struck up conversation again.

Yet in the night there had been a brief encounter. A male sidled up to the wire and said, 'Is Galliard really dead?'

Leon nodded without saying more, fearing that Maladon might hear this talk and come over and object.

'Did he have . . . a good life out there?'

'He found liberty too much for him,' said Leon, 'but he died a true wolf.'

'Oh,' said the wolf, nodding. He seemed a kindly animal, and a warm one, and he added, 'Galliard was born in the same litter as me. He was my birth-brother. He was always stronger than me. I just wanted to know . . .'

'Wolf, I can tell you more.'

But there was restless movement and before Galliard's brother could fade back into the anonymity of the dark compound Maladon appeared.

'There is time before dawn yet, wolf, and we are unseen and unobserved. Complete your story and tell us how Galliard came to die. You others – you may listen if you like.'

The others emerged once more from darkness, and the watching Jicin understood that this was Maladon's way of keeping them occupied through a time of waiting that might otherwise prove too much for some, and allow others time to lose their courage.

Leon took up the story once more:

'I have told you how we were allowed out of the cages only twice. Well, there was a third time, and it proved the cause of Galliard's death.

'It was two years after the time we were allowed into the field for them to clean out our cage, at a place called Zaragoza, which we called upon each year: a place with great Mennen roads and factories, and with smoke like that across these fields in the air, so black and thick that it caught at your throat.

'Galliard had not been well, and twice in previous months he had foolishly tried to bite one or other of the Mennen when they fed us.

The third time, which was a week or two before we came to Zaragoza, he succeeded in drawing blood from one of those who came to stare and point and even prod.

'"Don't!" I warned him when he growled and lunged, but he was not the wolf I had first known. He was ill and needed open air and better food and warmth. He was old, and needed patience. He was lonely, and perhaps he only needed death. "Don't!" I warned him.

'But he ignored me, and caught the hand or fingers of a Mennen child, which screamed.

'The Mennen came and dragged him from the cage and beat him then and there with sticks and the metal prod. Beat him until his eyes swelled and blood came from his rear. Beat him until I could not look at him any more. I thought they were killing him, but suddenly they stopped and threw him back into the cage with me and left him.

'I tended him, as did the Mennen too in a way, and the weather warmed so that he began to recover over the next few days. We came to Zaragoza, but we were not put where the Mennen could come and see us, but hidden away out of their sight. Two nights later some Mennen came to see us, shining lights in our eyes from beyond the bars, smelling of smoke and stale food, and of Mennen shit.

'A few nights after this, when the evening show was over and the animals were back in their cages and the visiting Mennen all gone, those Mennen came again and took us away. Our cages were covered with tarpaulins for travel and we were driven through the night out of Zaragoza and into the countryside. I was excited, but Galliard was frightened and feverish.

'"Where are they taking us?" he kept saying. He seemed to have forgotten my name.

'It was still dark when we stopped in a place that smelt of bulls. You could hear their roaring, and their thumping massive weight against walls and padlocked metal doors.

'The cage was uncoupled from the vehicle that towed us and pushed by Mennen into a closed place. Its walls were wooden, and round, and blinding lights came on up in the night sky, more powerful than the stars, nearly as powerful as the sun. Flies and moths flew across the lights, and there was laughter and the hush of a good many watching Mennen. It was like the circus – but there was savagery in the air.

'Our cage was opened, not by the keeper we knew best but another, one of those Galliard had tried to bite. While prongs were used to keep me in my place, others forced poor Galliard out. He was afraid, so afraid that he did not answer when I tried to reassure him. There was the smell of the blood of bulls and death in that round-walled rising place into whose lights he went.

'He stood with his back near me, thin and shivering, made to seem yet older still by the shining lights. He tried to retreat but the Mennen stood by the cage to stop him coming back into it, or hiding beneath it.

'There was a Mennen shout followed by a silence; then came a bellowing, and with thunderous crashing a gate opened at the far side of the place and a young bull, huge-horned, charged out. It was black in the night, though brown-black closer to, its coat shining, its nostrils huge and its speed and power utterly formidable.

'Galliard was prodded towards it, and only then did I see that blood and shit were dripping from his anus. Galliard was already dying before my eyes. He was my only friend, my teacher, my wolf-world.

'He dragged himself towards the bull, guessing perhaps that its initial charge would slow before contact, which it did. The bull charged and stopped, Galliard stopped and growled. Then, quite suddenly and at a speed that must have taken even Galliard, wary as he was, by surprise, the bull renewed his charge.

'It was looming and thunderous and Galliard barely twisted to one side before the bull's horns raked his flank and tumbled him, bleeding. The bull wheeled, sharply as a hunting dog, and even as Galliard hobbled to his feet in an effort to turn about and face it the bull was on him again, and gored him in his flank and raised him flailing and screaming into the air, a bloody, spewing arc of dying wolf caught in the light. He was my friend.

'There was a Mennen roar and I saw Galliard falling with a violent thump, thump on to the ground, head thump, legs thump, guts trailing from the gaping wound. The bull stood still, surprised at its own success perhaps. Galliard began to crawl and then to run on three legs away across the circle of sand and sawdust towards the gate from which the bull had been released.

'He got near enough for Mennen to come and prod him out towards the bull again, the trail he left being one of blood, and the dragging of his left hind foot. To my surprise I could see that his eyes were clear and that he was *thinking*. He seemed no longer in pain, nor even much afraid. He looked towards my cage and seemed to say, "Watch!" and "Be ready!"

'I watched as the bull charged down upon him once again; this time his sidestep was better timed and he ran forward, straight towards me. The bull turned, stared about to find him, battered at the sandy earth with a hoof and, as the watching Mennen roared him on, charged after him.

'I watched as Galliard sought hard to reach me, so slowly, so draggingly now, as the bull began to catch him up, began to lower its head and twist its horns in aim and in preparation for the final death-gore of my friend.

'Then . . . "Run, Leon! Run to where I reached, and then straight on!"

'I heard Galliard shout those words to me before the bull caught him up and his body was taken up by the bull's horn, and I heard the crack of bone, and saw the spew of blood, as he flew up into the blinding lights a final time.

'I think the Galliard that I knew did not come down, though his body did. But the Galliard I loved saw the stars beyond the Mennen lights, and he saw a wolfway in them which was his own, and which he might take at last and journey to stars more bright, more permanent, more compassionate, than those the Mennen make. Galliard's body lay still upon the ground before me, but Galliard was not there, nor suffering, any more.

'Then, when the bull had been driven back to its starting point, they came back to the cage and opened it, and prodded me out.

'"Run," Galliard had said, and run I did, without waiting for the bull to begin his charge. I heard the Mennen shouts of surprise and I heard their laughter die, I felt the lights upon me all along, and I ran straight as death at the Mennen who stood behind the bull.

'The bull began its charge but I ran on, even when I saw it approaching, huge, with its heavy protruding tongue, and burning eyes. I smelt its odour just before I swerved, too fast for it to catch me, too fast, and I ran on straight at the Mennen, thump! Galliard's poor body had crashed to the ground hard enough, but mine smashed and tore into the cruel Mennen I hated much harder. I wanted to kill them and perhaps I did, I know not. I tore a Mann's face, I tasted his blood and when I reached the gate I saw what Galliard hoped I might: an opening off behind the Mennen, a false wall of wood, more Mennen there, their dark faces and white shining eyes, wide with surprise and fear. Behind me the watching crowd was silent.

'Thump! I tore, I scrabbled, I bit, and pushed and then I ran, down into darkness, between stone walls, past panicking horses, between bulls, through gates, up and over a wall and on to a low metal roof and out into the sudden stretching darkness of the Meseta beyond, out and away to liberty, just as Galliard had himself done years before. Because of him I escaped.'

Leon looked at them, panting and breathless from the telling of his awful tale, eyes staring, mouth agape.

'Dawn is almost on us, wolf,' said Maladon, her harsh voice ending Leon's tale. 'Go to your positions, all of you . . .'

CHAPTER NINETEEN

As Maladon of Brive thrives on liberty and leadership,
Jicin decides she should stay away from the Heartland no longer

BY NOW it was becoming alarmingly clear that Maladon had such an inclination to dominate others, and had been so long in charge of submissive wolves, that she could not help behaving as if all wolves in her orbit, including even Jicin and her friends, were part of her pack and under her command. Jicin felt herself slipping back into a passivity and obedience she had not known since her days in thrall to Dendrine. Plainly, this was something she would have to find a way of dealing with if the escape was successful, but for now she and the others followed Maladon's orders willingly enough and took up their places in the shadows near the metal gate.

The ground was wet, the air filled with drizzle, so that though dawn soon came upon them, it was still murky when the sound of a vehicle was first heard. It began by starting up and roaring loud, and then it fell quiet and idling for a time, and finally it began a slow circuit of the cages by the path whose lights had just gone out.

As the dawn light advanced Jicin and the others finally saw what manner of wolf Maladon was, and she looked even more formidable than she had seemed at night, leaving no doubt that she was not only ledrene of the zoo pack, but its effective leader as well.

She was large – nearly as large as Aragon. She was well muscled, and her fur was thick and glossy, a silver-grey that helped turn the dew that formed on it into shining morning light. Her eyes were wide-set, her expression was permanently frowning and angry, and her flanks and paws and face were scarred by fights. All in all, Jicin told herself, she was a wolf who had kept her youthful looks remarkably well. Perhaps being cared for by Mennen could have its compensations after all.

Jicin saw that Maladon moved with a certain heavy grace made all the more impressive by the obvious fear of her felt by the other wolves in her pack, males and females alike. Nor were some of these males mere weaklings, which made Maladon all the more fearsome to those outside. Some were larger than her, some of stronger build, most healthy of fur and eyes, yet all showed deference to her.

The circling vehicle passed the compound fence slowly before disappearing beyond it to other parts of the zoo. The dawn advanced, the sky lightened, and a couple of the zoo wolves shifted nearer the metal door which the Mann would, they hoped, eventually open.

Maladon was some way back.

'I always charge when he comes, always,' she had explained. 'I charge to the ditch and then stop, as I did when you came to the fence. He expects it.'

Silence had fallen since Leon had ended his tale, but now Maladon suddenly addressed him, her voice no more than a rasping whisper.

'When we are outside which of you shall lead?'

'I led the way here, but Jicin is our ledrene and she . . .' said Leon.

Maladon cast Jicin a brief dismissive glance and turned back to Leon.

'You know the way away from Mennen then,' she said. 'Follow it and do not hesitate; never hesitate.'

'It is what Galliard taught me,' said Leon with a smile.

'It is what I taught *him*,' said Maladon. 'As for the attack on the Mann . . .'

She turned her gaze upon the other three, and settled finally on Jicin.

'*You* shall make it, wolf.'

Jicin stared at her, full of fear, but curious as well. She knew she would do as Maladon asked, and understood the reason for the she-wolf's choice. Maladon must have seen at once the weakness and inexperience of Egro and Ronera; she had seen as well the certainty in Jicin's eyes that like it or not – and she did not like the role of attacker of Mennen – she had faith that Maladon would be freed.

'Do not fail me, Jicin,' said Maladon proprietorially, as if she were free, and Jicin the captive needing to escape.

'Nor should you fail us,' said Jicin quietly, something of her true strength returning to her voice, and for the first time a brief glimmer of respect showed in Maladon's face. It did not last long.

'*Silence!*'

Maladon said the word as if it had been the others who had begun the conversation and not herself, yet silence instantly fell among them.

Sounds of a Mann whistling; sounds of a Mann's feet on a gravel path; sounds of metal keys, a door opening, more whistling, a curse as something fell, the sudden sweet scent of the Mann, sixteen wolves watching . . .

The Mann approached the inner door, the one that opened out on to the compound, and he called out a word or two of morning welcome to his pack. His back was now to the door he had just opened, and there was the jangle of keys in his hand. A pause while he fumbled, and Maladon rose majestically, pricked her ears, and waited for the second door to open. She had said he was always cautious, careful to keep it just sufficiently ajar for him to deal with the food he carried, and turn on taps for fresh water.

This was the moment to wait, the moment to be still. This was the moment when a lifetime of waiting might be thrown away by over-eagerness, so wait a little longer . . .

The keys jingled once more, the door scraped and opened a fraction, and Maladon barked her command to Jicin and the others and simultaneously began her own charge.

Leon, Jicin and their companions rose out of the shadows; the Mann's gaze was upon the approach of Maladon, which made him laugh as usual. Leon led the way to the first gate, Jicin scented at it briefly and then remembered the command not to hesitate.

Now was the moment, *now*!

The gate swung open at her push, the Mann half turned, and Jicin was suddenly up and charging at him even as beyond him in the compound Maladon turned nonchalantly away, and then swung suddenly and fiercely back towards him.

No hesitation then, not from Jicin nor Maladon. The one crashed her paws upon the Mann and, grasping at him with her teeth, pulled him back. The other charged, leapt over the ditch and at the gate, her paws and head crashing it open, straight into the face of the falling, struggling, shocked Mann.

'Now!' she called, turning back to look at her own pack. '*Now!*'

The Mann rose struggling, seeking to strike Jicin from his back, and Jicin remembered what she had been told to do: retreat, retreat swiftly so that the way was not blocked, retreat outside and wait.

As she turned she saw Maladon swing round, stare down at the Mann, and then as the other wolves began their charge she saw the great wolf leap towards his flailing arms and face, stifling his cry with the crushing, bloody grip of her jaws, sending him straight backwards to the ground, to fall where moments before Jicin had been.

A wolf standing over a Mann, a wolf tearing at a Mann's face, a strange stifled cry, drowning away in blood, and a sight yet worse: Maladon, massive now, seeking to drag the Mann out of the way by the face and head. She only half succeeded, for he proved too heavy and awkward for her, his clothes catching at an obstruction. She turned from him, her face bloody, spitting out his teeth and gore, and came calmly out to join the others.

Then the drumming of wolves' paws, the rush of wolves through the gates, the batter of a swinging gate against a fence and one by one they all came through.

'Eleven,' said Maladon.

'Fifteen, counting us,' said Jicin ironically. She could not but look between the two gates at the Mann upon the ground. He was not dead. A hand moved, and then an arm, reaching for the face that was no more, moving to where a mouth that was a torn wound sought to speak, or cry out a warning perhaps. The arm fell back against the gate.

Behind in the compound a wolf's cry, weak and pathetic.

'Maladon!'

It was the wolf she had chastised and punished in the night; he was striving in vain to climb out of the ditch into which he had fallen or been pushed.

'Maladon! Ledrene! Take me with you – I meant only to speak a warning!'

Weak and pathetic . . .

'Come, you others,' she said, turning her back on the compound, and casting barely a glance about the near-silent zoo, where the only noise was a vehicle slowly doing the rounds, and the nails of the Mann's hand, scratching at the metal of the gate. 'We are all ready. There are no more.'

Then they turned to follow Leon and get as far as they could before the Mennen knew that they were gone. Behind them the wolf in the ditch howled, for he would never now be free.

Even before they had crossed the road outside, left the environs of Brive behind, and found again the cover of wild woodland, Jicin had made a few decisions regarding herself and her group, and Maladon and hers. She would stay apart, she would not be made subordinate. She would see that their duty was fulfilled towards these others – to get them to a place of safety, to make sure that they could fend for themselves, and then ... then ... Jicin did not yet know.

The nagging feeling that she was required for other, different tasks would not go away, nor the urgent sense that it was Klimt who needed her. Perhaps she should go to the Heartland *now*? 'But ... I cannot ... my duty is *here*.'

But at least something soon became very clear indeed to Maladon – to survive, she needed Jicin and the others. Arrogant and dismissive she might be, brutal and haughty too, cruel and unlikeable, but she was not a fool.

Within hours of their departure, when they first became aware that the Mennen were already in pursuit, and getting close, Maladon began to realize several important things. The first, and most obvious, was that a lifetime in a compound had not fitted her wolves for hours on the run, let alone days, let alone ...

Very soon a gentle uphill climb that Jicin and her wolves barely noticed became a desperate scramble for Maladon's pack; soon, too, they learnt that in a world of unfamiliar sound and scent they were uneasy, and stressed. They needed the guidance of the wolves who had rescued them.

When the hours stretched into two days without food many of them discovered hunger and thirst for the first time in their lives. Wolves who had been dominant in the compound now began to lose their composure and their influence; others, who had never been well placed, it seemed, and had learnt to survive on less, began now to come to the fore.

A pack less brutally led than Maladon's might soon have broken up in disarray, but this one did not. Maladon saw what must be done and did it – attacking those who showed weakness, or were mindful to complain; rapidly showing Jicin and Leon the greater respect that they were due; and understanding much sooner than the others the need to follow Jicin's advice on matters of lying low, or masking scent with routes through water, and not marking out the trees as territory every twenty paces.

Many have said that the escape of the wolves of Brive under the leadership of Maladon – it is always her name that is mentioned first, and rarely the names of those who made it possible, least of all Jicin – was one of the boldest of several escapes of wolves from captivity that took place at the end of the Dark Millennium, in the era of the Wolves of Time.

Others were cleverer perhaps, others owed more to chance, but none gave so many wolves liberty, nor brought into the domain of wolfkind so powerful a wolf as Maladon. Yet it was not the escape itself that was remarkable so much as the survival of all but three of the wolves in the determined pursuit by Mennen that followed. For rarely in the long and bitter history of wolfkind and Mennen can a wolf hunt have been so persistent and ruthless as that which followed their escape.

In the woodlands of the Corrèze the chase began, Jicin taking over the lead from Leon, for of them all she best understood the need to get as far from Brive as they could. For three days and nights she drove them on until they came upon the first of the massed barriers put up by the Mennen.

Trapped by the narrowing topography of the upper Dordogne and forced to flee on to the more open ground of Cantal, and then driven to retreat south and west and skulk for a time near Cahors, the wolves twisted and turned in their search for an escape route, but only seemed to bring the Mennen's squeeze upon them tighter.

Mennen and dogs, dogs and guns, guns and aircraft overhead . . . and while Jicin used her skills to find places to hide, and to mask their scent, Maladon kept the wolves going, driving them, and finally, when it became essential, sacrificing them.

At Labastide she crippled one of the slow ones that he might be found and slow their pursuers down.

At Rodez she refused to stop when one of her daughters cried out for the others to help her out of the mud of a river.

At Entraygues she stopped the others killing a Mann who had shot and wounded one of the pack.

'Let him be. He can take the wolf he's hurt and gloat, while we continue our escape.'

Then, at Lozère, quite suddenly, the pursuit stopped, and the wolves found themselves climbing steadily into the High Causses country, in which, Jicin remembered, Lounel had been raised. Time to pause a while, and listen to the guns of Mennen war to south and west, a war to which, perhaps, they owed their liberty, for it had diverted the Mennen from the chase.

Throughout all this Jicin had been forced to protect 'her' wolves from Maladon. At first they had been fitter than the Brive wolves, but as the days had passed, and the weakest Brive wolves had fallen away and the others gained their strength, Jicin and Leon had seemed to grow weak by comparison. Then too, as Maladon rapidly learnt the survival arts, a task made easier by the seeming retreat into their own concerns of the Mennen, the she-wolf's inclination to dominate and subjugate – as natural to her as breathing was to other wolves – came to the fore again.

There was a period of a week or two when she and Jicin managed to get on as equals – a period in which Maladon made it her business to find out as much as she possibly could about the Wolves of Time, about Klimt, about the Magyars, about the Heartland and the wolfways in the stars which were the means to get there.

Jicin might not like her, might still be afraid of her, but with each day that passed she could not help feel astonishment at Maladon's capacity to learn. She was a wolf hungry for success and triumph; a wolf filled with hatred for the Mennen who had imprisoned her; a wolf utterly ruthless towards any who got in her way.

'The only thing she seems unlikely to ever be able to do is have more young!' observed Leon in a moment of respite from the demands of Maladon, when he and Jicin had crept off to a discreet overhang of limestone in the High Causses where they now lived.

Here, the Mennen completely gone it seemed, they had come upon a flock of trapped, unguarded, dying sheep. They had decided to linger awhile, the sheep a natural larder, and for the time being even Maladon was content.

Jicin nodded: 'Yes, she is older than she looks and past rearing young. But nothing about her would surprise me.'

'Will you take her to the Heartland? Is she not fitted to join Klimt's pack?'

Jicin conceded that she probably was, and that perhaps she ought to lead her there.

'But not yet, and perhaps not me. You see, Leon, she may survive here awhile in safety, for we are not harried by the Mennen here and there is food enough for many wolves. But that will change in time – and it is better they learn their strengths and weaknesses here than trying to move on across the Mennen ways, by lower ground where Mennen are prevalent, and likely to take up the chase again. And there is another thing.'

'Yes, Jicin?'

He spoke sombrely, for he had sensed through the frenetic days and weeks just past that Jicin had been harbouring thoughts and fears quite different from any engendered by the escape from Brive, or by Maladon.

'Wolf,' she said, 'when I first saw Maladon I knew in my heart that she was destined to reach the Heartland. She will do so without my help.'

'And without a good many more of her "pack" if it suits her need to do so!' observed Leon with a certain grimness.

'Quite so,' said Jicin.

'But there's something more, isn't there?'

Jicin nodded and replied, 'I have said little of Klimt . . .'

'Little, but enough,' said Leon quietly. 'And your friend Stry told me something of it when I briefly met him. Klimt is a wolf you love, as I loved Galliard.'

'And if you heard Galliard's call, and thought he needed you?'

'I would go to him at once. I owe him my life and must always answer his call, however and whenever it came. But why . . . ?'

Jicin stood up. 'I have heard Klimt's call,' she said quietly, tears beginning to come. 'I have heard it as clearly as I hear your voice now.'

She fell silent, for some way below them they saw the form of Maladon, climbing up towards them through the outcrops. She could not have seen them, nor scented them, but on she came, inexorable, potent, fearsome. They pulled back, watched her approach and then pause and turn to survey the landscape, and the wolves, below. There was about her the look of one who was impatient and restless, wanting more than she had, always more.

Not knowing she was observed, she raised her head and howled very softly, a howl not of triumph but of ambition; not of satisfaction that she had found a world of liberty, and beauty – but a howl that expressed the greed of a wolf who wanted more.

'And this might be one of the Wolves in the Heartland?' whispered Leon.

'I am certain of it,' said Jicin, a chill stab going right into her heart.

Below them Maladon looked this way and that, and then she turned back to go down to her wolves again. They saw one come running towards her – Egro. Prancing, light-footed, showing off. Then Ronera, subservient, glad it seemed that Maladon glanced at her and nodded, happy to be noticed. Jicin had lost two wolves to Maladon.

'You were saying?' said Leon heavily.

'I was saying that I have heard Klimt's call, and sense his need for me. I feel I am in the wrong place. I feel my exile should be over and that I should now go home, but . . .'

She looked downslope towards Maladon and the others, who were roaming northward on a hunt for prey. Maladon had said they would be doing so that day, and had told Jicin not to forget.

'You mentioned Galliard,' began Leon a shade diffidently. 'Well, you know what he always told me, and it was what Maladon taught *him*, as she has made plain to us.'

'Do not hesitate?'

Leon nodded. 'He meant when a wolf was in danger, but –'

'Klimt is in danger, and perhaps if I stay with Maladon much longer *we* shall be in danger.'

'So?'

'I should leave.'

'And Egro and Ronera?'

Jicin looked across the country of the Causses in the direction they had gone.

'Perhaps I am learning something from Maladon. I have a feeling they have already found a new leader.'

'And me?' said Leon.

She looked at him and knew suddenly how much she liked him, and respected him, and did not want to lose him. And she felt something she had not felt for many years – the sudden pang of desire.

'Klimt needs me,' she said, quite without double meaning or irony. Desire for Leon she might feel, and she was glad of it, but her need to answer Klimt's call made that other desire as nothing, nothing but the bending of dry grass to the wind.

'You should not hesitate, Jicin, not a moment longer.'

'You will stay here, or come with me?' she asked.

'My heart and mind and way is not with Maladon,' he said. 'When do we leave?'

Again she looked downslope across the fell. Maladon and the other wolves were all gone from sight.

'Now,' she whispered. '*Now!*'

He nodded, they touched paws briefly as if to wish each other luck in their new enterprise, and then rose from out of the shadows of the rocks and turned eastward in the direction of the far-distant Heartland.

'*I am coming home to you, my dear,*' she whispered, and she knew

Klimt heard, she knew it, as she knew that what she was doing was right; and tears wet her face as she went, like life-giving rain across a parched land after long years of drought.

'I am glad you are coming with me, Leon,' she said with feeling, 'and glad you are my friend.'

'It seems you have many friends, wolf,' said Leon wryly, 'while I have but one. You must tell me how you do it on the way!'

'I'm not sure I really know,' said Jicin, laughing, and off they went to find the best and safest route back home to the Heartland.

Home to the Heartland ... Home to the Mann ... Time to go ...

'*Where is my home now?*' *the shaman Matthius Wald asked himself, brushing from his beard the light snowflakes that fell gently among the pine trees of the Bavarian forest up through which he climbed.*

It was four months since he had left the Black Forest and he and his assistant's first great push towards the Heartland in their search for the ending of his father's story had petered out. A chance encounter led them one way, fear of retribution from a people who lived in the ruins of München forced them in another, and finally they had taken refuge in the forest lands north-east of the upper Danube.

Choosing to be alone for the day Wald had left his assistant by their encampment and he now climbed slowly through a rise of trees no different from a thousand others.

Except they were different, and he had been here before, some time ...

'*Some time ...*'

He had the sense that time was running out, and that he was not moving fast enough along its wolfways to reach the place – the time – he needed to if he was to know the truth of the story his father had begun. Maladon, Galliard, Kobrin, the Pechorans, Klimt – their names meant more to him now that he had met them, or they had come from their Otherworld to meet him, and guide him on.

And Tervicz ...

That early visit from the oldest survivor of the Wolves, who Wald suspected was even now still confined to the mortal world, waiting, waiting, waiting for something he, Matthius Wald must do.

He should not have left his assistant on his own in such a place except that he must learn to let him journey alone, even if he tried to go too far too soon. Even if ...

Wald stilled, and his spine thrilled at what he saw: a young wolf, too uncertain to be a guide, up ahead through the trees.

'Wolf, what is your name?' Wald found himself asking in his mind and knowing the answer, caught between his assistant at the camp and this wolf not far ahead, the same, the same.

Then Tervicz was there at the youngster's side, a Wanderer and his assistant.

'Don't leave me,' said Wald, bereft to see them rise and turn and go on upslope, 'only let me follow you . . .'

As he followed and found their trail, their paw-steps filling up with snow even as they went, the winter air carried the strangest of scents for such a season: thyme and tarragon.

'The scent of the Wanderer,' whispered Matthius Wald.

Only much later, when dusk was falling and he had lost their trail to the falling of the snow, did he turn back, the scent still in the air, strong on his hands, strongest on his clothes, as if he himself might be the Wanderer now.

Far off, from the easterly direction in which Tervicz and his assistant had gone, a wolf's howl came, and then another, and then a third to meld and spiral up with the first two, and then a fourth.

Wald stood listening, snow upon his beard, glad he could hear his assistant hurrying to catch up for he had no intention of going back. It had been a poor place for an encampment anyway.

'Listen!' he commanded, as the youth arrived.

'What are they howling down?' his assistant asked, most sensibly. The youngster was learning.

'Jicin is returning to the Heartland but her Klimt is not there, though he will hear her call and start the journey home. Listen!'

They stood together in the gloaming, high in the Bavarian Forest, until the snow had stopped, and the wind began to clear the night sky of the clouds, little by little, and showed a wolfway that shone as bright as day from out of Russia, home to the Heartland, which was home to Klimt.

It was only Klimt's stolid self-confidence, and uncomplaining stance despite his own injury, that kept the five Pechorans in the Quarry ready and waiting at the great metal gates which prevented their escape, and through which he had hoped to find a way. The barrier was well-made, its iron mesh impenetrable to wolf, and the path beneath it tarmacked and too hard to dig into. At its sides the Quarry's walls rose nearly vertically, and no wolf could climb them. There seemed no way out.

Yet so confident did Klimt appear that escape would eventually be possible that way, and so unfussed as the days went by and nothing happened, and there seemed no prospect of ever finding a way out, that they were inspired to trust him, and their complaints and doubts withered in their mouths.

'You can smell their vehicles' fumes all the way down this track,' he said, 'which means they come this way sometimes and have done so recently. When they do they'll have to open up the gates.'

'And then? You know the Mennen will be ready for us with guns and –'

'Not if they have not seen us waiting here,' said Klimt, 'so keep out of sight. As for any Mennen, the longer our delay the fitter I shall be to deal with them, for I am not sure you –'

'You would not *attack* the Mennen, would you?' they asked.

Klimt smiled grimly and it frightened them.

'Attack and kill as well, if I must, just as I have before,' he said. He left the rest to their imagination and waited, praying to Wulf that He would find a way out for them; and trying not to think of Solar, who surely had not escaped, and Lunar, who might not have had the speed or courage to do so.

'*Klimt . . .*'

In the long, hungry hours of waiting voices travelled the wolfways of time to him, giving him succour and hope.

'*Klimt, I am coming home to you, my dear.*'

He assuaged the throbbing of his healing wound by imagining it was Jicin who spoke to him, and tried not to regret the years they had lost; tried not to dream of their coming back together; tried to subdue the yearning he felt, the old desire for her lost touch.

'*Klimt, my dear,*' and a single tear trickled down his face, unseen by any wolf, which he tried to blink away, '*my love . . .*'

Would they never open up the gates again?

The Mennen and their machines worked beyond the gates without pause, their lights coming on at dusk and not going out until sunrise. They would appear from time to time on the cliffs above and shoot into the bodies that had fallen, for sometimes one or two would still be alive after they had been tipped over. But the Mennen simply liked to kill, so that rooks and rats and anything that moved were their victims too.

'An opportunity will come,' said Klimt, 'and we must be ready to take it. These gates *have* been opened before, and they will be again.'

Klimt stared at the sky as he said this, thinking wryly that it would be good if Wulf appeared there for a brief moment, just to acknowledge that his prayers would be answered. Except that Wulf was not in that Otherworld above, but here and now in mortality, in the form of Solar or Lunar.

'Hmmm!' growled Klimt to himself, not for the first time doubting whether She who appeared at his sons' birth had really done so.

On the Quarry edge above their heads there was sudden guttural cursing as two men appeared there, and the sharp crackling of their guns.

'Look!'

One of the Pechoran wolves pointed to the bodies, the great mound of bodies piled up the Quarry wall to their right, and they saw movement. One of the fallen Mennen, half naked, had risen out of the corpses, been shot at, clambered down to the level ground and had started to run.

RATATAT TAT!

He ran, he crawled as shots thudded about him, dust rising, until he reached that same small shelter Klimt himself had found.

Vehicles starting, more shouts, and the rattle of chains at the gates. Yes . . . oh, yes!

'Wait for my command,' growled Klimt, and those who now followed him knew that if they disobeyed it would be them this strange and fearful wolf attacked, not Mennen.

'Keep low – wait . . .'

As the gates swung open a great vehicle rushed through, but not before Klimt had time to glimpse the one who had tried to hide rise up from his shelter, stand still for a moment, and then run back towards the corpses. It was most terrible. The Mann scrabbled at the bodies and delved in among them and then was gone inside that stinking morass of death, like a rat to its feed.

The Mann . . .

And even as Klimt's view was cut off by the vehicle thundering past, he caught the scents of thyme and tarragon amidst the stench of the Quarry, and knew who that Mann was, and where he had seen him before, and felt compassion that he was outcast of his own kind and no better now than . . .

'Us,' Klimt whispered to himself. *'Now!'*

As he rose the Pechorans rose with him and they were through the gates before the two Mennen lingering beyond, in the shadows of the rock walls on either side of the steep track, saw them.

'Run and scatter and head north-west,' cried Klimt as he bore down on the first of the two Mennen, buffeted him aside, and leapt at the second, whose sweet scent of fear he could smell even as he flew through the air.

The Mann fell, and the gun he held clattered down at his side, and Klimt turned to follow the others who had scattered but not flown as he had commanded.

'You'll not be as fast as us, Klimt,' said one respectfully, 'and Pechorans do not leave their friends behind.'

Then the wolves were off once more, running in the shadows of buildings, hearing the shouts of Mennen, past the rumble of machinery and on, on towards the open fell. The *ratatatt* of guns followed them, and then more prolonged shooting was heard somewhere deep inside the Quarry.

The Mann, thought Klimt. Then he led the escapees on, hoping to get as far from the lair of the Kazakhs on the far side of the Quarry as he could.

So it was that Klimt escaped the Quarry in the same hour that Lunar and the other Pechorans began to arrive, so that the main Pechoran pack was doubly in debt to the stranger Wolves.

As darkness fell Klimt heard Lunar's account of what had happened, and had no doubt that Solar had made his journey to the stars.

'His stand saved me,' said Lunar.

'Then your life had best justify his sacrifice,' said Klimt bleakly. He stood apart and in silence for a time, and out of respect for his natural authority the Pechorans awaited him.

'Shall we seek vengeance on the Kazakhs?' they asked when he returned among them.

The great wolf shrugged and shook his head and said, 'Let Wulf decide.'

Then he rested until the dawn when they heard more shooting, and the jagged howl of wounded wolf.

'If it is revenge we seek it would seem the Mennen are doing our work for us,' muttered Klimt; 'but it is not, for we have better things to do than kill fellow-wolves.'

He sat down wearily, his shoulder paining him, but the indefatigable look of a natural leader on his face.

'Lunar,' he said, summoning his son to him, 'what would you do now?'

At that moment Lunar knew that his father had given up hope that Solar was alive and was transferring his hopes, and experience, to him now. Had he not taught Solar the arts of leadership in just such ways as this? And had not he, Lunar, often thought he was glad he did not lead, even though he knew the answers too?

'Well, wolf?'

'Some of the Kazakhs will escape. We should watch out for them and ask them to join us if –'

'See to it, wolf,' said Klimt brusquely.

Lunar found himself doing so.

'You five, go that way and bring any that escape here: you four, that way; do not take risks, do not fight the Kazakhs, return at once if danger threatens.'

The Pechorans set off to follow Lunar's commands at once and without question.

'Well done, my son,' said Klimt. The two Wolves' eyes met, and in each was the grey deep grief for the brother and the son they had lost.

Within the hour all the Pechorans were back, bringing with them five Kazakh wolves, two wounded.

'Continue,' said Klimt quietly to Lunar.

'We shall leave at dusk,' he said, 'and those that cannot keep up with our leader will be left behind.'

Which was no wolves at all, for when Klimt finally rose once more he moved but slowly, limping and in pain. But there was not one there who would have dared challenge for the leadership, such was the sense of strength and purpose in his gait.

'Where are we going?' whispered one of the Kazakhs to a Pechoran, afraid to ask Klimt himself.

'To the Heartland,' said Lunar, overhearing him, 'to reclaim it for us all.'

CHAPTER TWENTY

Aragon returns to the Heartland,
and the Magyars show their strength

THE LEAVES of the silver birch had long since turned yellow, and been scattered by unseasonably cold autumn winds through woodland and forest before Aragon and his companions reached the Bavarian uplands, and the last leg of their journey home to the Heartland. It was late October, and they were tired, for the route Aragon had chosen to take after leaving Jicin in southern France had been demanding, and stressful. He wanted to take back to Klimt as much information as he could about the distribution of Mennen and wolves across southern Europe.

Of Mennen, the facts were plain enough. The city ruination they had witnessed in Toulouse was repeated many times along the way to the Southern Alps, and then in the northern plain of Italy. The great river called the Po, which Elhana had crossed with such danger and difficulty some years before, was as polluted and foul-smelling as she had described it, perhaps more so for it was filled now with all the foetid and oily detritus of Mennen war.

Bodies without number, stinking, carcasses of livestock too, all mixed in with the chemicals and pollution which they observed accompanied the breakdown of Mennen life.

They had thought the war had started where they first came upon it, at Toulouse, but now discovered that it must have devastated North Italy a year or two earlier, because already there was evidence of the advance of weeds through the ruins, and upon the roads. Such Mennen as there were had vacated the towns and lived now in isolated villages well guarded by their guns and dogs, whilst much of the countryside, once well farmed and occupied, was now burnt, abandoned, and laid waste. Often they came upon stray animals; cows, and sheep and pigs, often weak and sick and easy prey. But here and there, as in the foothills of the Alps, these same animals had begun to turn wild, the weaker ones long since dead, the stronger now learning how to wander and forage across landscapes which had previously contained them, and where food and pasture had been provided.

In one place Stry had very nearly been killed by a huge tusked boar guarding a litter of piglets which he had thought ripe for the taking; there were no Mennen about. In another place they had watched while two Mennen, seeking to restrain a feral bull, were chased off and injured. It began to seem that in those parts, at least, Mennen were losing their direction and their supremacy.

Thereabouts too they came upon a group of Mennen, blind and sick, herded along by other Mennen as if they were cattle. To the wolves these Mennen seemed mortally ill, for the stench of them hung in the air long after they had passed by, and clung cloying in their muzzles, and made them retch.

Of wolves, Aragon and the others learned something too for it seemed that south of the Po the Apennines were being re-occupied by wolves from the south. He would have liked to have spent time finding out more, but the Po crossing had proved difficult, for Mennen guarded the bridges and the waters were too noisome to swim.

But the forced diversion was rewarded by an encounter with wolves who revealed that the spread northward had been led by wolves of the Benevento pack, directed to explore by that pack's ledrene Pescara, Elhana's daughter, and the one who had displaced her. Aragon and the others had very nearly been coerced into journeying south to meet her but felt that their task was to get back to the Heartland without delay. As it was, the Beneventoan scouts, as they were called, were so insistent that only by dint of swimming back over the Po did Aragon and his friends escape. In consequence, they were all ill for some weeks afterwards, and their return across the Alps was delayed sufficiently that they ran foul of the first heavy snows.

They therefore reached the Bavarian forests with some misgivings, for they greatly feared that snow would have begun falling in Slovakia by the time they got there, making their task of ascending to the Heartland more difficult. They were further delayed by injury and accident, and the winter weather had long since overtaken them by the time they finally set foot upon the Magyar-controlled Fell once more.

They had had hopes of making a speedy and safe passage across into the Heartland and the protection of their old pack, but ill fortune turned to disaster. Just as Aragon and Stry had been chased off the

Fell by Magyars when they had left three years before, now they were being harassed by their old enemy once more, and if Aragon gave one final call for help that night, as the Magyars and their leaders closed in, he had no great hope that help would come, nor any way of knowing that Kobrin and others were close enough to give support if only they could reach him, and the wolves he led, in time.

Aragon and Stry had long been aware of the dangers of trying to cross the Fell, remembering as they did the excellence of the Magyar watchers. They made the dangers known to the three wolves who followed them – Srena and Gallega, two females, and Huete, a young and haughty male who took orders badly, but had the initiative to make decisions on his own, and the courage to sniff out opportunities for routes and food however near the Mennen might be.

In the days before reaching the Fell they discussed long and hard how best to make their final approach to the Heartland. Naturally, after so long they could not know the disposition of the Magyar wolves, or those led by Klimt, and they had to assume that both groups were still extant and active.

Now that winter was advancing, and the Wolves of Time had probably left the high Scarpfeld in favour of the lower ground of the Forest and Vale, it seemed sensible to approach from the south-west, which would allow them to skirt the Fell by ground they knew from the early days of the formation of the pack.

Then, too, it seemed wise to try to reach the area before colder weather brought heavier snows, and for that reason they had been hurrying for days past, and perhaps hastening too much and so becoming tired and careless. Soon after they had crossed the Danube one of their number, the she-wolf Srena, was injured leaping a wire fence, her inner back leg badly torn, and soon turning septic. They were only slowed down at first, but the group was finally forced to stop when Srena could limp no further. They saw the weather worsening by the hour and knew that their chance of reaching the Forest unobserved and without mishap was growing less and less.

Three years before in such a situation Aragon might have left his injured companion to her fate, arguing that the pack's welfare was more important than the individual's. It was a decision many leaders have had to make throughout the history of wolfkind. But times had changed for Aragon; he moved a little more slowly these days, he thought a little more deeply, and he cared more for those who followed him whilst still making the calculations of risk all leaders must.

'We'll stay by Srena,' he decided in quiet discussion with Stry, 'for she's served us well on the way here and been stalwart in fighting and watching, and sensible in travel. In any case, she knows things we do not know about southern Spain, and her loss will diminish the knowledge it is our task to bring back to Klimt. We've already lost the advantage of the weather and a few more days' stoppage now will not harm us.'

The decision was made all the easier by Srena's doughty insistence that they should *not* stay, and her vain attempt, when the first snows came and she realized what delay meant to the rest of them, to wander off and be lost, so they might be rid of responsibility for her. But she was soon missed, and quickly found, for she had only been able to crawl a short way before collapsing against a wall she was too weak to climb.

'If you try that again, wolf, we'll leave you to your fate at once!' said Aragon not unkindly, for he liked and admired her. 'Now listen, we've not all travelled this far together to abandon each other now, so lie low and keep warm, and eat the food we bring. There's water nearby, so you'll not thirst too much. Just get better, wolf, that's all I ask.'

Srena looked at him with gratitude and respect.

'This wolf who exiled you . . .'

'Klimt?'

'The leader of the Wolves of Time.'

'What of him?'

'If one such as you serves him, Aragon, he must be powerful indeed.'

'He is, and worthy of all our respect. Therefore, get better now, for the sooner you do so the sooner you'll meet him.'

'You are confident that after so long he will still be in the territory where you left him?'

'It's not just a territory, it is the Heartland. There is no other territory in which the pack he leads will wish to live permanently. The Heartland is our destiny.'

'And will he accept into his pack a wolf such as me, who has been foolish enough to rip her leg on wire she should have seen?'

'That's not his decision, wolf, but Elhana's, his ledrene. You might decide you do not want to stay in a pack of which she's ledrene . . . who knows? Now, *get better.*'

He looked at her with genuine affection. She was a lean wolf, and had the pale buff fur of the wolves of central Spain. She was a fighter born, and knew no words better than loyalty, faith, and good humour. Aragon would not leave her to die.

But it had taken a week for Srena's blood to begin to clear, and a week more before she was strong enough for the pack to move off again. By then the cold weather had come from the north to drive their prey underground, or off to inaccessible hills and forests, and the snows had fallen to impede their progress.

'We're certain to be seen if the Magyar spies are still as efficient as they used to be,' said Stry as they finally approached the west flank of the Fell.

'If we haven't been already,' responded Aragon darkly, for the day before they had come upon a marking scent, and a pair of fresh wolf tracks in the mud and snow along the banks of a river, the bold and steady prints of watcher wolves confident of their territory and who now and then marked it to warn others away, a warning Aragon would happily have heeded if there was a way to the Heartland which did not involve crossing the Fell, but there was none. It was simply a matter of time before they were seen again, and a matter of luck, or bad luck, just how soon, however carefully they went.

'If we sneak and skulk we take too long, and make our discovery all the more likely,' Aragon declared irritably, the Fell now straight ahead. 'If we make a dash for it then we'll certainly be spotted, but such might be the surprise, and the advantage of our speed, that by the time the Magyars gather sufficient numbers to feel safe in attacking us, we'll be across their main territory and near or on to Klimt's.'

They decided on the latter course, and an early start that might give them the advantage of sufficiently visibility to see their way, but not to be so easily seen from a distance. The wind was across them, which was better than behind them but not ideal, and though it was not too strong, the day looked changeable.

'Come,' said Aragon when dawn broke, 'and stay close together. We have a long hard way to go but between us Stry and myself know the territory well enough not to go too far wrong.'

Stry nodded grimly. The peaks ahead were swathed in cloud and the air was cold and fretful, the breeze likely to change.

'Srena, are you ready?'

She nodded.

'Huete? Gallega?'

Their acknowledgements were quick nods and grunts, their eyes on the way ahead.

'Come then, and may all gods be with us . . .'

Did the clouds darken then in acknowledgement of how uncertain was the outcome likely to be of that historic return of Aragon on to the Fell? Did the wind whisper warning that the risks might after all be too great? How soon after that did those running wolves, who never stopped for more than a moment, never talked but in quick rasps and staccato barks, find time to pause for a moment at some black reflective pool of water in the peat, and concede that they had seen and heard and scented wolves as fleet as they themselves, no, faster because fitter, following close behind, and certain to catch up?

Perhaps, had the weather stayed as it was when they began, they might have made it across the Fell in one fast run, but the weather changed, and changed terribly. The wind veered and harshened, bringing battering hail and rain which froze on tired wolves' faces, and sapped tired wolves' aching limbs.

So, running desperately, they ran into disaster. Srena's injury began to hurt once more, and the wound began to weep; Huete split a paw when his feet slipped on lichen-covered rock; whilst Stry breathed in particles of heather and began to choke, catching at his breath as he ran, eyes watering, body slowing finally. As they stopped they saw that three wolves were on their heels, watching; and they heard the quick howls and barks to summon reinforcement, that they might all go in for the kill.

'There's a chance we've so surprised them that their call for help will not be swiftly answered,' rasped Aragon. 'Those three won't take us on as they are – they'll be content to harass us from a distance until others come to help them – that's always been the Magyars' cowardly way. For which reason, with Magyars, it's best to take the initiative and attack at once, for then they fall back and re-group. Stry, are you fit enough now for a bit of fighting?'

Stry nodded, not for the first time reassured by Aragon's calm resolution in the face of threat. Wiping his face and eyes, coughing still to clear the small fronds that had got into his throat, he came to stand at Aragon's flank.

'Huete?'

'I'm cold, hungry, tired, and angry – just give the word!'

Aragon smiled briefly, glad to see that one as awkward and recalcitrant as Huete could be relied on when things became difficult.

'Srena, we're going to attack. When we do you stay near me as best you can – I won't be going far. Gallega, you stay with her, *right* with her, to protect her rear. Now follow me, and keep to my pace, which will seem to weaken and slow. Be ready for my turn back on them, for it will be very sudden . . .'

They set off again, aware that the Magyar scouts, who had slunk out of sight for a time, would soon be up and after them. Sure enough, it was not long before one of the Magyars showed himself, and shortly after that Aragon began to slow, and then slow some more, and then speed up again and then slow again, so lulling the Magyars into believing the whole group was weakening that the three scouts all came out into the open, and closed in.

'Now!' thundered Aragon.

He turned, Huete at his right flank and Stry a little behind, making sure the two females did not lose touch.

'Now!' he said again, and charged straight at the nearest Magyar, Huete feinting off to his right before slowing to switch across towards one on the left.

They were fast and vicious assaults, combining sufficient surprise and ferocity to speedily destroy the Magyars' confidence and make them flee.

'They always retreat like that at first,' said Aragon, as the others joined and circled about, watching for a counter-attack or other Magyars they had not observed before. 'But then they come back, again and again until their quarry begins to tire. Remember, Stry?'

'I remember,' said Stry, who had been in a chase like this before with Aragon, and not so far across the Fell from here.

'Come, we've gained some time so we'll start forward again before –'

He was going to say before the Magyars sent out warning howls, but now they heard those, loud and sharp. Support was being summoned.

'We could chase after them and finish the job,' said Huete, who was feeling the energy of anger.

Aragon shook his head. 'Save it, wolf, for you'll need it in the hours ahead. We're not quite as far on our way as I would have liked, but we're on it, and we're still moving forward fast enough to give us a chance of reaching the Forest and support, or respite. Srena, how is your injury?'

'All right,' she said shortly, though evidently in pain. 'It aches but it's holding.'

'And that paw, Huete?'

'Now you mention it, Aragon, it hurts as well.'

Aragon acknowledged his rueful good humour. Huete was definitely a wolf worth having at one's flank.

'Stry? Gallega?'

'Let's go,' said Stry.

Then they were off again, lucky to find a shallow straight stream to follow for a while which would make the Magyars' job of finding their tracks again a shade harder; luckier still when they veered off it to find another, and then a run of wet rocks which caught the wind, and would disperse their scent better than heath, which plucked at fur and held a wolf's scent.

Sensing the need for rest, and seeing they had gained an advantage, for there was no further sign of Magyars after that first skirmish, Aragon led them up through broken rocks to higher ground from where he might have the advantage of sight and scent, for now the wind had veered easterly and would bring any following Magyar scents to them. The afternoon was already darkening, the day seemed suddenly short, and hope of reaching the respite of the Vale in daylight hours was all but gone. But at least they could now see the rise of the lower cliffs of the Tatra, a black scar across the Fell.

'That is the beginning of the Heartland,' said Aragon, and the others gazed upon it with awe and relief in their eyes.

'It looks so near,' said Huete.

'Almost near enough to touch,' echoed Srena.

But their respite was only brief for quite suddenly they saw Magyars ahead, two of them, and heard them behind, the barking of intimidation.

'Come,' commanded Aragon grimly, calling the bluff of those ahead and making straight at them.

The Magyars seemed surprised; they hesitated, then decided to double-bluff and stand their ground, and were rewarded by the full force of Aragon's assault.

If the Magyars had thought they were but a bunch of vagrants, to harry and hassle for a time, they knew different now. This time Aragon sent the first rolling, his shoulder torn, but the second he decided to kill.

'Take the others on!' he cried to Stry, as he charged down the fleeing wolf, turned him over, and closed his jaws upon his throat. A weak wolf, terrified; screaming as Aragon ripped his throat, and dying by the time he rose bloodily from him. Aragon looked back, saw the original three hesitating, started for them, and they retreated out of sight once more.

'Stay clear of us, or I'll leave you all like this,' he cried after them. Then he was gone, his mouth hurting from the power of his own assault, and his muzzle warm and sweet with another's blood.

'Come *on!*' he shouted, catching up the others as a leader should, urging them on as he overtook them, hoping that his example would help them once more find the strength to continue to run.

Until . . .

'Stop! Yes, here . . . we can take a moment's rest.'

Blessed respite; lungs aching in their in-out reaching for air, and a snatched drink through the dirty ice of a frozen pool. Just time enough for Aragon and Stry to glance ahead at the gently rising fell-land that was all that now remained before they reached the pastures of the Vale.

'There – we can see the Forest now. May Wulf grant that Klimt has moved down there from the Scarpfeld, so that he is there to give us help and support when we arrive with Magyars on our heels.'

Wearily he rose up again to continue the flight, realizing that the route directly ahead offered only the prospect of difficult, haggy ground that would now tire them very fast. It seemed plain that the best path lay downslope where a road might be, *must* be . . .

'Huete, you're doing well; Gallega, well done! Srena?'

'I am all right. It hurts, it is bleeding now, but I . . . can . . . run!'

In such moments wolves' bonding deepens into something afterwards understood only with difficulty by others who were not there and did not see the courage needed, and feel the pain that had to be endured.

'Stry, are you ready?'

Stry nodded, and Aragon rose once more, and the group with him.

'Think of the dream that lies ahead, not the danger that seeks to overtake us from the rear,' cried Aragon, and then he led them off again.

A shrill bark and summoning howl came from close behind, answered by one some way below where the road they were heading for ran; the bark again, and the howl repeated, and far, far ahead an answer.

The Magyars were closing in behind and below, and drawing in support far ahead, and now the wolves could only hope that the course Aragon had chosen was the right one. The wind flurried icy snow in their faces once more as they ran off downslope, from hummock to hummock, through peaty puddles and in the shadows of rock outcrops. Down, down, their paws slipping in peat, and chilled by the water that oozed out of it as they went. Down, nearly falling at the small ditch before the road, a final struggle up its bank and on to it.

A momentary pause; aching, pumping lungs.

The rough never-ending wilderness of the Fell had been suddenly reduced to a thin flat tapering line of road, its surface shiny white with flattened snow over which, towards them, small flakes chased and swirled, turned and rose, flew and fell. It was an empty-stretching road, on which there were no other wolves behind or before, and they felt that it could, oh yes it *would*, lead them to safety.

Tired, tired limbs, and the sound of approaching Magyars.

They started then, running northward along that lonely road, running that they might travel far enough down it unmolested that when the time came to veer right, and break off upslope into the Vale and towards their own territory, they could get away.

On and on along the centre of that road they ran, and it seemed that the light of the moon shone upon it, and brought it a radiance the dark hummocks of the Fell on either side did not possess; and yet there was no moon. It seemed that each of the swirling flakes of snow had caught in its crystals light from the stars in the night sky from which it had fallen; and yet there were no stars.

A strange road then, and one which had begun as a friend, and now turned into an enemy. It seemed to the fleeing wolves to grow steep, though it ran ahead as level as at the start; and that it grew dark and dangerous, though it seemed to catch the light no less than before. It seemed in their growing desperation and despair of ever reaching the freedom that lay ahead that it was a road on which shadowy wolves waited in front, and at the verges, and came up behind, though as yet there were no shadows . . .

The sound of Magyars on the Fell on either side of the road.

'Look only at the road, wolves, think only of that,' rasped out Aragon, his breathing heavy and painful now, the effort of each step ever greater. But believing that what was hard for him must be harder for those he led, he drove himself on, unwilling and unable to betray their faith and trust in him, until all that remained was the heavy patter-patter of paws in his ears, the throb of his heart and blood in his head, the growing ache of his body, and the road ahead, and ahead, and ever more ahead, and the Vale, seeming never to come closer.

Then sudden as an unexpected squall an ambush of Magyars came from right and left, and thundering up from behind. No time to look back, for to do so was to stumble, and begin to fall and feel the strain that came with getting aright again, and running on.

'Aragon, I . . .'

It was Srena, and he slowed so that she was fractionally ahead of him. He could see the blood streaking down her right flank now, the old wound open once again, and her tongue was beginning to hang at her desperate mouth as she steadily weakened, feeling that she could do no more than she had and must fade back now to the Magyars' claws and jaws, and be gone from all their future.

'Oh, Aragon –'

'You . . . must . . . try!' he cried, his own heart feeling it would burst. 'You . . . cannot . . . give up!'

There was a burst of movement at his shoulder and Stry pushed past, to give what he still might to keep them going on, the snow fading now as if they were outrunning it, and the wind veering eastward to give them a marginal respite.

On and on they went, but slowing ever more now, weakening all the time, whilst the Magyars seemed untired; some were now weaving in and out alongside them, as if to show they had strength in excess and were readying themselves to take the wolves, just . . . when . . . they – . . .

A wolf, a Magyar, dashed out of the shadows to the right and nearly tumbled Stry, Aragon speeding forward and snapping at him as he went back into shadow.

Ahead, not so far ahead, those shadows on the road, so long merely imagined, suddenly took on form and shape and dreadful solidity: wolves waiting, wolves ready and waiting, wolves whose bodies and minds were not tired with running.

A quick look sideways from Stry, the first sign that he might be giving up; a gasp from Srena and a stumble, and Huete calling, 'Watch out ahead!'

Then Gallega, suddenly slowing, too tired now to repress any longer the fear she felt, and the relief she would feel if she could only yield up to it now, to give in to her tiredness, to lose her pain in the darkness that closed in upon them all.

It was surely then, as they slowed still more with the knowledge that they were outnumbered and already surrounded, that Aragon saw ahead of them for the first time a huge wolf bestriding the road. He was one whose parentage, and whose disposition, and whose cruel and wretched tribe Aragon knew, though as yet he knew not his name.

He might never know his name, for now the road that had raced beneath his paws so long began to stop, and the shapes that had followed on right and left took form as his companions slowed, and he knew they had not strength to fight, nor to seek escape into the alien Fell, nor any hope of reaching now the Vale that lay just ahead, and the Forest above them to the right.

He saw now how near, how very near, were the shadows beneath the rising cliffs of the Tatra whose waterfalls he could faintly hear, and whose gulleys were black scars down the faces of the starlit cliffs.

Stars, and the snow was gone behind them.

Moon, and the clouds had broken away.

Magyars, and they were circling around them, one so much bigger and more fearsome than the rest.

It was in that moment of impending defeat and death that Aragon raised up his head and howled for help. Not of gods, for they were lost in time and distant, but of mortal wolves, wolves that might be near, wolves that had fled these parts a millennium before but might now be coming home.

It was a howl that made the Magyar leader smile.

'*We* are here, wolf,' he sneered, chuckling and leering at his pack. 'Yes, we are here,' his wolves echoed, the claws of their paws clattering impatiently on the road.

As Aragon's wolves gathered about him, each seeking to guard the others and finding there were not enough to guard all, he raised his head and howled again. For friends he howled, for help, and to the lost wolves that were his ancestry.

'No need to howl so loud, wolf, for we can hear you well,' rasped the Magyar leader, growing tired of the game and readying himself to signal a concerted attack by all his wolves. It would be a massacre.

'We can hear,' his pack concurred, their heads hunching forward, their eyes fixing on one of the wolves, their paws beginning the forward slide that was preparatory to killing cornered prey.

A third time Aragon raised his head to howl, his front paws already flexing to withstand the attack the huge Magyar leader was about to make. Massive he was, and frightening, and as Aragon began his howl he knew it might be his last.

Patter-patter ... patter-patter ... the sound of wolves running towards them through the night. Patter-patt–

To see what wolves they were the Magyars pulled back from attack, then a ripple of laughter spread amongst them as two of their scouts advanced down the road, slowing as they approached, for they were not sure what awaited them.

'Well!' chuckled their leader while they were some distance off, and then turning to Aragon he said, 'and are these the answer to your call for help, or help for me? Eh, wolf?'

The two wolves came forward hesitantly.

'We came as soon as we could, Führer, we came –'

'Be quiet and still, be *quiet*!' he commanded, turning from Aragon and looking past the new arrivals and out into the dark.

Patter-patter ...

More wolves, but the sound of their paws was different, heavier, more formidable than those that had just arrived. *Patter-PATTER!* and the deep warning bark of a wolf who knows his business and has heard a summons and is confident of answering it.

Who, or what, was coming down the road Aragon did not know, but he could see the stars behind once more, and hear the stir and rush of the falls over and up beyond the Forest off to his right, and knew they had gained more than a fraction of time, they had gained surprise once more.

He caught Stry's eye; they nodded, for they had seen the only chance they had, and each turned on one of their own – Stry to Gallega, a bite, and 'Run!', and then Aragon to Srena, a nip, and 'Now!' – and then all three males together, Huete, Aragon and Stry wheeled and charged as one into the turned back of the leader, to tumble him, to confuse his pack, to run past him towards the help that came now out of the darkness, into the light of the stretching road.

A wolf larger even than Führer; a wolf who in his time had out-faced, out-fought, and killed more wolves than were assembled, friend and foe, on the Fell that night.

Kobrin had come, and Kobrin alone it seemed.

Kobrin, of all the Russias, the only one of the Wolves of Time, not excepting Klimt himself, who could match the Magyar leader for weight, for size and for ferocity.

One, as well, who could more than match him for experience.

Kobrin charging, himself seeming a whole pack of wolves.

Kobrin, war-lord wolf, wolf of war.

As Führer was buffeted and off-balanced from behind by Aragon and the others, Kobrin veered to the right, turning the focus of all of them away from the rising ground to their left.

As he did two wolves came down from the terrace on that side, down a wolfway they had followed, down together as if they were but one: Elhana to one side, Lounel to another. Into the sudden mêlée they brought their extra strength, turning, confusing, charging, as the Magyars turned this way and that, unsure now, their leader by-passed, their quarry fleeing not to right or left or straight ahead but all about, all running, veering, turning and at Aragon's urging heading finally out on to the Vale towards the Forest above.

Then Kobrin turned back, attacking the first that came.

Then Aragon, as Kobrin retreated past him, great Aragon now, his blood-stained jaws snapping at the next Magyar who tried to approach, and turning that wolf over.

Then Lounel, as Aragon retreated, took his turn to lunge at the approaching angry Magyars.

And then . . .

Then a single, staccato, shrill female bark, and the Magyars stilled and stopped as one.

A solitary female, haggy and old, coming to Führer's flank.

She laughed into the night and said, 'Follow my love, and you shall find – but not yet; find my dear, and you shall know – but not tonight; know, and you shall make these wolves flee like chickens before the fox. Not now, but soon, that their defeat is all the sweeter!'

But even Dendrine and her crude cackle of a voice was not what put the feel of a shaft of ice into the hearts of Aragon and Kobrin and those who now gathered about them, upslope on their own territory. It was Führer, squatting at her side, staring and unflurried, apparently amused. He rose slowly, he trotted with grace and ease up those slopes the others found so steep and hard until he stood at the head of Magyar pack, staring upward at wolves and territory which were not his own. He stared at Kobrin and Aragon, prudence overcoming his evident desire to attack them once more.

'Your name, wolf?' said the Magyar, as if he spoke to a flea-ridden vagrant, who had dared come within the circle of the pack.

'I am Kobrin,' growled the great wolf, 'and these wolves are in the protection of our pack and our leader Klimt of Tornesdal. This territory is ours. And *your* name?'

'He is my son,' said the she-wolf Dendrine, her teeth as yellow as her eyes, 'he is the Führer of the Magyars.'

'Your name?' repeated Kobrin, taking a single step forward so purposeful that the Magyars all hunched a little more as if ready for attack.

'Hassler was my father, wolf, and Klimt and you killed him, did you not?'

'Your name?' said Kobrin again, his voice as thin and harsh as stretched wire.

'I am the Magyar leader, and Hassler's son, and Dendrine's child.'

'Your *name*?'

'I am Führer, and in me are all the leaders past and present of the Magyar race. I *am*.'

He said it slowly, his voice and meaning carrying the force of blizzard snow.

Then, pointing at Aragon, he said, 'Today this wolf of yours killed one of mine. For this we shall take four of yours. One for four ever more won't make the Wolves of Time last long, eh, killer-of-my-father? Eh, mother?'

Dendrine laughed, taking pleasure in her son's good cheer.

A final drift of snow swirled in the narrow space that separated the two enemy packs while Kobrin said nothing, nothing at all. He signalled to right and left and one by one, in their own time, his wolves retreated upslope and into the dark of night.

'Kobrin!'

'Wolf?' responded Kobrin coolly.

'Tell your leader Klimt, who dares not show his face this day, that since he was first in this place of all of you, then he shall be last of all.'

'Last for what?'

'Death,' said Führer, smiling in the great lopsided way he had.

'Would you like to tell him yourself, now?' said Kobrin.

There was a moment's uncertainty on Führer's face, and on Dendrine's as well. This was not a risk they seemed to wish to take.

'We shall choose the time and place,' rasped Dendrine.

Kobrin smiled coldly as Führer turned from him and was gone with all his pack downslope, the pitter-patter of their paws fading down through heath and over heather, and back down the road that led beyond the Vale out into the winter-bound Fell.

'And where is Klimt?' asked Aragon a moment later, before they had even had time to greet each other. 'Up in the Forest?'

Kobrin and Lounel shook their heads.

'No, he is not, and nor are his sons.'

'But you told the Magyar that –'

Kobrin shook his head again and said, 'I told him nothing, wolf, but let him think a great deal. Klimt is not here, nor his sons, nor hardly any other wolves.'

Then glancing at those with Aragon, Lounel said, 'Aragon, your coming with these wolves has doubled the size of our little pack. You are most welcome!'

'You mean those Magyar wolves could have . . . ?'

'They could have taken us all,' said Kobrin, 'had they realized. Now come, to the Forest, where we can welcome you properly, and begin to hear your story, as you must hear ours . . .'

CHAPTER TWENTY-ONE

*Elhana discovers old passions never die, and the Magyars
begin to reassert themselves*

'**K**LIMT DEAD!' cried Aragon the moment the Magyars had
departed.

'Follow me, wolf,' said Kobrin urgently, seeking to hurry
him away at once lest the Magyars return in force to try to catch them
unguarded. The truth of his subterfuge concerning Klimt could wait.

'But where are Solar and Lunar?' demanded Stry, as troubled as
Aragon.

'*Come*,' said Lounel reassuringly, 'things are not quite what they
seem, nor as bad.'

'And what's this about retreating back into the Forest, and away?'

But Kobrin and the others did not tell the new arrivals the full story
until they were back in the safe haven of the rocks about the Great
Cleft, with the Fall a muffled roar nearby, and Aragon and the others
were well fed and rested, their wounds and sores attended to.

Kobrin told how Klimt had left with his sons for Khazaria, and that
it might yet be some weeks or months before they returned. 'Hopefully
with reinforcements. We have managed to keep the Magyars at bay,
and in that have been helped by their seeming indifference to this
part of the Heartland territory.'

He waved towards the Forest that stretched away beneath them,
Aragon rightly guessing that his brief account of 'keeping the Magyars
at bay' was a modest understatement.

In fact the group's survival under Kobrin's direction through the
long months since Klimt's sudden departure had been a masterpiece
of prudent withdrawal and retreat. That Führer and Dendrine were
unsure of Klimt's whereabouts showed just how successful the original
subterfuge had been, and how diligent Kobrin's guardianship and
deployment of the others had been since, keeping the remaining
Wolves out of harm's way.

'Führer might huff and puff about killing us,' said Kobrin wryly, as the two groups of Wolves had this first sharing of their news, 'but he has shown little interest in sending his forces over the col from the Scarpfeld into the Forest to search for us.'

'So you have a clear run of the Forest then?' asked Aragon.

'Not quite,' said Kobrin, 'and anyway we do not stay in one place very long. We come here regularly, if only because we believed that one day you might return, just as before long we expect others back.'

'You mean Klimt?'

'Not only Klimt,' said Kobrin, who had explained the reasons for Klimt's expedition to Khazaria, 'but Tervicz and Rohan as well.'

'Ah, Tervicz . . .' murmured Aragon with some relief, for he had not heard that loyal wolf's name mentioned until now and had feared the worst. Tervicz might not be the strongest of males, but he had about him something of the pack's final destiny, as befitted the legendary Bukov wolf.

'Elhana, explain about Tervicz,' said Kobrin, who as acting leader needed to see how these two approached each other after so long apart, and remembering that it was likely that Aragon himself had fathered Elhana's cubs, for which reason, and the love the two had shared, Klimt had banished him. Kobrin hoped that the flames of their old love would not be re-kindled now, but he feared his hoping would be in vain. He was too old not to know that some passions do not die however much time passes, or however the protagonists might change. So he watched with resigned curiosity as Elhana moved from the shadows where she had been lurking out into better light, where Aragon might see her.

Elhana had aged visibly these past months, partly for worry of what had happened to Solar and Lunar but also because Kobrin had kept the Wolves constantly on the move and she adapted less well than he to so nomadic and stressful a life. Her face was thinner, almost gaunt, and her fur had long since lost that sheen it held when Kobrin first met her years before. Her eyes, once so full of light and hope, held now the shadows of a wolf whose life has not been quite fulfilled: confident enough, intelligent always, but not quite happy. A ledrene who had done her duty by the pack, who had raised young and seen them to maturity, and was not yet willing to give up her role, but who had not known the full love and trust of a leader to complete her life.

'Aragon . . . welcome home.'

Her voice was a shade nervous, her glance quick and uncertain, as if waiting for his reaction. She managed a smile.

'Elhana . . .' he said, turning then to look at her. His voice, too, betrayed doubt and uncertainty.

'Elhana . . .' he said again, his voice deeper and stronger as if regaining control over himself.

They saw that he too had aged, his certainty in life long gone, its difficulties and ambiguities heavier upon him, the responsibilities of his years of exile somewhere in the frown that had settled in his face; and in his eyes, too, was the look of one who had done his duty but as yet found no fulfilment in doing it.

'Tell him where Tervicz has gone,' said Kobrin, looking from one to the other.

But try as she might, Elhana could not. She found herself staring into Aragon's gaze and rediscovering there the wolf she had once known, but older now, and wiser: the inner wolf she had always loved. He had aged, but the years had sloughed off the arrogance and vanity and replaced it with something simpler and far stronger. But what held her mute was his gaze upon her, for he saw beyond what she seemed to have become, and that the shadows that beset her could be – were being even now – removed by the light of his love.

'My dear . . .' she whispered impulsively, as if others were not there.

'Elhana . . .' he said a third time, laughing now, indifferent to all else, yet in no way disrespectful to old Kobrin, or those all about.

He went to her and they nuzzled face to face, then flank to flank, and it seemed that the dull roar of the Falls faded away, and the light from the drear winter sky was grey no more; and Kobrin knew that nothing had changed, nothing could change – and knew as well that the Heartland was better for it, much better.

He allowed himself a growling chuckle, as if to say he was not quite pleased, yet not displeased, but rather he wished the world would get on and let him be sometimes!

'What must be must be,' he said dryly; 'meanwhile, Elhana, would you please . . .'

Elhana laughed as well, the first time she had done so in months, and went to Kobrin's side to make it quite plain that she too recognized him as acting leader.

'He's gone back to his home territory,' she said, 'with Rohan for company. Klimt wanted it.'

'A reward,' said Aragon matter-of-factly, settling down. All there knew that Tervicz had never had a partner, and was too loyal ever to have taken Rohan to mate here among them, even had she pushed herself forward upon him.

'Yes, a reward,' Elhana concurred, 'and, too, to satisfy Klimt's need to know if the Magyars' occupation of the Carpathians has reached as far as Bukovina.'

'Klimt knows how to get the best out of everything.'

'Yes,' said Elhana dryly, 'he does.'

In the weeks that followed, as the winter's snows deepened and water-courses froze, the Wolves stayed close by the Forest, though at its eastern end, away from the Fell and possibility of a surprise attack from the Magyars.

The short days and long nights were cold and windswept, and when the wind died the dark, enshadowed trees rumbled to the sound of ice-falls and avalanches in the mountains and cliffs above. The Fall was the last water-course to freeze, its great roar softening to a muted rippling of sound until, one night, it stopped altogether; it had become a strange, rising mass of grey-white flows and waves beyond the Great Cleft into which its flow normally disappeared before issuing in a rush at the base of the cliffs and running down through the trees.

The Wolves explored the inner depths of the Cleft, now dark with shadows and ice-cold, the patter of their paws, their brief barks of warning to each other not to climb too high on the verglas-covered rocks, echoing above them and joining the endless round of cliff-noise the chamber caught – rocks falling, snow sliding, wind howling.

'A place into which to retreat if all else fails,' said Lounel.

But Kobrin disagreed. 'A place to get massacred in, by Mennen or by Magyars,' he said, for he always liked at least one good line of retreat.

Here it was, with Kobrin and the others turning a blind eye, that Elhana and Aragon renewed their love, and mated once more. They had lost too much time to want to waste more, and things had changed. They were older now, more discreet, and the impulse for their mating was more for comfort and mutual affection than to procreate.

'Anyway, my love, I'm surely past that now,' Elhana told Aragon one afternoon as, their desires satisfied, they lay by the frozen Fall warming their snouts in bright winter sun, and talking of their years of separation.

'You know that when Klimt returns –'

'I know,' said Elhana resignedly and with respect.

Aragon had learnt his place and would never split up the Wolves of Time again.

'You are sure he will come back, aren't you?' said Elhana.

Aragon nodded, needing to say nothing. There was an inevitability about Klimt's destiny that made those who followed him quite sure that when he said he would be back, he would be.

'He is the greatest wolf I have ever known,' said Aragon, who these days never talked of his youth, or the sense of high destiny that had been behind the impulse that first brought him to the Heartland.

'Solar and Lunar are surely your sons,' murmured Elhana, who by then was convinced of this and wished to remind Aragon that if it were so, by that fact alone he had fulfilled his destiny.

'Hmmm,' growled Aragon, pressing his flank closer still to Elhana's, 'I wish that I *felt* my destiny was done, but I do not. There is more for us to do yet, my dear, before you and I can ever take the wolfway to the stars knowing we have achieved what we must.'

Elhana could only nod her head, but though she felt the same she could not then quite say what it was.

But two months later, one harsh February day, a tiredness in her limbs and an unwonted reluctance to move from the warm comfort of her Forest den to spend a little time at Aragon's flank told her that she might be with cub once more. The prospect appalled her, and she lay quietly alone all day, eschewing company and food, and finally moving only to lick at some snow to ease the dryness in her mouth.

Nor did she reveal her condition for several weeks, not until the thaws set in; the cliffs and Forest were a-roar with the run and rush of meltwater through innumerable runnels and temporary falls, and the sun began to shine once more. But by then the others had guessed, and Kobrin had long since agreed with Aragon what they must do, which was to retreat eastward along the base of the cliffs and out of that part of the Heartland and find some safe secure place where Elhana might have her young.

'We have not strength as a pack to defend this place against the Magyars if they come in force,' he said. 'We must get away while Elhana can still move comfortably and hope these births go unnoticed by Führer, or, more particularly, Dendrine, who will surely wish to put a brutal stop to them. For if others hear that the Wolves are increasing their numbers naturally, and it turns out that the Magyars under Führer are only doing so by aggrandizement, you may be sure that many will feel that Wulfin favours us, and seek to join our pack.'

Aragon agreed, no more pleased than Elhana that she was to have more young. It would not help matters when Klimt returned, however much his absolute authority was acknowledged by all. He would surely not welcome an addition to the Wolves in such circumstances.

'We shall wait a few more days before we leave,' said Kobrin, 'for we shall have streams and rivers to cross and this is not the time to do it. Meanwhile, we had best double our guards, especially to the western side from where the Magyars are most likely to come. I doubt that they'll come in force until they know we're still here, so most likely at first they'll only send patrols. If we see any we'll be off at once, meltwater or no.'

The pack was made uneasy by Elhana's unfortunate news, and bad-tempered too, and only Lounel saw it in a better light: 'Wulfin smiles upon any female that gets with cub, however it might be, and if we keep our heads good will surely come of it. I wish I felt more certain that Klimt would soon be with us, but I do not. Only silence from that quarter, and strange uncertainty . . . the omens are neither good nor bad but troubling. Yet others will join us soon, for by night the constellations turn and turn above our heads as if wolfkind is gathering its strength.'

'You mean others will come before Klimt?' said the matter-of-fact Kobrin.

Lounel grinned, rose and stretched his lanky limbs: 'You can put it thus if you like, Kobrin, but the stars put it more poetically and it is with their voice that I speak.'

'Tervicz, most like,' grunted Kobrin, who since Klimt had been gone had come to like and understand Lounel rather more, and to trust his counsel.

'Could be,' said Lounel ambiguously, leaving them to wander amidst the scree that littered the bottom of the cliffs.

'Where does he go?' asked Aragon, watching after him.

He had affection for Lounel, and felt a certain awe as well, for though the gangly wolf seemed to do so little, being neither fighter nor hunter, nor even much concerned with pack-talk, his spirit held the very essence of the Wolves' spiritual dreams.

Kobrin smiled respectfully after the French wolf, for though he was less appreciative of Lounel's unique gifts he recognized his courage and route-finding skills in wandering alone into enemy territory.

'He likes the Scarpfeld and its proximity to the WulfRock. That's where I think he goes, despite the Magyar threat, and he's never been caught yet.'

Three days later Lounel's prediction that it would be Tervicz who re-appeared first proved correct. They heard the greeting of a traveller's howl one evening, and then another wolf's as well, and there, suddenly, he was, Rohan at his side.

If anything his journeying had thinned him, and his face was more lined, and perhaps it was the snow still on the mountains above that gave his coat a hint of grey; or simply a new maturity. Rohan, too, looked older, and her face had that good grace that Elhana's was wont to have when she was younger, which had returned a little since Aragon had come back.

Their greetings were many, and the Wolves talked long into the night of all their news, and listened as Tervicz described his home-coming to Bukovina, to discover that his father Zcale was long dead, but to his joy his sister Szaba and crippled brother Kubrat were still alive.

'No wolves ever venture up into the highest of the Bukovian mountains,' explained Tervicz, 'so they are safe enough from the Magyar threat. Even as it was, and though I knew the territory, it took me days to track them down, eh Rohan?'

The two looked fondly at each other, and it was plain that Tervicz had found a good deal more than his siblings in the weeks he had stayed in his home territory. The love the two felt for each other was palpable and touching to see.

'You might have stayed,' suggested Kobrin, who always tested the loyalty of those in his care.

'Szaba wanted it,' said Tervicz sombrely, 'more than anything. In us she saw a last chance that our ancient pack might not become extinct. But . . . my loyalty is to Klimt and to the Wolves of Time.'

'And mine as well,' said Rohan.

It was a considerable sacrifice, for the impulse to produce cubs is strong, especially in one of so prime an age as Rohan, and Tervicz must have felt the urge to stay with his siblings.

'Szaba wanted to come back with us, and Kubrat too, but his condition makes so long a journey difficult and dangerous, the more so when the Heartland is controlled by the Magyars.'

'Tervicz had to stop them following us forcibly,' said Rohan.

'And even then they only stayed where they were because I promised that one day I would come back for them and bring them to the WulfRock. It is Kubrat's greatest desire to bring himself before it in the presence of the Wolves of Time. He knows that his condition surely prevents him from being one of us, or of any pack, but ... his was the spirit that first impelled me to howl down the Wolves and take up my role as the Bukov wolf. Somehow or other, when times are better, I shall go back for them or ...'

'Or if you cannot then I shall,' said Rohan fiercely.

'Meanwhile, we have come back to serve the pack as best we can, and give this warning. We have seen many a wolf on the trails westward out of the Ukraine over the Carpathians travelling to join the Magyar hordes. The name of Führer is known, and of Dendrine too, and many wolves talk of them as if one day they will be gods!'

'Humph!' grunted Kobrin dismissively.

'Whether it be true or not, it is what wolves want to believe, and they are coming to the Heartland to join them. We pressed on through the snow and ice to be here before those wolves. As the snows finally melt and spring begins, they will be arriving in numbers on the Fell, and Führer's strength will be greater still. If the Wolves are to lead wolfkind to better ways our time is running out. So ... have you no news of Klimt?'

Kobrin and Elhana could only shake their heads.

'He will be back,' said Tervicz fiercely, as if others doubted it, 'and he will know what to do. Meanwhile ...'

'Meanwhile, my friend, we shall keep our heads,' said Kobrin calmly, 'and see that Elhana reaches full term with her cubs in safety and comfort. How Klimt will react to them I don't know. We must hope that since he accepted that Solar and Lunar and you others might not be his, I suppose ...' Kobrin shrugged. He too trusted Klimt to put the pack before his own feelings, and only wished he felt more certain that things would turn out well. For the best, perhaps, but at what cost? It was a heavy burden Klimt carried, almost too heavy for mortal wolf. 'Now, I know a place where Elhana can go and be safe, if she's willing.'

'Why should not I be willing, Kobrin?' said the pack's ledrene.

'Your daughter Merrow died there.'

Shadows passed over Elhana's face. She still missed Merrow. They all did. She had been the pack's joy, the pack's grace, the pack's laughter. Tare was its anger, its fierceness, its ledrene-strength, but Merrow had been the source of future pleasures.

'I know the place,' said Elhana, who already had it in mind as a sanctuary in which to give birth. It was that ruined building safely eastward of the Forest which bridged a river, and which had been inhabited by Mennen centuries before. Merrow had died in a Mennen battle there, lost when the structure crashed in upon her, leaving Lunar staring helplessly, and grieving afterwards for so many months.

The Wolves thought of the place as the 'Ruin', and had passed by there from time to time. Yes, Elhana knew it.

'I'll look at it again and see if there is somewhere there to hide away where my young will be safe, with water nearby and food to hunt. Aragon will come with me.'

So it was agreed, in the easy way the pack had adopted since Aragon's return, with none seeking precedence over others, but all acknowledging that until Klimt returned Kobrin would make decisions that affected them all.

The bulk of the pack now shifted eastward out of the main Forest to be nearby the ruin when Elhana started her cubbing, but Kobrin kept guards posted in the Forest itself, as far as its western edge, where they might easily watch for sign of Magyar up on the col or off across the Fell. Though a good vantage point, it was isolated, so he insisted that wolves watched there in pairs, or near enough each other that one could not be caught out alone and ambushed before another might come to their aid and help them to the sanctuary of the Forest. Once there he felt certain that their detailed knowledge of the terrain would ensure their safety.

'It's a risk,' he explained, 'but we must let the Magyars know we are about, for if we do not, they may conclude the Forest is abandoned and spill over into this territory with their new recruits, making it all the harder for us to recover it once Klimt rejoins us with reinforcements.'

Elhana's cubs came suddenly on a clear cold day in early March, at twilight. She had not grown as large as with previous cubbings, nor felt as well, yet on the last few days a calmness had come over her before the final restlessness; she had climbed upslope the day before to see the rushing streams that came off the cliffs and through the screes, to sit awhile with Tare at her side, and to stare eastward towards the main part of the Forest where she would have preferred to be. She knew she would cub soon, and said as much to Tare.

'You'll know, too, my dear, when it's your turn.'

'It'll never be . . .'

'Yes it will, and Rohan's too perhaps.'

'There won't be room for two of us,' responded Tare, frowning and aggressive. She and Rohan did not get on, and she had reimposed her authority over her gentler sister, and made it difficult for Tervicz to show his love and affection for her. Yes, Rohan and he had sacrificed a lot to loyalty.

'The day is coming when wolfkind will need all the young it can create,' said Elhana softly, 'and there'll be room for more packs than there has been since the start of the Dark Millennium. The Mennen are dying now.'

'Hmmm,' said Tare doubtfully.

Elhana had let her prepare the birthing-place beneath the Ruin, where Merrow had died. They had entered in alongside the stream that ran there, their feet scrabbling through water before they climbed up into the maze of secret places between fallen masonry, and girders, and still-standing cellar rooms all arched and ancient.

There had been a moment both had shared, which sent a frisson of recognition and horrified understanding down their spines.

'Merrow's scent!' whispered Tare. 'But that must mean she survived.'

'Yes,' said Elhana, exploring forward with Tare close behind, and finding places where Merrow had made a burrow for sleeping. The dark enshadowed places roared and echoed to the sound of running water, loud enough that they had to shout sometimes to be heard, and though the air was cool – cooler than outside – it was not especially damp. There were gaps and fissures in the fallen masonry and the place was well-aired.

'Why didn't she . . . ?'

'She must have been injured, she must –'

They both froze. There was a slinking of movement off in the shadows, and the odour of rats as eyes blinked and were gone.

'She must have fed on those,' said Elhana.

She felt relief, enormous relief, for if there were such indications here of her survival, and no sign of her mortal remains, then surely she had survived and prospered well enough to escape. Then . . . well, there might be a hundred reasons why she had not returned to the pack. Had not Elhana herself deserted her birth-pack? Shock and injury may change the way a wolf sees the world.

'May Wulfin be with her,' said Elhana. 'If this place saw her back to health it will surely give protection to my cubs. It will do . . .'

So it proved, and the day after Elhana and Tare had climbed to the screes Elhana felt the first constrictions and brief pains, and retired back to the Ruin, none but she and Tare knowing their true significance.

'Why tell the pack?' she had said. 'Let Klimt be the first to know, for Merrow was his daughter, was she not?'

Well, no, probably not, thought Tare, but in pack terms he was leader and therefore Merrow's father, as her own.

'Yes,' whispered Tare, who had learnt to hold her tongue better than before, 'of course.'

Now only Tare was allowed into the Ruin, and then not to the place where Elhana gave birth to the three cubs that came suddenly one afternoon, quietly, with barely pause to think of pain or discomfort but time enough to clean herself and them as each arrived.

Tare watched from a distance, warned off by her mother, permitted only to tell the others that the three were born.

'They want to know their names,' Tare said, 'when you choose them.'

'I have chosen them,' murmured Elhana, licking her young, easing them to her teats, content in their possession and occupation of her love and life.

'They still want to know their names,' said Tare some days later.

Elhana only smiled.

It seemed an age after that before Elhana began to emerge, to stare at the sun, to briefly watch the advance of spring before returning to her demanding young, whose eyes had opened, whose questing for her milk was unceasing except in the dead of night, when Elhana lay encircling them, loving them in a way she had never quite been able to love the others.

Within three weeks, towards the end of March, the cubs, two males and a female, were showing their snouts at the sunlight that shafted through the trees down to the watery entrance into Elhana's birthing-place, and wondering about the great shapes of wolves that went back and forth, and the eyes that stared, and the huge dark male who was allowed by their mother to come near them, and stare at them; and the old, grizzled male, huger still, who stared from across the water, his eyes softening a shade before he turned away to go about his work.

Until one day, the cubs more or less still, the sun upon their eager snouts and slanting across their soft downy faces and into their blue eyes, she told the pack their names.

'Of the three far places are they named, from where I their mother, Aragon their father and Klimt their leader came in days long gone . . .'

She howled the making of their names rather than spoke of it, as if in their birthing she had re-discovered something she had lost of a past before the Wolves of Time came to the Heartland, a time of hope and innocence.

'The first-born of these three is named Umbrio, after a wolf who loved me true when I was young and lost his life to the wolf who became leader of the Benevento pack, of which I rose to become ledrene. Acknowledge him.'

It was an ancient rite in which a pack accepts its new-born cubs into itself, and each adult utters the cub's name as if to seal it into their familial heart.

'Umbrio, Umbrio, Umbrio . . .' their voices repeated.

Umbrio looked wide-eyed at them all, a dark cub, playful, with the broad good looks of Aragon.

'My next born was –'

The female cub ran to her flank and tried to nuzzle at her teat.

'. . . is this ungainly, rushing thing. Just like her mother once was said to be! Too eager by half for everything!'

Laughing, Elhana turned to Aragon and said, 'In remembrance of your mother, who loved you true and gave you the stories that you tell of Spanish wolves, I have named her Jimena.'

Aragon smiled, his eyes glistening with memory before he went gently to Jimena to nuzzle her as she retreated before his bulk into her mother's flank.

'Acknowledge her.'

As the pack uttered Jimena's name Elhana's last-born stared at them all, aware that he was next to be talked about. He was fairer than his brother, and perhaps a shade smaller, but there was a strength and maturity in his gaze that the others did not yet have, and his eyes were paler and cooler, and though this time there was no doubt of the cubs' paternity yet the gods seemed to have put into his whole demeanour a hint of the Nordic tundra from where Klimt came.

'Klimt, our leader, came from Tornesdal, and in his honour I have named my last-born male Torne. Ack —'

But the pack had already begun to acknowledge him, for he came forward and stood proud at his mother's side, nudging away the playful Umbrio, smaller for now but stronger, and the pack felt compelled to say his name.

'Torne, Torne, Torne . . .'

Until Lounel came forward and said, 'They are well named, Elhana, and honourably named. May the gods endow these three with the gifts and strengths of their ancestry, and show us how best to teach them all we know, and all we forget that we know.'

Jimena stayed close by Elhana; Umbrio turned head over heels and ended in a heap amidst Aragon's great paws; while only Torne stood still and alone, staring about at them all, and then at the trees and cliffs beyond, and then turning from them to go down to the river and drink of its icy water.

'We knew we had a past, and have struggled to survive the present,' said Lounel; 'now we know we have a future.'

Kobrin nodded his agreement, and the naming rite completed, the pack dispersed, feeling a new mountain had been climbed, and a new horizon seen.

Meanwhile, there was work for Kobrin to do, and all the others too. The Magyars had been spotted across the Fell, in larger numbers than before, and scouts of theirs up on the col that led over to the Scarpfeld.

Lounel and Tervicz went scouting up there in their turn and reported that so far the Magyars had not re-occupied the Scarpfeld for the summer.

'Hmmm,' mused Kobrin, 'it might be worth pretending to re-take it for a time, to force them to "recapture" it themselves so that we can retreat back down here to the Forest leaving them feeling there are still more of us than they realize.'

'And Elhana?' said Aragon.

'Tare can watch over her, and one or two of the others. I doubt that the Magyars would venture this far before re-occupying the Scarpfeld; though . . .'

'Yes, Kobrin?'

'Unless they knew she had given birth. Then . . .'

Kobrin looked sombre. If they knew that, or even suspected it, they would surely come in force.

'They cannot but think our pack might try, especially if they believe Klimt is close.'

'Trying is one thing, having them a long way off outside the Heartland another; but having them here, but a day's trek from the Scarpfeld, right under their noses, that's another thing again. Dendrine and Führer would not countenance it, and we know Dendrine's cruelty, and her son's partiality to eating young.'

'So ... we might create a confrontation with them over the Scarpfeld?'

'Why not?' said Kobrin, the glint of battle in his eyes. Their numbers were strong enough for such games now, and they might set a scene that Klimt – assuming he came back – could capitalize on. There is nothing like a pack's gaining victory to promote complacency in the months afterwards. Yes ... 'We must choose our moment well – to show the Magyars how vain we are, how stupid, to lull them into thinking we are weak, and that Klimt is a spent force.'

Aragon understood and felt honoured to be in Kobrin's company. The old wolf knew more about fighting, whether personally or as a pack, than any wolf he had ever met.

Then, a few days into April, the Magyar threat returned in earnest, and the moment for the feigned confrontation Kobrin wanted to set up came nearer.

Rohan had taken up her watch at the east station of the Forest in mid-morning, having relieved Tervicz, who had been there since before dawn. Other Wolves were out and about in the Forest, while others still hovered about the Ruin, watching over Elhana's cubs as they began to find their feet beyond their birthing den.

The watchers where Rohan had taken up her stance used an area of open ground, slightly elevated from the sward adjacent to it and well clear of the Forest itself. It gave views right along the Forest's eastern edge, and down to the easternmost part of the Vale, where it ran on to the Fell. The ground comprised moist sward with occasional tufts of heather, dramatically broken up by a field of boulders, one or two as big as conifers, which a million years before had broken free of the cliffs above and rolled downslope. Perhaps in those far-off days the soil had been hard-frozen, for now the fall of boulders was far clear of the cliff itself, and the scree beneath it, and where they had run down the slope a rough scar of a channel had been etched into the ground.

Now the boulders were covered with moss and lichen, their nutrient-rich crevices filled with ferns and lady's mantle, and the upper parts of one or two of the larger boulders were host to the winding roots of mountain ash and birch.

In winter the rocks hummed and whistled with the wind, and their northern sides grew shiny with grey verglas upon which birds, eagle and buzzard, raven and rook, would strive for a time to get a grip, slipping about and flapping their wings to keep balance, before moving off to somewhere where perching was easier.

In spring the rocks gave shelter to delicate sorrel and saxifrage which grew where the sun was warmest; and in summer rabbits scampered out of their subterranean homes amongst the rocks, whilst marmots emerged from the screes upslope.

Only eastward was there no view, for there the land rose steadily to a low outcrop beyond which it dropped away towards the Fell once more. To this spot, watchers would often go, though it was too far from the Forest, and too exposed, for wolves to feel comfortable there alone for long – something the Magyars felt as well, for this spot had become the natural buffer-zone between the two territories, the males from each side making their way there at different times and marking their side of the hill . . . and 'the Hill' is what the Wolves had dubbed the place, the watching-ground near the Forest below it being called Eastern Rocks.

Rohan liked that watching duty very much, for it was much less exposed than the Tree, and while the winds could be harsh when they were north or southerly, when the sun shone there was usually a nook somewhere which a wolf could occupy for shelter and still retain a view, knowing he or she could only be seen with difficulty, even from the Hill above. She took up her duties that morning with some pleasure, for the sun was bright and warm, and the thaw so far under way that everywhere she turned the ground was moist and shining, whilst the air was filled with the running and rilling of a thousand streamlets, and the distant roar of waterfalls over the edge of the cliffs above. Indeed, so far had the thaw progressed that several of the gulleys that ran down through the Forest and were normally dry for most of the year, were now running and frothing with water, and the whole place felt alive.

Rohan picked her way over the rushing streams and amongst the trees towards the bright light of the sky where the Forest thinned, and called out to Tervicz she was there. At his answering call that all was well she bounded out into the sunlight, scenting at the spring air, alive to the waking of new life about her.

By way of greeting the two wolves nuzzled at each other, for they had become close companions on their journey west, and though Tervicz was shy of females, especially younger ones such as Rohan, he had learned to relax with her.

'I heard cows bellowing right down in the Vale, so Mennen will probably be preparing to bring them up into the pastures before long. There was scent of alien wolf from the Hill but when I went to investigate I found no recent signs or scent of wolf. Perhaps a Magyar or two came up to stretch their legs today as we're doing – and watch the ground upslope, it's still frozen underneath and dangerously slippery on the steeper slopes.'

Rohan only half listened to his report for her attention had been drawn by the shrill call of eagles and, though it took a little searching, she finally caught sight of a pair of them gyring up the grey-black face of the cliffs above, crossing and re-crossing higher still the white water of the falls.

'Rohan, did you hear what I said?'

But she only nodded vaguely, for the sun was warm on her thick coat, and seemed good all about the world.

'Well, anyway, watch yourself, for there'll be Magyars about today, if I know them.'

'Tervicz, you always worry so much; why not stop and talk to me awhile if you think I need protection?'

He grinned and shook his head. 'I've been here since before the moon faded and now I'm tired.'

Then he was gone back to the Forest and after turning for a moment to stare at her, he disappeared into the shadows. Yet Tervicz did not go far. He closed his eyes all right, but quite close to the Forest edge, where he could hear and respond all the sooner if Rohan gave warning that she had seen movement or danger about.

For her part Rohan watched him go with a smile on her face, for she liked Tervicz and trusted him, and was touched that he should show concern for her. She knew him well enough to guess that having scented Magyar earlier he had probably not ventured very far into the Forest before settling down to rest.

Few wolves were more selfless than Tervicz and, she knew, especially towards herself. It was just a pity he was not younger and more . . . more like . . . more like who?

She lay in the sun on the sward with the rocks behind and a clear view downslope, musing on males and on Tervicz, listening to the shifts in the breeze, scenting the moisture in the mild air, the wakening earth, the droppings of a rook.

The breeze turned for a moment into a wind, and shifted, and she heard a sound upon the Hill; her ears pricking, she was immediately alert, all thoughts of males gone. She stared and stayed quite still, before retreating into shadow and settling down once more. Colder, she stood up again, glancing across at the Forest edge where two rooks flapped in and out of the trees. A buzzard call across over the trees and out of sight, the sun bright, the breeze . . .

Rohan impulsively moved out into the sunlight once more, though keeping the rocks now about her, and she picked a way among them over towards the Hill. Slowing, cautious, contouring to the right to get better benefit of the breeze in case there were alien wolves above. Nothing, but . . . nothing. She looked back at where she had been and paused a moment, surprised at how far she seemed to have come.

'Not far,' she reminded herself, for she was always surprised at how a short climb upwards made all below seem so far off. The Eastern Rocks were bright in the sun, their lichen and moss green, their shadows almost black, not the murky greys of winter. She glanced to her left, up towards the cliffs, and watched the descent of a tranche of white water in one of the bigger falls. Slowly down it came, bright against the grey-black rock as across it a raptor flew. Eagle; two of them.

She sighed with pleasure and resumed the short upward climb towards the top of the Hill, contouring left as the breeze shifted, cautious, glancing back at her line of retreat, back to the rocks, and back from them to the Forest. Below, across the Vale, a cloud's shadow moved, and then another, not coming her way.

She rounded the Hill, avoiding the top so that she did not break its line in case Magyars were watching. Through a patch of long grass, by a rock, and then round on the other side, the Forest disappearing from view behind her as the Fell came into sight. It was a view she loved. The ground dropped away from her towards a patch of trees, not a continuation of the Forest but a stand planted by Mennen, dark green, nearly black in their shadowed parts.

She continued round the Hill, dropping height a little, enjoying the feeling of being in territory that was no wolf's, her own being back behind the Hill, the Magyars' spread out beyond the plantation and thence far out of sight to the west. She sat down, groomed herself a little, scented at the clean air, sniffed about and then made her way to the boulders that formed a thin spine dropping off towards the trees below. She turned back at the last moment, for here the ground was uneven and enemies might easily hide.

She moved upslope abruptly, suddenly uneasy at having been out of sight of the Rocks so long, took a few steps and stopped dead, her hackles rising at the scent of alien wolf in the breeze. She turned and saw him standing among the rocks, absolutely still. He was Magyar, wiry and with dark, rough fur, unpleasant. She barked quickly, a warning bark for her own pack and a warning to him, but the breeze was shifting and blew the sound back in her face. She knew suddenly she had made a mistake in coming so far, for she was in the wrong position to be heard that day.

She headed upslope immediately, even as he broke his stance to come purposefully towards her, and she started to canter up the Hill, trying not to seem unnerved.

The horizon of the Hill against the sky above her was broken darkly by the form of an advancing wolf: female, older, not quite Magyar – the sky was too bright behind to see more. Rohan speeded up immediately, not too nervous yet but anxious to get back over the Hill and within sight and sound of the Forest. On her travels with Tervicz she had trained for such a situation, and instead of turning left away from the two wolves she turned right straight between them, began a fast run, turned the wolf above her and then swerved sharply left and straight past him over the Hill.

It was neatly done and gave her time to bark another warning which she knew would be heard before she turned back to face the two wolves, this time on a level with the female. Rohan saw a wolf who was more than Magyar, more than female . . .

'Greetings,' said the wolf in a voice that chilled Rohan's heart, and she found herself looking into the yellow eyes of Dendrine, the Magyar ledrene. Dendrine looked past her at the advancing male, nodded, and stepped to one side as another came hurtling up the Hill from the rocks below.

'Hurt her,' Rohan heard Dendrine say, and with barely time to give a quick sequence of warning barks towards the Forest in the hope that Tervicz or one of the others might hear, she found herself attacked from two sides at once, and retreating slowly, snarling and threatening all the way, that she might gain time, and find a better spot from which to defend herself.

CHAPTER TWENTY-TWO

*Dendrine threatens the life of Rohan and Kobrin
decides it is time to act*

ROHAN WAS NOT unduly worried by the Magyars' approach,
at first. Two wolves can rarely so corner a third that he or she
cannot flee if matters get too serious, and the spot she chose
to defend herself from had plenty of lines of retreat.

She kept her head, gave loud warnings of trespass and howled down
her need for back-up and soon after became embroiled in a turning,
ripping fight with the interlopers. She was tumbled, bitten; rolling, her paws flailing, her barks and howls for help continuing the
while.

But then, as she conducted her defence with the confidence of a
wolf who knows others of her pack will soon be with her, she caught
the scent of another wolf coming fast upslope from the rocks. She
turned and saw a female coming, a Magyar, old and raddled, her
face mean, thinned by age and malevolent thoughts. It was Dendrine
again.

Rohan now knew she must get away, and fast.

'If you become seriously outnumbered, and there are males much
stronger than you there, go for the weakest you can see, a female if
you can,' Kobrin had once told her.

'*If you can!*' Rohan found herself thinking, for there was no way
she would ever get past these males to reach Dendrine, even if she
dared.

She was so focused on her challengers that she felt no pain from
their attacks, and no more than an awareness that one of them was
going for her from behind again, as her jaws locked with the other
and she rolled him over.

'*I must get away. I must turn him and flee down to the edge of the
Forest, I must –*'

It was then she caught a glimpse of Tervicz down by the edge of

329

the wood, and as she deliberately rolled downslope, flailing her paws again, she saw him howl and bark a command to others to come to their aid as he ran swiftly towards her up the sward.

'*Stop!*'

The command was Dendrine's, for she had seen Tervicz's approach and heard his summons. Her own wolves obeyed at once, disengaging and backing off to stand at their ledrene's flank.

Breathing heavily, and feeling the warm wet taste of her own blood in her torn and broken mouth, Rohan stayed where she was as Tervicz joined her, unwilling to give ground, but glad to see the Magyars retreat the few yards to the top of the Hill, their eyes glancing back and forth along the Forest edge, obviously uneasy at the Wolves' swift response.

Tervicz took a stance in front of Rohan preparatory to protecting her against further attack before their reinforcements came. She knew not to retreat, for that would leave Tervicz isolated and both of them vulnerable, but she was beginning to tremble from shock, and her head and neck were throbbing.

She turned to look towards the Forest and wondered why none of the other Wolves had come at her call, not realizing that but moments had passed since she first encountered their enemy. She felt so weary, it seemed like hours.

'Your names?' demanded Dendrine imperiously.

There was a cruel indifference to her voice that put a chill in Rohan's heart and she looked more closely at the Magyar ledrene. Thin and haggard she might be, with unhealthy-looking patches of fur-less skin at her flanks and joints, and terrible mating scars on her back, but her gaze was formidable: cruel, malevolent, utterly ruthless.

Tervicz thought he remembered seeing her only once before, upon the steep and narrow route up from the Fell to the Scarpfeld. Dendrine had been waiting up there with Führer four years before when Klimt defeated Hassler and led them to take the Scarpfeld.

Then . . .

Then he . . .

Then Tervicz had stared at her and not known who she was, or quite what she was . . . but then he had forsaken all his past and all his memory of it to run with Klimt and the Wolves of Time.

But now, reluctantly, he began to remember. His chest began to heave and now he . . . now he trembled at the sight of her, now. . . .

'Tervicz,' gasped Rohan from behind him, for though the Magyars were not advancing and the skirmish had turned into threat and posturing, the danger subsiding, she saw his paws were fretting at the ground, and he seemed to be readying himself for attack.

'Wolf, *your name*!' Dendrine snarled, eyes narrowing on him alone, and advancing fractionally. The two males with her were now beginning to come forward once more as well.

Rohan looked around desperately, hoping that one or other of the Wolves would appear, wondering why they were late, wondering what had come over the normally placid Tervicz that he had not backed off and calmed the situation. Instead he advanced a fraction more.

'Tervicz, *don't*!' she begged, reaching a paw to him.

He turned, gazed at her, and she saw he seemed both dazed and angry at once, as if confused.

'Tervicz, be careful,' she said more gently, looking anxiously at the Magyars and relieved to see that they had paused in their advance, and were themselves looking towards the Forest, and then beginning to back away once more. She turned again and saw that two of the Spanish wolves, Gallega and Huete, had come, both spoiling for a fight as they advanced upslope, snarling and baring their teeth. Suddenly, to Rohan's relief, they had the sense to pause and stand off, simply watching towards where Tervicz and she stood.

Rohan's mouth throbbed, and the taste of blood was in it still. The sun rose high. The rilling of streams came to her ears. A fly buzzed past her, and settled briefly on Tervicz's flank, which shivered instinctively and sent it off again. She saw that there was one thing Tervicz was not, and that was afraid. Angry, yes, more angry than she had ever known him be, and his chest was still heaving as he sought to control himself.

'They've made their point, Tervicz, and we've made ours, now they're going to go,' she began.

Suddenly he nodded and relaxed and said very softly, 'It's all right, Rohan, it's just that I saw in her –'

'She's *Dendrine*,' said Rohan, thinking that was quite enough for anyone to be.

'Oh, she's rather more than *that*,' he said calmly, and with a menace that was quite as unexpected as the wild power of his sudden anger had been, 'she is something more than *Dendrine*.'

A flicker of surprise and curiosity at his tone crossed Dendrine's face and she stared at Tervicz curiously, quite unafraid, her mouth contemptuous.

Tervicz advanced a step or two further and said, 'You want to know my name, wolf?'

'*Ledrene*,' she said, 'that is what underlings call me.' Her smile was arrogant and cruel.

'You don't know who I am?' asked Tervicz matter-of-factly.

The question evidently surprised her, perhaps because it came with such fearless disregard for her and her position that it seemed she ought to know.

She laughed and turned to glance at the males by her side as if to say 'And why should I *care* who he is?'

Yet there was unease in her now, and she scanned Tervicz's face as if in search of something she almost recognized there.

'Should I?' she said. 'Know you?'

'I am Tervicz of the Bukov pack, the son of Zcale . . .'

Her slight unease turned now to an absolute surprise which she could not mask with mockery or contempt, at least not immediately.

'. . . and of Amish born . . . *your sister*.'

Behind him Rohan stared, herself surprised, and trying now to remember what Tervicz and his siblings had told her of the demise of his pack and mother – never very much. It had been the one thing he did not speak of. But it was all too clear that Dendrine knew the names and hearing them now had taken her utterly by surprise and discomfited her.

Again Rohan turned; seeing that Gallega and Huete had advanced further, and sensing it best they stay where they were, she shook her head briefly. Let Tervicz himself finish the dialogue Dendrine had begun.

'Amish . . .' whispered Dendrine with a mixture of unease, fear, disdain, and as she did, and Rohan stared from her to Tervicz and back again she saw something that shocked her too, utterly. She saw that the flecked grey of his fur was like the flecked grey of Dendrine's; she saw that the set of his shoulders and the stance of his paws were *hers*. She saw that Dendrine might easily be close kin.

'You killed your sister, wolf,' he said quietly, in a voice as sharp as wind from across a glacier, 'and thereby you killed my mother. A wolf will kill you one day, though it shall not be me, for I am not the killing kind. But I hope I shall be there to see it, to know that your life is over and you are a curse on the living no more.'

He paused again as if searching for words from a realm of revenge and hatred he was not used to travelling in.

'Do you know what my father said of you?' whispered Tervicz, going nearer still and now in a stance so like hers that the resemblance between them was even more clearly to be seen.

'Zcale? A weak wolf that one!' she said, her mockery not quite convincing. It was plain she was getting angry in her turn.

'My father said of my mother's killing by the Magyars, "I saw Dendrine among them. I saw sister rip out the throat of sister." That is what he told me. And then, "I saw my love killed." That's how he remembered it happening in the Bukovian mountains, when you led the Magyars under Hassler into our territory and betrayed our kind, and killed your own kin.

'"I saw the eyes of evil..." – that's how he remembers you ... *aunt*. Now you're Dendrine, ledrene, mother of Führer, and Zcale's son looks into those same eyes my mother and my father knew and distrusted, and he sees the eyes of a wolf who does not change, and never has changed; the eyes of a wolf who might easily have killed another female, here, today, and one who is my friend.'

He indicated Rohan behind him, and only then did she understand the reason for the depth of his anger, his rage: he had caught Dendrine in the act of doing to *her* what she had done to his mother.

'And so you have come to the Heartland to avenge the death of my dear sister Amish,' said Dendrine, laughing suddenly, adopting a light and mocking tone.

'No,' said Tervicz pulling back from that dark place of hatred he had briefly entered. The wind whispered in the grass between them, and among the Rocks behind. 'I have come to the Heartland in the quest of an ancient dream of Bukov and wolfkind, before which the Magyar curse of which you have chosen to be part will fade, and fade, and then be gone.'

'Dreams!' she cried. 'Weak dreams. Just like your father!'

'Dreams, yes,' he said with a self-deprecatory irony and ambiguity which characterized the Tervicz Rohan knew, 'but not weak. They are as true as the fact that you will age and die when a wolf does to you what you did to my mother.' Then he turned away dismissively and said, 'Come, Rohan, let us leave her where she is.'

'Be warned!' Dendrine screamed after them.

'Of what, wolf?'

'That what we began to do today to this wolf at your side we shall do to all you other so-called Wolves of Time. Four of yours for one of ours, so my leader vowed, but it will be worse: all of yours and you as well will die before the year is through. Klimt may not dare to show his face these days but when he does my son will crush him; and if he does not, but continues to slink about the place well out of sight, we'll hunt him down. Better fulfil your destiny with the Wolves of Time quickly, wolf, for soon there will be no Wolves to *have* a destiny.'

'Better to die of old age soon, aunt, than to be eaten by another!'

Tervicz turned away contemptuously, quite unlike his normal gentle self, and led Rohan downslope and made his way without a backward glance towards Gallega and Huete, and then on to the safety of the Forest. When they reached its edge and looked back the two Magyar males had gone, but Dendrine was still there, staring down at them from the Rocks.

The moment Kobrin heard what had happened he understood the implications of the Magyars' appearance, and knew that the time had now come to move more aggressively against them if they were to be kept within bounds until Klimt's return. He had been troubled for some time about the timing of such a move, feeling that now Elhana had given birth he must be solely concerned to protect her cubs, at least until Klimt's return, or failing that until the late summer when they would be able to travel a little with the pack.

But at the same time a restless mood had overtaken him, for he felt that each day that passed without the Wolves showing their strength was encouragement to the Magyars to advance. Such vacillation was unusual in Kobrin, who saw issues clearly and made decisions swiftly. But he had the growing feeling that there was a tide of change and history bearing down on them now which would carry each of them towards a destiny which was as unstoppable as it was yet unknown – and that a move too soon might hinder it.

All his life he had fought and struggled, using brute strength when he was young to win his way, and later an ability to draw others to his side to help him wage the battles that had taken him to supreme power over the Russian packs. Then, when he had lost the taste for power and the trivialities and burdens it places upon those who wield it, he had felt impelled to travel to the Heartland and give what support he could in the struggle for wolfkind. He brought intelligence and cunning, combined with an immense experience of fighting, all of which made up for the onset of age, and a loss of strength and stamina, and the weakness that comes with loss of leadership. He was the perfect deputy to Klimt in such a situation as this, the more so because he had found in Klimt the only wolf he had ever respected enough to want to follow, a wolf who knew how to use the strengths of those around him. In Kobrin's case all those strengths had been needed when Klimt had left him in charge, and he had guessed that these months would be a final test: with so few Wolves at his command he had to make their limited numbers count, and give the superstitious Magyars the impression of far greater strength than they really had.

But since Aragon's return, and then that of Tervicz and Rohan, a new sense of destiny had overcome him and it took him beyond his natural intelligence and cunning into a realm of faith and trust in the gods he had not dare journey into before. He had become filled with doubts about this irrational faith he wanted to pursue, and had consulted with Lounel, feeling foolish in doing so. But Klimt's spiritual adviser had listened, nodding his thin head, and then listened some more. They had found a spot away from the others, where they could talk without being overheard.

'Well, wolf?' the exasperated Kobrin had finally growled, 'and what am I to do? The Magyars need a show of strength from us if they are to be kept in check until Klimt's return.'

'Klimt is coming back, is he?'

'Of course he is!' said Kobrin impatiently. 'But we ought not to leave Elhana alone, and yet whatever the outcome of that something tells me that she will be all right, and yet – dammit, wolf, you're grinning.'

Lounel did more than grin, he laughed. 'Kobrin, what do you feel you should do?'

'Be myself!' said Kobrin stoutly.

'Which means?'

The old warrior paced about, glowering downslope at where others were watching them and no doubt wondering what the two old Wolves were talking about.

'I began my life fighting and I want to end that way, but I do not want to take others on a journey that is for myself alone.'

'Have you ever met a wolf you feared?'

'Only one, and he not physically. Klimt I fear, and . . .'

'Wolf?' murmured Lounel, pale eyes clear.

'One of his sons, I suppose . . .'

'Which one?'

Kobrin stared at the ground, quite unprepared for the fact that Lounel could lead him so swiftly to things he had never dared express before, nor barely think.

'You *know* . . .' said Kobrin, retreating from saying it. He was referring to the possibility that only one of Klimt sons would be chosen to lead them on to the very stars themselves.

'Oh, *I* know,' said Lounel, smiling blandly, 'but do *you?* '

'It's Lunar, isn't it?' said Kobrin suddenly.

Lounel looked surprised, as if he had not expected Kobrin to have surmised which of the brothers carried the burden of immortality upon his shoulders.

'And you fear him?' said Lounel ambiguously.

'His wildness, his unpredictability, the risks he always took, the routes he found, the – I feared where he might lead us.'

'Yes, it *is* Lunar,' conceded Lounel.

'Well then . . . and why have you made me talk of this?'

Lounel shrugged. 'Perhaps when he returns we must each teach him what we are, and what we can be. Perhaps if we do that he will learn the most, that one day he will be able to make the journey that will return wolfkind to precedence. So . . .'

'So I had best leave him something to think about, eh?' said Kobrin, almost ruefully coming back to the point in question: should they move against the Magyars now, or continue waiting for Klimt to come back?

'I think so,' said Lounel. 'You're a warrior, Kobrin, and have always been so. These months past you've had to be a fox, a very clever fox, but a fox all the same. You've thereby kept us all alive, and the name of Klimt and the Wolves remains feared by the Magyars while Klimt seeks support. Well now, he's on his way home and your task is almost done. Perhaps you can risk being a warrior again, to give us all something to dream of and strive for.'

'And Elhana?'

'I shall watch over her, and Tare should stay behind, and there are three other Wolves will not let her down.'

'Meaning?'

'Her cubs. They'll be all right, for the stars shine over them. Go and do what you must on the Scarpfeld, Kobrin, and give the Wolves a memory of courage and warriorship out of which they can begin to make a myth that will not die, that the Magyars of this world can never vanquish.'

Kobrin stared at him a long time, frowning and uncertain. Then his eyes cleared and his face relaxed, and his old body seemed to gain new strength of stance and purpose.

'You're a wolf and a half, Lounel, and I never knew it before.'

'I'm lanky, that's true,' said Lounel, and the two chuckled and laughed together before parting, like old friends.

Thus had they talked, so that when the incident between Dendrine and Rohan took place and suggested the Magyars were beginning to advance again, Kobrin saw in it a confirmation that he must act, despite the risk of leaving Elhana and the cubs vulnerable for a time.

'No doubt Dendrine came trying to find out where we are,' he said to Lounel, 'having already sent scouts up to the Scarpfeld and found that we are not there. Well then ... it is best that Aragon, Tare and Huete go straight back to the Eastern Rocks to resume the watch there. We shall make our presence felt out on the Hill itself, so that the Magyars think we want to retaliate *that* way. Meanwhile, I shall send Stry and you to scout out the Scarpfeld and see what Magyar watchers may already be posted there. Then, tomorrow night, or soon thereafter, we shall re-occupy the Scarpfeld and lie in wait for when Führer and the others begin their ascent up to it for the summer.'

He summoned the pack and told them of his plans.

'Tomorrow night?' said Rohan uncertainly.

'All of us,' said Kobrin, 'but for two, who can watch over Elhana and the cubs. Lounel, you be one; Tare, you be the other.'

'Surely, we need Wolves stronger than these two to watch,' said Stry.

Kobrin nodded sympathetically and said, 'I understand your fears, wolf, but the Magyars will have other things on their mind than exploring through the Forest as far as the Ruin. In any case, if there was an emergency, I would trust Lounel's wisdom and Tare's anger to avert disaster.'

'And Elhana's love,' added Aragon quietly.

'That too,' said Kobrin. 'Now, we must prepare, and you, Stry, must do a little scouting, with Lounel to protect you!'

There was the excited light of battle in his eyes as he discussed his plans, and it seemed that years shed themselves from his old and ragged body.

It was the following afternoon when Stry and Lounel came back and reported that there were six or seven Magyars up in the Scarpfeld.

'Shivering, miserable, wretched they are,' said Lounel, 'showing every sign of not wishing to be there. They will give us little resistance.'

'Good. Then we leave tonight, if you have strength enough for it, Stry. Lounel will stay behind.'

The Wolves nodded and rested up for the afternoon. Then as twilight fell, and chill came to the air and low clouds drifted across the cliffs above them, they set off, Kobrin looking like an old warrior, going into his final battle.

'Kobrin!'

It was Elhana at the entrance to the Ruin, the three cubs ranged at her flanks.

'I wanted them to see you leave,' she said.

He turned back briefly, and came to them, placing a great paw on each one's head in turn.

'I am a wolf of Russia,' he said gravely, 'who found a last home in the Heartland under the greatest leader I have ever known. You will meet him, for he is coming home to the Heartland.'

'Is he greater than you?' asked one of the cubs.

Kobrin smiled, his grey-furred face creasing in a thousand places, and he nodded.

'He made me understand that the Heartland is my home, as it is yours. In your lifetime you shall see his work completed, and make it home for all wolfkind.'

'Will they all come here?' said another of the cubs.

Kobrin chuckled and nodded, saying, 'In their hearts they shall come here eventually, every last one of them, but only a few of each generation will make the journey in the flesh as I did. Yet Wulf will see there are always enough Wolves to keep us to our destiny.'

'Is Wulf coming here?' asked the third, the one they called Torne. He said it timidly, and pressing his flank to Elhana's for comfort.

The stars were beginning to show and Kobrin looked at them. 'He too is coming home. Honour him, and trust him, and . . .'

His voice seemed to deepen, as if he feared he might not see them again, and his eyes grew sombre and troubled. He looked at the brightening stars again, as if to help him find the words he sought.

'Wolves,' he said, smiling to see how each stood a little prouder to be called so and not mere youngsters, 'watch over Wulf when he comes among you, even if there comes a time when he seems to fail you. Trust him, as I have trusted Klimt. Trust him as surely as you know the day will follow this long night. Then when others desert him, when he is weak, when he has given all he can and he seems to have nothing left to give, you be the ones to stand by him as we shall stand by you until you are strong enough to travel the wolfways all alone. Will you do that? Eh?'

Eyes wide, Kobrin now a vast silhouette against the evening sky, one by one they nodded, all three, the offspring of Aragon.

'Now, we have work to do.'

With those words great Kobrin was gone, and Elhana began to think she might never see him again; and she knew also that the world was changing about them that night and they were caught in a pattern of destiny that put strange words in an old battler's mouth and memories in the minds of cubs which they would never forget.

Then, as she watched him and all the others leave but for Lounel and Tare, Elhana understood that her time too was short, and her mortal task very nearly done. No wolf lives for ever in the mortal world.

'Wulfin, give me courage and fortitude to the very end,' she whispered to those same stars at which Kobrin had looked.

'What did he *mean?*' asked Torne as she led them back into the protective darkness of the Ruin.

'Let me try to tell you,' she said, knowing it might take all night.

CHAPTER TWENTY-THREE

The ageing Kobrin leads the Wolves into the Scarpfeld,
in the hope of delaying the Magyars' inexorable advance

AS KOBRIN LED the Wolves through the darkness up the old familiar way to the Tree his expression was sombre, but his thoughts were calm.

There were eight of them in the assault party, including himself: Aragon, Gallega, Huete, Srena, Tervicz, Rohan and Stry being the others. This was a viable number, the more so because all were reliable pack members, and most very strong and sensible fighters. Meanwhile, Elhana and the cubs were hidden well away in the Ruin, with Tare nearby in the shadows, and Lounel out and about to keep watch.

When Kobrin reached the Tree he stopped and looked back; the Forest beneath them shrouded in darkness, the sky above clear and bright with stars, and a half-moon just beginning to rise.

'We shall go up in close formation by our old route, for Stry here reported this morning that it is safe, though not entirely free from ice and snow – but at least we all know it. The wind was favourable to this approach earlier today, as it is now, but we cannot rely on it to stay that way. If it does not, and we find that it is shifting behind us and likely to carry our scent down into the Scarpfeld, or seems about to, then we shall make our assault at night and in two groups of four, headed by myself and Aragon. Stry, you be a runner between us, for you know the territory well; Gallega, Huete and Srena, you stay close by us others, for the Scarpfeld is confusing terrain, full of echoes and rockfalls, not to mention ice-slips for the unwary, and none of you have been there.

'Tervicz, I want you taking no risks, none at all. You're not a fighter by nature, never have been; and if any of us fall I want the other Wolves to hear an account of how it happened, and why, and you're the best storyteller among us. Why, wolf, you could howl the stars out of the sky if you tried.'

Tervicz nodded his assent.

'And don't look so worried about Rohan, wolf – she's more than capable of looking after herself, just as Srena here is, and anyway she'll be close by me.'

Rohan glanced affectionately at the great wolf, though all she could see in the dark was the bulk of his head against the night sky, and the shine of moon and stars in his eyes and on his snout.

'And if the wind remains in our favour?' asked Aragon.

'Then we shall explore the Scarpfeld by the higher ways at the very first light of dawn, and deal with any scouts that may be about before establishing positions from which we can see the disposition of the Magyars on the Fell below.'

'Shall we kill the scouts to stop them returning to the Fell?' asked Stry matter-of-factly.

The younger wolves grew silent and serious with the sudden realization that it was more than a skirmish they were involved in.

Kobrin considered the point.

'Either way, the Magyars would be alerted. The best thing is to scare them and send them back thinking there are many more of us than there really are, and that we're fierce and ruthless. If there are three or more we'll kill one of them and seek to injure another – that should be sufficient.'

Kobrin looked at the night sky, which was dark and cloudy.

'Now, we had best move on. We cannot judge the wind from here as it will be up on the Scarpfeld, and for us the easiest thing will be to wait till dawn and see how things are. We must stay closely in touch with each other and each of you must remember not to try to carry the attack beyond the Scarpfeld itself. That is a short cut to death.

'Do not underestimate the Magyars, or Führer and Dendrine. They have conducted their pack well enough these months past – surprising us several times, doing well enough in the encounters we have had. We must take seriously Führer's threat against us to take four lives for the one we took. The recent venture against Rohan looked to me like no more than a studied insult, and an attempt to so hurt our pride that we attempt an assault on a place we ourselves know to be as nearly impregnable as any summer quarters can be. I do not think he can expect us to attack as early or in the way we intend to, and I have little doubt that the assault on Rohan, and the threat to come back "very soon" was a way of keeping us on our toes down here about the Forest while his wolves undertook a re-occupation of the Scarpfeld.

'By our action now we shall see of what stuff his wolves are made, and he will be left with a sense of the true strength of the Wolves, even if we ourselves do not yet know what that strength is. Let each one of you now strive to represent one hundred wolves, which are the Wolves that will follow you as a result of success now, your descendants, the offspring of your courage. Let them have reason to remember you, and howl down your names in the years and decades to come when packs gather and celebrate the brave actions of these years.'

The wind whispered at the rocks above their heads, and dark clouds began to move across the stars above. The Wolves' faces were grim and purposeful as Kobrin gave some final instructions, and each affirmed they knew what they must do.

'I shall lead up through the cliffs as far as the main approach to the Scarpfeld,' said Kobrin. 'Thereafter, Stry shall lead the way down from the col below which the Scarpfeld runs. Then we can see how the wind blows, and decide what next we shall do. Stay close; stay silent; and have faith that we shall win what is our right.'

The eight Wolves set off immediately, silent and purposeful, Kobrin's pace deliberately slow and steady, as was always his way at the start of a climb. Though he himself could still climb much faster, and there was certainly some urgency about their journey that night, he was careful to observe the principle that the slower members of a pack should not be discouraged by too swift a pace at the start.

When they reached the cliff-line above he paused by a stream that they might recover their first wind, and quench their thirst. The Forest already seemed distant and no longer theirs, while the Scarpfeld over the col might never again be held by them. There came then to many of them the sense that they were suddenly not quite anywhere, but betwixt and between, and a better understanding of why Kobrin was taking so very seriously the Magyar threat to re-occupy the Scarpfeld.

What is a wolf without a pack? What is a pack without a territory?

'We shall press on again now,' said Kobrin, interrupting their thoughts, 'and there will be no talk at all until I myself give the word, or Stry at the rear feels we are going too fast at the front. Are you all comfortable with this pace?'

Rohan was still limping slightly from her fight with the Magyars, but she nodded along with the others.

He smiled in acknowledgement of her fortitude and the others' purposefulness, rose, checked they were all ready one last time, and took up the lead again.

It was dark, but not so dark that they could not make out the shapes of rock outcrops on either side of the snowy way. Then, just when their lungs were beginning to burst from the effort of climbing, there came a point quite suddenly when the ground ahead levelled off and they found themselves with an enemy other than their temporary fatigue – the full force of the wind. It bore down on them and made all talk impossible until, advancing further, its powerful blasts became more sporadic, and there were times when their route took them out of it, when their ears seemed assaulted by the sudden lull in sound, and hummed and whistled with the wind in rocks above, and across slopes below.

Then into it again, colder now, and a new difficulty – the dank, damp clasp of light mist. Each wolf could only see the one ahead; each wolf hunched his head down now; all plodded on alone in their thoughts, wondering and doubting what might be in store for them in the hours ahead.

They stopped suddenly, one by one, turning a little from the wind, huddling closer to the ice-bound sward, seeking shelter while Kobrin deliberated.

'Stry? You know this place, wolf?' asked Kobrin.

'Well enough, I think,' said Stry, scenting about. 'It'll be a little while longer before we can judge the run of the wind over the Scarpfeld. Just here it tends to cut across the path because the ground over there is cleft that way.'

'You shall guide us on now, wolf,' said Kobrin, yielding up the lead to him, 'but keep the pace steady for in these conditions it is easy to lose track of each other.'

The change in Stry's manner as he was given this responsibility was remarkable. He stepped forward, scented at the air, moved one way and then another to get a sense of the ground all about – though to those watching him it seemed that all that was visible was a murky darkness, fleet skeins of mist in their faces, and racing, lurid clouds above.

'May I talk to the Wolves who do not know these parts?' said Stry, moving to Kobrin's flank. 'For there is a part of the route later that may prove difficult for those who have not navigated it before.'

Kobrin gathered the Wolves together so that Stry could speak to them.

'I'm going to lead you off the main wolfway we've been following, for in this wind there is part of the route that is too dangerously exposed and icy underfoot. But stay very close to the wolf in front, for the way takes us along a scree at the foot of a steep cliff, and the stones there are small and inclined to shift, which might give warning to any wolves below. Tread carefully, and keep your balance well, for if you slip here you are unlikely to survive. There is one other thing . . .'

'Yes?' said Tervicz, always a wolf who took such details seriously.

'There is a part of the way along the cliff where a jut of rock makes it impossible for the wolf behind to see the wolf in front – a corner that can leave the wolf behind feeling exposed and vulnerable, perhaps even lost.'

'I remember the place!' said Tervicz. He did not add that in daylight, when the view could be seen, a wolf needed steady nerves to take that path, such was the height of the sheer drop to the jagged rocks below.

'Well, then,' continued Stry quickly, perhaps relieved that Tervicz did not elaborate, 'when you others reach it, be sure that the wolf in front moves on sufficiently that the one behind can negotiate the outcrop without finding his path blocked as he rounds the corner. It is not a place to stop still for long. Yet the one in front should not go so far ahead that the one behind feels he has lost touch. As for the path itself, it is narrow, but not too much so. Keep your left shoulder hard against the cliff edge and you'll be all right. After that the path widens, and we can re-group a short way ahead in the lee of the col that runs above the western end of the Scarpfeld. There we can assess the run of the wind.'

It was well and confidently said, and those wolves who had never journeyed with Stry at night began to see why it was that Kobrin and Aragon put their trust in him for this part of the venture.

'Ready?' said Kobrin.

Stry nodded, moved into the lead, and they were off again, heads down, following the one in front by sight, sound and scent.

The climb that ensued was a long one, and tortuous, and soon there was not one among them but for Stry himself who was quite certain where they were. But he plodded steadily on, pausing now and then to scent at the wind and the ground as if to find his way. Time had flown by and the night sky was beginning to lighten towards the dawn.

Then the ground levelled once more and they cut off to the right through some boulders. The path contoured along a slope that became steeper and steeper, until suddenly there was only a cliff-face to their left shoulders, and a dark and swirling void of cloud to their right, with a path that was no more than a broken ledge, and occasional screes and stone chutes.

One by one, and always suddenly, they came to the awkward corner Stry had warned them of – and one by one they experienced a moment of sudden panic and loneliness as the wolf ahead, whom they had been following so long, suddenly disappeared, and it was impossible on so narrow and steep a way to turn for comfort to see the one behind.

One by one they went, the wind whipping and dragging at their fur, their paws tentatively outstretched as they felt for a good grip ahead, and their shoulders pressing hard into the wall of rock on their left, for comfort and direction. The worst moment of all came as they reached the turn and they seemed to be stepping forward into nothingness.

'Oh!' cried Gallega into the wind, which snatched away her cry of alarm.

And ... 'For Wulf's sake, *Stry*!' from Tervicz, who had to urge Srena on and found himself feeling more isolated than the others, since he was last; when he made the turn he found no Srena there at all, and for a moment feared that she had gone plunging into the void below.

Then he too was round and moving safely forward again to catch Srena up and reach where the others had grouped on ground that was blessedly flat and grassed, where they could lie down and catch their breath, and recover their nerves as well.

'The wind is against us,' said Stry with considerable relief, as he stood with Kobrin and Aragon near the top of the col, facing east across the Scarpfeld. 'From here the way down you will know.'

Kobrin nodded, his face a study in impassiveness though he, like the others, had been shaken by the sense of high exposure Stry's unusual route had given him. Still, here they were, though rather later than he had expected.

Kobrin and the others paced about, peered into the dark depths below, checked the routes to right and left of where they were and conferred with each other. Then some huddled close by Rohan to keep her warm, for the climb had been hard, and Tervicz joined them and sat laughing with Rohan at some shared memory of their journey to Bukovina which had known moments like this, the lull before the storm.

Kobrin decided they should all rest awhile, and each showed tension in a different way: Stry could not settle, and was up and down all the time. Tervicz was unusually silent, though this was perhaps more a sign of the troubled feelings he had suffered since he had met Dendrine. Gallega was calm enough, but then she was that kind of wolf, while Srena frowned and snarled at Huete, whose studied calm and indifference could not quite conceal his nervousness. Even Aragon kept going to the edge and looking down into the void, impatient for the time to pass, while Stry rested his head on his paws and tried to doze, but could not keep his eyes closed for very long. Only Kobrin was in complete control of himself, an old warrior knowing he must rest and be still for this waiting time if he was to think about the next move clearly, and be at his best when his best was needed.

It seemed a very long while later that the drifting clouds above began to lighten, heralding the first rays of the dawn sun. The pack divided as Kobrin had earlier commanded, the group led by Aragon setting off to take a path downslope some way further along the col, while Kobrin's group paused awhile before beginning their steeper descent on to the Scarpfeld so that they did not arrive too soon for Aragon's party to be in position.

Finally, at Kobrin's signal bark, both groups fanned out and began their sweep from the cliffs across the Scarpfeld, with Stry and Tervicz lagging behind to pick up any Magyar scouts that tried to lie low, or ran counter to the direction of the flushing-out.

'Go hard for any that you come across who stand their ground,' Kobrin had ordered, 'but if they flee do not try to overtake them – simply chase them to keep them running. We are aiming at a rapid ejection of these wolves, not their massacre. They will serve us better if they panic and run down the gulley to the Fell and impress upon the Magyars that we are up here in great numbers!'

Their barks echoed back and forth, just as Kobrin intended, giving the impression of a large pack and finally flushing out two of the Magyars' scouts not far from where Aragon advanced. He did not hesitate to charge them, and the two wolves stood their ground for no more than a few moments before they turned and fled, giving warning barks to their still-hidden colleagues.

It was the crucial moment of the assault; Kobrin, recognizing this, ensured its success by bounding on to a rocky rise and roaring his angry intent. At the sight of this fearful visitation two more of the Magyars rose into view, turned and fled without a sound, while a third was seen briefly at the entrance to the gulley before turning tail as well.

'Which leaves one more,' growled Kobrin, eyeing the terrain they had just crossed as the Wolves converged on the stony flat ground before the gulley descent. Then they saw him, zig-zagging his way towards the col, up the very cliffs they had just descended.

'If he sees our strength . . .' muttered Kobrin, glowering.

But they saw Stry suddenly chasing after the wolf, turning this way and that to cut him off, forcing him leftward across the cliff-face to its steepest part.

Up and up the two wolves ran, finally in the sunshine, and the others watched as the Magyar, realizing his mistake, was forced to turn and face Stry. It was an awkward movement to have to make in so steep a place and Stry took full advantage of it by charging as the wolf turned, catching him low on a hind leg and flipping him off balance. But he did not let him go, for the slope was not so steep that he might not easily survive the fall. Rather he held on to the leg of the helpless wolf, worrying at it viciously until the breaking of bones and snapping of sinews could be heard across the Scarpfeld. Only then did Stry hurl him powerfully down, and they watched as the wolf, unable to slow or stop his accelerating fall, thumped sickeningly on to the rocks below.

'It was well done,' acknowledged Kobrin when the bloodied Stry rejoined them.

'He had seen our numbers,' shrugged Stry, 'and had to be killed.'

The Wolves now turned their attention to the gulley and reaching its head were surprised to see the Magyar scouts below them, ranged in a line as if they intended to fight. This was not quite the helter-skelter flight of panic Kobrin had hoped for and the Wolves had themselves to advance down in to the gulley, but slowly, for the ground was steep and difficult, and there were places here and there where other Magyars, had they been minded and ready to, could have waited in ambush.

As the Wolves approached near to the Magyar line their enemy retreated once more – and then a short while later slowed, turned and massed; and again the Wolves had to pause and assess.

'They're more disciplined than I expected,' murmured Kobrin, not without respect in his voice.

'It's almost as if they have been trained for this kind of action,' said Aragon, 'which suggests that Führer is no fool.'

Kobrin agreed. 'I do not want to risk another charge on them, for it will be all the further to climb back up again and we're already as far down the gulley as we should go.'

The two groups stood off from each other, the Magyars plainly confident that they could escape again if the Wolves charged.

'Look!' said Stry.

He had seen movement below, far beyond the Magyars they were chasing, down where the gulley turned and turned again and opened to a patch of ground a little above the Fell. A line of wolves climbing steadily.

'Come on,' said Kobrin, 'we must charge them down one more time!'

Then down they went, resolute and determined now to make the Magyars finally turn and flee for good. Down and –

'*Kobrin!*'

It was Tervicz, and his shout of warning was enough to halt them all. In any case the Magyars seemed finally to have decided to flee down to their friends, worried perhaps that support was so far below them that it might not arrive in time. The bluffing was over.

The Wolves slowed and stopped and Kobrin turned to where Tervicz stood and then looked high above to where he pointed along the cliffs into which the gulley was cut.

'I thought I saw a Magyar up there, no doubt trying to contour round above us towards the Scarpfeld.'

'There is surely no way for a wolf to run up there!' said Kobrin.

'There is,' said Stry suddenly, turning and beginning to climb back upslope, 'for this is not the only gulley that cuts up into the cliff. Lounel told me of these routes once.'

As they looked back behind themselves upslope – and how steep it seemed, how far they had come, how hard it would be to climb back up quickly – they heard a far-distant howl of triumph and saw more clearly the wolf Tervicz thought he had seen.

'That's *Führer!*' cried Kobrin in alarm, astonished that he should risk being so isolated from the wolves he led. 'Where's Huete?'

Far from stopping where he was, Führer bounded along the terraces above them and with a roar descended to where Huete had been ordered to wait with Rohan. The Wolves had been outflanked by another who knew the territory better than they, and though no commander could ever blame himself for so unexpected a turn of events, or feel the position of his pack could be threatened by a single wolf way out of natural bounds, yet Kobrin was appalled. He had presence of mind enough to order three of the Wolves under Aragon's command to stay where they were and watch the Magyars below, while he and Stry rushed back upslope to give Huete and Rohan support.

Even as they advanced back to the boulder field they heard a dreadful howl, and the sounds of a struggle. With one accord the two Wolves redoubled their efforts to reach the top, their legs aching now, their lungs painful and bursting, their hearts cold with the possibility of what they might find.

'Come *on*!' cried Kobrin, knowing they had been outflanked and outwitted; and . . . 'Faster!' He was very fearful now at what might have happened above. The climb seemed endless, the silence above ominous, but for the cawing of ravens at the continuing rise of the sun.

They reached the top of the gulley almost together, ran on to the flat ground where the Magyars themselves had stood earlier and stared desperately forward. There was Huete lying in front of Rohan, where he had fallen to Führer's onslaught while defending her. Führer, so visible but moments before, had now entirely disappeared, and they at first thought he had retreated back to the gulleys and cliffs that led down to the Fell. But there he suddenly was, back on the high terraces above the gulley, unreachable.

He turned and stared at them and roared, 'Four of yours for one of mine, I said. So I promised, and so it shall be. This is just the start: and that coward Klimt, who sends you out to do the work he should do, will be the last. This is my birthplace and my territory and I shall re-occupy it as and when I wish, and punish those who dare claim it as their own!'

With that he surprised them once again by doing what he had done when they had first met him years before in the gulley: he charged down on them. Faster and faster he came, his head like a great rockfall, his legs as swift as a deer's. Faster and faster, straight at them, and so great was his power and speed, and such his advantage with the slope in his favour that they could only stop and stand still, hoping they might tumble him as he rushed between them – hoping as well he did not kill them as he went.

But he was too strong to tumble, too clever and too swift for that. He feinted one way and then another, and then a third, and as he broke past and back upslope they heard his panting, and saw where the blood of Huete stained his mouth and paws.

They turned back after him but did not move, for he was already swinging down and at them again, huge and strange, magnificently awful. Then he was past them once more and up among the terraces once more. Then he was gone from sight, down some gulley and through some cleft of whose existence he had learnt as a cub when Dendrine had raised him in these parts. No doubt he felt he had made his point and was returning to the Fell; there was no doubt he was right.

Kobrin ran over to Huete and Rohan and saw at once that the one was dead and the other still in shock. He calmed himself and moved to the gulley top to summon the other Wolves back up. His face was set in cold calculation: each side had lost one but the Wolves had made their point, and made it well. So had Führer. Honours even.

'We have done what we had to,' said Kobrin heavily, 'and we will stay here through the day making ourselves visible to the Magyars below. Aragon, you will take two wolves and secure our retreat up the col so that we cannot be cut off down here should the Magyars try to outflank us by coming up through the Forest. At dusk we retreat and make ourselves scarce. After that, we shall lie low, and wait for Klimt's return, for Führer is a wolf too bold, too clever in his evil, for an old wolf like me to overcome with limited resources. But Klimt — he will know what to do, and whom to inspire. He will know. The work he left us to do is done.'

The Wolves left the Scarpfeld that night and by dawn were heading back down towards the Forest. But the trees below seemed ominously quiet, the Fall strangely muted, the dawning air filled with strange despair.

No sooner had they paused at this sense of foreboding than they heard a signal bark from the shadows below, and then a howl.

'It's Lounel,' began Kobrin.

Aragon ran downslope to greet him and they all saw at once the shock and sadness in his eyes.

'It's Elhana . . .' began Aragon.

'It's all of them,' said Lounel, 'all of them.'

And it seemed the cliffs above them echoed with the savage howl of triumph of a wolf whose energies and deeds were beyond one of wolfkind's ablest generals, and beyond imagining.

Then the Wolves followed Lounel to where they had left Elhana and the others, to find what new outrage Führer had committed.

CHAPTER TWENTY-FOUR

*Elhana finally seeks her wolfway to the stars,
and Dendrine declares Führer Lord of All*

THE UNSETTLING MIXTURE of destiny and foreboding that
Elhana had felt for the past day or two began to deepen as
she watched Kobrin and the others set off for their assault
upon the Scarpfeld.

Tare came to stand with her for a while, but there seemed nothing
to say and eventually she wandered off on her rounds into the gloom,
leaving Elhana at the entrance to the Ruin with the river waters
rippling by. Lounel appeared briefly among the trees on the far side
of the river, nodded amiably in her direction, and then disappeared
to watch higher upslope.

'He's probably gone up to the tree-line to sit and watch the night
settle across the cliffs above,' she told herself; and she was right. In
their different ways they would both watch over her until Kobrin and
the others returned, to warn her if danger approached so that she and
her three young could secrete themselves away in safety within the
Ruin. It was best they stayed away at a little distance so that if intruders
came they could lead them away from where Elhana and her young
lay hidden – after giving a signal bark to warn them to lie low.

Elhana watched on into the night until the scent of the departing
Wolves was overtaken by the cool breezes that blew hither and yon
about the river water, and into the tunnel entrance to the Ruin. Then,
suddenly feeling the cold, she turned into the subterranean darkness
of her den to check her young, that they were asleep, or if restless
to find what might comfort them, or if irritable to scold them into
quiet, though they were getting too old and big for such admonish-
ment.

They *were* restless that night, sensing Elhana's own disquiet. Jimena
feigned going to her mother's teat, though they were all long since
weaned. Perhaps it gave her a kind of comfort, some echo of a safer

past, and Elhana's gentle touch was enough to send her back to her sleeping-place and settle down.

Umbrio tossed and turned, grumbling that the sticks and stones of their den were sharp on his flank; declared he could not breathe; aped dying of breathlessness; laughed as Torne copied him until he too dropped off to sleep.

'Elhana? Mother?'

Torne was wide awake and wanted to talk. Or rather, he wanted Elhana to talk. He liked to listen, he liked to learn.

'Mmm?'

'When *will* Klimt come home?'

'Soon.'

'Is he the strongest wolf you have ever known?'

'No.'

'Is he the biggest?'

'No.'

'Is he the cleverest?'

'Possibly.'

'But he is the greatest?'

'Yes. Now go to sleep.'

'Have you been to Tornesdal where he came from?'

'No.'

'I want to go there.'

'Perhaps you will one day.'

'I definitely will.'

Elhana smiled at his youthful certainty; smiled too at something else: he was like Aragon, yet with Klimt's Nordic strength and purpose; and he was like Klimt, with Aragon's southern joy in life. She loved him as she had always tried to love her young: fully, so fully.

'I feel . . . nervous,' whispered Torne.

'Come here, my dear,' she said. 'Now . . . why?'

'Because Kobrin's not here, and Aragon's not here either. They've all gone.'

'They'll come back.'

'Not before.'

'Before what?'

'The dark wolf comes.'

The dark wolf was the one her three young had invented stories about when they were small cubs, and sometimes still did. The dark wolf was the one Klimt had long since gone to get help to defeat. The dark wolf lived just beyond the circle of their pack. The dark wolf was the roaring of rockfalls and the cawing of ravens in the cliff; and the dark wolf sometimes stared up at them from the still, peaty deeps of the river when they went to drink.

'There is no dark wolf.'

'Yes there is.'

'No there isn't.'

'What shall I do when he comes?'

'Hide until you are strong enough to fight.'

'But if he finds me?'

'Protect the others as the pack has vowed to protect you. Think what our leader Klimt would do, and do that.'

'Yes, mother,' whispered Torne, eyes closing at last as he tried to form an image of the leader he had never met, and managed to make an image greater by far than the dark wolf, 'yes . . .'

Elhana guessed that of all her young he was the one who would try hardest, he was the one after Solar and Lunar who would take up the Wolves' destiny and fulfil it.

'Torne?'

It was as well he was asleep. A youngster does not need to know too much about the future. It is enough that he must learn the lessons of the past so that he knows how to survive in the present through to adulthood. He can begin to worry about the future then.

But Torne was right and Elhana wrong: the dark wolf did exist.

He came the following night, hulking through the Forest, carefully staying downwind of them and any watchers they might have. He guessed wolves were there but not who or what, just *knowing*, quite certain in his malevolence. The dark wolf was Führer and he came, alone, with the blood of Huete barely dried in the fur about his mouth and neck.

Führer came as a wolf *does* come who knows no fear, and believes a quarry lies ahead. The Wolves up in the Scarpfeld had been eight in number; Klimt was not among them, nor was there a sign of any ledrene. So thinking that Klimt had stayed behind in some secret place across the Forest to protect his ledrene, who probably had cubs, Führer had gone on a solitary hunt, the kind he liked.

It was not hard to find the Wolves' scent up on the col, fresh as daisies it was, light and quite heady to Führer. The Wolves smelt good. He grunted and slavered at the thought of what he might find at the end of the scent trail and followed it down as far as the river that issued from the Fall. There he lost it, as Kobrin intended intruders should, for the Wolves had used the stream-bed for a time, and crossed and re-crossed their tracks to mislead until they had felt it safe to go on.

This made Führer angry, for he was eager for the pleasure of putting Klimt to death and supping off his flesh, and that of any offspring he might have, eager and . . . disturbed.

There was a tranquillity in the Forest that reminded Führer of something he had lost. There was a sense of lupine order which the motley mass of wolves who called themselves Magyars and followed his lead upon the Fell just did not have, an order he could not himself inspire. He liked the smell of peace he found up in the Forest, which is why he liked their scent; he wanted relief from the chaos of his life. It was that desire that made him leave his followers where they were for a time, and set off on his nocturnal hunt.

After killing the wolf he had gone up into the terraces, gone back to where he was born, where he had been solitary lord, where Dendrine was his mother and had been young, not his ledrene as now, and old.

He paused in the Forest and raised his great sad head in the dark of the night and, forgetting the Wolves' clever back-tracks and false trails, sought out something else: order, peace, quietness, a stilling for his mind; and he knew which way to go and where he thought Klimt must be. It was stronger than any scent.

Across the stream from the Fall he leapt, on through the trees, a great ugly silhouette of a wolf, bitter and lonely, sad and desolate, yearning for the peace that lay ahead and thinking that if he could not take it back with him he would destroy it. Hunger for flesh had become hunger for something of a different kind, for which he had no name; a deeper yearning. He was ravenous for something he had long since lost and might never know again.

Huge though Führer was he moved with grace, and in silence, creeping towards Tare without her knowing. She scented good, and looked good too in the moonlight. He ogled her for a long time, saliva drooling from his loppish mouth unhindered. He feared that if he lapped it back she might hear the slap and slobber of his tongue.

Tare grew suddenly restless, mortally afraid, which fear he scented. He did not hesitate: indeed the smell of fear was good to Führer, a drug which turned him savage, made him kill.

Tare suddenly scented the evil mounting in the shadows, but so quick was he that she barely had time to give a warning bark before he was on her, over her, ripping her life out almost before she had a chance to feel pain. As her blood spilled darkly on to the Forest floor, and her last breaths faded into the thick air of his scent, he moved on indifferently to find a stream and wash himself of her blood, and of the one before. He scented purity in the Forest air and sensed he should purify himself. He found the stream and pressed on, the scent trail clear as day, the smell of young wolves all about, maddening, alluring. He must move on before they understood the strangled signal the female watcher had barked out and fled. Perhaps they had done so already? No, no, he would have heard them.

He raced massively out of the trees and, seeing the Ruin, stopped short. He saw a female in the moonlit arch of a tunnel over the river there, the stars and moon in her fur. She had been in the act of secreting herself away but now, hearing his coming, she turned to face him, the light of a ledrene's fury and purpose in her eyes. She was so beautiful it stilled his heart, her movements were of such elegance.

He tried to slow his panting breath, to mould his great mouth and tongue into something less grotesque.

She advanced upon him even as another wolf appeared on the far bank. His fur was pale as well, but with age, and his legs were brittle sticks in the moonlight.

'Lounel, stay where you are!' he heard her order in a ledrene's voice. 'Leave him to me.'

Führer listened to her voice and thrilled that it was as beautiful as her, and she as magnificent as her own courage. He missed completely the second command implicit in her words – that Lounel should find opportunity to slip away to the youngsters, to keep them quiet, to get them away if he could.

Führer simply relished the anger in the female and grunted his desire for her as she advanced to challenge him.

'Where's the Klimt wolf?' he said, by way of conversation.

'Not here. Gone to the col. Just me. We are not upon your territory.'

'Where is he?'

Führer's anger mounted with his desire, for he liked not to be denied.

'Gone.'

Lies or the truth? Truth, thought Führer. But . . . so many questions, and still she came and the smell of her confused him.

Her scent . . .

He moaned at the loveliness of it, so different from Dendrine's ancient familiar odour.

Anger in him now. Hit out. Destroy what he could never have.

'Where . . . ?'

She went for him but he barely needed to move, but for a paw that buffeted her so hard she fell on her side. Less beautiful now, she was, and he felt powerful, his control coming back.

She rose once more, caught by the starlight, visibly shaking now with shock. Yet still she tried again, gaining time.

He took her right shoulder in his mouth, softly at first, mawing it as she flailed helplessly against him. He rose up, taking her full weight in his jaws as he lifted her paws off the ground. Then he tossed her towards the river in one great sweep, keeping his teeth just tight enough in her flesh that her shoulder ripped open from the power of his throw.

Führer went to where she had fallen in the river, the blood from her wound a sudden dark swirl in the starlit water.

'Didn't mean to,' he said.

She lay half in, half out of the water, and he stared down at her, huge and terrible and breathing heavily and quietened by her silence, stilled by her remaining beauty. He reached out a great rough paw to touch her and ignored the movement he heard in the ruins that over-arched the river. That other wolf, perhaps. Youngsters, maybe.

Now she was quiet and still, now she was not attacking him he could be near her, which was all he had wanted at first. If only she could stay so for ever, yet breathing still; if only she had not tried to attack him.

He lowered his great muzzle towards her, snuffled his snout across her body, tasting her, enjoying her, and then grasping her unhurt left shoulder in his jaws gently heaved her out of the water that he might snout at her some more; then, timidly, he licked and half-sucked at her protruding teats. Scent of milk, sweet and distant; taste of blood, fresh and foul. The admixture of his youth, and it made him angry and confused.

He remembered the brother Dendrine forced him to eat alive; then came a memory from before that, a moment of the blessed time, a time of peace before the darkness of his life began, when Dendrine had no name but mother, and mother seemed a blessed thing. There had been a moment of peace in Führer's life then, the only one he remembered, when for a brief while his brother had stared at him with eyes bright with trust. That moment was the best ever, when someone liked him, and needed him.

'Eat his leg,' Dendrine had said, and ... and he ... and Führer had. No peace ever since.

Elhana had stirred and moaned when he shifted her, and now, dazed and in shock she could only stare at him from where she lay, his face a vast cliff of troubled light and dark above her, his body a whole mountain range. She looked round to where Lounel had been and saw that he was gone to do her unspoken bidding and protect her young, except ...

Elhana struggled up for a moment or two, putting her weight on her good shoulder, before the pain and hurt of her injury forced her down on to her haunches once more. She could snarl, or bite a wolf within range, but she knew she could do little more. Führer could literally walk circles round her now. The injury was too deep, the blood loss too great and she was gravely weakened, and weakening still more.

'Pity them,' she said quietly. 'Kill me but do not harm them.'

He stared at her, feeling a sense of intimacy at being so close to so beautiful a wolf, and pondered what next to do. He was used to resistance, and to crushing it, used to inspiring terror, and now her clear and fearless stare, her gentle voice, made him apprehensive and uncomfortable. He tried to get angry again, rising and growling and looming over her but ... he could not ...

'Eat his leg,' Dendrine had said, and her voice came back to him now, bringing anger as he thought of it.

Out of the darkness that descended he raged at Elhana again, doing to her the kind of thing he had sometimes wished to do to Dendrine. He picked her up and ran at the river with her, turned from it, shaking her, feeling her fur and flesh rip and the pathetic scrabble of her paws before she began to go limp. She was a grey pigeon in a fox's mouth; she was a cub in a mother's mouth; she was his own to hold and take and destroy, and her blood flowed through the fur of his lower jaw; she was beautiful and he was afraid of her beauty and wanted to be rid of it.

Thus caught in a world of doubt Führer held the dying Elhana in his jaws and stared at the dark void of the Ruin and saw ... or thought he saw ... he saw his brother coming out into the clearing.

Shards of fear burst into his heart and he lowered Elhana to the ground. The youngster stared at him with wide eyes, without trust, and behind him, from out of the subterranean shadows, the old wolf came, the one he knew they called Lounel.

'Where's Klimt, he's the one . . .' Führer tried again.

'He is not here, wolf,' said Lounel. 'Only his ledrene whom you are killing now, only me who fights no wolf, and this youngster who will fight you now.'

Führer stared at Torne in utter disbelief as the youngster advanced, growling as best he could, trying to seem a great deal bigger than he was.

Führer stared down at Elhana as she murmured, 'Do not harm him. He is yours to love.'

Führer stared in wonderment as Torne's young paws flailed at him, snowflakes in the starlight trying to fell an oak.

He is yours to love. The words seemed to Führer as beautiful and otherworldly as the dying wolf who uttered them.

He is . . .

'Won't harm him, not again,' he said.

Führer opened his great jaws, rose and turned, growled as gently as he could, and in one curving, turning sweep caught Torne by the scruff of the neck and heaved him off the ground, paws and all. He stood briefly there, Torne helplessly threshing his legs, before turning back towards the Forest and the Fell and the troubled darkness of his life.

Elhana strove to rise, to follow after him no doubt, but Lounel restrained her.

'It is well, my dear,' he said. 'He will not harm Torne.'

'But Dendrine . . .'

'Yes,' said Lounel, staring after Führer into the darkness, 'yes, she might try to harm the youngster. But she will not. It is well, Elhana, very well, and ordained that it should be so. It was Torne's own thought to do as he did, not mine. He is the wolf who will take forward our destiny.'

'And the other two?'

'Unharmed,' said Lounel, as Umbrio and Jimena emerged into the lightening darkness, 'and there will be no more danger now.'

'No . . .' whispered Elhana, turning to look across the river and upslope towards the clefts that ran into the cliff, the sound of the Fall now lulling, now loud with the slow awakening of the dawn breeze.

'Look, Elhana, you are not alone.'

She was on the sward among the fallen rocks beneath the cliff above them, She who had come at the time of the birth of Lunar and the others. She howled Her summons now, for it was Elhana's turn to go to Her own realm.

'Help me across the river, Lounel,' whispered the dying Elhana, 'and you as well, my dears. You two shall come with me to help me to the end, and you, Lounel, will go to meet Kobrin and Aragon and tell them what has passed.'

'Elhana . . .'

'She has come for me now,' said Elhana, 'and I have felt Her coming for days. The youngsters must help and see where my wolfway to the stars begins, and remember it.'

'Elhana . . .'

But she said no more as he helped her into the water, its icy cold cleansing her wound and so numbing her that she regained something of her strength. Umbrio stood downstream of her, lest she needed support against the water's flow; Jimena whispered encouragement to her mother to keep moving. Neither quite understood how gravely she was injured. Above them, in the shadows, though seeming brighter than the dawn that rose about her, Wulfin awaited them.

'Go now Lounel, let me see you go.'

He embraced her, released her broken body into Wulfin's care and turned away, his clear eyes filled with tears. It was ordained, it was her destiny, it was her triumph, yet he wept. Torne's destiny was to be taken, yet Lounel shuddered to think what might yet come to pass.

So had Lounel come to meet Kobrin, Aragon and the others and they had hurried back to find the bloody evidence of Elhana's brief struggle. They followed her scent up towards the cliff, and thence along its edge, a scent that mingled now with that of the youngsters, and as well with that of thyme and tarragon, which was a holy sign, and found its end in the cleft from which the Fall flowed. Into the cleft's darkness had they gone, up and up amidst the rocks, where one by one the Wolves found they could follow no further, and only Aragon remained, struggling on.

'Come back, wolf, it is too dangerous without the guidance of the gods,' roared Kobrin, but his voice was lost in the thunder of the water, but even had he heard it Aragon would not have listened. On he struggled, through clefts and voids, and over rocks made treacherous and slippery, calling for Elhana, calling for his young, calling and calling until he was too weak, too defeated to crawl further or call more.

Then he slept, while the Wolves waited at the cleft's entrance, heeding Lounel's advice, wanting to believe his reassurances. Had they not waited once for Solar and Lunar when they went to the WulfRock, and had they not returned?

'Not for days and weeks as I recall,' growled Kobrin wearily.

'Which is nothing when set against the long hard years of the Dark Millennium,' said Lounel sharply.

There were times when Kobrin's doubts troubled him: a little faith went a long way towards making a pack more trustful. Then Lounel added, 'We'll wait until Aragon's first grief is done and he comes back, then return to the Ruin to wait for the youngsters to come back. And if they do not do so soon I'll go and get them myself! They had best be back before Klimt's return!'

'Oh, so *he's* coming back too, is he?' grumbled Kobrin.

'Very soon,' said Lounel, closing his eyes and shutting himself off from their doubts and fears, 'very soon indeed.'

'And what of Torne, eh? We're just to leave him to his fate, are we?'

'Yes,' said Lounel, eyes still closed, 'we are, if you want no further deaths. He will come to no harm. He will learn much. It was meant to be thus.'

Muttering, grumbling, uneasy, the pack wandered restlessly about by the Fall while Lounel slipped into blessed sleep.

Yet long before either the two youngsters or Klimt returned from their different journeys to prove Lounel right in his predictions, the Magyar wolves under Führer did what they had threatened for so long, and advanced. They were like a huge sweep of autumn leaves across a treeless landscape, except it was early summer and leaves do not take prey. Across the Scarpfeld they came, and in to the Forest, out over the westward edge of the Fell, and eastward too, and up into the hills and vales of the Carpathians, in the name of Magyar, in the name of their leader and ledrene, Führer and Dendrine.

Their long wait was over, their hour of triumph at hand and their hordes swung this way and that, scattered here and there, spilling out of the Heartland they had taken down towards where the Mennen places were, to feed on their dead, and their half-dead, to prey on what they found in the chaos and anarchy of the Mennen wars.

While at their centre, at their heart, the heart of the Heartland, Führer was, Dendrine swearing and violent at his flank, and at *their* heart, the still centre of their love and hatred for each other, the youngster, the one they thought was Klimt's.

'Eat the little shit or I will,' snarled Dendrine when Führer first brought the youngster to her, hoping she would accept him.

'Won't,' said Führer, who always grew nearly speechless before her. She made him thus.

'We could gobble him up together,' she insinuated, licking at Torne until Führer pulled him away.

'No,' said Führer, stubborn.

'Take me then,' said Dendrine, sliding her hindquarters into him.

'Yes,' sighed Führer, not yet weaned from incest it seemed but pausing in the middle of the grotesque act to think that he didn't like it any more, and that whatever Dendrine commanded he would never eat or gobble Elhana's male youngster. It would be different from how it had been with his brother.

Meanwhile Dendrine lost herself in his familiar, habitual, comforting embrace, certain she would have him do her bidding with the youngster in the end and meanwhile enjoying repossession. She would not yield up her loveling to a cub, and she revelled in the prospect of restating her power over Führer by making him destroy his new toy so that he might return wholly to her.

Torne watched their sport, not knowing what he saw, thinking they were playing, not understanding how a wolf who was older even than Lounel, and even weaker-looking, could bear the weight of Führer upon her; nor quite believing how her cracked, horrible voice turned sometimes when they played into a youthful scream of pleasure.

So far innocent, Torne stared, and was not afraid. The dark wolf had come and taken him and not killed him. Rather he had carried him gently as his mother had been wont to do and had run wildly up through screes and cliffs, the world all topsy-turvy and exciting. Torne had never flown like an eagle before, but that's how it had been with Führer when they swooped down the other side.

Nor had he been to the Scarpfeld, but here he was, nor ever allowed to run a stone chute as huge and long as that which ran down the length of the gulley, but now he did it, with Führer nearby to save him from his own exuberance when he began to slide too fast and lose control.

Nor had he ever dreamed of a land as huge as the Fell, where no trees were but only heather and peat, and confusing pools of black water that tasted strange and old, like drinking the earth itself. Cold, dead water that gave a wolf life.

'Don't like the Scarpfeld,' conceded Führer one day when they had come down to the Fell, 'not any more.'

Torne knew this general disenchantment included the dark wolf's mother, Dendrine. He didn't like her either. Her eyes were puckered red. Her teeth smelt. Along her stomach hung a set of ancient teats, split and calloused by clambering over the Scarpfeld rocks. He was scared of her and she was beginning to appear in his dreams, which were becoming nightmares. Always she was going to eat him up and she was as predatory as a raven, as unpredictable as Mennen. She had put a new face on the dark wolf in his mind and it was foul and old and cruel and wicked. She was going to do worse than eat him up; somehow, worse . . .

Elhana had said he was to protect the others as the pack had protected him and he had tried to. The dark wolf had come and began to play with his mother to death and he had stared from the ruins wondering, having ordered Umbrio and Jimena to stay in the shadows, and then forced them back into crevices and ways too small for adults to get into, especially one as big as the dark wolf.

Then Lounel had come and they had watched together until Torne began to understand that soon the dark wolf would want to play with Lounel to death as well. The blood on his mother's body told him that, for she was strong, as strong as mountains, and Lounel was old and weak.

'Protect the others,' Elhana had ordered him, and he saw that must include Lounel as well.

The wind had whispered at the entrance to the Ruin and it was like the voice of gods he had heard them talking of, and he was reminded he must behave as Klimt might do. Klimt would fight, that's what he would do. Torne's heart beat faster but he was not *so* afraid: the dark wolf was not as dark or big as he was in his dreams, and nor was he anywhere near as big as Klimt must be. The wind whispered what he must do and he had advanced upon him out of the Ruin's protection, to kill him, or to pretend to. The dark wolf had stared at him and laughed and that made Torne feel better. Then he had left his mother alone, promised not to harm him, and taken him up and away; and Torne did not feel a thing.

'You won't eat me like Dendrine sometimes says, will you?' asked the youngster now, out upon the Fell.

Führer looked down at him, his eyes full of horror and therefore frightening.

'Will you?'

Führer half shook his head, uttered a thick sound, bending down to pick Torne up by the scruff of the neck as he had the first time, except now Torne was heavier and Führer grunted with the effort and paused a moment to regain his balance. Then, more terrible still, Torne was carried and dragged in a wild rough race into the gulley, and then up its sides among outcrops of rock to a secret place that overlooked the gulley, the Fell off to the south and the Scarpfeld to the north; a cave, with the dried bones and pelts of prey, smelling like a long-deserted birthplace.

Here Führer deposited him, staring at him strangely, mouthing at him, slobbering on him as he began to weep, hitting him sometimes as he howled and roared, bruising him, hurting him, caressing him, protecting him from himself, from two wolves; one dark, the other light.

'*Will* you?' whispered Torne, beginning to recognize his strength over this great trembling hulk of a wolf.

'No,' said Führer finally, weakly, exhausted by grief for the brother he had been forced to slowly kill, 'won't, won't, won't.'

'Nor let *her*,' said Torne, feeling stronger and more certain still.

'Not ever,' said Führer, turning broken from the youngster whose weakness was his strength, whose innocence was his power, whose ability to shock and persuade Führer lay in the shadowy and uncertain clouds of fear that came into his eyes from time to time, assuaged only by Führer's inexperienced gentleness, and blown clean away by his unaccustomed sense that he must now defy his mother Dendrine, whose final hegemony over Führer was the trust he at last dared place in him.

'Won't ever harm you or let you be harmed.'

While Dendrine, lurking below near the gulley, knowing where Führer and the brat were, watched from a distance, hearing the roaring and tears, seeing no sign of the youngster, and trusting that her darling was eating the little bastard this time, paws and all.

Such was the pitiful nature of the wolves at the heart of the Heartland as the long-laid plan of Führer and Dendrine to reclaim the Scarpfeld came to fruition with the retreat of the snows across the Carpathians and the rapid advance of spring into early summer.

'You must travel about, my dear,' whispered Dendrine to her lover-son, 'to see that the different packs and groups of Magyars are following your commands.'

'Won't leave him with you,' said Führer, whose interest in the Magyar advance had all but died since Torne's arrival in his life.

'I wouldn't suggest such a thing,' said Dendrine blandly, 'though we cannot keep him thus for ever. The Wolves will want him back. We must use him while we can. He cannot always live, just as he cannot always be so pliable a friend of yours. You will have to decide one day, won't you?'

'Yes,' concurred Führer.

'And soon, or otherwise those who love you, those who follow us and lead our packs will become dissatisfied. Remember, Führer, Klimt killed your father Hassler, *killed* him. You shall avenge your father through Klimt's son, shall you not?'

'Might, but –'

'But don't worry about it now. Take him on your travels. Let him see the world of the Magyars. Let him not out of your sight lest some harm may befall him. Maybe it is better you find his wolfway to the stars for him than another does it cruelly. But no need to worry about that now. Go, my love and my leader, leave us for a time. Fulfil your tasks and do not worry if you decide to come home alone. None shall blame you, for you shall be Lord of All.'

'Lord of All,' whispered Führer, who liked the ring of it. It seemed a certainty beyond the uncertainties Dendrine's words created.

Sometimes the youngster gave him a headache. But . . .

'Won't hurt him, never,' mumbled Führer as he left, his charge at his side.

'Of course you won't,' purred Dendrine as she watched them go, the hatred in her bitter eyes softened by the smugness of belief in her own power over him she had named Lord of All.

'Führer!'

'Mother?'

'Tell the Magyars you meet that we are already victorious.'

'But Klimt still lives and the Wolves –'

'Tell them, and it will become true. Indeed, it is true. We are victorious. Say it.'

Führer did more than say it, he howled it so that those he left behind knew it, and those he was about to visit along the way might hear it in advance.

'That's more like my love,' cackled Dendrine approvingly.

'What's victorious?' asked Torne as they finally left.

'Not sure,' said Führer heavily, glowering at the wolves who followed dutifully in his wake. 'But today you'll see a killing.'

'Who?' said Torne.

'Don't know,' muttered Führer, increasing his pace and leaving Torne struggling along behind.

'Come *on!*' cried Führer, galloping back to him, horse-like in his play.

He said it like an older brother and Torne tried to hurry up, just like a younger one.

'Feel good,' said Führer that evening, looking back down towards the part of the Fell over which they had travelled.

'So do I,' said Torne, staring at the rising of the moon and somehow knowing suddenly that he might not have long to live, 'so do I.'

CHAPTER TWENTY-FIVE

The shaman's journey to the WulfRock faltering,
he accepts guidance from Leon of Spain, friend of Jicin

MATTHIUS WALD woke with the dawn to the crackle of the ice breaking across frozen puddles, and the scuttering of the hooves of a herd of deer as they crossed the Fell below the Scarpfeld. He shifted uneasily, awed by a sudden change in the cloud-shadows up about the cliffs to the east, which seemed . . . if not to move, then to open and admit something in, before they closed again to mortal view.

Having dallied for long winter months down in the lowlands he had broken free of the doubts that beset him and come up to the Fell with the spring. Here he had lingered for days, feeling he was being watched, though whether by wolf or man he did not know. Man probably. Yes, man.

Or the spirit of a man, perhaps.

That was hardly surprising. There was something brooding about the Fell which gave a traveller the feeling that he was trespassing. In a sense he was, though across boundaries surely long since abandoned and forgotten. Nevertheless, there had been something curiously forbidding about the extraordinary barrier of wire fences, and the maze of trenches, that he and his assistant had to negotiate on their way up to the Fell.

The fences must have been raised at the time of the last great wars, decades before; but for what purpose, against what enemy? The trenches, and the inviting gaps between them, were still mined, and there was evidence enough of the quite recent deaths of animals – a deer here, a wolf there – to make him wary, very wary indeed.

When they finally came through safely, and were within sight of the cliffs, where they believed a gulley would take them up to the fabled Scarpfeld, they found evidence that the place was occupied; but by whom? It was hard to pin it down: prints of naked feet; a blackened *fire circle in the peat, not so old; and then, one morning, far off, a single gunshot: bang!*

They had lain low, watching, and after several days they saw the most compelling evidence of all: a man up by the base of the cliffs. Old, very old, judging by his white hair, but agile and fast. A man who had long since given up the world of men and cast them all into the mould of Mennen. A man who watched, but did not want to know.

Now another cold morning had dawned and Wald glanced at his assistant and looked away again. He felt suddenly restless, and finally anxious to get on.

'How many days have we been here?'

He sounds almost as usual, his assistant told himself, and his grief and anger at Elhana's passing seems to have softened. It was the first time he had spoken normally for days.

'Five, Master.'

'Which of the Wolves have come to see me in that time?'

His assistant did not answer, because he knew it was not a question. His master was thinking, reviewing, beginning to see the end of the end, and he was searching for a new way ahead. Though his assistant had had faith that this moment of arrival would come, with the Scarpfeld in their grasp and the resolution to move on, his latest journey with the Wolves had taken far longer than he had expected. Indeed, he had almost left Wald where he was, had been tempted to desert his master, who had continued muttering and dreaming long after he had stopped the journey drumming from sheer fatigue.

'Eike, Eike . . .'

The assistant smiled, glad to be called by his name. Wald was returning to the mortal world.

'Master?' he said affectionately.

Of course he would not have left, not ever. They were on the final part of a journey few men could make, or would ever make again.

'How long have we been travelling? What year is this?'

'Nearly two years, Master. It is the sixty-fourth Year of the Wolf.'

'Do I seem older? I feel it!'

'You are a little greyer, Master, and your hair is thinner, but I think perhaps you look younger.'

'You look younger, Eike, each month you look younger. We are near the end. That's the gulley across the Fell. We must climb up it.'

'Are you afraid to journey on up there?'

'I am looking for a special place upon the Fell. We cannot go on until we have found it.'

'What place, Master?'

Wald looked surprised, as if it was obvious what he must be looking for.

'The place where Klimt's life was fulfilled.'

Eike, in his turn, looked surprised.

'He is to come back then, and Lounel will be right? I had thought perhaps –'

'No, no, he is nearly home, very nearly home where his heart is.'

'But Jicin . . .'

'She's near too,' said Wald, taking a few steps to a nearby rise of heather to stretch and look about. The wind tugged at his ragged trousers and at his grey hair. His face was spare, his eyes keen.

Wald had taken to drinking at a little pool of water through the long days of his latest vigil, but had eaten hardly at all. He had slept. He had wept; and latterly he had muttered Jicin's name a good many times, and Leon's, trying to invoke them perhaps. No, definitely trying to.

It was Torne who worried Eike. What wolf was he to be exactly, and where had he gone?

'Perhaps he is myself,' muttered Matthius Wald, and Eike nodded, no longer surprised his master read his thoughts. But who else could understand the nature of the world they had succeeded in journeying into through these long years? A place of physical hardship and wonder; of austerity and summertime indulgence; of discipline and abandonment. Of occasional illnesses that shifted into periods of well-being and new health, so that for journeyers of these wolfways it was hard to say what was ill and what well. Each turned about the other, and each was part of a single whole. Yet always the Wolves came back to be their guides when they were needed, just when they were needed.

But lately something else had tagged along: this Mann they had seen, wandering about, here before them on the Fell. Eike did not like the thought of him so near, shadowing them perhaps.

Vagrants had followed them before, and gangs of them had robbed them, attacked them, given them trouble. It had been Wald's fearsome stare, and the sense he had about him now that he was blessed by the Wolves and was of their number that protected them. That, and (it must be said) Eike's young man's strength and fierceness in defending his master, and willingness to threaten to use a knife and club if he was forced to. The two now made a formidable pair.

The deer whose running had woken Wald now startled them again, this time rising as one from dead ground just before the entrance to the gulley and entering into its shadows, to pick their clunking way up the stone chute there, pebbles scuttering down behind them as they went, their passage only seen in occasional glimpses here and there between the rocks of gulley walls as they rose higher and higher.

They both lay low and saw that it was a young male wolf that had disturbed the deer, who in turn had been disturbed by an old man stalking him.

Both wolf and man – or Mann – Wald and Eike now saw quite clearly across the Fell. The man turned away suddenly towards the gulley and in his turn disappeared down into the dead ground where the deer had been, while the wolf wandered along the bottom of the escarpment between Fell and Scarpfeld.

Wald ignored the man and followed the wolf, which was not so hard, for the animal was evidently very tired and kept losing his footing and pausing for breath. Then he hurried on as best he could, looking back sometimes as if in fear, as if he were being chased.

He was too dark and too large a wolf to be of local Magyar stock; too weak from fatigue to pose much threat to any living thing. They set off to follow him and as they began to catch up it became plain that he was injured in the left shoulder, which was red-raw, the fur below the wound matted brown-black with blood and dirt.

Then he saw them and stopped dead. He studied them, across a dip in the undulations of the Fell, with a little stream between them, and a rise of rocks beyond. The wolf stared from the top of the rise where he had stopped, and the two men stared back. Then with one accord, all three of them turned to stare together at the gulley, from where they heard again the sound of sliding scree.

The Mann they had seen earlier, who had been following them for days, stood there looking their way, shielding his eyes against the bright sun that caught his white wild hair, and glinted too upon something in his right hand.

The wolf moved first, turning and slipping away back towards the base of the escarpment into rougher ground wherein he could easily hide, and across which it would be hard to follow him.

Then the Mann moved, back into the shadows of the gulley and on up towards the Scarpfeld above, eager it seemed to get there first. Or *so they thought. For suddenly, shockingly, there was a phut and a spurt of earth between them and the wolf, and a shatter of stones followed by the echoing crackle of a shot up through the gulley. The man had fired between them.*

It was most strange.

The wolf fled, and Wald dropped down towards the stream, which came from the direction of the escarpment and whose water was clear and cold. He waded across and made his way to the rocky outcrop where the wolf had been and pointed to the caves and shelter he found there.

'The wolf guided us here, having misled that Mann. This is the place I was seeking. This is where Klimt found his life's fulfilment.'

'What wolf was that?' asked Eike, his face betraying awe and wonder and some alarm at being in such a place, and now so near a completion of their journey to the WulfRock, with a wolf and man and Wulf knows what besides watching them.

'The wolf was Leon, friend of Jicin,' said Wald matter-of-factly. Then, his face becoming grimmer, he added, 'But you might better ask who that Mann is.'

'He is very old.'

'I saw that he carried a gun before he fired it. Did you see that?' Eike nodded unhappily.

Wald shrugged.

'He's a hunter . . .' Eike murmured, 'and we seem to be reaching the end of the same chase he is pursuing.'

'We'll make camp here for today,' said Wald, 'so that the Mann knows where we are, and we may discover something more of Klimt's last days. Then we'll move on under cover of the night.'

'Up the gulley?'

Wald shook his head. 'The wolf Leon led us here. Let us follow on in his steps along the escarpment and round by way of the Forest. We can more easily reach the Scarpfeld that way without being detected. That Mann probably means us ill, as Leon knew. I shall sleep and you will watch. Wake me before dusk while we are still visible and you shall provide cover for a journey by beginning to drum for me. Continue into the night, so that he thinks I am here; but I shall travel on ahead of you.'

'Yes Master,' said Eike obediently.

'Your drum shall be our answer to his gun.'

A faint scutter of stones at the gulley top and the herd of deer broke cover and stood briefly in the sun, taking Eike's attention for a moment. The deer stared down the way they had come, down towards the old Mann who had been following them, the likes of whom had followed them through all the aeons of time. Then they turned as one, to try to lose themselves in the Scarpfeld, to escape the Mennen's Mann.

Following the Wolves' retreat from the Scarpfeld Kobrin decided it would be unwise to leave the vicinity of the Ruin despite the dangers posed by the Magyars' advances even beyond the Scarpfeld to the western Forest, so they lay low and hoped they would not be found.

'Perhaps, after all,' said Kobrin with a rueful shrug, 'the main and unintentional result of our venture to the Scarpfeld was to make Führer and Dendrine think we are not worth bothering about.'

He accepted Lounel's opinion that Führer would do no harm to Torne. Lounel's views prevailed as well in the matter of Umbrio and Jimena, for Kobrin accepted his argument that the gods would watch over those they led up into the heights – as once they had guarded Solar and Lunar – and the two youngsters would surely return safely at the moment the gods judged best.

'Probably they'll come back the way they went, by the Cleft through which the Fall flows, so provided we have a watcher there at all times to make sure the youngsters do not unwittingly attract the attention of any Magyars in the Forest we shall have done what we can. They *will* return.'

'Like Klimt will,' grumbled Stry, who was not so sure that Lounel's confidence was justified.

'Like him, yes,' said Lounel firmly, his sharp eyes twinkling.

Yet strangely, though there was no more evidence than before of the likelihood of Klimt's return, something had changed since Elhana's ascent to the WulfRock, and a new faith in the future had come among the Wolves. Their harrying of the Magyars had been judged a success and even Aragon accepted that Elhana's passing had the mark of destiny, and was part of the recovery of the Wolves' dominion. All was in change, all coming to a crisis, and there was an exciting sense of completion in the air; a sense very amply confirmed a few days later by the unexpected arrival of a stranger among them – a stranger to all but one of them.

He came up off the road in the valley beneath the Forest, a large, dark, tired wolf, and one whose body spoke of a great journey, and whose eyes told of his hope that he had finished it. Warned of his coming by a watcher on that side, Kobrin stared in astonishment as the wolf approached calmly, not stopping until he called out a warning to him to explain himself. He looked no Magyar, but these days one never quite knew. Then Aragon cried out in recognition and ran forward to greet the wolf.

'Leon of Spain!' he cried, even as the wolf came to a halt, his tired legs trembling and beginning to give way under him.

'I . . . am . . . Leon!' he answered, unable to stand any longer, 'and I . . . I have come . . . she . . . we . . .'

'Are the Magyars after you, wolf?' said Kobrin urgently, as the others advanced past Leon, their eyes scanning the slopes below the Ruin.

'They . . . I ran . . . and lay low in the valley below us for days. They did not find me.'

But he could say no more, no more at all, until he had rested for a short while, and they had led him to the river to drink, gasping between each gulp, his chest heaving, his eyes wild.

The first words he said when he was able to speak again were, 'She . . . she is . . . he . . . they have . . .'

'Who is, wolf?' said Aragon.

'The Magyars chased us . . . they nearly caught us, but she knew a way, a place . . . she is . . .'

'*Who* is, wolf?' growled Kobrin urgently.

'She . . .'

'Who?' said Lounel, pushing through to him and speaking with a gentleness that calmed him.

Leon breathed deeply, and said to Aragon, 'Jicin; she wanted to come home to the Heartland. I have travelled with her all the way, but when we reached the Fell she was injured escaping the Magyars.'

As the others glanced at each other in astonishment at this unexpected and most welcome news, he broke off, trying to catch his breath.

'Which one of them is Klimt?' he asked Aragon quietly.

Aragon explained that Klimt was not there, and that Kobrin was acting leader.

'Where did you leave her, wolf?' asked Kobrin.

'I . . .'

'Tell me, *now!*'

Never in their lives had the other Wolves seen Kobrin quite so serious, or ever heard his voice so softly dangerous, so awesomely threatening. Next to Klimt himself, Kobrin was Jicin's closest friend. Doubt had fled from him; hesitation was all gone; indecision did not exist; his mood of uncertainty was now but a dead leaf blowing away on an icy wind.

Leon stared at the great wolf, eyes widening, as if the Magyars that had chased him over the Fell were preferable by far to the wolf he found himself facing now.

'A stream, we crossed that – some trees, mountain ash. She knew the place.'

'How far from the gulley above?'

Leon did his best to say. Then he told how Jicin had been injured and unable to run, the Magyars chasing them.

'But she knew the place well, so well, and where to hide, where to lurk ... and we hid in the lee of a peat bank in the hope her paw would mend, near a stream.'

'South-west of the gulley?' Again it was Kobrin who posed the question, for he too knew the Fell.

Leon hesitated, still not sure. 'She told me to try to get up here to the Scarpfeld, and for two days now I have tried. First by the gulley, but it looked too dangerous, a place where I could too easily be trapped. Then I tried to skirt the cliffs southward but there were Magyar watchers and I could see it would take too long. Then ...'

'Then, Leon?' said Kobrin.

'I saw a wolf, an extraordinary wolf – his head foul and huge, his eyes vile.'

'Did he see you?'

Leon shook his head. 'I saw him descend by a way to the south side of the gulley, a dangerous way, but ... well, I took it. Through dark and dripping places, with echoes and the sound of wolves chasing me and ... and shadows, huge dark shadows whose blackness gave me cover when that wolf came back for a time, and whose mists seemed like my friend. I ... then I broke cover and ran, almost into him and he should have taken me, but ...'

'Well?'

'There was a female, a hag of a wolf and they were, they were ... preoccupied. They did not see me.'

'Did not *see* you?'

'They were mating.'

Three brief words, but on his face a look of disgusted incomprehension, of distaste, of revulsion – Dendrine and her huge son, mating in the dark and dripping shadows of a secret place.

'*They* did not see me,' said Leon. 'Though another one there did. A youngster, their cub, I suppose.'

'Pale grey of fur, intelligent of eye?'

Leon nodded indifferently, too lost in his tale to take note of the significance of their interest in a young wolf, or to wonder how they could have known . . .

'Torne,' murmured Aragon in a voice betraying both relief that he was still alive and anxiety that he should be in a situation so very dangerous.

'Then I ran on up that strange way, up and up, not caring that my paw-steps echoed down, not caring because I never wanted to look back, to see that one thing, horrible, those two had become. She was a hag, more dead than alive, and he was huge on her. It was from that thing I ran, and because Galliard told me never, ever, ever to give up, ever – but there was no way out that I could find. I lived for days up there, terrified they would come on up and find me trapped, but they never did. I lived off the drips of water that trickled down the cliffs, and warmed my shivering flanks in the brief show of sun at midday.

'Finally, when I knew I could not survive a single night longer I retreated downslope ready to die. But by then the foul wolves had gone, and I escaped westward along the base of the escarpment until I was able to climb over its lower end and into the Forest.'

'You saw no Magyars there?'

'A few, two-wolf patrols mainly. Not hard to evade for one who has travelled so far as Jicin and I, and been hunted and harried by all manner of creatures, Mennen and all.'

Leon gave a wry smile and Aragon said approvingly, 'When you hear the full tale of this wolf's life you'll understand why a few Magyars in a forest would not deter him!'

'Jicin told me to seek out the scents of thyme and tarragon, and this I did. So . . . I have reached you here and my first thought is not for myself but for Jicin, who lies weak and injured and in need of help.'

'Tell us again where she is, wolf, and take it slowly. The Fell is wide and the places in it many where a wolf might hide, but if we are to rescue her we need to be able to find her swiftly,' said Kobrin, restraining the restless Aragon who had no intention of not going to the aid of so old and trusted a friend as Jicin. Yet was it not just like Jicin to arrive on the Fell in the midst of the Magyars' resurgence, and be injured as well!

'She said Klimt would know the place, and Kobrin too. There are rocks there, and mountain ash, and places to hide, and she said it was where you were once alone with her, the last place. She said –'

'Is there a little stream there, which issues across undulating ground from the escarpment above?' said Kobrin quietly.

Leon nodded, relieved that these wolves so quickly recognized the place.

'It is where she and Klimt knew happiness for a time, a perfect place for a fugitive,' said Kobrin, sitting down calmly and nodding to the others to do so. 'There is water and small prey, and the undulations of the ground, and the caves there, make the winds flukey and a wolf's scent is hard to track down. You have left her in as safe a place as it would be possible to find. You have done well.'

'But we must go at once,' said Leon, rising suddenly and looking from one to another in alarm, for he detected in these wolves a certain reluctance to move.

'Leon, my friend,' said Aragon, who had himself calmed a little now he knew where Jicin was, 'there are good reasons why we should not mount a mission through the Forest and out on to the Fell just now. For one thing . . .'

He explained about their waiting for Umbrio and Jimena, and for Klimt as well.

'But they might never come,' said Leon when he had heard Aragon out, 'and meanwhile –'

'Did Aragon ever let you down?' asked Kobrin quietly.

Leon stilled and shook his head, saying, 'Nor Jicin either.'

'Quite so,' said Aragon. 'It is better we leave her where she is, relying on her good sense and the Magyars' apparent eagerness to advance into the Tatra heights as the warmer weather continues to advance. We must wait for the two lost youngsters, and we all believe in Klimt's return; and then when we have numbers enough to risk such a venture we shall go to Jicin's aid.'

'Meanwhile,' declared Lounel, 'I think that Jicin herself may play a final part in giving Klimt the strength to come home. She may never have been his ledrene, but she was always his true love, and if ever a wolf deserved one, having put duty before pleasure, it was he.'

'What do you mean, "giving Klimt the strength"?' asked Kobrin.

'I said he would come back, not that he would come back as the wolf he once was,' said Lounel shortly. 'There is, however, one thing we may usefully do this night. Tervicz! A word with you!'

'What's he about now?' growled Kobrin to Stry.

Stry shrugged and they all turned to listen to Aragon's questioning of his friend Leon, to hear of that wolf's early life with Galliard, and then to learn of the escape of the Brive wolves, and later of the long journey with Jicin from the Auvergne.

Yet stirring though these tales were it was Leon's account of the growing disarray of the Mennen in the lands through which he had travelled that caught their immediate attention, and raised most questions. Since he and Jicin had taken a similar route to Aragon comparisons were possible, and it seemed that more Mennen settlements had been ruined, more bridges destroyed, and the ills and plagues that beset both Mennen and their livestock were now more virulent and widespread than formerly.

'Time after time the stench of death hung in the air adjacent to their settlements,' Leon told them, 'and even out in the countryside away from where they normally lived we came across great masses of the dead, and the dying living in their own filth, under attack from their own starving dogs, each eating the other.

'For wolves there is no shortage of prey on which to feed, for those things we eat like rabbits and deer, and the food we like to eat but formerly avoided, such as cattle and sheep, run wild now in many places, unchecked by the Mennen as they used to be.'

It was a bleak picture, but an exciting one too, for the Wolves had faith that their renewal would come with the end of the Dark Millennium, and that was already well advanced.

'The time is coming when we must finally secure the Heartland for ourselves,' said Kobrin, hearing Leon's account of things. 'But we will have to defeat the Magyars once and for all if we are to achieve that aim. It is my belief that so disparate a mass of wolves is most easily vanquished by dispatching their leader and ledrene, and being seen to have done so. But who will lead the Magyars after that . . . well, I doubt that Klimt will want that task.'

'Will they not simply disperse once more?' said Stry.

Kobrin shrugged. 'They might, and possibly cause a great deal of trouble doing so. A strong leader, sympathetic to us Wolves, would not go amiss among the Magyars!'

The Wolves' discussion might have continued in this vein had not

Tervicz at that moment, dusk being near, and at Lounel's suggestion, begun a howl of entreaty and summons. It was but brief at first, to get them all in the mood for it.

'I suggest we ascend as one to the col,' said Lounel, 'for we know the way by night well enough, and better than the Magyars. We may have chosen not to fight them directly yet, but we can intimidate them with our howling. And more than that, we can give a signal to any that can hear us that they are in our thoughts.'

'The youngsters, you mean?' said Aragon.

'Them, and Jicin too, for the wind is right for our howling to carry over the escarpment and out on to the Fell. She will know it is us. Then there is Klimt, perhaps he will hear our summons too!'

It was a very long time since Tervicz had led a howl as he did that night, and the Wolves who heard him were regretful that he had been silent for so long. For this was the howl of the Bukov wolf and it carried a sense of age-old purpose, spreading out across the Forest and mountains as a song of ancient longing and the craving for home-coming that lingers in the air of ancient places, and long unused wolfways which await their turn again.

He howled as well a summons to those who could hear the right purpose of the Wolves, and had courage to pursue it whatever their circumstances, and as the others joined their voices to his lead, he howled a message of hope to those beset, as Jicin was, and those confused, as the youngsters might be.

But last of all he howled encouragement to those who had faltered on their way, who needed new courage and hope, howling high into the night air, up towards the stars and moon, that the different winds up there, which rose and blew beyond the mountain-tops, might take their howling to those that needed it.

'Look!' whispered Aragon much later, pointing at the moonstruck clouds that earlier had drifted southwards, out across the Fell.

With Tervicz's final howling the wind had died before shifting eastward, towards the highest of the peaks, taking their howling up and beyond it.

'Listen!' said Kobrin as one by one they fell silent, but for Tervicz himself.

For below them in Forest and Scarpfeld they heard the low, tremulous howls of frightened wolves, of Magyars who believed it was the gods themselves that howled, in wrath that their territory was invaded.

While from far further off, as if from all quarters of the earth, but mostly from the east, they heard or seemed to hear the howling of a thousand wolves, perhaps a thousand packs, as if they sought to answer the summons of the Bukov wolf and say, 'We are coming now, we come.'

That night above them in the skies, where the clouds swirled and turned in the starlight, the Wolves seemed to hear and see the tide of destiny begin to quicken in their favour, and though none dared say it then, they knew that now it was that Klimt must come home.

Yet one did dare say it later, as the Wolves turned off the col and back towards the safety of their hiding-place.

A solitary howl they heard, sweet as summerlight: from off the Fell it came, not an answer to their call but rather affirmation of it, from one who loved to one she loved; two Wolves so long apart, coming closer now, in whose union and reunion destiny might find its most loving grace.

Kobrin heard lost Jicin's call and said, his face fur wet with unwonted tears, 'If he does not come home to lead us soon I shall go and rescue her myself!'

The Wolves nodded their approval, grinning at each other at Kobrin's sudden show of sentiment. Then he growled at them, and buffeted a few, that they might come to order and follow him back to the Ruin before the dawn light became too bright.

CHAPTER TWENTY-SIX

*Klimt brings new supporters back to the Heartland
and Lunar discovers the difficulties of leadership*

THE RETURN OF Klimt and Lunar from Khazaria with the Pechoran wolves was delayed principally by the continuing weakness of Klimt himself following his escape from the Quarry. Outwardly he had seemed well enough, considering what he had been through, and the gunshot wound to his shoulder had healed satisfactorily.

But inwardly he was troubled and weary, and spent days and nights in silence, barely willing or able to move on. Rather, he wanted to talk, about the past, present and future, and all three at once, often in a way that seemed confused to Lunar, so used to a father who was clear-cut in all he said and purposeful in all he did.

There had been a time too when he seemed almost delirious in his desire to return to the Quarry to make sure, he said, that the Mann they had seen still alive in it and trying to escape had succeeded as they had.

'But he's just one of the Mennen,' said Lunar, puzzled.

'He's the Mann,' said Klimt, in what seemed to the others a moment of delusion, 'the one who was there before when I escaped from Sweden, and there again when I reached the Heartland and first met Elhana and her father Ambato.'

'Surely he's just a Mann,' repeated Lunar, 'and they are all the same?'

'Are we?' said Klimt, his head falling back in weakness. 'Are we just the same? May Wulf protect him, for I am not yet able to.'

'You, father?' said Lunar in astonishment.

'If not I, then you shall do it.'

Had it not been for the Pechoran wolves' continuing loyalty and support for one who had given leadership to Kobrin, their greatest scion, and who had entrusted the Heartland to Kobrin's care, things might have gone hard for them all through this troubled time when their leader was sick.

Nor were those few Kazakh wolves who followed Klimt and Lunar westward out of Khazaria after their defeat loyal to their new masters for long. They had picked up more of their kind along the way, including that patrol of powerful wolves who had first accosted Klimt and the others on their arrival in those parts, and thus strengthened in numbers the Kazakhs did not fraternize with the Pechorans, despite Lunar's attempts to mix them up and make them work together.

'I can teach you nothing but what you will learn by doing it for yourself,' Klimt told Lunar, who had sought advice about how to deal with the continual sparring and bickering between the Pechorans and Kazakh wolves, which threatened to spill over into serious violence, and an attempt to wrest the leadership from the still-weak Klimt.

'You can tell me what *you* would do,' grumbled Lunar, who felt he was not ready for such problems and challenges as these.

'Find them a common task, wolf, and even better, point out to them a common enemy, for nothing makes a pack forget its differences more quickly than that.'

'There is no common enemy,' said Lunar, surveying the vast dry desert lands across which they were returning, 'except a lack of water, and stretches of land in which I fear there may be too little food to sustain all of us.'

'Quite,' said Klimt wearily, 'hunger and thirst are your enemies; now make the wolves fear them, and get them to find ways of combating them.'

So, a reluctant leader, Lunar learnt what he must do – describing the perils ahead to the wolves in much worse terms than he remembered them from his earlier journey from the west.

'The lack of water will turn the strongest of you mad if you are not careful, and hunger is a demon sent by the gods to harry at your stomach like hornets at your face. The main party will therefore journey only by way of those water-courses and pools I remember, but I shall split you up into smaller groups of Pechorans and Kazakhs together, each of which can explore to north and south in the hope of finding water and prey. Whichever group performs this task best of all might be judged most worthy to be going to the Heartland in the service of the gods.'

Klimt could not but help giving a wry smile of sympathy at Lunar's attempts to engender some discipline and competition among the wolves. It was better than doing nothing.

Yet despite these ruses the journey continued with Lunar in a situation he was not quite ready for, and Solar, had he still been alive, would certainly have dealt with it better. For one thing, the Khazarian wolves were of the type who respect a physical show of strength above all else, the more brutal the better, and several times Klimt observed situations where, had he been fit and well, a swift assault upon a recalcitrant Kazakh wolf might have cut all argument short; while a single killing would have sustained them a good deal further on the journey.

'They will continue to grumble and argue for a time, testing us out to see how steadfast we seem,' observed Klimt in a whisper one day, 'and a moment will inevitably come when they try to defeat you and kill me, or the other way about. I can cede the leadership to you, Lunar, but that will only turn their frustration at my weakness on you – and perhaps their wrath as well for the way you succeeded in fooling and defeating them in their own territory. You must find a strategy of survival.'

'What would you do, father?'

Klimt shrugged and turned away.

'You know what to do, don't you?' cried Lunar angrily.

Klimt sighed. He did, yes he did, but if Lunar was to lead he must discover what worked best for him.

But Lunar had one friend in whom he could confide, and that was Utin, the Pechoran he had fought and later saved from the Kazakhs.

'He knows, but he won't tell me,' complained Lunar.

'What would Solar have done?' said Utin.

'Solar?' repeated Lunar in some surprise, frowning, snarling at another wolf who came too near. 'Why, he . . . he . . .'

'Well?' said Utin. 'You always say he was stronger than you and knew how to lead better. And what of Kobrin, what would *he* do?'

'You're as bad as my father,' said Lunar morosely, 'always asking questions and giving no advice. Well, I am not the weakest wolf amongst them, which is a start, nor yet the strongest. What would Solar have done? Found allies. And Kobrin? Analysed, worked things out, assessed his enemies' strengths and weaknesses. Yes . . .'

Utin grinned as his friend talked to himself about his problems, teasing out a solution.

What would Klimt have done? Found allies, analysed . . .

'Lunar!'

It was Utin, and it was dusk.

'There's trouble!'

Two Kazakhs had taken on a Pechoran wolf and the others were ranging to support their kind. They had observed that Lunar was off in the distance sitting apart and there was talk of his being too irresolute and weak to settle the dispute.

Lunar padded quietly over towards where the wrangling continued, getting worse all the time. Klimt was not far off himself, and evidently glad to see Lunar arrive. But his son did not immediately seek to quell the disputing factions, but instead assessed the situation, as Klimt himself would have done – and had been doing.

Lunar remembered how when he was a youngster his father would sometimes ask Solar to assess a situation and decide how best to act. He looked across at Klimt now, and guessed that though silent he was asking the same question now.

Allies, that's what he must be sure he had.

'Utin?'

His friend nodded.

'Get three Pechorans, like . . .' Lunar named the ones he had in mind. 'Tell them to break away from this fray and form a protective group in front of Klimt. This fight is not quite what it seems.'

Utin nodded and went to do Lunar's biding.

Analysis . . .

No, it did not feel quite right, quite real. The Kazakh wolves were giving him as much attention as they were their foes, and the tussle was not developing as fast or viciously as it would have done had it been genuine. Other wolves were hanging back, watching too. It was a test, but by whom and for what? From the corner of his eye Lunar saw that one of the three Pechorans he had named was not going with the other two, but rather staying close by the Kazakhs. Hmmm . . .

Resolute attack when least expected, that was Klimt's preferred way: intimidate the opposition, be ruthless, utterly.

Silently invoking his brother Solar's name, and Wulf's as well, Lunar rose suddenly, that all might see, and began a charge straight at the mêlée of wrangling wolves, just as he would be expected to do. He saw the others tense, looked around to see which seemed calmest and most still, and picked out one of the Kazakhs as the most likely organizer of the incident. A big wolf, but somewhat slow. Lunar knew him well enough. Still going for the group, he charged faster, one against several, one who might very easily be outnumbered.

Attack, and be ruthless.

As he began the final leap that would bring him to the quarrelling wolves Lunar felt the power of Klimt's will in him. This was how his father felt: cold, so cold of purpose; certain, so certain of his right to act; exhilarated, so –

Lunar landed but a step away from the troublemakers, steadied himself with all the poise he knew, glanced up to look beyond the fight to its creators, and to one yet more poised than the Kazakh wolf he thought was its progenitor: the Pechoran who had refused to go with Utin, smiling and benign, but the real enemy. The one.

Lunar gathered all his strength and resolution and leapt again, right over the whole group and straight towards the one he had picked out.

Attack, and be *utterly* ruthless.

If surprise had a name it was that Pechoran's, and if anything convinced Lunar that his analysis was right it was the mingling of astonishment, fear, anger and embarrassment to be so detected that crossed his victim's face; there was not one shred of outrage that he was being wrongly accused by Lunar.

Lunar did not waste time on words or niceties. He had seen Klimt in action thus and did the same himself: straight for the face, a bite and crunching grip to make the other's jaws powerless. Then the turning pull and a sudden push and shove that had the wolf wrong-footed and tumbling down, his paws' grip lost, their power weakened, even as the yelping scream of shock and pain began.

For a moment he felt the Pechoran's more powerful body begin to rise and push and muster all its strength. Pechorans are trained to fight, Utin had said, and Lunar knew he had but moments to complete his task before he lost the advantage of surprise and risked losing all.

A flashing memory of Solar once, when his brother had pulled him down and might have taken pity on him, but had not. Instead he had gone in harder still and Lunar remembered the bitterness he felt as he saw his father nod approvingly at Solar's brutality.

He saw Klimt staring now, he saw the nod again, but this time he understood why, and it left no room for pity. Hard into the Pechoran's neck, a ripping bite, and then up, twisting in the air, a spray of the other wolf's blood from his mouth, and he went straight and hard at his genitals.

It was over in a moment. Screaming, scrabbling away, his tail between his legs, blood dripping from face and under-parts, the Pechoran escaped, and Lunar stood suddenly proud, his back to Utin and the two Pechorans who guarded his father; the sham fighting of the other wolves had ceased.

'If any other wolf wishes to question the ascendancy of Klimt, who is my leader and yours too, let him do so now and leave in peace. If any other among you plots against Klimt, he plots against us who stand with him. Are there any such here?'

Silence, but for the nervous panting of a pack of wolves.

'Are there any here who do not accept Klimt's leadership?'

Silence, but for the pad of two or three Kazakh wolves who slipped away.

'Will you all swear fealty to him through the howl?'

Silence, waiting, and a certain awe at Lunar's new control over them, and reluctance to show they had no idea what 'the howl' really meant.

'Humph!' said Lunar, wishing Solar was there to share the joke. He had no idea either, having just that moment made it up.

He pushed his head forward and then raised it slowly as he began a howl which told of leadership and Klimt, and spoke of the Heartland to where they were going, as one, as one – that might as well be what 'swearing fealty through the howl' meant.

Nearby, the grim lines of Klimt's face cracked into a smile, as he began to understand Lunar's ploy. He was beginning to believe again there might be hope after all, for Lunar was showing a strength he never thought he had, and the ability to be prudent and to learn. He might yet be the chosen one.

As the howl proceeded Klimt gave thanks to the gods, and asked if he would be spared long enough to witness Lunar's ascendancy over others. Hearing the howl, seeing the slow work of pack-building beginning to bear fruit, Klimt really expected no answer then and there from the gods to his silent prayers; so he was surprised to hear whispers in the distance, a far-off howl in answer to the howl, the stirring of a summons home, and a sudden and unexpected pang of longing for her he had missed so long, whom he had not thought of for weeks.

'Jicin, are you too journeying home, my dear, and will I feel your touch one more time?'

Klimt's hope for the Wolves found a sudden counterpart in hope for himself, that his task of leadership was nearly done, and that after it, before he journeyed on to the stars above, he might know again the bliss of union with Jicin, the only true mate he had ever known, his true love, and find the fulfilment that had so long eluded him. To turn his back on duty and give way to pleasure – it seemed so wrong!

'Jicin, my dear . . .'

'What is it, father?'

It was Lunar close by, with a worried frown; he had seen the glisten of tears in Klimt's grey eyes, and heard the murmur of Jicin's name.

'I miss her, wolf.'

'I know,' said Lunar; he had never met Jicin, nor known his father peaceful with a mate, and could not quite imagine it.

Seeing Lunar and Klimt then, in the privacy of night and of a communal howl, a watching wolf might have asked which was the father, which the son?

'I'll see you get well again, and home as leader of this new pack of ours if it is the last thing that I do!' said Lunar.

'Not the last thing, I trust!' said Klimt in mock alarm. It was the nearest Klimt came to levity throughout that long journey.

There were no more threats to Lunar or Klimt after the fight with the Pechoran, and all agreed that Lunar had acquitted himself as a budding leader should. Indeed, it had been very well done, and the outcome was the better that Lunar did not claim leadership as he might have done – and as Solar probably would have done.

He knew he had much to learn and had been lucky. Better that Klimt was given time to recover; better that in the weeks ahead before they got within striking distance of the Heartland the wolves about them learned to work together as a pack must; better to find which wolves among them could be relied on in a crisis, as Utin clearly could.

'Just provided we can keep the troublemakers at bay until you are strong again,' Lunar told his father some days later when an invigorated Klimt insisted on resuming their long journey once again.

'Well, maybe,' grunted Klimt; Lunar took his new-found ill-temper as a sign of frustration at not being fully fit, and an indication that he was finally getting better. 'But remember, one day I shall not be here at all, wolf, so you had best look to your future strengths rather than rely on declining ones like me. Oh yes, I may make it back to the Heartland, and there have a glorious few months as leader once the

Magyars are defeated, but my work is nearly done and others will replace me. I trust those others will include you, and you shall become pre-eminent. It is what Wulfin herself ordained all those years ago.'

'Humph!' said Lunar, who preferred to ignore such talk. The great destiny of the Wolves of Time he could accept, but he felt himself to be merely mortal and that it was absurd to talk of him or any other wolf becoming a god. Those were his father's dreams, and the fabled visit of Wulfin at the time of his and Solar's birth was surely only a chimera.

'They are not dreams, Lunar my son, not dreams at all, but the righting of past wrongs, the learning of lessons, the beginning of our new supremacy, the turning of the years and centuries back to what we were before Wulf fell to earth and mortality. Now . . . no, do not hurry on so! Listen! *Wolf!*'

But Lunar did not like to listen to talk of coming gods. It was all nonsense, it was . . . it was . . . and it frightened him.

'Lunar!' cried Klimt, catching him up, 'I was simply going to say that we do not have to hurry back to the Heartland as fast as this. Something tells me we can trust in Kobrin to keep things under control a little longer.'

'They must be anxious to see us back,' said Lunar. 'The warmer weather will be advancing even on to the Scarpfeld by now and with it the Magyars will surely begin their advance back into the centre of the Heartland.'

Klimt nodded, suddenly claiming to feel tired again. Perhaps he did, or perhaps he was using such devices to slow things down.

'He thinks I have much to learn yet,' grumbled Lunar to Utin, his confidant.

'Maybe he's right; I know I have!' said Utin disarmingly.

So they continued to pause here and stay there, to turn north from their westward trek in search of prey, and then south again in search of clean water. Sometimes they rested awhile where the water was good and prey were abundant to recover their strength and hear each other's tales.

Yet these delays brought certain benefits, as wise Klimt knew they would, and one of the most valuable was the final defection of those wolves who became disenchanted with the slow progress, and so showed they might not be suited to the great task Klimt inspired the rest to undertake.

Such wolves sometimes slipped away into anonymity and were seen no more; at other times their fate was not anonymous at all. So it was that when two wolves left the main group in search of water in the desert of the Ukraine the main party later found grim evidence of their fate in the form of their decaying bodies caught in Mennen snares. Lunar had not seen such wire traps before and insisted on going back to study them, his distaste and distress at the malodorous condition of the bodies overridden by his desire to know how such thin pieces of wire could have so easily entrapped powerful wolves. It took him a while to work it out, and to see how the two wolves might have freed themselves had they not pulled away from the wire and instead pushed against its cutting loop and so loosened it.

The snares suggested that Mennen had been lying in wait for whatever creature came along; but it seemed probable that the intended prey had been rabbits, not wolves, for there were extensive burrows thereabout, all now deserted, though from the sweet, dry smell that came from them no rabbits had died within for a long time. On his way back from this morbid examination Lunar found something more, led to it by the flap of buzzards' wings in the dusk, and the scurry of rooks on higher ground.

Dead Mennen were there, a dozen of them, in stinking tarpaulin shelters formed in the lee of a vehicle of the kind used in the Mennen fights along the Forest Road. It seemed these Mennen had been driven out from some distant settlement and, running out of food and water, had died. The snares had been a last desperate attempt to survive, taking their prey when the Mennen were too weak to benefit from the catch.

It was soon after this distressing incident that the wolves entered a less arid area of the Ukraine, and now began to see how great was the devastation of the Mennen war in those places they had passed through months before. Instinct and common sense kept them well away from the centre of the towns and cities. In one place they came upon a population of blinded rats, their eyes seeping a white viscous fluid, their lives reduced to a vicious internecine struggle and decline as they fed upon each other. They stood poised and still when the wolves came by, listening with ears whose hearing was impaired, feeling for vibrations through paws that had gone numb, squinching their snouts in alarm as the wolves wended their way past, through the ruins and the Mennen corpses.

They reached the river where Solar had fought to defend Lunar. Then it had been clear; now it was red with spuming pollutant, and out of it, as it flowed on its congested way down south, heads of blinded cattle emerged, the feet of Mennen, the slowly arcing legs of a dead horse, rising out of the red pottage before sinking below its surface again.

There was the pervasive smell of annihilation, of decay and loss, of a river choked with the detritus of a desecrated, barren land, flowing on into another devastated long since. They found a Mennen bridge and crossed it, staring upstream and down, almost wishing there were Mennen there, and so normality. The stench made a wolf retch; the acrid, contaminated air made eyes weep.

Nothing moved across those dry lands but the slow red-brown river of death beneath them, and their own troop as they journeyed on eastward.

It was only some weeks later, in April, when the wolves reached the western and higher part of the Ukraine that things began to return to normal. Smoke rose from the chimneys of little settlements, as it had in the old days, and at dawn Mennen led horses out across the fields, tending to new crops, carrying feed to livestock, clinking and rattling back along the narrow highland tracks at dusk with creaking carts and harness, observed by the wolves, unseen.

It was now that they heard news of the Magyar advance on the far side of the Carpathians, towards whose great mass they were already beginning to climb. They came across vagrant wolves, mainly in ones and twos, though occasionally in larger groups, fugitives from the Magyars or Mennen, and sometimes both. Most told the same story of how Magyar emissaries had come to them the previous autumn and spoken of the Magyar leader Führer, mighty, wise and proud, who would be advancing back into the Scarpfeld, the very centre of the Heartland, with the coming spring, there to explore the fabled WulfRock and reaffirm the true destiny of wolves.

It sounded promising, but mountain wolves like to stay close by their own territory and did not relish the 'join us or be against us' approach of the lowland Magyar wolves who came so boldly up among them. But those who did not respond to the Magyars' summons found when the new spring began that they were victims of persecution by zealous Magyar hordes from south Ukraine, and from other members of their pack who were setting off in support of Führer.

Worse still, these same wolves, who had lived alongside Mennen for centuries without much conflict – the Mennen had long since gained ascendancy over the wolves on the richer, lower ground – now found themselves persecuted once more.

'The Mennen come with guns and dogs. They chase us and shoot us, or take our weaker ones alive and torture them so that we hear their cries and are afraid . . .'

There were many such reports and about half the wolves they met were too frightened by what they had seen to linger with Klimt's group, or yield to their persuasion to come along with them. They preferred to remain fugitive and flee, and it was no good telling them that the land they fled to was ruined now.

The other half of the fugitives felt reassured by the order and purposefulness Klimt and Lunar had worked so hard to impose, and were inspired by their talk of a coming destiny for wolfkind. In any case, a sensible wolf could see that there was safety in numbers against both Magyars and Mennen, and a security and purpose not likely to be found by wandering on alone.

So it was that by May, when they were up in the foothills of the Carpathians, their numbers had swollen considerably. By now Klimt had regained most of his old strength and all his great authority. His shoulder still ached on steep climbs and caused him to limp a little when he was tired, but Lunar had been able to relinquish day-to-day control of the pack to him, and was thankful for it.

Two or three days from the Heartland, Klimt decided to split the pack into two, putting most of the Pechorans under Lunar's leadership, for they all got on well and had built on the trust established at their first meeting. As for the rough, tough Kazakh wolves, and some of the more difficult elements of the vagrants who had joined them, Klimt relished the challenge of imposing control and leadership on them all, a task made easier by the fact that some of the newer recruits had heard his name spoken with awe by the Magyars, and but brief acquaintance with his formidable presence told them what they had heard was true.

'Lunar, take your group on ahead of mine, for you exercise authority over them and have made them work as one, with Utin as worthy an assistant to you as Tervicz always was to me. You can travel faster than my larger group, and in any case I need a day or two longer to get our latest recruits into order. Therefore, push on ahead now as fast as you can to the Forest, and re-establish contact with Kobrin and the others. Tell him I shall be no more than three days behind, and that I shall come by way of the Ruin where Merrow was lost so long ago.'

Lunar nodded bleakly at the memory.

'So . . . whatever else he and you may decide to do, make sure there is always a watcher there to guide us on to where you may be. I shall try to muster more wolves before we arrive, which will not be difficult since Führer seems to make enemies of those he fails to impress or intimidate. Like father like son, it seems!'

They talked some more, and made what other arrangements they could to ensure that they might more easily be in touch if need arose, and then Lunar led his pack away towards the higher Tatra, to find a safe way through the late snow to the Forest, his heart beating all the faster to be home at last.

CHAPTER TWENTY-SEVEN

*Homecomings, and the beginning of the final confrontation
of the Wolves with Magyars, and with Mennen*

SOME NIGHTS LATER, with a light frost crackling underfoot, and their white breath caught by moonlight, Lunar and the Pechorans finally reached a place he knew, and he felt the breathless surge of homecoming. They were in the Vale that lies two hours from the Ruin where the three travellers to Khazaria had originally parted from Kobrin and the others.

He felt a strange happiness, and knew the reassurance of clear purpose. The stars were so surely set in the sky above, and his command of the wolves who followed him felt complete at last.

'How far before we might make contact?' asked Utin at his shoulder.

'Two hours, not much more.'

'Excited?'

'Very.'

The two had become close friends and had that easy trust that Klimt and Tervicz always had. Lunar understood with a sudden pang how great his father's sacrifice had been in leaving Tervicz behind. Had he missed him? He must have done.

Lunar's sense of Klimt's greatness had grown powerfully over the past few days. His dream had held the Wolves together, as it held him now in its spell, powerful as the stars. He never betrayed any doubt that Kobrin was safe, and that he had seen to it that those who had stayed with him had fulfilled their task.

Some, perhaps, had died. Lunar felt it must be so. He could almost smell it in the air. Things had changed but their destiny was still intact. But while some had gone, others were surely coming home, like they themselves.

'Come on,' he said when they had rested enough, and drunk from a stream that tasted of the mountain water he knew so well, 'we're nearly there.'

'Will Kobrin *really* be waiting for us?' asked one of the Pechorans.

'Yes, I believe he will,' said Lunar. 'He was always there for *me*, from the moment of my birth, and I'm not a Pechoran! The gods will surely have seen to it that mighty Kobrin will be there to welcome the courageous Pechorans who have trekked so far to take up the great work he helped Klimt begin!'

Lunar had always had a talent for words, and now he used them in such a way that made other wolves want to follow him.

'Come, my friends!' he said, and led them on.

They did pause one more time. A Mennen helicopter, lights flashing, flew over their heads, not towards the Scarpfeld but along the safer line of the valley bottom, up its soft gradient towards the Fell beyond. Lunar watched it go, wincing a little at its harsh roar and wondering at Mennen ways, glad to have his paws upon the ground as the silence of the mountains came slowly back to the ground.

They decided to approach the Ruin slowly, taking the advantage in scenting that the wind from the mountains gave them, and circling away from the Forest to rougher, rocky ground only as dawn advanced. There were too many conflicting scent tracks all about, both Wolves and Magyar, for Lunar to risk exposure yet.

He paused awhile by a conifer whose surface roots were shiny ochre in the early light, and had been nibbled at by deer. He knew the spot and scented all about.

'Stry's been here,' whispered Lunar softly, 'and another wolf.' But he could not recognize the scent except that it was female.

Having gained a point of vantage they waited until full dawn, the air dank and heavy with the nearby stream, which ran on down to the Ruin itself. They listened to the movement of creatures through the undergrowth, and the howling barks of wolves off to the south: Magyars. Then, when the wind began to shift behind them, as it usually did thereabouts as the sun rose, Lunar stood and shook himself. Nodding to Utin to take charge he signalled to two of the largest Pechorans to accompany him.

These things were best done carefully, for if others had already joined the Wolves under Kobrin, and knew him not, they might attack. It would be so much easier if the first he saw was one he knew, and safer to have guards with him.

Lunar's heart thumped in his chest as he dropped softly down the slope among the trees, the river to his left. It was not just the natural nervousness of coming back that troubled him, but the memories of all those times before his journey – times that seemed so long ago – the worst and chief of which was the loss of Merrow in this very place.

He saw the flank of wolf, grey-brown, and then another but moments before they saw him. All froze, then shifted a little to get a better view through the obscuring trees. An eye, another flank, the rising hackles on a back, and the fleet soft run of paws below and around them, ready to ambush or to flee.

Lunar and his companion advanced a step more that they might be the better seen, and then he barked to identify himself as one of them. Then he gave a short rill that said they were no danger, and then he made further advance towards the stationary Wolves.

Then suddenly there was Stry, coming from behind two trees where he had stayed close hidden.

'Stry! Wolf! It's me!' cried Lunar.

The two advanced upon each other, wary for a moment, and then circled touching shoulders, cheek to cheek, rough-tumbling in the way Stry himself had taught Lunar when he was young.

'Lunar! By Wulf, it *is* you!'

They stood looking at each other, relief on both their faces.

'By Wulf, there's much we want to know, but . . .'

Stry looked past Lunar at the strangers and seemed perturbed.

'Where's Klimt?'

Lunar took Stry to one side, that others might not hear, and quickly explained the size and disposition of the forces they had brought, and that Klimt would be with them in a day or two.

'And not a day too soon!' muttered Stry.

'Why, what's wrong?' responded Lunar.

Stry quickly described the recent advance of the Magyars into the Scarpfeld, and how since then Kobrin had insisted that the remaining Wolves lie low, trusting in Lounel's prediction of Klimt's return. He told as well of Elhana's grievous death, though Lunar's face expressed his relief that she had surely made her way to the WulfRock and beyond to the stars.

'So now you're waiting for the return of the two youngsters, this other wolf, Torne, having been lost to the Magyars?'

Stry nodded. 'Kobrin's been up by the Fall where they disappeared since last night, though it's not his turn to await their coming until this morning. Lounel says they'll come back that way. Aragon's there too –'

'Aragon!' cried Lunar with astonishment.

'There's so much to explain, and so little time,' said Stry. 'We believe Jicin's out on the Fell at that secret outcrop where she and Klimt once lived together for a time. Now, we had best summon Kobrin back, I'll send –'

Lunar smiled and stayed him for a moment.

'There is a better way to summon him than that!' said Lunar, looking about the Ruin and the trees around it, then beyond to the cliffs above. The Wolves' time was coming now, it was right here with them, and all were returning as they must that the last assault upon the Magyar could begin.

'How *is* Kobrin?' asked Lunar.

'Well enough, but Klimt has been away too long and Kobrin has aged. He has barely rested for weeks, perhaps months past, watching and worrying, planning and manoeuvring – none but he could have fooled the Magyars into thinking there is a full pack of us down here so long, and kept them believing that Klimt was nearby. Just lately I think they have realized our numbers are low.'

'Excellent!' cried Lunar. 'My father always likes to give his enemies unpleasant surprises.'

He called over a Pechoran wolf and commanded him to go and fetch Utin and all the others at once.

'We shall give Kobrin a summons and a welcome of a kind he must have decided he would never hear again, one that will greet him as the great wolf he is.'

A short time later the Pechorans began to file into the clearing by the Ruin and mingle with the others, testing and snarling, scenting and quietly barking, before settling down. When Lunar announced that Kobrin was nearly the Pechorans fell silent, and several looked awestruck.

'You know how to greet him?' asked Lunar softly.

'With honour and respect,' said Utin, taking the lead among his own. He raised his head and began a strange high howl, as when a tundra wind catches in frozen undergrowth, and with a hint of the swirl of dry snow swept out across a frozen lake.

The other Pechorans slowly rose and took their places by him, their voices melding with his into a softly mounting howl of the northern wastes whence they had so long since set forth in search of the Heartland, in search of the one whose example had so long sustained them.

'*Heuren Sie!* Listen now!' whispered Lunar to Stry and the others, for their howl was a telling of decades of waiting, and of the many who had never lived to make this journey, though often they had dreamed it; a telling of the courage of the few who had now done so, and wished to greet the greatest wolf ever born to their tribe, and in that greeting say that they too were ready to join their strength and courage to the search for a fulfilment of wolfkind's destiny and for the recovery of Wulf to immortality at Wulfin's flank.

Old Kobrin had shivered all night at the entrance to the Great Cleft in the cliff through which the Fall flowed. He had not quite known why he had come, for it was Aragon's watch through to morning, and he could have stayed by the Ruin and kept warm. But the sky had been clear in the gloaming, strangely clear, and the stars as bright as ever he remembered, and the changes that had been gathering pace seemed imminent about him, and right across the sky as well: great rafts of stars rarely seen, a cold night wind, and echoes and cries from the Cleft itself, from which Aragon had come to join him.

But by dawn Kobrin had grown despondent, and his and Aragon's conversation had been sporadic as they waited for what Lounel had promised would come to be.

'Where *is* Lounel?' asked Aragon, stretching at first light.

'Gone up towards the col, to howl in the hope that Jicin might hear, to tell her we shall come to her aid now whether or not Klimt returns. All is changing, wolf, the old world is ending, and I am old and have served my time. Let others complete this task!'

Aragon looked at him, and it seemed that the frost on the ground had also settled on Kobrin's face, and down his thick, patchy legs, so grizzled and grey was he. His fur hung off him now, and his manifold scars seemed ever more prominent across his face and body; he was losing weight, and strength.

'Kobrin . . .' began Aragon, wishing to find words of reassurance, but finding none that seemed to help. Then he said, 'The echoes in the Cleft were eerie last night. I swear that if there was a night for the youngsters to return it was the one just past. But now dawn's here –'

It came to them then, sudden and strange – a howl so faint it seemed but the whispers of a tundra wind, and the whip of snow across an icy lake.

'Listen, Kobrin, what's *that*?'

But Kobrin *was* listening, his wrinkled eyes widening, his ears pricked, his great maw opening in astonishment as his tongue flicked across his dry mouth.

'What is that howl?' repeated Aragon.

It became louder, then faded, then swelled louder still, just as the tundra winds will come and go through forest trees, now drawing the branches forward, now seeming to suck them back. Formidable it was, and spoke of endless days and nights in which a wolf survives only by a self-belief, and dreams of better things as he huddles in what cold shelter he can find.

'Kobrin . . . *Kobrin!*'

The great wolf had stood up now, his eyes and mouth open wide still, and his breath coming out in strange gasps as if he could not quite catch up with events, or with what it was he heard, and all it meant.

Louder still the howl, bolder too, eerie and strange, travelling past them along the scree, winding down the slopes, all along, perhaps even where Magyar scouts lay low, struck dumb now and much afraid.

While behind Kobrin and Aragon, whose hackles had begun to rise in simple fear and awe of what he heard, the howl journeyed to the Fall, and then into the Cleft, echoing there, powerful in its stark strength, purposeful, louder by far in its echo than the Fall itself. So loud and reverberant indeed that the howling provoked a rockfall, for there was a scatter of stones on to the grass above them which made both turn.

'Kobrin –!'

But Kobrin saw them too, up among the shadows in the Cleft – the two youngsters so long lost, grubby and wet from their journey down through Wulf knew what strange twists and turns, but strong enough to cry, 'It's us!'

For a moment the two adults forgot the howling they had heard and ran upslope to grab Jimena and Umbrio, lest to leave them there meant they risked being spirited away again.

'Where have you been?' cried Aragon, the senseless question of a father who knew not what else to say.

'What's that howling?' asked Umbrio. 'We heard it and we came . . .'

Then they were running off downslope towards the Forest and thence along to the Ruin, ahead of their amused father, faster than the grumbling Kobrin, towards the howling, which echoed and vibrated louder still, its winter winds dying and fading into spring as they approached, joyous now and welcoming.

'What is it?' asked Jimena, nuzzling up to a laughing Aragon.

'Yes, what is it, Kobrin?' asked Umbrio, a little more in awe.

They had stopped a little way short of the Ruin to let the adults lead them in.

'It is the howl of my tribe, a howl of greeting which tells that the long season of dark waiting is over, and spring is here, and summer coming fast. A howl of contentment in the present, and confidence in the future, which tells those who hear it and are allies that a whole tribe is with them.'

'And those who are enemies?' said Aragon softly, glancing towards the Magyars far down-valley of them, and on the slopes below the col.

'That they are doomed,' growled Kobrin.

'Well, should we answer it?' said Jimena.

'We should go and join it, wolf,' said Kobrin, his face gentle with happiness and relief. His long wait was over, a wait that journeyed back those long years to when he had first left Pechora. Pechora had come home to him.

'Come on then,' said Umbrio, setting off once more, 'come *on!*'

Aragon and the youngsters covered the last few yards swiftly, while behind them Kobrin took his time, much moved by the joyous sight he saw. Huge he seemed, and absolute, and somehow younger than those who knew him well had ever seen him look.

Then, as he finally reached the place where the wolves were, the howling slowly died in the Pechorans' throats as one by one they saw the greatest of their tribe looking across the clearing at them, no wolf prouder, no wolf so strong, no wolf so venerable.

Utin came forward and said, 'Kobrin, sir, we bring you greetings from your homeland . . .'

Kobrin sighed and nodded, his eyes full of glad tears.

'. . . and from those who could not come. We honour those who started out with us but fell along the way. We offer ourselves now to you, weak and few though we must seem, to serve you as you command us, which is and always was our good fortune and our destiny. And I . . . I . . .'

'Yes, wolf?' howled Kobrin in the way he had, coming closer to Utin and making the younger wolf seem smaller.

'. . . I never thought, I never dreamed, that we would make it!'

Kobrin laughed, deeply and generously, and said, 'Wolf, I often doubted that you would!'

CHAPTER TWENTY-EIGHT

Klimt of Tornesdal returns home to the Heartland
and inspires the Wolves to follow him into a final battle

As KLIMT OF TORNESDAL, Wolf of Time, reached the last hour or two of his long journey back from Khazaria, he felt his age and dared hope that his great task of leadership was nearly done. The truth was his shoulder still ached from its injury in the Quarry, and probably always would. Then too, those he was leading pressed close behind in their eagerness to get on to the Ruin and a confrontation with the Magyars, making him feel harried and breathless.

Twice he slowed, twice they steadied down behind him, but a wise wolf knows he cannot hold back youth and that, one day, it will overtake him, and then leave him far behind with barely a second glance. So Klimt led them now, trying to keep calm at the prospect of meeting Kobrin and Stry, Elhana and his daughters and all the others again; and Tervicz too. Especially Tervicz, whose advice and company he had so often missed.

Then too . . .

But he shook his head to drive away the thought, stared ahead to see they had not far to go, looked round to see who was close behind and if he could remember all their names, and then carried on.

Then too . . . *nothing*.

Oh, but there was.

Then too, there was Jicin – no good pretending. She was the one he had missed most of all, and who he most feared never seeing again. Sometimes it had been the thought of her, and not dreams of the destiny of the Wolves of Time, that had kept him going on the long trek home.

Their route turned a corner amongst the rocks and they climbed over a last watershed into a tributary of the valley along which the Forest runs. He caught again the familiar scents of pine woods and mountain rivers and found new energy to hurry on. Now he went faster than before, and this time it was the younger wolves who had to hurry to keep up.

Should they be wary?

Probably, but Lunar had gone on ahead to alert the others that he would be coming. If Magyars or Mennen were about then the Wolves would have got a warning to him, or he would have begun to scent the danger. On he went, yet faster now, reaching a path they had used when they had left, into territory he knew and finally, and he sighed with relief to hear it, within the range of a sound he had forgotten was so familiar.

'What's that?' several of them asked as he paused, cocking his head to listen to the distant roar.

'The Fall,' he said tersely. 'Before that we'll come to the Ruin, and there, if Lunar has done his work, there'll be a watcher awaiting us.'

He went on steadily, hardly turning to look upslope when he heard a signal bark from a watcher up among the screes, nor stopping when he saw another below them by a tree.

Then a third, coming towards him – and beyond that one the Ruin and a wealth of wolves.

'Stry! Lunar! Rohan, my dear . . .'

They came to him respectfully, those who knew him well coming to touch their heads to his flank, others who had never seen him hanging back, standing off a little.

He was leaner, he was grey, he was more lined of face, but he was Klimt.

'Lounell!'

'Welcome back, Klimt of Tornesdal!'

They came about him then, frisking, tails all over, paws touching, laughing, a mass of wolves and welcome, of laughter and great hope.

'Where's . . . ?'

Kobrin appeared, and did not hang back at all.

The two old friends went for each other with a strength of affection and relief that had both of them tumbling and growling for a time, almost into the stream, before Kobrin stood off and, bending his great head in obeisance, made all there understand who was leader now.

'Elhana?' said Klimt softly, knowing immediately that she was no longer alive. 'These two youngsters?'

A sudden tension descended as Klimt went up to Jimena and Umbrio and stared down at them.

'Hmmm,' he said, puzzled, before staring around until he caught Aragon's eye, a wolf he had not yet greeted.

'You?'

'Me,' said Aragon lightly, in his old way, smiling.

'Some things never change,' said Klimt a little curtly, leaving them guessing his true thoughts.

The Wolves stood about uneasily, for many a homecoming is spoilt by revelations.

Some things never change . . .

'What did you expect, Klimt, if you will stay so long away? Eh?'

The voice was light and came from the trees just beyond the clearing, from the watcher who had seen them first. He came now towards Klimt, a little shyly, and it was clear he was close to tears.

'I mean,' he continued, his voice breaking, 'you have been away a very long time!'

'Tervicz,' rasped Klimt, 'I . . .'

Then Klimt looked at Aragon half smiling, and he reached a paw to the two youngsters and said, 'Do you know who I am?'

Jimena said, 'You're Klimt.'

Umbrio shook his head and said, 'No, he's our leader.'

'Something else . . . I'm your father's friend, and friend to all these wolves, and a friend to Tervicz here.'

It was enough to break the tension, and have them all talking excitedly once again as, in the next moment, he had gone to Tervicz and embraced him.

'I missed you, wolf,' he said.

'Klimt, there's –'

'I missed you very much.'

'Klimt . . .'

But for a time there were no words for Tervicz to say.

Klimt did not let the greetings go on too long. It was quite apparent from the expression on the faces of senior Wolves like Kobrin, Aragon and Lounel and the others that there were decisions to be made and work to do.

He called a council at once, Kobrin and the others forming an inner circle, while any other who wished to listen could do so. As was his custom, Klimt listened to what the others had to say, learning of the Magyar advance from Kobrin, of the latest disposition of their forces from Stry, and of their various strengths and weakness in numbers of force from Lunar, who had had time since he arrived to check the position with Kobrin.

'With those you have brought today,' concluded Lunar, 'we have a fighting force that may not quite match the Magyars in numbers, but which has experience and strength. The Pechorans have recovered very quickly from the journey and want to see action now, preferably under the command of Kobrin and myself. Your own wolves may need a rest.'

Klimt nodded and said, 'A day will suffice, two at most. We did not over-hurry for I guessed we would very soon be needed. In any case, we cannot expect to hold so many wolves together here for very long. Our numbers and whereabouts will soon be accurately known to the Magyars if their watchers do their job, and Wulf knows where we would find food for such numbers.

'We must strike soon, and strike hard, and take sufficient territory that the Wolves, for all those who honour us by fighting alongside us are surely such, have enough food and water for their needs. Now, to the question of Jicin, whom Leon here was forced to leave out on the Fell.'

'It was the only thing I could –'

'I mean that as no criticism, wolf. Jicin knows the Fell as well as any Magyar, since she was raised on it. She would have a better chance of survival alone than with you there, that I know! I am loth to base our strategy upon her rescue, but –'

'We both know where she's most likely to be,' began Kobrin.

Klimt nodded. 'What is your advice, old friend?'

'They'll expect us to attack by way of the col, and I suggest we do not disappoint them. I doubt that they can know that we have so many supporters and I suggest we surprise them by using the cover of the Forest to go down into the Fell by way of the Eastern Rocks, the watching place where Rohan was recently attacked. A third force, for we have enough, can –'

'That might work,' said Klimt interrupting, 'but if instead we were to . . .'

As the two Wolves debated their campaign strategy the other senior wolves listened with mounting interest, offering their own thoughts where they could, answering any questions Klimt and Kobrin raised.

The more the debate went on the more it became clear that this was to be no ordinary fight between packs, and these were no ordinary wolves who planned it.

The discussion went on so long that the light began to fade. The two Wolves took a break, Klimt having a rest while Kobrin went among the new arrivals, talking with them, asking them questions, finding out their worth. There was not a wolf there he did not make contact with in one way or another, and not a single one but felt more confident in themselves and the Wolves as a result.

Klimt and Kobrin might be old Wolves now and past their physical prime, but together they made as formidable a pair as any wolf there had ever seen.

'If I was Klimt,' said one of the Pechorans, 'and it was my consort lost out on the Fell I'd be out there rescuing her right now, not having a kip.'

'But you're not Klimt, wolf,' grunted Stry, who overheard the remark. 'Klimt thinks before he acts, and he gathers about him Wolves who do the same. You'll see he was right.'

The Pechoran accepted what was said with a smile.

'When will we be setting off?'

Stry shrugged. 'Soon enough,' he said. 'Too many of us to stay here long.'

The Wolves huddled down in groups, each group having been given a different time to find prey and feed, their movement in and out of the area around the Ruin creating a growing sense of excitement about what would soon be happening. There was a low murmur of talk, which fell silent when one of Kobrin's scouts came in to report.

'Magyars on the col . . . three watching by the Tree . . . howling on the Fell, the usual . . .'

Snatches of information, tension rising, and in the middle of it all Klimt of Tornesdal, resting.

When at last he rose, and went down to the stream to drink, silence fell. It was early evening; the clouds had come in low in late afternoon, and obscured the upper cliffs. There was light enough still, but the clouds would make for a dark, thick night, and a dank and misty one up on the Scarpfeld.

Klimt settled down with Kobrin, Lounel and Tervicz, having given instructions to Aragon and Stry to sort out the other Wolves into groups larger and smaller, seven in all. These were gathered about the Ruin, some on one side of the stream, some the other, while Klimt strode into the stream itself, his back to the arch of the Ruin. A cold breeze blew out at him, and Kobrin came to his side.

'Wolves,' he said, 'by now most of you know Kobrin, and all of you know me. We are going to begin a battle this night which we believe will end the long struggle with the Magyars and allow wolfkind once more to reclaim its ascendancy over the Mennen, our true enemy.

'So . . . we do not wish to kill the Magyars, merely send them back to their territory, as one day most of you will have to return to yours. The Heartland cannot sustain so many wolves for long and nor should it.

'But we had to gather here in the name of Wulf, and seek to reclaim what is all wolfkind's. We shall do that better in our hearts and minds than through our bodies, for it is there the Mennen long since destroyed us. Tonight, and in the hours thereafter, we shall assert our ancient right to inhabit the Scarpfeld, and those of us who are chosen, who are known as the Wolves of Time, may perhaps journey on to the WulfRock itself, to where none but Wulf and Wulfin have ever truly been, and those gods who serve them.'

The evening was darkening fast, and from out of the Forest to the east, and from off the col, came the howling of Magyars, triumphant and vulgar, made that others, such as the Wolves, might hear.

Klimt paused a long time then, listening to their howling and seeming to think what he wanted to say. Had it been any other leader his listeners might have said that he seemed irresolute and uncertain. But in Klimt, such apparent doubt was thoughtfulness and prudence, and the Wolves waited in respectful silence.

Finally he continued thus: 'My friends, while it is true that I want to lead you in a great cause for wolfkind it would be less than honest if I did not also say that in my heart I have another cause which means much to me. The name Jicin will not mean anything to those of you who have most recently joined our ranks. But those of you who travelled with my son and me from Khazaria will know already something of her, and that she is a Magyar who most bravely came over to join our cause some years ago. A few of you who know her, and remember her, will agree that she is a worthy wolf, and one who would lay down her life for those she serves, those she loves, those put in her care.'

Kobrin nodded, as did Stry and Tervicz and Lounel as well, indeed all those who knew Jicin of old.

'Well then, she is the wolf I love and at this moment she is out there on the Fell, hidden away in a place she and I know – and Kobrin too. But probably she is injured, surrounded by Magyars, and in mortal danger of her life.

'Leon here was forced to leave her in that little sanctuary and come on to the Forest in the hope of getting help. Now, Wolves, no leader worthy of the name would ever risk many lives for one, or lead his packs into a war in the name of one great cause whilst secretly hoping merely to save the life of the wolf he loves.'

Klimt's voice was low and he found it difficult to talk so personally, and so openly; yet nothing could have made more clear to those who did not already know him that this was a wolf who truly put duty before love and perhaps had paid a heavy price for doing so.

'Some years ago, in the interests of the unity of our pack, I was forced to send Jicin into exile with Aragon here. When I did so something of my spirit died. I am not a wolf who talks openly of such things but I will do so now, for if you are to give your support this night in the coming battle, you must understand the reasons for the action I have decided we must take.

'Jicin taught me to love. In her I found that the desert that was my heart might after all see new life. She gave me strength to return to take the leadership from Aragon, and without her example, and her support, I would not be here now to lead you back into the Heartland.

'She is but an ordinary wolf, and one you would not notice in the crowd. But that is her importance. For as she waits out there in the Fell tonight, as she has waited for long days and nights past, she will have prayed to Wulf and Wulfin that help may come, and her prayers will have joined the many, the thousands, the hundreds of thousands, which through the decades and the centuries other lost wolves have offered up, and not always had answered.

'Jicin *is* wolfkind this night, waiting, hoping to be saved. We are the Wolves whom time and destiny have brought together now, here, to help. Think therefore, as you battle against the Magyars, and dare to risk your own life, not of many wolves and great causes, but of the few, the one perhaps, whom your actions can save, as I think of Jicin.

'Yet there is more. I have no desire to massacre the Magyars – though Wulf knows we have right and might upon our side – no wish at all. Our enemies are Führer and Dendrine, and not the wolves they so foully lead. I believe that if the gods are with us, if we keep our nerve, if we keep as our objective the saving of one life and not the destroying of many, we shall end the coming battle quickly and simply.

'In ancient days leaders of rival packs fought each other for supremacy and did not let their whole packs fight. This night a battle will begin that I shall strive to end by challenging Führer himself, and Dendrine too if I must. I shall seek to fight for the life of one wolf, against one wolf, and thereby save the lives of many.'

The Wolves listened in stunned silence as Klimt not so much offered as insisted that he would seek to fight Führer on behalf of all of them.

'Our first objective, then, is to secure the Heartland for all wolfkind; and our second is to be seen to save the life of a single wolf, and use that diversion as a way of further securing our positions elsewhere. For you do not imagine, do you . . .' – here Klimt permitted himself the glimmer of a smile – '. . . that you will all stand about idly while I fight Führer for Jicin's life! No, no; that shall be seen to be *my* objective, and thereby confuse the Magyar leadership into thinking it is *our* objective. Let the rescue of Jicin be a feint and diversion which gives the rest of you time to secure the Heartland for wolfkind; thereafter, when you are successful, and Führer is vanquished, let Jicin's rescue travel forth into the hearts and minds of wolfkind through the stories you tell of this battle's work, that others know we Wolves are able, and always will be, to think of one when we think of many.'

It was a brave and extraordinary strategy, in which Klimt would be seen to risk his life for one *and* all, an act of bold courage that seemed all the greater because any who had ever seen Führer, and all who knew his reputation, could hardly doubt who the victor must be.

It was now that Kobrin came forward and said in his gruff way, 'Believe me, my friends, I have tried to dissuade Klimt from this course. He was always a good fighter, perhaps at one time a great one, but he has slowed and weakened, and his injury has left him lame.'

'He mustn't do it then,' cried several then, 'or surely there are others can stand in his place!'

'Do you not think I have offered to do so?' cried Kobrin. 'As has Lunar here, and Tervicz, and every single one of those Wolves who know and love their leader. *You* try and dissuade him, for we cannot!'

There was a moment of silence before Kobrin added, 'And anyway, the gods have always smiled favourably upon Klimt, and I have never known his strategy to be at fault. Perhaps, after all, they will favour him one last time.'

Kobrin seemed to raise himself high then, and he looked at Klimt with a gleam in his eye.

'Shall we follow him?' he cried out.

'We shall!' thundered the Wolves in reply.

'Have we faith in him?'

'We have,' they roared.

'Are the gods with us?'

'They are . . .'

And none could doubt at that stirring moment that if ever there was a god of war in mortal form it was surely Kobrin himself: huge, grey of fur, still powerful of body, his scars bearing witness to the many fights he had fought and won, and utterly loyal to the leader who stood at his side.

'*Heuren Sie*, my friends, listen now!' said Klimt when the cries of support had begun to subside. 'The battle we shall fight will be won through the courage and faith of each one of you. You who can afterwards say you were here, having come to put your strength and courage at the service of wolfkind, will journey home one day and tell those lucky enough to call themselves your friends, your kin, your descendants, that you were a Wolf and a true servant of Wulf.'

'Now then – those in command of your group will give you your orders when you are in position. Obey them, trust them, have courage to see them through. But if as the night passes into day, and that day back into night, you find the orders begin to fail, or that your leaders fall, then take their places, use your initiative as Wolves, have courage to find your own wolfways.'

'Our first base will be here, but by this time tomorrow our strongholds will be the col that overlooks both Forest and Scarpfeld, and the stonefield above the gulley that leads down on to the Fell. Only one order shall override all others, and demand that you obey it.'

The Wolves watched in silence as Klimt nodded to Tervicz to come to him.

'Mark him well, for he is the Bukov wolf. He shall ever be at my flank. His howl, from col or from stonefield, from gulley or from Fell, shall be the signal to each of you to come, and bring whatever others are with you. For then shall be the climax of our struggle, then shall you be most needed. If he howls not it is because the gods have granted our strategy their grace and favour, and our victory is won. But if he does then answer his call, and swiftly! Stry . . . Lounel . . . Aragon . . . Rohan . . . Lunar . . .'

Klimt ran through the names of the senior Wolves a final time, sending them to their groups and then off to their positions with a brief touch and nod. Tervicz was to remain at his side, with the group of mainly Kazakh wolves he was to lead.

'What about us?' asked Umbrio and Jimena, excitement in their eyes.

Klimt nodded seriously and said, 'It is right that you see something of this battle, and remember it. For safety's sake you shall stay apart. One of you shall travel with Lunar and the other with Rohan, so choose which it is to be.'

'Lunar,' said Jimena at once.

'Rohan,' said Umbrio almost as quickly.

'If all wolves were as sensible as you,' said Klimt, 'there would be no need for wars! Now off you go, and may Wulf be with you!'

Then Klimt watched as all the groups dispersed, but for those that were to stay for a time at the Ruin.

'Come,' he said to the Wolves he was to lead personally, 'follow me.'

A few moments later he, and those he commanded, set off westward into the darkness of the Forest, and the night.

CHAPTER TWENTY-NINE

*The Wolves join battle with the Magyars, while Jicin
must confront her mother Dendrine once again*

JICIN LAY NOW not far from where Leon had been compelled
to leave her days before, knowing she was beginning to die. It was
the dawn following the commencement of the Wolves' campaign
against the Magyars, and though there were howlings and signal
barks near and far as the two groups began to skirmish, and Magyar
patrols ran hither and thither not far from her hiding-place, she barely
noticed them.

She could not stop the shivering of her flanks and the chattering
of her teeth from the cold that seemed now to have reached right
inside her, though the sun showed promise of rising bright. Nor could
she stop the dull thud, thud of the pain in her injured paw; the cuts
were oozing blood and pus now, and the poison was beginning to
travel towards her heart. Oh, how long since he had left her, her
friend, her good friend Leon. Even now, even so weak, tears came to
her eyes to think of the last lingering look he had given her before
he left, as if to say that in trusting him to reach the Scarpfeld by
himself, and to find help, she was entrusting him to save the very
world itself, which was *her*.

Klimt she loved, and loved with a passion that could never die;
Aragon had become a friend like none other she could ever have; but
Leon . . . why, he had become the brother she was never allowed to
have; a wolf who loved her simply for herself, and had said often on
their long and dangerous journey from the High Causses of the
Auvergne that he thanked the gods above each day when he woke up
simply because they had let him come to know her.

So . . . when he had finally left her in a last attempt to get help he
had stared back at her, as if half guessing that she did not believe he
would be able to. But how else could she have persuaded him to flee

to safety and leave her alone? Never, not ever – he would not have left her side.

'They'll be there – they will!' she had said. 'The Wolves of Time are always there, always . . . up in the Scarpfeld. Klimt himself will come. Look! You can see the cliffs that form its southern edge. There are ways up it, but beware that main gulley for there are always watchers there. Go my dear, go; it is the only chance we have. Go . . .'

So finally, and only half convinced, fearing he would never see her alive again, but knowing it might be the only hope they had, he had gone, and she had been left alone.

The place they had reached was the same where years before Klimt had first found her, and it was good terrain to go to ground in. There was the same patch of scrubby trees the Mennen had planted years before, a stream stained brown-black by the peat hags through which it ran, and the fissured cleft of rock where Klimt and she had mated. Here she had known the happiest moments of her life, here their love had been no-one's and no-pack's but their own; here, if anywhere along the wolfways she had travelled, she would be content to die.

There was the sudden drift of alien scent, and her head came up alert, and her heart began to thump. Magyar, almost certainly. She stayed absolutely still, her view of the stream some way below partly hidden by the tufts of coarse grass that grew on the ground in front of her cavern.

She doubted that she could be easily scented out, and certainly she could not be seen; but there seemed much activity all about, and she thought she could see a massing of Magyars up on the stonefield at the top of the gulley.

But that alien scent was closer, *too* close. Quite suddenly two wolves came into view down on the far side of the stream. They were quartering the ground methodically. Both were young, and one most certainly Magyar from the smaller size of its form, and the rough darkness of its fur; the other seemed alien, but plainly was under orders from the first.

'Shall we cross the stream?'

A shift in the breeze brought the sound of the water, and Jicin could no longer hear their words, but their meaning was plain enough. The two debated whether or not to cross as she prayed they would move off another way. But over one of them finally came, sniffing about, gazing up and along the rocky outcrop in one of whose fissures she lay hidden, then dropping his muzzle again and checking out the ground.

She had avoided approaching her hiding-place that way, wisely coming over the rocks, and sending Leon back off that way as well; but the wind was gusting and flukey and the wolf might easily . . .

He paused and stared again towards the area where she lay before coming nearer, evidently puzzled. He shook his head and then turned, but stared back once or twice before rejoining his friend on the far side of the stream.

The wind shifted and she heard one wolf say, 'We ought to go. Führer's sent another party of wolves up to the Scarpfeld and there's rumours that the Wolves . . .'

The wind snatched his voice away again as a moment of hope, and of longing, stilled her at those words, 'the Wolves'. The two conferred a while longer, and then seemed to look her way a final time before shaking their heads, and continuing their search further upstream.

She would not risk venturing out until the night, though Wulfin knew she was thirsty, her tongue so dry it stuck painfully to the roof of her mouth and her teeth.

Wolves searching for her . . . Mennen . . . life itself harrying and chasing her . . .

She found peculiar comfort in simply lying where she was, for all her life she seemed to have been on the run in one way or another, or trying to get to somewhere other than where she was. Her cubhood with Dendrine, when cruelty was the norm, when the slightest questioning of her mother was punishable disobedience: first offence, a buffet; second offence, thrust out into the cold away from warmth and companionship; third offence, a biting, or, as in the case of one of her brothers, death by the crushing of his skull.

That was Jicin's first clear memory, Dendrine killing one of her sons in Jicin's litter, and his look of isolation, growing panic, and then strange and shocking distortion as Dendrine's mouth closed on to his tiny head, and the blood, from every cranial orifice, which seemed to chase after Jicin as she tried to flee. Hassler caught her, and flipped her back to Dendrine, whose maw came down upon her too.

'My sweet,' Jicin remembered Dendrine whispering, tongue and mouth gore-red and wet with her sibling's blood and brain, 'do not be afraid. If you're good I won't have to punish you. If you're bad it'll be no good fleeing because I'll catch up with you in the end, and –'

Dendrine's teeth had clamped on to her tiny skull and begun to squeeze, until Jicin felt the pressure, the pain, and her eyes lost focus. Then Dendrine let her drop to the ground. From that moment on, Jicin felt now, as she lay in hiding in a place where later she had found brief love with Klimt, she had been fleeing all the time.

Except for that time with Klimt, *here*.

Jicin looked about the dank, dripping, slanting cavern, not much bigger than herself, and felt gratitude that once in her life at least she had known such love.

But then, the inevitable defeat by Elhana, and Klimt's necessary decision to exile her with Aragon and Stry. Years on the run after that, but years of final peace and strange contentment. Jicin smiled, remembering the sun of Spain, and Spain's son Aragon – she was so proud to have been part of it.

Then it was over, and Aragon gone back to the Heartland, and she had been ledrene enough to lead Leon and the others to Brive, to rescue Maladon, who began to assert her extraordinary authority during the weeks and months that followed. And then the final parting, when Jicin knew it was time to commence the long journey home with Leon.

Jicin sighed, shivering, eyes aching, and did not deny the pride she felt in what she had achieved, nor the loss she felt now in the knowledge that the gods had not after all granted her reunion with Klimt.

'My dear . . .' she whispered, 'oh my dear . . .'

No one, least of all Dendrine, had taught her how to love; no one had showed her how to reach out and touch, and feel love returned. No one had taught her to close her eyes and feel his peace, and release, and all they had shared. Except each other.

'Here,' she whispered in wonder, *'here . . .'*

She would die content; regretful for what might have been, yet content in what had been. Despite the cruelty of her upbringing something of her had survived her Magyar youth and all Dendrine had done, something Dendrine would never have, and there was perverse comfort in that too.

She was so thirsty – but was it worth the risk of going to the stream? She moved so slowly now, all hunched up and old. She stared at the stream, at its cold dark water, and realized she was beginning not to care. No, she must not risk it . . .

She woke with a jolt, the sound of water loud in her ears, and found she had fallen unconscious by it and must have ventured out without knowing and never returned to her hiding-place.

A wolf barked nearby, and she turned in a panic back towards the cleft and slid thankfully into it and into almost instant sleep. She *was* beginning not to care, sleeping for moments, waking to the mounting cries and the sound of battle, and the blur of light and shadow, and of wolves once more down by the stream.

A blur of dark dreams and fancies, of old fears and new, and of the throb, throb, throb of pain, and terrible sickness.

'Wolf!'

A wolf's head silhouetted against the sky outside the cleft.

'Wolf!'

A voice towards which she tried to struggle, out there in the world of light and consciousness.

'*Wolf!*'

And a shooting, shocking pain in her right leg, and right into her heart, as the head grew bigger, the eyes dark-bright, and teeth grasped her leg and pulled her bodily from where she thought she was unseen and undiscovered.

'She stinks, ledrene.'

Jicin opened her eyes into shock and a horror all the worse because only slowly did it dawn on her it was real.

'Hello, Jicin; hello, my dear.'

She found herself staring into the cruel and narrow eyes of her mother Dendrine, whose mocking tone affected warmth and such a greeting as a wolf might make who had last seen the other only yesterday.

Then: 'It's true,' said Dendrine matter-of-factly, 'you do stink. You've shitted yourself. You've been sick where you slept. Your foot's so rotten with filth and pus it looks to me like it ought to be bitten off. Ha, ha ... So ... this foul thing is what the Wolves are seeking, is it? There can be no explanation for their little group sneaking out on to the Fell to the north unless they know she's here and are trying to rescue her. What fun, and what a blessed little opportunity for us to finally wipe them out. I trust Klimt will be with them, because Führer wishes to kill him.'

Musing thus to herself as she stared down at Jicin, Dendrine began to laugh, and Jicin tried to understand her words and comprehend what was happening. It made no sense. She felt helpless fear and sadness and knew that her death was going to be painful, and by torture.

She lay where Dendrine had dragged her, utterly exposed. Magyars looked down from the rocks above and up from the bank of the stream below. There were others all about, staring, eyes full of cruel hatred. Not a few looked like Dendrine their mother; not a few like Jicin, too.

Jicin had been found and pulled out into the open by her own kith and kin, and in that moment of terrible waking she knew that terror was palpable, and that she did not want to die, not like this, and not here, here of all places in the world, not here . . .

'*Not here!*' she screamed.

'Clean the bitch up and bring her back, right here!' said Dendrine. 'And summon Führer at once. Let him send reinforcements to the Scarpfeld if he must but *this* is what the Wolves have showed their frightened faces for, and this they shall have when I have finished with it. Then when they come for it we shall finish with *them!*'

Two grinning males dragged her unresisting to the stream, right into it and under, the water as shocking in the pain it caused as their brutal teeth. Noise in her ears, choking in her throat, fighting for a life she could not hope to save, terrified, broken with panic, in those moments Jicin knew nothing else but fear. They dragged her out of the water just as she began to drown, and laid her back at Dendrine's feet. Her mother's eyes were even more cruel than she remembered.

'What are you?'

Dendrine leaned forward, brushed aside Jicin's vain attempt to thrust her away, and caught her left ear between her teeth, and jerked. The pain was sharp and violent.

'Bitch! Little bitch for leaving us!' screamed Dendrine as she pulled away. Blood poured down Jicin's face, and the ear felt torn and broken, with deep pain inside.

'Bitch!' screamed Dendrine again. 'I should have crushed your head when you were young.'

The horror mounted as Jicin saw the bloody spittle at her mother's mouth, a clot of torn and bloody matter that was her own fleshy skin: part of her ear. Jicin began to shake with fear, and to weep for loneliness, for where she was being taken was a place of no hope, no love, no comfort, and there would be no respite upon the long slow way to death.

Then worse yet: the sky darkened behind Dendrine, and Jicin saw the huge distorted form of her brother Führer appear, his eyes redrimmed and chilling, then focusing on her and curious.

'Oh my love, my son, my sweetling,' purred Dendrine at the feel of him behind her, and his breath upon her old, thin, hag's head, 'here's a wolfling I want you to meet: your elder sister, dear. Her name is –'

'Remember *her* and need no name,' he said, his voice reluctant, as if he was resentful of speech. She had been born in the litter Dendrine had before the one he came with, and she was its only survivor.

'Mother, Dendrine, my ledrene . . .'

He spoke with a touch of pleading in his voice, like an over-attentive lover, not a son.

'Mmm?' Dendrine giggled, sounding like a female courted.

Jicin tried to crawl away, tried and failed utterly, as Dendrine giggled again and shook her head, partly to tell Jicin that she must not even try to escape, and partly to tell the great, foul, stenchy Führer to stop harrying her and join in the fun.

'Mother, there are Wolves about.'

'There are a few, a puny few, and this vile bitch is what they've come for, sneaking round by the cliffs.'

'Some seen on the far side of the col, ought to –'

'Must do if you must, beloved,' said Dendrine. 'Go and tend to our rightful territory and take that little bugger with you.'

Dendrine turned to point and for the first time Jicin noticed a youngster standing at Führer's shoulder, watching. His fur so young and glossy, his stance so proud, his eyes . . . intelligent, watchful, glancing at Dendrine with fear and at Führer with a curious trust.

'Torne, come with me,' growled Führer, 'nothing for you here. Race you up the gulley. Got work to do.'

The wolf called Torne stared at Jicin with pity and then turned to move off as he had been told.

'She can't be your sister,' Jicin heard him say.

His voice was so young, so innocent.

'Won't be for long,' said Führer, 'not now Dendrine's got her.'

Jicin felt the panic coming back, and with it strength, and tried to flee again. She raised herself, and turned, scrabbling at the rough grass, getting away among some rocks, the stream's noise off to her left. Each step, each yard she made, was a world of pain beyond which, somewhere across the Fell, Klimt was awaiting her if only, if she, when –

A thin, scratchy paw stamped at the sward in front of her and brought her to a halt and Dendrine whispered in her wounded ear, 'Time for food, my dear.'

'Oh Klimt,' whispered Jicin, strength leaving her, and the sound of laughter and pursuit behind, '*you* are *my* dear.'

For he was clarity, he was purity, his love could cleanse her of the filth that was her mother and take her for ever to another place.

'Jicin, my sweet, please don't leave us, *please* don't be so rude . . .'

Dendrine smiled down at her, her thin haggish face calloused and warty, her eyelids sagging, her smile pure sadistic malice.

'I gave you sustenance when you were young, now you shall give me sustenance, and the leftovers your brother Führer can gobble down when he comes back; and that brat he goes about with, he can have some too.'

Dendrine approached nearer still. Her mouth stank of rot, and her muzzle too, but inside, flicking like a snake's, was a pink, wet tongue, lascivious between her broken teeth. Jicin tried to turn from her but Dendrine put a paw on her shoulder and held her down, as if she were a cub again, and she the mother. Her tail was flicking back and forth.

Jicin snarled at Dendrine, and sought to bite her face.

'Now, now,' Dendrine whispered, 'it's my turn to do the biting, not yours.'

Jicin snarled again, quite unable to move for the weight and strength of her mother's paw, and suddenly her head was jerked back and to one side by the smash of that same paw that had held her down, and the rocks above seemed to jerk back and forth, and she felt her mother's tongue at her torn ear as she tasted her, and grunted with satisfaction, and mounting eagerness. Wolves stared, some grinning, some fascinated, a few seeming shocked.

'Sweet, sweetling?' said her mother, who was upside down against the bright sky.

She pulled away, her breath foetid and heavy with the smell of her daughter's blood, then down again and a strange sound, worse than any Jicin had ever heard. She was sucking at her wound to taste her more.

It was then, exactly then, that Jicin ceased to be the wolf who lay beneath her mother as she began her foul perverted meal, and turned instead into a disembodied wolf, who saw herself, and Dendrine and the stretching southern Fell, dispassionately. Already beyond hope, she moved on in that moment beyond pain, beyond fear.

'Sister, I am sister, Dendrine's son's sister, and my mother's food.'

Perhaps she only thought the words, yet they drummed in her ears to the sound of the sucking and the rasp of her mother's tongue, and

the unexpected scrape of her lower teeth up her cheek, 'I am sister
. . . I am daughter . . . I am, I am . . .'

The words, repeated over and over, as she began repeating them
then, might have become a prayer of sorts, and the beginning of a
journey not into death, but towards the stars, for soon there remained
just that final whispered affirmation, 'I am . . . I am . . . I am . . .'

Then Dendrine pulled away quite suddenly, startled by something,
moving off a step or two and turning to stare, and this pulled Jicin
back to present reality.

There had been a summoning bark from the direction of the gulley,
some commotion nearby, and most of the wolves about them turned
and left, leaving Dendrine almost alone.

'Ledrene, you should come . . .'

'Some of you stay while I finish my meal, some of you stay.'

Then fear returned fully as Dendrine came near.

'Oh do not shake so, Jicin,' crooned her mother. Then, more harshly,
'And do not snarl at *me!*'

Jicin's head fell back, her ear wet and flooding with blood and her
mother's spittle. She wept. She shivered. She was in her hurt and
frightened body once again and nowhere else.

'Don't make such a meal of it, my love, ha-ha-ha,' cackled Dendrine,
rising suddenly to piss into the grass, her own thin flanks shivering
and shaking when she had done, 'leave that to *him* . . .'

From the direction of the gulley came the sound of howls, and
barking, and a scream: wolves fighting. Then more commotion nearby
on the far side of the rocks. Klimt? Wolves? Hope?

'I hoped your friends might come, my dear, and it does sound as
if they are trying to. Führer will kill them and eat you, gobble you all
up, you little bitch!'

Dendrine's grinning, maddened face came near, the yellow spikes
of teeth showing, and the tongue, reaching out towards the other ear,
and Jicin felt the first clench of maternal teeth upon it, the first
stressing of paws upon the ground to begin to jerk, to pull, to tear,
to disfigure on that side too, so that later, when he returned, Führer
would have something more to taste.

'Oh . . . *no!*' screamed Jicin.

It was then, as she felt her head and ear caught hold of that Jicin
finally knew from what she had been running all her life. It had not
been pain, nor death; not even the torture that her brother Führer
was shortly to mete out to her.

It had been *this*, the ultimate betrayal in all of life, when a mother begins to kill the cub to which she has given birth. Worse, to do it cruelly. It seemed to Jicin then as clear as day that from the moment of her birth, everything her mother had ever done for her and to her had been directed towards this terrible culmination. To do this, or something like it, was what Dendrine had given birth to her *for*.

This foul mouth, this hatred, this stench of malevolent cruelty, *this* was evil . . . and this, *this* vileness was what had happened to all other siblings but for Führer.

Always until now Jicin had found the will to live and survive. Somewhere, deep inside her heart and mind, there had been something secret and untouched, which was her true self, what she really was. That true self Klimt had discovered, and had loved and been loved by it; that true self gave her pride; though it seems so vulnerable it is in fact the very essence of a wolf's strength, and might be called the rock within – it was to her true self that Jicin turned in this final moment of Dendrine's betrayal.

Her body was hurt and dying, all hope seemed gone – no, *was* gone – and fear was palpable and real within her, and about her, but . . . but she turned now from all that to her last reserve of strength, her only respite.

'NOOOOOOO!'

Wrenching her head and ear away from Dendrine's teeth she turned upon her mother and closed her jaws upon her face, upon the left jawbone, upon the left cheek, the incisors into the left eye. Into that final moment of discovered strength she put all the anger she had ever felt, all the sense of betrayal, all the feeling of unfairness, all the impotent rage at so many rebuffs, all the darkness her mother had ever made her feel. And there was more.

For her lost and tortured brothers she did it; for the sisters she never knew; for the Bukov wolves whom Dendrine had betrayed, and for the gods, who ask that wolfkind seeks out the light, and finds the strength to destroy the desecrating dark: for those gods she did it.

She felt her mother's mouth straining to scream at the sudden, unexpected onslaught, struggling to rid herself of the jaws that had clamped upon her, and filled an eye with blood. But the daughter-jaws shifted and locked tighter still with her struggles, the teeth cut through to older teeth and began to break them with such pain and then held deeper still. As Dendrine tried to scream out her agony the only thought she had was this: the more she sought to break free the more she hurt and the greater the void of horror into which she found herself falling. Jicin did not let go, even when she felt her own teeth breaking with the power of her grip.

Then, as other paws seemed to try to stop her, and her strength began to fail she felt her mother's own grip weaken, and her whole being falter. Words of Leon's came into Jicin's mind, words he had learned from Galliard: 'Once you start do not stop . . .'

Jicin plunged back into herself for more strength; she felt her mother begin to fall towards her, she dared release her jaws and then, terribly, slid them beneath Dendrine's jaw and thrust her teeth into her throat. Skin, fur, sinews, the desperate in-out rasp of choking, sudden softness, sudden flowing warmth, and Jicin tightened her bite and felt fear, and terrible release, as her mother began finally to die.

Jicin turned a little, for Dendrine's blood was spurting into her throat and choking *her*, and tried to free herself. But her mother's weight was too much, thin old hag though she was, and Jicin fell back, putting her last strength into worrying at the throat between her teeth, back and forth, back and forth as rapidly as she could, and felt the death of life as she herself sank back into the heather, her mother across her, their blood between them both, so much that she felt their bodies slipping and sliding against each other, as her last strength gave out and the sky grew dark, and her pain fled back into the earth beneath her.

Shouting, voices, and the plashing sound of Führer's paw-steps back over the river brought her round, as well as her own choking with her mother's blood and filth that was in her mouth and throat.

She tried to heave off her mother's body, to turn to face him, even to begin to do to him what she had done to Dendrine – but she had no strength left; all was gone.

She could see his huge paws now, hear his heavy breathing and his gasp when he saw them both, his cry of outrage when he saw what she had done to Dendrine as she stirred a final time, no more than a tremble, though her blood flowed on.

Then Jicin relaxed, relaxed utterly, for she had done what her innermost being had so long wanted to do. She had rid herself of Dendrine, and there was nothing Führer, or the world, could do about it.

'Oh . . .' she sighed, 'oh . . .'

She felt Führer sniffing at her, his great head at her lower body, and she heard him begin the deep growling-howl of loss for Dendrine, and sensed the sudden tensing of his paws against her as he thrust at Dendrine to move her, to slide her off, that he might get finally at Jicin.

And that strange deep howl, so terrible to hear, so full of loss . . . Did he love Dendrine as much as that, did he truly?

But he did not lift Dendrine away, nor pull her off, he did something far more violent, far more extreme. He pulled back from them both with a roar, he thrust forward and down into Dendrine's shoulder, and she saw his great jaws close and tighten, and then with a massive pull and jerk Jicin saw Dendrine fly away from her, wheeling through the air, jaw, and loose bloody face and eye, legs, tail, haggy back all turning, turning above her, away from her, out and towards the stream downslope of them, flying high, high before she began to arc back downward, down, down and out of sight on the rocks and grass below.

Then Jicin, half blinded by the bright light of the sky, turned her gaze to Führer, utterly spent.

'Jicin,' he said, and thrust his great head and jaws towards her, 'Jicin my love . . .'

She stared at him, and the sky darkened once more, his head seemed to sway slowly, there was a ringing in her savaged ears.

'Jicin . . .' whispered Klimt, his voice breaking.

'Oh . . . oh . . .' she sighed. Then she wept as from out of the far, far distance, like the coming of warm spring air and sunshine across a wide and verdant plain after a narrow, dark and besetting lifetime of winter, he came back to her, and held her, and she knew that never now, not ever, would he leave her again.

'Oh my dear,' she sighed.

'Yes,' he whispered, his deep voice shaking not so much at the sight of her, bloodied and broken, as because, though she had seemed past saving when he first saw her, she was still alive, and knew him.

But more than all those things, from the look in her eyes, of relief, of trust, and of a slow returning from the hell in which she had for a time been cast by the present, and the past, he knew how much she loved him, and their long wait was over.

'Jicin,' he whispered once again.

'Klimt . . .'

Then, battle or no battle, for a time there was no world but theirs.

* * *

419

Across the Fell had they come, sneaking, just as Dendrine said. But only after positioning themselves in the dark of night, and taking advantage of a cold and misty dawn, and when the other groups had signalled from their barks that they were in position too. Then Klimt and the Kazakh wolves who went with him, and Tervicz too, had come across the Fell, taking care they were seen, not making directly for where they hoped Jicin was, drawing attention to themselves.

Magyars began to appear and challenged the little group. Then, when a fight had started, the Wolves' reinforcements had emerged from the heather and charged, keeping the momentum going, drawing yet more Magyars that way.

Meanwhile, up near the col, Lunar's party kept well out of the fray, though some were seen. Führer was drawn that way, hurrying up the gulley, but he hastened back when he saw what was happening below. More Wolves than he had imagined, spreading across the Fell, heading towards that outcrop where Dendrine was with the Jicin wolf, just as she had said.

'Mother's often right,' he told Torne, 'so we'll have to turn back.' Suddenly irresolute, he finally commanded the Magyars who were guarding the stonefield above to come down to help drive off the Wolves who dared to come out upon the Fell – and so the Scarpfeld was left unguarded.

Watching from a vantage place Stry saw it all and chose the moment to give Lunar the signal his group had waited for. Slowly they came up the Fell, in two and threes, ready to take on the guards up there – their numbers now weakened by the need to replace those who had left the stonefield.

Then, 'Charge!' and Lunar led the attack at the col and over it, while Kobrin, his own force hidden by the lower cliffs, stayed back, ready for Stry's further signal to charge the gulley when the Magyars had left it to follow Führer's command.

Thus were the Wolves poised to grasp the initiatives of position and surprise, while Klimt, oblivious for a time, tended Jicin, and held her close.

'Klimt! *Klimt!*'

The urgent cry of Tervicz brought Klimt back to the world of the battle.

'Klimt, wolf, look who comes!'

Klimt stood by Jicin, his own guards closely about him, others further off forming a protective circle as from the direction of the gulley Führer charged. Wild and dark he came, thunderous, behind him a stream of Magyars, eager for a fight but undisciplined.

Klimt nodded to others to watch over Jicin as he took a step or two towards the stream. Lean he was, large, not young, his fur grey, in his eyes a piercing light and around him, behind him, up on the outcrops, his Wolves, fewer than the Magyars yet a force somehow more formidable.

'Führer!' he roared.

'Klimt,' came the gruff reply as the Magyar leader slowed and stopped on the far bank. Silence, but for the breeze in the heather and the stream's low murmur.

Führer stared at them all, taking in the scene. Then he saw his mother lying where Klimt had hurled her, half in, half out of the water, much as Elhana had once been.

All remained still and waited as Führer, gangling and ill-shaped, loped down to look at her, and touch her. Then he sniffed at her, and cocked his head and stared down, like a cub puzzled by what he saw. But it was not a cub whose head rose up, nor a cub's eyes that stared.

'Must kill you Klimt for this. Can't let you live.'

'Kill me for the Heartland,' said Klimt evenly, stepping forward. 'Kill me to prove to all these wolves that you are Lord of All. And if you don't –'

'Will,' said Führer, 'must.'

'. . . and if you don't, and I survive, then I shall be . . .'

'Lord of All?' said Führer, coming closer still, readying.

Klimt shook his head and shrugged. 'Let our fight settle it.'

'For ever and ever,' said Führer, his paws fretting at the ground.

'Yes,' murmured Klimt, leaning forward with the slope, steadying himself, and moving into a sudden charge, down and down towards Führer, down and towards . . . teeth and claws ready as they joined each to the other in great splashes and spumes of spray in the middle of the stream. 'Yes . . .'

CHAPTER THIRTY

Lord of All

A S KLIMT AND FÜHRER began to fight, and the rise of spray
caused by their first clash turned into the falling of shining
droplets caught in the summer sun, it seemed that time began
to slow. Then, to those watching, even before that first clash was over
and the two wolves pulled back from their initial testing of each other,
it seemed that time had almost stopped.

Strange and misshapen though he was, Führer moved with a curious
grace and beauty, his huge paws carefully placed, his body all of a
piece; his glances about to see where the stream was, where the land,
and to check if others nearby might dare impede his progress, were
measured and calm. He was a wolf for whom movement seemed to
take him beyond himself, leaving the awkward heaviness of his body
and mind behind.

Klimt's stance was more stolid, less mobile. Where Führer circled
he simply turned or backed, where Führer moved smoothly round
obstacles of sward and rock, Klimt seemed simply to override them;
where Führer seemed to look everywhere, Klimt's clear eyes settled
on their quarry and stayed there.

The second charge they made on each other brought them both
tumbling and snarling on to the far bank, away from Klimt's supporters,
who instinctively moved forward, stilling only when Klimt commanded
them to do so. This was his fight, his alone, and the prize was Jicin,
and all wolfkind.

But the Wolves, and especially Tervicz, only relaxed when Führer,
after one of the Magyars made as if to join in the attack on Klimt as
well, turned on him and said, 'Him and me, wolf to wolf, like brother
fighting brother.'

It was an odd allusion, perhaps unnoticed by all but Klimt himself,
in a moment whose greater interest lay in Führer's clear acceptance
of Klimt's rules: this *was* one on one; this was a fight to establish

supremacy, in which one would be left vanquished and the other the victor and the Lord of All.

As the fight began to settle down to charges and to feints, to wrestling, snarls and biting, and the tangle and scrabble of paws, it seemed that the two were more evenly matched than the Wolves had at first feared, and the Magyars had initially hoped.

True, even in the earliest moments of the fight it seemed to those who watched, whether Magyars or Wolves, that Führer had clear advantages. Klimt's limp was pronounced, and fierce and powerful though his personality was, and frightening the ruthless sense of purpose he conveyed, Führer was the quicker, the cleverer, perhaps even the more imaginative. Indeed there was almost a sense of play in the way he darted in and out, raced round and back, paused and stared, and then charged again, which made him seem the lighter, the swifter, the better.

Yet as the fight wore on, and the early snarls became grunts, and the warning roars mere growls of effort, the concentrated ruthlessness of Klimt began to show itself. When, at one moment, Klimt slipped and made himself vulnerable, Führer danced about, mocking, almost laughing, and missed an opportunity. But when a little later Führer over-reached himself and began to pull back Klimt grabbed the moment and went straight and hard for his exposed underbelly. From Führer's angry cry of pain it seemed that Klimt had found his mark.

Then too, when Führer sought to pause for breath Klimt drove the harder at him, forcing him back into the stream once more, and at times he lost his grace and stumbled, falling to his knees or on his side, squirming to get away.

These moments gave the Wolves cause to think that Klimt might win, though his body began to show the bruises and the bloody wounds of the encounter, more so than the swifter Führer. Worse, that shoulder injured in the Quarry yet long since healed now opened up once more, the result of a terrible savaging Führer gave it during one of their more violent clashes. Then too, Klimt began to lose his power, and something of his earlier speed, so that he moved more heavily and his lunges were less jarring in their effect than they had been at first.

The sun had risen to its highest in the sky and now began to slope down towards the afternoon, the two embattled wolves fighting on, their pauses longer, their wrestling sometimes an opportunity to recover their breath.

Of all the Wolves two suffered visibly to see great Klimt's strength beginning to fail. Tervicz began to wince and strain at every setback his leader suffered, his eyes wide in horror to see such injury to one he so revered; while Jicin, tended by the others and regaining a little of her strength and alertness, began to see that the one she loved, to whose flank the gods had so recently granted her return, now might lose the struggle, and thereby his life.

'No . . . no . . .' she whispered, knowing none there could intervene, unless it be the gods themselves, 'now my love, try . . . no . . .'

There came a moment indefinable when all there knew that Klimt was beginning to fail. At first it was a subtle change: a weariness in his turns, a deeper gasping after breath, a wildness in charges that earlier had been clear and direct.

Then, worse still, the focus of his eyes began to go, as if after so many years of leading others he was losing the will to lead himself in the greatest fight of his life, even losing hope. While Führer, sensing this change, gained strength, new purpose, and a sharpened focus.

Until, worst of all, suddenly Klimt's shoulder gave way utterly; he staggered to the ground and tried to use his leg to rise but could not, and as he backed to the outcrop of rock to give himself a better chance, it seemed that he must finally lose.

Führer thought so too, for now his steps resumed their early playful dance, his paws found their balance once again, his red eyes took on a terrible brightness.

'Mine now,' he cried, looking around as if for praise before he went in for the kill.

'Klimt . . .' cried Tervicz.

'No . . . no,' grunted Klimt, eyes never leaving Führer as he advanced, 'it is between him and me alone.'

'Yes, yes,' roared Führer youngster-like, 'him and me, him *for* me!'

He seemed to laugh aloud as he charged once more, upslope towards the cliff where Klimt now lay, good paw forward, eyes defiant once again, jaws set at the ready to cause what damage they could.

'Will be Lord of All!' he roared, prancing towards Klimt.

It was then that out across the Fell, from the stonefield at the gulley head, there came a howling of a kind that might send a thrill of horror or triumph through a wolf who heard it, depending on who or what they were.

So strange and striking was it that all turned to look, Wolves and

Magyars alike, including even Führer; they saw a press of movement on the cliffs above. A mass of Wolves, at their head Lunar, leading a howl of triumph and possession, of victory.

Ruthlessly had Klimt begun the fight he seemed about to lose, ruthlessly he now ended it. Führer had turned at Lunar's howl, to glimpse, to see, to wonder at such confidence above when down below he, Führer, would-be Lord of All was about to –

Like a rolling avalanche of rock, Klimt hurled himself at Führer's head, catching his throat at its most vulnerable, catching and clamping on. Attack, analysis, surprise – it was Klimt's method from the start; waiting for the moment, which had now arrived.

As Führer's roar became a choking sob of incomprehension Klimt held on and stood before him, his left leg good, his wounded shoulder strong, all pretence of serious injury abandoned.

As he gripped he pushed, using his last strength to gain advantage as he sought to heave the younger, heavier wolf off his feet. For a moment Führer's front paws lifted and scrabbled at thin air, and it appeared quite certain that Klimt must win, and Tervicz's prayers seemed answered.

But then Klimt's straining lift faltered, and Führer's superior agility began to show; he relaxed his front legs, rolled back towards the river, taking Klimt with him, and as they tumbled he pulled himself free of Klimt's jaws. Free, but not free to do much more.

Nor Klimt either.

Both rolled now in the river, the gravity of their injuries plain to see as the water turned red with their blood, from throat and shoulder, from haunch and leg, from belly and from hindquarters, though whose and which none could tell as the blood mingled in the water, and turned it from brown to black.

No victor then, both vanquished and fallen now, unable to fight more, gasping where they fell, the stream swirling around them, their blood flowing out across the Fell.

Yet there was a difference, and it lay in the spirit and demeanour of their followers. Several of the Magyars came forward to stare down at Führer, seeming angry he had failed, and they might have moved in on the helpless Klimt had not the Wolves grouped immediately about him.

'One to one,' growled Tervicz, 'and that is how both wished it to be. Neither is the victor and we shall look after our own.'

But his words were overridden by further triumphant howling from the Scarpfeld, a signal that Klimt's strategy had won the day: while the two leaders had fought upon the Fell, the Wolves had taken the heart of the Heartland almost unopposed.

As the realization that this was so spread among the Magyars their glances at the fallen Führer became more cursory still, and they turned their attention from Tervicz and the other Wolves ranged with him towards those Wolves who now stood so proud at the edge of the Scarpfeld.

Suddenly irresolute, they abandoned all concern for Führer to talk and argue among themselves about what they should do, and had not Klimt and Kobrin made it so clear that a settlement rather than a massacre was what the battle must finally be about, the Wolves might have been tempted to charge, and take advantage of the Magyars' disarray. Instead, they felt constrained to stay where they were, and watch a new drama unfold, and a new danger threaten.

Perhaps Lunar had sensed from the silence of the Wolves with Klimt that he had fallen, and was gravely, perhaps mortally wounded, for the howling on the Scarpfeld suddenly ceased. As it did so, and as if in some way a reflection of this, the sun that had been so bright upon the Fell now faded and was lost beneath a drift of cloud, while upon the Scarpfeld its rays shone out, bright and brighter yet upon the spot where Lunar stood.

At the same time the air upon the Fell seemed to be shaken by a chill tremor, and the wolves there grew hushed and still. Then Tervicz and the others saw Lunar begin to descend, Kobrin and a few others with him – descend straight towards the mass of Magyars standing silent and nervous on the Fell by the gulley entrance.

'Surely we cannot let them come down unsupported,' said one of the Wolves.

But Tervicz, remembering Klimt's earlier commands, and awed now by the strange mood in the air and the fading of the light about them by the stream, stayed the wolf with a look.

'Klimt,' he said, kneeling where his leader lay gasping from the fight and the wounds he had received, yet beginning to recover a little, 'shall we go to Lunar's aid?'

Klimt shook his head and rasped. 'See where he comes and how he comes, Tervicz. See, the sun lights his path, and great Kobrin, my general for so long, goes by his side now.'

'But that's only because –'

Klimt shook his head wearily and said, 'No, wolf, it's not just because

Kobrin's there, it's because perhaps Lunar's time has come to assert himself upon us all.'

'But he's not ready, Klimt. He's still too young –'

'Do not the old always think those younger than themselves *too* young?'

'Well then, there are too many Magyars for him to take on with so small a force. All that we have won may now be lost. I beg you, let me send reinforcements to the gulley, or howl down all our wolves as you said you might order me to do.'

Klimt smiled and shook his head. 'Not yet, Tervicz, not yet. Let Lunar show the strength he has. For me you might have howled, but I have done what I could, and our strategy has won the Heartland, and given Lunar his chance. For myself –'

'Leader –'

'Tervicz!' said Klimt harshly, 'you talk too much. Once the Bukov wolf in you howled down the Wolves of Time and we obeyed that summons – the time to howl them back into the stars is not yet come. Wulf is still a mortal, His life not yet fully run. See now how he comes, how Lunar comes, to try to assert himself over both Wolves and Magyar, and so unite us all and thus set an example for wolfkind. Save your howling for the day he grows too old and needs our help.'

'But Klimt,' whispered Tervicz, not quite understanding it.

'Save it for the time to come, and support him, wolf, as you have supported me. Now, help me up to Jicin's side. Rohan, you help as well. Help us both, for we have been apart too long and shall never be separated again.'

Rohan came from Jicin's flank, and together she and Tervicz helped Klimt up the slope to be with Jicin.

The two wounded wolves reached out to touch each other, smiled, gazed upon each other, shifted nearer, licked each other's wounds with no need for more words than sighs of contentment to be together, and the whispering of each other's name.

The light faded further, the clouds above mounting dark before a cold, cold wind, so that the sunshine where Lunar was, which stayed with him as he came down the gulley, seemed brighter still.

'Where is Klimt?' he cried as he boldly advanced upon the growling Magyars. '*Where . . . is . . . he?*'

They fell back before him, muttering, none ready to make the first attack, awed by the light that seemed upon him, and the presence of great Kobrin and two of the larger Pechorans at his side. But though they were cowed for the moment, and unwilling to take decisive action against Lunar yet, they did not show much respect either.

'He has fallen where Führer fell,' snarled one of the Magyars, his contempt for both the leaders as obvious as the hostility he felt towards Lunar and those with him.

The Magyars did not willingly part to let Lunar through and he had to push between them, past some bigger than himself. Without a doubt, as he crossed the open Fell to Klimt, had the Magyars shown spirit and resolution they might have wiped out for ever Lunar and his friends, and gone on to destroy the Wolves protecting Klimt. Perhaps it was the fact that the Wolves had so cleverly secured the higher reaches of the gulley and the Scarpfeld beyond that prevented them; but there was as well that sense of moment and destiny that Lunar so bravely conveyed from within himself.

However it was, Lunar broke through the Magyar ranks to the stream and there saw Führer lying on the ground, weak now from loss of blood, and mumbling and muttering to himself in a choking, rasping way as if he no longer understood where he was, or what had happened to him. No Magyar stood nearby but rather all stood off, talking anxiously among themselves. Not even when Führer managed to drag himself further from the stream did they turn to him, so that his retreat was all the more noticeable because all his supporters appeared now to have deserted him and none went near. It was as if he had never been, or no longer existed.

While closer by, huddled in the heather and muddy grass by the stream, seeming now no more than flotsam brought down by the waters in spate, lay what had once been Dendrine, her blood-soaked fur stiffening against the breeze, her malevolent evil reduced now to almost nothing.

What she had been – feared ledrene and cruel destroyer of innocence – lived now only in the eyes of those Magyars unable to keep their glance from straying to her body, at which they gazed with morbid fascination and the gloating triumph of those ordinary wolves who revel to see an extraordinary wolf fallen, one they need fear no more. She whom they had been too timid to confront in life, they now surreptitiously dared face in death.

Lunar took in this sorry scene only briefly before moving on to the stream and staring at that very different sight he saw there: Klimt and Jicin as solid in their position now together as the Wolves who had instinctively gathered about them were in the protection they would give. Outnumbered they might be, the shelter of the temporary truce Klimt had made with Führer now running out, but none could doubt that they would defend Klimt and his Jicin to the very last.

'Now, why don't you take your injured and leave this place,' cried one of the braver Magyars from the far side of the stream.

It was enough to encourage others of his kind to shout more threats and abuse, and worse still, to begin those little steps and gestures of advance which in a single wolf betrayed his timidity, but in a mob gave hint of more violent and concerted action.

Still Lunar ignored them, and splashing to the stream went straight to where Klimt lay, concern upon his face, and love in the way he said, 'Father, I –'

'Lunar, my son, worry not for me. My shoulder, already lame, is now too badly hurt ever to support my weight with ease again, but I shall live. More importantly for me now, Jicin here will live as well.'

Lunar reached out a paw to her, as he might to his own mother. If she had ever doubted his acceptance of her she could do so no longer, for his clear eyes were smiling and gave welcome in their warmth, and sympathy in their quick glance across her hurt and battered body.

'May Wulfin bring a healing to you both,' he said, even as the Magyars, mistaking the attention he was giving Klimt and Jicin for a reluctance to face them out, advanced to the stream's very edge and began to shout more insults and abuse.

'Now, father,' said Lunar calmly, 'what was that about time running out for us Wolves of Time?'

'Lunar, my fighting days are over, and my desire to be leader all but gone, for I have done what I could and borne my duties and my responsibilities as a wolf should.'

'Father,' said Lunar, 'you are my leader still; only give the word and we Wolves will do your bidding and fight.'

Klimt shook his head, struggling to sit up a little higher, but only able to when Lunar from one side, and Tervicz from the other, helped him. He stared at the horde of Magyars and then at Lunar.

'I yield the leadership of the Wolves of Time to you, Lunar. I have taught you all I can, and I have a feeling you have learnt yet more! If I could fight you for the leadership I would, if only to prove to myself and the other Wolves that you are worthy of it. But . . . I cannot. I yield it to the only wolf I know who can stand proud among us and say, though the phrase is not felicitous, and is one the Magyars like to use, that he is "Lord of All".

'Let me watch you unite us all, my son, that I may know that I was right to believe that the wolf who visited us in the days following your birth was who She said She was.'

'If it must be so, father,' said Lunar softly, those nearest him remarking how his paws trembled, and his breathing quickened as if he was uncertain if he was yet capable of so great a task, 'then as Lounel was wont to say, it *will* be so!'

The Magyars, seeing Lunar half turn towards them, began to fall into silence, waiting to see what he would do.

'Lounel *still* says it,' said a thin old voice from the rocks above, and Lounel came to stand at Aragon's side. 'Now wolf, pray do what you must do, for I am hungry and a little tired but I cannot very well . . .'

Despite the awesome nature of the moment, Lunar could not help but smile: wolves might come and wolves might go but Lounel stayed the same, and always made him laugh. Never had Lunar felt surrounded by such love as then.

'Kobrin,' he commanded harshly, the smile fading on his face, 'and all you others, the words I shall speak to the Magyars are intended for you too. Act on them as you feel you must, without fear or favour to myself or Klimt, who has yielded up the leadership that another may take it.'

He stared around at them fiercely, waiting to see if any of the Wolves would take his words as invitation to mount a challenge to his authority. But all watched in silence, and some like Tervicz and Stry, and even Aragon himself, nodded their heads as if to encourage him. As for Kobrin, he had already given public acknowledgement of his deference to Lunar by the way he had accompanied him down the gulley. Now he looked on with interest, as a fighter as experienced as he might well, to see how Lunar dealt with the Magyars and the challenge they seemed certain now to make.

With a brief nod to his supporters, hardly less austere and curt than those had been inclined to give when in their prime, Lunar turned to face the Magyars. His lighter fur, the boldness of his step, and the forthright way he gazed upon the Wolves' enemies, marked him out as a worthy adversary, and one only a confident wolf would cross.

He went down to the stream's edge alone and stared unwaveringly across at the mass of wolves on the far side. For a moment down there, with the mobbing Magyars thick on the far bank and the rise of ground beyond, he looked vulnerable. But as soon as he raised his head and began to speak, his grasp of the moment and his authority were all too clear.

'Fellow wolves,' he cried, 'my name is Lunar and I am the son of Klimt, who has proved himself the equal of your leader this day, though no more.'

The Magyars quietened, perhaps surprised by Lunar's immediate acknowledgement of Klimt's failure to win the fight.

'I stand here now to take up the challenge Klimt first made Führer, to fight as one wolf to one that the lives of many may be saved. Let the victor take possession of the Scarpfeld.'

This offer caused the Wolves considerable disquiet, excepting Klimt, who might have been expected to be most alarmed by it, for why should Lunar risk losing all the Wolves had gained? Yet Klimt showed no sign of worry, but rather seemed inclined to nod his head in agreement with Lunar's words.

However, the Magyars were not quite convinced: 'You're not telling us that if one of our number defeats you, puny son of Klimt, your lot will withdraw from the Scarpfeld which you've occupied today?'

'I am not only saying it,' said Lunar, 'I shall prove it. Send what guards you choose back up there now to stand by my own. Let whichever leader emerges victorious today take command of both sets of guards.'

As the Magyars took up Lunar's offer he watched carefully to see which of them would take command, now that Dendrine was dead, and Führer fallen. Three bigger Magyars began to do so and before long had sent some of the tougher-looking guards back up the gulley, with Rohan to accompany them and explain matters to Utin, the Pechoran wolf Lunar had left in charge of the Scarpfeld. This done, the Magyars seemed to have settled down somewhat.

'Now,' said Lunar, 'let us see what you Magyars are made of.' He took a few steps forward until his paws were in the stream and continued, 'Well, and which of you is it to be? You over there? Or *you*? Or . . .'

With each of these verbal challenges Lunar took a step further across the stream until by the fifth or sixth he was on the far bank, and by the seventh or eighth he was head to head with the front rank of the Magyars.

'So – you can be brave together, but by yourselves you are irresolute. Let me therefore chose my first foe for myself.'

He smiled slightly, and turned impulsively, almost playfully, to one of the smaller Magyars near him and advanced. The wolf retreated at once, as did many of the other lesser ones, leaving Lunar confronting those who were more determined, and more experienced, including that triumvirate of Magyars who had conferred together before sending their representatives to the Scarpfeld.

Having successfully weeded out the weaker of the Magyars Lunar's mood now shifted into something more serious, and the watching Wolves could only be impressed by his courage and nerve.

'Well,' said he, 'and which of you is it to be?'

The three wolves growled and muttered, their paws fretting on the ground, for the moment remaining indecisive as to which of them would attack. All were as large as Lunar, one perhaps more so. While all about them the other Magyars' hackles rose, and they paced about glancing at Lunar as if they too were thinking of taking him on, yet . . .

The first charge came suddenly from one of these, who had been holding back and guessed this might be the best chance he would have. The other Magyars, including the three most obvious candidates for leadership, fell back to watch what Lunar made of the one attacking him, and, too, to assess his strengths and weaknesses.

The bout was ferocious and swift, and Lunar took the wolf full on, ducking under his guard after a few moments of a heaving tussle and lifting him bodily off the ground. As he fell Lunar rose and turned in the air and landed as he did, but with his jaws open at the other's throat. With a half-howl of defeat and a scrabble of paws the wolf turned tail and ran back among his fellows.

Almost immediately, too soon perhaps to give Lunar a chance to recover himself, the largest of the three attacked Lunar from the right flank, quite brutally. This was more serious, and for a time, as each took the measure of the other, the two were circling and trying to get a hold, weight against agility, youth against experience . . . except that very soon, Lunar proved he had experience as well, and extra speed. With a final snarl and attempted bite the second combatant retreated.

Another of the three was next, this time more cautious and, as it proved, cleverer. He succeeded in turning Lunar twice, and once brought him to his knees. But always Lunar rose again, and each time went forward with more ferocity, as if to tell the other that he would always meet like with like, and more. Then, in a distant echo of a game he had played with Solar, Lunar turned and seemed to flee and the attacker foolishly followed wildly after him. Not for long. Lunar chose his moment and his ground, and as the wolf tried to right his step on the awkward slope he had allowed himself to be led to Lunar turned and took him hard, very hard, and the fight was over in a moment.

Perhaps had Lunar not begun to show signs of tiredness he would already have done enough to prove his supremacy. But it is a wolf's prerogative to try for the leadership at any time, and a leader's duty to meet any challenge whenever it comes, and from wherever.

So now other wolves essayed a challenge on Lunar, who for a time seemed to grow more tired, panting for breath at moments of respite, and recovering himself less and less with each new challenge that came along. These were strange and unusual contests, for in such a situation most wolves will hold back knowing well that if they win they will have done so against a weakened wolf, and may themselves have to face a challenge before ever they have time to impose their authority as leader.

For this reason it was the Wolves' turn to abuse the Magyars, saying they were cowards to so harry a wolf who had proved himself. But Lunar himself silenced them, saying, 'If the gods are with me this day, and judge that what I do is right, then I shall not be forced to yield and Magyar will make peace with Wolf. Therefore –'

But he had no time to say more before yet another challenger tried his luck.

So it was that on that famous day when Lunar sought to take forward his father's challenge and his work, and unite all wolfkind by bringing together the Magyars and Wolves under his sole leadership, he took on Magyar after Magyar, until twelve had been repulsed, though none injured badly, for Lunar defeated them by agility and by winning such a position at their throat or underbelly, and sometimes at their eyes, that he might easily have killed them or maimed them permanently, so they yielded to the better wolf.

With this last, the twelfth, it seemed that finally Lunar's great challenge was over. The darker clouds had began to disperse, and as the afternoon advanced the sun returned across the Fell. Lunar's fights had taken him far from the stream and the Magyars had dispersed about him, none daring to take up the challenge for themselves as he went from one to another, seeking and finding obeisance, until he circled back towards the stream. His route unwittingly took him near where Führer lay, far now from where he had fallen, yet seeming still too badly injured to do more than raise his head sometimes and groan, speaking words too slurred and thick for others to quite make out.

Thus it was that as Lunar turned at last to address the Magyars as a group once more, Führer lay close by, staring malevolently at the new victor, his breathing a rasping, his maw a wounded, ragged thing.

'Magyars,' began Lunar once more, 'I say again and finally, if there is still one among you who wishes to challenge my claim to leadership of Magyar and Wolves both, let them –'

'Wolf!' grunted Führer from the ground, '*wolf!*'

Lunar turned to him, as Führer intended that he should, and he saw that great wolf rise, bloodied though he was. Rise and lunge, lunge and reach forward with his jaws, reach and take a grip.

Of all the horrors on the Fell that day this was the worst. So sudden was Führer's attack, so absolute in its murderous intent, that all there gasped, Wolf and Magyar alike, and many instinctively came forward, for there was something untoward and terrible in Führer's subterfuge, something illegitimate.

Yet not one wolf went to Lunar's aid, for in a fight for leadership even such a challenge as that must be met, perhaps all the more ruthlessly.

Lunar fell before Führer's fierce onslaught, and the great wolf was on him, his head thrusting hard at Lunar's underbelly, so hard indeed that he let out a winded gasp and turned and tried to crawl away.

'No!' roared Führer. 'Want you to play with me!'

It was mocking as it was ruthless and it seemed that Lunar in the moment of his victory might now suffer more than defeat, for this was not a foe who would grant him that same mercy he had shown his twelve opponents.

Somehow Lunar turned and twisted from Führer's grasp.

Somehow he found sufficient footing to hold fast against Führer's next attack.

Somehow he found strength and courage to take the initiative back again and charge Führer down, down into a mêlée of paws, down into the ground from where he had risen, down into the void of weakness and painful suffering whence Führer had for a moment managed to rise up.

Down, and down, fighting him back, until the great wolf began to seem weak again, his lunges containable, his growling ineffectual and his huge head unable to rise from dropping low, low to where Lunar had brought him, which was back to the flank of his dead mother Dendrine.

'Nooooooo!' cried Führer with his last strength, 'not . . . no . . .'

It was the cry of a youngster who seeks escape from the dominion of cruel parents; the sobbing, helpless cry of one who knows he is returning back to hell.

'Only wanted . . . only want . . .'

As Führer tried to speak to Lunar, simply to speak, the Magyars all about began to chant, 'Kill him! Kill him! Kill him and be our Lord of All! Kill!'

Lunar looked down at the stricken wolf and saw what others could not see. He saw a frightened wolf, more badly injured than his last bid for victory would suggest. One eye was gone from Klimt's fearful last assault, and the flesh about his jaw was so badly ripped that it hung loose, his teeth showing. His flanks were torn, one of his legs seemed crushed, and yet he strove for life.

'Only wanted to . . .'

'What did you want, wolf?' said Lunar softly, bending to him and ignoring the clamour of the Magyar wolves for death.

'Wanted to play . . .' whispered Führer, his voice a cub's, 'like you did with *your* brother.'

'*My* brother?' said Lunar in astonishment before looking up briefly and signalling Kobrin and the others to keep the Magyars back.

'Watched you,' said Führer, 'sometimes when you played with him.'

'But . . .', began Lunar, 'but . . .'

'Helped you find your way home. Just wanted to play but she . . . but Dendrine made me . . . she . . .'

Slowly the light of understanding came to Lunar as he realized who it had been who had led him and Solar to safety that time the Mennen came to the Scarpfeld with their guns. It had not been a god that watched over them, nor a god that saw them safely home, but Führer, who had been raised on the Scarpfeld and knew it better than any wolf.

'You . . . ?' said Lunar.

Weakly, Führer nodded, and from his good eye a tear came and was lost on his mother's flank.

Lunar pulled back from him and stood astride him in a stance that was protective, not triumphant.

All fell silent.

'Wolves,' he said, 'I shall not begin my leadership of you with death, but with life. Now . . . is there not one of you who will stand surety for this injured wolf?'

Silence, but for the quiet running of the stream.

'Is there not one who will tend the wounds of one who once led you?'

Silence, but for the breeze in the heather.

'Is there not one of you here, Magyar or Wolf, who will forgive this wolf those things he has done, and help him?'

Silence, but for the rustling of a wolf's paws across the Fell, and his voice; 'I will stand surety for him, and tend him, and help him.'

The wolf came forth from among the Magyars into whose midst he had come but a short time before. He had hidden up in the terraces since dawn, as he had been told to do. He had seen the advance of the Wolves, first one way and then another, and he had watched in horror as Dendrine had sought to kill Jicin, and then met her own death.

Horror had overtaken him too as Klimt and Führer had fought, and tears beset him when both of them had fallen, and both seemed dead. Then he had watched Lunar's great challenge, and seen him defeat twelve wolves in a contest for leadership that would be an inspiration for all wolfkind.

Then when Führer had risen once again, and seemed to seek to kill Lunar, he had laughed, for he understood that Führer wanted to play. But play it had not been, and Lunar had fought back and defeated him and then, as the Magyars cried out for his blood, Lunar had seemed about to kill him.

Only then had that wolf risen from his hiding-place, and, disobeying the strict instructions Führer himself had given him, began to slide and run down the gulley as fast as he could, faster and yet faster lest he be too late.

Is there . . . ?

Yes, yes he was coming.

Is there not . . . ?

Yes, he trusted Führer.

Is there not one . . . ?

Yes, there was one whom Führer could call a friend.

That wolf came now, hearing Lunar's call and answering it, boldly: 'I will.'

As the youngster approached Lunar pulled back in astonishment, for if ever a wolf looked as Solar had when he was young this was he. The gods themselves had answered his appeal.

'What wolf are you?' said Lunar, as the youngster went to Führer and stood by him, appalled to see the injuries he had sustained. 'What is your name?'

'I am Torne,' said the youngster, 'and my mother is Elhana and my father Aragon and my leader . . . my leader is . . . you are my leader.'

'He's Lord of All,' mumbled Führer.

'Then what are you?' said Torne in puzzlement.

'Me?' said Führer, who had never known. 'Me? Know what I *was*.'

'What were you?' said Torne, with such gentleness that Lunar knew that Führer could find no better healer than this.

'Long, long time ago I was a brother,' whispered Führer to the wolf who stood above him, bending his head now to lick his wounds for him, helping him.

'You are still,' said Torne.

'No!' cried Führer terribly, 'no . . .'

'Yes!' said Torne, quite firmly, as certain of himself as day follows night, 'yes you are!'

Lunar grinned, for Torne sounded like a brother himself, one who thought himself older and a little wiser, almost as Solar had liked to sound.

'Well then,' said Lunar speaking to them all, 'would you call me leader or Lord of All?'

His eyes were clear and bright, and on his face was that lightness of expression, that good humour and fancifulness that had made all like him when he was young, excepting sometimes Klimt who did not always see the joke.

'You choose,' said Kobrin coming forward, and the Magyars nodded their heads.

'Well then,' said Lunar, 'tomorrow and in the days and months and years thereafter, so long as the gods grant me strength, let me be your leader; but today, when we shall celebrate our union, and the beginning of wolfkind's union too, let me be Lord of All.'

V

THE SEEKERS AT
THE WULFROCK

CHAPTER THIRTY-ONE

Matthius Wald

WALD AND HIS ASSISTANT EIKE sat in the sun, watching the flow of the stream where Lunar had fought for the future of wolfkind. Their backs rested against part of that unremarkable outcrop of rocks which had once given sanctuary to Jicin.

'It's time to set off for the Scarpfeld,' said Wald.

Eike nodded, at first unable to react to a decision he had awaited for so long, and which marked the beginning of the end of their historic trek from the Schwarzwald, which had been years in the making.

The old man with white hair and a gun had not been seen again, though they sometimes heard the sound of shots echoing in the cliffs above, and down the gulley walls. Nor was there any sign of Leon, the wolf of Spain who had first led them to Jicin's hiding-place.

In the days they had been here Matthius Wald had explored all along the cliffs as far as the road to the north, which dropped down into the valley alongside which the Forest ran. The wolves there were undisturbed by his presence, and followed him discreetly up through the trees when he trekked up to the Tree, and from there along the screes to the Fall. Someone, the old man perhaps, had erected strange multi-coloured drapes, no more than a metre or so high, hanging like curtains right through the Forest across the routeways out and in.

'Nobody would believe they stop wolves,' said Wald, 'but I think they do. Though the fabric merely hangs, the wolves refuse to cross through it and so are hemmed in. Hunters used them in the old days when they wanted to eliminate wolves from a forest, frightening them along the nets into a cul-de-sac, and killing them when they began to panic. It's strange and worrying that we find them here.'

He had returned to where Eike and he had made an encampment and there, for days past, meditated upon what he had seen, and jour-

neyed to the sound of Eike's drum, seeking the Wolves' further guidance.

In his heart he knew there was not much more for the Wolves to show him, and only one place left to which he must journey – the WulfRock – and one survivor of the original Wolves of Time left who might guide him . . .

Then there came a dawn when that Wolf appeared, the same ancient vagrant wolf who had first led them out of the Schwarzwald when their pilgrimage began, and who often, Wald fancied, had been watching over them on their journey, sometimes letting himself be seen. Now he had shown himself again, grey-white of fur, slow of paw, standing by the gulley, waiting.

'He has chosen to be our guide at the end, just as he was at the beginning,' said Matthius Wald. 'He wishes us to be seekers at the WulfRock now, as so many wolves and one Mann have been before us.'

'Your father?' said Eike.

'Yes, I think this was the final journey he made,' said Matthius, who had journeyed far enough in his father's footsteps to be more certain of what he had done, and who he had been. 'I think if he had lived after reaching the WulfRock he would have come back to tell the tale, and bring to an end his story of the Wolves of Time.'

Eike said, 'When I first saw that old man I thought he might be . . .'

'My father, Jakob Wald?' said Matthius, shaking his head. 'He never carried a gun in his life.'

'I don't like old men with guns. You know who I now think that man is, don't you!'

'I have a good idea,' said Wald grimly. 'He was always a survivor, that one. Don't worry, Tervicz will protect us, for he is the Bukov wolf.'

'But I do worry – and he's so old,' whispered Eike, who had been awed by the sight of the wolf, as of the man, 'far older than when we first saw him in the Schwarzwald. I thought he was ancient then! How could he possibly live on?'

'His task is not yet done.'

'Whose? Huntermann's . . . ?' said Eike with bitter irony. 'He would have to be very old to have lived this long.'

'Here in the Heartland time is different.'

'Yes, but why is he here at all? Anyway, when I learned about the

last great wars it was always assumed that he was dead, killed by his own supporters.'

'Maybe that's what he wanted people to think. Maybe, too, he wishes to be a seeker at the WulfRock.'

'Taken him long enough – but then I suppose it does take time to know what to go looking for.'

'You are learning, Eike.'

'I am,' said Wald's assistant with a wry grin. 'Enough to know that only a foolish man or a wise one –'

'Or a wise wolf . . .'

'. . . risks being a seeker at the WulfRock.'

Wald laughed. 'Let's agree to be foolish then, and see what we can find,' he said, leading Eike away from the stream. He turned to look back a final time at where they had been encamped so long. 'I don't really want to leave this place,' he said, 'because it feels like it has known a happiness that lives on in the weathering of the rocks, and the swaying grass, and the sound of the stream – happiness, and joy, and a final fulfilment. And you know why?'

Eike nodded, and they finally set off.

Klimt and Jicin

That long summer after Lunar took up the challenge of leadership, and began his journey towards immortality, Klimt and Jicin found their love again. There by the stream, and sometimes in the shade of the terraces and rocky outcrops, they lingered for three months, their wounds healing as well as they could, their hearts rejoicing. There was food enough for two, and for three or four when others joined them.

Klimt's face began to relax and his eyes softened, and he talked of his past, of the summons of the gods, of duty, of leadership, of responsibility. But mostly he said nothing, for there were no words to describe the love he had found again, and the wondrous and strange world it led him to explore.

For a time, however, their peace was disturbed by Mennen, as was that of all the Wolves. The Mennen came first to the far southern edge of the Fell and there completed that vast run of high fences the

Magyars had seen going up over the last year or two. Two lines of wire fencing were erected, thirty yards apart, with razor wire and other obstacles to discourage Mennen crossing through.

However, the Mennen made it easy for animals to pass through. There were tunnels underneath big enough for wolves to use but too narrow and small for Mennen. Elsewhere there were no fences at all, just trenches which the deer soon learnt were safe to leap across but fatal to fall in, because the bottoms of them were mined.

Then the Mennen came with great transporters on the Fell, and helicopters, working non-stop, their activities illuminated by lights at night, to make . . . structures, mostly underground, most strange. Four altogether, miles apart. Each with a grey-white propeller on a tower which turned with the wind, thrump, thrump, thrump almost endlessly.

When the work was finished there was the sound of gunfire, a burst for each of the structures, and concrete pits from where the scent of Mennen corpses came.

It left Klimt and Jicin uneasy, even when, come September, the Mennen went, leaving the structures and the fences in place. For now the silence was broken by the thrumping of the windmills, day and night.

Klimt tried to shut them from his mind as he and Jicin lived out their last days of summer, and finally did so. They were becoming indifferent to the doings of the Mennen.

'My dear . . . I missed you,' he said one day, waking up and finding her not right there next to him.

'I was only down by the stream, never for a moment out of sight.'

'Still . . . you seemed to be gone from here.'

'I was watching the water in the stream, and wondering where it came from.'

'The WulfRock.'

'Yes, my love, I believe it does.'

Silence, thinking, flanks touching all day long, and then evening sun upon their faces.

'Jicin?'

'Mmm?'

'My body ached today, that's why I've hardly moved.'

'I know.'

'Have to leave here soon if I'm to have the strength to climb the gulley and get to the Scarpfeld and lead us to the WulfRock.'

'I know,' she murmured.

'We are going together?'

'Of course, my love.'

'There'll be healing for our aches and pains at the WulfRock.'

'There better be! Now, come on Klimt, get up and come down to the stream and drink,' she said, rising, 'it'll do you good.'

Klimt rose and tried to stretch, but it was getting hard. He stumbled stiffly the short way to the stream.

'Jicin my dear, we'll watch the stars tonight.'

'As we do every night.'

'And Lunar will come by . . .'

'And he'll make you talk and weep . . .'

'And you as well . . .'

'Yes,' sighed Jicin, 'I still weep. But I weep for joy too.'

'But we must leave soon my love, though I daresay the gods will tell me when it's time to go as they have instructed me in so much else. Tomorrow? The next day? The day after? Soon . . .'

Klimt shrugged and sighed.

It was indeed the day after that there was a sign, or so Klimt thought.

A Mann appeared up in the gulley, a Mann who moved slowly now: the Mann whom Klimt knew.

'He's injured as I am,' said Klimt, watching the Mann's slow descent of the gulley. It took him nearly a day to climb down. When he had he simply sat and stared across the Fell, towards the endlessly turning propellers of the windmills. Only Lunar dared to go near him, to check him out.

'I'm sure he's the one you thought he was,' he reported to his father. 'He has the same sweet scent of thyme and tarragon you noticed in Khazaria. It took him longer than us to get back to the Heartland!'

'If he goes back up to the Scarpfeld I shall follow him,' said Klimt. 'He's another seeker, just as we are.'

'Maybe he needs a sign from *you*,' said Lunar.

The Mann seemed set to stay where he was for the night, huddling down into the heather for warmth.

Klimt said more than once, 'Maybe he does need a sign, maybe . . . Now, let's talk, Lunar, for time is running out at last. Let's talk.'

Of Klimt's life they talked, and then of the Heartland. Of Elhana and Aragon. Of Mennen, and of all the triumphs and the tragedies they had known. Other Wolves came by to listen, stopping far enough away that they were hardly seen.

Twice Lunar shed tears, and Jicin and Klimt comforted him: for Solar, whom he had known and loved so well, and for Merrow, lost before she had a chance to play a full adult part.

'Your mother Elhana believed she did not die, for there were signs in the Ruin of a wolf having lived there for a long time. She said she recognized Merrow's scent.'

'After so long?'

'Do I not know the Mann's, after so long?'

'Merrow alive . . .' whispered Lunar doubtfully, weeping again for what might have been.

That night was indeed the last in their sanctuary. Lunar left before dawn, and when Klimt finally awoke the sun was already up and warm.

'How are your joints today?'

'Better,' said Klimt in some surprise, for they were. 'Much better.'

He rose, he saw the Mann over by the gulley, he felt in himself a reserve of energy, but not much. Just enough, in fact . . .

'My dear,' he whispered, reaching out for Jicin, 'let's go.'

For a moment she looked afraid and she too rose, found it was her turn to feel old and stiff, and sank down again.

'It's a long way,' she said, craning her neck up towards the top of the cliffs, 'and that Mann . . . ?'

'He'll do us no harm. Rather, he needs a little guidance. *Come!*'

There was something of the old command to his voice and it made Jicin rise again despite her pains, which were far worse than she ever let Klimt know.

So, as simply as that, they set off for the gulley.

The Mann barely moved as they went by, and nor did he smell of fear when Tervicz and Lunar came after Jicin and Klimt, except the awe all creatures must feel as they begin their final journey to the WulfRock. As they went up, others began to gather and journey with them, for there was a finality about Klimt's gait that spoke of a longer journey than a mortal one.

Tervicz appeared quite suddenly from nowhere as it seemed, and said he was there to lead them up the gulley. He picked as easy a way as he could find among the screes and boulders, stopping often so they could catch their breath. Lunar followed after them, and others were waiting at the top, Kobrin, Aragon, Stry, Rohan, and many more.

The Mann picked his way slowly up behind them, and at Klimt's command he was ignored by all the Wolves.

The Scarpfeld was warm, the white clouds high, the sky so blue and bright it made the rock-faces shine, and the streams and multitude of little waterfalls sparkled and glittered.

Klimt said few general words, but to each he knew well he spoke individually, saying his farewells, while to many others he gave acknowledgement. Torne was there, but not Führer, who was off and about up in the gulley terraces, or somewhere across the Fell, a vagrant who talked only to Torne, but whom no wolf now feared.

Klimt's slow farewells stretched into the afternoon and the sun began to decline towards the west. Finally, with a nod to Jicin he asked that Tervicz lead them on. Then they were off, their final words for Lunar, new leader of the Wolves, words of farewell.

Tervicz led them up the rough ground towards the cliffs and then to the boulder which marked the entrance to the little gulley which led to those great labyrinthine gorges wherein the WulfRock rose.

How old Klimt seemed as he climbed the last few steps towards the entrance, but at the last he had to turn back to help Jicin on, for she was slowing now. Haggard their fur and gaunt their flanks; yet their eyes shone with hope as they turned at last from the Wolves they loved, and the world they knew.

'Tervicz . . .'

'Klimt, leader . . .'

'Watch over Lunar to the end, until his moment comes.'

'It is my task and I shall fulfil it, however long it takes.'

'We shall be waiting for you, Tervicz, where this world ends and the next begins. We shall be waiting for you, dear friend, most loyal of all those who have followed me. So, too, will all the Wolves, for it is your destiny to be the last, when you have led He who shall be Wulf again to his new wolfway to the stars.'

'Farewell, farewell!' cried Tervicz, and his words followed after them as they went on into the gorge, echoing up and away.

Then he turned to those watching from the Scarpfeld below and howled not of history or destiny fulfilled, but of loss for a wolf he had loved from the moment they first met – farewell, he howled, farewell – and the greatest wolf of his time had gone from them for ever.

Yet . . . the sun still shone, the white clouds still drifted by, and the cliffs were golden reflections in the peat pools on the Fell. Time went on.

∘　　∘　　∘

The Mann had watched this final rite, and now he encamped upon the Scarpfeld. He wandered off, picking clean the bones of a rabbit he had snared and cooked; and he wandered back again. He had come to stay.

Three days after Klimt and Jicin took the wolfway to the stars, early one morning, the drone of a helicopter grew louder over Scarpfeld and Fell. The Wolves went to ground, as did the Mann, as they waited to see what it might be, and if it was coming down to land.

Strange, but the wind died over the Fell and the windmills slowed and stopped, leaving a silence that seemed forbidding as the helicopter came nearer still, roaring yet nearer, its shadow swift across the undulations of the Scarpfeld and the gulley walls.

Then it was gone out across the Fell to land, and the Mann was the first to rise and stare, and wonder, and then retreat, as discreetly as a wolf.

Merrow

Merrow, lost sister of Lunar, awoke to the sound of explosions and gunfire, and her master coming home.

She rose, sniffed at a half-eaten Mennen chop, and stared up at the angled window, trying to make out stars, and wolfways.

Then she prayed to Wulfin with the passionate faith that had kept her sane through the eternity of her captivity.

'Wulfin,' she cried, 'set me free.'

Then she was silent. Huntermann was back.

Huntermann

Few dictators in Europe's long and troubled history ever planned the last days of their power, or their final escape, with quite such mastery and equanimity as Huntermann.

Perhaps, after all, he really was unique among history's more geno-cidal heads of state in recognizing from the first that his days of power would be numbered, and that it might be wise to have a vision to pursue after his power had gone and he was alone once more.

That vision he had shared with no one, not Schlitz, his bodyguard and aide, nor his wife, always his unquestioning supporter, nor even his beloved darling, his daughter, whose embraces in the night were ever his final sanctuary from the affairs of state. To her alone he yielded up his power and knew the peace of utter subjugation, but he did not surrender his final secret until he really had to.

'Where and when,' he had once asked himself, before ever the dream of ultimate power became real, 'have I been happiest?'

The ordering of the question was deliberate: for Huntermann place was important, and throughout his ruthless quest for power and these years of orchestrating the escalating collapse of Europe into a pandemic of war and plague, he never felt happy if he was too long away from mountains, which for him meant the Carpathians. So much for the 'where'.

The 'when' was more problematic and shifted with the years. Once it had been the day when he first walked the hills alone above his north Ukrainian home; later it had been those exhilarating hours that followed his killing of the men who had caught him in the Forest, especially the last, so slow, and his escape up to the col that led on to the Scarpfeld.

He had lain on the gritty sward on the col and watched the villagers find three of their menfolk dead and one dying, and had then watched on as they began to try to find where he had gone, some heading off towards the Fall, others up towards where he lay. He let them come, enjoying the solitary power of seeing without being seen, and then he retreated into the clefts and caves of the Scarpfeld cliffs and hid away until they gave up searching.

It was during that time that he had discovered a way up into what might be that place Carpathian folklorists called 'The WulfRock'. He had explored up a cleft in the cliffs, found where it opened out into an extraordinary gulley, and would have gone up but for the swirling mist, so dank and cold, and sudden his awesome fear of the shapes that the protruding rocks above seemed to make as the mist came and went. Not one wolf but many, and all against him. So he had turned back before he reached the end, telling himself that one day if he had the time and opportunity he would come back to seek out the secret of the WulfRock, if there was one.

Afterwards, emerging into the sun of the Scarpfeld, he saw that his pursuers had given up hope of finding him and he had sat near the entrance to the cleft, by a boulder above some scree, which he would use as a marker to find the place should he ever have time and opportunity to return.

Sitting there that day in safety, with the wide world and a whole life before him, Huntermann had known happiness.

In the days that followed he snared rabbits, not wishing to risk the sounds of rifle shots. He drank of the icy streams. He watched stars far brighter than townies – citizens – ever saw. He hunted deer, and studied the one creature that threatened his hegemony, the wolves. Huntermann caught them, and having cradled and nurtured their cubs, and caressed them towards adulthood, he tortured them for their desire to break free, which to him was ingratitude.

Or with those that became pliant, and bonded to him, worthy animals like himself, he committed acts of bestiality under the bright stars, shuddering at the secret pleasure of it, admiring their indifference. Not many men ever mate with female wolves, but Huntermann did.

How much he learned from the wolves! It was their strong image that he used as the symbol for the terrorist organization and political party he later led.

The 'where' and 'when' of his happiness thus answered, it was a vision Huntermann held on to through his years of power, and all his planning for the escape that must one day be inevitable had as its minimum objective to get him back to the Scarpfeld in good health, with the one person before whom he could be abject if he wished: his daughter. It would be a retirement into a paradise of montane purity for a man who had practised the terror he had preached, and known most of the depravities humans know, and broken most taboos.

To stand again on the col with the Forest to one side and the Scarpfeld to the other, and know he had rid the earth of many of its fools and he was master of its Heartland, Lord of All, was Huntermann's final vision and objective.

In the year 2013, the tidal waves of chaos Huntermann and his party had created from their base in Prague reached the outer limits of their range in Europe, bringing down the embattled governments of Portugal, Greece and Norway. Like waves that crash against great cliffs, or granite harbour walls finally too strong for them, and turn

back on themselves to overturn, submerge and drown those last little
ships of state at Europe's heart, that moments before had seemed safe
and proud and upon the crest.

Until, the waves' power not quite spent, the hiss and rush of their
last turbulence turned on Huntermann himself, bringing treachery
among his loyal civilian followers, who finally realized he was the
diabolic architect of all their woes; then to his private army's generals;
and finally, the last spumes and surges of the waters reached his closest
aides and his most trusted guards and turned them against him.

Huntermann sniffed the putrid air of plotting and treachery, and
of his own likely assassination, in the heart of his bunker building in
Prague's back-streets, right where it all began, and could not but smile
. . . he was prepared.

By then Huntermann had authorized the release of the chemical
weapons which several of the European states, France and Britain
among them, and Russia too, had so obligingly developed, ready to
fall into the hands of whichever head of state one day took ultimate
power and decided to use them.

These vile killers Huntermann had released among Europe's masses,
who turned fugitive and fled, spreading disease and disaster worse by
far than any that ever went before, and far more apocalyptically
magnificent than Huntermann had dared expect. An arsonist needs
light only a single match to see the forest burn, but Huntermann had
ignited several boxes of them, and scattered them across ten thousand
miles, for plague is a fire, and its tinder is the frailty of the human
body.

One place only did he secure: the Scarpfeld. End to end, the ring
of fences he set up, and the mass of guards, might have rivalled the
great wall of China. Inside was literally no-man's-land, though the
nomadic wildlife like the deer and wolves was given leave to move
freely back and forth by way of certain gaps and holes Huntermann
designed himself. He was no fool: if he was going to live there, he
needed prey to feed on.

His design for this last resort also included several well-stocked
bunkers, planned and built to the last detail. In addition, at one end
of the Fell he had a curious concrete pit constructed, covered with
reinforced ceilings but here and there open to the wind and rain, and
winter blizzards. He placed it where once he had peed on to the grass.
That was his private joke.

Each team of architects and builders of each bunker were shown *this place, discovering its purpose only as they fell into it, shot off their legs by Schlitz. If they were still alive when they had fallen they discovered too why there was a bulldozer down there, for the last thing they saw was its slow advance upon them as it shovelled them with their colleagues into the darkness under the ceilings to be concreted in, and there die. Others whom Huntermann had cause to do away with were dispatched by train in batches of four hundred to the Quarry that lay across in Khazaria. Huntermann much enjoyed the notion of a death-camp train, Gestapo-like, and even more that its miserable occupants, unlike many of the Jews who preceded them on similar journeys seven decades before, knew exactly where they were going. Huntermann liked to inflict the suffering on a man that comes with knowing he is going to die and possibly how. Of course, the carriages were sealed, blacked out but vented to give air, with enough food for half to survive in comfort, or whoever first worked out what was what in the darkness and defended it against the others.*

Towards the end, when the trains were running more frequently and on time, Huntermann sometimes had Schlitz fly him to the Quarry terminus, to watch arrivals and departures. Often he had his daughter-woman with him. Sometimes, especially in the final months, she it was drove the trucks to the Quarry edge and pulled the lever to release the load into the void.

The victims were not numberless, and never rivalled the scale of the Holocaust, but they were large enough that when Jakob Wald was finally caught and put upon the train and survived the journey by lying still and letting others do the killing in the dark, father and daughter did not notice him pass them by as he was shovelled on to a waiting truck and driven to the Quarry side.

But they saw his escape below all right, and were utterly incensed, as such people often are, that someone should dare attempt to defy the system. This was not escape but the heavens being put out of joint by a sinner. Daughter commanded the guards to find the man. When they failed, the Quarry being vast, its cliffs and rock-piles, ruined buildings and machinery unexplored, she asked her Daddy to kill them all, so furious was she. Huntermann obliged, but then he was going to kill two of them anyway: they had been fools enough to shoot two wolves.

'They're pests round here, sir,' the guards had said by way of explanation, 'and anyway, they're the cause of the plague.'

This to Schlitz who passed it on to Huntermann, who asked that the two men be pointed out to him. His grey eyes registered nothing at all as he gazed at them. He was thinking of their deaths. Perhaps he would have them thrown over into the Quarry, or better still . . . but then the fuss over the escapee distracted him.

'He'll die in no time down there,' said one of the foolish guards by way of excusing himself for not finding him.

Schlitz shrugged and went over to Huntermann while the guards watched nervously. It was then that Daughter demanded their deaths. Huntermann let her do it herself. She shot them, and enjoyed it, as she always enjoyed such things; Daddy's girl.

The guard's assumption that the wolves were plague-carriers was common currency, and not surprising since there was a direct correlation between the mounting deaths by war and the plagues of recent years and the resurgence of the wolves, who had become bolder and bolder in their invasion of areas where people lived, and in their preying on corpses along the roads and in the fields. Their breeding cycles had shortened, their litter sizes had increased, and man's old fears and revulsion at the sight of them seemed reborn overnight as the wolves began to spread back across Europe.

In response to this wolves were caught and burnt alive; pregnant females were disembowelled, their foetuses kicked about; wolves were blinded, or their paws cut off, or they were nailed by their genitals to old church doors, an act of blasphemy against an institution that had failed utterly and was in alliance with the devil (or the Wolf) himself.

Inevitably this superstition about wolves, and the fear and hatred at their resurgence, rebounded on to Huntermann's Party, which had so long used the black image of a wolf's face with the same effectiveness as the Nazis used the swastika. It was a backlash Huntermann could not escape, and nor did he wish to. Certainly it did not take him by surprise. He used it to eliminate the lower orders of his party – blaming them for failing to uphold the good name of wolves – and then when the final anarchy came in the middle months of the year 2013, he allowed the vagrant survivors of the wars and plagues, in towns and cities where they were organized, to lynch his party members to their hearts' content.

Huntermann's downfall, as so often in such cases, was swift and sudden. One day his daughter was rude and offensive in public once too often and Prague's masses revolted against Huntermann's presence in their midst. The inner cadre of Huntermann's private

*army became rattled, and last days became hours, and hours turned
to minutes.*

'Time to go,' said Schlitz.

Huntermann was not so predictable as to use the helicopter on the
roof, deliberately placed there long since to focus a ravening crowd's
efforts on getting in. The little party slipped away by corridors and
tunnels long since readied by workmen and officials killed to keep
them secret. Down to private quarters near the river they went, in what
looked like an old museum building, while the Party's headquarters was
already disintegrating half a kilometre away in the fire and explosions
planned beforehand. The mob was attacking, and cheered when the
helicopter's blades began to spin and the whole craft seemed to rise
before it turned and fell right out of sight, burnt bodies already in
place. Other people's. A nice touch. Schlitz's neat idea.

Huntermann lingered only minutes at his unknown, unidentified,
private place, there to do three things: to change his clothes and ask
his wife and daughter to do the same; second to spring a sweet surprise
on wife and Schlitz (whose goings-on together Huntermann secretly
enjoyed, watching them on tape with Daughter) and kill them both;
goodbye, my dears.

The third act in this moment of escape?

To release his pet, a wolf, by taking her to a street door and letting
her free.

'What's her name?' asked Daughter, as the wolf slipped out into
the violent night.

'Wolves don't have names,' he said, watching Merrow, Klimt's
daughter, go.

'Where did you find her?'

'Some of my men found her injured and sheltering in a ruin in a
forest north of the Tatra.'

'Will she try to go home?'

'Probably. Now . . . we had best get out of here.'

It was dusk and they climbed up through the empty building like
an eloping couple. Well hidden by clever camouflage, yet in a space
clear enough to take off from, stood a helicopter.

'I didn't know you could fly,' said she in some alarm.

Huntermann grinned. 'Nor did Schlitz, or your mother.'

'I thought that between them they knew everything about you.'

'So did they.'

They climbed in and waited awhile for dusk to grow into night. All around them, beyond the walls and nets that hid them, Prague was bursting into a final joyous conflagration at the fall of Huntermann.

Like a god he rose then slowly, the roar of the helicopter barely noticed, and its lights not seen at all.

'Father! Look!'

It was the wide sweep of the River Vltava that she saw, lit up by fires on either side, and a sky that was filling up with explosions and stars, one of which, had any noticed them from down below, they themselves would have been.

Huntermann turned south-eastward.

He had health.

He had a lifetime companion who desired him.

He had a goal.

He had far more than most men ever did.

Oh yes, he had earned his retirement, Daughter as his mate, with a kingdom all his own to call his home, and time to explore it, to know the delights of Forest and Fell, of Scarpfeld and mountain, of river and heather bank.

Huntermann felt happiness approaching.

He looked across at his daughter, and she at him, and they laughed conspiratorially, with the smug assurance of those who are quite sure they have won the race, though it is true that they have not yet seen the finishing tape, nor had their medals hung about their necks.

'Father, what are you doing?'

'Destroying it,' said Huntermann, pulling his daughter back yet further as they waited a few moments more before the helicopter flared into an explosive burst of flames.

'But –'

Against the great Fell, and the Tatra mountains that rose beyond it, the flames and smoke of the craft's final moment seemed as nothing. They felt a flash of heat upon their faces, they saw the helicopter's cockpit briefly illuminated in its own flames before it buckled and imploded; the blades described a half-turn before the whole machine slewed sideways into the heather. Then the last flames shot up as the fuel ignited, and one of the blades shifted and pointed to the sky.

'Couldn't you have just left it as it was, since it saved our lives?' said Daughter a mite testily.

'I wanted you to know the past is over, and see our last link with it is done. Now . . .' Huntermann turned from her and looked about, vigorously breathing the air. 'How about a change of clothes?' he said, nodding towards the entrance to the bunker they had chosen as their home for a short time.

'Good idea,' she said heavily, her hand seeking his; then coyly, sweetly, sickly, she glanced at him and said, 'We're Adam and Eve now, aren't we?'

He nodded and felt aroused. If any of his victims could have seen him then, the thousands, the tens of thousands, the hundreds of thousands and the millions, the horror of their dying would have seemed as nothing to the horror of this: Huntermann had forgotten them, all of them, and in his eyes was a look of adventure as when he was a lad first seeking out the hills.

The past really was behind him, no more important than the smoulder of the embers of a helicopter destroyed upon the Fell, whose ashes would be washed away by the first rains, and whose remnants would rust and decay through coming winters until one day they were lost for ever among the heather and the peat.

They had left the past behind, and it lay in all its ruins right across Europe, beyond the labyrinth of wire fences and mined trenches that Huntermann had made to keep it well at bay.

'Adam and Eve,' he murmured, repeating his daughter's little joke, 'let's go and see if we can find an apple.'

At that soulless moment, when lost humanity was forgotten in an incestuous jest, it really seemed that Huntermann had won and that the Christian god was defeated; almost, that there was no god at all.

Merrow II

Behind them in the chaos of Prague, her ears battered by the final Armageddon of the last whole city in Europe destroying itself, Merrow was a shadow sniffing at the air, frightened and yet not overwhelmed by fear.

After being shoved out into the cold street, she had tested the air a good few times, and cocked her head against the breeze to get some kind of natural scent, but it was the stars above that calmed her. The night was cold and cloudless, but the city lights and the flashes and flames of Mennen war prevented her from seeing the sky clearly.

Instinct took her across a bridge over the great river, towards a darker place where the lights were fewer; a park, but it proved not yet dark enough. She hurried on, glancing up at the sky now and then, scenting at the gutters and the buildings that she passed, wary but increasingly excited, eager to put the Mennen city behind her. On and on she went, in among some trees, towards the darkness of a great stretch of open ground.

She looked up once more and finally saw the sky more clearly. Behind her a city burned, before her the night sky opened out, its stars unobscured by Mennen lights. She saw a thousand wolfways in the sky and gave thanks to Wulfin that she was free. Then she looked again, and found the wolfway that she sought, the one that would lead her back to the Heartland, back to her home, back to her kin. Then she found another. She was not yet ready to go back, or be a seeker at the WulfRock, not yet . . .

She rose up, shook herself, and began to lope towards the dawn and a life of freedom.

Friends

The winter after Klimt and Jicin died, great Kobrin's strength began to fail. No wolf had journeyed so far in life as he, once leader of all the Russias, now old, revered, but living past his time.

He had wanted to see that Lunar took up the leadership successfully, and by late November, when the snows were beginning to thicken, and the deer to drift down to lower ground, he was satisfied.

'Lunar,' he said, 'I swore fealty to you as to all the Wolves.'

'You did Kobrin, and few Wolves' loyalty is so highly prized.'

'Do *you* feel your age sometimes these cold mornings? Eh, Lunar?'

Lunar laughed and said he did. He had never used to, but now . . .

'It's been like that with me for many years, Lunar, since before you were born. Well, I'm tired of it and want no more of it. I'm ready to make my last journey, because my strength has gone and my will to fight for a longer life is weakening.'

Lunar could only admire his father's old friend, his own mentor in many things, for his characteristic bluntness.

'If there's nothing more I can do for the pack then if it's all the same to you I'll –'

'Oh, but there is,' began Lunar with a smile.

In spite of what he had said, and his weariness, the light of battle brightened for a moment in Kobrin's eyes.

'Tell me,' he growled.

Lunar waited awhile until Lounel appeared and settled down, and Stry as well; then Aragon sauntered in, and finally Tervicz and Rohan.

'You've been waiting for me!' said Kobrin. 'This has been arranged!'

'Yes, we have,' said Lunar honestly. 'Now listen, we need your help, and your advice. I have been thinking, and consulting too, for even though he's getting deaf, and his fur is almost falling off his body now, Lounel here still has strong beliefs and good ideas!'

Stry laughed and he and the other old Wolves gazed upon Lunar with affection and respect. He had a lighter touch than Klimt, but when it was needed he too could impose his authority. He had shown the quality of his fighting skills the day when he gained the leadership, and since then he had not been found wanting when resolute action against another wolf or group of wolves was needed.

A new order and calm had been imposed across Fell and Scarpfeld alike, and the Magyars, like the Wolves, were beginning to disperse once more in ordered packs, to spread forth, as it were, into the New Millennium, taking the fullest advantage of the Mennen's decline. While it had been Klimt's task to lead the Wolves to the Heartland and secure it for the future, it was plainly Lunar's to oversee the promulgation of the Wolves' belief in the coming ascendancy of all wolfkind.

'Well, then, Lunar, and what can an ailing has-been like me still have to offer?' grunted Kobrin.

'In the past months, since my return with Klimt from Khazaria, the word of our achievements has spread and more and more wolves are coming to the Heartland – too many in fact. Our need is no longer to convince wolves of our faith in wolfkind's future by attracting them here, but rather to spread the word outwards, to the very ends of the world we know.'

The others nodded.

'My friends,' said Lunar, 'I do not want to see you all decline in health and begin to struggle for a place against younger wolves, becoming injured and embittered, and finally outcast.'

'It happens to us all in the end,' said Lounel, 'whoever we may have been.'

'It'll happen to me no doubt,' growled Lunar. 'Meanwhile, here is what I would like you to do. The surplus of wolves hereabout includes many who would like to journey further afield than nearby valleys and hills, and some whose destiny is no doubt to establish great packs of their own, in places and along wolfways which have not heard the howling of wolves for centuries past. These wolves need leadership for a time, and example as well. Stry . . .'

Stry nodded, looking serious. He, for one, was ready to hear Lunar out.

'You came over the Tatra to join my father, journeying with your brother Morten. The young Magyars look up to you, for they know you as a mountain wolf, a Carpathian. Choose ten of them, male and female, and lead them north-west through the mountains by the route on which my father first journeyed here.'

'I am a follower, Lunar, not a leader,' said Stry uncertainly, 'so I'm not sure . . .'

'*Do it*, wolf,' said Lunar impatiently. 'You have served at Klimt's flank as we all have – you'll find you know more than you think about leadership.'

'And when a younger wolf better fitted for that kind of thing comes along?'

'Give him a hard time,' said Lunar, 'make him earn his leadership from you.'

'And then?'

'Then your task is done,' said Lunar coolly, 'and then you may give up. Meanwhile, I trust, you will have fathered young of your own by a worthy ledrene and told them tales of the Wolves that they may proudly spread the word that their father was himself a Wolf. Do it, Stry, in memory of your brother and of us all.'

'Well . . . well . . . I will!' said Stry heartily. 'You're as irritatingly persuasive as Klimt coud be, Lunar!'

Lunar laughed and said, 'I take that as a compliment! Now, Lounel . . . you came from the Auvergne in France where we know that the wolf Maladon was establishing herself at the time that Jicin and Leon left those parts. Leon is willing to go back, and I want you to return with him. Tell the wolves you find there about our work, and what we are. Advise them.'

Lounel nodded and said he would, though his legs were too thin for much journeying, and he could not hear the whisper of the wind any more. Still, if Leon was willing to help him, he would do what he could to further the cause of the Wolves.

'And Aragon too, you travel with Lounel, for did you not first journey here with him?' said Lunar.

'I did,' said Aragon gravely.

'Then return with him, taking Wolves of your own choosing with you. See that Lounel's thin legs get him back to his old home, and then continue on to Spain to tell *them* the tale of Klimt and all the Wolves. Perhaps Leon here will journey on with you – that's for you to decide. Our time for expansion has come, so grasp it, all of you!'

Then he turned to Kobrin.

'Kobrin, you –'

'I know, I know. You want me to go back to Pechora and there –'

'Something like that!' said Lunar. 'There are many Pechorans who want the honour of journeying with you, for they have achieved what they can in the Heartland. Go with them, inspire them, talk to whatever wolves you meet along the way, teach them the wolfways as you taught me, teach them to howl.'

'I'm old,' said Kobrin, 'but not so old that your words do not inspire something in me. In any case, I'm fed up with these mild winters! A real wolf likes to freeze once in a while, and I miss the tundra, and its winds which cut through to the simple truth of things. I'll go if I must!'

'And you'll go grumbling!' said Stry, buffeting his old friend.

'Humph!' said Kobrin.

Lunar finally turned to Tervicz.

'Dear friend,' said he, 'how can I command the Bukov wolf? I cannot! My sister Rohan is your companion now and brings you happiness. Journey forth or stay, Tervicz, the decision is yours.'

Tervicz smiled briefly, his thin head thinner than it used to be, the burden of the years upon him, his brows white.

'I'll wander back and forth,' he said, 'I'll rove and roam. I have only one task left but the time has not yet come. When it does, be sure that I shall fulfil it, Lunar.'

'Which is?'

'To see that *you* reach the WulfRock when your time is come.'

'You'll be there before me!' declared Lunar in surprise.

Tervicz slowly shook his head. 'I won't,' he said. 'Klimt commanded me to howl the Wolves to his side if all their help was ever needed. He knew it was ordained that one day the Bukov wolf would perform that service to the leader of the Wolves. Well, I did not need to, did I? Not for him at least, because you were there to take the leadership forward. But I might have to summon support for you at the end, Lunar, for your destiny is different, perhaps more difficult. You might need us, all of us, wherever we may be if you are to seek out the WulfRock. So . . . I shall wander, and roam the many wolfways, and finally return when I am needed.'

'Lunar's right,' said Stry, 'you'll be too old!'

'The Bukov wolf is as old as time,' said Lounel quietly.

Tervicz smiled gently and said, 'So I was told when I was young. If it is true, may the gods help me to survive until I am needed to howl down the Wolves a final time.'

'But what of *you*, Lunar, left here alone when we are gone?' It was Lounel who spoke.

'Not quite alone!' said Lunar. 'I shall have Utin at my side, as Klimt had Tervicz here, and others will join us, as you joined Klimt. As for loneliness, which is what perhaps you mean, do not all leaders suffer it? Did not my father? Why, wolves, I do already. I have missed my brother Solar almost every day since he died in Khazaria, though now I see our task beginning to be fulfilled I become a little easier. But to run with him again upon the col – to hunt for prey with him nearby – I am sometimes sad that can be no more . . .

'Then, too, there was Merrow, whose loss leaves a different gap. I confess that were I to choose the wolf I most want to meet again and have nearby, it would be her. She understood my words, listened to my tales, laughed when I did, and cried as well! But . . . the gods cannot answer all our prayers, and nor should they. It is such losses as these, and how we learn to live with them, that make us mortal, make us wolves, and finally teach us to be compassionate to others. Have not each of you suffered such losses as these? Stry? Lounel? Kobrin?'

'I lost my sister too,' agreed Kobrin, 'but the gods granted that I found her again, and was able to return her to our pack, there to live in old age, and die surrounded by what she knew. May the gods grant that Merrow returns to you, Lunar!'

Lunar shook his head sadly, close to tears at that memory, and murmured, 'It can never be. But I've got young Umbrio to train, and Torne to watch over as he stands by Führer, and learns of Magyar traditions and territory which he can teach to me, all of which will stand him in good stead when I am gone.'

So did the old friends listen to Lunar, and accept his commands. In the days that followed they left the Heartland one by one, with those wolves they chose to take, setting off against the winter winds. Surely, the gods would be with them and see that they made it back to their homelands, to tell of the Wolves and to show by example the nature of true leadership.

'Send word,' said Lunar to each of them as they left, 'that is all I ask.'

Until, when December came, all the original Wolves of Time had gone upon their wolfways home, to spread the good news that the Dark Millennium was over, and wolfkind in ascendancy once more.

While Lunar, now without these old supports, sought to forge new friendships, and bring forth the strengths of a new generation of wolves. Though sometimes in the months following, and finally the years, Utin would find him sitting alone up on the col, or out on the Scarpfeld, or down by the Ruin, remembering different times and different wolves, who he said had taught him all he knew.

'Oh, Utin . . .' he would say, there being no other words to express his thoughts, and no other wolf to whom he could show his weakness.

Then would Utin stay close by, as Tervicz was wont to do for Klimt, wishing he could help more than he did.

'Help him, Wulfin,' Utin would sometimes pray, 'for he is lost in a place to which I cannot go; help him.'

The Boy

Some months after their arrival on the Fell, Huntermann and Daughter began to fall out with each other. She grew irritable, and untidy, and was no longer minded to climb up to the Scarpfeld as he liked.

For his part Huntermann was suddenly tired of her, and puzzled by her seeming dullness, her lack of fun, her . . .

'I'm pregnant,' she announced one day during their first spring. The

Fell was alive with the rippling sound of the streams, and the sky wild. 'I'm going to move out and have the baby in one of the other bunkers.'

He was appalled by the pregnancy, but not surprised by her desire to leave. He sought to persuade her to abort the child but on such matters she was as strong-minded as he was on most others.

'Fathers and daughters do not make ideal parents,' he said.

'If the baby's deformed I'm going to kill it,' she said.

The baby was a male, and *was* deformed, but she did not kill it. It was not that bad: a misshapen head, grotesquely oversize upon so puny a body. So from the first the look of him suggested he might not have his father's intelligence or his mother's looks. Then too, his hands were larger than seemed natural, and his feet as well. He was not normal.

But Daughter would have none of it, having delivered the baby in another of the bunkers further off, doors locked, all by herself, tribeswoman-like. Down there the baby's hands had reached for her, as hers for him, and plucked from her mind any intention to kill.

Alone with the child for days before emerging into the sun, which she did with a handgun lest her doting daddy sought to kill the child, she bonded with it. Worse, she almost immediately transferred her rampant affections to the child, leaving Huntermann feeling excluded. He was not unduly upset, and anyway, there was a compensation: she moved permanently into the bunker where she had given birth, to continue living in that disorder which she liked, leaving Huntermann to practise his obsessive tidiness just as *he* liked.

Thus separated by a few kilometres father and daughter forged a new harmony. When he felt like company Huntermann strolled across to see his daughter, and his growing boy. When he did not he avoided them. For her part she had need of adult company only rarely, and then because she needed sex. Then she went and demanded it of Huntermann – not that she had to demand very forcefully. It was often so good out upon the Fell that afterwards they said they should do it more often, but then they went their own ways once more and the weeks and months went by without another bout of violent intimacy.

By the time the boy was walking, and growing, his deformities began to seem normal since they had nothing else to compare him to. His head seemed always bigger than it should be for his age, the wide mouth hanging open, the squat nose running, the eyes askew and red-rimmed. His hands and feet began to seem less large and cumbersome once he was ambulant, for he went barefoot, and was always carrying things: rough tangles of heather, rocks, larger and heavier as he grew older, dead birds, whatever animal droppings he could find, bits of the burnt helicopter, the detritus left by the builders of the bunkers – in fact, anything that was portable and appealed to him. These, and the natural history of the Fell, were his toys.

His speech was slow, laborious, and slightly slurred because of the malformation of his mouth; and also because there were long periods when his mother did not talk at all, and others when she talked and shouted non-stop and did not allow him the chance to speak.

He became used to her violence, and knew when to stay outside and huddle in the heather. The cold and wet, the sun, the blizzard nights, these were better than her storming rages and vicious slaps and punches, which, when over, were replaced by smothering physicality: 'My love, my darling, didn't mean it, my *wolfling* . . .'

Yes, by the time he was nearly five she was calling him that, for by then the boy had begun to run with wolves, or rather not run *away* from them when they came sniffing about. He had ample opportunity to meet them since he spent as much time outdoors as in, in summer, the more so as he grew older, and his parents left him to it.

He first walked the distance between the bunkers when he was three and came to no harm, and after that did it often. Huntermann liked to have him on his own and the boy enjoyed the orderliness of his father's home and its gadgets; the windmill made a deeper sound than the one he and his mother had and it pleased him.

He would sit under it for hours, listening to the 'thrump' until it became a drumming in his head, which took him far off the Fell, beyond the mountains, to where once other Mennen lived and might live still.

By the time he was six the boy was as strong as a twelve-year-old, and knew the Fell and the Scarpfeld, and right up to the col, as well almost as the wolves whose tracks he followed, whose scents he learnt, whose howls he sometimes shared, knew them more intimately than his father.

By then he had discovered he had a friend, who might well be a god, and whom he thought might live up the little gulley past the rock, where the gorges were, where his father went and stared into the beyond, where the WulfRock was.

'You don't go there, never,' said Huntermann his father, 'or your mother will eat you.'

Maybe it was a kind of joke, but it terrified the boy and he never went up there. But the god lived there because where else could he hide who was here one moment and gone the next, but by the WulfRock?

The god was the Mann and the boy knew his scent which was of thyme and tarragon. No other was as sweet. The boy was not frightened of him, but would stare down at him from up there in the cliffs.

One day the boy knew his god had need of help, he just *knew*. He set off in search of him, and found he had fallen down a cliff. He licked his broken leg with his great mouth and tongue, warming him as wolves did, and he brought him food. He was seven then and the Mann talked to him and told him all he knew of the names of the wolves, and the stars, and the plants, and where the wolves lived, and why the deer would come from where they did, and when.

'Where do you go?' asked the boy, meaning when the Mann disappeared.

'Beyond the fence, but *you* mustn't. It's dangerous for now. Leave it a few years yet. Things are getting better out there and settling down.'

'You don't live in the WulfRock?'

The Mann laughed.

'Not dangerous?'

'No,' said the Mann.

'Dad said don't go there or else, or else . . .'

The boy's misshapen mouth trembled and he looked at his great odd feet and said no more.

'You'll go there one day, when you're ready,' the Mann told him. 'We all will. Boy, does your father know I'm here?'

The boy shook his head vigorously. He had never told. He knew by instinct what to say and what not to say to his parents.

'Good.'

That year, the boy's eighth, was his happiest. He had a friend, he learnt things, and he knew the world beyond the fence, which he journeyed to in his head with the thrumping of the windmills, was 'settling down' and that he would be able to reach it one day when it was not dangerous.

Then, one terrible day, his dad glimpsed the Mann, and loaded his gun.

'That's for killing,' said the boy.

'Yes, killing vermin,' laughed his father and went off up the gulley to the stonefield to hunt down the Mann as if he were a deer.

Twice he tried to stalk the Mann but the boy found him first, using secret routes, scenting him out, warning him with howls to go away. The howls were an attempt to conceal his complicity from his father. But he suspected. So the third time, when the boy was nine, Huntermann locked him in the bunker and then set off. There was the same look in his father's eyes as in his mother's sometimes, and it was murderous: the boy didn't worry for himself, but the Mann was getting weaker and he might mind a lot.

The boy was so frightened of what was going to happen, so fearful of the enclosing bunker, that he howled his anguish. The wolves came and howled outside to keep him company; his mother heard this and came and let him out.

It was nearly dark but he ran straight up the gulley, up and up, sniffing the ground, finding where his dad had peed, finding where he had picked up the Mann's trail. He listened, and might have tracked them along the many paths they had trekked trying to outwit each other, but there was no need: he knew the Mann had been forced to flee finally to the Rock, and then to the gorges, and then . . . then on in . . .

The boy went up there, fearful lest his father saw and told his mother and she ate him. But he dared go no further than the entrance.

He sat on his haunches and listened, and heard the rifle shot. It echoed and echoed a thousand times, now back and back, now forth again. The shot seemed to come right out of the distant past, and then right back from the future. And then again, a second shot, terrible in its brief finality.

Jakob Wald

In his last, stumbling steps through the ravines that led to the Wulf-Rock, Jakob Wald felt himself ready to die. He had been fleeing from Huntermann all his life, or someone like him, just as all Europe had; now he was the final victim and it did not matter.

It . . . did . . . not . . . matter.

Huntermann's first shot had caught him in his thigh, and the blood poured out between fingers that tried to stem the flow in vain. Pain? Perhaps.

But just as it began to be a throb too great to bear the mists shifted yet again and ahead he saw the rising of rocks, huge and sombre and overhanging in great dark jags and thrusts, turning above him, spiralling up towards a distant sky.

The sound of Huntermann's booted feet on scree.

Wald turned to face him and then propped himself up. He found himself where countless men and women, children and wolves had been before: facing death, too far gone to care.

Huntermann stood now, far enough off to make the shot difficult and therefore a challenge.

Behind him Wald felt the hard rock stir, and knew the touch of protective paws, and felt his leader's breath: warm, comforting, the scents of thyme and tarragon.

'Yes,' he whispered as Huntermann tensed, stilled, and squeezed.

The rocks that rose above him turned and turned, spiralling into wolves, and the sky in the heights beyond darkened slowly and filled with stars whose light came nearer, and then nearer still.

'Release the Mann,' said Wulfin then, and it was a command to all the world, and all that had protected him.

The Mann rose up and followed her upon his wolfway to the stars, and left himself behind.

The Boy II

The boy waited and waited, shivering through the night, until at last his father came out of the little gulley the next day. He looked, he looked ... he looked as he did after he mated with mother on the Fell, like that. The boy did not know the verb 'to gloat', or indeed what a verb was.

His father went back home and the boy shivered and knew the Mann was in trouble. The Mann did not come out of the gulley, not that day or the following night. So the boy did the bravest thing he ever did: he risked going through the gulley entrance and on among the gorges. There was mist and the shapes of wolves, and each step was fraught with fear.

He called for the Mann but there was no answer but his own voice, a thousand echoing boys' voices, the sound of children, a sound he had never heard. He wanted to run to those children and play with them, and share his secrets. Then the boy wept for himself, and for the Mann because he knew his father had found him, shot him, and he was dead: gone to the WulfRock.

The Mann never came back, and the boy knew loneliness from that day on, each and every day, an isolation more painful the older he became. Sometimes he cried and his mother comforted him and took him to her bed. She made him mate with her. He forgot himself in her gasps and screams, roaring out his raging loneliness which was always worse afterwards.

She gave birth again; the baby died, and she buried it secretly before he saw it.

'It was a boy,' she said.

'It was my brother,' he said.

Time flowed like the streams out on the Fell; slow or fast, angry or quiet, without regularity.

There was the year he lived by the fence and wondered if it was still dangerous beyond. That was when he started the great task of his younger years: dismantling the fence.

There was the time his mother raged at wolves, and chased them naked over the Fell. By then the boy was big enough to carry her home. He washed her injuries in the stream and dried her skin with heather. He tended her because his father didn't and she might have died.

One day he said, 'Mum?'

Her mouth was open; her teeth were bad and she was thinner than a baby deer. She didn't like the Fell, or the Scarpfeld, or the wind, or the rain. She liked her stinking darkness and her own things.

'Mum? *Mum!*'

She did not answer and grew cold.

He left her in her bunker and closed the doors upon her, first one, then the next, then the one after that. He left her in the pitch-black down there, terrible.

He *couldn't* leave her there. Living had been her way, dead would be his.

He went down, was sick, wrapped her in blankets, and carried her out into the open, his eyes weeping at the smell of her, and he took her up to the Scarpfeld and left her by the rock, within reach of the gulley that led to where the WulfRock was.

'Mum,' he said, 'the Mann said everybody's time comes one day. This is your time.'

The boy wept for everything, the tears coursing through his beard; he lay in the Scarpfeld, roaring out his griefs.

How many days he remained there he didn't count. How long he slept he didn't know. One day he woke to find the wolves licking his face to wake him up. He was covered in white because the first snows had come and he was nearly cold as death.

He sat up and recited the names of the wolves as the Mann had taught him them: Klimt, Elhana, Ambato, Solar, Tare, Galliard, Stry, Kobrin, Tervicz . . .

Then, suddenly, Tervicz stood before him, an old wolf, older than his mother had looked in death. He had clear eyes, like the Mann's.

Tervicz turned and led him back to the safety of one of the other bunkers, and as they went the boy decided not to speak to his Dad again. Howl maybe, but not speak. Not ever. He would wait until the day came when the place beyond the fence was dangerous no more. He would go there, and speak to someone there – unless someone came up here first.

The boy felt better for that decision, nodded his great head to himself and decided he could hope.

The boy barked at Tervicz not to go so fast.

The boy felt good and howled his pleasure to be alive.

The boy felt strong.

The boy began to run with Tervicz, trotting and leaping, giving rills of pleasure, down to the Fell and halfway across it just for fun.

The boy had become a man who ran with wolves.

Führer

For many long years after his arrival on the Fell, Huntermann never shot a wolf. He had white hair and a gun and a scent like rotten apples. He followed the wolves as he had when he was young, gaining their trust though never their liking. He only killed to eat and not for the pleasure of it, or out of anger. So it was mainly deer he hunted.

Yet a rage began to emerge and a kind of madness as he began to slow and grow old. The boy had long since left those parts, journeying to where the fence was and occupying himself by taking it down. This angered Huntermann terribly, and the old man began to rant and rave obscenities, and say what he would do when he caught the boy.

Then, one day, Huntermann finally fell over a void in his own mind and set off to hunt down his own son and shoot him if he could. This would not be easy, for the boy could scent him coming two kilometres away, or (if the wolves were minded to inform him) even further still. In any case the boy was far bigger than Huntermann, faster, stronger. The only quality he lacked which his father had in abundance was the desire to control through murderous intent.

Two wolves in particular became the boy's friends: Führer and Torne. He had an affinity with both, and since no other Mann had ever come to give him companionship, these two were his special friends. Between them, they were what his father might have been.

One hot day – one very hot day – when the heather was dry as tinder, and the breeze parched the throats that breathed it, a fire began to spread across the Fell, its smoke thick and acrid, its flames quick and voracious. Führer smelt it first, then the boy, and finally Torne. The wolves looked to the boy to find a way out, for he could see further and always kept calm.

He led them this way and that across the Fell, beginning to run when he realized they might be cut off and surrounded for the strong wind was fanning the flames. The wolves trusted him, as he them, but without knowing it he led them into the trap Huntermann had set when he started the fire. There was one escape route, by way of a stream, and Huntermann was covering it with a gun. A machine gun, just for fun, from his bunker's stores.

Rat-tat-ta-tat-*tat!* it went as they ran past a certain rock; Huntermann was shouting: 'Rat-tat – you're dead!'

All were hit, but Führer worst of all. He lay whimpering in the heath and though Torne got away easily enough, the boy, himself wounded, had to carry Führer to temporary safety to try to heal him.

But the wounds were too deep, the blood flow too strong, and old Führer died in the boy's arms, Torne looking on. All wept and whimpered, their sounds of grief half-human, half-wolf.

Then Huntermann came and the boy retreated, leaving the body of Führer behind.

Huntermann took out his knife and cut off Führer's head, just as he had done to men in the old days. He put it up on a pole outside his bunker for the flies, and so the boy could see it.

'It's what the Mennen do who live outside the fence,' said the boy aloud, because the Mann had told him. He felt revulsion at seeing a friend so treated, and for the first time he began to think his father might be one of the Mennen too. Then the boy thought something else: that Führer did not look bad up there, with the windmill thrumping right behind.

'Maybe,' he told Torne, 'Führer's so tall now he can see beyond the fence to where I'll go one day, all the way there!'

Torne led the boy up to the cavern above the gulley where Dendrine had raised Führer, and they said goodbye to him there, staring across the blackened, smoking Fell, and down at the bunker where Führer's head stood tall. They saw Huntermann emerge, and he looked small.

They said their goodbyes to Führer and hoped that once he had come back from exploring beyond the fence he would make his way to the WulfRock and join Klimt as a friend. The WulfRock would make him whole again.

'Anyway, he was getting old,' said the boy, 'like Dad is.'

Lunar

Through the years after Huntermann's ranting madness began, when the boy began to take down the fence and learned how to explode the mines, Lunar continued to lead the Wolves.

He made one great journey in that time, to Tornesdal, Klimt's birthplace, and there made sure that the Wolves he took with him formed a pack that would survive. It was not difficult, for already wolves had spread south through the Nordic lands, the Mennen having nearly all gone now, their settlements in ruins.

Wolfkind's time had come again.

Utin travelled with him, and afterwards, the two drifted slowly home from the north, teaching of the Wolves as they went, inspiring others with tales of the Pechorans and of Kobrin, spreading the good word. By the time they returned to the Heartland Lunar knew that wolfkind's ascendancy was assured, and the long task was nearly completed.

He discovered too that he had aged, and he had to fight hard to regain the leadership when he returned, and suffered thereafter more and more challenges, the strongest from his brother Torne.

One day, matter-of-factly, just as Klimt had, he yielded up the leadership to Torne, though not without a final fight. There was no shame in it. He was simply past his prime.

'What are you going to do?' asked Utin, his old friend.

'What are *you* going to do?' asked Lunar in reply, licking the wounds his brother had given him. 'I think they see my destiny and yours as one. *My* defeat is yours as well.'

'I know,' said Utin soberly.

'Yet do not be downhearted: adversity has compensations, as Klimt might have said, but probably never did. Torne needs a good adviser, and you –'

'No, Lunar, I want to go with you!'

'But you have more to offer him now,' commanded Lunar firmly, 'and he wants you. For my part there is one journey I would like to make, though whether I shall ever come back from it to journey to the WulfRock, as is said to be my destiny, I rather doubt. I want to go to distant Lake Baikal, which was the home of the Wanderer. Indeed, Utin, it is my time to become a Wanderer too.

'There are memories that trouble me, times past I cannot quite remember, sadnesses to face out, joys to recall, and finally a peace to find. It is time to explore the wolfways of my past lives so that when I go to the WulfRock it will be only the future that I seek.'

'When are you going to make such a journey?'

Lunar smiled and shrugged. 'Today I yielded leadership to Torne. Today is the time to leave.'

'But –'

'Now, Utin, *now* is the time we do things.'

'But *Lunar* –'

'Now, my friend!'

Utin thought he had never seen Lunar so at peace with life, and with himself. Having laid down the burden of leadership, he was free to journey as he wished.

'But when will you be back?' called Utin after Lunar, for he meant what he said and had gone down to the Ruin one last time, and set off as dusk fell.

'When it's time.'

'I'll be hereabout,' said Utin.

'A part of my heart died here,' said Lunar, looking at the Ruin. 'More has died since. Perhaps it must all die before I am able to come back.'

'I'll be here.'

'And I,' said Tervicz, emerging from the shadows; 'the Wolves will be here.'

Lunar looked from one to another, loyal advisers both, and then at the Ruin where Merrow was lost. With a shake of his head he was gone, on a journey that would take him years.

'Will he come back?' said Utin.

'Have faith,' said the Bukov wolf, 'and find a wolf to love meanwhile. I did.'

Rohan came out of the shadows to his side.

'Me? I'm just a vagrant now,' said Utin. 'No female worth her salt would want a wolf like me!'

'You'll find one who will, my dear,' said Rohan.

Tervicz raised his head to howl, which was a rare thing then, and the others joined him. It was their farewell to Lunar, a real farewell, for no wolf ever became a Wanderer and came back home the same.

Eike

Eike followed Tervicz and Matthius Wald slowly up the gulley, stopping for breath rather more than they did. The old wolf moved rhythmically and with dignity, while Eike grumbled that he felt now too hot, now too cold, and expressed surprise at how dark the gulley was, how steep and damp the walls, what a contrast in terms of light and atmosphere to the Fell below.

'Yes, yes, Eike,' muttered Matthius Wald a shade testily, for he had little strength for conversation. Indeed, he suddenly seemed to have no strength at all to keep up with Tervicz, who went steadily on ahead, always seeming on the verge of disappearing from sight.

The air was moister when they reached the stonefield, the ground flattened out, and it was far colder than on the Fell below. A dank mist was blowing from the north in rolling billows which obscured the cliffs and the mountain beyond them on the far side of the Scarpfeld.

'We're not going to see much,' said Eike, disappointed.

'Maybe we were not meant to yet,' responded Wald shivering, pulling his outer garment from his bag. He was sweating with the effort of the climb, but could feel the cold already eating into him.

Behind them, in the gulley, or perhaps up among its terraces, a scatter of rocks fell.

'What was that?' said Eike, turning quickly. He was suddenly jumpy and nervous.

'Huntermann,' said Wald, 'finally. Come, let's follow the old wolf in the hope he'll lead us away from the old man.'

They followed over undulating ground, the mist tantalizing in the way it drifted across their path, now thicker, now fading, never quite allowing them a sense of where they were, or where they were going.

Tervicz turned and came back to stare at them, head on one side. They were near one of the innumerable peat pools and he stood on a little plateau of rock above them. Then he turned, looked westward towards where the col must be, his ears pricking. They heard the muffled sound of shooting. With a last look that seemed to command them to wait where they were, he was gone, his grey-white fur quickly melding with the mist.

'What now?' said Eike.

'Get out your drum,' said Wald, sitting down.

'Now?' cried Eike in disbelief. 'That old man will hear and come and shoot us, and the wolf –'

'Huntermann is otherwise engaged. Can't you feel his evil, Eike? The tension – can't you hear it?'

Wald's brows were wet with mist and in his eyes was the look of a man on the edge of a void.

'Help me, Eike,' he said, lying down. 'Cover me. Drum for me. Drum me to the Wolves that I may run with them, for they are near, so near . . .'

Eike covered him with a blanket, placed stones about it to hold it down. As he did so the wind whipped up, harsh and sudden, and for the first time ever in their experience the stones were more than symbolic. Without them the blanket would have been snatched away, as Eike's hat was, off into the mist and lost to sight.

'Drum for me . . .'

Eike unhooked his drum from his shoulder in something like a panic, for the wind was getting stronger, the droplets of the mist stinging on his cheeks; his hair was blowing, and the blanket, flattened now around the form of his master, shifting and moving, hard to see, almost as if, as the drumming began, his master was not quite there.

'Faster . . .' came Wald's voice, but it was not from the blanket, nor

from anywhere identifiable. It was from everywhere, from beyond the
mist, the voice of the drum itself, the voice of time.

'Faster . . . for the fear is coming now.'

'Master, I am afraid, mortally afraid.'

Wald sat up quite suddenly, and as the blanket fell off him Eike
saw that his eyes were wide.

Fear.

'Come on!' he said, 'it's now, now . . .'

Then they rose, and began to run into the mist, stumbling across
the scattered rocks and rough sward, running out of fear, and so into
it.

'Master!' cried Eike, 'Master . . .'

But Wald had gone on ahead, and Eike was alone.

Lunar

Lunar was old now, old and nearly forgotten. Oh, they knew who he
had been, or thought they did; and at first they supposed his stories
must have a grain of truth in them. They let him live in the Ruin,
and take what prey he could find. Rabbits too old to dodge him; voles
too stupid not to get caught. The husks of pine cones; the soft slime
of old mushrooms dribbling down his chin.

Some said he had been everything, even a Wanderer once. Some
said he was great Torne's father. Some said he had always lived alone.
Only a few of the older ones remembered that when they were young,
very young, there was a female lived there with him. Old like him,
and grey; thin and spindly and hardly able to walk.

'Remember them? Of course I do! They used to laugh until they
cried, cackling like corncrakes!'

It was true enough.

Lunar had come home those long years later, and Merrow was there
. . . *Merrow had come home to him.* She, and Utin, together. Rohan
was gone to the WulfRock by the time Lunar came back, but at least
she and Merrow had shared a little time in which to talk before
Rohan's end.

Lunar wept when he saw her but then said that Wanderers often
did. Did not the world weep?

'A bit of laughter does no harm, Lunar,' said Merrow, which for some reason made him smile.

They chose the Ruin as their own place, harried only occasionally by the younger Wolves, for old though they were they still had a measure of authority then. Every day until the time when Merrow died they laughed about something, except for four days, and those were the four times the old man came.

'Huntermann,' whispered Merrow, snarling through broken teeth. She could tell a few things about him.

They watched him wandering about, peeking and poking about, and pissing down the stench of rotten apples in dribbles. Took him an age. They cackled about even that afterwards.

'You're not much faster at it these days yourself, Lunar,' said Merrow, starting their laughter again. Four days is not so much out of so very many, each a joy, each a bonus.

Utin died, and then Merrow soon after, and Lunar was alone, lingering and suffering; and in those weakening years, when new generations forgot who he was or were never told, past memories came back to him which he had never known before. But he was Wulf in mortal form, condemned to live so many mortal lives until, if he lived nobly and found courage, he might attain to immortality once more, and affirm wolfkind's new ascendancy.

He suffered his past lives unnoticed, but for his mumbling, his sudden barks and shouts, his snarling at enemies unseen, his madcap fights with enemies long dead, circling about a wolf who was not there.

Sometimes two or three of the younger Wolves would want to drive him away but always there were others there who showed compassion and let him stay.

'We'll be old one day, and forgetful, and maybe years ago he was one of us, a Wolf; maybe a great one. What's his name?'

Many names and one.

'Wulf,' he would sometimes say when asked, 'my name was Wulf!'

Then they would laugh and leave him to it, to cackle and mutter to himself as much as he liked; to fight wolves who were not there; and one day soon, the gods willing, to die. But – Wolves who were born when he was old, grew old themselves and died, and still he was there, alone now, utterly alone.

Once they found him trying to climb up through the screes towards the col, struggling step by step, saying he wanted to go home.

'Where's that, wolf?' they said. 'Or should we say Wulf!'

'The stars,' he whispered.

'Come on, it's cold. We'll show you the way back to the Ruin where you live.'

'Don't want to go back there. She's gone, they've all gone and I'm too alone down there.'

'Come on!'

They had to be quite firm with him, and he wept when they brought him back.

Once, years later, he howled as if calling for another to come to him.

'Who *is* he?' that generation said, staring at the stars, awed by the sound he made, which spoke of wolfways beyond their imagining.

'Just an old wolf who should have died a long time ago,' they said. 'Let's take him some food in the morning.'

So it was that Lunar, son of Elhana, brother of Solar, successor to great Klimt, journeyed through his final years, back and forth, now and then, weeping now and laughing then, his words seeming jumbled, his thoughts confused, his life so seemingly bereft that new generations of Wolves wondered what kept him alive at all.

Why could he not just lie down and die?

But fallen gods do not die; they can only wait and suffer and strive to wake up out of their mortal punishment.

'Wulf, Wulf . . .'

Sometimes he heard the wind whisper his name, and seemed to see the female wolf whose voice it was.

'Merrow? Elhana? Jicin? Rohan?'

He could not yet remember who Wulfin had been, and that she was his love, as Jicin had been Klimt's. She was the one he had sought all his many lives, and never quite found, though his sister Merrow had come near.

They heard him calling names that held no meaning for them now, calling up towards the screes, or standing and trying to out-roar the Fall with his weak old voice, legs trembling with the effort, one eye beginning now to cloud into blue-white.

Wulf, Wulf.

How could he know that she was watching over him to the last, weeping for his tears, for the suffering of the many lives he lived and died through the Dark Millennium, in the last of which he was dying now.

'Wulf, my love, can you not yet hear my call? Wulf . . .'

The wolf who had been Lunar could not hear her call, nor have seen her clearly had she come, but could only lower his patchy head to his feet and pick at his scabs, and try to rid himself of fleas and search the ground for something he had lost, something he must do, or find, if he was to raise himself for ever once again.

'How's Wulf today?' they laughed.

He turned away, slipping on the rocks in the stream, and went to the darkness of the Ruin which had become his home.

'Wulfin,' he prayed, remembering her name but not who she was to him, 'help me, show me what I have lost.'

He was getting near the truth at last.

The fear, when it came, was palpable.

It hung over the Forest like polluted mist; it crept up to the col; it slid its horrid way down into the Scarpfeld, and then across to the gulley. There it paused awhile, cloying now, impossible to remove from fur and eyes, or from between the claws where it found its way, or out of ears and snouts and throats; then it rolled down to the Fell and there became unspoken terror.

The Wolves knew it was there but not what it was, except it was thickest where the Huntermann was, so thick it was like darkness, and heavy, and made even the bravest Wolves slip away, their hackles rising, their eyes haunted.

Only Lunar, in his Ruin, stayed impervious to it. He who had seen so many things, suffered so many horrors, known so many joys, had no energy left to respond to fear, with fear.

They came to ask him if he knew what it was.

He smelt it and knew the answer: 'Mennen, all the Mennen in the world. What a stench they make, alive or dead!'

So, fearful now, they watched helpless as Huntermann went about for weeks, slowly dragging things, or digging things. He set things up, whistling tunelessly. Now at the Forest edge, now on the col, now somewhere across the Fell.

Nets, the red and white kind that wolves cannot cross, though they are only fronds of material, he set up day after day, until they reached right round the part of the Forest the Wolves used, just beyond the Ruin, and hemmed them in, leaving only one way to go, up the col.

Fear.

Explosives he dug in and laid down, they could smell them. Sharp their odour, and acrid, and dangerous because they kill wolves.

Fear.

Mines he laid, quite openly, and a wolf's back legs were blown off, who lived awhile, squatting immobile, another came to help and was blown up as well. Gore flying through the air, and landing near.

No wonder there was fear.

Pools he poisoned and deer died, and the Wolves who ate them.

Fear now wherever Huntermann went by.

Then, one day, from the col, four sudden shots and four Wolves lay dead by the Tree; the leader, the ledrene, and two of their four cubs.

Fear palpable.

The Wolves no longer ruled the Heartland. The Mennen were back in the form of Huntermann. Wolfkind might still be ascendant, but its heart was being ripped right out and soon it would die.

Fear.

Then respite for days. Nothing. The Huntermann was down in his den, lying low.

It seemed two Memnen had come whose scent was good, clear. Was this what old Wolves called thyme and tarragon, was this the scent of Wanderers?

'Ask the old wolf in the Ruin: he's the only wolf around here who's forgotten everything!'

Laughter, of a kind. But perhaps he had been right about the stench being the Mennen . . .

Then Huntermann was back, up in the Scarpfeld, carrying a gun, shooting at ravens as he had done in the old days. The Mennen who had come had made things right. Things would be all right. Things would be better now.

Things suddenly went wrong and the fear was back, redoubled like an echo in a dark place.

At dawn he started, old and wild and white, scrabbling up to the Forest from the Fell and setting up the last few nets to guide the Wolves upward. One after another, right across the Forest.

Fear.

Then the explosions, bang, bang, bang, reverberating from one side of the valley to the other; the Wolves were confused, not knowing which way to go, leaderless.

Then, as they fled up towards the col, he began to shoot, and all became a mess of horror as Wolves fell, or worse, did not fall, but cried out and tried to crawl away.

Fear, as the shots continued, and Wolves continued to fall; and the terrible confusion as some turned back to run, and his shots frightened them a new way, right across the mines. Fear became an ice-cold lake into which Wolves began to fall and drown.

Fear utter and total, for Huntermann was coming down from the col, shouting, raving, ranting: the Mennen personified, Mennen incarnate, and the Wolves' hegemony beginning to break into parts, and fall, piece by piece, tumbling down through the gorges of fear like so many leaves blown into a quarry upon the blizzard wind of Mennen's hatred.

He woke up to it sometime then, did the wolf who had once been Lunar. He smelt the fear coming, and saw the frightened Wolves who carried it, running hither and thither, fleeing from the gunshots on the col.

Wulf!

He rose slowly, head up, astonished at how sweet the sound of her voice was.

Wulf, they need your help.

The odour of fear was so foul it cleared his head.

Wulf, rise now!

The panic of the Wolves about him increased as their warnings came: 'Huntermann's come down to the Forest. He's coming this way. He'll kill us.'

The shots came now and then as confirmation, intermixed with the cries and screams of panicked, wounded Wolves.

Lunar stood staring, wondering why he felt so old, and where he had been.

'Where shall we go? There's nowhere to go!' they cried.

'Where's your leader?' he asked one and then another. But their eyes were crazed and Huntermann was coming nearer, his scent ahead of him, nearly as foul as the fear he instilled.

'Where's your leader?' he said again.

None heard him at first. None saw him immediately.

He stood in the clearing by the Ruin as they ran all about, unable to go far because of the nets Huntermann had laid, one after another through the weeks, the gaps now all filled.

'Where is your leader?' he asked. 'Where is your ledrene?'

'We lost them,' they cried out, 'we lost them all.'

Wulf, you are their leader, only you. See how they need you.

Lunar saw and understood, but felt too old to help. For these were not just the Wolves here and now, but all wolfkind, desperate, lost, unguided throughout the Dark Millennium. Nor was Huntermann just one of the Mennen, but all of them, all coming back. It seemed too much, and yet he supposed that he must try.

'Follow me,' he cried, his voice so old and cracked that none heard it above the panic and the shouting, 'follow me.'

Then Lunar raised his head and peered up the long trail that led to the col, further than he had been in years, and knew what he must do.

No prayers. No words at all.

Just one thing: he must lead.

Wearily, as one who begins a trek he believes he will never finish, Lunar took another step forward. Then a third. Each one feeling like a life, like a friend lost, like a day of pain; each step a time of torment he had lived.

He did not look back.

He ignored the shots that followed him.

Ignored Huntermann's shouts.

Ignored all but the desire to show there was a way, and its freedom lay in conquering the fear.

'Look!'

One or two had seen him, now up beyond the Forest edge, now past the Fall, now across by the Tree, now beginning the steep ascent towards the col; *'Look!'*

They saw in wonder that the old wolf was showing them a way, and though many doubted, and preferred the shadows of the Forest to the clear light of day, a few had faith and followed him.

He went on slowly, step by painful step, though intermixing now with the torments were a few memories of joy, brief sensations of happiness remembered; but more than all of this, what drove him on and on was a clear memory of one whom he had loved, and lost; not Merrow, not her but another, a Wolf of all Time.

'Wulf!'

He had faltered and looked back, and hesitated, because of those who had followed him many had been shot and had fallen and only a few remained.

'Wulf, hurry now!'

'Come,' he called to them, 'have faith and follow me . . .'

On he went knowing she was there ahead, waiting as she had for all the centuries for him to find himself again. But her name . . . still he could not remember it.

Another shot, closer this time, and fragments of rock stung his face. He looked back and saw that Huntermann was coming, white hair wild, his rantings and ravings and anger, and his fear – that of all Mennen always.

'Come on, come on,' cried Lunar, daring to pause and hurry the few Wolves who had followed him upwards and on.

They reached the col but hardly paused for breath, for Huntermann was closer behind them, shouting, swearing, beginning to catch up.

'We don't know the way,' they cried, panicking again, for the mist had come down.

'I do,' said Lunar, 'come . . .'

Over the top of the col they went, by way of the routes Stry had long since taught him, and then down to the Scarpfeld, into the billowing mists, so weary now, and so nearly home. Then, as the mists cleared and they climbed the last few steps towards the rock at the entrance Lunar stopped in his tracks, as did those who were still with him.

'A Mann,' they cried.

'Yes,' said Lunar, 'but *he'll* not harm us, only come to harm . . . *come!*'

Then Lunar lead them past the Mann, past the rock, and into the first of the gorges, and on to find where the WulfRock rose.

Wulf

Matthius Wald did not know where he was until the rolling mist cleared, and he found himself near the entrance, by a rock above some scree, with Wolves coming towards him. They were led by a wolf as old as Tervicz, but a little larger, a little thinner, a wolf who looked near death.

The two stared at each other and then the wolf barked a command in a cracked voice and pushed on past him, as if he wasn't there.

Then, as one by one they came, Wald saw the Huntermann following behind them, gun in hand, another across his shoulder; a wild, lawless creature, no better than a smelly feral goat, as evil as sin, getting ever nearer.

As Wald stared in astonishment the old man raised his gun and fired, and the bullet spun Wald round to face the entrance, towards which he began to run, just as his father had before him, just like him.

Time present and time past came together in Wald's cry of pain, and his calling for help to the gods, and in the fear he felt as Huntermann crashed up the scree behind him towards the entrance. When Wald's hand clutched his shoulder it was warm and wet with blood. So this was it, past and present both at once as Wald fled from them into the future which was, and is, and would yet be, the WulfRock.

He ran into the first gorge, trying to catch up with the Wolves, trying to find the one who led them, seeking out His help; and to get away from Huntermann.

'*Wulf* . . .' he beseeched.

The voice that answered was gentle and light and beautiful as the sunlight high, high above. But then . . .

'I'm coming after the lot of you bastards!'

It was Huntermann, closer still, his second rifle clattering on the near vertical walls of the narrow gorge as he tried to catch Wald and the wolf, to kill him, as so many years before he had killed Jakob, his father.

Time present and time past were both now hurrying to be at one with time future, for good or for ill, for wolfkind or for Mennen. A turn, another, a fork, a third, which way, any way, somewhere . . .

'*Heuren Sie! Listen now!*'

Wald stopped; no one behind, no wolf in front. He listened and heard the running of all his life, the fleeing of his feet, the thunder of a fearful heart.

'This way, Wanderer!'

This time, it was Tervicz, ahead, then to the left, old, so old, limping. 'Hurry, Mann, for you are needed now.'

On and up, another turn, lost in the labyrinths of time and place, while ahead, not far now . . . not far . . .

The gorge widened, the mists came down again, clammy and clinging as they swirled. Then the shapes of wolves were all about them, dark and getting darker. They were awaiting them ahead, where the gorge stopped and turned into a clearing about which rose a vast amphitheatre of cliffs and rocks, sheer, rising to a distant portal on the sky itself. While in the centre of this holy place, a stack of riven rock, slanting, faceted, shining damp and sheer at the very foot of which . . .

But even as the hurrying, desperate Matthius Wald understood he was almost within touching distance of the WulfRock itself, and the secret of what lay still and suffering in the shadow of its protection, he saw his way was barred by a wild and living decoration: Huntermann.

His back was turned on the approaching Wald, for his focus was inward, towards the rock, as he sighted his rifle upon the vulnerable form that had led the Wolves out of the forest up to this last sanctuary: Lunar, nearly his time, near the possibility of immortality again, near the end of his Dark Millennium of punishment.

As Wald ran forward it seemed he saw Lunar, the Wolf, in the same cold sights that Huntermann had levelled. He saw that while Lunar lay still, his amber eyes staring with utter gentleness, the other mortal Wolves of Time stood uncertain of what to do, terrified of Huntermann.

Wolves, Huntermann, the Mann . . . an eternal moment in which the only sound was the drip, drip, drip of water down the wet cliffs, which became the stream that flowed out into the world beyond.

'Nooooooo!' Wald cried, pushing Huntermann and his gun aside as he ran past that living vileness to take his place with the Wolves. He had killed a boy once when he was barely been more than a boy himself and never again had Wald taken another's life. He would not try to do so now, not here, where the silence was ancient, the power for good quite palpably the power for life.

'Nooooo!' he cried as Huntermann regained his stance and began to squeeze the trigger to take the old wolf's life before he found a wolfway to the stars in his own time, 'noooo!'

It was the shocked and desperate cry of one who sees an act of desecration at its beginning: a desecration that lay in not just the killing of a holy wolf, but a killing in a holy place. In Wald's awful cry was all the horror of the cries and screams that once he, like his father, had heard in silent memory in Oradour, in a little church where Mennen who were the Huntermann of that time had killed the women and the children: 'NOOOO!'

Oh, it had happened before so many times and the world had been dying for so long.

It had happened before, here, then as now, to Wald's father, the Wald before, and Matthius Wald now found himself looking at his coming death as it prepared itself in the muzzle of Huntermann's stock-still gun, first Lunar the Wolf, then Tervicz, then himself; as routine, eternal, ageless and unremarked as the drip, drip, drip of the water that broke the silence, and echoed softly about, the rising, broken rocks and cliffs almost shaking with the gentle sound.

But a gun shot? Wald found that here and now time had slowed and he had time to ponder.

When his father had been killed had it been that shot which brought so many rocks tumbling down and formed the litter of rock-fall that partly filled the amphitheatre in which they now waited? Could such a place bear another such violent sound?

Wald, who had not felt fear until now, looked up and saw the looming juts and abutments of rock above and did feel fear. The certainty of death from Huntermann's gun seemed as nothing compared to the fearful chaos into which the world might plunge were these fragile, hanging rocks, their shapes so like the heads of ancient Wolves, to be brought tumbling down upon them all.

A shaft of sun, a finger of bright accusation from the distant sky above, came pointing down upon Huntermann, catching his wild, white hair to set it starkly against a backdrop of wet, dark, fractured rock. And his smile, triumphant; and his cold, cruel eyes, self-satisfied in these moments of final immutable control.

Huntermann fired, but not at the wolf.

As Wald felt the searing pain near his neck, but not so near as to kill him – so deliberate, the shot of a torturer still – and as he fell spinning to one side, he heard the roaring blast, and the roaring retribution of its echo coming, mounting, frightening. He hit the ground and felt it begin to shake, as above him the WulfRock shifted and began to disintegrate, its wounds far greater, truly mortal.

He stared and saw rising above him, past the Wolf's head, on and upward, right towards the skies which lightened with day and darkened with night, again and again and again, rose to where the stars were, to the very sun, he saw and knew he could do no more.

He must give up the hope of life itself. He must put his trust in Wulf. He looked over to where Huntermann was and saw him steady the gun again, this time towards Lunar himself, the wolf who would be Wulf. There was a residual Mann in Wald as in vanity and conceit that he could help a god he struggled to pull himself across the wolf's body and heard instead the whisper of the mounting wind, which was Wulf's own voice: 'Listen, look and learn is all I ask.'

Far off, Huntermann smiled, all folly and blindness, for the roaring of the breaking, cracking cliffs was almost on him, down, down upon the shaft of sunlight even as the sunlight went right out, blocked by their thunderous descent.

As Huntermann's gun burst into the sudden flame and smoke of his last shot, as the bullet came slowly, so slowly out of time towards the wolf, turning in the air, slower by far than a shining stone hurled looping up into the air by one boy at another, old Tervicz rose.

He raised his head into the Bukov howl, to summon all the mortal wolves to stand by the dying Lunar, to summon too all the Wolves of Time that ever were, that ever might be, here and now to witness the last mortal moments of a millennium of punishment, and the reincarnation of a god.

Tervicz howled down the Wolves of Time, and they were as the breaking of the vast cliffs and rocks above, the transmutation of the dark echo of the Huntermann's shots into a summoning in retribution and in triumph.

Wald felt his god's embrace, protective against the darkness falling down. He saw the slowly spinning bullet caught in the falling rock, buffeted, struggling to come on, then beaten and falling, its last strength spent, lost, a source of fear no more.

He heard the howling of the Wolves, and the running thunder of their paws, and the piercing lightning of their eyes as the shapes of the walls of the place he was in bulged and shifted, broke forth and began to fall, huge rocks turning, Wolves emerging, and the roars and snarls of faith, of those who will not have their leader die.

Huntermann looked up and saw, and he stared in horror, and fear, for the Wolves were coming now, howled down about him, ranging and raging, and one by one forming, shaping, becoming all that he most feared, most tried to control.

His last shot was lost in the huge mêlée of the Wolves; it was harmless, it was nothing now. Then his guns were torn from his hands by the winds that blew about him, tugging and pulling him this way and that as he saw them staring at him, the Wolves he had failed to kill, the Wolves of Time, whom Lunar, so old, too weak to move, saw now were come back to help him on.

His leader Klimt, his father Aragon, his mother Elhana, Lounel . . . Stry . . . Morten . . . Rohan . . . all were there.

'. . . Solar, my brother; Merrow, my sister,' he whispered, and . . .

Leon was there, and Galliard; Torne and Führer, Ambato, Jimena and her namesake Aragon's mother – more and more, all the Wolves of Time he had ever known.

'One more, where is she, I lost her . . .'

'*Wulf,*' the blasting winds of time roared and then turned gentle, to whisper in dying Lunar's ears, '*Wulf my dear, Wulf* . . .'

Then was She there before him in welcome, Her eyes the sky above, Her eyes the sun and moon, Her eyes the stars . . .

'*My love* . . .' She said, and Lunar remembered and knew what once he had lost and now reached out to know again.

And Wulf began his journey to the stars, with Wulfin at his flank, and the Wolves of Time about them, old Tervicz with them now, yet old no more.

Wald watched them go away from him, above him, into the nights and days beyond the WulfRock, into immortality.

He lay and watched, helpless, unable to move the great rocks that lay across him, unable even to raise his head to see who it was who called so weakly: 'Help me! Help *me!*'

It was Huntermann, his voice from a hell of his own making.

Then Wald saw the sky obscured and human eyes looking down at him, red-rimmed. He felt a rough hand touch his face, and grunted with pain as the pressure on his leg was suddenly released, and then the rock across his arms was moved away as well.

Bearded was the man who helped him, wild-eyed, and with a mouth that was misshapen. The man knelt down and licked his wounds. The man gave him water. While all about them, not one hurt by the great rock-falls that were now finally still, though all were grubby with rock dust and muck, the Wolves stared, shifted, watched and howled. And Wald howled, and the man who had come as well, all howling as one, Wolves, brothers, at one in a healing world. The man fed him while the Wolves kept him warm for two long nights, and saved his life.

Days and nights when Wulf watched over him and the voice from the void nearby still cried for help.

'Come on, get up, ready now,' said the man at last. 'We can't stay here. Wolves need food.'

But Wald was too weak to move.

'Carry you then until you're well,' said the man. 'You're the Mann come back to life and I knew you would one day. Come on.'

As he was raised, and turned, Wald saw a terrible thing. He saw the glimpse of a face trapped inside a cage of fallen rocks, each of which seemed in the mist that came about them to be the head of a Wolf.

The face inside the dark impenetrable void was Huntermann's, and he was still alive.

'Help me,' he cried, nearly voiceless now, 'don't leave me alone.'

'Can't,' grunted the man who carried Wald, 'can't shift those rocks. Too heavy for me.' Thus, on a cruel practicality, was Huntermann abandoned by life while still living.

A hand reached out for Wald, for life, but then it was left behind, left in the mist, left for ever alone, dying.

Then Huntermann cried out as he never had, and then he began to scream.

Screams which began as horrible as deepest pain, yet when they rose as echoes into the indifferent rocks and cliffs above, lost themselves as whimpers, abandoned and as insubstantial as the mist that died before the sun that began to shine again, down to where Huntermann reached out his hand in mortal fear, helpless, control quite gone, punished and pissing himself in terror.

As Wald and the man and the Wolves left him behind, to trek down through the gorge to join themselves to the life of the world again, Huntermann screamed more. Had his victims in their hundreds and thousands, their thousands and millions, heard him they would have known that now, too late, he knew the tortures of unrequited suffering, and they were themselves avenged.

As the light of the day brightened the path ahead, the Wolves, and Wald carried by the man, stumbled out onto Scarpfeld once more.

The man said, 'Told the Wolves that one day the Mann would come back.' His greying beard was warm on Wald's cheek. He was laughing.

Then they were in the sun and Eike was there, looking like death.

'Master,' he said, 'I was too frightened at the end to follow you, but he –'

'I know that fear,' said Wald, reaching a hand to Eike, 'I know it well.'

They lingered for days on the Scarpfeld while Wald recovered his strength. The Wolves were their constant companions, for the man was of them, and would howl with them. So in the end would they.

'When are we going?' Eike asked Wald finally.

They were standing on the stonefield, looking right across the Fell. 'Now.'

'Where?' asked the man.

'Home,' said Wald.

'Beyond where the fence was?' There was delight in his voice and wonder in his eyes.

'Yes,' said Wald.

Then, picking their way carefully down through the screes, they went: three men with the Wolves to see them on their way, and watch over them in all of the Years of the Wolf to come.